What Passes for Wisdom

Also by C. H. Lawler:

The Saints of Lost Things

The Memory of Time

Living Among the Dead

What Passes for Wisdom

A Novel

C. H. Lawler

Walrus Books

New York·Chicago·New Orleans·Pierre Part

ego sum vitulisque marinis

This is a work of fiction. Names, characters, places, and incidents are either the product of the author's imagination or are used fictitiously, and any resemblance to actual persons, living or dead, businesses, companies, events, or locales is entirely coincidental. Any and all resemblances to persons living or dead are purely coincidental.

ISBN # 9781721563500

Front cover background: *May Night*, Willard Leroy Metcalf

National Gallery of Art, Washington, D. C.

For those who perform heroic acts, unrecognized on earth and recorded only by God. Among them are the teachers who taught us, particularly on days that we had no interest in learning.

"And the herald proclaimed aloud, 'You are commanded, O peoples, nations, and languages, that when you hear the sound of the horn, pipe, lyre, trigon, harp, bagpipe, and every kind of music, you are to fall down and worship the golden image that King Nebuchadnezzar has set up. And whoever does not fall down and worship shall immediately be cast into a burning fiery furnace.'"

Daniel 3:4-6

Sammy, 1956

He was eleven years-old, an age at which anything is possible.

Outside, through the four-paned windows, the moon threw ghost-shadows on the live oaks and the lawn. Inside, it threw pale shapes on the walls and the dresser and the bed. He pulled the covers up around his chin and looked up to the ceiling. Above it was the attic, the place where his sisters said her ghost slept. Through the four-paned windows and out across the silver lawn, was the ice barn where they said she spent her days lurking in the shadows. And he believed his sisters because they were older than he was, and so they should know.

They sat on the edge of his bed. Marilyn was in her nightgown. She was too old to dress up anymore, but Charlotte was still dressed in her costume, a cat. Marilyn had painted divergent whiskers over her sister's cheeks. Candy wrappers were scattered on the floor and his comforter. The girls spoke with a flashlight that they passed from one to the other, each one taking a turn placing it under her chin.

"*She stalks Mount Teague at night,*" Charlotte spoke solemnly as Marilyn made rushing noises like the wind by pursing and unpursing her lips. "*Even though she died over a hundred years ago, on this very spot, her spirit is restless, wandering eternally but finding no peace. None!*"

The girls snickered for a brief moment and then feigned ghostly weeping. Their little brother pretended to be unaffected, though his smile looked a little forced. Marilyn unwrapped a Milky Way and took a bite as she passed the flashlight to Charlotte.

"*Yesssss,*" Charlotte hissed as she positioned the flashlight under her chin. Her eyes fell into hollow shadows. "*On nights like this very night, when the moon is full, she wanders as a pillar of flame, seeking vengeance on those who have harmed her in her former life.*" Marilyn stopped in mid-chew of her Milky Way and moaned a plaintiff note. Sammy inched under the covers. Charlotte's character broke for a moment.

"Scared yet, Bubba?"

"No," Sammy lied defiantly, his crewcut hair like a brush against his pillow.

"Okay…" she scratched through a pile of wrappers and put a candy corn in her mouth, "*It was in a fire in the fancy ballroom where she died a young woman, when her whole life was ahead of her. And as the flames rose higher, she appeared in them, clothed in black, in mourning lace, beating on the locked window, begging for someone to open it. Until…until…her fancy dress caught on fire…she was consumed in flames, and the ballroom crashed in on her….*"

The girls put their faces together and moaned even more in the flashlight. Marilyn turned the beam to the window. The girls cackled as the pane glowed in a yellow circle. Behind it was a shadow, just the crook of an oak limb, he told himself, but his courage was failing rapidly. He swallowed to force his resolve to stand its ground.

"There! There she is!" Charlotte hissed, "Looking in the window! The Burning Lady is looking inside at you!"

His eyes dilated at the image in the window. Maybe it was the moon-shadow of a limb. But maybe it wasn't. All courage, all resolve collapsed.

"Stop it! Stop it, Sissy!" His bawling face was twisted red. His cheeks quivered, and his eyes broke like a dam, unleashing tears in a sobbing torrent. He whimpered and wept, disconsolate. He put his head under the covers, but his sisters pulled them back.

"Look! She begs you to look at her! *Look upon me, Samuel Teague!*" He shut his eyes against the image that was surely looking at him through the window. The hand-blown glass of the windowpanes quivered. He couldn't help it, he sniveled. His sisters, the cat and the non-cat, had hit their mark, and they rejoiced.

"Titty-pie, titty-pie, Sammy is a titty-pie!" they teased.

"Am not—am not—am not!" he blubbered, red-faced in the darkened room.

Charlotte's cat-whiskered face smirked and whispered into his ear, "Titty-pie."

Heavy footsteps pounded the stairs, and she appeared as an immense shadow in the doorway. Her silhouette reached inside the door and eclipsed the light. She flipped the switch, and the room was illuminated again.

"You girls stop teasin' that baby! Y'all ought be shamed!"

"Oh, it's Halloween. We were just having some fun—" Marilyn exhaled, rolling her eyes to the ceiling in protest, "Miss. Della. Mae."

"You scarin' yo brother," Della Mae said, "y'all get on to bed, now, and I don't want hear no noise. When yo mama and daddy come back from they party, it betta be quiet as a tomb up in here."

Charlotte clicked off the flashlight. Marilyn straightened her nightgown, and she and her sister the cat scampered to their rooms. Miss Della Mae picked up candy wrappers and put them in the pocket of her apron. She was still fussing, *po' beeby*, as she clicked on the lamp and clicked off the room light. Her black face glistened in the lamplight, a squatty rectangle of kindness. She sat on the edge of Sammy's bed and pulled the covers up around his chin and put her dark hand, as wide as the blade of a boat paddle, on his chest.

"Verily, I says unto you, Sammy Teague, though weepin' endure for the night, joy come in the moanin'. Das right." She squinted dark rolls of skin over her eyes and raised a hand, palm outward. "Lawd Jesus, proteck dis baby from all harm," she whispered softly, "from ghostes and spirits and spectors and all sech. Help him be a good soul cause he show a purty chile and he gone be a good man one day. Show is. Amen. Now Mist Sammy, Miss Della Mae gone be rat downstairs. Don't you be worried no how."

She turned off the lamp light and got up. The door slowly wheezed shut after her. In the moonlight that seeped in through the window, his mind still hummed with Halloween candy, and he couldn't sleep. He became angry with himself for having been scared, and his sisters for scaring him, and then he became bold, just to show himself and them. He got up and went to the window and looked out on the building that everyone called the ice barn. The longer he watched them, the more the shadows seemed to whir and shake and blend. And then he saw her or thought he saw her, or maybe he saw her or he didn't, or then yes he saw her but no, out there on the lawn under the oaks, a pale blue shadow in the gray-green, oak-filtered moonlight, floating with a serene graceful movement. His mind played the Moonlight Sonata he was learning on the piano as it coasted in the confusing, restraining space between terror and fascination.

He collapsed under the window as a branch from the live oak scraped the pane of glass. He knew that if he got up and looked out of it, he would see her through the window. Her face, glowing white, rippling like a flame, would be looking into his. So, he cowered low under the sill and waited. He sat paralyzed under the window, certain that her image was above his, looking in, a quivering wash of white and yellow. His mind could almost see her, a glowing face emanating rays like the fiery petals of a flower. He sank down and clutched his knees to his chest.

He woke the next morning under the window and its curtain and the bright light of All Saints' Day. Someone had put a blanket over him.

The days were cooler now. They had played all afternoon with the imaginations of boys, his friend Jimmy Chauvin playing for LSU and Sammy playing for Ole Miss, two boys who would surely grow up and wear the purple-and-gold and the blue-and-red and greet each other at the end of the game with handshakes as their teammates made for the locker rooms. But today, since they were still eleven, Jimmy Chauvin had just left on his bicycle, waving goodbye to Sammy and hugging the side of the highway to stay out of the way of traffic. Tractors and trucks were returning from the fields, pulling behind them trailers shaggy and tall with cane stalks. The roads were littered with the yellowed debris of them this time of year. Car and truck tires mashed them into the pavement of state highway 308, into carelessly woven patterns.

Sammy waved back to Jimmy and watched the trailer-loads of cane stalks disappear into the sheds where the machinery would chew them up. He knew that eventually it all would become sugar, but he didn't know exactly how. He just knew that it was so, and that there would be great mounds of it, white like snow, and that was what his family sold to other people. Sugar. Great mountains of it.

He turned back from it and teed up his football. The crossbar, the thick horizontal limb of a live oak, stretched out across the lawn of Mount Teague.

"This should be the last play of the ballgame, folks. The Rebels trail Alabama 14 to 16 with one tick left on the clock. The ball is spotted on the Crimson Tide thirty-five...." He revised the degree of heroism, "*...make that the forty-five yard-line....Teague waits for the snap....and here it is....The ball is placed, and here's the kick....*"

His foot hit the ball, and it sailed away in a pathetic, tight, sideways spin, well under the crossbar-limb, out in the direction of the tenant house. It skittered and bounced across the grass, and he ran after it. He stopped to retrieve it where it came to rest, and, when he did, he saw her. It was perhaps the closest he had ever been to her. He had been warned against it by his mama.

The girl was making a clicking noise and broadcasting feed from an apron to the chickens that pecked the ground around her. Her feet were bare on the bare ground. Her hair and her eyes were black; her nose and cheeks were lightly freckled. He and the girl exchanged a quick look, a glance that said everything and nothing. He retrieved the football and went back to the spot on the lawn and the oak with the perfect crossbar-limb. He teed it up again.

*"Wait....there's a flag on the play...offsides Alabama! It looks like Teague and Ole Miss will get another chance. The ball is spotted at the forty-five....*He forgot to mark off the offsides....*make that the forty....the snap, the kick....*"

The ball ascended in a perfect end-over-end trajectory, well over the mossy, oak limb-crossbar. He leaped into the air with his little boy arms extended up. "*Ole Miss wins, 17-16! The Rebels clinch the Southeastern Conference championship!*" In his celebration, he caught a sidelong glance of her, watching him, just before she went back into the tenant house. He paused for a moment, waiting for her to come back outside.

When she didn't, he went to find his football. It had careened off the root of an oak and the trunk of the ancient magnolia and rolled into the ice barn. He got as close to the old building as his courage would allow.

At the edge where the weeds grew up around it, he peered into its darkness at the shadow of his ball. There were other shadows in there, and, among them, her shadow, the queen of all shadows.

So, he left the football inside the ice barn, with the homerun ball he had hit for the Cardinals to win the World Series the week before. Maybe his daddy or Miss Della Mae would get it for him.

Sammy, 1982

It began with a spark, as it always begins. The dragging scrape across a rough surface, the small tentative droplet of flame falling into tinder that lay innocuous and unaware and ready. The drop of flame became a puddle and then a weightless mound, a burning hillock, a fiery haystack. It flickered and danced and spread out, horizontally and vertically, following its appetite like its ancestors had done in the caves of ancient men, in the hearth fires of peasants and kings, in the rock rings of pioneers, in the fires that devoured Chicago and San Francisco, London and Rome. Every one of them the offspring of a single, small, gasping spark.

This flame, in an abandoned outbuilding on a Louisiana plantation, was much the same as the one that erupted in almost the same place over a hundred years before. It raced along eaves and probed gaps in the sagging roof. Smoke boiled out gray and blue and black into the twilight. It cackled and spat and divided and reunited with itself, even bigger. The flames tumbled out windows and chattered over the eaves. Cataracts of orange and yellow rose, waterfalls turned upward. Swaying points poured up and out and around corners, the specks of embers whirling in updrafts under the limbs and leaves of the oaks. In the amber light, mice and wrens fled from the building to join the crows and squirrels that lived in the boughs of the adjacent trees. Golden sparks swarmed under the green canopies and over the fire trucks, up into the sky with the silver specks of stars.

He sat alone on the root of a live oak tree with his arms on his knees and his fingers interlaced, golden-faced in the darkness. He looked for her silhouette in the carnival of flames, thinking he saw her apparition here, and then there, only to see that it was merely a beam or door jamb or a windowsill listing at an angle before slouching over and crashing down. But he knew it was empty–he had emptied it himself, wheeling out an old carriage and farm implements no longer useful, until there was only rotting floorboards and bare earth. There were no living creatures in the old ice barn, except for rats and mice and birds. And now they were leaving.

The firemen watched the blaze like a lion tamer watches a lion, waiting for it to cross an imaginary line to be knocked back with the spraying whip of a firehose. Their silhouettes moved in the roaring backdrop of the blaze. Some sat on the roots of the neighboring live oaks, and some stood on the running boards of the firetrucks, polished to a meticulous red. The radio squawked as the men smoked and chatted and watched the fire continue into a mass of flaming geometric shapes. In the morning, some of them would go back to their jobs at the chemical plants, welding shops, and crewboats bound for the rigs offshore. But this evening, they stood guard, making sure the fire didn't overstep its welcome and consume anything else. Every so often, one or two of them would spray the bright undersides of the illuminated live oaks, powerful blasts that recoiled the hoses and set the men straining in wide stances, as if they were wrestling the tentacles of a sea serpent. When the blast was done, the hoses suddenly relaxed, and crystal drops fell golden from the limbs and leaves in the firelight, and the men lit another cigarette and resumed their conversations as the smoke emerging from their outlines rose with the twisting flames. The winter night sky burned cold blue and the old building burned intense orange and the shadows of the live oaks danced between the burning heavens and the burning earth. The old building which had stood for over a century was giving itself up into the flames of a single night.

It had once been called the ice plant, and then the ice house, and then the ice barn. Over a century, generations of Teague children had played in the building. When he was a boy, he had asked how old the building was, and he had been told it had been there since "just after the war," though they were never sure if it had been the war that had occurred there in St. Matthew Parish or the one in Cuba or the ones in France. And when he was a boy, he had been teased by his older sisters, sometimes to tears, with stories of the ghost that lived in the old ice barn. The girls would dream up elaborate tales and underscore them with pranks–moans they would send up late on moonlit evenings like this one, floating lanterns that would swing from fishing line, sounds of lost souls wailing in penance, or for succor, or for retribution.

As a boy, on long, lazy summer days, the shadows of castoff plows and carriages and implements conspired in the afternoon darkness, coalescing into monstrous profiles, hulking shapes that threatened to march out of the ice barn and onto the lawn of Mount Teague and give him chase. The shadows breathed stale, dusty air, the breezy sighs of the malignant creatures that lurked inside the darkness, waiting for his back to turn before ambling after him with mismatched, dangling tentacles shaped like abandoned traces, horsewhips, and cane knives. In dreamy horror, he would look out his bedroom window and see her in the moonlight, or imagine he saw her, a fiery shadow on cold nights, an icy shadow on warm nights. But when he gathered his meager courage to look again for the ashen ember of the woman, there would be only the bulky form of the ice barn sitting on the distant edge of the lawn of Mount Teague. These memories were imprinted on his childhood in restless, sleeping terror, and, even as a grown man, he was careful to avoid the old barn, the ice barn, especially at night.

But on this night, the flames continued to curl and swoop and dance like the golden hair of a mermaid swaying in an ocean of fire, and he thought of her, the principal character in the same plantation-tour-of-homes legend, the same specter in the same tall tales and campfire ghost stories and unsettling bits of lore, whispered by grinning older sisters, faces up-lit by flashlights in darkened bedrooms late at night.

Alice, The Burning Lady.

Around midnight, the firemen sprayed down the blackened ground. Sammy shook hands with them and thanked them for standing by. The clearing under the oaks was dark again. The embers had floated off and burned away, and the only lights in the midnight blue were stars. The trucks of the volunteer firemen crunched down the oyster shell pavement between the alley of oaks to Highway 308 and turned toward town, and the children who had watched from the back gallery, far away at the big house, were shooed upstairs to bed. He turned one last time to look at the space where the ice barn had been. In erasing it, he had finally gotten free of her, Alice, the Burning Lady.

That's what he thought.

The morning air was fog-damp and smoky. Vibrations agitated circles in the black surface of his coffee cup as the diesel engine muttered. He took a long, rippling sip to bring down the level, so he could cradle it in his lap without spilling it. The engine grumbled and the flap on top of the exhaust pipe opened as the bulldozer moved forward, chains jangling on the plow that pushed the charred earth and timbers forward. He lifted the metal trough and retreated and brought it down again. Burnt timbers bunched together in a blackened jumble. He retreated again, and the bulldozer shuddered to a pause and then moved forward once more. The twin tracks stamped row after row of shallow, bar-shaped impressions into the cold, wet ground. The wood of the old ice barn, reduced to charcoal, snapped and fell into the muddy black ashes.

This time forward, the bulldozer shuddered as metal hit metal and a small tongue of coffee vaulted over the ceramic rim. He threw the gear shifter back and withdrew, and then he shifted and went forward again. The plow hit with a scraping, iron blow that he could feel through the corrugated steel floorboard of the bulldozer. He retreated again and turned the key, and the engine quieted in the silent buzz of the fog. He stood to see over the yellow engine housing and took a sip of coffee, then he set his cup on the hood of the bulldozer and climbed down.

There in front of the plow was a dark, square something in the blackened rubble. He retrieved a shovel from the back of the bulldozer and carefully tapped the box with the blade. When he struck it a little harder, it gave out a ring of metal on metal, the sound of a ship's bell in the mist. At the edge of the dome of fog, the sound jarred a snowy egret into flight. It lifted, up into the wet haze, disappearing after three gentle wingbeats. The shovel spooned away the ashes and blackened debris, charred bones with square nail holes that dissolved into cinders with each strike of the shovel. Everything was quiet except for the shuffling through the ashes and the fall of them as they were tossed away. And then, there it was.

He leaned on the shovel and looked at it. He struck the metal with the shovel again, and a cascade of dry, black soot fell from it. *Barn-* was revealed. He touched it with his work gloves, the back of his hand first. He pried the fingers off the right glove and touched it with his bare hand. It was iron-cold. His fingers slapped away the thin layer of ash on the top and on the front door. There, written in big-block-long-ago letters:

Barnes Safe and Lock, Third Street, Pittsburgh, Pa., and under it in fancy, sweeping letters, *FIREPROOF.* Below the lettering, a small metal plate bore an embossed inscription, *Burke & Barnes Fireproof Safe Co., Pittsburgh, Pa 129 and 131 Third Ave., Fire and Thief Proof Safes.*

He sat on the tractor plow with one glove on and considered the safe. Who had left it there? How had he missed it when he emptied the old ice barn? Where had it been? Behind a false wall, hidden away in a secret compartment? Certainly, it must have been; he and his son had emptied it completely. If the safe had been hidden, then why?

And, the biggest question of all, what was in it?

At last, he got up and retrieved his coffee cup from the hood of the bulldozer where it left a wet ring on the yellow metal. After a cold sip, he threw the rest on the ground. He started the bulldozer again and gingerly maneuvered the plow under the safe. The plow was raised, and the safe fell into the concave of it with a loud crash that shuddered everything. He slowly trundled across the yard, keeping an eye on the raised plow with the safe in it, lifted to heaven like an offering. At the entrance to another, more modern shed, he lowered the plow and sprayed the ashes from the safe with a hosepipe as the bulldozer popped rhythmically in neutral. The safe seemed to become denser, blacker, as the ash was washed away.

He vaulted back up into the cab of the bulldozer and shifted it forward, into the fluorescent light of the shed full of trailers and cane harvesters. Inside, he lowered the plow and the safe down onto the concrete floor gently, gently, until it teetered and grated on the concrete, back legs-front-legs-and then all four. The bulldozer retreated outside and went silent. Inside the shed on the concrete floor, the safe sat dripping under the fluorescent lights.

Sammy examined it. It was about as big as a small refrigerator a student might use in a dorm room at college. The lock required two keys.

He pushed at the top of the safe to see if he could tilt it back on its edge, but it was too heavy. He sat back on the plow again. Outside the shed, the fog hung in the air, and a crow sat in a cypress somewhere and cawed into it. The sky was only a vague idea as the air swirled with the fizz of tiny water droplets. Despite the cool of the day, his hair was wet.

The children inside the great house were still asleep, and his wife had gone into Thibodaux to make groceries. He eased the backdoor shut behind him and looked in a kitchen drawer, through spare screwdrivers, flashlights with batteries, flashlights without batteries, old butter dishes with rubber bands and paper clips and safety pins. He took off his left glove and put it on the kitchen counter with his right glove, and a slight sift of ash fell. He scratched through another drawer, looking for a set of two nineteenth century keys, though he knew they wouldn't be there. There were ballpoint pens, a menagerie of old papers, children's drawings, scotch tape dispensers. But no keys. He thought for a moment.

His boots pounded on the floorboards of the central hallway, past the portrait of his great-grandfather, old Sam Teague, the ancient patriarch in his Confederate uniform with a hand resting on a book. Old Sam Teague was portrayed in such a way that his eyes followed passersby, and again Sammy felt the disapproval of the great man from his portrait. In his great-grandfather's study, which was now his, Sammy went through the ancient mahogany desk that had always been the beating heart of Mount Teague, a place of ledgers and registers, contracts, documents, invoices, and reports, since the days of the subject of the portrait in the central hallway. He looked through every drawer, but there were no keys.

Sammy's heavy footsteps pounded softly through the central hallway past the portrait again, the ancient man with the same nickel-gray eyes of all the Teague men, even Sammy's son Quint, who at fifteen was asleep upstairs on this early Saturday. The old stairs creaked under Sammy's work boots. He took off his old flannel coat and put it on the knob of the bannister, and another sift of ashes fell on the wooden floorboards of the landing. In the master bedroom, the curtains were open. Outside the windows, there were green leaves, gray oak branches, and a blanket of white fog.

He went through his nightstand. Louis Lamour novels, *The Farmers' Almanac*, the December 1981 issue of *Scientific American* with an article about how barn owls hear, and several old issues of *Louisiana Conservationist*. He paused a minute, looked to the door, and then looked through his wife's nightstand. *Today's Missal*, a small white plastic bottle with a gold cross on it that said *Holy Water*, a paper clip of coupons, an assortment of prayer cards, and two or three Rosaries, though he couldn't tell from the tangle of beads. There was a small, brown pouch with a leather string, bearing the inscription, *The Scapular Promise of Our Lady of Mount Carmel*. He held it in his hands, turning it over and over. He looked outside to the patch of black earth lying cool and wet in the fog. Something clicked in the stillness of the sleeping house. The bedroom door eased open, and the face of his youngest, Judee, appeared. She pattered in short strides to him and pulled her pacifier from her mouth.

"Daddy, you dusty like that chimney *sleep* on Mary Poppins," the girl whispered, touching his shirt and hugging him. He brushed the ash off her nightgown.

"Go back to bed, now, my baby," he said, and he kissed her on top on her tousled head, black hair like her mama, the smell of some fruity shampoo the little girl and her sister adored. Her footfalls drummed lightly and then ended with the squeak of a bed and the rustle of sheets.

Sammy returned the leather necklace with the Scapular Promise back to the drawer with the prayer cards and the Holy Water and the Rosaries and the coupons. There were no old keys in either drawer. But he had figured that would be the case. He walked out on the landing, past his flannel coat on the bannister knob and the small layer of ash on the floorboards, heavy boots touching softly on the stairs. Downstairs, he began the search again for every spare or mismatched key, through junk drawers, from nails hanging on the insides of seldom-used closets, even in the attic on the surfaces of rafters. But the keys had apparently long been lost.

Back in the shed under the fluorescent lights, he picked at the lock for the better part of an hour with a set of Allen wrenches and picks on a lanyard. At last, he decided that the lock had melted in the heat anyway.

He slouched back in a folding chair, his arms folded across his chest. The laces of his boots had become undone, the leather strands limp as spaghetti. His lips pursed, and his chin twisted as he wondered what could be inside and how he could get there. The iron fortress sat across from him on the cold-hard floor, silent and knowing, the great sweeping letters of Mr. Burke and Mr. Barnes' safe with the taunting inscription, *Fireproof & Thiefproof.* The black box pulled from the rubble, like the ones they put in airplanes.

When he heard the dog barking at the house and the crunch of tires over the oyster shells, he looked down at his watch. An hour and a half had passed without him even noticing it. He got up and brushed off his pants and started for the great house.

He kissed her in the driveway over a paper bag and then helped her bring in the groceries while the dog, the same kind of red, mismatched dog they had had before, a dog of many dogs, barked around them. The dog bounded up the steps with them, slipping through the screen door as they went in, wagging her tail and smiling in the kitchen as each bag was set on the counter.

"It was raining hard in Thibodaux," she said as she reached into a bag and opened a cabinet.

"Store crowded?"

"Nah, I think I beat the Saturday rush. Just old people, mostly." She folded an empty Delchamps bag and put it in a drawer with others. "You got much done, bay?" She opened a cabinet and reached in another bag.

"Got it leveled off. Not much left of it." He pulled out a five-pound bag of rice and a bag of potatoes and turned to put them away.

"Leave them out," she said. "I'm gonna make a gumbo for the firemen and bring it down to the station. For comin' out."

He left them on the counter. "Yard looks funny without the old ice barn there. Kinda empty."

"You the one wanted it gone," she said, folding over another empty bag. She put her arms around his waist and kissed his cheek before returning to her work.

For a moment, he was sorry he had done it, but he didn't say anything. He sat in comfortable silence and watched her start her roux. The way she pulled up the sleeves of her long-sleeved New Orleans Saints T-shirt. The way her blue jeans still fit her. The way she pulled her black hair into a ponytail and tied it back. The way she tapped the spoon on the edge of the pot. The way her black eyes studied the pot while she leisurely hummed a song that he knew to be in French. He and the dog watched her.

She set water to boiling in a Magnalite pot and began cutting potatoes for the potato salad. At last, he got up and kissed her on the cheek. She turned, kissed him on the lips, and resumed stirring the roux. He went back to the shed and the safe. He had meant to tell her about it but hadn't.

The rain was indeed moving in. The morning was slowly turning dark, and the limbs and leaves and branches were twitching and swaying. In the gathering dark, a light flared from inside the shed. It flashed and glowed, on and off, a miraculous white light like something painted on a prayer card. The rain began coming down. He paused for a moment and then pulled his coat up and ran toward the light in the shed.

Inside, a man was using a blowtorch to cut off the end of a bathtub. Along his left forearm, his name was tattooed, *Teeter*, the result of the slow cooking-down of the nickname his parrain had given him as a child, *tête dur,* hardhead. Beside him was a three-foot concrete statue of the Blessed Mother, hands clasped, and head tilted beatifically in blue and white. She stood passively at his side, her concrete hands supple and lithe, her eyes closed softly in a benediction. The fierce blue light blared orange across the tub as Teeter finished the cut and pushed away the offcut end with his workboot.

"Say, baws-man," he said as he lifted his visor. His face was mostly nose–everything else was an afterthought. He pointed to the bathtub and the statue. "I made mama 'n 'em a grotto for Christmas. Now my nanny wants one. I had to drive all over the Parish, but I finally found an old tub in somebody's trash." He pointed to the black iron safe with the silent brass nozzle of his torch. "You knock over a bank, baws-man?"

Sammy snorted a quick laugh. "Nah, I found this where we burned that old ice barn last night. Must've been behind a wall or in the attic or under a floorboard."

"I tried to move it," Teeter said, "Mais, it's some heavy." He looked at the writing on the front of the safe. "And fireproof? That's for true." He looked to Sammy. "You got the key, baws-man?"

"Nope. Long gone, I guess."

"Hmp," Teeter pulled his mouth tight and grunted in agreement.

Simultaneously, they both glanced at the torch and exchanged an understanding look. Teeter struck it to life. It gave a small, hoarse roar.

"Well, I guess we gonna have to talk a little French to it, then," Teeter said. He put a cigarette to his lips, peered down it, and lit it with the torch. Taking a puff, he flipped down his visor. Wafts of smoke boiled out from under it with each exhalation.

Baws-man, Teeter's voice was muffled by the visor and the cigarette in his lips under it. *Baws-man! Mist' Sammy!* Teeter tapped on his own visor and pointed to another one on the work table behind them. *Comme ça.* Sammy put it on and flipped down the visor.

The blue splendor of the torch began cutting, and smoke filtered up from the metal. Suddenly, Teeter stopped cutting and pointed the flaming nozzle away.

If it's Lafitte's treasure, we split it fitty-fitty, say baws? His voice was dampened and small. Their visors were expressionless as they looked at each other like two robots. Teeter put out his free hand.

All right, Sammy's muffled voice yelled back from under the hood, and he shook Teeter's hand.

The blue comet seared into the metal, encompassing the lock and leaving a trail of smoke that lifted lazily into the air. The iridescent flame swept around like a second hand until it completed the circle. The flame fell silent, and they lifted their visors. Teeter reached a finger to touch the lock and quickly withdrew it.

"*Poo-yi-yi*!" He shook his finger. "Shit, tha's hot!" He put on a glove and touched the cutout disk again and lifted it from the hole he had cut. He placed it on the concrete and reached into the opening and pulled. The door swung open.

Sammy looked over Teeter's shoulder. They peered into the safe.

"Well, ain't no treasure, no," Teeter said with mock dejection. He hadn't expected any. "Mah! Jus' a bunch of old papers and shit. All yours, I guess, baws."

Sammy took a quick look as Teeter returned to the grotto and picked up a grinder to file smooth the cut edges of the bathtub. Sammy put the papers back in the safe and went to help Teeter by steadying the tub. All the while, he kept looking over his shoulder at the safe sitting across the shed from them. Sparks flew across his vision. The door was still open and proclaiming the century-old boast, *Fireproof & Thiefproof.*

When Teeter was finished, he ran a hand over the edge to check for smoothness. Then they loaded the tub-grotto and the Blessed Mother into the back of Teeter's old Ford. The rain had slackened, but Teeter put a tarp over the truck bed out of respect for the Mother of Jesus. Sammy lifted the gate and slapped the side of Teeter's truck.

"Say baws!" Teeter shouted over his shoulder and out the window of the truck. "If I don't see you, Happy Mardi Gras!"

"Happy Mardi Gras!" Sammy shouted back, and Teeter waved in the rearview mirror and drove away.

Sammy turned back to the shed. The rain continued a rhythm on the metal roof. In the massive shed, half a dozen green-and-yellow cane harvesters rested and waited for the fall. A few feet away from them on the floor of cold concrete under the pervasive hum of the fluorescent lights, the safe sat passively, forgotten by time for a hundred years and now remembered again.

He sat and looked at it. He felt as though it were looking at him, too. They sat and looked at each other as the rain pattered on the aluminum roof and the air turned a little colder. Finally, he pulled up a pressed plastic chair and sat next to it. He hesitated for a moment, then pulled out the contents, a hodgepodge of papers, and put them on a worktable next to the welding visors. When it was empty, he sat on the table and shuffled through them.

The first was a yellowed document, the weight of poster paper:

Baptised into the family of God this 23rd day of May 1853,

Holy Trinity Church, Guildford, Surrey,

Alice Victoria Elizabeth Lamb

Suffer the little children, and forbid them not, to come unto me: for of such is the kingdom of heaven.

The paper slipped from his gloved hands and floated to the concrete floor. His breath steamed into a cold cloud as he clumsily picked up the baptismal certificate with padded fingers and set it aside. There was a Church of England *Book of Common Prayer*, with the inscription, *Alice Lamb, Ancoats, Manchester.* And under it, sheet music. Chopin. Liszt. Beethoven. He held one of them up. *Sonata in C#m.* It was the Moonlight Sonata he had learned as a boy. He hummed the notes of a few bars as his right hand stroked them in the air as he thought of those days, days of practicing in the central hallway as breezes funneled through, legs dangling from the piano bench with feet that couldn't quite reach the pedals of the ancient piano. He replaced the pages in the safe.

Under that, an ancient edition of Audubon's *The Birds of America.* Inscribed on the first page was,

For Papa, Christmas, 1869

"All things bright and beautiful
All creatures great and small
All things wise and wonderful
The Lord God made them all."

-your loving daughter,
Alice

And in the pages of Audubon's book, a sheaf of papers written in a different hand, "A Description of the Serpents of southern America," and, "A Treatise on the Choupique, or, Shoe-Pick, of the Louisiana

Bayous." Sammy thumbed through them and then set them aside. In the very back of the book were several rejection letters from something called The Linnaen Society in a place called Burlington Hall, The Strand, London. They were addressed to a Rev. Arthur Lamb, St. Matthew Parish, Louisiana, America. He opened one. The writing was that of a hundred years earlier and a little hard to follow.

"*Dear Reverend Lamb*," it began, "*we have received your submission for publication. It is with modest regret that I must inform you that the committee has agreed that whilst there is some tepid interest in its subject, there is insufficient interest at present to warrant publication. It is our opinion that your time would be better served in the devotion of your energies to ecclesiastical matters rather than scientific ones. Furthermore, any subsequent submissions shall be returned to you without consideration….*"

Sammy refolded the letter and tucked it back in the envelope that said in embossed letters,

LINNAEN SOCIETY, BURLINGTON HALL, LONDON.

He held it up to the light and ran his fingers over the raised letters, and then put it on the workbench. Next, there was some sort of document that read The Confederate States of America. He read the title and thought of the uniformed man in the portrait in the central hallway. Shame welled up in him again, and he set it aside when he saw a card with the name *Musson*, and the address, *372 Esplanade, New Orleans, La.* He put it in Audubon's book, with the rejection letters, the document issued by the Confederate States of America, and the baptismal certificate.

There were two books, *Mrs. Beeton's Book of Household Management* and *The Young Wife: Or, Duties of Woman in the Marriage Relation* by a man named William Andrus Alcotts. He set them aside and reached for the remaining thing in the safe. It was a book, a girl's diary, with the inscription on the inside cover:

If this book is found, the bearer is kindly asked to return it as promptly as is practicable to:

Miss Alice Lamb, 25 Pewley Hill,
Guildford, Surrey

Sammy sat on the worktable and looked around the shed. The light hummed and whirred in bright fluorescence. The rain had slackened into a slow, cold simmer, and his breath was a chilly vapor. Like a thief, he gathered everything he had taken out of the safe, pausing halfway through to hastily remove his gloves. He found a white plastic five-gallon bucket with the red letters, Pierre Part Store, on the side. Gingerly, he placed everything in it and snapped on the lid. Then he lugged it up to the house in the steady rain, picking around puddles, and placed it in his study on the floor by his desk, the old mahogany desk of every Samuel Teague since the first one over a hundred years ago. And then he waited for the courage to read through them, the rendered testimony, a trail of paper, the witness of a specter, the woman who had always haunted him.

At last, he sat down with the diary and opened the cracked leather cover. His eyes strained to read the century-old handwriting. It began when she was eleven years old, an age at which anything is possible.

Alice Lamb, 1864

Guildford, Surrey, England

1 AUGUST 1864. This diary is a gift from Mama and Papa. Papa says that it is a great undertaking to begin an account of one's life and he sees no reason why I cannot begin one now. He is a vicar and says that it is what the apostles did when they wrote down the life of Jesus. Mama says that I should want to grow into a sensible young woman happy and useful as I am named after two queens and a princess. My namesake is Princess

Alice who is twenty and is a Hessian princess and has a new baby Princess Victoria Alberta named after her mother the Queen and also her father dearly departed Prince Albert who the Queen misses and still morns [*sic*]. I am also named after two queens Elizabeth the old queen and Victoria the present queen.

4 AUGUST 1864. Across the street on Pewley Hill Road lives our neighbour Mr. Phillips. He was in the Queens Hussars and was sent to a place called Crimea. He smokes on his doorstep all day and receives a pension whilst his sister works. Papa says it is doubtful that he shall ever work again. If he sees me when I leave my house he yells hallo to me from across the street and I return his hallo. He sits in the heat with his waistcoat open and his hair wild and shaggy and smokes on the steps of their house which is down from ours. Sometimes he talks to himself as he waves at flies that are swarming around his head. Either no one else can see them or else they are very small. His sister is at work all day in a shop on the High Street.

8 AUGUST 1864. Mama says that I have cousins who live in Australia. They are not first cousins but rather second or third cousins. We share a common grandfather and grandmother on Mama's side, perhaps Mama's grandparents. Mama says that she has not seen them since she was a girl but sometimes she receives a letter though it has been a very long time since she has and she prays that they are well. Mama says that it is always hot there for Christmas and there is seldom any snow on Christmas or any other day. We hoped to get a card from them last Christmas but we did not. It would be a good thing to have a large family with which to play and share secrets and big dinners at holiday time, but it is only Mama and Papa and I. Mama says that it is God's will for us but perhaps one day He shall grant us a larger family. I think I shall pray for one, for Papa who is a vicar says that God hears earnest prayers, especially those of children.

13 AUGUST 1864. I have a trinket box which is an old tobacco box. I have a goose feather and a duck feather and a peacock feather which

seems to have a great staring eye upon it. I also have a gemstone that I found at the beach at Brighton that I am sure is a saffire. Papa says it is possible but hasn't taken me to see the jeweler on the High Street in Guildford though I have asked. I keep the box under my bed next to my church shoes which are fancier than my school and play shoes. I have had the saffire since I was very small and I have shewn it to no one except Papa and Mama and Mrs. Sullivan who keeps the vicarage.

15 AUGUST 1864. Mr. Phillips our neighbour is frightened of many things. He is frightened of horses. He is also frightened whenever there is a loud noise such as the fall of a large object like a box or a crate being unloaded. How very sad for him! Mama believes that it is because of something dreadful that happened to him when he was in the Queens Hussars in the place called Crimea. Somedays he likes for me to read to him. I read to him from Roderick Random and The Tales of King Arthur. Sometimes he sings and sometimes he cries. It is a very sad thing to see a grown-up cry. Sometimes I can manage a smile from him if I tell him a clever riddle but usually he sits on the steps of the house he shares with his sister who works in a shop on the High Street.

18 AUGUST 1864. Papa has a great chest made of oak in which he keeps all of his sermons. It is very handsome indeed and sometimes I sit upon it when I visit him in his study. It is perhaps my favourite place to sit in the whole world. Papa's sermon this morning was entitled God is not our servant, we are His. Papa is a very good speaker in front of other people which is quite a good thing as he is a vicar. It was a warm day and the windows of the church were opened and I confess that I looked out them a good deal at the birds that flew past. A jackdaw landed on the roof of the house opposite the church and strutted upon it before flying away. Mama pulled me up when everyone had stood to sing and I had not noticed.

20 AUGUST 1864. Today was a Saturday and Papa and I ambeled among the haystacks and Papa said that this is exactly the kind of ground where all manner of serpents might lay in wait for mice but we do not

have many serpents in England or anywhere else in Britain. Still I kept my eyes on the grass that reached my knees and Papa's shins and I put my hand in Papa's as we went along. Papa says that a snail carries his house upon his back as does the tortoise. He says that even though they are very slow God has made them very wise creatures indeed. Sheep and geese are not very wise. I collected some interesting stones for my trinket box.

22 AUGUST 1864. Papa says we are to go into the city this Friday for a visit before I begin my term in school. It shall certainly be an adventure as London is a place where there are many magnificent sights as well as robbers and pickpockets. Our housekeeper Mrs. Sullivan says so. She says that I should mind myself and avoid talking to strangers as there are many who would like such a dainty morsel as me.

26 AUGUST 1864. Today was a grand day for we took the train from Guildford into London. Papa brought with him a satchel of papers and took them to a place which is called the Linnaen Society. I know this because it is chiseled in stone on the front of the building where it says LINNAEN SOCIETY. The keeper summoned a man in a tailcoat who came down. Papa said that the man in the tailcoat is the secretary of the Linnaen Society. Papa gave him the papers and he (the secretary) behaved as if Papa had given him the gift of an unwanted kitten or puppy (Papa told Mama) but the man thanked Papa though I do not think he meant it. Papa was in great spirits when we left. We walked a while and went to High Holborn Street to the Hamley Toy Shop which is as famous as it is big. There was a doll I fancied and Mama said that perhaps Father Christmas shall bring one much like it in December if I am good. I wonder if by 'much like it' she means that I might have a brother or a sister which is the thing that I should like more than anything in the world. Perhaps that is it and I shall keep wishing for it to be so. In Covent Garden we saw a street magician. He wore wool gloves with the fingers cut off and pretended to pull a coin out of my ear. He shewed it to the crowd of us gathered, closed his hand and then opened the brown glove and it was gone again. Thence to our amazement he produced it

again from his mouth! We children looked up to our parents and there was polite clapping. A man in a top hat muttered that there must be some trick to it and the street magician winked at me as we moved on. In Trafalgar Square there is a tall pillar with a statue of Lord Nelson. Below it there was a Punch and Judy show. Mama was reluctant for us to stop, for she wanted to go into the National Gallery which is a very stately building Mama says. Papa said oh let the girl enjoy the show with the other children as there were many boys and girls sitting on the lawn in front of the small theatre with striped roof and a scene of countryside painted behind the stage within the booth that is the theatre. Mama let go of my hand and I sat next to a boy in a blue suit and a girl in a pinafore and I arranged my skirts over my legs and petticoat. Punch the puppet and Judy also a puppet had long noses and red cheeks and little arms. Punch would become angry with Judy and the constable and the clown and thrash at them with a stick which he held in his little arms and we children laughed and laughed and I saw Mama and Papa smiling at me. When the show was over a man came from within the booth and collected a three-pence from each of us and put it in his hat. The girl in the pinafore hadn't a three-pence and so Papa paid for her as well. Did you enjoy sitting with the other children? Mama asked. Yes I said because it was true I did.

Sammy, 1982

When he looked up from the diary to the clock, the round dial was dissected by a horizontal line, a quarter to three. A cold afternoon rain was falling on the knee-high cane and the oaks and the roof of Mount Teague. And under that roof was a man with a young English girl's diary, a girl who would grow up to be the ghost that would haunt him.

He hooked the clasp and set the diary in the top drawer of his desk, the mahogany throne of the Kingdom of Mount Teague. It bore the wear of a hundred years and needed refinishing, but he didn't want to remove any of the sacred patina, accumulated by the generations of great men, and one in particular, a warrior who had ridden off on horseback to fight blue-coated invaders and then had returned to become a champion of agriculture and industry. Sometimes Sammy felt unworthy to even sit at the desk of the original Samuel Teague, a learned man with a library filled with books, a soldier and scholar who seemed to scowl at him in displeasure from the portrait in the hall just outside the study.

Sammy rose and put on his red flannel work coat, keeping his eyes on the cypress planks, away from the portrait on the wall and its judgment. On the front gallery, the air was cold and dense and wet, and breath became a steamy chill. He put his hands in his pockets and walked under the cover of the oaks to the highway. Out in the fields, the cane was coming up. As soon as the ground had dried, he and Teeter and the other hands would have to plow up the roots of the recently-cut second ratoons, cane that had grown and been cut through three seasons and would no longer yield enough sugar to make it worthwhile. The older hands called the plowing of the roots of spent cane "busting stubble."

At the end of the lane where it met the Thibodaux Road, a St. Matthew Parish school bus passed on the wet pavement, the big tires making the sound of a wave on a beach. Several hundred yards down the road, the bus slowed and stopped at a trailer house, and the airbrake belched, and the signs deployed. The bus released a few children, so far away that he could see them but not hear them. The lights played red-and-yellow on the pavement, and then the sign collapsed to the side of the bus and the lights faded away from red-and-yellow, and the bus grumbled down the highway.

The road fell silent again under the weight of the sky. He turned and walked down the lane of oaks, his workboots crunching on the white shells of the drive. On the porch, he tapped his boots, one on the other, and went inside his house. The portrait of his grandfather scowled down at him in the central hallway. A small, bright voice chirped, "Daddy, look. Mardi Gras colors."

His daughter Elizabeth held up a picture she had drawn in purple, gold, and green. He appraised it under furrowed eyebrows and said, "Mardi Gras colors. Is that a fact?" as if he hadn't known it.

"It's the Krewe of Jupitre," she said, and her little finger pointed to the picture. "Look you're the king!"

"Wow, that's pretty good," he said, though he knew that, unlike the gray-uniformed subject in the portrait on the wall, he would never be the

King of Jupitre. He, Sammy Teague, the great-grandson of old Sam Teague, the original King of Jupitre, had abandoned his duty by dodging the draft and going to Canada and so had become the parish pariah, the subject of whispers and clicking tongues.

That evening, he had gone to sleep in his study with the diary in his lap and had woken up just enough to make it upstairs. It took a while for him to summon it back, but sleep finally came to him as the cold settled on the house and his family. He dreamed of a girl with golden hair on a bus, a St. Matthew Parish school bus, full of dark-headed children, both black and white, except for this one girl with golden hair. He couldn't see her face, only a fleeting side view. He had to see her, though he didn't know why. In his dream, he followed the bus everywhere, over bridges and on ferries across the river that only took seconds to cross, under oaks and down Canal Street and Rue St. Sulpice in Montreal and along the highway to Grand Isle amid the yellow marsh grass. Every time he pulled even with the bus and almost saw her, she would look away, and when, in the inertia of his dream, he would fall back behind the bus, he would see her looking at where he had been. The golden hair shimmered in the monochrome of his dream.

He awoke to the sound of a dog barking. His sleep was so deep that, at first, he thought it was the neighbors' dog on Rue St. Zotique, in Montreal, and then, as layers of slumber fell from him in gray sheets, he realized it wasn't the neighbors' dog. He looked at the windows and the door. *Oh, that's right,* he thought. *I'm home again. This is the house I grew up in. My house. My dog.* Even after almost five years, it was hard for him to believe that he was no longer in exile.

The clock glowed in green vertical and horizontal matchsticks, *1:07.* Sammy toed into his slippers. Betsy was still asleep, black hair fanning out and twisting among white sheets. He drew his robe around himself and then carefully, quietly went down the stairs. The dog was outlined in moonlight on one of the front windows. She was called Pongeaux, named by his daughter Elizabeth after the Disney Dalmatian, even though the dog was female and reddish-brown with a curled over tail like the dog that had sired her, Chanceux, but at night she was only a shadow, like every living and non-living thing is at night. She glanced back at her owner with the purposeful look a dog has when it's doing its duty, and she looked back out the window and launched a quick bark.

Shh! Pongeaux! He shushed, *hush, girl. Hush.* She blinked and licked her lips apologetically. Out on the highway, a set of headlights sped away, followed by the red glow of taillights behind them, all to the accelerating roar of an engine. Sammy grabbed a flashlight.

He opened the door and went out into the moonlit front porch. Pongeaux curved her body to go through the door around him. Sammy shined the beam back to the front of the house. Everything looked normal. This time.

He and the dog descended the front porch. Sammy scanned the outbuildings, dark shapes in the pale moonlight. Pongeaux went directly to Sammy's truck, her nose fanning back and forth, gathering clues. She followed them to the driver's side and sat there on the white shells.

He picked through the puddles in the yard and shined the light. It had happened again. This time it was his truck and not the barn or the house.

There scrawled on the door panel in jagged letters was a message similar to the ones before:

DODGER.

And under it, another:

PAS BON. *No good.*

He went back in and to his study. There would be no sleeping now, so he went to his study in his robe and slippers and opened the drawer with the diary.

Alice, 1864

2 SEPTEMBER 1864. We have returned home to Surrey and I went across Pewley Hill Road to visit Mr. Phillips. He says that a goose can crane his neck but a crane cannot goose his neck. What silly things Mr. Phillips says!

4 SEPTEMBER 1864. At church today Papa prayed that the war in America should be over soon. Mr. Phillips was in a war in Crimea. Mama

says that I am not to speak of it to him as it is said that he saw many dreadful things.

5 SEPTEMBER 1864. School begins today as Papa has paid a subscription fee for me to attend the Guildford School so says Mrs. Sullivan. We begin our day with prayers and then we sing a hymn and then we sing God Save the Queen and we take lessons in Arithmetic, Reading, Grammar, and Penmanship. At lunch we are permitted an hour to go home though some girls bring a pail from home and that is what I do. Some girls live in the upper rooms at the Guildford School and they are called borders *[sic]*. We begin the afternoon with drill lessons. We march in place and bend our knees. Some of the girls giggle and it causes the rest of us to do so and we are scolded by Miss Goodforth who is our teacher. We skip around the room single file until we are almost out of breath and then we return to our desks and our slates and our chalk for history and geography lessons.

8 SEPTEMBER 1864. There are several girls in my form at school who are named Alice. They are Alice Latham, Alice Holloway, Alice Macfarlane and me, Alice Lamb. Alice Macfarlane is called redhead Alice or sometimes Red Alice. I am sometimes called Golden Alice because of my hair which is much like Mama's though hers has a little grey in it. Papa whispers that I am not to mention it. He says that Mama is rather vain on matters such as her hair. In my form there are also two Louises (Davies and Pidger) a Victoria, a Helena, and a Beatrice. We are all named after the Queen's daughters though there are girls in our form who are not and are named after old aunts or their grandmums or ladies from the Bible. Many of the boys in our town are named after the Queen's sons and some are named for their fathers or for men in the Bible. We are all girls of eleven but it is hard to imagine that in less than ten years' time that we should have husbands and babies. For now we are girls and have our favourite dolls and treat them as if they are babies though some girls have forsaken their dolls as they have baby brothers and sisters to tend. Many of the girls have large families but I am not to envy them as it is not a Christian virtue, Mama says.

12 SEPTEMBER 1864. At the Guildford School we wear skirts that would keep our knees cold were it not for our stockings. We also wear pinafores and frocks with puffed sleeves as well and straw hats with blue ribbons about the crown which is the top of the hat. When we begin the upper forms girls may wear beautiful long skirts with blue spencers and bodices underneath that are more fitted. I look forward to the day that I shall wear one. On Tuesday and Wednesday afternoons we study French which is taught by Miss Latour who is from Paris and is quite pretty. She is also ever so nice and is patient with us. I find the French language comes quite easy for me especially the pronunciation. Miss Latour says that some of the sound must pass through one's nose. Or as she says it nooze and some of the girls snicker but I do not. It is quite easy to learn things from her as she has a pleasant manner and encourages us. We write in chalk on slates but the upper forms are allowed notebooks and inkwells. Miss Goodforth says we are not to be trusted with paper and ink. When we are in the upper forms we shall get to wear longer skirts and fitted bodices and spencers and we shall also get to use pen and ink as well.

14 SEPTEMBER 1864. Papa received a letter which made him rather sad. Mama stood behind Papa with her hand on his shoulder. It seemed to help his spirits for at last he managed a smile though the smile was still rather sad somehow. Apparently to them I am a man of no importance, he said. Well then dear you are of the greatest importance to me, Mama said and she kissed his cheek. He smiled again though he still looked unhappy. His hair has turned almost all white and he looks very much older to me. Mama still looks rather young and sometimes those who do not know them think they are father and daughter. Mama seems more distressed by it than Papa. Later I ran and sat in Papa's lap and put my head on his shoulder. My beautiful daughter, you are both a pride and a pleasure to me, he said, and he kissed me on my forehead.

18 SEPTEMBER 1864. This morning I rummaged in Papa's desk a thing I am not to do and I found the letter. It was from the Linnaen Society at

Burlington Hall. It is a sientific *[sic]* society that Papa wishes to join but he is not allowed to do so as he is only a vicar and is thought to not know anything about sientific matters.

19 SEPTEMBER 1864. When I run it is as if one foot is trying to step on the other and the other girls say that I move about like a pigeon or a goose. It is hurtful but I shan't show it. Mama says that I shall have long legs one day like her family and a fine figure but that it shall take time for me to grow into them and until then I should mind how I get about.

20 SEPTEMBER 1864. If I had a sister or perhaps a brother we could read and tell ghost stories late at night whilst Mama and Papa jump about on their bed, though we my sister and I would be scolded for doing so.

21 SEPTEMBER 1864. In French hello is bonjour unless it is night and then it is bon soir. Miss Latour says that I have very good pronunciation and that someday soon she and I shall be able to have a conversation in la belle langue as she calls it which means the beautiful language. It of course is French.

23 SEPTEMBER 1864. Alice Hedges is one of six she always says the youngest save one. Alice Macfarlane red Alice is one of seven second most and she goes on about changing nappies and feeding her younger siblings who are twins a boy and a girl. The boy is named Bertie after the Prince. The girl's name is Victoria after the Queen. Louise Davies is forever going on about how difficult it is to be in a large family and wearing the outgrown dresses and shoes of her sisters. I envy them plainly but envy is a sin and I am not to indulge in it.

24 SEPTEMBER 1864. Saturday again and Mama took me to sit in the scale of the poulterer on the High Street and I now weigh seven stone and stand well over five feet tall. I think I shall be tall like mother and that is also what Papa thinks. Two hundred and twenty yards a furlong makes. The weather has cooled and I must wear a scarf and jacket on days such as this.

26 SEPTEMBER 1864. Miss Goodforth has us recite together:

Farthing, ha'penny, penny
Penny six, a sixpence makes
Six pence two, a shilling makes
Shillings five, a crown makes
Shillings twenty, a pound makes
Shillings one-and-twenty a guinea makes

The sweets at Mr. Reynolds the confectioner on the High Street cost half a sixpence. They are a favourite of Papa's and I like them as well.

28 SEPTEMBER 1864. Today as we were skipping rope after lunch Alice Latham said her Mum says they shan't have anymore. Anymore what? I asked. Babies, she said as she picked up the end of the rope. It was my turn to skip and I became entangled in the rope and fell with a hole in my stocking and a skinned knee. Miss Latour ran to see to me as I was crying though it did not hurt so very much.

30 SEPTMBER 1864. Alice Latham says that she heard that Mr. Phillips' sister kisses men for money. I said that is a dreadful thing to say when you don't know if it is true or not. She says dreadful or not it is what she heard and that it costs two shillings. I shan't repeat it for whether or not it is true it is not our affair and a horrid thing to say.

1 OCTOBER 1864. Papa and I took the train into London for the day. We visited the Kew Gardens and saw the orchestra of a man named August Manns. I thought it funny that there is a man named Mr. Manns. Mama scolded Papa a little and said that I was being indulged and that a vicar's stipend wasn't enough for it. Oh, but Winnie, the girl enjoys it so, he said, Let her have a little enjoyment. It can only be for her betterment. The violin sang the first note and all the other instruments sang with it to keep them in tune. That is what Papa said. The orchestra was like an animal menagerie to me, a string section of violins and cellos, bows

stabbing in the same direction like the quills of a porcupine, kettle drums like the steps of an elephant, the double bass groaning of the tubas like hippos and the blare of trumpets like the hoarse call of birds in the jungle. And set in the middle of the strings a harp like a swan with graceful neck.

6 OCTOBER 1864. As I was crossing the street today I was thinking of the orchestra and was almost struck by a carriage. Mr. Phillips grabbed me at the last minute and pulled me away. Child, child, innocent child! Mama shreeked *[sic]* and then ran across to hug me and kiss me. She thanked Mr. Phillips heartily. Mr. Phillips went back to his door stoop. He wears a coat now with the cooler weather though someone his sister perhaps has had to patch the elbows where there were holes from wear.

7 OCTOBER 1864. Today by the stone wall on the green we were skipping rope and singing rhymes. These are my favourites.

> Lady Bird, Lady Bird, Fly away home,
> Your house is on fire, your children will burn
>
> Sing a Song of Sixpence, A bag full of Rye,
> Four and twenty Naughty boys, Baked in a Pie.
>
> There was an Old Woman, Lived under a Hill,
> And if she ain't gone, she lives there still.

We sang and chanted the rhymes whilst the rope slapped on the cobblestones and our feet kept time with each jump. The leaves are turning yellow brown and orange some of them.

8 OCTOBER 1864. Mrs. Sullivan and I made biscuits for Mr. Phillips and I brought them to him in a basket with a bow. He seemed to not know what to do with them and retired inside with them without saying thank you.

12 OCTOBER 1864. Today Miss Latour had me lead the class in the reading of the French lesson in which Pierre and his Ma-ma go to see the great museum in Paris which is called the Louvre. Miss Latour says that my pronunciation is effortless or eff-fare-less as she says it.

13 OCTOBER 1864. I was scolded again today by Miss Goodforth. Miss Lamb! Stay to your task!

I cannot help it. Later, I am last to come from the cloak room. I neglect my shoelaces. I forget my bonnet for chapel. Then I sit in chapel and my mind wanders again. I believe I should like to play the harp.

14 OCTOBER 1864. Papa and Mama tell me that I am to receive a present soon. I hope it is news that I shall be a sister. Whilst Mama helps Mrs. Sullivan cook downstairs I think of names for our new baby for certainly that is what it shall be.

15 OCTOBER 1864. The present that I have received is a piano. It is a handsome one made by John Broadwood and Sons, Great Pulteney Street, Soho, London, as it says over the part which is the keyboard in lettering which is in gold and is quite fancy. I sit and lightly strike a key and Mama says that it is excellent that I have found middle C. Then she explains the flats and sharps and octaves and the notes which are all named after letters though only up to G. There are pedals, one called a damper and one called una corda that are pushed with one's feet to change the sound. I have a hard time reaching them when I am seated. Mama shows me how to play the things on the piano that she knows which she says isn't much.

19 OCTOBER 1864. Alice Holloway has a new sister. This is her third and with two brothers as well. I have none neither brothers nor sisters. I have cousins in Australia (Mama says they are distant cousins really) but they are not brothers or sisters. The Queen has many children. Mama says it is because she and Prince Albert were very much in love. It is sad that he is dead and the Queen is left to mourn. Certainly there is more to

having children than being in love for Mama and Papa are clearly in love and have only me.

22 OCTOBER 1864. I rose early and practised softly so I would not wake Mama and Papa. Papa rose anyway and came to the sitting room in his dressing gown and cap and sat in a chair. I played the few things I know and he could recognise all of them.

24 OCTOBER 1864. The leaves are turning from green to yellow and orange. Mama says it is her favourite time of the year.

26 OCTOBER 1864. Miss Latour and I had a very long conversation in French today after class and she only had to correct one or two words and only had to supply another two or three that I stumbled over. Alice Latham asked how I get along so well in French and that certainly I must have an aunt or uncle who speaks French and I said no it is just easy for me.

29 OCTOBER 1864. Papa has hired a piano teacher whose name is Mr. Nesbit. He wears spectacles and has a hook of a nose and hair parted in the middle. He looks rather like an owl. When I play he seems surprised that I play as well as I do as if I have cheated or been caught in a falsehood. As he left today he told Papa the girl has a natural inclination. But he is very sour indeed.

5 NOVEMBER 1864. Guy Fawkes Day was today. It is a day that is celebrated in all of England in remembrance of the day on which Guy Fawkes tried to explode a great amount of gunpowder under the Parliament and the King which is why some call it Gunpowder Day. A band on the square played God Save the Queen and Rule Britannia and then there were fireworks exploded across the River Wey and all the dogs of our town Guildford howled at the fireworks which were spectacular. Then there was another howl and it was from Mr. Phillips. He was on his steps curled up in a ball shrieking and shouting out FOR THE LOVE OF GOD AND THE MERCY OF THE ANGELS!

7 NOVEMBER 1864. I missed school today as I am ill or under the weather as Mrs. Sullivan says though this makes no sense to me as we are all of us continually under the weather as no one is ever above it! She makes a tea with brandy and cloves and I sleep well.

8 NOVEMBER 1864. I am well again today and Mrs. Sullivan and I made gingerbread for Papa. He put his nose to it and sniffed and took a dainty bite and rolled his eyes in pleasure. Then he took a bigger bite and pronounced it capital.

12 NOVEMBER 1864. Mr. Nesbit tells me to mind my posture as I practise the piano. Sit well to play well he says.

19 NOVEMBER 1864. I taught myself to play Jesus, Lover of My Soul which was quite easy really. Sometimes I think the notes are colourful birds that are flying out of my piano, birds of all sorts that circle about one another and sing.

20 NOVEMBER 1864. Papa's sermon this morning was on the topic There is but a letter's difference between fasting and feasting. Mr. Phillips was not on his door step today.

23 NOVEMBER 1864. The days are getting shorter and colder. Both the collier and the sweep came by today each quite as much black and covered in soot as the other. The collier filled the cellar whilst Mrs. Sullivan supervised him and the sweep attended the chimney. When they were done Mrs. Sullivan escorted them into Papa's study. Papa rose from his writing and went to shake hands with the men. But the men shewed their sooty hands and so they exchanged small bows. Papa gave each his wages with a little something extra for good cheer as he likes to say. The collier an older man who is rightly called Mr. Black questioned Papa saying Reverend Lamb sir I believe you've given us sixpence more than we've coming. Papa said Take it my good man and use it in good health and to the glory of God. Each of the men pocketed his sixpence with

profewse *[sic]* thanks. Later Mama who had overheard Papa and the men said Arthur do you mean to break us? O, Winnie, kindness and generosity are the flowers of heaven, said Papa. Mama said I do hope they are edible flowers and she turned and left the room. Papa laughed silently to himself and dipped his quill in the inkwell and turned back to his writing.

25 NOVEMBER 1864. Today as we girls sat on the stone wall by the green Alice Latham said that for a woman to have a baby her husband must put his willy in her hoo-hoo and jiggle it about. I hadn't an idea what a willy was and I was too embarrassed to ask so I pretended I knew. When I got home I asked it of Mrs. Sullivan. She was removing ashes from the stove. She looked from inside the stove to me and got up and wiped her hands on her apron and bade me sit with her in the kitchen. She said Well it's the thing boys has got what we girls ain't got. It hangs there until it's in a state of excitement and then it stands up. I exclaimed that I should never like such a thing inside of me! She pursed her lips and said Well then dearest perhaps you won't and we'll just see then but it certainly ain't a matter for today. Then she excused herself to the backstairs for she had developed a fit of coughing.

28 NOVEMBER 1864. I am in trouble again with Miss Goodforth for daydreaming. I begin well but soon an idea pulls down invisible lids over my eyes and I began thinking of how the haystacks in the fields look like old women or where the water in the River Wey comes from and whence it goes or how a cloud can change shape so slowly as to make one wonder that it even did so. And then I was awakened by the slap of a ruler on my desk and I looked to see the faces of the other girls looking at mine, some aghast and some pleased. Miss Goodforth sent a note home with me. Mama read it and was quite displeased and I was sent into the rectory. Papa let me sit on his sermon chest whilst he wrote and quite a long moment it was. At last he looked up and said What's this I hear, then, my beautiful daughter? I was daydreaming, I confessed. He leaned back and made a look of surprise and said Daydreaming, then? He pressed his lips together and his eyes seemed to try to look down at them. Then he looked to me again. Were you disturbing others in your daydreaming?

No, Papa, I said to the floor, and rather meekly. And it is true that I was disturbing no one, until Miss Goodforth slapped the desk with the ruler. Well then, henceforth, endeavour to do better Papa said. Stay on task. There was a pause, and he resumed writing again. You are dismissed, he said as he dipped his pen in the inkwell. I rose again and was at the door when he spoke once more and I turned. He didn't look up from his writing and instead smiled down to his pen as he dipped it in the inkwell and moved it over the paper. But remember also my beautiful daughter that God sends the best of man's ideas in the form of daydreams.

5 DECEMBER 1864. Mr. Nesbit came today. He told Mama and Papa that he is astonished by my playing which he pronounced remarkable and extraordinary.

9 DECEMBER 1864. When our teakettle sings it is a low E note, two octaves below middle C. Our doorbell is the D two octaves above it. The jackdaws on the telegraph lines remind me of notes and I think it would be something fanciful if they chirped the note on which they sat.

12 DECEMBER 1864. The churchwarden Mr. Winston visited with Papa today and brought me sweets. I played Good King Wenceslaus without any mistakes at all.

17 DECEMBER 1864. My classmates have all departed to their homes elsewhere in Surrey or to the homes of relations in Kent and Plymouth. Alice Latham and her mother and father and all of her brothers and sisters boarded the Great Western train for Bristol. There were so many bags and cases that Papa said that they look like Napoleon's Army setting off for Moscow. Louise Davies has gone with her family to her grandmum's house which is in Swansea in Wales. Papa and I stood at the station and I sent them off with a hearty wave and a brave smile. But there was envy in my heart but it is a sin and I am not to indulge in it. It was a cold walk back home in the snow with Papa.

21 DECEMBER 1864. We have a nativity set up in the church yard though the characters are not full size but the size of children at most. There is a donkey and also a camel that are the size of dogs perhaps. There is a Christ child that reminds me of how much I would like for us to have a baby. I would ask Father Christmas for one but I know that he doesn't bring such things as babies. That is a task for the stork.

CHRISTMAS DAY 1864. Father Christmas has come and has left me new music, a looking glass, a book called Foxe's *Book of Martyrs*, and some penny sweets. For Christmas dinner after services there was a goose and dressing and a pudding. There was a bit of snow this afternoon and it was quite cozy inside with Mama and Papa and me.

26 DECEMBER 1864. Boxing Day today. We put up several parcels of my old clothes that I have outgrown though they are in excellent shape as I have grown quickly and did not wear them very long.

1 JANUARY 1865 New Years Eve. Papa and Mama and I stayed up late with hot cocoa. As the old clock struck midnight Papa said Well it is the new year 1865 and I kissed his cheek and Mama's.

3 JANUARY 1865. Foxe's *Book of Martyrs* says that St. Albans was a saint whose head was cut off by the Romans in Hertfordshire. It is said that a spring of clear water broke through the ground where his head fell. I do not think I should like to drink from it though.

7 JANUARY 1865. A very grey day indeed. I played the piano and read all day and then helped Mrs. Sullivan in the kitchen. She does not sing very well at all but I shan't tell her for it would be impolite.

10 JANUARY 1865. Mr. Foxe in his *Book of Martyrs* says that 'I fear neither death nor fire, being prepared for both.' I told Papa that Mr. Foxe must have been a very brave man. Yes Papa said Or else death and fire were very remote at the time he wrote it. Mama laughed and scolded

Papa.

12 JANUARY 1865. I have been at my looking glass today. I hope this is not the sin of vanity which one can commit with a looking glass. My mouth is somewhat small quite like the Queen's mouth, very lovely, Mama says and my hair is yellow & fine & stringy. Some of the other girls are getting figures but I have not & I fear I shall never though I do not know what I should do with one other than strut about with it.

14 JANUARY 1865. A letter came for Papa from the Linnaen Society with the papers he gave them. He is rejected again.

Sammy, 1982

The old travel trailer sat in a skirt of weeds next to Teeter's mama's house. With time, weeds would grow in a skirt around the half-bath tub sheltering the Blessed Mother. Her paint was still new, light-blue and white. Next to the grotto, she appeared again in a faded plastic nativity with her husband Joseph and their baby boy. They had been there since before Christmas. The light inside the decoration had long since gone out.

Inside the house, the blue light of the television flashed on a woman reclining on the couch in her housecoat and smoking. Teeter's mama was watching *Magnum P.I.,* which she called *Magnum pu-yi.* Teeter and Sammy stood in the driveway by Sammy's truck. Sammy pulled the duct tape off the door to reveal DODGER and PAS BON scratched in the aqua paint of the driver's side door. Teeter put his cigarette to his lips and squinted as he approached the door, hitching up his pants on his small frame. Scraggly hair that was not quite shoulder-length fell around a face that even Teeter's mama said was *tout nez,* 'all nose.'

"I can do it, yeah," Teeter said around the fuming cigarette, "but you ain' gotta pay me, bawsman."

"I'm gonna pay you, Teeter," Sammy said. "A man works, a man gets paid."

"I jus' appreciate you givin' me another chance," Teeter said, and he took the cigarette from his lip and shook Sammy's hand. There was the shine of a tear in Teeter's eye as he looked off to Sammy's truck. "I can sand this out, *droit-là*," he said, running his finger over the scratched-in message. "Match the paint. Mais, you won't even know. Just like that ol' barn they marked up last time. Ain' nobody gonna know the difference."

He ran his hand over the scratches again with the smoking cigarette still in his fingers. An indolent plume lengthened and curled and faded.

"Gimme a day or two. I'll get it fixed up, bawsman. Let me keep it till then. Come 'ci, I give you a ride home."

Teeter's old Chevy was steeped in the smell of years of cigarettes and had yellow foam protruding from rips in the upholstery between strips of gray duct tape. A 1981 calendar was adhered to the peeling dash over the tape deck with the eight-track of *Journey- Evolution* in it. Teeter palmed the wheel with the curves in the road, and the cigarette smoke floated like incense. A Rosary hung from the rearview with a scapular of Our Lady of Mount Carmel, the same kind that Betsy had in her bedside drawer at home. With each turn in the road, the Rosary and the scapular leaned and returned to plumb, and the white smoke scented the cab, dimly lit by yellow dash light.

They passed the moonlit, pillared ruins of the old Parris place, dead winter grass encroaching on steps that led up to nowhere. The highway wound with the bayou in sweeping curves under leafless branches and the cold sky. If the trees were thinking about budding out, they weren't showing it. Teeter turned onto the long tunnel of oaks that led up to Mount Teague.

"Come inside for supper?" Sammy asked.

"No thanks, bawsman. I think mama got somethin'."

Inside, the gumbo on the stove put a rich smell into the air, and Sammy realized how hungry he was. After supper there would be baths to be given and stories to be read, and then the talk about nothing he would have with his son Quint, an inconsequential talk that fathers and sons have, the kind of talk that will be forgotten by the father and remembered forever by the son. And then, when everything was done, he and Betsy would enjoy the full, glowing blessing of the quiet of a peacefully sleeping household before retiring to bed themselves.

After dinner and baths and bedtime stories, he thumbed through *Louisiana Agriculture*, waiting for the noises from his children's rooms to quiet so that he could return to the diary. He set aside *Louisiana Agriculture* and reached in the white plastic bucket and pulled out the sheet music entitled Liebestraum by Franz Liszt. He wondered what "Liebestraum" meant. It was German, he was pretty sure, but beyond that, he had no idea. Maybe it was someone's name. The notes perched on the five lines like birds on a telephone wire. He studied them, each one a sound, a chirp.

He took the music into the central hallway and sat at the piano and played as softly as he could. He wondered if Alice's fingers had done the same on the ivory keys of the old piano, which was ancient and had been destined for the junkpile until Sammy's daddy had talked his mother into refurbishing it. Sammy was glad, and it was as much a part of Mount Teague to him as the columns or the lane of oaks. His fingers gingerly traced the melody as his eyes studied the music, and he became so absorbed that he didn't hear the quiet footsteps or the creak as she sat next to him on the bench. He was peering into the lines of notes, listening to them say their names as he pressed the white and black keys.

"That's beautiful," she said as she put her head on his shoulder, just like her mother always did. "Daddy, I'd like to learn to play."

He was concentrating on the sheet of music, but he managed to smile as he followed the circles and staffs. "Maybe when you're just a little older, baby."

She slowly melted into his side, absorbing the scent of his work clothes, a scent she would recognize as home and would look for in the man she would marry one day. Her eyes struggled to keep open as he played softer and softer. Finally, his fingers left the keys, and he scooped her up and took her upstairs, her arms knowing to drape around his neck, even as she slept. He laid her into the bed next to her big sister's who was already curled into a ball under the covers.

Betsy was asleep in the light of the nightstand lamp, *The Autobiography of Miss Jane Pittman* by Ernest Gaines open in her lap. He put her bookmark in to keep her place and put the book on the nightstand and turned out the light. His light steps on the stairs squeezed out quiet squeaks and moans. Downstairs, in the study, his fingers opened the clasp of the diary, just as Alice's young fingers had done over a hundred years before.

Alice Lamb, 1865

12 JANUARY 1865. Mama sat on the corner of my bed today where I was reading Foxe's Book of Martyrs and bid me close the book and she paused as she looked at the wall opposite my bed. She said that I shall soon emerge into womanhood like a beautiful butterfly from a cocoon. It is hard for me to imagine and sometimes I feel that I shall only be a moth. Downstairs I heard Mrs. Sullivan use the coal scuttle to set the fire in the kitchen for afternoon tea. Mama said that I shall one day perhaps soon get a figure and then I shall have a certain issue of blood every month. She says that is part of God's plan just as the phases of the moon and the tides and that it is because Eve bade Adam eat the apple. Adam and Eve ate the apple and so we have the tides? I asked her. No, she said, the issue of blood. I asked her if this to happen to both boys and girls, for both Adam AND Eve ate it. No, only girls, she said. That don't seem fair, I said and she said, doesn't. Doesn't, I corrected myself. She said that I might run and play now and she kissed my forehead and I have the feeling that she is quite relieved that our talk is done. I now put my looking glass in my coat and go to the Down as it is a fine clear day though cold.

24 JANUARY 1865. Mr. Phillips was out again today. I shouted hallo but he did not return my hallo. I crossed the street carefully this time and sat next to him and he stared far away. He was dressed as always in a waistcoat that was unbuttoned with a blouse under it that was dingy white from want of washing Mama says. I asked him if he was cold but he didn't say anything. I asked him what he was regarding over there past the housetops. He said he saw the devil and that he sees him all the time. The devil? I asked him. Yes he said. I paused and then I asked him, well then, what does he look like? Mr. Phillips said the devil wears a red velvet suit and slippers with the toes curled up like a Turkish pasha. Mama

called me inside and I told her what Mr. Phillips told me and she said perhaps I should avoid the society of Mr. Phillips now on.

27 JANUARY 1865. Mr. Phillips emerged from the house he shares with his sister who might kiss men for two shillings if Alice Latham is to be believed. He was naked and shouting and Mama and Mrs. Sullivan came to see what was the matter and one of them put her hands over my eyes and called for Papa to come quickly. Other men joined him in an instant and threw a blanket over Mr. Phillips who was taken inside and someone was sent to the High Street to fetch Mr. Phillips' sister who might kiss men for two shillings. I only saw Mr. Phillips' willy for a moment and I do not think it was in a state of excitement but it is the first time I have seen one. Mrs. Sullivan made tea and put a dram of brandy in it for herself and then Mama wanted some in hers as well.

4 FEBRUARY 1865. The weather is cold and grey and I read constantly though there are many words whose meanings I don't know straightaway. Bless me soul how that girl reads! Mrs. Sullivan said and then she and I made scones and ate them with currant jam and treacle. She says that my appetite is prodigious indeed and that I have grown a half a foot since Christmas if I have grown an inch. Mama says she will have to add to my dress for me to remain decent.

6 FEBRUARY 1865. There was a great fire last night across the street where Mr. Phillips lives with his sister. Bells rang all over Guildford including the big church bell on Quarry Street and horses came pulling engines with big pumps. I wanted to watch from the front steps but Mama and Papa sent me upstairs. I watched from the window in their room though. Papa threw his great coat over his nightgown. Still with his nightcap on he ran with our other neighbors across Pewley Hill Road. I saw fire in the windows of the upper storeys and the fire brigade pushed up and down on pumps to spray water on it. It took quite some time but the fire became smoke and then it was out. Then I saw Papa help some men carry something out in a bedsheet. It was black with soot. Thence some men brought out Mr. Phillips who was also black with soot. He

twisted in their grasp like a caught fish pulled onto a riverbank. They put him in a carriage and thence down the street toward Sydenham Street.

7 FEBRUARY 1865. Papa left very early this morning. Mama was up early as well even before Mrs. Sullivan and made a breakfast of pudding for me as she knows it is my favourite. I asked her if Mr. Phillips is all right and Mama stopped what she was doing and sat right next to me and Mrs. Sullivan turned her back and shook her head a little. She said that Mr. Phillips' sister has died in the fire and that Mr. Phillips will have to stay at the asilum *[sic]* in St. George's Fields that is called Bedlam. I asked Mama if we can go and visit him and she said she was sorry but it is very doubtful as the asilum at Bedlam is not a proper place for a young lady to visit.

8 FEBRUARY 1865. Today was the funeral of Mr. Phillips' sister. Papa performed the service. I stayed home with Mrs. Sullivan. Everyone wears black as it is the colour for mourning.

10 FEBRUARY 1865. Workmen arrived as I departed for school. When I returned a great deal of the Phillips' old house is removed. Bricks and burned wood remain in piles.

11 FEBRUARY 1865. I have mastered all my new music and I would like to learn more pieces as Mr. Nesbit calls them. Perhaps I shall receive more for my birthday in April. I wonder if Princess Alice plays the piano. Mama says she doesn't know but that it is possible as it is said that all of Queen Victoria's children are quite accomplished.

14 FEBRUARY 1865. Mrs. Sullivan hummed a tune she knew as a girl called The Rose of Donegal and I picked out the notes and then she sang with me as I played it. She does not at all sing well but her heart is quite into it and that is something Papa says that we should sing loud and make God sorry for the voices he gave us.

18 FEBRUARY 1865. Papa and Mama and I sat in the parlour and read on this cold grey day. Papa read humorous stories from *Punch* aloud to Mama, who pretended to blush and said O! Arthur! I fell asleep and woke to Papa putting me in my bed. She is almost too heavy for you to lift Mama whispered. Nonsense said Papa and he kissed my forehead and I was asleep again.

21 FEBRUARY 1865. Papa asked me to come to his study this morning and I sat upon the sermon chest. He looked up from his desk and removed his glasses and smiled at me. He looked away and his smile was broad like a sunrise. He slipped his glasses into one of the compartments of his desk. Well, my beautiful child, I suppose it is as you wished. What is it, Papa? I asked. I could feel my face rising and opening like a morning sun. But then I said nothing. If it was what I was expecting, it would be too wonderful to express it lest it not be true. So I waited for Papa to say it. He said, You are to be a sister at last! I ran to him and embraced him and he took me into his arms and lifted me onto his lap though Mama says I am getting too old for that. Mrs. Sullivan says it also.

25 FEBRUARY 1865. I spend a great deal of time reading King Arthur Tales for I think our new baby shall like them as I do. If I should kiss a boy I fancy that it would be one like Sir Galahad.

27 FEBRUARY 1865. Mama sleeps great lengths of time. Mrs. Sullivan brings her tea and toast. I am learning to play Brahms's lullabies for our new baby though it shall be sometime before we shall see it.

4 MARCH 1865. While Mama sleeps Papa and I go and walk along the River Wey. Papa says that clouds are cumulus or serious *[sic]* and they are shaped by the wind. I remarked that I fancy that they are shaped like animals and ought to be given names such as hare-clouds and horse-clouds. I didn't mean to do it but I was gladdened in making Papa laugh which he did for quite a long time.

11 MARCH 1865. Mr. Belcher came with his black satchel to look after Mama. No one smiled today and there was no mirth in our house. Mrs. Sullivan tended the fire. I played the piano but Papa asked me to stop as Mama needs her rest.

12 MARCH 1865. Mr. Belcher stays late at our house and I am confined to my room though I am given penny sweets from the confectioner on the High Street. The house feels very unsettled. Late last night it rained and pattered against the roof and the window panes. I thought I heard someone wailing last night but I believe it was a dream. A nightmare rather.

13 MARCH 1865. Mama was up today and taking tea with Papa. I was on the landing listening to them, a thing I am not to do. She and Papa spoke softly and I had to listen closely to hear them. Why, oh why, did I not keep it a secret from her? Mama said. O, it will crush her Papa said. He stared at the rug at his feet. Mama did too. Papa's voice was low and weak and he said it's not your fault dear you just wanted to share our happy news. Mama said, Arthur I suppose there is no help for it. But our dearest one will you tell her? O! I cannot bear it! You must be the one to tell her. I shall Papa said but it will break her heart and then mine again.

14 MARCH 1865. I am not to be a sister after all.

15 MARCH 1865. I was allowed to stay home from school again today as I had no heart for it. Papa says that God is aware of every sparrow that falls and is quite heartsick about it. We are very sad still.

16 MARCH 1865. Louise Pidger goes on and on about changing nappies dirty and wet ones. She wrinkles up her nose and makes faces and the other girls laugh and laugh. I do not wish to hear of it but do my best to remain polite as it is the Christian thing to do.

20 MARCH 1865. Papa would like for me to begin playing piano in church. He says that I have become quite proficient on all the old

standards. The regular accompanist Mrs. Clarke is down having had a baby. It is one thing to play in one's own drawing room for one's own family and quite another to play in front of others in church. To say it plainly I am not a little frightened.

26 MARCH 1865. I made my debut on the piano today but my embarrassment almost would not allow it. I sat at the bench and looked over the top of the piano to see Papa smiling back at me from behind the pulpit. I tried to smile back but I found it very difficult. So I looked out to the congregation and the smiling faces. Papa told me of a trick that he was taught in seminary and that is to imagine the audience as animals. I saw a man who looked like a walrus and his wife who was a sea lion and children like kittens and puppies. My fingers stopped sweating and I began to play as I knew how Gentle Jesus, Meek & Mild and when I was done the people in the congregation were like people again and not animals and they exchanged glances of approval and Papa gave me a small smile. And it was the most magnificent of days.

1 APRIL 1865. I climbed the highest tree on our street the old chestnut down by the Brumlees. Mama shouted up for me to take care not to rip my petticoats and that I was getting too old to climb trees anyway. Papa happened up returning from the High Street and I could see him talking to Mama well below me. They spoke for a moment and when I looked back down again Papa was climbing up after me. Arthur! Mama shouted. That is Papa's Christian name. And YOU are certainly too old to be climbing trees! She said up to him. Papa smiled as he grasped each limb. His white hair had come uncombed but it seemed the closer he got to me the broader was his smile. When he was almost there he winked at me and then we were at the top of the tree. Far below us through the green leaves Mama looked up with her hand shielding her eyes and her other arm across her waist. We were as high as the bell tower of the church and we could see the River Wey and the fields beyond and sheep and horses and cows and people who tended them as big as ants because they were so far away. What a wonderful world God has provided my beautiful

daughter Papa said. See all the green? Why the earth is renewed! And the wind sang to us. Or so it seemed.

3 APRIL 1865. Papa has taken Mama on the train to Bath to take the waters as did the Romans. Perhaps Mama's health shall be set right again so that she may be able to have a baby. I am left in the care of Mrs. Sullivan. Whenever Mrs. Sullivan talks to me she leans in and then she sits up again when she listens. Mama says it is the way of the Irish.

7 APRIL 1865. Papa and Mama have returned from Bath. Mama seems much the same to me.

8 APRIL 1865. Mama and Mrs. Sullivan and I went to Mrs. Poole's shop on the High Street. The dressmaker Mrs. Poole goes about with thimbles on some of her fingers and carries a yard measure under her arm. I was to be measured for a dress for summer which shall be soon. It is to be the first bespoke dress that I have ever had. In a room in the back of the shop I tried on the sample dress from the shop window. Mrs. Poole said It quite becomes the girl as she is beginning to come into her figure especially the bust. Mama asked that Mrs. Poole leave a little extra hem turned under so that Mrs. Sullivan can turn it out as I am sure to grow yet. Just so! Mrs. Poole said. Then she put a measuring tape to me including my bust and hips which embarrassed me.

10 APRIL 1865. The London newspapers say that the war in America is almost over and will probably be concluded by summer. Papa prays that it shall be so and that all wars begin with the sin of pride.

12 APRIL 1865. Papa in saying grace thanks God that the war in America is over. I think of Mr. Phillips. I do not think that his war shall ever be over.

15 APRIL 1865. Papa took me fishing in the Wey and we caught five fine trout! Papa shewed me the exquisite colour and the gills and fins. They

have a tail fin a dorsal fin and two pectral *[sic]* fins. Then Mrs. Sullivan prepared them and we feasted like a king and his court.

18 APRIL 1865. My feet now easily reach the damper pedals of the piano and I can span the entire keyboard with hardly any leaning over. My hand can almost extend over an entire octave. Mr. Nesbit said that I can go on to more difficult pieces if I please.

22 APRIL1865. I have almost mastered a composition by a Hungarian composer who is named Liszt. It is called Liebestraum which means love dream and has a lovely flow and is a dream to play and sounds delightful. Mr. Nesbit only sat in a chair and listened to me play. He seldom offers any advice now.

25 APRIL 1865. I am twelve today. There was cake and new music. I asked Papa and Mama if I could begin it straightaway and they said yes and I went to the piano and played. It was the Sonata No. 14 in C sharp minor by Beethoven and a beautiful piece. Mr. Winston the churchwarden gave me half a crown and I put it in my trinket box for safekeeping.

29 APRIL 1865. As I am twelve now I am allowed to run about Guildford with my friends for the first time. On the green playing were some boys whose trousers were too tight or else too loose and hanging from braces. Some of the boys wore the uniforms of the Royal Grammar School. They stopped their play at marbles and cricket and watched us run past and some of the girls were shouting and giggling. We ran down High Street under the Guild Hall clock and down to the High Street bridge and then we stopped to look at the old Guildford Castle and then we were off to the ruins of the chapel on St. Catherine's Hill. There we sat on the old stone wall and looked up at the old chapel. Alice Latham asked what do you suppose happened and Louise Pidger said that perhaps it was sacked by the Vandals. I asked who the Vandals were and she said that they were hairy men from Prussia with big clubs and that her mum has a book with their picture in it. I said that I like to believe it was

burned by a princess who was held captive in it. We became silent as we thought upon it and Alice Holloway sat down in the grass and began making daisy chains out of clover and then we all did. As our fingers worked the green stems Alice Latham said that she might like to kiss a boy one day but the other girls said that they should not. I think I might like to. Just to see of course. But I did not say so for the embarrassment that might come of it. We wore our spring necklaces and danced in a circle like fairy princesses. Then down in Guildford the clock tower struck and we were off toward town again over the High Street bridge and past the White Stag and the Guild Hall clock over the High Street and I was faster than the other girls because of my long legs. A flock of sheep scattered as I ran through them and I took delight in the way they scampered and bleated. When I turned to see my friends I found that I had outrun them and they had each taken off to their homes and their families to brothers and sisters and lively conversations over a busy supper table. All, save me, Alice Lamb.

3 MAY 1865. Today someone left a nosegay of wildflowers in the ring below our door bell. Papa said that it looks as though our girl has a gentleman admirer. I felt my face redden. If I am to be plain about it I am a bit bashful on subjects such as gentleman admirers.

6 MAY 1865. Sometimes boys fly kites on the Down and we girls sit at a distance and watch them. Alice Latham says again that she should like to kiss a boy and not for a shilling but for the kiss itself. Fewer of the girls say that they should not like it. I believe that I may. Just to see of course.

8 MAY 1865. Mr. Nesbit told Papa that he can do no more for me as I have exceeded all he knows. He suggested that Papa look for a more experienced teacher in London or perhaps Paris. Mama said she would never allow me to board away in any such place as those and that at any rate we cannot afford it. I suppose you are right Winnie Papa says.

10 MAY 1865. A man called the Bishop came to visit with Papa in his study. They talked quite a long time with the door closed. Mama told me

not to play the piano or make a peep otherwise. When the Bishop left he and Papa shook hands and the Bishop said that I hope you shall consider it Arthur. Arthur is Papa's Christian name.

11 MAY 1865. Papa prays this night in his study for guidance. Mama says that he is considering an important matter. She rather than Mrs. Sullivan brings him tea and he does not depart from his prayer. She only sets it on his desk and kisses his forehead before departing the room.

12 MAY 1865. Our physician Mr. Belcher has suggested a change of air for Mama and the Bishop has arranged for Papa to be a vicar in India and so it is that we are to proceed there in a fortnight. Mrs. Sullivan is sad as she cannot go with us and so am I.

13 MAY 1865. Papa says that we are to have a great adventure. We are removing to a place in the mountains of India called Darjeeling where Papa is to have a church. It is sad for me to leave my friends and Mrs. Sullivan but Papa and Mama think that the climate may help with Mama's health and that perhaps God will favour us with a baby there and this makes me happy although it is sad for me to leave my piano but Papa says we cannot afford to bring it with us on a vicar's stipend. Mama says that Papa wants to study God's world and perhaps find a subject that shall grant him admittance into the Linnaen society. Papa again says it shall be good for Mama's health and perhaps if it is His will God shall grant us a larger family there. India is a place much talked about. Perhaps I shall see elephants and tigers. For once all the other girls are envious of me Alice Lamb.

14 MAY 1865. Papa announced to the congregation that we shall be soon be departing for India. There was some weeping and after service was over there was more weeping and hearty handshakes as Papa is quite loved here.

16 MAY 1865. In packing for our new life in India I am permitted only a portmanteau. I must leave behind my small trinket box. In it are a

feather from one of the geese on the River Wey and one of a peacock that I found from a great house on the Down and a small piece of blue glass that I gathered years ago at the beach in Brighton. When I was a much smaller girl I was sure it was a sapphire and begged Papa to let me keep it. I am wiser now and I know it is only blue glass from a chemist's bottle. I shall leave the trinket box on the window sill and perhaps another girl or boy shall want to keep it from now on. I leave my piano behind as well though I shall bring the half-crown with me to India.

18 MAY 1865. Today we depart for India. Before we boarded the train for the port of Southampton I sat and played my piano for the last time. Liebestraum by Mr. Liszt which means love dream.

Sammy, 1982

There was a blank page after that. He looked a page ahead where the handwriting changed to the more elegant script of a lady. It was as if the little English girl had disappeared.

Elizabeth was sound asleep again, nestled in to his side. He scooped her up, and she absently put her arms around his neck. Her small body and the little arms around his neck were wiry like a monkey's. He looked over the sweet scent of her hair at his feet as they ascended the stairs, slowly and carefully taking each step until they reached the landing and the door to the girls' room. He tiptoed around the scattered Barbies and crayons on the floor and laid her in her bed, the one next to her sister Judee's. Outside their window in the moonscape, light filtered through the big, waxy leaves of a magnolia tree and threw shadows on the grass at the base, and it looked like a cluster of sheep had gathered there.

Later that night, he found himself looking for her. His daughter Elizabeth was out here somewhere in this black-and-white scenery that was neither day nor night. Above him, the canopies of the oaks spread out under a blank sky, the ancient oaks that had seen everything and remembered all of it but could speak none of it.

And then, there she was, behind a massive trunk. She came from around it and balanced on a root. He couldn't see her face for the wide brim of her hat. A ribbon fell from the crown, and her hands toyed with the ends of it. Her dress was white and lacy, with pale legs under the hem and the black, ankle-high shoes of another century. She darted across the shell lane, her clumsy, graceful legs pushing under the frills, her shoes gliding noiselessly over the white shells of the driveway.

Elizabeth, why did your mama dress you like that? he tried to say, but his mouth wouldn't move, and he could only think it. His legs felt light but immovable as he followed her. The girl pushed her hand down on the crown of her hat as she ran noiselessly down the driveway. The faster he floated, the faster she did. Her hat flew off, and, despite the monochrome, he knew the ribbon on it was blue. The girl's hair wasn't black like his daughter's but blonde in the gray light, though he couldn't see its color either. She was getting farther and smaller, and then he heard her footsteps on the shells, the running footfalls that became louder with each quick step. At the end of the oaks, off in the distance, the girl turned and spoke to him. It was as if she were right next to him, and her voice was that of a grown woman.

"*Sammy...Boo…*" she said as someone touched his arm.

He blinked his eyes. He was standing in the middle of the drive between the alley of oaks. The shell driveway glowed in the moonlight. Above the oak canopy, the sky had stars in it again.

"Bay, how you got out here?" the woman said.

"I…I don't know," he said. He had been following someone, but he was rapidly forgetting who it had been.

"The last time you walked in your sleep was when we lived off Rue St. Sulpice," the woman said, and then he saw that it was Betsy, and he remembered that night. He had awakened on the sidewalk in two feet of snow as a city bus rumbled by at three in the morning. A Montreal policeman saw him and walked him home. It was the night that his daddy had called him to tell him his mama had died.

Betsy took off her housecoat and put it over him.

"But you'll be cold," he mumbled in protest.

"You just gonna have to warm me up when we get to the house," she said.

They walked back to the great house, huddled together under the stars that burned hard in the cold sky and the moon that made everything glow. She wore her big fuzzy slippers, and he wore her fuzzy housecoat. Their steps crunched on the shell driveway.

A shadow moved and paused by a tree trunk and then scurried to catch up with them. It was Pongeaux. The dog bounded up the steps and into the porch light and was reddish brown again. Sammy held the door for Betsy and the dog, and, as they slipped into the house, he looked back. The lane of oaks was empty except for starlight, night air, and moonlight.

At the top of the landing, they paused to check on their daughters Elizabeth and Judee. The floor was still an explosion of dolls and stuffed animals and Mardi Gras beads. Two girls holding hands were drawn on a chalkboard on an easel. One was smaller than the other, but they had identical flipped-up hairdos. He looked up from the portraits to the girls they portrayed, two sleeping lumps, two tangles of favorite blankets and ruffled hair. One day they would be beautiful women like their mother. Moments like these warmed his heart and broke it at the same time.

Sammy and Betsy went to their room, and, behind a door locked against toddlers, the man and his wife warmed each other. Afterward, she fell asleep naked against his bare chest. He lay there thinking of trinket boxes and 'saffires' and willies and hoo-hoos. Though he was relaxed, he still couldn't sleep. He slipped from under her, and her breast brushed against his chest. She turned to her other side, and he waited to see if she would wake and suggest he make coffee. But she went back to sleep, and he rose and dressed in the cold and went down to his study and the diary, which he had put in the top drawer of the old mahogany desk, the one that had belonged to his great-grandfather Sam Teague.

He settled into the Campeche chair that was also as old as the desk and Mount Teague. There was a small shuffle of noise, and he looked up to find a little girl there. Her hair was in disarray, and her eyelids were heavy, and she had a cape of blanket draped around her. He beamed at her, and she ran to him with a tickling patter of tiny bare feet and climbed up into the chair with him.

"Good morning, Judee bug," he whispered, "where's sister?"

"She still sweepin'," she said. "Daddy…"

"What, baby?"

She cast her eyes to the ceiling and sang in a small voice, "*Mama called da doctor and da doctor said...*" she put out a little finger that was a diminutive exclamation mark for each word that followed, "*...no more monkeys jumpin' on da bed.*"

He looked past his chin at her small face that was looking at the pages of the diary he held. She was too young to read them, too young to know what they meant. He found his place, marked with a deposit slip from the St. Matthew Parish Planters Bank. He tucked it back into the pages of the diary and began again with a sleepy girl nestled into his side. The handwriting was different now–even, graceful, flowing. The penmanship of a lady.

Alice, 1869, Manchester, England

15 November 1869. In these leaves, my story commenced when, as a girl of eleven, I began this account. I read these prior pages now and reflect on my school-days. How simple I was then! And how life could ever be otherwise than simple and happy! But I was just a foolish child then, and I have since put away childish things, as the Apostle Paul exhorts us. This volume has returned again after having been several years parted from me. It was found among the things in the safekeeping of our housekeeper when we lived in Surrey, Mrs. Sullivan, a woman whose memory is as cherished as it is vague to me now, almost five years hence. It was sent to me here in Manchester by Mrs. Sullivan's son after her passing earlier in the year in old Guildford in Surrey where we once lived, before our time in Darjeeling in India. It arrived with my old trinket box with a peacock feather and other feathers and a piece of blue glass. I found it necessary to read the diary to remember why I had kept them. I thought of tearing out the pages that were written here years ago by my younger self and dashing them all into the fire, but I rather think that I shall leave them as a testimony and instruction to me, my now older self. Because there are only a few pages with entries and the rest is blank, I fancy I should begin placing entries in it again as it is. And so, it is also a practical matter to avoid the purchase of a new one. Welcome back, old, leather-bound friend. I trust we shall get on splendidly together.

16 November 1869. Our old situation in Guildford has long been taken by a young vicar from Basingtoke, a man who has a large family 'as numerous as the children of Abraham,' Papa jokes. Papa and I have located here to Miles Platting, Manchester, a place where, though the sun might shine occasionally, it never takes the trouble to warm anything. We get on well enough here, though St. John's Church isn't near as prosperous as our old church in Guildford or even Darjeeling. I feel our move here has been ill-circumstanced, but Papa and I are resolved to make the most of it. The weather here in the north of England is not at all salubrious, and Papa's health and vigour suffer from it, though in degrees. Our new position has no provision for a housekeeper and so I am pressed into duty. I wait here in the vicarage during the day and read and play the piano, and then I prepare for Papa as I consult a house-keeping book and try a turn in the kitchen. Today I roasted a joint of mutton with parsnips and carrots. Papa blissfully pronounced it first rate though I confess I found the centre rather underdone.

19 November 1869. Papa was called to the bedside of a child of no more than ten who was caught in a loom at the Victoria Mill. The child's mother sat up with the patience of Job and prayed the Rosary. Papa, to his credit, didn't ask where the Catholic priest was. Disease brought on by the weather, primarily pneumonia but also consumption, has stretched all the clergy thin. The spinning rooms with their shuttles and flying jennies and spinning mules and carding machines make a riotous noise which can be heard throughout the town and join with the other mills in Miles Platting and Ancoats. Many of the stations in the mills are attended by children performing the same monotonous tasks. The clacking, clattering hum is like a modern, more musical version of Dante's inferno. It is thought that the child shall live, though greatly effected and unfit for further service in the mills.

20 November 1869. The Bishop's carriage passed today, a fine brougham with a pair of smoke-coloured horses pulling it. I did not see the Bishop inside, as the curtains were drawn. I have heard that he has been ill. As it made the turn onto Varley Street the driver shouted, 'Make way there, you. The Bishop passes!' Common people scrambled to the edges of the street as the fine horses tossed their heads and clopped against the stones of the street. Heads canted as eyes tried to find a space in the curtains for a glimpse of the man inside, but the red velvet was drawn tight and seamless, and curiosities were left unsatisfied. I remarked to Papa that the Bishop certainly goes about in a fine carriage. 'Yes,' Papa leaned into me to whisper as we crossed the street in his wake, 'A case of pomp and splendor passing for wisdom.' It startled me. Papa so rarely speaks ill of anyone.

24 November 1869. The weather is beyond cold now and has fallen into bitterness, a harbinger of an even deeper winter. The smoky, metal air of Manchester does nothing against it. I read by the fire, and I confess caught myself staring into the orange coals, imaging they were glowing gemstones. Papa came in and asked the object of my pensive demeanor. Trying to keep his spirits up (for I know that they naturally sag this time of year), I told him that I was enjoying how cozy it was to be here with a book and the fire for company. He smiled and patted my shoulder, pausing to release a complicated cough before removing his scarf and cape. Of course, my little confidant, the room and its fire would be so much cozier with others, a family, with which to share it, but I do not speak of this. It is a topic that is old and stale, and Papa and I have lost much for the want of a family and the attempt to get one.

26 November 1869. We were paid a visit from the Bishop today, who arrived in his fine conveyance. He appeared quite frail as he descended from his carriage with the help of a liveried attendant. 'You are quite accomplished on the piano, I hear,' the Bishop said to me on entering, as Papa took his coat and scarf. Modesty prevented me from answering in the affirmative. 'Why, on the piano, she is the very thing, sir!' Papa said, to which the Bishop replied, 'Perhaps you can come by the Bishop's

Palace and play, then.' Perhaps so, I said, as politely as I could. The Bishop slowly sat down in a chair like a hen setting on a fragile egg, and I made tea for him and Papa. As I came in with the tray of tea-things, I overheard the Bishop say, 'I need not remind you that this is the Queen's church, and we are to administer first and foremost to its followers and eschew any semblance of papist trappings.'

'Respectfully, sir,' Papa said, 'many of these poor souls who work the mills are Irish and Catholic, and vestments and incense and candles are welcoming to them. The Bishop raised his voice to Papa, and I was surprised that so frail a man could do so with such force, 'Let me make myself clear, Lamb. If they are Roman Catholic, then let their own priests attend to them.' Then he graciously thanked me for the tea and helped himself to sugar and cream for it. He seemed as comfortable with his statement as if it had been a comment about the weather. Papa had his look of pleasant concern which I have come to recognize as inwardly stricken. 'But there are so many of them,' Papa said, 'The Catholic priests are stretched thin, your Eminence—'

'—it is their affair,' the Bishop interjected. A small spot of cream clung to his jeweled ring, an enormous thing that made the teaspoon look like a snuff spoon. He didn't notice it, the spot, I mean. I excused myself at this disagreeable juncture. When I returned, the Bishop had finished his tea and risen onto his cane, which functioned for him as a spindly, mahogany leg with a bejeweled knob on the top. He wrapped his scarf around his neck and pulled his great coat around himself and left as Papa held the door for him and bid him, 'Good day, your Eminence.' The bishop plodded forth and didn't waste the effort to look at Papa as he said, 'Good day, Lamb.' As the Bishop left in his carriage, all pomp and splendour, Papa remarked under his breath, 'I fear that the Bishop's copy of the Bible is missing a page, and that is the one in which our Lord states, *I was a stranger and you welcomed me.* Perhaps it was left on the bookbinder's floor and swept out with the other rubbish.'

29 November 1869. I visited the stationers this day for envelopes in case a reply to Australia is necessary. I only do this to please Papa, as I have long since given up the notion that we should ever hear from our cousins there. It is more of a ritual than anything else, but I do it for Papa if it will keep his spirits.

1 December 1869. In Papa's study, there is a ledger in which the names of parishioners who are sick or dying or both are kept. Whether they get well or whether they die, their names are crossed off just the same. The fickle wind pushes at the window panes as Papa and I play at whist.

4 December 1869. The people, men, women, children, blow warm breath into their mittened hands, mittens riddled with holes where pale skin shows. Shabby children, shabby adults. Newsboys sell the *Guardian* which surely few of them can read. The bootblacks are poorly shod. Children run in the streets, bundled in ancient, worn scarves and hats, and oft-patched trousers and coats sizes too big or too small. I wonder if each has both parents living yet. They seem happy enough, but perhaps that is how a family works, 'happiness shared, multiplies, and sorrow shared, divides.' The wives of the mill proprietors go about in great fur cloaks and matching hats whilst most here in Ancoats haven't a sixpence to bless themselves with.

5 December 1869. The vicarage is in want of washing, but it must wait until the spring which, here in Miles Platting and in the rest of the north of England, could be in May. Papa's sermon today was entitled, 'Suffering is the Ache of Redemption.' If this is so, then Papa and I should be quite redeemed by now.

9 December 1869. I spent most of today, a Wednesday, at the piano here in the vicarage. The D just above middle C does not serve and gives only a faint tap, so I transposed Schubert's *Impromptu No. 3 in G-flat major* up half an octave to avoid it as much as possible. I sing the missing note when I must.

10 December 1869. The sweeps are busy this time of year, sooty men going about with ashy carts loaded with black brushes and grey brooms. Their faces are blacker than the darkest African and when they squint their eyes and open them again, they seem wide-eyed in astonishment. They are a cheerful lot, offering ashen waves to Papa and me.

13 December 1869. Papa was called to see the Bishop in Manchester, as his eminence's health doesn't allow him to get about any longer. Papa insisted that I go with him 'to take a little air,' though I do not see the point with the belching breath of the mills. I go rather to keep Papa company, so he does not lose heart. Indeed, the Bishop did not seem well. He took a snuff-box with a trembling hand and brought some to his nose, which elicited a most thunderous sneeze. 'Pray be seated, Lamb,'' he said as the same quivering hand sponged his nose with a handkerchief. 'Will you excuse us, Miss Lamb?' he asked me. I excused myself to the sight of Papa's plaintive eyes begging me not to go. In the adjoining room, I scanned the gold-printed spines in the Bishop's library whilst I only heard small portions of the conversation within: *'If the matter is given to scrutiny, Lamb,'* and *'positively awful,'* and *'her majesty's church,'* and once, the Bishop exclaimed so that there was no need to strain to hear it, '*BAH! FLUFFERY AND NONSENSE!*' When the Bishop was finished with him, Papa emerged frowning but on seeing me straightened his countenance into a more neutral expression, though it appeared to take no small effort. I am sure this was for my benefit. Papa and I were quiet as we walked in the direction in which Ancoats and Miles Platting and the mills rumbled like a herd of great beasts lumbering about. At last, Papa only said, 'We must remember our Old Testament duty not to bow down before idols.' I am not sure if he meant the Roman Catholic Pope or the Bishop of Manchester.

15 December 1869. Papa has taken to referring to Bishop Lee as the noisy gong and to Rev. Fraser as the clanging cymbal. I am somewhat surprised at Papa's candor on this subject. Whilst he may bear uncharitable feelings, it has never been his way to express them.

17 December 1869. Papa has again submitted papers to the Linnaen Society in London and has again been rejected. The submissions committee says it is widely known that a vicar is unlikely to be competent to speak on scientific matters. Papa no longer expresses dissatisfaction, only resignation.

19 December 1869. Sunday. Church attendance today, five-and-twenty, many of them awake for the whole of the service! Papa's sermon (delivered through the congregation's circus of rattling phlegm), 'Beware the Ruiner of Men's Souls.'

20 December 1869. Papa was dispatched to find a man at the insistence of some of his more sober friends. When Papa asked one of them where he might be found, the man replied through a mouth with less than a full complement of teeth, 'Lord, bless me soul, but 'e's amongst them as is drinkin', vicar, sir.' And so, I accompanied Papa through streets lined by dingy-aproned shopgirls and full of fatherless, 'come-by-chance' children. We entered one of the public houses on Cotton Street in Ancoats where we were told he was last seen. Everywhere were men who commit rough deeds, men who drink in these taverns between shifts at the mills, men who beat the tabletops with their empty cups and fondle the maids who replenish them. Men who suddenly tumble forward, insensible from the drink, and are carried off neck-and-heels and thrown outside into the gutter where their families, often their oldest children, come to gather them. It is a brutal way.

I sat at the front of each public house as Papa searched the back for the man, a Mr. S-, and I observed the inhabitants quite as a scientist might. The air was filled with the roar of the slurred conversations of drunkards and the thunderous laughter of tosspots. Faces were half-dark and half-lit by the fire in the hearth and the shadows it struggled against. The tavern maids cooed at the men and addressed them as 'my love' and 'you clever boy,' even the old ones and, perhaps, especially the old ones. When a hand wandered, it was allowed a short sojourn before a smart, small slap with a girlish giggle which set it right again. As I waited, a patron staggered over and sat next to me and slurred a greeting which was carried on the foul breeze of his sour breath. I gathered my skirts closer to myself and told him that I was waiting for my father, the vicar of St. John's in Miles Platting. The man at once began singing a bawdy tune about the vicar's daughter and several others joined without looking up from their porter or away from the cleavage of the lewd women who attended them. I myself looked away and waited for Papa and prayed it would be soon. Papa returned with the news that Mr. S- was not here, and we ventured out to the Crown & Rose. There we found him, slouched in a corner of a back room thick with tobacco smoke and coarse laughter and dim, honey-coloured light. 'Is this man Mr. S-?' Papa asked.

'Aye, 'tis,' someone said. Some of the patrons lifted Mr. S- onto Papa's shoulder, they themselves perhaps half an hour from needing carrying-off as well. I scolded Papa for shouldering such a load and at his age. Papa told me to think nothing of it, that God would make his burden light. As we made the corner of Blossom Street, the man vomited down the back of Papa's great coat. Accompanied by the bitter smell of the man's vomited wages, we pressed forward down the darkened streets to the man's abode and family. Perhaps both Papa and I had expected a reception in the style of the prodigal son, but the man's wife simply said, 'Put his sad arse there in that chair until the drink be done with 'im.' Papa eased the man into the chair, and then, rather than thank Papa, the man's wife said, 'sorry for your trouble, reverend, sir, but next time, 'e may as well go to the deuce.' Papa and I set off for home, with a stop at Mrs. Tilley's on Henry Street to have Papa's great coat laundered. It was a cold walk home for him from there.

23 December 1869. Papa and I hired a carriage and went out into the countryside to gather greenery to 'do up' the church for Christmastide. A horse-and-gig was selected for us, and Papa presented the old mare with an apple which he had hidden in his coat. Her black lips reached for it eagerly. The stable hand, who had an amiable way about him, remarked, 'Why, reverend, I believe this horse has as much appetite for the old apple as Eve did!' He and Papa laughed in the bright sun, made brighter off the snow, and then we were off to the countryside to collect greenery. On the way in, we purchased candles and red bows from Mr. Newman's on Oxford Road. After several hours of work in the cold, mangy old St. John's was transformed into a festive haven. Perhaps we shall have enough coal to keep it as inviting as it appears in its mantle of green and red.

Christmas Eve, 1869. Papa and I persuaded Mrs. Tisdale and Mr. Crump to join us in caroling, for Mrs. Tisdale has a fine soprano (when she can be persuaded to sing) and Mr. Crump's baritone is quite passable. On Blossom Street, we were met with a lump of coal thrown at us during 'Good King Wenceslaus.'

'My husband's been up all night at the mill, so shut your noise the lot of you!' the woman shouted. She was small and wiry, with a swath of white hair down the middle of her hair, much like a badger might look if portrayed as a person. 'Why, madam, we only wanted to wish you a Merry Christmas!' Papa called to her. Then she lobbed the lump of coal at us, barely missing Mrs. Tisdale, who was quite shaken. When we scattered, the woman went out into the street to retrieve the coal from the snow. We, for our part, adjourned to the vicarage for mulled wine.

Christmas Day, 1869. This morning Papa and I exchanged gifts, a new set of pocket-handkerchiefs and a book, Audubon's *Birds of America*, for Papa and a lovely green satin parasol for me. In the box was a second gift, music from Chopin. Christmas services this morning were sparsely attended, and I have been at the piano all afternoon with the gift of Mr. Chopin. The sound of it cheers us on such a day as this, the missing key a small matter. Later, Rev. Hill came around with his family, a precious brood equally mixed of boys and girls. He pulled Papa aside as Mrs. Hill and I sat and read to the children. When they had left, Papa informed me that Rev. Hill brought news that Bishop Lee died last night. We said a prayer for the Bishop and for the repose of his soul. And then we thought of what was to come next, though neither Papa nor I said anything, one to the other. He fears that Rev. Fraser shall be appointed bishop, and he shall be no better than the departed Bishop Lee and may God rest his soul.

Sammy, 1982

He had not been sleeping well at night, the same troublesome dream of blurry red lights set against yellow and the churning slap of a pendulum and sheep under a magnolia tree. He awoke suddenly from an exhaustion-fueled nap to see her in the doorway. The diary fell from his lap to the floor, and, rather than betray to her that it existed, he left it for a moment.

"Sammy," Betsy said. "There's another one."

She didn't need to say what or where. He laced up his boots and walked down the lane. The early morning air was bright and clear. The oaks filtered it and threw dappled shadows on the wet earth below. As his footsteps crunched the shells of the lane beneath the oaks, he strained his eyes and saw it up near the highway, a white blur in the distance floating from a cord that he could just barely see in the distance. It hung from a limb of a different oak this time.

He cut the cord that dangled the chicken and picked it up by its claws. His fingers laced around the wiry feet, and the white feathers of dead wings splayed out in an upside-down prayer. He looked to the north and to the south, but 308 was empty. Sammy crossed the highway and flung the bird into Bayou Lafourche.

That night, he sat in the yard. Flames rose in orange and yellow shifting tendrils against the backdrop of the house. He slouched down in a lawn chair and tucked his hands into the sleeves of his red flannel coat. The fire crackled in the huge metal cauldron, and he wondered if this was the same sugar kettle that had given his great-grandfather his scar. The days of the old "Jamaica train" process for boiling cane were long gone, and now the sugar kettle was just a fire pit.

The red-orange and orange-yellow coals broke and changed from rows and columns of squares into single cubes. Pongeaux lay blinking with her head on her paws and the fire dancing in her eyes as the glow popped and hissed. A figure approached in silhouette, a moving shadow holding something in each hand. He found himself hoping it was her, the apparition from his childhood. If it was, he would ask her something, though he didn't know what. The shadow spoke.

"You used to be terrified of the dark," his daddy's outline said, and it emerged into the light of the fire. "Now look at you, sitting out here in it by yourself."

He took a beer from his daddy and twisted the bottle cap and tossed it into the fire. "It's just a nice, cool night," Sammy said. "The warmth of the fire is nice. Heat'll be on us soon enough. You must've just gotten in. So how are my sisters?"

"Jesus Christ," his daddy said, shaking his head. "It's a crown of thorns and a trip up Calvary every time." He turned up the brown bottle and leaned back into the lawn chair by his son's. "Still squabbling over your great-grandmother's sapphire pendant. Both say that your mama gave it to them. You haven't seen it, have you?"

"No sir. I don't think I've ever seen it."

His daddy turned up his bottle again, and then he looked into the fire and said, "I don't think I've seen it since I was a boy or a young man, in the thirties. But each of the girls is convinced the other has it. They both want it because it was a gift to your great-grandmother from your great-grandfather Teague, their Confederate war hero."

Sammy watched the fire pondering their forefather, the great Confederate war hero, the patriarch of Mount Teague.

"What did you know of your grandfather?" Sammy asked his daddy. "Did you ever meet him?"

"No, he died around the time I was born. If I ever met him, I don't remember it. And from what they say, he wasn't the kind of man to take a baby in his lap. But he knew how to make a dollar. Built up all this. And you didn't cross him. That was common knowledge."

"What do you know of his third wife?"

"She was British or Scottish or something like that. There're no pictures of her, but she was uncommonly pretty, is what they say. Died in a fire in the ballroom back of the house there." Trey pointed with his bottle and then sipped from it.

"Accident?" Sammy asked.

"I suppose so. That's the family story. Believe I heard that it was being expanded when it went up. Maybe some paint or turpentine or linseed oil caught fire." Sparks whirled up into the darkness as a glowing log settled into the orange coals. "Must've been hell for him," his daddy said.

"Hmm," Sammy grunted in agreement as he watched Betsy's shadow move in the lights of the house. He felt sorry for his great-grandfather, though, from the portrait in the hallway, Old Sam Teague didn't seem to be a man who needed or would accept pity. "Must've been real lonely for him, losing his wife, so young and beautiful, with her life ahead of her," Sammy said.

Trey Teague leaned back into his lawn chair, his face bathed in dancing yellow firelight. "I know how hard it is to lose a wife," he said, "and it's hard." He paused and looked up into the night sky filled with stars and embers. "Your mama died ten years ago next Thursday. The worst day of my life." His daddy sipped from the bottle. Father and son kept a gaze into the fire.

More out of sympathy than anything else, Sammy stated the obvious. "You still miss her."

"Oh yeah. Leaves a hole in a man. To lose your mate. Or anyone so close. A man's not meant to live alone. At least, I'm not."

His daddy's bottle tilted again, and he smacked a small smack. He looked at the label and seemed to address the bottle. "I know about loneliness. After your mama died, this place was like a vacuum. I missed you then. Would've missed Betsy, too, if I had known her good."

"You ever thought about getting married again?" Sammy asked.

His daddy chuckled and reached down to stroke Pongeaux. "Who? Who would want to come and live in bayou country with an old cane farmer like me?"

They sat and nursed their beers as the light in the kettle danced and the little dog rested her chin on her paws and watched it, enjoying something primal, the simple fireside companionship with its people that a dog enjoys almost as much as anything.

"Betsy said they hung another one from the tree by the road," Trey said at last.

"Yes sir, third or fourth one. Joke's getting old."

"People are like that, son. Everyone needs to feel morally superior to at least one other person. No exceptions. Self-righteousness is as common and necessary as oxygen for some people. Maybe for everybody. You made your choice, son, but like every choice it's not just the chooser that has to live with it."

The words stung Sammy a little, though his daddy hadn't meant for them to. Trey may have sensed it, so he changed the subject. He sat forward with his elbows on his knees and gave a small shake of his head with a forced chuckle.

"But your sisters and that god-damned sapphire pendant. Each one thinks the other one has it, and they think I'll referee. You're the only one who doesn't give me trouble anymore."

Anymore.

Sammy knew that he was an embarrassment to his sisters and his daddy, that he had committed a vast departure from duty, a plummeting fall from the warrior painted in the hallway of the house that lurked in the darkness away from the firelight. Sammy wanted to ask his daddy if he was proud of him. His daddy wanted to tell him that he still was. Sammy wanted to talk about why he had evaded the draft. His daddy would have told him that he didn't agree but that at the end of the day, he was glad that his son was alive. But neither of them said anything. Instead, they gazed into the fire, each holding an empty brown bottle and silently pondering the obscure but certain truth that you can love someone and still not approve of what he's done.

Another log shifted in the fiery sugar kettle, liberating a whirl of embers into the cool night sky. Father and son watched them twist upward. At last, they returned to the house. In the central hallway, they looked up to the portrait of the ancestor whose name they both bore. He looked down upon them, three sets of nickel-gray eyes. Sammy looked for grief in the eyes of Old Sam Teague.

"Well, I'm turning in, son," Trey said.

"Goodnight, Daddy. I've got some reading to do. *Louisiana Agriculture* came in today," Sammy said. But the reading he had to do wasn't from the *Louisiana Agriculture.* He went to the study and pulled the diary from the desk drawer.

Alice 1869

26 December 1869. Boxing Day, though we have but little to box and give away. Nor do the children of Ancoats and Miles Platting, who amuse themselves by taking turns rolling each other in an empty barrel or throwing stones at each other and running away.

28 December 1869. Mr. Liles visited today and examined Papa. He is of the opinion that Papa's health would benefit from a more vigorous lifestyle in a climate closer to the sun. I, for one, wish he would consider it. If I lose my Papa, then all is lost.

30 December 1869. At my insistence, Papa has been looking through the *Guardian* and the *Times* for opportunities elsewhere. I am inclined toward Australia, but Papa said that it is twice the fare of anywhere else, save the moon. I suppose that it is just as well, for I would fear for Papa's health in such a long passage. Papa favours America, as he has become enamoured with Audubon's book, *Birds of America* and speaks of the place as if it were the Garden of Eden.

1 January 1870. There was a knock on our door tonight and who should it be but Alice Latham from my Guildford days. Quite surprised to see her after all this time, I exclaimed, 'Alice!' But she did not seem to be the same carefree and spirited Alice Latham that I once knew. Her face was pallid and drawn, framed by an old shawl which she had wrapped around her head and shoulders against the cold. 'Hello, Alice,' she said rather flatly, 'Is your father the vicar around?' Papa appeared at my back and put his hand on the edge of the door. 'Papa, it's Alice Latham from Surrey,' I said. Papa welcomed them in with a hearty, 'Well, come in, come in.' A man (a boy, really), with a basket was lurking under the eaves. Papa beckoned him to come in with a sweeping gesture, 'There now, you as well.' Then Alice Latham, in a tone that was rather hushed, said 'I was wondering if you would marry us, Vicar Lamb, I've–' she looked around herself '–we've had a baby. A child. Bertie and me.' Papa said certainly and that it would be an honour. I pushed away the blankets to see a pink face, eyes heavy with sleep and a diminutive tide of breath sliding between parted lips. Papa and I pulled on our coats and scarves and followed the path to the church with Bertie and Alice Latham, though I suppose now she is Alice Pennywaite. I played the wedding march, although Alice and Bertie were already at the altar. The baby stayed in his basket on the bench next to me, all of us remained wrapped up in the cold church. Afterwards, there were a few perfunctory congratulations, though all Alice Latham could say was, 'you play well, Golden Alice.' How odd to hear my childhood nickname after so many years! Papa asked where they would go now, and Bertie replied that he had found work on the Great Northern and that he meant to make a railroad man. 'Very admirable,' Papa said, and another odd silence followed, and then they left into the snow, taking their basket and its small occupant with them, and I am left wondering if I shall ever see them again. It is unlikely.

4 January 1870. Rev. Fraser visited again today. He is an austere man of no uncertain opinion, a man who it seems is physically incapable of smiling. He seems an expert on the subject of eternal damnation and at one point said, rather joyfully, 'It shall be, you understand, Lamb, a frightful thing when it happens, the end of the world.' Papa replied with the Biblical admonition that surely no man knows the day nor the hour when the world shall end. Rev. Fraser seemed taken aback by this, as if he had expected to find the date on the church liturgical calendar. His eyebrows undulated, and he regained his composure. 'Yes,' he said, 'Perhaps it is so. But nevertheless, mark my words, Lamb, but the world shall end as surely as it began. And it shall be positively frightful.' He seemed to be quite looking forward to it, as if he would watch the end of the world from a private box with opera glasses.

5 January 1870. Rain sweeps in from the sea, and men, women, and children move about briskly in it. Hats are pressed down on heads, and bonnet strings are pulled tight under chins. Some people struggle with umbrellas which snap outwardly, abruptly like the sudden burst of a bloom. Smoke from the chimneys flees on the icy wind. Winter seems so much more unkind here than anywhere else we have been.

6 January 1870. Papa came in from home visits and sat by the fire, in turns rubbing his hands and rubbing the cold from his legs. I took his scarf and hat and greatcoat and hung them on their hooks by the mantle. As the firelight faded in the silence, I lit a taper for Papa, though I knew he would soon be asleep in his chair. How many times have we repeated this ritual! As the day's light faded, he said, 'Your mother and I waited so long for you to be granted to us, that somehow we became old. And now I am older than I have ever been, but then I suppose we all are.' He smiled in his wry manner. His face is lined so with wrinkles, and his hair is so very white. He seems to have aged twenty years in a mere span of five. Then he again spoke the words of the Apostle Paul, 'my grace is sufficient for thee.' He is resolved to bear it and so I must also be. I keep my grief for my dear Mama within my own breast. Surely Papa does as well.

11 January 1870. Sunday last, during morning services, there was a clatter of metal rubbish bins in the alley outside the church and a shout as Papa prayed the Prayer of Consecration. An Irish voice declared so loudly that it was clearly heard and understood in the silence inside St. John's, 'I'll cut your *f–* Limerick tongue out, I will!' Glances of the congregation sought the floor as the scuffle rattled outside in the alley. Papa serenely raised his voice with the chalice. Then he did what he does so well, delivering the soothing rhythm of prayer, well-metered praises and supplications. And the tempest in the alley was forgotten. Today, Papa has received a reprimand for raising the host during consecration. He bears the reproach as stoically as Our Saviour. 'We must take the fat with the lean,' he says.

14 January 1870. Papa says that Mr. S-, whom we rescued from the Crown & Rose and who vomited on Papa's great coat, has been found dead in the Rochdale Canal. It is thought to be an accidental drowning as a result of the drink.

16 January 1870. Half of the congregation has just returned from the pubs, and the other half is going there straight away after. The bells in Manchester thunder so that we can hear them in Miles Platting, while our much smaller bell simply clangs, cheerfully enough, but reduced and tinny in comparison. The church is draughty in winter, but Papa refuses to wear a scarf or a great coat during services. He believes that to do so would fail to present the appearance of a welcoming church. Adding to the sound of my piano are the great fluttering chorus of coughing and sneezing of the parishioners in our half-filled church. Papa himself had to stop in the middle of his sermon and then again in the Creed to cough and catch his breath. He keeps a pitcher of water, his only concession to my remonstrances about his health. He has lost weight in the last month. There is a great deal of sickness in the mills, and I have asked him not to visit them. He says, however, that would not do if one is to follow the example of Christ. The offertory song was 'Come Now Font of Every Blessing.' I feel as though I could play it in my sleep.

17 January 1870. As Bishop Lee has died Christmas Eve, those who might assume the bishop's chair have become active in pursuing it. And so, we received another visit today from the interim bishop, Rev. Fraser, who has made no secret of his desire to become the rightful bishop. As I brought in the tea-things for Papa and him, I came upon Rev. Fraser browsing through Papa's small library. 'What is this book, Arthur?' he asked, to which Papa replied, 'Darwin. *The Origin of Species*,' to which Rev. Fraser exclaimed, 'Ha! Poppycock! We are descendants of Adam and Eve, purely and simply. Anything else is merely a matter of faulty logic–merely guesses, conjectures, and inferences resting upon remote analogies. If I were you, sir, I would dispose of this nonsense, as it is unbecoming a clergyman of the Queen's church.' With that, he tossed the book onto the desk, and rather roughly. Papa said that he would see to it, though, knowing Papa as I do, I find this doubtful. When their visit was concluded, Rev. Fraser rose, and Papa rose with him to get his hat and coat. As Papa opened the door, the cold rushed in and Rev. Fraser turned and said, 'Really, Lamb, do you not fear God?' Papa replied, 'Aye, I fear him, though I sometimes wonder why I should fear a loving God who means well for me.' Rev. Fraser seemed to fall further into exasperation, sighing and shaking his head before saying, 'I bid you good day, sir.' With that, he huffed through the door and into the cold. When we could hear the clop of hooves and the rattle of the traces of the Reverend's carriage,

Papa rapped on his desk with his open palm and shouted to the ceiling, 'But I will tell you whom I do not fear, and that…is the BISHOP. OF. MANCHESTER!' I have never seen Papa in such a state. He took Mr. Darwin's book and put it on the highest shelf, then sat on a chair and rubbed his chin. 'My beautiful daughter, whilst I certainly have no aspirations of it myself, there is word that Rev. Fraser is to take up the bishop's crozier permanently,' Papa said with no small amount of resignation in his voice. He paused, trying to regain his composure, a gesture which I have come to recognize. At last, he smiled his wry smile. 'Well, we must take heart, my beautiful daughter,' he said as he got up to retrieve Mr. Darwin from the shelf, 'that not all the Pharisees perished with Old Jerusalem.' We read by the fire, he and I, the rest of the afternoon.

14 January 1870. Rev. Anson paid a call to Papa with news that charges for departing from the liturgy of the Queen's church are being considered against Papa. He said that a vicar in Dorset has been imprisoned for similar departures. 'How can this be, George, when surely the church belongs to Christ and his children?' Papa said. To this, Rev. Anson said, 'No matter, Arthur. If I were you, I would reform or vacate.'

16 January 1870. Unexpected visitors to church today, most certainly sent by interim Bishop Fraser. Papa officiated a much more conservative service, most likely out of fear of censure. Or, perhaps, imprisonment.

18 January 1870. Papa has received a fortunate offer to become a vicar in America, in a place called St. Matthew Parish in the province of Louisiana at a church called St. Margaret's, a flock that is seeking a new shepherd. It is quite a journey, but I feel I am to be quite gladdened by it, for myself and for Papa. Anywhere he can enjoy good health and preach the Gospel without the fear of imprisonment.

20 January 1870. Papa and I spend another winter's evening in the vicarage. I play for him as the wind coos and swirls outside. I am sleepy and long for bed, but I know he is lonely for Mama. As I am. And so, on I play, until the candle burns down to a bare stub.

21 January 1870. It has quietly snowed all morning, and people and carriages leave muddy tracks in it. Occasionally a drift will slide off the eaves and land with the sound of a snowball finding its mark, a small, muffled crash. Papa is out visiting parishioners. The widow O'Rourke is ill. Two of the Clancy children as well.

23 January 1870. Papa's last day in an English pulpit. He did not speak of it to the congregation.

25 January 1870. And so, we have embarked, boarding a vessel called the *Chrysolite.* As we stood on the deck, it began to snow once more, the grey sky whirring in a feathery blur of icy ashes. Despite my gloves, my hands ached from the cold as we waited for the fog to lift and the tide to take us out. The bells of the channel buoys clanged unseen in the mist like the strike of a shovel on iron. I again leave behind a piano to our late dwelling, just as I did in old Guildford. In the years to come, who shall play them, I wonder? The tide wandered in and began to lift us, and we bade adieu to the cold and coal-smoky air, farewell, dirty old Manchester, a town where so many die so young and are glad to do it. Farewell, her dour, tight-lipped sister, Liverpool. We sail on the hope that we are leaving behind disappointment and gloom and shadows. As we were borne away, the snow fell heavier, and Liverpool shrank behind us and England as well, shrinking and sinking into the sea. And the ocean inhaled us to the other side of the grey world.

Sammy, 1982

Her handwriting was elegant, but there was something about the way she formed her letters that made his eyes begin to tire. He looked up at the shelves of books and wondered how long it would be before he would need glasses. The gray of February was sharp and cold out the window. He looked out at it and stroked his beard, hoping a short pause would let him read a while longer. The old grandfather clock in the hallway chimed the hour.

Though he always dreaded going and enduring the silence that reeked with judgment, he couldn't put off a haircut another day. Maybe Mr. Clyde could trim up his beard a little, too. It was finally looking as if he was intentionally growing it, rather than having forgotten to shave. Growing it was not as easy as he thought. It itched and looked awful at this stage, but he told himself that, if it would just grow a little more, a week or two, he would begin to look like the hero in the portrait in the central hall.

He paused as he opened the door to his truck and ran his fingers over the hood. The paint was smooth and gleamed in the morning light. Teeter had done a flawless repair, but he wouldn't take payment for it, so Sammy had given it to Teeter's mama, Miss Vessy.

The truck crossed Bayou Lafourche and the still, brown surface clouded with green and yellow duckweed. The sun broke free from the clouds and threw his shadow before him, a tall, thin driver outlined on the pavement ahead of him. He passed by St. Margaret's Church, the red brick seeming to darken each time he passed it. Behind it, the rows and columns of headstones and crypts lounged in the winter sun. Among them was that of Reverend Lamb and his daughter Alice, the Burning Lady. He wondered if they ever thought they might come to rest there when they left that gray day in Liverpool.

In Mr. Clyde's Barber Shop in Napoleonville, old men read *Field and Stream* and *Sports Illustrated.* Conversations in French were punctuated with *Astros* and *Tigahs* and *Saints.* Combs marinated in glass containers of clear blue disinfectant. A calendar courtesy of Shannon Hardware in Morgan City announced that it was February 1982, and a pretty woman in a skimpy red bikini held a large crescent wrench. *The Tool You Can Trust* was written in perfect cursive under her stilettoed feet.

Mr. Picquet was there, not for a haircut, but to hold court among the other old men. The square face laughed under his ball cap, dark blue and lined with gold piping, *NAVY, USS Midway.* His eyes met Sammy's, and his animated expression fell. He murmured something under his breath as Sammy came in and sat in one of the black chrome-and-vinyl chairs.

Then he fell silent, sullen, stony, and Clyde skillfully changed the subject elsewhere, sports, fishing, petty crime in the Parish.

When one man was finished, there was a shaking pop of the black cape, and a cascade of graying hair fell to the floor. A fishing for a wallet in loose fitting khakis or overalls. Money exchanged, the rumble and ting of an old cash register, a little in a tip jar. A kiss of friendship on each cheek, *merci beaucoup, podnah.* A bell's tinkle and a cool flash of air with the opening of a door. The radio playing softly, songs sung in French to the wail and wheeze of an accordion and a fiddle. The DJ announcing between songs that Monsieur Alan Thibeau *en Lock-poort* had a flatbed trailer for sale; interested parties should call a number, which was given in English and then in French. The KCs of St. Anne Catholic Church were holding a jambalaya supper as a benefit for a family who had lost their trailer in a fire. *Allon, allons, come get you sohme,* the DJ said. And the sweet-strong smell of Vitalis and Brylcreem and Clubman talc lingered over all of it. The pop of the cape again, "Awright, Mist' Sammy."

Mr. Picquet continued to sulk and occasionally stare at Sammy. He mentioned something about Sammy's beard, *barbe*, and scowled and muttered a word in English because it had no French equivalent, *Hippy.*

Sammy heard it and understood it, but he didn't say that the beard was inspired by the man in the painting in the central hallway, the war veteran and learned man, the first Samuel Teague. The radio struggled with the uncomfortable silence, so Mr. Clyde pitched in to fill it with the off-color joke about *Monsieur Puce*, Mr. Flea, and how *Monsieur Puce* had somehow traveled from Boudreaux' beard to Thibodeaux' beard via Marie, and everyone laughed, though they all had heard it hundreds of times.

Sammy eased into the chair, and Mr. Clyde rotated it a quarter-turn to face the old men seated along the wall, old men who had received their haircuts but had stayed because they had nowhere else to go. To Sammy, it had the odd feel of a jury. Through thick glasses, one of them read an old copy of *Baseball Digest* from the previous season. It sat propped on his paunch with the cover proclaiming, "*Dodgers on Fire!*" The word *Fire!* was written in yellow and orange flames.

To help the radio fill the silence, which was gathering again, someone else said, "Hey Clyde, you hear 'bout that trailer caught fire back of Labadieville?"

"Mais, they all right?" Mr. Clyde removed the metal lid and fished a comb out of the blue water.

"Yeah, but they loss ever-ting, them."

"Oh, man, tha's sad," Clyde said to the back of Sammy's head and the scissors and the comb. He raised the chair one pump.

"They got one dem relief funds down yonda the Planta's bank," another old man said.

Voices in French and English became distant. The chesty cape of the twelve-point buck mounted on the wall blurred. The click of scissors, the play of the comb, the click, the pull, a soft brush and sweet talcum on the back of his neck. *Fire!* written in flaming letters. The click of scissors, hair crunching between blades. *On Fire!* it said. And then from the depths, Mr. Clyde's voice.

"Awright, Mist' Sammy. I did my bes' widdat animal on your face…say, boo…you awright?"

"Yessir." A blurry pause. "Yessir."

The black cape was pulled back, and sandy hair slid down onto the black and green and white tile. He fished for his wallet and paid Mr. Clyde. A little went into the tip jar.

"Merci," Mr. Clyde said without looking as he brushed hair from the vinyl seat.

"Merci beaucoup," Sammy said, and he left the old men reading about things on fire.

Mr. Picquet had excused himself from the barber shop and sat on the bench outside, as if the talc and hair tonic scented air had been polluted with something else when Sammy walked in. As Sammy walked by, Mr. Picquet's voice muttered from under the dark blue cap that read *Navy.*

The voice said, *capon.*

Coward.

Sammy kept walking without saying anything.

His workboots still had a little dried mud on them as they entered the lobby of the Planters Bank, but, then again, so did every man's boots.

Inside the doors, the strange, cool calm of banks lingered, with pens on chains and neat stacks of deposit and withdrawal slips. The smell of the talc from his haircut was intensified in the chill.

Over a microphone, a teller was talking in loud, bemused French to an old woman in the drive-thru lane, explaining to her how to operate the pneumatic tube. Across the lobby, a woman with feathered bangs and a business suit sat at a desk and talked on the phone. She looked up to Sammy and smiled and held a forefinger up to him. When her call was done, she hung up and rose at the same time and shook his hand.

"Hey, Mist' Sammy," she said. "How you doin', Boo?"

The truth was, he had not been sleeping well.

"Oh, just fine, Miss Delores," he said. "Listen, how much that relief fund for the Landry's have now?

"*Pauvre bête*," she said as she pulled a ledger from a desk drawer and opened it. "Them poor babies. A little over eight hundred."

He sat down, took out his checkbook, and began writing. He signed his name and folded the check and gave it to her. She read it and shook his rough, cane-farmer hand with her lithe, soft banker's hand.

"You know, you write real nice for a man."

"Thanks," he said sheepishly.

She got up to follow him to the door.

"Mist' Sammy, why evva time there's a fund for a sick child or an accident or a house fire, you always come in to match it? And don't never let us tell nobody?"

He narrowed his eyes and looked around the bank lobby and put his finger across his lips. Then he just shrugged his shoulders and left. Outside the St. Matthew Parish Planters Bank, the breath of the southern wind whipped the American flag, and the blue Louisiana flag rippled under it. On it, the mama pelican's breast bled to feed her babies, Union, Justice, and Confidence. Two men sat on a bench in a patch of sunlight. They were talking, but as Sammy passed on the sidewalk, they fell silent and stared at him. He drove home, away from their silent accusations and the judgment of their conversation. The radio prattled something low, and he turned it off, too.

Pongeaux met him at the highway and was glad to see him, launching herself down the lane of oaks alongside his truck and barking a welcome home. He got out of the truck and stroked her flank, and she rolled over, and he stroked her underbelly, studded with small stubs like the bars of a xylophone. They climbed the steps together, and she shook stray hair in a blur of half-rolls as he ran his hand through his hair to release stray hairs. She squeezed into the door when it was barely a crack and followed him into his study to lie in a patch of sunlight while he read.

Alice, 1870

28 January 1870. Our third day at sea, and I must say it has taken me this long to overcome the *mal de mer*, though I am doing so and my stomach has kept to itself since morning yesterday. Papa seems to have adapted well to the sailing life, with no ill-effects whatsoever. He would make a fine sailing vicar, if there were such a thing. The sailing men are sun-browned and ruddy-faced men who spend a great deal of time in a fairer climate. They are quite nimble and move about on the tilting deck as if it were dry land.

29 January 1870. Papa and I have finally gotten our 'sea legs,' and so we took the opportunity of the fine weather to walk about the deck. The ocean is such a limitless, immense thing, rolling as far as the eye can sea. Yes, a pun, my little companion. It scents the air above it, which gathers in winds that snap the canvas of our sails and spirit us along. Papa and I were silently contemplating it all when we were approached by the master of the vessel, a Captain Gill, who asked, 'Pardon, might you be Reverend Lamb, sir?' Papa broke from his reverie and said, 'I am.' Captain Gill narrowed his eyes and regarded Papa as he asked, 'And might you be related to our late Prime Minister, Sir William Lamb, Viscount of Melbourne?' Papa said 'Yes, though distantly.' The captain took Papa's hand and, pumping it emphatically, remarked most heartily, 'Well then! Pleased to have such a distinguished gentleman aboard our humble bark! I am at your service, sir!' Then he begged leave of us to attend to other duties. After he had departed, I remarked to Papa, in a low voice, that I never knew of our kinship with Prime Minister Lamb. Papa winked and said, 'Certainly, dear. We share common ancestors.' He gazed out on the blue horizon, then glanced back at me, and added, 'Adam and Eve.' O, Papa!

30 January 1870. Papa conducted services on board under blue skies. Hymns were played on an accordion, perhaps a first for the Church of England. What would the bishop say!

31 January 1870. Winds are brisk and favourable under a warming sun, away from bishops and mills and pubs. A sky-blue ocean and an ocean-blue sky, and I can see how some men might elect a sailing life. I have begun reading Rousseau's *Confessions,* in French, as I am told that it is a language one hears in Louisiana as commonly as English. I think fondly of Miss Latour from my Guildford days.

1 February 1870. Capt. Gill had us to dine in his cabin this evening. I must say that he sets a fine table for being at sea, though it is a table that tilts with the gentle roll of the ship. Papa asked how the ship came to be named, and Capt. Gill said that she is named after the gemstone Chrysolite, which some call peridot, greenish things, 'as green as absinthe,' he said. The wife of the ship's factor, a Mrs. Putnam, is quite fond of them and comes aboard in Liverpool from time to time, 'fairly dripping with them, like a peacock, she is.' There are certainly touches of green everywhere, in the trim, the rings of green painted around the bottom of each mast, and the name of the ship, *Chrysolite*, painted on the bow. Even the eyes of the woman-figure on the bowsprit are the same emerald green. As green as absinthe, as Captain Gill says.

2 February 1870. The morning was filled with the jabber of the voices of the Irish children and the patter of their steps. The sea rocked us all and occasionally a hiss of spray launched over the railing and spattered on the deck, to the delighted laughter of the children at the expense of the one who was most dowsed. The whole lot scrambled down into the hold, small voices still bubbling, little girls in worn dresses and bonnets, boys in trousers much too short, all as happy as larks. I found myself in a daydream which broke when I was startled by a voice. It was Papa who said he would give me a penny for my thoughts. The breeze was freshening, toying with my hair, and I pulled a strand of it from my face. Whilst pushing my closed eyes into the wind, I told him that I was daydreaming. Papa said that he has always considered daydreaming a form of prayer, the highest form, perhaps, as surely it is simply listening for what God has to say. I put my temple into his shoulder, and he drew me near to him as we gazed out at the ocean. It was so peaceful, so comforting. He asked me, 'pray tell the subject of your daydream,' and I told him that I was daydreaming about the ocean, how endless it appears and how it seems to slumber so. But of course, my little confidant, that was not what I was daydreaming about at all. So much better to admit to daydreaming about the ocean than to admit that I was daydreaming about a family, brothers and sisters, great boisterous holidays and houses filled with the noise of voices, young and old, and tables set ringed with relatives and holding hands during the blessing and plates and serving bowls passed and sharing our voices in song around the piano after. But I did not say it. We have both suffered supremely for it, Father and I. He has lost a wife and I, a mother, in the mere attempt for a family of just one more, not to speak of a horde.

3 February 1870. Just as in Manchester, the vice of smoking is taken up by even the youngest of the sailing men. The captain's cabin steward, just a boy, also engages in it. He was in the wind-shadow of the wheelhouse, cupping his hands around a match and the cheroot he was lighting. He shook the match and threw it up into the air and the wind took it away and out into the sea. I asked him, 'how old are you, my friend?' He said, 'twelve, ma'am, if I'm a day.' I found it difficult to believe that he is but four years younger than I. Though he appears younger in height, his manner is that of the other sailing men, that is to say, older. With a hand on my chest and a slight bow, I introduced myself, and he took off his cap and introduced himself as 'Tommy Haskins, ma'am.' I asked him how long he has smoked and he said as long as he has been to sea, which was when he was eight. I then asked him if he had a home in Liverpool, and he told me that there is a lady there who keeps him for half-a-guinea a month, when he's in, 'which ain't regular, ma'am.' I asked him if he had parents and he said nay, and his manner seemed to slacken a moment, and he took a long puff and blew it out into the wind. I braced myself on the railing, in a wide stance. He scarcely needed to. He stood as nonchalantly as if he were standing on dry land. His countenance brightened as he told me of the places he had visited, New York, Tenerife, Santiago. He had been through the new canal in Egypt (the Sue-ease, he pronounced it), and Sidney in Australia, and 'why, San Francisco and Old Calcutta!' At this, I remarked, 'So have I!' as I struggled with the wind to keep my hair out of my face and mouth. He replied, 'Why, on my soul, yes ma'am! They've a many a thing there, ain't they?' I replied that they most certainly did, and I wondered if he knew, at his age, of the bawdy houses and opium dens and prostitutes. Surely he does. The seafaring life does not hold back those things, even from a boy.

4 February 1870. Dinner with Capt. Gill, who again lavished us with hospitality. Papa and Capt. G imbibed a great deal of brandy, and Tommy Haskins was sent below to gather another demijohn. At last, we parted company with Papa offering a final toast, a favourite of the Irish in Manchester, 'may you be in heaven half an hour before the devil knows you are dead,' to which the good captain replied, 'and you, my good sir! And to you, Miss Lamb!'

5 February 1870. A day of reading with the chatter of families about us. I practised French with an old woman who is returning to New Orleans. Tonight, the majestic spell of the sun setting into the water under the ship's bowsprit.

6 February 1870. Services on deck again, this time under a cold mist. The sailing men do not attend, perhaps because they worship some sea-God rather than Christ. Neptune, perhaps.

7 February 1870. The passengers from steerage, or 'tween decks' as the more common sailing men call it, gathered on deck today to enjoy the pleasanter temperatures. Most of them are Irish trying to escape life in the mills. The Irish do not speak of their anxieties but rather wear them on their faces when they are alone and looking out on the sea. Perhaps Papa and I do as well. With the afternoon sun painting a yellow-gold streak in the water off our bow amid a freshening wind, there was dancing, which Father and I were compelled to join. What a joyful occasion it was! And to the squeak and croon of the fiddle. Father's new health served him well, and he and I took a dram or two of their whiskey. Several of the Irish men pronounced Papa a 'swell fellow' and 'the genuine article.' As for me, I was addressed as a 'fair rosheen,' and a 'comely garl.' At sunset, the party broke up, though even now as I write, I can hear the singing below deck.

8 February 1870. We dined again with Capt. Gill, and again, after another ably prepared repast by the ship's steward, glasses were raised and toast after toast proposed as we drank the health of Parliament, Mr. Gladstone, and the Queen. I adjourned myself to the bay window seat of the captain's cabin and fell into the trance of the swaying ship and the window pane and the jagged lines of moonlight on the sea rocking around us and below us, into a nameless dream, vivid and forgotten, then Papa's hand on my shoulder slurring his gentle words, *rise, my beautiful daughter, rise.* The bones of the ship croaked quietly as I made my way to our cabin, one hand balancing a candlestick against the darkness, one hand bracing against the passageway, on legs unsteady from sea and sleepiness.

9 February 1870. A family named Corcoran has a new baby, less than a year old. I was allowed to hold him, and it was a great treat, his small pleasant weight nestled against me. Little Mr. Corcoran then, 'Messed his diddy,' as the saying is in the mill slums, and his older sister retrieved him from me to remedy it. I believe her name is Maureen, though I don't remember. The Irish have great hordes of family, everyone seemingly related, as all are addressed as aunt, uncle and cousin.

10 February 1870. The days lengthen rapidly as the earth tilts toward its equator and nudges us toward the sun. Papa reads old copies of the New

Orleans papers and quizzes any Americans he encounters about the habits of our new home. I continue with Rousseau's *Confessions.*

11 February 1870. Off our port bow this morning was a rather remarkable sight, a whale, and I was among the first to see him. It quite took my breath away, and, at first, I couldn't form words and was transfixed by his great blinking eye, larger than a man's head. He staid right where he was, calmly moving his flippers about and blowing wet draughts of air through his blowhole and staring at me. Perhaps he was as transfixed with me as I was with him. It was truly a wondrous thing, and I wondered how a man like Jonah could live inside. To my younger self it was so simple to understand, Jonah sitting and smoking his pipe in the darkness among a great cathedral of ribs, seated on a stool, perhaps. Soon the deck was crowded with us beholders, straining at the rail, parents lifting their children so all could see. And then, with one more blink of his massive eye and a turn of a gigantic flipper, he submerged into the deep, dark blue, a shadow of himself, and then we saw him no more. Papa exclaimed that he was a magnificent creature and asked one of the crew if it was a Right whale. 'Aye, and correct you are, sir,' the man said, 'but if you sees a whale, reverend, sir, then *shorely* it means weather ahead and rough weather, that.'

12 February 1870. This morning on the horizon, a ship appeared. She hailed us and drew near. It was the *Fire Queen* headed in to Southampton. The sun was shining, but the sea was beginning to heave in rolling foothills of cobalt blue saltwater. She seemed to have been the subject of great distress, and the sailors on the *Chrysolite* remarked that in the days of sail, without steam boilers and propellers, she would have been stranded and likely lost. Shredded sails hung from her spars and masts like the graveclothes of Lazarus. Men were dispatched in a launch that dove and rose with a slow pull of oars to the *Fire Queen.* After a time, they returned with the news that there was indeed significant weather ahead. Several casks of drinking water were sent over with some other supplies and eatables for the *Fire Queen.* Papa asked if were to go around it or not.

Capt. Gill said that we can't go around it, only toward it or it will come toward us.

13 February 1870. There shall be no services this sabbath due to rough weather.

15 February 1870. Toward the end of the day on Sunday, two days ago, the sea began to convulse, the gentle, rolling plain transforming itself into hills, and then great mountain ranges. The sea slid under the ship, lifting it up, and the ship slid down the sea raising a deafening, roaring splash before being lifted up again. Outside our cabin window, where there was once a grey sky, there was suddenly grey ocean, and then sky again. The sky darkened so that one couldn't tell if it were sky or sea. Then the sea began to lift and fall even more violently. Soon it became apparent that we were in danger of becoming a catastrophe of the sort that vanishes and is only to be supposed by those in the ports that we have left and were headed. Right became up, left became down, and then the reverse. The steward came through the narrow passageway, beating on each door with the heel of his hand, shouting over the wind and water with an unequivocal message: put out your lanterns and candles, lest they topple and we catch fire in the midst of all this water. In the dark, my portmanteau tumbled over and slid with Papa's sermon chest, rasping across the planks of our cabin floor, and then, right and left exchanged their roles of up and down, and it slid back again, scuffing and rotating along the planks again. The mountainous sea sent jagged waves, one after another. Below us, I could hear children crying 'tween decks and mothers and fathers singing to them, interrupted by sudden changes in what was up and what was down. With each brief pause in movement, the singing began anew. And then right became up and left became down again. It was too rough to write, lest the inkwell topple, and I pen this several days later.

16 February 1870. Weather improved today. A calm, sapphire sea with an azure sky and a bracing north wind. Everything is bright and crisp. The Irish and their bountiful families take to the decks again.

17 February 1870. Capt. Gill says that with another two or three days of sailing we shall be in the Gulf of Mexico. A brace of porpoises escorts us off our starboard bow, vaulting into the air with grinning faces. Birds appear in the air, which is a source of hope as the voyage has grown tiresome to most. Perhaps it was the same with old Noah.

18 February 1870. 'Fiddle' music on deck again with the clap of hands. How I would enjoy playing the piano, even one which is missing a key.

19 February 1870. The colour of the water has changed to a green. The sailing men say it is the colour of the Gulf of Mexico.

20 February 1870. Sunday, fewer 'parishioners' attend services. Perhaps the amusement of it has grown tiresome. Capt. Gill says that this shall be our last sabbath at sea.

21 February 1870. Monday. The sea has long since grown tiresome, and there is no land on the horizon. Capt. Gill maintains that we shall have arrived within a week's time.

23 February 1870. At the mouth of the Misisipi *[sic]* A tug is given us, and a new pilot taken aboard to assist our captain. The land is low and grassy among the many outlets of the river, which is many times wider than the Thames. Families crowd the railings. An alligator was spotted today off the port railing, a fascination for both young and old. The animal is much blacker than I had supposed, rather than green, and as knobby as an old log, which is part of its ruse for prey, Papa says.

26 February, Saturday. New Orleans and America at last.
At last we land in New Orleans, a place that is heard before it is seen. The Irish passengers in steerage are greeted by a wealth of family, men in limp braces (suspenders, rather, here in America), women in stringy hair and uncovered heads, many of their mouths lacking their complement of teeth. But they welcome their relations with great embraces and adoring

appraisals and laughter, and they filter away into the city like the Manchester fog under a midday sun. I watch them with nostalgia, feeling our bonds breaking, though my shipmates have already forgotten me. Even Tommy Haskins, the cabin boy who is kept by the woman in Liverpool, moved along with the older sailors as a sort of mascot, a pet for them. I called to him, 'Tommy! Tommy Haskins!' and he stopped and looked up to me where I stood yet, at the rail of the ship. He shielded his eyes against the sun to find me, and he seemed even smaller to me against the profile of the city. I called down that perhaps I could write to him. He called back that he moves around so, and "sides, I don't read much, ma'am.' I do not know if he doesn't read or can't read, but I suppose it is all the same. I wonder what kind of man he will grow to be. The kind of man who frequents the taverns and bawdy houses of the port cities of the world? The sort of man who gets tatues *[sic]* while nursing a head that is stinging from strong drink and opium? Surely I shall never see him again, and this sets me with a bit of melancholy. I looked again, and he had disappeared into the city with the Irish who have gone off to be Americans. I sit on our bags and write now whilst we wait to be received.

27 February 1870. Sunday. Yesterday, it was quite a while longer when we were greeted by a man named Mr. Morris, who is of middle height and friendly bearing. He seemed to know us straightaway when he arrived, but, of course, surely it helped that Papa was the only vicar on the levee in front of the *Chrysolite*. Mr. Morris begged our pardon for his tardiness, saying that he was expecting a younger man. We introduced ourselves, Mr. Morris taking my hand with a slight bow. When he rose from his bow, he kept his gaze downward. 'Might I say, but that's a fine-looking chest,' he said. 'Beg your pardon, sir?' I said, somewhat aghast, and he pointed to the chest with Papa's sermons in it. I was a little embarrassed by my presumption that he meant my bosom and I admit to blushing. Papa thanked him and told Mr. Morris that they were his sermons, the sum-total of his life's work, as it were. A man loaded our things into a wagon as another man, a light-skinned negro named Lorenzo if I recollect properly, helped Papa and me into a separate carriage, a fine one, with a white silk canopy and woodwork that Papa whispered was mahogany and as fine as one would see in London. The tufted velvet seats faced each other, and Papa and I rode in the rear seat, and Mr. Morris rode facing us, with his back to the driver. He offered Papa a cigar and lit it, and then lit his own. The dense smoke trailed behind us in the bright air as our carriage moved forward in the rumble that is New Orleans. As we rode, Mr. Morris said that he and a Mr. Howard in the city were business associates in 'a certain venture' with our sponsor in St. Matthew Parish, and that this person had instructed them to spare no expense toward our comfort. Mr. Morris said that after a day or two in the city to get our 'land-legs,' we are to take a steamer upriver and then down a Bayou Lafoosh *[sic]* to St. Matthew.

The principal high street of this city is Canal Street, as wide as any avenue in Manchester or London. Greeting visitors is a statue of Henry Clay, the Great Compromiser, though Papa said that on the subject of compromising, he wasn't quite good enough. 'Yes, I suppose you are right,' Mr. Morris said, and our horse's head shook as if in agreement, the magnificent feather in his harness swinging to the clop of his hooves on the street below, this Canal Street. High above Mr. Clay's head on the brick façade was written '*J. Levois & Jameson,*' two of the many merchants who hold shops on Canal Street. Mr. Morris said that it is the division between the French-speaking part of town and the American, English-speaking part of town. Our carriage paused in a gentle veer to let a mule and its trailing omnibus pass, and then we turned onto a different street. Two Negro women walked by engaged in animated conversation, unconcerned with the baskets of laundry atop their colourfully wrapped heads. They wore large hoops from their ears, much like the drawings of pirates I have seen in book tales. I turned back to look at them recede into the distance, my palms pressed into the soft velvet. A steam whistle launched a hooting shriek at our backs, far off on the river. After no more than two or three streets, the driver stopped in front of a grand edifice with six enormous columns and helped Papa and me down. Mr. Morris escorted us to the marble steps as negro porters took our things. Mr. Morris and Lorenzo took their leave, and Papa and I entered the hotel and waited in the lobby among the massive columns rather like those of a

Greek temple. The lobby was crowded with guests who conversed in a torrent that swirled around the marble. Whirlwinds of conversation flitted by in English and French as the stony space baffled the sounds into a resonant babble.

Papa approached the register where a pair of clerks attended the desk and a third placed messages in the cubby holes behind them. I waited on a circular settee, tufted in rose-coloured damask. Papa's chest and our baggage were clustered at my feet like a small outpost of our lives. People came and went between Papa and me in the bustling echoes. Finely dressed children with negro nannies. Handsome men and elegantly draped women. White-gloved porters who handled the baggage of these people with effortless, herculean strength. The scent of roses from the enormous arrangement behind me. The sounds of that street, St. Charles, coming and going with the opening and closing of the gigantic doors. It was a tableau that begged the question, *how did I arrive here, and why?* Papa's voice startled me with the news that the clerk had told him that our lodgings were the 'compliments of St. Matthew Parish and our benefactors at St. Margaret's Church there.' He seemed rather puzzled, as did I. I looked down to discover that our bags and Papa's chest were gone. Quickly, I stood and looked about. The rush of people continued, but with new faces. I looked about for anyone who might have borne our belongings away.

A man approached who introduced himself as Charles Howard, friend and partner of our St. Matthew benefactor. Papa said that we seemed to have misplaced our bags, but Mr. Howard told us not to worry for our bags and that they were already in our room. He is a man with a rather wan face and a small beard that he strokes like a pet. We followed him up the great marble staircase down a hallway thickly carpeted in rich red and yellow. Gaslit sconces leaked an amber light into the passage, and we cast multiple, incongruent shadows in it. After a few moments, we found ourselves in one of the most opulent rooms I have ever been in, the one in which I now write these lines.

Mr. Howard opened the tall glass doors to a balcony, and a breeze stirred the curtains, as sheer as gossamer. He said it would be an excellent vantage point to watch the procession which is to take place on Tuesday.

We didn't know of what he was speaking, and he seemed surprised that we didn't. 'Why, Carnival. Mardi Gras,' he said, rather incredulously. As he departed us, he said that until then, the city is ours, and that wherever we dine or shop, to tell the waiter or clerk that we are guests of St. Matthew Parish, and that shall settle the matter. With that, he shook Papa's hand and kissed the white cotton of mine and left. Sleep came quickly, though I still feel the rocking of the ship and wonder how long I shall do so. I finish this entry in our palace, as I must dress for church services, our first in this new land and this new life.

28 February 1870. Monday. The newspaper was delivered at our door this morning without any need for requesting it, and I amused myself with a leisurely morning of reading it with tea, which is also brought up unrequested with a breakfast service of toast, butter, and marmalade. The intelligence in the foremost newspaper of this place, the *Daily Picayune*, of yesterday, says that the steamer *City of Boston*, bound for Liverpool from Halifax in Canada, is missing and presumed lost, and I wonder if it was the same storm that tormented us in our crossing. Two blocks of the Texas city of Galveston were consumed by fire, with the result of a million and a half American dollars in losses. A train accident in Mississippi has killed fourteen. Interspersed amongst these parcels of bad news is an advertisement for Moody's on Canal & Royal, where one may buy costumes and theatrical hosiery for merrymaking. But among news good and bad, there is no news of Parliament or other English matters, though I suppose that I should not have expected any. Papa and I took a sojourn today into this strange new country. Everywhere there are soldiers of the occupying army, part of 'Reconstruction' as it is called. They are on every other street corner, as well as the coffee houses and public houses, called saloons here. Also in no small number are the dissolute women who attend them. It is much like Ancoats and Miles Platting except that the weather here is so much more clement. After a diet of relatively simple ship's fare, Papa and I have certainly feasted like royalty. Oysters, trout, beef, sauces, gravies. The menu at M. Antoine's was in French, and I was compelled to order for dear Papa. He seemed proud and delighted that I did so. Later, I was taken by Mrs. Morris, wife of Mr. Morris whom we met on Saturday, to a shop, Braselman & Co. on Magazine Street, another of the High Streets of this city. An evening dress was purchased for me by our benefactor in St. Matthew Parish for a ball to be held tomorrow night. It is a brilliant green trimmed in black and fits perfectly. I have never had such a dress as this. I wear it as I write now. My vanity yet prevents me from removing it! Our anonymous St. Matthew benefactor has also arranged for tickets to a performance of the 'Flying Dutchman' at the St. Charles Theatre, a benefit for a Mr. Hill, as the finely printed programme indicated. I am too exhausted to attend, as is Papa, as he has spent all day at the Crescent City Museum on St. Charles just down from our hotel. He saw a great many curiosities there today in the company of Mr. Morris and has been writing furiously at the desk here in our elegant quarters.

2 March 1870. A Wednesday. Shrove Tuesday yesterday, or, locally, Mardi Gras. The *Daily Picayune* had a frontpage article on Carnival, *Carni Vale*, or in plainer language, *adieu to the flesh.* Everywhere the streets were prepared for the type of carnival that the crew of the *Chrysolite* spoke of in the same reverential tones as the carnival of Rio de Janeiro in Brasil. Every conceivable colour was worn, men wore masks and leggings and were dressed in such costumes which were as numerous as they were varied. There was singing and shouting, and handkerchiefs fluttered from balconies. On the matter of balconies, the newspapers earlier in the day reported that one such balcony collapsed last year on Camp Street with the loss of life, and there have been admonishments concerning the risk of overcrowding. Nevertheless, there was quite a throng on all of them facing St. Charles as the Krewe of Comus passed below us. Among those present on our balcony was Mr. Howard. Far from jubilant, he seemed distant and despondent, almost bitter, particularly when asked by Papa if he had ever considered participating. He asked it of Mr. Howard innocently enough, while waving to the procession. Mr. Howard replied in a rather annoyed tone that Comus would not admit men like him, nor would the Metairie Jockey Club, with the reason (according to Mr. Howard) that they are 'new money.' His language was as slurred as it was candid as he took a sip from his tumbler and then looked at it. In fact, he held it up and, for a moment, it appeared as if he might throw it at a wagon with revelers passing below. But he paused and placed it down gently and went inside, petting his beard thoughtfully. As he went inside, I thought I heard him mutter, 'They'll see. All those old money boys. They'll see.'

The procession passed gaily below us with torch bearers called flambeaux accompanying the wagons with men dressed as actors on them. At last the final wagon crept by, pulled by magnificently liveried horses, and we were off to a ball held at the Odd Fellows' Hall, tickets secured by none other than our sponsor from St. Matthew Parish. The darkness of the big ballroom was punctuated by the amber beacons of gaslights, we dancers like shapes in the underworld. Men and women smiled behind masks, a gathering of half-faces in the glowing gloom. Meanwhile, the orchestra played a great many airs which were quite suitable even for those like me, less gifted by Terpsichore, the Muse of Dancing. Papa favoured a chair on the periphery of the immense room, near the punchbowls attended by the finely dressed servants who were quite attentive to his thirst. Masks were presented at the door of the ballroom by a committee of ladies who also wore them. The smell of cigars and roses and perfume and lilac weaved through the gathering which Papa estimated at several hundred. And as the god of merriment, Dionysus, laughed and glass after glass of punch performed its work, I danced with a succession of partners, names all forgotten, faces half-remembered.

One person, however, I do remember. He was tall, and in the dim gaslight, behind his mask was the trail of a scar, shaped like a comet or a sickle at the corner of his sparkling paper façade. He walked with a limp, which he said is from the 'late war' as it is called here, though he is not the only one to possess an uneven gait. And then in the murky light, we found ourselves a pair, my white-gloved hand in his, my eyes on his eyes, our masks concealing all else. The tip of his scar parted his beard and moved down behind his mask. The orchestra was far away, the conversations of everyone else nonexistent, the servants and dancers and Papa and the orchestra all far, far away. It was not at all comfortable, but rather, held a certain tension. I spoke in attempt to subdue it, telling my dance-partner that he was certainly an agile dancer. 'Despite my limitation, you mean?' he answered. I stammered that I didn't mean to draw attention to it. He said that it was no issue and that it was all in the service of 'our late country.' The music called for a change of partners, and he bowed to me and I to him, and the musicians favoured us with another air. And with the brush of taffeta, the denizens of the darkened ballroom seemed to return. Several times in the night, when we were dancing with other partners, I felt his gaze on me, even without seeing it. I would follow its strange energy and see him move away with a turn of his partner into the depths of the ballroom, his height and limp betraying him as the man with the scar. A continued succession of brandy and rum-imbued punches made the evening take wings and we revelers moved through the tawny light of the dim ball room. Today, the bells of the many Catholic churches ring penance, and the mark of ashes is upon the face of much of the population. The Bishop of Manchester would be quite beside himself among all these displays of 'popery.' Now our things are collected as we leave the city for the journey to our new home.

3 March 1870. We arrived last night at our new home in St. Matthew Parish, St. Margaret's Church. The vicarage appears to be quite cozy, and we are afforded all the domestic comforts that we might hope for. From the steamer *Henry Tete*, which was tied to a cypress tree in the bayou, hired men unpacked our trunks and moved them up and into the lovely red-brick cottage behind the church and bell tower of the same material. Papa helped one of the men carry in his sermon chest, declining any offers of help. We found the house stocked with barrels of flour, etc., a whole side of some sort of salted meat, another barrel of corn meal, a bushel of oranges and a smaller basket of lemons, all courtesy of the St. Margaret's Ladies Altar Guild. There is also a generous cannister of Darjeeling tea, a most thoughtful surprise. When we were unpacked, the committee took us inside St. Margaret's. There is a very fine piano next to the pulpit, and I could not help but to sit and play, 'Jesus, Lover of My Soul.' One of the committeemen, a Mr. Parris, I believe, remarked that he had no idea that they would be getting a pianist in the bargain and that Sam had outdone himself on this one. Now as I write, it is just Papa and I, enjoying a quiet morning after all the greetings and hullaballoo of our arrival yesterday.

Sammy, 1982

There were footsteps in the hall, a light, familiar patter. He put his bookmark, a deposit slip from the St. Matthew Parish Planters Bank, in his place between the pages, in the spot about an English vicar and his daughter starting a new life right here in St. Matthew Parish, halfway around the world. He held the book in his hands, thinking of a tearful Irish housekeeper holding it in hers as she thought of the little girl and her parents who had had to leave her, and then her tearful son finding it among her things when she passed away, and then Alice herself being reunited with it and remembering her childhood confidant, an Irish housekeeper called Mrs. Sullivan. Now it had fallen into his hands.

Elizabeth's small face appeared in the doorway to his study. He put the diary into the top drawer of the ornate mahogany desk of four generations of Teague men and pushed away from it. His daughter and her big grin trotted to him and crawled in his lap. She put her head under his chin and said, "Daddy."

"What, baby?" he asked.

"You take me to the li-berry? It's gonna be story time."

He kissed her forehead, which meant yes, and he put her on her own two feet and took down his flannel coat from the rack in the hall. He kept his eyes from the portrait on the wall.

They drove past the fields where the cane was sprouting in thin, green parallel lines all the way to the trees bunched along the bayou and the canal. Within a month, it would be time to off-barr, to pull the soil away from the plants and into the rows, so the sun could warm the roots and stimulate the stalks to grow. Teeter was getting the three-row machines ready, and Sammy hoped he would stay clean for it.

The buildings of town began to appear, a convenience store called the Gator Stop, the post office, the brick walls and aluminum awnings of St. Matthew Elementary. Out front, a sign with a diminutive, doe-eyed horse said, *Home of the Ponies.* They passed Mr. Clyde's barbershop with the red-white-and-blue spirals on the pole. Mr. Picquet was outside looking across the road and the bayou. After they passed by, Elizabeth asked, "Daddy, what does this mean?"

Sammy looked over and his daughter was making the middle-finger salute, looking at it herself as if it had just appeared on her hand.

"That's not a very nice thing to do," he said. "Where did you see that?"

"That man sittin' outside did it," she said, "so I did it back to him."

He tried not to smile and managed to say, "Well, baby, don't do it again, even if someone does it to you. It might offend them."

"O-fend them?" she asked.

"Hurt their feelings," he said.

Oh, her facial expression said. She seemed to be trying to figure out why the man in front of the barbershop was trying to hurt *their* feelings. They always tried to be nice to other people because Jesus said so. They pulled into the white-shell parking lot of the St. Matthew Parish Library.

The St. Matthew Soldiers and Sailors Memorial stood on the lawn between the library and city hall, surrounded by a semicircle of camellias with crimson bursts of flowers amid dark green leaves. Tapped into the granite were the names of the two men killed in the war against North Vietnam, the four killed in the war against North Korea, the twelve killed in the war against the countries of Germany and Japan, the one killed in the war against Spain, and the twenty-seven killed in the war against the United States. He wondered how close his great-grandfather had been to having his name etched with them, if a bullet meant for him had grazed his arm or hit the man next to him. Back in the hallway of his home, the war hero and scholar had a faint touch of reddish brown on one sleeve, a detail which was always pointed out to visitors on the Spring Pilgrimage Tour by his mother when she was alive. But through luck and turn-of-events, Old Sam Teague had lived and avoided having his name etched into the granite façade. And equally through chance, four more Samuel Teagues had been born.

Elizabeth pulled her daddy's hand, and they moved from the granite marker to the library. Inside, Miss Robin, the librarian, was just beginning the story of *Clovis the Crawfish* to the semicircle of children gathered before her. Elizabeth let go of Sammy's hand and sat with them on the carpeted floor.

Sammy sat at a table in the background and listened to the story for a while, but soon he got up and browsed the shelves. From within them, he could hear Miss Robin's voice ask, "And, den what you tink happen nex?" Small hands went up in the air, and small voices gave her possibilities about what was going to "happen nex."

He floated down the aisles and came to a room marked *Archives.* Inside was a desk with a microfilm reader and a metal cabinet. He slid open one of the thin drawers to find little boxes that read, *St. Matthew Parish Compass, 1858-1865.* He opened the drawer under it and found boxes that said, *St. Matthew Parish Compass, 1866-1875.* His finger followed the labels, *1868*, *1869*, and then, *1870.* He pulled out the little box that said, *February 1870.*

It took him a few minutes to figure out how to load the roll of film into the reader. At first, it was upside down, and then it was backwards. Finally, he loaded it correctly and turned the knob, and history scrolled past in a blur. Dates cruised past, under the bulb and projected onto the blank white screen. He slowed when the date appeared and scanned the two-sheet newspaper of a small, nineteenth century town. There it was among advertisements for liniments, corsets, and carriages, in a column called *On Dit–,* or, "It is said–"

> St. Margaret's Church has welcomed a new vicar, Reverend Arthur Lamb and his daughter, Alice Lamb. They have arrived hither from Manchester, England.

Such a major event in the lives of two people, a perilous transatlantic voyage to the other side of the world, reduced to a two-sentence paragraph. He scanned the rest of the February and March 1870 issues of *The Compass* and found the familiar beacon of his name:

> Persons with knowledge of the whereabouts of Paulina "Polly" H. Teague, late of Mount Teague Plantation, St. Matthew Parish are kindly asked to contact S. M. Teague via *The Compass.*

He was scanning further into March 1870 when he felt a tap on his shoulder. It was Elizabeth. The story of *Clovis the Crawfish* was over, and story time was concluded. He gathered her hand in his, and they went home.

Alice, 1870

3 March 1870. How strange it is to wake up in a new bed in a new room in a new place on a new continent. This morning as I look outside my window at the live oak that shades the churchyard, I see squirrels undulate and prance in silhouette on the limbs large and small. There is the smallest shake in leaf-shadows against the pale blue sky as the little creatures leap from one limb to another. One limb arises from another and is distinctly curved so that it looks rather like a scythe such as the grim reaper might wield. Yesterday, after the previous day's unpacking and the beginning of putting this place in the shape of a home, there was a knock on the door. Having just risen, Papa straightened his collar in the looking glass in the hall and went to open the door. Standing there was a dark woman with greying hair, like the glass plate negative of an old daguerreotype. Her hair was in two long ponytails like plaited grey bullwhips. She introduced herself as Mozie Cousins, 'yo' house girl,' though she was at least Papa's age. She carried a basket of things, among them an enormous loaf of bread, some eggs and a crock of cheese or perhaps butter. The end of a portion of bacon protruded from under a towel. She took off her shawl and placed it on a hook by the door and proceeded to make us a breakfast of biscuits (American) and bacon (streaky–also American). Having fed us, she cleaned the dishes from the table, and then cleaned the kitchen and started on the rest of the house.

4 March 1870. First Friday in Lent. Mozie fried fish and baked bread, and half as much would have been ample enough to feed the multitude. There are small fritters as well, made from the immense barrel of corn meal. The paper of this place, The *St. Matthew Parish Compass*, and the French version, *La Boussole de St. Mathieu*, carry a condemnation of the refusal of the occupying army to allow the annual procession of Mardi Gras here, the Krewe de Jupitre.

5 March 1870. The flowers of this place riot cheerfully, explosions of white, pink, magenta, and purple azaleas, tulip trees percussing in pink, redbud trees, white snows of bridal wreath, all quite out of step with Lenten penance. The ground sprouts hillocks of clover with tuffs of tiny orbs of delicate white flowers. A garden also grows here, attended by Mozie. It appears to have been growing all throughout the winter, a miraculous thing after the stern cold of northern England.

6 March 1870. Papa's first Sunday in an American pulpit. The church here has a bell-tower of sorts with two flights of iron stairs that lead to a platform made of the local wood, cypress, and a bell with a rope on its clapper like a jellyfish with one tentacle. Papa ascended the steps and rang the bell to signal the hour of services. After the gathering hymn, Papa thanked the generous people of St. Margaret's Church for the opportunity to serve as their vicar and hoped that his accent would not be a barrier, as he had not mastered American English yet, to which there was a scattering of polite laughter. I played 'When I Survey the Wondrous Cross,' and 'Jerusalem the Golden' for the offertory song. Church service was well-attended, though Papa thinks it may be from curiosity about us, rather than a need for repentance and thanksgiving. Afterwards on the steps, the reception line was long, as it seemed we shook every hand in St. Matthew Parish and received the well-wishes of all. Among them was someone who was vaguely familiar, and after he had introduced himself, I realised he was the man with whom I had danced several nights before in New Orleans at the carnival ball. Specifically, he was the man with the limp and the scar. I think he said his name was Teague though I cannot be sure due to the lengthy procession of introductions.

7 March 1870. Mozie arrived early and began the wash, which is the custom here on Mondays. When the wash was hung in the warm sunshine, she started a 'pot of beans,' which is also the custom here on

Monday. Her energy is dizzying, hands moving from task to task, wiped on an apron or hem in between, frequently with a song on her lips.

8 March 1870. In going through the last of my packed things, I found a recipe for scones that was Mama's. I showed the recipe to Mozie and asked her if she could make them. She said she could if I would read it to her. I was puzzled by this. Read it to you? I asked. 'Yes ma'am,' she replied, and then she said, 'Ain't none of us ol' Mount Teague *n*– can read.' I asked that she not refer to herself in such derogatory terms, and then we set about remedying her illiteracy. I spread flour onto the bread board, and we began with her name. She had no idea how it was spelled, so I spelled it how I might. I traced the letters slowly, M-O-Z-I-E. Her old crooked brown finger traced the letters in the powdery white, and her grey-ringed pupiled eyes looked to me. 'That's my name? Mozie? 'Show-nuff?'

She regarded it as one would regard a diamond found unexpectedly in a chest or a 'pearl of great price' in the stony crags of an oyster shell. I brushed it out, and we went on to other simple words. We sounded out letters and combinations of letters. We spelled the names of her children. We spelled the things in the kitchen. *Sugar. Flour. Lard. Bacon.* The scones emanated a warm scent from the oven, and when they were done, we ate them with Darjeeling tea and treacle (called molasses here) whilst we practiced with more letters and numbers. Her old brown finger with its gnarled joints and callouses pushed through the flour awkwardly as she traced the loops and lines that make the written word. She is an enthusiastic student, and I fancy myself in the very same mold as Miss Latour from my Guildford days.

9 March 1870. The Union soldiers garrison this place like the Romans in Judea, bored and passing time. Many are negroes. Mozie believes that the men who are stationed here from 'way up nawf' conserve their strength for the coming of the heat and the steam which surely shall not be long in arriving but shall tarry greatly in departing.

10 March 1870. The paper here, the St. Matthew Parish Compass, carries this announcement:

> Persons with knowledge of the whereabouts of Paulina "Polly" H. Teague, late of Mount Teague Plantation, St. Matthew Parish are kindly asked to contact S. M. Teague via *The Compass.*

Certainly, this is the Mr. Teague of our church, St. Margaret's. I read this to Mozie, and she was quite beside herself on the subject. She said that 'Marse Sam's' first wife died having the third little girl and then his second wife, this Polly Teague, 'up and left' her husband and her stepdaughters. 'Shame, shame!' she said as she took down a rolling pin that she used to flatten dough. She said that Polly Teague had the gardener, a man named Luther, take her to the river landing in Donaldsonville and put her on a steamer for up north. All the while, Mozie shook her head at the shame of it and spoke down to the rolling pin as it worked the mound of biscuit dough. Her brown skin was white with flour to the elbows, her fingers were thick with dough. 'Miss Alice,' she continued, 'Miss Polly just turn her back on them girls and Marse Sam. Bless they hearts!' She took a teacup and began cutting circles and lifting them out onto a baking pan shining with butter. Her gaze never departed from the circles of dough, and it might have seemed that the tale was intended for the biscuits and not me. She said that 'Marse Sam,' as she calls Mr. Teague, never lets anyone see his true feelings, but that it hurt him deeply to be left by her, and for his girls to lose another mother. As I write this evening, I find it incredibly heartbreaking for Mr. Teague. Papa has lost one wife, but Mr. Teague has lost two, one in childbirth, one by abandonment. It must certainly be a tremendous burden he bears.

13 March 1870. Services again today, still robustly attended despite rain.

14 March 1870. Papa and I have been furnished a fine chaise with a handsome white mare (named Sugar!) to pull it, this after a seemingly innocent remark after services Sunday by Papa about wishing to see more of the countryside. It is by no means as fine as the carriage of the Bishop of Manchester, but it is certainly a luxury to us. Mozie's nephew Simeon showed Papa and me how to hitch Sugar into the traces and then showed us how to care for her. She is a handsome thing with glassy black eyes that blink thoughtfully. I think we shall get on well, Sugar, Papa, and I.

16 March 1870. We made a trip into Napoleonville with Sugar and our chaise. The talk in town was general in nature, though particular to this part of the agricultural world–acreage, rainfall, yield, and so forth. This evening, over dinner, Papa and I discussed the day's news. He says that he heard from none other than Mr. Teague himself that his wife Polly Teague suffered from mania. Her torment must have been great indeed to abruptly leave in such a manner, Papa says. She must have been quite like Mr. Phillips in Surrey, a man who used to talk to himself on his front stoop and whose sister was consumed by fire.

18 March 1870. The weather seems to grow more pleasant each day, and Papa and I take advantage of it to get about our new home. There is something quaint about St. Matthew, though the buildings are either hovels, quite abject in their lowness, or else grand structures. And none so grand as the place on the Thibodaux Road known as Mount Teague. It is simply a showplace which rivals the finest manor houses in Surrey and Kent. It abounds with outbuildings, appearing from the road to have its own dairy, cooperage, blacksmith shop, and commissary. These we could identify from the road, though there were other buildings and industries further back which we could not. Papa says that Mr. Teague lives alone with his daughters, but that is all he knows.

21 March 1870. As I played in church, I glanced at the congregation, as is my custom. The attendance was still robust, though not as well-attended as our first Sunday, as for many, curiosity has been sated. Some closed their eyes in rapture, though some of the men feigned rapture for the purpose of a catnap. Among those who did not close their eyes was Mr. Teague. I found that he was watching me, and each time I finished playing and everyone's eyes were turned to Papa, his were still upon me. I must admit, my little confidant, it was both stirring and unsettling. Papa preached on the loaves and the fishes, and I played 'God Moves in a Mysterious Way' for the offertory. The weather today is pleasant, and the windows were opened for the whole of the service. The cane emerges from the ground beyond the dense oak-shadows of the churchyard.

25 March 1870. Men work with mules in the fields behind the vicarage, pulling soil away from the earth to warm the roots of the sugarcane so that it may grow more vigorously. Papa says that it is called 'off-barring' and that it may serve as a spiritual analogy for us in some manner.

28 March 1870. Sunday dinner on the grounds today, prepared by the Ladies' Altar Guild, or rather, their 'hired girls.' It was an immense feast served on fine china with exquisite silver under the oaks and magnolias.

2 April 1870. Papa came into the kitchen today to find Mozie and I practicing her reading and writing. We were reading from the Psalter, Psalm 119. Papa asked, 'What is this, then?' I told him that Mozie was learning to read, and he said, 'Most excellent! Reading is freedom. The first step in subjugating a people and ensuring them thus is to prevent them from reading.' I am not sure if Mozie understood his words, though I am sure she knew what he meant by them. She progresses daily.

3 April 1870. Papa decided to change his sermon this week to Psalm 119: 'Your Word is a Lamp unto My Feet, and a Light unto My Path.' Thus, I have changed the musical selections to reflect it. 'Zion, the Marvelous Story Be Telling.'

5 April 1870. A lovely day today, and Papa and I went fishing on Bayou Lafourche, much as we used to do in the River Wey in Guildford. The spring breeze pushed the new green leaves into slow, swaying dances. Papa was placing a worm on his hook. As the worm squirmed to avoid its fate, Papa remarked that a fish doesn't feel the point of the hook nor the sting of the barb until it is too late. 'And so it is with sin, my dear,' he said as he wiped his hands together, 'and so it is with sin,' he repeated, and he threw his line into the water. We enjoyed an idyllic day and returned with a pail-full of fish. On returning, Papa asked Mozie what sort of fish they were and if they were eatable. 'They all eatable, just depend on how hungry you is!' she laughed with a semi-toothed smile as she looked through the pail of fins crowding together in the dark water. Her brown hand fearlessly grabbed each fish from the splashing jumble. None could long elude her grasp as she pinched behind the gills to hold each up and assign it its name. Sac-a-lait, catfish ('French folk calls 'em bar-boo,' she said.) She came to one she called a shoe-pick. I do not know why it is called thusly, but Mozie said never to put your finger in its mouth. She pressed down on the lower jaw to reveal rows of white, needle-like teeth. 'Oh my,' Papa said as he gazed inside the fish's mouth, 'That is absolutely pre-historic.' Mozie said, 'Show is,' though I am doubtful she knew what pre-historic meant. She said that the shoe-pick can crawl on land when the weather is hot and dry. We ate the fish after she had fried them, except for the shoe-pick, which Papa dissected on a plank in the churchyard, his sleeves rolled up and his coat hanging from a tree limb. As I write, he scribbles feverishly in his study, but not on a Sunday sermon. I fear it is a fish story which shall be rejected by the Linnaens.

7 April 1870. I received a rather unexpected amusement today. The newspaper, the *St. Matthew Parish Compass*, today carries an advertisement for a baker in Thibodaux, but there is a small error of great consequence: Through the simple transposition of one letter, instead of offering the *nicest* cakes, the bakery carries the *incest* cakes. Oh my! I feel as though I should write the editor of the paper, but I don't want to appear to be adopting an air of superiority. However, if the error is repeated, then certainly I shall!

9 April 1870. The *Compass* reminds its readers that the late war concluded five years ago today, though the presence of the soldiers reminds us that the anger simmers yet.

10 April 1870. Palm Sunday. This morning as I played the gathering hymn, 'All Glory Laud & Honour,' Mr. Teague limped in. He is rather handsome, in that rugged, American way, with a sandy-brown beard. He was alone but seemed to pride himself on keeping his posture straight and his head up. But as he sat upon the pew, he winced. Certainly, his wound from the late war must give him great trouble yet. Would it trouble him less if the cause for which he fought had succeeded? While Papa prayed, I watched Mr. Teague as he bowed his head with the rest of the congregation. Such a shame for a man of his pride and character to be left by his wife! Surely, he must feel very much humiliated. As I was thinking thusly during Papa's prayer, Mr. Teague looked up and I'm afraid our eyes met again. I quickly verted mine to the safety of the white-and-black keys. His eyes seemed to be on me every time I glanced out on the congregation.

11 April 1870. I awoke late last night (or early this morning, rather) to the flash and crash of lightning and thunder. Objects were suddenly and briefly illuminated. A hair brush. A book. The mantel and fireplace in my room. A clock that said half past three, before vanishing again in the darkness. I gathered my dressing gown about me. Papa was awake also and looking out of the window of his study. The rain was falling with the murmur like that of a crowd awaiting the start of a performance. 'She loved thunderstorms,' he announced to the window and my reflection in it. 'That she did,' I said quietly. I drew near him, and we watched together, the churchyard and the sugarcane that encroached upon it and everything else here. Like a photographer's flash, the oak and the graveyard and the church and its bell tower, all were suddenly revealed and then taken away again. I asked him if he ever thought of marrying again. It is a question I have not asked before. He answered, 'Who here would want the affections of an old English vicar? And a poor one at that?' The downpour drummed on the roof, and the lightning revealed and took away its revelation. Then he said, 'It may rain equally on the just and the unjust, my dear, but it doesn't rain riches. Only rain.' And then he looked up past the eaves to the starless sky and said again quietly, 'Only rain.' The rain slackened and then dribbled for a while, and we listened to its pattering dance on the roof and the ground and the stones in the graveyard. Finally, Papa said to the window and the darkened churchyard. 'Well, my beautiful daughter, it seems as though the Creator's performance is over, and we may go back to bed for a time.' I returned to bed, but sleep took its time returning to me. Nor did it return to Papa. His sporadic cough betrayed that he was still in his study, and the light reflected in the hall betrayed that he was at his desk. And then, like a thief or a magician, sleep returned to me.

12 April 1870. The amendment of the American Constitution to give the right to vote to all men, regardless of colour or prior servitude has caused quite a bit of consternation here in St. Matthew. Talk among the men in town seethes with disquiet. It is also so with the women of this place, though they still cannot vote. 'Most of them can't even read!' is the bitter muttering. Well, then, perhaps we should teach them, I say, though not aloud. The sentiment here precludes it, and we are still new to this place. The *Daily Picayune* carries a notice for the Louisiana State Lottery, and a Charles T. Howard is listed as its president. Surely, this is Mr. Howard, our host when we arrived in New Orleans, the man who is bitter at the 'old money boys.'

13 April 1870. Papa has found lovely specimens of an iris of a lovely purple colour as well as a small blue flower of the phlox family. He previously has not heard of either. He says that there seems to be two of every kind of creature here and exclaims that Noah could have anchored his boat in Bayou Lafourche and loaded them all aboard. I laugh with him until he announces that he shall write to the Linnaens and perhaps this shall be his admittance. I do not discourage him, though my optimism wavers. His exuberance on the matter is beyond my control and cannot be tempered. I fear, however, that it is a prelude to more disappointment.

14 April 1870. The English language is spoken here, but some of the consonants frequently go missing (missin'). As well, some of the humour I find nonsensical and obscure. Whilst in Aucoin's Dry Goods today, I overheard this riddle. I do not think they knew I was so close as to hear them, for it was told in a somewhat hushed tone. One man said to a second, 'Here's one: What is the difference between a bird and a man?' The second man replied, 'What, then?' The first then said, 'Why, a bird can whistle through his pecker, and a man can't!' They both laughed heartily, though I must admit, I fail to discern the meaning. Perhaps it is some sort of nonsense-joke with no intended meaning. Nevertheless, they laughed in fits that rose in gusts with a great deal of bending forward and slapping of thighs as each repeated, "*and a man can't!*" I have thought upon it all day but do not find its meaning.

15 April 1870. Good Friday services were held today. Papa read St. John's account of the Passion, and I played 'Alas! And Did My Saviour Bleed.' Afterward, in the vicarage, we spent the day quietly, as we have done on all Good Fridays since I was a girl.

16 April 1870. When all other subjects are exhausted, the town-talk of the common folk is of Mount Teague, and the abrupt departure of Mr. Teague's wife. It is said that she is a vivacious redhead with a remarkable figure and was last seen on a steamer headed upriver, perhaps for Memphis or her native St. Louis. Certainly, it is difficult for a proud man like Mr. Teague to endure the shame of being left in such a manner and becoming the butt of town-talk in the wake of it. Gossip is as much a cruel pastime here as elsewhere.

17 April 1870. Easter Sunday. He is Risen. St. Margaret's was arranged beautifully with flowers gathered from the countryside, and Papa wore a white vestment made for him on the direction of the Ladies' Altar Guild. Papa's sermon was one I have heard before, 'Roll Away the Stone from Your Hearts.' In the afternoon, there was a great deal of visiting at the vicarage, most of whom are members of the congregation. Late in the afternoon, the party departed, leaving us a tremendous ham and other eatables. The animal from which it came could be assumed to be as large as a hippopotamus! Papa is presented an Easter gift of cherry brandy by one of our parishioners.

18 April 1870. Papa and I fished on the banks of Bayou Lafourche. The water here, whether in the bayous, canals, or swamps, is in no hurry to go anywhere, and I believe that St. Matthew is every bit as green as the Irish in Ancoats say their home country is. Never have I seen such glowing colours in nature, azalea blossoms as red as rubies, gardenia flowers as white as ivory, all set amongst emerald foliage as green as absinthe. As we fished, waiting for the citizens of the world beneath the surface of the water to greet our hooks, my mind wandered, as it has since I was a girl. Trees overlooked the water and were mirrored in it, a flat version of them. Circles appeared, from fish and from turtles, and oval rings from the knobby snouts of alligators. Perhaps Papa is quite in the right in saying that this place rivals the Garden of Eden in the matter of beauty.

19 April 1870. This in the New Orleans *Picayune*, last week's edition, just arrived:

> *WANTED*, a young woman of good character to serve as governess and tutor for three fine and well-behaved girls, and to aid in their formation as young women with the teaching of French, Music, and Mathematics. Position to commence, May 1870. Candidates should apply through *The Compass*, St. Matthew Parish, Louisiana.

I would apply, if it were not for the necessity of keeping Papa company. The days, though beautiful, tend to drag. It would be nice to share the society of three 'fine and well-behaved girls.' Perhaps we would get on as sisters, almost, a welcome diversion and an answer to my childhood prayer for siblings.

20 April 1870. Another day of fine weather called for fishing, and Papa and I adjourned to the banks of the Lafourche. After a morning's work ending with a pail full of several fine perch, called sac-a-lait here, we discovered a snake swallowing a mouse at the bayou's edge. The snake was wide-eyed, its jaw hinged over its overmatched opponent. The tiny, wiry feet of the mouse kicked against its fate until at last it became merely a tail and then a bulge in its captor. 'Poor mouse!' I cried. 'Why must it be so?' Papa replied that it is the Creator's way, for if not, we would be knee-deep in mice. 'Remember, my beautiful daughter,' he said, 'even the Garden of Eden had a snake in it.'

21 April 1870. Mozie and I read the newspapers again today, and I find that she has made steady progress and can now read increasing amounts of the stories with less help from me. In coming across the recurring notice requesting information on the absconded Mrs. Teague, Mozie shook her head and made a clicking noise of regret or disgust or both. 'Shame, that woman,' she said. Then we read the notice the *Picayune* carries for the situation as governess for 'three fine and well-behaved girls.' Mozie said that it is for Mr. Teague's daughters, who have lost their mother and been abandoned by their stepmother.

24 April 1870. Sunday again, a day of rest, unless you are a vicar and his daughter. Mr. Teague made his usual appearance, finely dressed in a top hat and silk cravat, but this time with his daughters, who have been visiting Mr. Teague's mother in Misissippi *[sic]*. The youngest is only four or five or so and has a face that seems to be all rosy cheeks and a headful of ringlets, a fine little cherub. She fidgeted a great deal, swinging her legs and making shadow-puppets on the pew and staring through the window as I can remember doing when I was but her age. The middle girl of about nine or ten, I presume, toyed with her little sister's sandy hair, but also tended to contemplate what lay out the open windows. The oldest, whose name is Jenny, sat next to her father and dutifully participated in the service, kneeling at the communion rail between her father and her sisters whilst raising her eyes as Papa presented the Eucharist to her. It is said that she plays quite well upon the violin. I spy on them from behind the piano and find myself wondering if they have acquired their governess. On the steps after services, Jenny introduced herself and her sisters, Ida, the middle and Lucy, the youngest. Papa asked Mr. Teague if the position of governess has been filled, and Mr. Teague said yes, it has. Then he bid me good day and departed in the carriage with his daughters. His manner is so gracious.

25 April 1870. I am seventeen today. Mozie made a cake which we enjoyed with our tea. I think of all the Alices and Louises and Victorias from Guildford. They are seventeen also. What has become of them? And what of Alice Latham and her baby? Are they both well, I wonder? One thinks at that young age that the world is constant and that our friends shall always be our friends, but in the meantime, this celestial ball turns and tilts and the seasons advance and decline, and our friends drift away to the corners of the earth. And I am in this corner. In which corner are they? A warm breeze comes today from the Gulf, which is to our south. Mozie predicts rain: 'Wind from the sout' got rain in her mout'.' As the first drops of rain spatter the churchyard and its cane-field neighbour, she and I sit at our flour-board and practise our words. She learns prodigiously.

26 April 1870. A negro rider in fancy dress approached the vicarage today with an invitation to a ball-masque to be held at Mount Teague next Wednesday evening. I have had no small amount of curiosity about the grand palace on the Thibodaux Road. I shall wear the green-and-black gown from the ball at Mardi Gras, as it is at the head and front of my wardrobe. I hope no one has seen it before. I am relishing the change in routine, and, I admit to you, my little confidant, the chance to satisfy a little curiosity.

28 April 1870. Father's health improves in the clean, clear air, and he is certainly in fine fettle. Gardenia and sweet olive scent the air, which warms every day. Papa writes in the evenings. I hope he is writing sermons and not another treatise for submission to the Linnaen Society. I fear that another rejection might reverse the gains his health has made. I would tell him that the work that God has for him is surely the church and his flock, but I don't want him to feel that I am in sympathy with the Linnaens.

30 April 1870. The days are beautiful but pass slowly. I spend much time in the sanctuary, apart from the society of others, playing the piano in the dark solitude. It is warm enough now to open the windows, and almost warm enough to wish for a breeze. Mozie is some company, but she sets us to our day and then leaves to attend her own family, which is immense and so, no small task.

1 May 1870, the Sabbath. On Sunday afternoons, the spectacle of Panama resumes now with the passing of Lent (It is suspended during this time). There are horseraces and prizefights and a relatively new game much like cricket called Base Ball. The devotion the people of this place, all colours, have for these Sunday afternoon games borders on the religious. But it is a welcome respite from the toil and sweat of their weekly labours. The Northern soldiers participate in the fighting matches under the bayou oaks and the horseraces in the lanes between the cane-rows. A great deal of wagering occurs among them and the local people. It is a great diversion for them to attend the spectacle. Their commanders discourage it but do not stop it.

3 May 1870. There was great laughter this afternoon from Papa's study, and he called me to go there. I sat again as I always have since I was a little girl, upon his chest of sermons. 'My dear, my dear! Listen to this,' he chuckled, 'The *Compass* passes along congratulations to Mr. and Mrs. Thaddeus Browning of Plattenville, who will soon *celibate* fifty years of marriage.' He showed me the paper, pointing to the article. I held my face for a moment but soon fell into laughing, and then Papa did so again. 'Celibate fifty years, my dear!' he howled, wiping the tears from his eyes, 'How dreadfully dull for them!' O, Papa!

4 May 1870. I have finished Rousseau's *Confessions* once again, this time in its original French. M. Rousseau's candor is both astonishing and refreshing, and as a diversion, it was quite pleasant. I admit, however, my little confidant, to no little preoccupation concerning the Planters Ball this evening at Mr. Teague's residence on the Thibodaux Road.

5 May 1870. The Planters' Ball was held at Mount Teague in the spacious ballroom, the largest in the South according to the awed and whispered conversations of some of the guests. Music was played by a finely attired quartet set up in a corner of the ballroom, and there was an abundance of libations and eatables set out on tables and sideboards in the central hallway. When Papa and I arrived, a negro butler (also finely attired), greeted us and announced, 'Reverend Lamb and daughter, Alice Lamb!' Such an introduction, fit for a duke and duchess! Dancing was already in progress, but our host, Mr. Teague, excused himself from a waltz with a much older woman with a slight bow and a smile. He grasped Papa's hand in both of his and said, 'Reverend Lamb and Miss Lamb! I am so pleased you could join us!' Then he put his lips to the white linen of my glove. Yes, my little confidant, I blushed. Mr. Teague loped through quadrille after quadrille, waltz after waltz. An older lady said that he was shot in the hip in the last days of the war and that his leg does not answer well. He seemed to have to will the leg to move, which he did most valiantly. Poor, dear man. Mr. Howard attended with his wife, Flora, I seem to remember she is called. She is an amiable woman, descended from an old New Orleans family. Their younger two children were in tow, and, though I saw them very little, from time to time I could hear their thudding play upstairs where they presumably kept with the Teague girls under the eye of an old negro woman.

I danced with several of the gentlemen, but always found myself in the end as the partner of Mr. Teague. At one point, he remarked, 'I once was a fine dancer, if you will bear my boasting, Miss Lamb. I'm afraid this limp betrays my old wound.' I replied that it was a shame that the old war was fought at all, and he said, yes, and particularly the outcome of it. Despite his limp, he was still among the better dancers and certainly better than Mr. Morris, who cast no aspirations of being a fine dancer. 'As if I have but one leg,' he joked. My own legs grew tired, and I rested at the periphery of the tableau and visited with Mrs. Pugh and Mrs. Anderson. Rather than talk of art and literature, the conversation revolved around acreage, field hands, and money. Mrs. Anderson asked how we liked Louisiana and where we would spend the summer months. I did not quite understand her meaning and said, why, here, I suppose. The women seemed rather surprised, Mrs. Pugh exclaiming that summer is the fever season and surely Papa and I must get away to a more healthful climate, the mountains or the seaside, or Europe, perhaps. She said that her husband the colonel and she generally remove to Biloxi in the summer, and that perhaps Papa and I might return to England for a time until the heat has passed. I remarked that we had no relations in England to visit and that certainly it would fail our Christian duty to abandon our parish, fever or not. Their faces assumed smiles that seemed forced, and just then, the quartet played a waltz, and Mr. Teague approached.

'Miss Lamb, would you give me the pleasure?' he asked with a slight bow and one hand outstretched to me and the other behind his back. 'As you wish, sir,' I replied, and I took to my feet, leaving Mrs. P and Mrs. A whispering to each other behind their hands. The other dancers and onlookers whirled through my view over Mr. Teague's shoulder, our reflections in the windows cast reverse images of ourselves against the dark night. The quartet rendered the waltz splendidly, and it was all quite lovely, a moment of fairy-tale enchantment, such as a younger girl might imagine. I noticed then the scar on Mr. Teague's cheek, vague under his beard like a bit of country lane winding through a forest of sandy brown as seen from a hillside. My eyes kept straying to it as I was lost in the music and wondering how he had received it. 'This old scar?' he said as if he had read my thoughts. 'I had a run-in with a hot sugar kettle during grinding season years ago. One of my hired men was about to fall in it. Would've killed him.' 'And you saved him?' I asked. He smiled but said nothing, which I took as an unspoken yes. It was a chivalrous modesty befitting King Arthur and his knights. Then he said, 'I hope you will acquit me of any selfish designs, but you might be the loveliest lady in St. Matthew Parish tonight. Or on other night, or any other place.' I blushed, and then the music called for a change of partners, and he and his limping step moved away to Mrs. Pugh, and Colonel Pugh moved to me.

Later, word circulated that I was quite proficient on the piano, and I was called upon to play for the gathering. I chose Liebestraum and a selection of Chopin, and a few of the popular airs I have heard. Jenny Teague, the oldest of the Teague girls, joined me on the violin, and there was a great patter of applause as we finished each one. She has the same nickel-grey eyes of her father, but the rest of her features are presumably from her mother, who I am told was Mr. Teague's first wife, and who, like my mother, died in the process of giving birth. Jenny plays remarkably well, with exceptional tone and tempo. All she lacks is the ability to read music, and perhaps I may help her with this. There was discussion of the impending heat and several men talked about an ice making apparatus. One of the men said that it is the mark of a first-rate operation, to have the capacity to generate one's own ice, and not depend upon 'Yankees' for it. Mr. Teague sat thinking, his fingers combing his beard as he listened. He seemed completely lost in thought, as though a thousand miles away. From the adjacent parlour, there were peals of laughter and singing, and I was asked to play again and Jenny to accompany me. It was morning before the last of the carriages departed, ours among them. Papa had become quite overwhelmed by cherry brandy, and we were driven home in our chaise by Mozie's nephew Simeon. We have slept late this day.

Sammy, 1982

It had never been an easy thing, but he found it harder than ever to sit in the central hallway and look at the painting, done by some nameless itinerant artist long ago, a man, or a woman, perhaps, vanished from the earth without even signing his or her work. The ancient man within the elaborate frame, the stern warrior in the Confederate uniform, the learned man of letters who had left behind a library full of books and a mythological air of military exploits and duty served and satisfied, though in a lost cause. Sammy stood up and looked closer at the reddish-brown stain on the sleeve. He wondered if it had come from clutching the bullet wound in his hip.

Alice, the Burning Lady, had always scared him. Old Sam Teague had only intimidated him, and now Sammy felt it more so having fled in the face of his responsibility to his country. After sitting out the Vietnam War across the border in Montreal and then being pardoned along with the rest of the dodgers and shirkers, Sammy had crawled back into town and become the object of whispered derision and disapproving glances.

He himself could bear it. It had been his decision, after all. It was the teasing his family endured that troubled him. They were innocent.

But now, the great-grandson saw a hidden pain in the man in the painting, a secret sadness in his great-grandfather's gaze, a thorn in the Great Man's pride. Sammy stroked his beard and compared it to his great-grandfather's and then rose and turned to the mirror across from the portrait. In it, Old Sam Teague looked over his great-grandson's shoulder. Their nickel-gray eyes were the same, but Sammy's beard hadn't reached the same nineteenth century fullness of his ancestor. He had made it past the itchy-scratchy stage, the phase in which it feels like ants are crawling over your cheeks and neck. The beard was growing and was almost comfortable now, but it still needed to grow. He sat down and stroked it, as if it might stimulate its growth, and the tall clock clacked evenly for the two men.

The afternoon light came rushing through the transoms and sidelights of the front door. And then the door opened, and Judee came rushing in with it. She stopped to lean into the big cypress door to shut it and then ran to her daddy sitting across from the portrait. She jumped into the settee next to him, and they looked up into the man in the painting and his metal-hard stare.

"Daddy," Judee said in a small chirp as she looked up to Old Sam Teague. She turned to her daddy and ran her small hand over his emerging beard. "You got *whispers* like you great-grandfodda."

"What do you think?" Sammy asked her, moving his chin this way and that.

"You look like the rugarou. Tha's what Nonc Claude says."

Sammy made a small howl for her, and she giggled. She settled into his side, and they looked at the old patriarch in the rectangular frame.

"Daddy," she whispered.

"What, baby?"

"Was he a mean man?"

"No, baby. He was a fair man. Hard but fair, they all said," and Sammy smiled up to the uniformed man in the painting, who did not smile back.

Judee looked from Old Sam Teague to her father, Samuel Teague the fourth, and back again. Her small hand stroked her daddy's beard like it was an animal that was fascinating but that might bite, and then suddenly she laughed and said, "It's the rugarou!" And she jumped up with her hands in the air and scampered up the stairs.

Sammy looked around and found his home strangely animated by occurrences of a hundred years before. The floorboards creaked with ancient footsteps. The walls echoed with silent conversations held long ago. The ceiling bore witness to gatherings of people long gone from the earth. People great and people humble had passed through the doorways, all of them vanished from the surface of the earth and laid to rest within it.

He imagined his great-grandfather greeting them with a hard expression on his face and a firm handshake for the men, and an eloquent word and a polite kiss on a gloved hand for the ladies. He had moved with a limp from a war wound, and his face bore a scar from a 'run-in' with a hot sugar kettle. But there were no paintings, no photographs, not even a cloudy daguerreotype of Alice, the Burning Lady. But she had been in this house, too. She had danced and eaten and drank and played the piano in this very house. She had darkened these doorways; she had mourned her mother and hoped for siblings, a family, a confidant. She had enjoyed the blessings of music and rest and a cool breeze. And she had died young, in a frightful death. He knew that much.

Alice, 1870

8 May 1870. There is a rumour murmured on the steps of church that the elusive wife of Mr. Teague was seen in St. Louis, living under an assumed name. When discovered, she quickly removed elsewhere, Kansas City or Cincinnati, perhaps, though that is presently unknown. It is said that she lives lavishly wherever she goes, and all at her husband's expense. Why does he not divorce her? Perhaps he is too proud. Or perhaps he hopes for a reconciliation.

9 May 1870. I received a visitor today at the vicarage, the oldest of the Teague girls, Jenny, who is just a few years younger than me. She was driven by an old negro who sat patiently on the buckboard in the shade with a dappled mare in the traces. Both the mare and the negro swatted flies, each in a different way. She held her violin case like a small portmanteau and said that she wanted to pay a call, perhaps to play music. I was delighted to have the monotony broken by a visit, and we adjourned to the sanctuary, where we went through a number of selections. She is quite proficient, really. After a delightful afternoon in her society, she and the negro and the mare departed, leaving me with an open invitation to visit her at Mount Teague.

10 May 1870. I ventured forth boldly today, determined to see the countryside of our new home and to master the driving of our gig in the process. I sat as erect as I could behind Sugar's bouncing white flanks and mane. All around us, fields of yellow wildflowers crowded the banks of the bayous and canals, small, cheerful faces floating on a knee-high cloud of deep, brilliant green. The dogwoods have given up their Easter white, but the myrtles have taken it up behind them and added burgundy and violet as well. The trees glow green, the grey trunks mottled with sunlight and shadow. In the expansive fields of sugarcane, insects are beginning to buzz when the day warms sufficiently. At last I found myself at the long lane of oaks leading up to Mount Teague, the majesty of its white pillars rising upright and smooth against the rugged grey limbs and trunks of the trees. On a whim, I shook the reins, and Sugar clopped a jaunty rhythm over the white shells of the lane.

I followed the sound of a violin, part of a nocturne by Chopin, and halloed for Jenny. The playing stopped, and she emerged from the side porch, violin in one hand, bow in the other. 'Alice!' she exclaimed, 'This is a pleasure indeed! Let me have Ruthie prepare us refreshments.' She handed me her bow but kept her violin and opened the front door. The galleries of the house were clothed in the sweet smell of something blooming intensely and in abundance. Inside, the house had a peculiar, strained silence, broken only by the slow, staccato clack of the hall clock.

I listened for the younger Teague girls but there was only this silence and the clock that attended it. I surmised that they were in the process of naps. The sound of someone blowing his nose came thundering from within another room, and then Mr. Teague emerged from his study, wiping his red eyes and wet nose with a handkerchief. He looked very much disturbed and seemed stunned to see me and murmured something on the order of, 'Pardon my state, ma'am, but she bedevils me yet,' or the like. It is sad to see him so emotional for a wife that has run away from him and all he gave her. Surely, he still holds out some hope for her return. How lost he must feel without her! Jenny and I adjourned to the shade of the gardens and the statue of Venus that presides over them in marble stillness. The grounds are in fine fettle and scent the breeze with an air that is soft and sweet. We enjoyed a happy afternoon in each other's company before I returned in our chaise to the vicarage. I feel that I have become quite the driver here, as one must get about in some manner.

12 May 1870. Papa and I walked today along the bayou, in the shade of the willows. Papa was exuberant. 'What did you come to see?' he exclaimed, quoting John the Baptist, 'A reed swaying in the wind? Surely this bayou is the River Jordan, and this place paradise!' We were treated to views of all the inhabitants of the bayou, turtles, snakes, an alligator floating like a log. Papa collected more specimens of the purple-coloured iris and a plant that he says is a species of blue phlox. It is lovely, glowing blue, cheerful and petal-faced.

15 May 1870. Church attendance has fallen off a bit. Mr. Teague attends faithfully with his girls, and we chat afterwards in the cool shade of the oaks. He is not so much handsome as attractive. Perhaps it is his demeanor which makes him so.

18 May 1870. Jenny Teague came for a visit today, and we adjourned to the sanctuary to play a variety of what Mr. Nesbit in Guildford always called 'pieces.' She favours the works of Chopin, and we played them together. We have worked on her reading of music from the printed page, and she has improved remarkably. Then, she played from memory several of the waltzes and reels that the local French-speaking people play. We practiced our French, but hers is much in the same way as the locals here, not at all the French of Miss Latour, though we manage, Jenny and I, in the old *belle langue.*

19 May 1870. The countryside abounds with blue-coated soldiers, waiting like Jonah waited to be disgorged from the whale. The heat mounts more every day. Papa goes about in his waistcoat.

21 May 1870. The *Compass* today carries another scalding condemnation of the new addition to the American constitution, the fifteenth such 'amendment.' The opinion of the *Compass* is that some men do not possess the mental faculties to perform the duties involved in the casting of a vote, namely men of colour. Papa says that one's colour is no indication of one's mental acuity. The constitution of this country also includes a bill of rights, including the right to worship and assemble and bear arms in a militia and speak freely. Papa says that as fine and robust as this young country is, perhaps it would be better served to also possess a bill of responsibilities, chief among them the responsibility to love and serve God by loving and serving each other.

22 May 1870. Today at the end of the Benedictory hymn, 'Love Divine All Loves Excelling,' Mr. Teague's gaze found me. Perhaps he thought the same of my gaze.

25 May 1870. An anonymous benefactor has acquired a pipe organ for the church, and workmen have come from Cincinnati to install it. They rest frequently, as surely they are unaccustomed to the heat. The immense sounds of it rattle dishes in the vicarage kitchen, which prompts a chuckling 'Oh my!' from Papa. He says that when I play it, perhaps I should be lashed to the bench to keep from toppling backwards.

27 May 1870. Jenny Teague visited the rectory today, and on a lark, she and I climbed up into the oak tree here at the vicarage. It was so much like the great tree down the lane from our house in old Guildford. We moved from spot to spot in its cool, dense shade, our skirts and petticoats gathered about us. Our feet slipped on the wet bark, and so we took off our shoes and watched them fall to the earth in a plummeting pause, meeting the leaves below in a faint rustle. She showed me how to bounce the limb up and down, and it began to sway. The waver of the limbs stirred the cool air and wafted the scent of the earth and the tree. Sunlight moved in speckles within the shady darkness with each long movement. At last we sat side by side. It was rather like being held by a giant. Papa saw us from his study window and emerged from the vicarage. From below the tree, in the shade of it, he called up, 'Two exquisite specimens! I must write to the Linnaen Society at once!' Jenny asked me what the Linnaen Society was, and I told her, though I did not add that Papa is excluded from it. Then I realized that I was holding on to the limb that looks like a scythe.

29 May 1870. The windows of St. Margaret's were open today by necessity. Fans fluttered in the congregation, most of whom have donned lighter colours. The men now wear linen suits.

31 May 1870. The myrtles are bursting in small, dense, frilly blossoms, white, pink, red, and the jasmine scents the night air, lemon-sweet. The sun shines differently now, intense and unrelenting. It is beyond mere warmth. Shade and breezes are welcome now. It is not quite June–how much hotter will it be? Jenny visited again today, and we talked of the places I've been, London, Calcutta, Manchester. She has only traveled to New Orleans. She can't believe that London or any other place is larger. In the relatively cool dark of the church, the workmen put the finishing touches on the organ. I want to play, but the head man, a Mr. Schmidt, says that the pipes must sit a day or two to get acclimated to their new home. As Jenny and I sat in the shadowy church, we began giggling as two schoolgirls might, watching the men as they bent and leaned, and Jenny made a joke about them attending to their organ. In our whispered titters, she said that another name for a man's organ of regeneration is pecker. A willy, in other words. The joke between the men in the general store is apparent to me now. Perhaps such topics are the conversations that siblings enjoy, along with the delicious giggling they produce.

1 June 1870. The fourth month of our new situation. Personalities have begun to emerge in the congregation, developing like images in a photographer's basin. Intriguers, saints, well-wishers, the gamut of human nature, including the self-righteous. Papa says that is the natural way of things for us to be enamoured with the perception of our own virtue. One may be quite content with his own gluttony as he derides the lower classes for the laziness that perpetuates their hunger, or unconcerned with the sin of gossip while whispering the news of another's sinful liaison with the spouse of another. Papa says that we are all quite tolerant of our own sin and that it is the sin of others we find abhorrent. 'My beautiful daughter,' he says, 'the congregation here, like all congregations since Jerusalem and Rome, has its share of intriguers. But that is a small matter which we must bear, for remember, my dear, even the Garden of Eden had a snake in it.' I believe it is a sentiment that he has expressed before.

2 June 1870. The organ is installed at last, and what a colossus it is! A bellowing bull elephant, trumpeting soaring anthems to the herd, an artillery piece of musical power and might, blaring fanfares as if blasted by angels with great muscular cheeks and bulging, squinting eyes! Even the old men of the congregation wake from their slumber when it is played. Papa says that if the Almighty cannot hear it, then surely He is deaf. Rumour is that the anonymous benefactor responsible for the organ is Mr. Teague.

5 June 1870. First Sunday services with the new organ. The old men of the congregation cannot rest because of its stormy blasts, eyes suddenly exploding open when I press the keys. I admit to taking delight in this.

6 June 1870. I have been asked to stay with the Teague girls whilst Mr. Teague travels on business. I asked Papa if he can do without me for two nights, and he said yes, though I still feel guilty in a subtle way, quite like the pain from a sore tooth that is forgotten until biting down. He said for me not to worry and that he has his submission to the Linnaen Society to get ready. O, how I wish he would abandon his hopes for acceptance into the Linnaen Society. But then I think that it is his hope and not mine, and our hopes, like our fears, belong to us and us alone. Nevertheless, I told him that I would not be gone long. 'My goodness, dear!' he exclaimed, 'You'll be but two miles down the road, not in Calcutta or Australia!' I kissed him once more and alighted into the carriage sent by Jenny from Mount Teague.

I was greeted by Lucy, the youngest, who was right behind the door when the old butler opened it. Jenny, who seemed to be waiting for me also, quickly relieved the butler and showed me in. Little Lucy stammered, 'Miss-Miss-Miss-' Then Jenny helped her sister with my name, saying, 'Alice. Miss Alice.'

'Miss Alice,' the little girl said, 'My mama ran away.'

'Lucy!' Jenny exclaimed, 'You shouldn't say things like that!'

I told Jenny that such honesty is to be expected from little children, and I took little Lucy's hand. Jenny whispered to me that their stepmother had been detained in Memphis and that Mr. Teague had gone to verify that it was her. I asked if her father hopes for a reconciliation, and Jenny answered, 'I fear so, but that is his matter.' Lucy then broke into our whispered conversation by announcing that her 'gubberness' Emilia Duplantier had 'left and she quit and she not comin' back.' Lucy shook her head in slow and emphatic agreement with herself. Jenny said, 'Now, sister, Father says that we're not to speak of her ever again.' In a whisper, I asked Jenny about it and she said that Mr. Teague had to dismiss this Emilia Duplantier, and then Jenny made tilting motions as if she were tilting back a bottle. Lucy followed us to the parlour where the tea-things were prepared. She said that I talked 'strange,' and I corrected her 'strangely' and told her that it was because I am English, from a place called Guildford, in Surrey, England, far across the sea and that there are many people there who speak as I do. The middle sister, Ida, joined us and I told them stories of England and India and they questioned me incessantly about it. And it was wonderful. We spoke of mountains and tea plantations and elephants that were trained to move very heavy objects like tree trunks. After tea, we played duck-duck-goose, and Puss-in-the-Corner, and we sang, and then we read from *Alice in Wonderland*, and Lucy asked me if the book was about me. I laughed and stroked her hair and said that no, Alice and her world were all imaginary. Then Jenny and I read to Lucy and Ida from *Stories for Children* by Cousin Sarah, and then from a book of fairy tales, stories of frog-kissing princesses and damsels in towers with long golden hair suitable for climbing. Our crooked fingers worked as puppets through the dramas, each shepherd's staff-shaped digit wiggling with a different voice, a falsetto or an outrageously low baritone, all borrowed from the Punch and Judy shows of my girlhood. We dined together and then read and sang some more and turned in for the night. As I turned down the lamp and the room gave way to summer moonlight, Lucy crept into my room and said, 'Miss Alice, I wish you could be our mama.' How is one to reply to such a heartfelt request? I told her, 'One day you shall have a very fine mama indeed, one who is both kind and beautiful, just like you.' She crawled into my bed and tucked her little head under my arm and her breathing slackened and her eyelids fell and her lips parted limply. She began to exude a tiny heat, and her small weight collapsed into my side like a sack of flour. And she slept the whole night in that manner. And it was wonderful.

Sammy, 1982

He knew the book, an ancient volume worthy of a book collector's trove. It rested on the same shelf reserved for the oldest of books, the top shelf, books that were either no longer loved and enjoyed or so revered as to be set aside on a high shelf and untouched. He stood on his tiptoes and carefully hooked his finger over the top of the spine and tipped it out. *Stories for Children* was embossed in gold on the spine lengthwise, and *Cousin Sarah* crossways. To his knowledge, he had never opened it, nor had anyone else still living. Growing up, Miss Della Mae had read to him, but mostly Uncle Remus and stories like those.

He opened it, and, among the stories, he found a lock of golden hair, bound in two red ribbons. His fingers felt the strands of it, wondering if it had been hers or one of the Teague girls. It was still as gold as a shock of wheat in summer sunshine. He replaced it exactly where he had found it, among the pages of a story about a lady spider who took great pride in her web. There was a picture of the spider with big eyelashes using two of her legs to sweep her web with a broom. He closed the book and replaced it as carefully as he had removed it, with a curator's light touch, rising on his tiptoes and pushing the book back into its place, high on the top shelf.

He eased down the stairs and out the screen door. It had turned out to be a beautiful day, crystal cold and clear, late winter in south Louisiana when green is not yet a color but just a feeling. Across the lawn, the white tank of the water tower rose proudly against the intense blue of the sky and looked resolutely across the fields and tree lines. The writing on the tank of the water tower proclaimed, *Cane-do!* He trudged through the yard to the chain-link fence around it. His fingers picked through his keys for the one to the padlock on the gate and opened it. The fence and the lock were a necessity after the cruel word, CAPON, coward, had been painted in place of *Cane-do!* He and Teeter had gone up in a cold winter wind to paint over it.

He planted a boot on one rung and then the next. The big house got smaller and smaller as he climbed hand over hand, rung over rung. The breeze picked up, rushing through the metal rungs of the ladder and rustling his hair. He climbed onto the catwalk and stood and leaned into the railing around it. It was even colder up here, and he paused to button his flannel coat. Down below him, fields of black earth slept, dreaming of the sun and their purpose under it.

Also down below, music played faintly from the big bay door of the metal shed that held the cane harvesters and trailers and the safe. The small figure of Teeter was just outside the door, repacking the bearings on one of the tires of the big machines. Sammy smelled the faint and distant smoke from the cigarette in Teeter's mouth as his black-greased hands worked with the wheel. Teeter was always good at taking things apart, and, when he was clean and clear-headed, good at putting them back together.

Sammy looked for all the familiar landmarks, the blank area where the tenant house had stood years ago and the smudge of black where the ice barn had been just a month ago. Sprigs of grass were emerging from the char like whiskers, like a green five o'clock shadow. Within a few cycles of mowing, the place where the ice barn and the safe had been would be identically grassy green to the site of the tenant house, simply part of the lawn, remembered only by those who had seen them.

He took inventory of all the places he had associated with her. When he was a boy, sometimes he would see her weeping. Other times, she floated over the lawn. Other times, she glowed fixed in one place, as if pensively deciding what to do. His imagination hadn't seen her in years, and he thought it was because only as children can we see the fantastic, and that as adults we become captivated by the commonplace. He had simply grown older, and the ordinary had taken root as the idea of ghosts, fairies, and phantoms had faded.

In the summer, all this is like a green ocean, Sammy thought. Even now in the southernmost fields, cane was sprouting from the black corduroy. It was still a miracle to him how a man's living, how a family's sustenance, how a community's prosperity, how all of it could emerge from the ground every spring. How dirt and rain and sun could conspire into bounty. It was regular, mundane, even, but it would always be a miracle to him. The wind cooed, and he could almost hear the voice of Rev. Lamb:

What a wonderful world God has provided, my beautiful daughter. Why the earth is renewed!

Off in the distance, the steeples of the churches in Napoleonville rose with the water tower for St. Matthew Parish Water District No. 2. The Twelve Arpent Canal ran man-made-straight, and Bayou Lafourche wound its natural path, both bordered by trees. And there among the churches across the bayou on the opposite bank, the church of his youth, St. Margaret's Episcopal. He had not attended it since high school and then only at the insistence of his mother. He would sit with his friend Jimmy Chauvin as the congregation sang all the old hymns, blandly and vigorously meted out to the ancient bellowing organ. In between the old standards, they would read from the Psalter and the Book of Common Prayer, reciting the Nicene Creed and listening to the Word proclaimed and taking the sacraments. Did they still sing the old hymns? Was the old organ still in place?

He looked back down at the blackened earth that had been the site of the ice barn and then back across the distant landscape at St. Margaret's. They were two places so crucial to the life of someone now gone from the earth for a hundred years. Someone who had laughed and cried and worried and loved and grieved. Though she had once terrified him, he had known so little about her. It now occurred to him that she would never have meant to terrify him, that it was only his older sisters and his imagination. His hands were in his pockets, and he realized how cold he was, so he descended the stairs again. The big house grew larger with each rung. He locked the gate behind him to prevent more graffiti that might blare out the advertisement of his shortcomings.

Alice, 1870

7 June 1870. After a late breakfast and then a long walk through the rows of cane to the banks of the Twelve Arpent Canal with the Teague girls, we returned to the great house for tea, which in the summer is generally served chilled and heavily sugared. There is certainly enough sugar here for it. When we were alone, I asked Jenny of Mr. Teague's war years, and she said that he was wounded at the very end of it and is very reluctant to speak of it. She said also that they are going to White Sulphur Springs in the mountains of Virginia during 'fever season' to see if taking the mineral waters there might help his leg. She asked if Papa was ever in the war, and I told her no, though the English were involved in a war in a place called Crimea when I was a baby and so I have no recollection of it, though we did have a neighbour in Surrey who was in it.

Jenny wears a small locket around her neck, and I asked to see it. I opened the elaborate brass to find the cameo of a woman who is the girls' mother. One can see a little of her features in each of the girls, the shape of her mouth in Ida, the shape of her eyes in Lucy, her dark hair in Jenny. By Jenny's account, she was a woman of angelic kindness and her passing in childbirth was a tremendous loss to her family. She said it occurred during Lucy's birth at the close of the war, sometime before Mr. Teague sustained his wound, as she can remember him carrying Ida without a limp and putting her in a carriage to take them to the Parrises that night. I told her that Mama died in the same manner, during childbirth when we were in India, and that I have always felt guilty, for a sibling is something that I have wanted more than anything. 'Well, then,' she said, 'we can be your sisters.' I was suddenly embarrassed by my tears and Jenny placed a hand upon my shoulder as I wiped them away with a trembling hand. Ida came and read to us, as she said that their father has instructed her sisters and her to read and practice their penmanship for an hour each day. She reads remarkably well for a girl her age–I should say as well as any English schoolgirl of the upper forms. I asked Jenny how she has come to read so well, and she said that her father has them read to him every day. How excellent for him to take such a keen interest in their development!

The afternoon passed into a dinner prepared by the servants. Then, in the midst of duck-duck-goose, Ida's hair fell, and I was delighted to be called upon to put it up again, and then Lucy shook hers loose and requested the same and that I do it also for her doll Penny, a gift from her former governess, this Emilia Duplantier. Penny has the blank, neutral expression necessary for a girl's play, an expression of neither happiness nor sadness. She also has what Lucy calls a 'bobo' behind her ear, a small chip in the porcelain, and I told Lucy that the first step in a doll becoming a real girl is to receive a small chip or a blemish such as Penny's. After a delightful dinner with these sisters, it was time for bed, and I told the girls to go straightaway to bed, 'quick-quiet as a mouse and off with you then,' which is exactly what Mrs. Sullivan was in the habit of saying when I was a girl their age. The crickets sing in the live oaks now as I write, and I lay down my pen to listen to their song through the open windows.

8 June 1870. I was on the back porch this afternoon, looking out on the exquisite gardens of Mount Teague. The shade is still tolerable, though barely pleasant, but the sun is accosting, and more so every day. A light-skinned negro, an albino, I believe, was on a ladder pruning the top of a wall of hedges that surround a magnificent statue of a nude Venus whose afternoon shadow fell upon the hedges in a darker patch of green. Everywhere, white was the theme of the gardens, gardenias and magnolias, everything planted with the purpose of synchrony. The sweet banana smell of the magnolias took advantage of any subtle breeze. A voice startled me, and I found that it was Jenny, coming from inside. She said that her father is surprised that she didn't take the garden and the statue of Venus with her when she left. Who? I asked, and she said Mama, with a roll of her eyes, that is to say, her stepmother, Polly Teague. Apparently, she insisted that the girls address her thusly. Out in the bright sun of the garden, the albino gardener climbed down off his ladder, repositioned it, and moved up it again. Jenny said that Polly Teague had a penchant for the colour green and for spending money and that she had expensive tastes. The gardens certainly show it, and apparently, she still has expensive tastes, as Mr. Teague still receives bills from her, according to Jenny. I remarked that the gardens are certainly beautiful and a delight, and I asked if the statue of Venus was her idea. Jenny said yes, as was the ballroom. I must admit that both are very well done.

According to Jenny, her stepmother was a demonstrative redhead with an enormous appetite, and that Mr. Teague thinks his absconded wife suffers from mania, and that this leads her to overspend. Jenny said that they could be heard at all hours of the day and night, her step-mother and her father. In what way? I asked, and Jenny replied, 'You know. Behind closed doors. They could not keep quiet. The marital act. Before I knew about such things, I thought they were fighting.' I remarked that they were entitled to it as husband and wife. It may have sounded like I was defending them, but I was only trying to be fair. Jenny said that was true, but the rest of the house wasn't entitled to hear it all. We giggled as two sisters might, and then she took my hand, and it was off to a reclining chair in the shade of the porch. We eased into it, our four bare feet lounging together as the albino gardener stood on a ladder in the sunny garden. His shears pruned away at the hedge, the clipping sound of them lulling us into naps. As I drifted away on the scent of magnolias, the naked statue of Venus surveyed her garden, and I wondered if she had heard the ecstasy of Mr. and Mrs. Teague, and if the Goddess of Love had been pleased by it.

9 June 1870. Mr. Teague returned to Mount Teague this morning with news that the woman detained in Memphis was not his wife, and so, Mrs. Teague remains at large. After fond farewells, I returned to the vicarage to find that Papa has been labouring over the description of his fish and drinking cherry brandy in the process of it. He appeared stunned as he stared at the manuscript. On his desk was a bottle of Whitham's Cherry Brandy. I lifted it to find it almost empty. 'Papa,' I admonished him quietly. 'Yes, a gift from a parishioner,' he slurred. His hair was askew, and he scratched his head and said, 'Yes, empty, empty as the garden tomb. Well, it must have gotten away from me, in some manner.' He will not say it, but he was lonely in my absence. I am sure of it.

10 June 1870. I was in the sanctuary going over this Sunday's music, and, I confess a few selections of Liszt for my own enjoyment. The windows of St. Margaret's were thrown open in hopes of gathering a little breeze as the air was hot and *listless.* Yes, a pun, my little confidant. The church door opened, and a wave of light washed up the center aisle, containing a long shadow. The door creaked closed and the light narrowed to a thin strip and disappeared. Running steps pattered and then in the light of a window I saw that it was little Lucy Teague! 'I missed you, Miss Alice,' she said, almost in tears. I asked if her father or her sisters knew where she was, and she said no ma'am. I said, 'Well, then, let me get my bonnet and I shall walk you home.' She asked if I would stay for lemonade and I smiled and said, 'how about tea, rather? And I shall read to you from the Nonsense Book. Wouldn't that be lovely, then?' She clapped her hands and I fetched my bonnet, and we walked in the afternoon heat, her small, sweaty hand in mine under the shade of the oaks and cypresses that line the bayou road.

11 June 1870. While Papa worked in his study, adding another sermon for his chest, Jenny and I played duets together in the sanctuary. Ida and Lucy walked upon the communion rail, and Jenny had to scold them. I let Ida play a few blasting notes from the organ. After all, her father is said to be its benefactor.

12 June 1870. On the steps after church today, Papa shook Mr. Teague's hand and asked how the new governess was getting on. I realised that I had neglected to tell Papa that the governess had been dismissed. Mr. Teague said that the position was vacant again, as he had to dismiss her not long after her position commenced. He then leaned in and whispered to Papa, though I was near and easily heard him say, *she was drinking my liquor.* Papa gave a headshake of disapproval and said that he would pray for 'God's poor creature.' 'Yes, please do,' Mr. Teague replied, before moving to me and taking my hand in the two of his. The gaze of his grey eyes holds a certain enchantment. One might easily become captivated by them.

13 June 1870. In what must pass for the cool of the morning, I took a walk among the sugar cane. I lost my way in the maze of green stalks, and soon it became quite hot, 'as hot as Calcutta,' as Papa is fond of saying. I was becoming rather anxious and a bit fretful that I would stay lost in the heat of the day. The sun was rising quickly and the heat with it. Then there came a rustle in the leafy green stalks and they suddenly parted, and there was Mr. Teague. My hand was to my chest in fright, and he apologised for startling me. He spoke from atop his mount, a horse the same brown as his saddle and with a black mane, a gelding who stamped rather nervously as if wanting to take again to the road to get out of the sun and into the shade and to a water trough. Mr. Teague announced that I was just the person he was looking for and that he was coming to ask me if I might be interested in the position of governess. He paid me great compliments, saying that his girls are quite fond of me and that I am good with them. 'I believe my judgment to be better this time,' he said, 'our last governess could not be trusted,' and I waited for him to add, *with my liquor*, but he did not. I said that I would have to think upon it, and he nodded and said, certainly. Then he vaulted down from his horse and said, 'allow me, Miss Lamb,' and he lifted me upon the great broad back of his chestnut gelding. He led us back to the vicarage as he loped along in the heat, quite a generous act of gallantry. The heat of the day between ten and four in the afternoon is certainly something to avoid.

14 June 1870. Today was very hot, I would say the hottest day we have had. Every creature blessed with mobility adjourns to the shade and keeps still in it. The *Compass* again carries the regular notice asking for information on the whereabouts of Polly Teague.

15 June 1870. Papa married a couple today, a beautiful bride and a handsome groom, both seemingly ready to burst with pride in each other and I am sure anticipation of a night of rapture. Papa peered over his spectacles and the open *Book of Common Prayer* he held, smiling kindly at the groom and then the bride as he asked them the sacred questions, 'Do you promise–?' He pronounced them man and wife, and I unleashed the organ in an arching, soaring, colossal fanfare as the couple faced the packed church, the polished oak pews decorated with green and white arrangements of jasmine and magnolia flowers. The older women fanned themselves against the heat and the emotion, and their husbands pulled at collars to admit a little air on their necks. Later, in the vestry, Papa was putting away his surplice. We were speaking of the couple and their future, and talk turned to my own future. Papa replaced the chalice in the sacristy vault and without looking up, addressed me. 'It is the springtime of your life, my beautiful daughter. Time for youth and the enjoyment of it,' he said. 'There are those in this place who have noticed you.' All I could say was, 'Yes, Papa, and I suppose you are quite right.' Of course, he is correct. But what will Papa do if I am not there to care for him? And who has noticed me?

16 June 1870. What sad news. The *Picayune* reports that old Mr. Dickens has died at his home in Kent, his latest novel unfinished.

17 June 1870. Papa is of the opinion that I should take the position of governess to the Teague girls. He says that for years, he and Mama prayed for me to have siblings, and now those prayers have an answer, though in a way very unexpected. He says that it is no secret how those Teague girls idolise me. I asked him, 'But Papa, what shall you do?' He said that he has reading and writing to do. He said that he had spoken to Mr. Teague, and that I may spend nights at home here at the vicarage, if I resolve to take the position. I am still undecided. I sit and look at the starry night sky for answers. I simply do not think Papa shall get on well without me.

18 June 1870. After a time of prayer and reflection, I have declined Mr. Teague's offer. I sent a letter to this effect, thanking him for the opportunity, but that I could not take on such a task and expect to give it my all. I sent the letter by courier, and a few hours later Mr. Teague himself came riding up on his chestnut gelding. He knocked on the door and Mozie admitted him, and he took off his hat as he came in. He gave Mozie a small package, a gift for Papa. I offered him a seat, but he declined and asked once more if I would not reconsider his offer. I told him that it is one thing to visit from time to time, and quite another to commit to a daily engagement. Then I lowered my voice and said, 'Simply put, Mr. Teague, I cannot leave Papa.' With this, Mr. Teague nodded with the dejection of a man who is seldom given no for an answer, and he rose and bid me good day. As I watched through the vicarage window, he galloped away, just as Papa came merrily down the bayou road in our carriage with Sugar in the traces. He tied up to the post and came to ask me the nature of Mr. Teague's errand. I told Papa that Mr. Teague had simply come to pay a call.

19 June 1870. Papa sweats profusely in the pulpit. All doors and windows are open, as all are desperate for a breeze.

20 June 1870. A visit to the Teague girls again, as Papa makes calls elsewhere in the Parish. As the girls and I read in the parlour, Mr. Teague came in from riding his fields, his heavy limping step on the wood floor announcing his entry. He graciously took my hand and told me what a pleasure it was to see me and how I light up his dwelling-place with my presence. Then he adjourned to his study and called for Ida to come and practice her reading to him. Initially, she did not seem to want to part from my company, but in the end, she dutifully left to go and read to her father for a full hour and was still reading when I left. She was reading from the *Picayune*, quite a feat for a girl of eight!

21 June 1870. The dogs of this place curl up under houses and sleep on their sides. Wasps float lazily under the eaves. The tree lines on the horizon throb in the heat. Nothing else moves. Rain falls in the mid-afternoon and then the heat returns anew.

26 June 1870. Attendance at church today was diminished by families that have left the heat for the summer. Talk on the steps is of the relative merits of the seaside versus the mountains. Some talk of Europe.

28 June 1870. Mr. Teague came today to invite Papa and me to accompany his family to the mountains in Virginia for several months. He is concerned for our safety with the onset of the fever season, and, though he is a man who does not plead with anyone, it was clear that he is concerned for our safety. He said that those who have the means must leave, and that it was as simple as that. Papa thanked him for the kindness of his offer and said there are those who cannot leave, especially the poor, and that he intended to care for them, as was his Christian duty. Mr. Teague said that it was certainly admirable, but it grieved him to think of the two of us becoming ill here. He repeated that all those who can should leave and that it was essential. Papa thanked him again but said that his promise to God was essential. Mr. Teague gave Papa a concerned look in return and said, 'Please, consider it, reverend. You and your daughter have become so dear to us here in St. Matthew.' Then he rose and took his hat, which he had been twirling in his hands, and he limped through the doorway of the vicarage, his tall figure eclipsing the light.

1 July 1870. I asked Papa once more if he would not consider leaving with the Teagues for Virginia and the mountains. I confess that it would be grand to spend time with my girls, enjoying the tranquility of the pleasant air. Jenny has mentioned more than once that the hotel possesses a fine piano in its lobby, and that she and I might play duets and perhaps entice the guests to sing. Papa was in his study, his shirt sleeves rolled up and his waistcoat open against the heat, and I said to him, 'It was kind of Mr. Teague to offer to take us with his family. He is so worried for our safety. Should we not reconsider it?' I asked. He dipped his pen into the inkwell and answered me thusly without looking up from his *Book of Common Prayer* and the notes he was making: 'I was sick, and you cared for me,' he said. I recognized it from the Gospel of St. Matthew, and I knew that as a Christian, he was quite in the right for not leaving and shall not do so. Nor shall I.

2 July 1870. A visit to the Teague sisters today, and a pleasant day of music, reading, and games. Ida and Lucy had us play ring-around-the-rosy and puss-in-the-corner and blindman's bluff until I had quite sweated-through my day-dress, even though it is of a light and airy linen, and I finally resorted to peeking under my blindfold and grabbing little Lucy. At last, Jenny said that surely Miss Alice tires and the games were concluded and we adjourned to the back gallery where a rather showy tea party was held.

The cool wind approached, the harbinger of the afternoon rain, and we went inside to the gentle push of the breeze in the central hall. We gathered on the settee and read from *Aesop's Fables*, and Lucy and then Ida fell asleep to the story of the wolf and the crane. What little loves, what sweet little creatures! I myself fought sleep, and in that hazy space between wakefulness and slumber, I saw Mr. Teague in the doorway of his study regarding us with a look of bemusement. I closed my eyes again, falling into a dream in which the Teague girls and I were searching for someone. When I woke with a start on almost falling, Mr. Teague had returned to his desk. As it drew time for my departure, I rose and paused to bid adieu to Mr. Teague, who was in his study looking out over the sugarcane, moving in feathery green for miles and waiting on the afternoon rain.

Perhaps I shouldn't have, but I said, 'Sir, it's a shame about Mrs. Teague. I hope that I am not out of line in saying so.' It seemed to startle him, and I can't tell if it was the subject or the suddenness that broke him from his private reverie. He turned from his chair and the French version of the Compass, *Le Boussole de St. Mathieu,* and asked, 'Mrs. Teague? 'Why? What have you heard? Do you have news of her?' He seemed rather hopeful, as if I knew where she might be, like a man clutching at debris in a flood. I, of course, had no news for him, and I wish I had not asked. But I could only go on, and so I told him that it was such a shame that she left the girls and him, and in such haste. I clearly felt that I had overstepped my bounds. But he was candid in his reply, saying after a pause, 'Yes. Yes, it's a shame she turned her back on these girls. And me.' Then he asked me once more if I would reconsider serving as governess to his girls, hoping that this time I would assent. He said that he would be 'mighty' appreciative and that I would be a credit to them and to him for them to turn out as lovely as I. To this, I blushed and found that I could only stammer, 'How would Papa get on?' 'Yes. Of course,' Mr. Teague said, 'Your Papa.' My carriage was readied, the bonnet pulled over against the first drops of afternoon rain. I took Sugar's reins from the old negro attendant and alighted onto the seat of my carriage and shook waves into the leather. Over my shoulder, I could see Mr. Teague in the window of his study, watching me as the road I took disappeared into the sugarcane and the rain began to fall.

4 July 1870. Independence Day was celebrated by the victorious Union Army, though not by the population who was denied theirs by the late war. The countryside remains dotted with soldiers, bored men wiling away the tedious hours, days, weeks, and months, dreaming of home and family, perhaps. I share their dreams of family, though my dreams are only pipedreams. Because of the Union Commander of this district, the Mardi Gras procession was cancelled in February, and there is quite a bit of discord here because of it, almost as if Christmas or Easter had been cancelled. There is a great deal of lounging about by these soldiers, though they occasionally drill in the public places. There is also gambling, drinking, and fistfights. They are not at all welcome by the people here and scarcely tolerated. Meanwhile, the sugarcane lounges about as well in the summer air, with an appearance as thick and soft as velvet. The air whispers with the sound of thousands of leaves and stalks languidly rubbing together in the vacant breeze.

6 July 1870. The French version of the newspaper, *La Boussole*, carries a society column called *On Dit–*, which is mirrored here in the English version, *The Compass*, as *It is said–*. It carries news of who has left and for where. The list grows longer every day. Among the news is that 'our dear Samuel Teague' shall be leaving with his three daughters for White

Sulphur Springs. Papa works in his study on Sunday's sermon, looking through his chest for examples of former sermons from Sundays long ago.

7 July 1870. I played the piano today in the cool shadows of the sanctuary, the open windows waiting on a breeze, my shoulders uncovered, trying to dispel the hot, dense air. During the second stanza of 'Come Now Font of Every Blessing,' the church doors opened and spilled a shaft of light and heat down the central hall. My eyes strained to see who the figure was entering the church. Upon crossing the threshold, he removed his hat and limped toward the front of the sanctuary. I stopped playing and turned on the bench to face whoever it was. My eyes strained against the darkness as I pulled a shawl over my shoulders. At last I saw that it was Mr. Teague. He begged pardon for the intrusion of an unannounced visit. As he approached the altar, the light fell on him, and I must say, he looked rather forlorn, like a man sagging under a weight. He asked if Papa was in, and I told him that he was out visiting in the parish and asked if he would like for me to tell him that he called when he returned. Mr. Teague instructed me to only tell him this, that he wished that at least I would reconsider quitting St. Matthew until cooler weather. He said that my well-being is so important to everyone here at St. Margaret's Church. I thanked him again and told him I appreciated his concern, but that I was sure that God shall watch over us and that His will would be done. He agreed and said that he hoped that it was His will to safekeep us from harm, particularly the trouble from disease that must be endured here each summer. He said that if money is an impediment that we should be assured that Papa and I would be their guests.

He does not seem the kind of man who finds himself easily or frequently vexed, and in general circumstances, he must be mild of temper and possessing a genial disposition. His way was so benevolent, his countenance so kind, as he talked of this place in the mountains, White Sulphur Springs, and how the waters are favoured as a cure for rheumatism and other maladies. He said that they were popular with his wife, and that he receives word that she makes an appearance there at other, more temperate, times of the year. Then he smiled in a rather wry manner, as if bearing up under a certain sorrow which is made worse by its nature and the fact that it is common knowledge among the people here in St. Matthew. I myself find his society not at all unpleasant, however reserved his manner may be. I thanked him as cheerfully as I could, and he bowed slightly. Then he limped down the aisle in the darkened church to the door, and the light and heat washed in as he opened the portal and his shadow's hand replaced the shadow of a hat on his shadow head. I felt badly in declining his offer. I removed the shawl from my shoulder and resumed playing, 'Come Thou Font of Every Blessing' on the piano.

Sammy, 1982

His way was so benevolent, his countenance so kind.

Sammy reread the sentence and set down the diary. In the central hallway, he looked up at the portrait of the man in the frame. It was a side of the great man that he had never considered, a hard man, but perhaps a hard man with a soft heart and a secret pain that he showed to no one. When Sammy was a boy, his older sisters had told him that he had been adopted, and he had tearfully believed it for a time. Lately, he had begun to entertain the notion again, that he had little in common with the noble man in the portrait in the central hallway. But the nickel-gray eyes and the sandy-brown beard they shared told the truth.

"You been spendin' a lot a time in front that ol' man, bay."

Betsy nestled down on the settee next to him, across from the portrait. With identical nickel-gray eyes, the man's scar-less, bearded face looked down on his great-grandson's scar-less, bearded face. Sammy was trying to read his great-grandfather.

"Hard but fair," Sammy muttered.

"What they say," Betsy said as she looked up at the original Samuel Teague.

"You ever regret it?" Sammy asked her while keeping his eyes on the portrait. "All the heartache we get for going to Canada?"

"Not even once," she said. "It was my choice, my only choice." She nuzzled the crown of her head into his neck. He smelled her hair, a sweet scent all its own. "If you had chosen differently, Boo, wouldn't none of us would be here. These kids wouldn't be here, no." She kissed his cheek.

Upstairs, a little girl's voice rose in anger. A door opened up there, and Judee came trudging down the stairs, one foot catching up with the other on each tread, her hand carefully steadying herself on the bannister as her face bent in sadness. She stopped halfway down the stairs and announced with a sniffle, "Mama, Elizza-bit fussed me."

Betsy rose from her comfortable spot with her husband in a patch of sunset light and sighed.

"Don't you think they should just work it out?" Sammy asked her.

Betsy's eyes looked up the stairs to the girls' room. "Firs', I need to show them *how* to work it out. So they don't end up like my sister-in-laws, grown women squabbling over a piece of jewelry."

She picked up Judee and carried her up the stairs. At the top of them, Betsy's voice asked into the girls' room, *What's all this? As if!*

Sammy looked up to the man in the portrait, the man who had given the piece of jewelry to his great-grandmother, the fourth Mrs. Teague. An exquisite sapphire pendant, the heirloom that Sammy's sisters Marilyn and Charlotte both claimed. They were not speaking because of it, this small piece of adornment.

The light from a sinking sun quit the central hallway, and night converged onto Mount Teague and St. Matthew Parish and Louisiana. Sammy rose from the settee and went onto the back gallery. Stars were speckling the midnight blue of the sky. Light from the bay doors of the metal barn reached out onto the ground and fell into a skewed rectangle. It was cool enough for a dew in the morning but not for a frost.

Sammy gathered two beers and went down the back stairs and stepped onto the cold night lawn. In the barn, fluorescent lights hummed, and a small cloud of bugs swirled around them, the first insects of the season. Teeter's boots were braced on the concrete floor in front of a cane cutting machine called a soldier harvester. He peered over the knock-down roller between the two vertical crop dividers, occupying the same position that sugar cane stalks do just before they're cut down. On the concrete floor was an aluminum pie plate with bolts and washers.

"You out here pretty late, Teeter," Sammy said.

"Hey bawsman," Teeter said over his shoulder as he narrowed his eyes to see into the darkness between the dividers. His cap was on backwards, and his hands were smudged black. He mumbled through the cigarette in his mouth, "Tryin' to get this roller rollin'."

"How bout a beer?" Sammy asked him.

"All right. You insist." He wiped his hands on a rag and took a beer from Sammy.

They moved out to the darkness to look up into the night sky. Breath turned to mist in the chill, too cool for the creatures who later in the year would croak and mutter. On a night like this, the only thing heard was the silence.

"Night sky always make me think that night I left California," Teeter said as he sipped his beer and looked up at the midnight blue.

"California?"

"Yeah. For ova-seas."

Teeter never, ever said the word *Vietnam.* It was always "out the country" or "ova yonda" or "when I's in the army."

"How is that?" Sammy asked into the mouth of his beer bottle as he brought it up to his lips.

"Dem stars up there? Remind that night we took off from California in that 130-C bird, big ass plane. Look down, them little lights way off. All us scared, but we all jus' boys, so we laughin' and jokin', tryin' not to show it, no. Took off, middle the night, see them lights on the coast out the window, lil' bitty like stars, like the world been flipped upside down."

He took a sip of his beer and stared out into the night. Sammy took a sip of his beer, too, but his eyes were looking up at the sky.

"And then all dat black ocean. Got real quiet all a sudden. I look up, ev-body else lookin' out dem windows. All the jokin' stop. All the talkin' stop. Jus' dead quiet. We all wonderin' if we evva gonna come back."

Teeter closed his eyes as his lips pulled at his cigarette. He blew out a long, smoky exhalation.

"Get ova yonda, and das where I met Madame Dope. Grass, smack, all dat. Especially junk. *Heroin.* You could buy glass jars a that shit on the side of the road from ol' mama-sans and papa-sans. Big smiles, like the pass-tru at McDonald's. We used to dip our cigarettes in it and smoke it. Easy to get and hard to avoid."

"How long were you over there?"

"Two years, five months, and seventeen days. I was all used up, so they send me home. Get home, ain' nobody glad to see us, no. Only people glad to see me? My mama and my parrain and my nanny. Das it. No parade, no nothin'. Jus' 'fall out sojah."

"Sometimes I wish…" Sammy said, but he fell silent with his confession half in and half out of him. He wanted to call it back, to inhale the words. Teeter looked up to the stars.

"Wish you hadn't run off, what you sayin'?" Teeter pursed his lips around the cigarette and looked off into the darkness. Sammy could imagine him like that in the jungle on a steamy night, squatting with his elbows on his knees and a fuming cigarette in his hand. "Oh, I know what you done. Evvabody know. Well, don' be sorry, bawsman. You ain' miss nothin'. Nothin'."

His lips pulled at the cigarette again, and the ember glowed orange in the darkness. He let out a mouthful of smoke and looked at the cigarette and said, "I wouldna gone I didn't have to." He sighed a tragic sigh and stood up.

"But I ain' no college boy, me. I had to go. Rish boys didn't have to go. They all had heel spurs and flat feet and daddies what knew people. Oh, I know what you done, bawsman, but das all right. I don' blame you, no." He let go a cloud of smoke with a facial expression something like a grimace. "But I seen things ain' never gonna go away."

He put his cigarette butt in the beer bottle, and it sizzled inside. He handed it to Sammy, and Sammy felt the diminished weight of the bottle in his hand as he watched Teeter go back in the shed, an emptiness to both Teeter and the bottle. Sammy looked up into the stars.

He thought about Teeter, and about Mr. Phillips in Surrey, and whether their horrors were the same horrors, or whether Teeter had new ones that didn't exist a hundred years ago, and whether Mr. Phillips had been tempted with smack or junk or whatever name it went by in the nineteenth century. He thought of what kept Teeter together that Mr. Phillips had lacked. He wondered if it was just a matter of time. Sammy left the bottles lying in the grass under the star-speckled sky and went back in the house.

Alice 1870

10 July 1870. Each Sunday the congregation diminishes. At this rate, by the end of summer it shall only be Papa and me, like a hotter version of St. John's in Miles Platting. I suppose the weather in the north of England is splendid now, though certainly the mills continue to belch smoke into the pleasant summer sky there.

12 July 1870. This today in the *Compass*: 'Those who can flea to more temperate climes such as the seaside or the mountains have done so.' Flea for flee. Our paper is found again with a misspelling. I am beginning to enjoy them and shall leave any notice of correction to others. Perhaps they are intentional. It is true, however, that many, particularly the more affluent, have left. However, as Papa and I have endured yellow fever, malaria, and other bilious fevers before, in India, we have elected to stay in St. Matthew. Mr. Teague and his girls have departed this morning for White Sulphur Springs, in the mountains. The Parrises have left for the seaside, Biloxi, setting off like the children of Moses escaping the pharaoh. Most of the big houses in St. Matthew Parish are left in the charge of the negro caretakers, who can neither flee nor flea.

13 July 1870. The rain approaches this afternoon with the brisk scent of metal and a wind that stirs the tops of the sugarcane like the palms for Our Lord entering Jerusalem. The breeze is welcome.

15 July 1870. The New Orleans *Republican* reports that recently in New Orleans and Memphis people have died of Yellow Fever. This place, St. Matthew, seems to be holding its breath. The blurred glare of the pale-white afternoon heat settles its weightlessness on everything, wagons, trees, sugarcane, outbuildings. Everything gasps in the hot, suffocating air.

18 July 1870. Papa preached the funeral of an old man, a Mr. J–, a veteran of the Battle of New Orleans, in which our general Packenham was driven from the field by a ragged collection of stevedores and pirates. Papa mentioned his bravery for his country and his devotion to his family. Afterward, Papa remarked to me how ironic it was that his funeral was preached by an Englishman.

22 July 1870. The *Picayune* says that France is at war with Prussia, the hairy brutes of which Louise Pidger spoke when we were children.

24 July 1870. Nothing moves in this heat. Great mountain ranges of grey clouds rise into the sky and empty themselves onto the sugarcane and the church and the vicarage and we are granted half an hour's respite from the heat. Then the mosquitoes set upon us. We give up after half an hour of fruitless swatting. They are too numerous for us.

28 July 1870. A letter from Jenny arrives today and is very much welcomed. She says that her father is taking the waters which are hot enough to turn one's skin red. She says that the noted General Lee of the late Confederacy was visiting, and he looks quite old and ill. They gather about him under the springhouse, and everyone fawns over him like he is Christ, including Mr. Teague, until the General espouses the idea of educating negroes. Jenny says that her father, Mr. Teague, is not at all in favour of that.

31 July 1870. Papa preached today on King Solomon, who asked God not for riches, but for an understanding heart. Then Papa prayed that God may grant us the grace to bear that which we must understand. Then I played 'Lord My Pasture Shall Prepare.' The congregation is scant. Most have vacated to the mountains, or to Europe, or to the seaside, Grande Isle or Biloxi.

2 August 1870. The air has become vaporous, and it is difficult to breathe freely in it. The only thing that moves is the sugarcane growing, which increases itself at a pace that is almost audible. Jenny sends another letter from the mountains. She states that it is necessary to wear a cover at night and to light the fireplaces there due to the cold. She says that she reads the papers and the reports of Yellow Fever and prays that we may be spared here in Old St. Matthew.

5 August 1870. The air sits and goes nowhere. The water sits and goes nowhere. Everything is the prisoner of inertia. And again, the sugarcane is the only exception and grows prodigiously. The sky above it glows white-hot with heat and light.

8 August 1870. I am now firmly of the opinion that St. Matthew Parish is all as hot as Calcutta if not more so. The cane grows as tall as a man's head. The *Compass* announces that Yellow Fever is found in some remote places along the river.

11 August 1870. Another letter from Jenny imploring Papa and me to quit St. Matthew for a while and join them. I write a letter in reply that she is not to worry as we are under God's protection.

13 August 1870. There is no rain today as much as I might wish for it. Papa sends a post to the Linnaen Society. I cannot endure another disappointment for him. May God help us bear that which may disappoint us.

14 August 1870. Several of the Union soldiers attend church in blue suits and grey trousers. Papa preached on Jairus' Daughter. I played 'As Pants the Heart for Cooling Streams,' for the opening hymn and 'Lord Dismiss Us with Thy Blessing' for the benedictory hymn.

15 August 1870. Yellow Fever has appeared here. We have seen it before in Calcutta and have no fear of it, if it is to be our fate. Thy will be done.

17 August 1870. Two deaths in Plattenville. One in Paincourtville. Several more in Donaldsonville. Letter from Jenny in Virginia. Old

General Lee has departed. Jenny and her sisters play at croquet. I have no time to respond to her letter, though I am glad to receive it.

21 August 1870. Sabbath. Papa's sermon today to a church that is three-quarters empty: 'Weeping Endureth for the Night but Joy Cometh in the Morning.' I could only hope it is a cool morning when joy cometh. More fever every day. Played "Eternal Source of Every Joy." Word after services is that the barracks has seen Yellow Fever now and suffers from it.

23 August 1870. Two parishioners sick. Papa and I attend them.

26 August 1870. Two funerals today. Many more are sick. Due to sickness, mail service has been suspended.

28 August 1870. Only three in church today, Papa and I excluded. Our health remains excellent despite our exposure to the sick. Played 'Salvation! O the Joyful Sound' for the five of us. Mozie is in excellent health also. There are reports that some of the servants looking after the finer homes of St. Matthew have ransacked the larders and wine cellars. There are also reports that they are aided in their thievery by the occupying soldiers.

4 September 1870. Papa welcomed several of the negro soldiers into the sanctuary for services this morning. It is said that newspaper service shall soon be suspended, as mail service has been. How I would enjoy a letter from Jenny. I began Rousseau's *Confessions* again, this time in English.

Sammy 1982

The next day, he drove to St. Margaret's. In the churchyard, Mrs. Armstrong, the vicar's wife, was in a flower bed next to the dark red brick of the vicarage. She was wearing a sunhat like a Chinese or Vietnamese woman might wear and pruning roses. Her green work gloves wielded shears that snipped away at prickly stems. She stood and greeted him.

"Well, hello, Mr. Teague."

"Hello," Sammy said back. He wondered how she knew his name. Was he famous or infamous?

"Spring will be upon us before we know it," she said, scratching her nose with her wrist. "Important to get these roses back to four or five canes now so we'll have nice blooms."

"Yes ma'am," Sammy said as he looked around the grounds of the vicarage. He found the tree that he thought might be the one with the limb that looked like a scythe and looked up into its branches. "How old is this tree, do you think?" he asked as he searched for the limb among the leaves and branches.

"This one? Oh, I'd say, at least two hundred years. It's magnificent, isn't it? Twice as old as anyone alive in St. Matthew Parish."

"Yes ma'am, it is. How long do you think it's been this size?"

"Oh, at least a hundred years," she said with her wrists on her hips as she wriggled her nose at an itch. Sammy kept looking up into the limbs, trying to imagine which ones that Alice and Jenny had been on.

"Do you mind if I look around?" Sammy asked.

"Feel free to make yourself at home," she said as she sat down on a little portable bench to continue pruning her roses.

He walked out to the highway to look at the historical marker the state had put up, *St. Margaret's Episcopal Church, established 1849 and consecrated 1850 by Bishop Leonidas Polk.* Sammy turned and walked back to the church belfry under the shade of the live oaks. He ascended the winding iron treads that had *Tredegar Iron Works, Richmond, Va.* stamped in them. In the belfry, a bird chirped from her nest in the rafters where a bell slept, waiting to be awakened by the rope cord that dangled down to a knotted end. He looked back through the tree lines to the tank of the Mount Teague water tower where he had just been, a white speck above the gray and green treetops.

From the belfry, the cemetery spread out behind the church in a space that had been carved out from sugarcane fields. White headstones and crypts extended in rows and columns, a village of the dead, people who had taken secrets and hopes and hidden pain and the love of their families with them, and the families who had done the same later. All of them were grieved for and then forgotten, as the ones who had grieved joined them later.

He wondered about the Teague girls whom Alice had tutored, an obscure and possibly withered branch of the Teague family tree. He had never seen their headstones in the cemetery of St. Margaret's. The Teagues were always laid to rest in the red-marble crypt in a copse of trees on the grounds of Mount Teague. He knew the girls from his great-grandfather's first marriage weren't there, and he wondered where they had come to rest. With their husbands' people, he supposed.

He spotted the graves of Alice and her father, the Rev. Lamb. They didn't scare him anymore. He felt he knew them now. Down in her roses, Mrs. Armstrong whistled cheerfully against the winter wind, and Sammy felt it against his beard as he looked out the portal in the brick belfry. The small figure of Mrs. Armstrong picked up her garden bench and placed it in front of the next rose bush. The bird in her belfry nest had been brightly chirping a warning the whole time, and Sammy left her to her young and descended the winding steps.

The epitaph on Reverend Lamb's crypt was worn and barely legible, *Most Reverend Arthur Lamb.* Sammy ran his fingers over the troughs in the stone. Below the reverend's name, only *Done* and *Good* were still clear from what must have been *Well Done my Good and Faithful Servant.* Next to him was a simple monument for his daughter Alice, with the date of her death and the simple inscription, *Gone from Sorrow.* Around them were the graves of those who had died in the late summer and early fall of 1870, fever victims, most likely, poor sufferers who had been attended to, perhaps, by the Reverend Lamb and with his daughter by his side. Sammy thought of how, as a boy, the mere fact of being here before these graves would have been an act of heroism worthy of a medal. That fear had mellowed into fascination. He turned to walk out of the cemetery, passing the graves of old people that Sammy had known or known of. Mrs. Armstrong was gathering up the thorny offcuts and putting them into a wheelbarrow. Sammy stopped to help her.

"Have you ever seen the silver tea service that your great-grandfather gave to the vicarage?" she asked. "It really is quite an item, though we never use it for its purpose any longer. As a matter of fact, there are a number of things he gave the church. He was quite a generous man. Let me show you." She took off her gloves and laid them on top of the spiny offcuts interspersed with red and yellow rose blooms from the months before and now faded by a winter in the cold.

The inside of the vicarage was dark and smelled old, the kind of building that Sammy imagined was typical of England. Mrs. Armstrong called out for her husband, "Bob? Bob?"

There was no answer, and she said, "Must be in the vestry."

She opened up a locked cabinet. "Here it is."

Their reflections gleamed in the silver, distorted and bulbous. Sammy thought of Alice's reflection in the tea service, her gloved hands pouring and then sipping, her English accent conversing with an American one of someone else, his great-grandfather, perhaps.

"Old Mr. Teague, your great-grandfather, gave this to the vicarage in…." Her mind searched.

"Eighteen-seventy," Sammy said.

"That's right," Mrs. Armstrong said. "Worth a fortune then, and even more now."

She carefully placed it back in the cabinet and locked it.

"Let me show you something else," she said. "Come with me."

They passed through the breezeway between the vicarage and the sanctuary. For a moment, the dark shadows of the church and the scent made Sammy feel as though he were eleven again. She showed Sammy the organ. On the wall was an embossed brass plaque,

Donated to the Parish of St. Margaret's by Samuel Teague in 1870

Placard placed 1906

"Now, that's an antique," Mrs. Armstrong said.

"Are you talking about me?" a voice called from the vestry.

"The organ, Bob," she called back as she winked to Sammy.

The Reverend Armstrong appeared in the vestry doorway in a white shirt and clergyman's collar. His soft hand shook Sammy's firm hand.

"Well, nice to see you again, though I understand you're a Catholic now," the reverend said. "Did you come to get a second opinion?"

"You might say that," Sammy said. He looked at the organ.

"Do you play?" Mrs. Armstrong asked.

"The piano. But I've never played the organ," Sammy said.

"Try it, then," Rev. Armstrong said with an upturned palm.

Sammy sat and arranged himself. He played middle C. The organ cleared its throat, a sound that might belong to the horn of the ferry boat in White Castle or a steamboat calliope. He played a few other notes, thunderous groans of the lower keys and hoarse whistles of the higher ones like the trumpets of angels.

"Play something," Mrs. Armstrong said.

He played the first thing that came to mind, the thing he had been playing with regularity over the past week, *Liebestraum.* It was a piece composed for the piano, and the organ bellowed it out clumsily.

"Ah, Liszt," Mrs. Armstrong said when Sammy was finished. Then he played a few more, including some of the old standards from his youth, the same ones that Alice had played. He could almost feel his fingertips touch hers through the keys as the organ rose and fell, soaring and diving in colossal fanfares.

"Well, the old gal's still got it after a hundred years or more," Mrs. Armstrong said as Sammy concluded.

"How do you mean?" Sammy asked as he rose and put on his red plaid flannel coat.

"The old organ," she said. "I call her the 'old gal.'"

"Oh," Sammy said as he shook their hands and turned to the door of the church. His mind wandered over the countless brides who had entered through those doors and left through them again with new last names, including Alice Lamb.

"Good to see you, Mr. Teague," Reverend Armstrong said, and, when they reached the steps of the church and the cold shade of the oaks, he added, "I want you to know that you're always welcome here."

There was something unsaid in what he said. Maybe it was, *it's unfair how people treat you around here* or maybe, *we've forgiven you because we're supposed to.*

But whatever it was, it was left unspoken. He returned to Mount Teague and his study where the diary was waiting in the top drawer of his desk. In the central hallway, he carefully avoided the gaze of his great-grandfather, the benefactor of St. Margaret's Episcopal Church.

Alice 1870

9 October 1870. Forgive me my little friend, my confidant, for neglecting you. There simply has not been enough time to write an entry of any length. The fever has done its worst and is thought to have abandoned this place with the cooler weather, which is welcome indeed. Papa and I have attended negro and white alike in its wake. Church attendance today was augmented by the return of the Parris family, who have been at Biloxi. After the benediction, at Papa's urging and in thanksgiving, I played works of Mozart on the organ, an impromptu recital. Those present stood and clapped, and I stood from the bench and bowed. Then at the door of the church, Papa and I received the congratulations and well-wishes of the returning parishioners. Talk on the steps was of those who have gone to eternity. Mrs. Parris asked Papa if he really believed that whites and negroes will share a common heaven. Papa replied that it is his belief that there shall be but one heaven, and in it all souls shall be the same colour, regardless of their earthly wrappings. Likewise, he said, there shall be but one hell, and in it everyone shall be different colours, and each minor difference in hue shall be the source of great agitation and violence. The smile fell from her face and her hand slipped from Papa's as she took her husband's arm and they walked over the lawn of the churchyard to where their negro servant attended their carriage. Later, Papa told me, 'If you want to anger the satisfied, my beautiful daughter, then preach the word of Christ to them. I can assure you, they will not like it, no more than the Pharisees did when our Saviour first preached it.' I asked Papa if he meant to anger them, and he said, no, he meant to preach the word of Christ to them, as he was called to do. Any anger with him or with the word of Christ is their affair, to be taken up with the Creator.

12 October 1870. A most wonderful day today, as Mr. Teague and his daughters returned from the mountains. Ida and Lucy were in great spirits and greeted me warmly. Lucy jumped in my arms and put her arms and legs around me. It was very good to see them all. Jenny told me that her father had a quarrel with a man named Roddey who was a general in the late war. They had quite a row over something and parted with great animosity. 'He fumed all the way home,' she said.

14 October 1870. Most have returned from their exile, as the air is clement now and more so every day. The sugarcane is as high as a man's head, if the man is on horseback.

16 October 1870. Papa was asked by several of the planters to pray for a good harvest. He did so but added in his prayer that the people of St. Matthew may reap as well the sweetness of generosity and ample kindness to those less fortunate. From my bench behind the great organ, I could see eyebrows raised from their prayer.

19 October 1870. The *Compass* brings the news that General Lee has died in Virginia on the 12th instant. Though the war has long been over, and the cause is lost, there is much sadness here. Some don the black attire of mourning.

22 October 1870. The *Picayune* reports that the Prussians have Paris under siege.

23 October 1870. In the vestry before services this morning, Papa told me to watch the faces of the congregation, for when he preaches from the Old Testament, particularly a case in which retribution is meted out, they are all smiles and nods and rapt attention. But when the lesson is from the New Testament, especially a case of turning the other cheek, they seem to be preoccupied with other business. And so, Papa preached his sermon, 'Take Up Your Cross and Follow Me.' It is one of his finest. 'Who wants these nails?' he asked, 'They are simple, even useful. But without them, there is no cross, and without the cross, there is no glory.

Everyone desires the robe and crown of Christ. Few desire the nails to pay for them.' And then he sat, and I played to the stricken look on most of the faces of the congregation. They all seemed uneasy, save a few, among them, Mr. Teague, whose countenance seldom speaks.

25 October 1870. Mr. Teague paid a call today to congratulate Papa on the 'fine sermon' Papa gave on Sunday, praising it as a 'champion effort!' Papa seemed gratified but said that he was afraid that he may have stepped on some toes. 'Oh, fiddlesticks,' Mr. Teague exclaimed, 'sometimes there is no way around the truth.' Papa thanked him again and excused himself for a moment, and when he did, Mr. Teague again offered me the job of governess for his girls. His way is so resolute and insistent! I told him, as politely as I could, that though the girls have become as sisters to me, I feared that Papa would not get along well without me. Mr. Teague said that he begged to differ, that he believes that Papa would get along quite well and perhaps find a new mate among the widows and spinsters of the parish. I myself can hardly imagine it. When Papa returned from the privy, Mr. Teague presented him with a gift of a 'fine American pony.' We looked out the vicarage window and there tethered to an oak limb was the horse in question. Calling this horse a pony is much the same as calling Kensington Palace a cottage. The horse, called Hercules, is a jet black, shining, muscular thing that stamped nervously and shook his head and flared his eyes and nostrils, pulling at the reins tied to the post outside the vicarage. I wonder how vigorous he would be were he not gelded. Mr. Teague told Papa that perhaps he could now get out and do a little courting, 'a young man like yourself' and that perched upon this horse he would certainly come off as a 'knight-errant.' Papa guffawed at this whimsical compliment. Though horsemanship has never been Papa's strong suit, he seemed intrigued with the gift and thanked Mr. Teague for his generosity, saying the he hoped that he and Hercules shall get on well together in time. Mr. Teague has also provided a saddle in the American style. As Mr. Teague bid us adieu and took to the lane and the bayou road on his own chestnut horse, Papa said to me, 'You see, my dear, there are generous and thoughtful people everywhere you go!'

28 October 1870. Word is that within the space of a few weeks, the sugarcane will be cut. It shall be odd to see the earth barren of it, like seeing a sheep shorn of its wool. Hercules must be tethered away from Sugar after biting a gash in her neck.

30 October 1870. After services, Mr. Teague asked if Papa had made any forays on horseback. Papa said that he had not yet had the chance, but afterward confided in me that Mr. Teague may feel rather slighted in his gift not being enjoyed.

31 October 1870. Papa and I stood at the fence and watched Hercules frantically race its perimeter. Mozie said, 'That hoss show got some pepper in him.'

1 November 1870. I have spent the morning watching Papa become acquainted with his new horse. At the edge of the churchyard, there is a vine that bears a sort of pear or apple called a mirliton. Papa has discovered that Hercules has quite a taste for them. The horse greedily nibbled the green mirlitons, his great slobbering lips grasping for it, his great black eyes blinking, until at last Papa had to quickly withdraw his fingers to keep them from being bit. He ran his hand along the horse's shining, black flank and it rippled as if repelling a fly. Then Papa tried to slip the harness over Hercules' head, but the horse would only shake his head against it. Finally, with the promise of another mirliton, Hercules accepted the harness and allowed Papa to lead him around the yard. After a half hour of this, Papa granted Hercules another mirliton and led him to his stall which is beside Sugar's. Papa says that tomorrow he shall try the saddle.

2 November 1870. With a great deal of negotiating, Hercules has accepted his saddle. Our mirliton tree is all but depleted of pears.

3 November 1870. Rain today, cold and hard, and so Hercules stays in his stall and Papa in his study.

4 November 1870. Though a cold, brisk, stunning day, it has also been a most horrible one. With no small amount of coaxing this morning, Papa was able to put the saddle on Hercules as Mozie held his leader. The horse took it rather more calmly than I had expected and even let Papa lead him around the churchyard. Hercules was most compliant, as docile as a lamb. Papa placed a foot in a stirrup and vaulted up into the saddle, securing his hat and smiling tentatively. Mozie stepped back as Papa shook the reins, but Hercules would not budge. When Papa pressed a heel into the horse's flank, Hercules reared back and took off suddenly, running as if pursued by wolves, and Papa was taken off at a gallop. He had to duck to avoid a large oak limb which knocked off his hat, leaving his white hair wind-twisted into a frenzy. Horse and rider disappeared down the bayou road, and Mozie shouted, 'They he go!' We waited for Papa to come back, but he remained away for quite a while, and I thought perhaps he had stopped to visit someone. When he failed to appear for tea, I became worried. I was just about to see if Mozie would take Sugar and get the carriage put to, when a man on horseback came leading Hercules, who was again stamping and prancing, but with an empty saddle. A wagon came a little way behind them, and in it was Papa. He was got into the house, and in a great deal of pain. The man who had led Hercules home rode into Napoleonville to get the doctor, who came after Papa had endured a great deal of pain and for quite some time. By the amber light of the lantern, the doctor set the leg and applied a plaster-of-Paris cast. Papa sleeps with the help of what the doctor calls, 'Lady Laudanum.'

5 November 1870. Today is Guy Fawkes' Day in England, though here it is simply called Saturday. Papa claims to have slept well, though I am certain I heard him groan in his sleep during the night. There was a knock on the door this morning, and upon opening it I found Mr. Teague, standing and twirling his hat and wearing a nervous look of concern. He inquired after Papa, saying that he felt horribly about what had happened, absolutely wretched. He asked if he might see Papa to offer his apologies, but I found Papa sleeping again. Mr. Teague said he would call again tomorrow and every day until Papa's health improves.

6 November 1870. For the first time since we came to this place, Papa was absent from the pulpit and I was absent from the bench. A vicar from Thibodaux was brought in to serve as Papa's replacement. Mr. Teague visits today with the gift of a ham and other eatables.

7 November 1870. Papa had a much better night and this morning was able to sit up in bed and take the breakfast Mozie brought him. Soon after breakfast, Mr. Teague appeared. I showed him to Papa's room, where I found Papa reading the *Compass.* I told him that Mr. Teague had come to pay a call, and Papa rustled the paper closed and took off his glasses and bid me send him in. Papa apologised for not being able to rise and greet Mr. Teague properly, but Mr. Teague said that it was he himself who needed to apologize for the gift of 'that fractious beast of a horse.' Papa joked that he had never been one to look a gift horse in the mouth, as the saying is. Mr. Teague offered to have the horse 'put-down,' but Papa said that there was no need and that Hercules is merely a creature of God, obeying his nature like the rest of us. Mr. Teague said that it was really no trouble, that it would be a small matter, but again Papa refused. Mr. Teague once more expressed how wretchedly he felt about the whole thing but supposed that we should take heart in the fact that lesser men would not have survived such a tumble. Papa replied with a small chuckle that it has been said that we English are made of iron and oak. 'I can see it's so, a most admirable quality,' Mr. Teague said with a raise of his eyebrows. They chatted a few moments, Papa again expressing his admiration of the place, St. Matthew, this Garden of Eden, vigorously trumpeting green, even now, well into autumn. Mr. Teague left with renewed apologies and the promise to return for a visit tomorrow.

8 November 1870. Papa still endures no small amount of pain in moving. Mr. Teague visited again today, proclaiming cheerfully, 'Why the patient seems to improve a little every day!' This was charitable. I do not see any improvement at all. He had with him a bottle with a bow around the neck, what he described as a 'tonic which should speed your recovery.' It was a bottle of cherry brandy, which Mr. Teague said he believed was a favourite of Papa's. Papa replied with a reference to Matthew's gospel, 'Well, then, I was thirsty, and you gave me drink!' but Mr. Teague only gave a confused smile and asked if that was some old English saying. Papa said that, yes, in a way, it was. He said that it was very thoughtful of Mr. Teague and asked him if he might take a 'wee-dram,' as a Scot might say it. Mr. Teague demurred, saying that he was a whisky man, himself, but that his mother would swear by cherry brandy to restore good health and vigor, if she were ever to swear, he joked. The two of them laughed, and then Papa had me bring two glasses and the decanter of bourbon from his study, for Mr. Teague's tastes. I fetched the glasses, and Papa held up his glass of cherry brandy, or cherry bounce, as some call it, and Mr. Teague held up his bourbon, and they drank each other's health. Mr. Teague added *and to a quick recovery to you, kind vicar.* It was followed with another and another, Papa smacking his lips and looking at his glass with the first few sips. After a short discussion of church matters, including who shall officiate in Papa's absence as he recuperates and an assurance that the church wardens have agreed that Papa shall continue to receive his stipend whilst convalescing, Mr. Teague rose from the chair at Papa's bedside and said he must be going. After another round of thanks from Papa, Mr. Teague replied that he hoped that the cherry brandy shall speed the patient's recovery, and that he should take a tablespoon for pain, or for sleep, and then another and then two and so forth, and to work up to small draughts. He said that his personal physician Dr. McKnight says that it brings excellent rest and refreshment. Papa said that he certainly shall and thanked Mr. Teague again. When Mr. Teague had departed, Papa had me bring him his small lap desk and his pen and ink, and I am heartened that he is working on a sermon for when he returns to the pulpit.

9 November 1870. Papa sleeps in today. Midmorning, he rose and called for me, and I helped him to the chamber pot. His bowels are in a flux, and his broken leg slows him. 'O, Papa, your poor dignity,' I said, but he only laughed wryly and said, 'It is well, my beautiful daughter. Dignity is a play we perform for others. We always get a view of ourselves from behind the curtain, backstage and from the wings.' I give him spoonfuls of cherry bounce, and he is able to take a little toast and treacle (molasses, rather, here in America) and then some rest.

10 November 1870. Papa does not look well today. I waited for him to call me to assist him in rising, but he staid abed late into the morning. I brought a tray of breakfast that Mozie prepared. Around noon he remarked, 'My beautiful daughter, you have been both a pride and a pleasure to me.' I replied that I shall continue to be one, with God's help. As I continued the conversation, I found to my surprise that Papa had fallen asleep.

11 November 1870. Mr. Teague called today and was taken aback by Papa's appearance. He called for Dr. McKnight, who arrived within the hour. He said that Papa has all the indications of cholera. The vicarage is quarantined.

12 November 1870. Dr. McKnight returned today, though Papa has slept all day. I, however, cannot. Papa's hair has thinned to mere wisps, and he does not look well at all. During lucid moments, he murmurs, 'Whitham. Whitham,' and I go to fetch the bottle of Whitham's Cherry Brandy, and when I return, Papa is fast asleep again. The bottle is now only a quarter full and I asked Dr. McKnight if he thinks more brandy will help. It may, he said, and that it certainly doesn't hurt in cases of cholera. He asked me if I have had any symptoms. No, I said, though I am tired. Certainly, it is because I have slept very little.

13 November 1870. Papa shows no improvement. Today he said, 'If only we knew how temporary we are, then perhaps we would do things quite differently.' 'Yes,' I replied, 'I suppose it is so.' Then he looked at me and said, 'Heaven cannot boast of a finer, worthier angel than you, my beautiful daughter.' Several of his teeth are loose. He then said that he would sleep for a while and asked if I would mind the vicarage. I told him I would, but he was already asleep.

14 November 1870. I sit and pray with Papa, though he is not aware of it. Outside the window, with each day, more of the fields are cut by men who swing knives and chant songs. Wagons set into the fields empty and leave packed high, and the earth becomes exposed again in bare, black patches. The stubble is set ablaze, and the smoke scents everything, and at night the fires burn under the stars so that it is not necessary to light a candle against the darkness. It is as if verdant-green heaven has become a black and smoky hell. Papa breathes so heavily, so loudly. I fear that his weary soul is taking flight.

15 November 1870. Papa was peacefully released this morning.

Sammy, 1982

He closed the diary and looked out the window of the study and into the darkness. She had lost the very last member of her already small family. Though he had never met her, he felt a pain, like it had happened to him. Down the central hallway in the kitchen, Betsy was talking to the dog, sweetly, patiently, the same way she talked to their children. He knew the dog was sitting and twisting her head this way and that, as if she were tuning a radio dial to understand better. Betsy's footsteps and the clack of the dog's claws came to the door of his study, and the three of them went upstairs. They checked on the children, all sleeping, even teenage Quint. Pongeaux tapped over the plank floor and curled up on her bed in Quint's room.

Betsy was asleep within minutes, the blessing enjoyed by someone who works a hard day and has no regrets at the end of it. Her dark hair was splayed over the pillow as her breath eased in and out of her, softly and silently. There were nights when Sammy watched his wife as she slept and wondered if she dreamed of her daddy. If he dropped into her sleep for visits. If his work-rough hands held his daughter's face as he kissed each cheek with a beaming grin. If he embraced her, pulling her to his work shirt, scented with perique tobacco and his toil, *Mount Teague* embroidered over one pocket and *Duplechain* over the other. If he told her just before she woke and he departed, *mais, I'm so proud a you, bay.* Betsy slept, and Sammy watched her and prayed that it was so.

Outside in the darkness, Winter and Spring wrestled in the night air, tumbling over the emerging cane, tussling in the boughs of the live oaks, brushing against the wind chimes that his daughter Elizabeth had made on a sunny afternoon with her mother, the latest Mrs. Teague, the one sleeping now in a tangle of sheets, clutching a pillow, and dreaming dreams of happy reunions. The chimes tingled in the night breeze, stirred by warm and cold air. He rose and looked out the bedroom window.

In the pale glow of a light bulb high on a utility pole in the backyard, he thought he saw her, a shadow in the amber light, cast by the swaying fingers of oak leaves, playing on the blank screen where the ice barn had been. He hoped it was her, that the imagination of his childhood would rekindle the vision of her. The wind slackened, and he knew that he hadn't seen her. He had only wished he had. His fear of her had been replaced with fascination.

He thought of the night his sisters had locked him in the ice barn and the cloying embrace of feathery cobwebs in the old barn, the caress of ghosts. But rather than casting the blame at the feet of his sisters, his mother's darling idols, he had blamed the old building itself and hated it like one would hate a person, like an inanimate school bully forever taking the lunch money of his self-respect. He had inwardly rejoiced when it went up in flames. Now he regretted it.

Behind him, the door to his bedroom creaked open, and the hall light crept forward in a lengthening triangle. The night window was illuminated, and he saw his own reflection in it. Something touched his hand, and then there was a scratching peck of paws on the window sill next to him. Pongeaux stretched up on her back legs and looked up to him and then out the window at the night. The reflection cast a dim portrait of a man and his dog. He scratched her head and got back in bed, and she leapt and curled up at the foot of it.

The next day, he gathered the papers, the academic descriptions of blue phlox and purple irises and choupique, things that were relatively commonplace to him, but to an English vicar of a hundred years ago were the object of scientific fascination. He thought for a minute and bundled them together in an oversized envelope and drafted a cover letter to accompany them, thinking, *why not?* All the old beards of the Linnaens were gone, and surely there were new ones now.

He drove into town and stopped at the library, greeting the librarian on his way to the room labeled *ARCHIVES*. He found the box labeled, *St. Matthew Parish Compass, November 1870,* and loaded the film into the projector. The light flipped to bright whiteness, and the news of the long-ago month scrolled by. And then, there it was.

Died

The Reverend Arthur Lamb

Last Monday, Nov. 15 at his home, the St. Margaret Church vicarage, of cholera. Friends and acquaintances are invited to attend funeral services for Rev. Lamb, to be held Thursday, Nov. 10 at 10 am at St. Margaret's Church.

Sammy looked at the papers in the oversized envelope, which contained the ideas of this man, written in his own hand. The obituary was two sentences, a meager paragraph for a man who had loved and served, who had humbly spoken his mind when he felt called to do it. Two sentences and a worn monument in a cemetery thousands of miles from where he was born and raised.

Sammy wound the film back into a roll, put it in the box, and then turned off the light. Outside, the sun was beginning to burn away the cold. He pulled onto the highway and, on passing the church, glanced at Rev. Lamb's monument in the community of other monuments behind the vicarage and St. Margaret's. He looked up just in time to slam on his brakes and avoid running into a car waiting to turn and cross the bayou. The car turned, and it took Sammy a moment to regain himself, and, in that moment, a truck honked angrily behind him.

At the post office, the lady behind the counter was sorting mail into plastic bins. The air smelled of paper and ink and glue and floor wax, the smell of all government buildings. Sammy waited in line behind an old white-haired lady. The clerk abandoned her sorting and came up to the counter. She patiently took her time with the old woman, explaining in French the amount of postage she would need to mail cards to her grandchildren in Jennings and Abbeville. After repeating the postage required for each, *vingt cents, quarante cents par deux, madame,* the woman peered through thick glasses into a coin purse and finally dug out four dimes to hand to the clerk. Then it was Sammy's turn.

"Miss Jeannie, I need to mail this."

He handed her the envelope, and she asked, "Where to, bay?"

"London," he said. "England," he added, as if there might be another.

"London?" She took the envelope and weighed it. "We gonna have to put an extra stamp or two on it, then. London's a long way down the bayou," she smiled.

As she pulled the postage out of a meter, he addressed the envelope, *Linnaen Society, Burlington House, Piccadilly, London, United Kingdom.* Then he had her put two more stamps on it. Just to be sure.

Alice Lamb, 1871

1 February 1871. Pardon my inattention, my little confidant, but I have not had the heart to write in you. Nothing interests me. Nothing soothes me. There is no relief, just sunrise after sunrise, sunset after sunset. I am sluggish with apathy. Nameless days slip by. Only you, my little confidant, keep me tethered to the world, lest I float away from the earth or be consumed by it. Mozie is here but only silently busies herself with the errands of the vicarage. Everywhere I look, I see him. Every sound in another room is him, rising from his chair, shuffling papers, clearing his throat, chuckling to himself. O, how can life go on, in such a vacuum?

2 February 1871. Mr. Teague came and sat with me today. He said that he must shoulder the blame and that he has had Hercules 'dispatched to Hades, where he belongs.' Mr. Teague also said that the cholera did its worst and departed St. Matthew and lingered in the neighbouring parishes of St. Mary and Terrebonne before quitting those places. I have heard nothing about any of it, as I have led the life of a recluse. I had very little to say to Mr. Teague and he left, doubtless still feeling as though the blame is his. Of course, I suppose his intentions were good and noble.

4 February 1871. People visit but I scarcely recognize that they are even here. I only sit with my hands in my lap and look out the window. Surely they are aware of my vacant gaze. Grief isolates me, as if I am invisible, or they are. When they leave, I open the old sermon chest and read Papa's papers. I can hear his voice from the pulpit, hear him by the firelight reading to Mama and to me, asking our opinion on some Biblical analogy or a matter of grammar. I can see his mannerisms as he gazes lovingly over his flock like a good shepherd. And then I catch myself staring into nothing and I replace the sermons, holy things because he touched them, into the chest just as lovingly as I took them out, and I close the lid like a coffin.

5 February 1871. The Sabbath today. Though I can hear the organ, I do not leave the vicarage. I have no desire for the society of others.

8 February 1871. I have been sleeping in a chair by Papa's bed, comforted by the scent of his chamber. At last, Mozie said we needed to wash the sheets. I knew she was right, but I sobbed. 'They, now,' she said tenderly, 'You come with me now and we do them together. We ain't gone say nothin'. Is the bess way to remember.' And then we reverently removed them from the bed. Our soapy hands kneaded them and wrung them out and I sobbed and Mozie said nothing. Then we hung them in the winter sun and the breeze nudged them and the shadows they cast came and went in waves on the new green grass. And I wept again, and Mozie said nothing, for there was nothing to say, and she was wise enough to know it. When they were dry we took them down as prayerfully as the disciples took Christ down from the cross, and we dressed the bed again. And when Mozie ran a flat hand over them, so did I, and I knew that she was quite right. It is the best way.

10 February 1871. St. Margaret's has had a succession of itinerant clergy, generally the rectors of the churches in Thibodaux and Donaldsonville, though services were conducted one Sunday by a Methodist circuit rider. This is through second-hand news, as I have not attended church in several months. In fact, I do not leave the vicarage. I view the world and the events of it through the black lace of mourning. Mozie is my only companion. She urges me to get out and take some sunshine, but I cannot. I fear I shall crumble, and then I fear I shall not, that I shall remain whole and aching.

12 February 1871. The organ sounds triumphantly in the sanctuary next door. Today must be Sunday, then.

13 February 1871. A letter arrived for Papa from the Linnaean Society, and after yet another tempest of emotion, I find the strength to read it. *Let me speak plainly with you, Reverend Lamb*, it reads, *I beg you, sir, please do not send any more submissions.*

As you wish, sir.

16 February 1871. Mozie tells me that she overheard that a committee of 'mens' has been assembled to search for a new vicar and that 'Marse Sam' is among them. They are in Memphis presently interviewing a candidate. Mozie reads slowly from the *Picayune* and the *Compass*, and I help her with words she cannot understand, which are numerous but fewer every day. The paper says that the siege of Paris has ended with a Prussian victory. The Prussians, those hairy men with clubs of which Louise Pidger spoke. It as if my Guildford days never happened, and Surrey is an imaginary place.

18 February 1871. The coldest day we have had in a while. Mozie keeps the fire up. I spent my time reading and playing the piano and the organ in the vacant church, and the darkness protected and consoled me. News from the outside world is old and stale. I receive visitors when I am up to it, though chief among my society is Jenny Teague. She came again this afternoon, bundled in a heavy coat, bringing word that another Mount Teague governess has come and gone. She didn't say if she was let go or left on her own accord. She said the new vicar is to be a reverend from Tennessee who served as a chaplain in the late war and that rumours circulate that he is tall and quite handsome and of a genial disposition. She brought her violin, and I tried to accompany her on the piano, but I had no desire for it. But Jenny was very patient and sat quietly when I asked her to stop playing. Laying down her violin, she came and sat next to me on a pew, and I looked up to the empty pulpit and grief stirred again. I turned, and her arms were around me. I trembled and put my head under her chin, and she whispered, 'That's all right. Hush, now. Hush.'

21 February 1871. The occupying army has allowed the people here to resume their Mardi Gras procession and has even furnished several regimental bands to accompany the merriment. Mozie returned from the parading of the 'Krewe of Jupitre' through the streets of St. Matthew saying, 'Marse Sam sit hisself up on dat throne on dat wagon! In dat mask and dem tight stockin-drawers! Now ain' dat a sight, now! And how did them chirren laugh at Marse Sam!' Beneath this black veil, within my black cloud, I am warmed by her delight. I would have liked to attend, but it would not be proper. And in this state, any amusement quickly becomes tiresome.

Sammy, 1982

Betsy's voice broke his concentration, "'These chirren want to go to their parade, Daddy."

The girls were dressed in purple, green, and gold with little plastic princess crowns on their heads. Quint had beads around his neck and his hands in the pockets of his jeans. Sammy closed the diary and put it in the desk drawer and got his jacket.

They parked the car along Highway One where the parade, the Krewe of Jupitre, would pass. Judee rode on Sammy's shoulders with her little hands under his chin in the shagginess of his beard. Elizabeth held Betsy's hand and looked up and down the street at all the people gathered. Quint seemed happy enough to be with his family, but Sammy thought that, when he was his son's age, he would be with friends. People were waiting along the highway, and the sounds of several marching bands competed in the air, each playing a different song. A St. Matthew Parish sheriff approached with blue lights circling atop his cruiser, driving slowly with a blaring whir and whoop of his siren, his tires turning over bits of cane stubble in the road. A band came marching behind a banner that read *Donaldsonville High School Tigers.* The brass instruments gleamed in the sun and trumpeted to the cane fields and the bayou to the rattle and boom of snare and bass drums.

In the wake of the band, a float made from a flatbed trailer and pulled by a tractor followed, filled with men and women in masks and purple and green wigs. The riders untangled strands of beads and flung them into the raised arms of the crowd in between sipping cocktails from plastic cups. Another band passed and then the floats of the Kiwanis, the Rotary Club, and the Knights of Columbus. The float of the St. Matthew Parish Farmers' Co-op trundled by with a sign that said, *Eat More Sugar.*

Another float passed, and someone on it blew soap bubbles. Quint smiled at his sisters as they popped them with hand claps. A band from a high school in New Orleans approached playing "Iko Iko," the air filled with the metallic blare of trumpets and trombones and honking tubas, lips on brass mouthpieces, eyes hidden under the bills of caps, horns swaying, knees marching high. In a sudden downdraft of sound, the horns fell silent and the drums fell with them and the young voices rose to fill the space with the old Mardi Gras standard:

My grandma and your grandma
Sittin' by the fire
My grandma said to your grandma
Gonna set your flag on fire
Talkin 'bout-
Hey now!
Hey now!
Iko, Iko un-day!
Jockamo fee-no ai na-ne, jockamo fee na ne….

Lips and mouthpieces reunited and horns were lifted and mounted a brassy shout, drumsticks found drums in rattles and thumps, and the music continued along and the parade surged forward, the air filled with music and a flurry of shiny, clattering beads. Young girls, every shade of brown, with elaborately braided tresses marched in high steps, pompoms on white boots, checking in sidelong glances that they were on cue and in step.

More floats passed by, pulled by tractors, and green and gold and purple and red and silver beads rained down. Masked riders pointed to spectators and threw them beads, and some were caught, and some fell rattling to the ground where they were swarmed by teeming children. The trees held shiny fronds of beads, hanging down like strings of berries, some hanging from power lines, some scattered on the ground with the dry stalks of cane stubble.

One whimsical float after another passed, and then the grand float of the King of Jupitre, pulled by a big green cane-cutter. The King smiled beatifically behind his mask, raising the ceremonial brass cane-knife-scepter with a white-gloved hand and nodding his brass-crowned head, but his short stature and big gut betrayed his identity as Mr. Picquet. Somebody in the crowd said that he looked like a cartoon king on a cereal box, and everyone who could hear laughed.

The King's Float receded past, and Sammy watched it go. Every Teague man had been selected to be the annual king, but Sammy knew that he would never be King of Jupitre and that his children would never watch him ride the elaborate King's Float pulled by the cane-cutter, big trampling wheels and chattering engine. He would never wear the king's mask and tights (*stockin' drawers*, he thought of Mozie) and tunic and brass crown. He had as much chance of it as the Reverend Lamb had of election to the Linnaen Society.

And then the last float passed, the Pas Bon wagon, a float known for its cutting satire, the exclamation point of the procession, the last float in the Krewe of Jupitre. For some, it was the highlight of the parade, ridden by the most drunken revelers, decorated with novel puns and double-entendre. There was a big cheer as the float edged forward. Beads rained down to the ground and in limbs, along with *Les Pas Bon's* novelty throw for Mardi Gras of 1982, plastic hand grenades in green and yellow and purple.

This year, the revelers all wore blue hats with *LA* on them, like the major league team, and blue shirts that said Dodgers. But Sammy knew that no one around here was a Dodgers fan. Everyone around here was an Astros or Braves fan. When he saw the Canadian flag, a piece of red-white-red painted cardboard with a misshapen maple leaf in the center, he understood.

"There's our house, Daddy!" Elizabeth shouted and looked up to Sammy as she pointed to the backdrop of the float.

And there it was, crudely painted on a sheet of plywood, but easily recognizable as Mount Teague. Elizabeth and Judee didn't get the joke about LA Dodgers and plastic hand grenades. They were too young. But Betsy and Quint did. Their faces wouldn't lie about something like that.

The parade lumbered down the highway, leaving a litter of beads and plastic cups. Sammy gathered his family, and they walked down the highway to their car, passing an Ascension Parish School Bus parked just up from them. Sammy stood and stared at it, as if he could see it somewhere else, as if it had some separate significance. It was raining, and there were red-and-yellow lights blurred in the rain.

Betsy's face appeared in front of his, and she said something that sounded underwater as she looked at the school bus and then at her husband. The sound of the bands that were reaching the end of the parade rose from the distance, and the Teague family loaded up and went home. And as Betsy fixed dinner and the girls played upstairs in their room and Quint caught up on homework, Sammy adjourned to the diary, in the study of a house that had been painted on plywood as a gag.

Alice 1871

28 February 1871. A milestone today. Through Jenny's gentle insistence, I was able to play the complete Mozart's Piano Concerto No. 21 without stopping. As the sound faded from the pressing of the final key, I looked up, and there she was, sitting in the first pew in the dim light. Her hands were in her lap, her knees together, her legs slanted to one side. Her eyes were closed, and her lips curved in a beatific smile. She quietly said that it was wonderful to hear me play again. Her way is so gentle. It is hard to believe she is a few years younger than I.

2 March 1871. I have lost weight, perhaps a stone and a half, so Mozie cooked all day and stood over me while I ate. The weather is mild. Rain threatens us with a soft grumble in the west and is felt in the downy air.

5 March 1871. Jenny persuaded me to attend services, and I went, but I did not play, and the congregation sang without accompaniment. Their glances were repelled by my veil, and I was grateful for the small curtain of black lace. The magnificent organ was silent, and it was a shame, but I have not the capacity for it. The rector of St. John's church in Thibodaux conducted services, a man with wooly side-whiskers and a voice quite like a carriage wheel on a shell road. The old hens of the congregation who have heard tell of the new vicar describe him as young, handsome, and gracious. A veteran of the late war and a bachelor, they say as punctuation. I can feel their scheming to make us a match, and me, still in mourning. Busybodies.

6 March 1871. The impending arrival of the new vicar has necessitated my vacating the vicarage. It is seen as improper that an unmarried young woman should share a house unsupervised with a single young man, vicar or not. It is certainly so and quite understandable. I must secure an alternate situation. Jenny, who visits daily, urges me to take the position of governess at Mount Teague, as it is vacant again.

7 March 1871. Mr. Teague himself visited today to offer me a room and the position of governess when I am up to it. He said that perhaps it shall help with my bereavement. His way is so kindly, and I, having no other prospects, shall accept it. I warned him that there may be days that I am not fit for my duties. He gently said that it is certainly to be expected and for me to perform my duties as I can, and no fault will be found.

10 March 1871. My last entry into you as an inhabitant of this vicarage, my little confidant, as today you and I must remove to Mount Teague. In anticipation of it, I float around the empty vicarage like a ghost. So much has happened here. So much life has seeped into these walls, in front of this hearth, at that table. Mozie promises to visit often, though she must stay to keep house for the new vicar. I gathered the papers from the desk in Papa's study. His last sermon was there, the one entitled, 'All Hail the Queen,' as well as his unfinished submission for the Linnaen Society, 'Treatise on the Choupique, (*or 'Shoe-pick,'*) of the Louisiana Bayous.' There are others, and I have put them all in my portmanteau. Later, when I feel up to it, I shall keep them together in the sermon chest and hold it as a temple to his memory. I have taken great care with its packing, and it is already in the wagon behind the driver. I look out the window to the east at the sun floating up into the morning sky, and I cannot help but to see Papa's silhouette in it, though the window is empty. In the live oak of the churchyard, the limb that sprouts like a scythe is covered over with new leaves. The morning glows with impending brilliance, and it shall be a spectacular day for those inclined to be about in it. In the graveyard, I stand before Papa's crypt, which is above the ground, not in the soil of England or in the rocky earth of Darjeeling next to Mama, but here, above the black ground of Louisiana. The azaleas are a few days from their peak, and nature shouts in emerald green. But I cannot hear her. Her voice is as distant as everyone else's. Mozie stands by the wagon and visits with her nephew Reuben, who waits patiently on the buckboard whilst I take one last look. In leaving, I seem to leave Papa behind as well. I cannot look backward, only forward. I ascend into the wagon and Reuben snaps the leather. And the vicarage shrinks away in the distance.

Sammy, 1982

A car honked behind him, and he realized he had been daydreaming at the only traffic light in town. He looked in his rearview and held up an apologetic hand. The school bus that had been in front of him rumbled down Main Street, lurching with each change of gear. Sammy put his truck in gear and followed up the street. The bus turned to cross the bayou at the next bridge, and Sammy continued straight.

The aqua green pickup pulled up into the parking lot of St. Margaret's Church. The scratched message on his door was unrecognizable now, though he would always see it there, as if it had been etched somewhere inside of him and not on the door of his truck. He reached into the bed of his truck to retrieve the weed eater.

The lights in the vicarage were off, and the Armstrongs' old Buick was gone. The house and the sanctuary seemed as empty as the day that Alice left it. Sammy stopped and leaned against the live oak tree that he was reasonably sure was the one that Jenny Teague and Alice Lamb had climbed that day. He looked up into it and tried to imagine two nineteenth-century girls sitting up there. The sun scattered through the branches, and he held up his hand against the light.

Sammy glanced to a window of the vicar's study. There were no faces in it as there had been earlier in the day or a year or a hundred years ago, just empty glass panes. He turned and walked back to the gravestone and crypt of Rev. Lamb. He put his fingers to the eroded inscription and felt the letters carved into the stone, *Done* and *Good*, the only ones recognizable in *Well Done My Good and Faithful Servant.* Above that, he thought he could feel the word *Cholera*, though he was less sure about this part of the epitaph. They were words hastily chosen by a grieving daughter, and Sammy imagined the conversation that might have taken place between the undertaker and the bereaved.

What would you like it to say, ma'am?

Oh, anything, she might have said, if she had said anything at all. Maybe she had just shaken her head and sobbed, and the undertaker had decided on his own, one of a dozen or so stock phrases he might have had on hand for cases like those. A person's life, reduced in the spur of the moment to a seven-word sentence, now worn down by the elements to two words.

The cemetery was a place from his childhood, when St. Margaret's was his church and the children of it were his friends. It always made him think of his childhood friend, James Chauvin, who, like Sammy, was also a younger brother to two sisters. The two of them would play, sometimes, in the graveyard of the church. James preferred to be called Jimmy, but his mother, a woman who doted on her only son, insisted on his full, Christian name, James. His family was not nearly as affluent as the Teagues, no family was, but the boy Jimmy was good company. He was a friendly boy with an easy, freckled smile and a giggling laugh, a boy who wore the same crew cut as Sammy.

Back then, the graveyard, and especially the grave of Alice the Burning Lady, was the second most terrifying place Sammy knew, right behind the ice barn. Jimmy knew it, too, but never teased Sammy about it. He was a kind boy who gently prodded Sammy, and himself, really, to venture into the graveyard at night while the lights of the Episcopal Church glowed with evening vesper service or choir practice or altar guild or some other social event. As night fell, he and Sammy would shine a flashlight on the lettered stones and suppose about the lives of the occupants of the graves and marvel that so many could die so young. They would search for the most ancient grave or the youngest or oldest person who had died or try to construct families from among the markers. When their courage was sufficient, they would stand in front of the graves of the Reverend Lamb, *well done, my good and faithful servant,* and Alice, *gone from sorrow*, and whisper about them, as if the occupants might hear them. And when Sammy could feel his fear pushing him to the breaking point, teetering on terror and ready to bolt out of the darkened cemetery, Jimmy would calmly move along, and Sammy would follow him to a less scary stone, the marker of Jimmy's grandparents, who had died within a month of each other in quiet old age, people from whom Sammy was sure Jimmy had gotten his kindness.

Jimmy was a boy with a heart that was big and good, and a benevolent face to go along with it. Without a word, they agreed that they would be lasting friends, he and Jimmy Chauvin. They would double-date in high school and be the Best Men in each other's weddings. But Sammy's mother had sent him off to boarding school in Tennessee with the children of the South's other Best Families, and, although he and Jimmy had promised to write each other, time and distance were forces too insistent for boys, and they had fallen out of contact. But their friendship remained tucked away in Sammy's memory, forgotten until stirred again by something as odd as a cemetery.

Sammy pulled the cord, and the weed eater rattled into a whir and then a whine as it clipped the grass around the white edges of the Reverend Lamb's crypt. Even the letters of the vicar's name were worn down, and anyone who didn't know who was buried here would have to trace the impressions with his fingers and then guess.

He moved over to Alice's grave, next to her father, her dear Papa's. He thought of the night that he had confided to Jimmy, there before her grave, of the terror she inspired in him. Sammy had never told anyone before, and he cried as he unburdened his little-boy heart. Jimmy said that it was all right, that everyone was afraid of something and that he wouldn't tell anyone. And as far as Sammy knew, Jimmy never had.

Sammy knelt and swept away grass clippings from the white tablet of Alice's grave. Then he put the weed eater across his shoulders like he had seen in pictures of American soldiers in the newspapers in Montreal, young men in slouch hats or helmets heading off single file into the jungle. He carried his weed eater back into the new part of the cemetery, his shadow looking like the silhouette of a soldier passing over the grave markers. He found the right spot and took it off his shoulder and pulled the cord again, and it trilled to life as he trimmed a perfect linear edge around the stone that read,

Pfc. James L. Chauvin
U.S. Army
Vietnam, August 26, 1970

The memory of a life reduced to a perfect, granite rectangle. Sammy paused for a moment and held the silent weed eater. Then he filed past the rows of stone markers, different sizes and shapes, remembrances of people who were all equally gone, past the church with its empty window and into the parking lot. He leaned over the side of the truck bed and carefully laid the weed eater into the bed among the scattering of dead leaves.

Alice, 1871

11 March 1871. I was welcomed here yesterday by Jenny and her sisters, with long, tight embraces. Lucy asked me why I had a little curtain over my face. I told her that I was in mourning because my Papa died, and I was sad. Somehow, telling this simple truth to a small child seemed to help a great measure. Lucy stammered, 'Miss Alice, my-uh-my-um-my mama died, too,' and she nodded solemnly at her little pronouncement. Ida shushed her, but Jenny stroked Lucy's hair. I told Ida, from within my black cloud, that it was quite all right, she is but a child, and that I would have said much the same thing at her age and that it is as true for her as it was for me. The servants put my things away in a corner bedroom that is to be mine, and then the girls and I climbed up into the magnificent bedstead. The emerald world outside the open windows was splashed with magenta and red and white and lavender as the wind caressed it and it swayed in response. Birds sang on the breeze and little Lucy sang quietly with them in her child-voice, *'hush, little baby don't you cry,'* and either Ida or Jenny (or perhaps both) toyed with my hair and I sank into the covers and eiderdown and fell into a magnificent sleep. It is the best I have slept in months.

12 March 1871. I woke this morning to the smell of breakfast in my room, placed on a magnificently carved table with a white marble top. Indeed, there was enough food to feed one of the field hands and, though I could manage little of it, I did my best. The hospitality of this place and my host cheers me. The sounds of others in the house warms me, especially the small voices of these girls, these administering angels. I hear them now as they return from church, which I have neglected this day.

13 March 1871. A walk in the gardens on a perfect day. They are simply exquisite, privet hedges, azaleas, wisteria vine, hibiscus, sweet olive. Everything is perfectly laid out and would stand in favourable comparison to any English garden. The gardener works diligently in keeping them, a light-skinned negro who falls in and out of the shadows in his labours. His way is so calm, but with a quiet industry, quite like he feels as though if he were to pause, the earth would swallow him and feed upon his labours.

14 March 1871. Of all possible calamities, I cannot find Papa's chest! I am certain it was placed in a wagon when we were leaving, but it has not arrived here. I feel as though I have lost him, or a large part of him, all over again. All those sermons! A lifetime of prayer and reflection. O, where is it? I have traced my steps and even returned to the vicarage and gone through the rooms. But they are empty, all is empty. More so than ever before. I asked everyone here at Mount Teague and finally Mr. Teague, who was in his study. He asked what was the matter, and I replied, almost in a shriek, I fear, that Papa's chest was gone. My hand was at my forehead as I stared to the ground, looking for the answer. I will admit to no small amount of agitation. Mr. Teague rose and stormed out of his study. 'Ruthie!' he bellowed to the house girl, 'Run out to the quarters and fetch Reuben and Simeon.' She flew out across the back gallery and down the stairs in pattering steps. I watched her fly across the lawn to the rows of shacks, hoping they would bring word of the chest, or perhaps bring the chest itself. They came from their abodes, pulling suspenders over dingy shirts and shoulders, trotting up at a pace between a run and a walk. As I watched them, I became aware of Mr. Teague at my side on the back gallery. He asked me to accompany him to his study. The two men were right behind us. 'We are missing a chest,' Mr. Teague said, almost in the way of an accusation. One of the men, Reuben, I believe, said that it was in the back of the wagon, and when he went back to get it, it was gone, and that he thought Simeon 'done took it up.' Mr. Teague calmly tapped his finger on his desk as he stared at the two men, who held their hats in their hands and stared at the floor and their worn boots. They didn't look up once, but one could tell they felt the stare of Mr. Teague. At last he dismissed them both and said to me, 'We will find your chest. Certainly, it was just misplaced. But if it was stolen, well, we'll recover it, and the *n*– that took it will pay, don't you worry.' My face was in my hands, but I managed to say, 'Please, Mr. Teague, don't refer to one of God's creatures in such terms.' He replied, 'Pardon me, then, Miss Lamb. It is our way here. But don't you worry. We will find it.'

15 March 1871. Still no sign of Papa's sermon chest. I expressed my concerns to Mr. Teague, and the men who moved my things from the vicarage, Reuben and Simeon, were sat in chairs again, almost as if on trial. Both said they thought the other had brought it up from the wagon. I fear that it is lost forever, but I do not fault either. Mr. Teague's temper seemed about to boil, but I quelled it by saying, 'It is no matter, and it will not bring Papa back. But if either of you two see it, please return it, will you?' 'Yes ma'am, show will,' they said quite earnestly. I do not think they have taken it, though I may be mistaken. What business would they have with a chest full of sermons?

16 March 1871. I have resolved that Papa's sermons are lost forever.

18 March 1871. The new vicar visited Mount Teague today. He was a chaplain in a Tennessee regiment in the late war, and he and Mr. Teague spoke of it. They seemed to get on well. We were introduced, and Rev. Givens took my black gloved hand in his. He is as handsome and gracious as they say, a tall, fashionably dressed man with a head of blonde waves. He seemed to look through my veil and see my anguish. He said that he has heard that I play the piano, all the old standards as well as classical pieces. I told him yes, though I haven't played much recently. That is understandable, he said, though perhaps playing might assuage my sorrow a measure and that he has found that music can be a balm for those troubled with grief. Perhaps so, I said from within my shadow. 'Well, then, Miss Lamb, in time, perhaps,' he said as he seemed to gaze into me. Mr. Teague escorted him to the door, and they shook hands and exchanged a small bow. Then the new vicar of St. Margaret's Church descended the steps and mounted Sugar. He pushed his hat, a silk topper, onto his head with its blonde curls and then pressed his heels into her white flanks, and she trotted down the lane of oaks. I watched through panes of wavy glass as he diminished to a small galloping point on the Bayou Road.

19 March 1871. I have returned to church as it is Rev. Givens' first Sunday in the pulpit. He gave the usual introductions and pleasantries of clergymen greeting a new flock, the same sort of thing that Papa did in India, Manchester, and here in St. Matthew. Perhaps they are taught such things in seminary. Rev. Givens has a fine tenor in leading us in song, perfect teeth in an exquisite mouth, eyes of the bluest shade and an erect bearing, even more so from the pulpit. Many fan themselves, though it is not hot at all. The older women, mainly.

22 March 1871. The state of North Carolina, part of the late Confederacy, has removed its governor, according to the *Picayune.* The sugarcane has sprouted almost knee-high. The misprints still occur in the *Compass*, but they no longer amuse me.

26 March 1871. The Rev. Givens is every bit as handsome as they say. What makes him more so is his gentle manner. I am certain Papa would have admired him and favoured his society. I find myself peeking from around my veil at him, to see him without the black lace. I wish I was not required to wear it—perhaps he would show me a little attention were I not. It is becoming tiresome, but etiquette dictates it to be so. There is no escaping convention, no more here than it would be in England. He is friendly with me, but, beyond that, he shows no special interest. Certainly, it is because of my mourning clothes. I am but a shadow, a black cloud. But it is only proper that I should continue to wear mourning and I shall persist in it.

2 April 1871. Sabbath. I whispered to Jenny how I should like to return to the bench and play. She whispered back that it is a shame that there is no piano at Mount Teague.

5 April 1871. Rain again today and I am consumed with melancholy. How long has it been since Papa has died? At times it seems like forever and at times it seems like only a few hours. I went to the cemetery today. Rain drummed on my umbrella. Grass has begun to grow around his crypt. How I should like to have his chest with his papers in it! What has become of it? I can hardly bear thinking of him sleeping out in the rain, though I know he sleeps peacefully in Christ.

7 April 1871. I have still not had the industry to begin plans for the lessons of the Teague girls. They mill about in boredom, swinging from the mosquito bars that are gathered about the bedposts waiting for hotter weather and the insects it shall surely bring.

9 April 1871. Easter Sunday. I suppose I should take heart that Papa shall rise with our Lord on the last day. I still miss him dreadfully. The Rev. Givens delivered a fine sermon, however, and commanded the attention of the congregation, the women in particular. His appearance is certainly no deterrent.

10 April 1871. I felt like getting about today and had Reuben ready the carriage so that I might visit Mozie at the vicarage. Of course, my little confidant, I confess to you alone of wanting a glimpse of the new vicar. But he was away to call on the convalescing, and Mozie and I read the newspaper in the kitchen as we have done before. She has continued to practice and now reads much more proficiently, though it is still slow but steady with a stumble now and again or a pause to discuss what she has read. The *Picayune* reports that the Royal Albert Hall opened in Kensington in last month with a speech by the Prince of Wales. The Queen was there but would not make a public comment. I understand her sense of grief in a way that I would not have appreciated a year ago. The account says that the Royal Albert is a magnificent structure, and it is said to possess the largest organ in the world. Mozie's finger stopped its slow tracing of the words in the paper and said that the Royal Albert Hall sounds quite like a man, boasting about the size of its organ. It was the first time I have laughed since Papa died.

14 April 1871. The *Compass* says that it is ten years today that the late war began at a place called Fort Sumter in South Carolina.

16 April 1871. Sabbath today. Rev. Givens gave another fine sermon, and though I cannot remember its topic, it was well-rendered. A girl of the parish was given a turn at the piano and I'm afraid her nerves got the best of her. I wanted so much to whisper to her that it would help immensely to imagine the congregants as animals, as Papa once told me. Nevertheless, Rev. Givens gave her a generous nod and smile when she concluded. She scurried down the centre aisle and sat on the rear-most pew and then departed the church before the conclusion of services.

17 April 1871. It is said that Mr. Teague has been cruelly served, abandoned by his wife who is a spendthrift and a gadabout. The servants here at Mount Teague are hesitant to speak at all of her, but when persuaded, they say that she was a buxom, vivacious woman with red hair and a penchant for peacock feathers. She has fled and now lives on the credit she exacts from her husband's money and good-standing. I wonder if she has any idea how much sorrow and distress she has caused, or, if she does, whether it concerns her at all. Jenny says that her father wonders at the debt she accumulates in his name and that it is a source of constant worry for him. It is also said that, at her insistence, Luther, the keeper of the magnificent garden, took her up to Donaldsonville suddenly and in the middle of the night and put her on a northbound steamer. He is an odd sort of man, an albino, lacking in pigment but with the coarse hair of the negro race, though as golden as mine. He spends the day serenely and keeps his own counsel as he clips and sweeps and prunes and plants. I try to make conversation with him but only receive terse answers. Yes, miss. No, miss. Thank you, miss. Nevertheless, he is a master at what he does. The gardens are exquisite, all centred around the masterpiece, the marble Venus, cool-white in the gathering heat, as she presides over her gardens. I wonder if he feels that in taking Mrs. Teague where she demanded, he betrayed Mr. Teague and now is embarrassed by it, and must work harder to keep in Mr. Teague's good graces. Something seems to make him retreat into his work. Mr. Teague does not at all seem to harbour a grudge. He only says that his gardener was in no position to tell her no, as she was his employer.

18 April 1871. I have begun to conduct lessons for the Teague girls, but only for an hour or so a day. Jenny helped with her younger sisters, and Jenny and Ida practiced their reading for their father, who listened attentively. The girls have persuaded me to remove my veil for lessons and I have relented. It has become tiresome.

21 April 1871. I had Lucy read from Maguffey's Primer whilst Ida practiced with her father in his study. I overheard her reading Latin to him. What a fine little scholar Ida is, to be reading Latin at her age! Mr. Teague must be quite proud, though he doesn't show it and adopts a stern tone with her. At each turn of Latin phrase, he monotones, 'Again,' and Ida repeats it. '*Nemo me impune lacessit,*' she read, which is the motto of old King James, *"no one can harm me and remain unpunished."* At this, Mr. Teague sounded delighted and had her repeat it, which she did at least ten times until he almost had it. I suppose that Latin doesn't come as easily to him as it is for some. After Lucy's lesson from Maguffey's, I rewarded her with selected tales from the Brothers Grimm, as much a treat for me as it is for her, as I enjoyed her small form pressing into me on the drawing room settee. As I read to her, in ever-diminishing tones as she fell into a nap, Ida continued her Latin lesson with her father, though I could hear fatigue in her voice as well.

23 April 1871. Rev. Givens wore a fine blue-silk cravat and matching braces, or suspenders, rather, here in America. I suppose I shall always be English when it comes to braces—suspenders. There was no music today, as the girl who played last week was either persuaded not to return or was too frightened.

29 April 1871. The privet hedges planted under the direction of the absconded Mrs. Teague begin to exert themselves, sweet and floral, much to the dismay of Mr. Teague. His eyes redden around grey pupils, and thunderous sneezes erupt like Vesuvius from his contorted face. 'She troubles me yet, that woman,' he muttered as he dabbed his handkerchief to his nose and eyes. He said that perhaps he should have those hedges cut back, and Mr. Luther replied, 'Just say de word, Marse.' But there was no more said of the matter, though Mr. Teague's sudden trumpeting erupts from time to time in the unsuspecting quiet of this house.

30 April 1871. Sabbath today with heavy showers, excellent for sugarcane but difficult to get about in. Skies were dark enough to necessitate the lighting of the church lanterns. Mr. Teague, who usually rides on horseback next to our carriage, rode with us under its bonnet. Rev. Givens preached on the subject of tithing and the widow's mite.

3 May 1871. Mr. Teague has informed me that the annual Planters' Ball is to be held tomorrow evening, and he has invited me to attend if I shall feel up to it. All the best people, he says, from St. Matthew and the surrounding parishes shall attend, and he gently admonished me to do so also. To be polite, I told him that I may, though really, I do not think I shall. Downstairs, workmen are busy installing something heavy. I must nap, however. Fatigue is never far away.

(later) Night has fallen and now, downstairs, the sounds of revelry, conversation, singing, a violin which is presumably Jenny playing for the gathering. I hear also the fine tenor of Rev. Givens, and I wish that I had accepted Mr. Teague's offer. I keep to my quarters, however.

4 May 1871. Jenny came up last night and persuaded me to come downstairs for a cup of cordial. I dressed as finely as time allowed, knowing that Rev. Givens might be downstairs. As I descended the stairs, I was greeted with upturned faces and eyes, and slight nods and bows, and then a round of polite applause. Jenny and I shared a cup in the kitchen, though to me it had but little flavour, and then I became overcome by the sudden press of society. Someone came to ask Jenny to accompany Rev. Givens on the violin. She assented and left, and I remained on the back gallery, listening to the music inside the house and thinking how much Papa would have liked such an occasion. And I became melancholy. It is so easy to do so these days. As the music and laughter resounded, I sat quietly on the back gallery. Across the yard was an outbuilding, a shed of some sort, and I wondered if Papa's sermon chest might have been misplaced there. I descended the stairs, leaving the sounds of merriment behind me in the great house. The night air was laden with the weight of an approaching storm. Insects whistled and croaked in it as I picked my way out to the dark block outline of the structure, wishing I had a lantern, like Diogenes looking for an honest man. In the window of the storeroom, there were several steamer trunks, and I entered and searched for the chest of English oak. The sound of music and laughter was small from within the yellow-lit windows of the ballroom. A woman in the window laughed at something a man whispered in her ear, and then she smiled and batted her fan as if to whisk away whatever was said. In the yard, the limbs began swaying and twitching and then the rain began suddenly, and I found myself trapped in the shed by it, lest I become soaked. Falling torrents roared on the tin roof. A match flamed against the dark, and I was startled by the thought of someone else in the shed with me. 'Who's there?' I asked the tiny speck of orange light set against the dark, and then I smelled cigar smoke. An ember flared and there was another gust of cigar smoke as a male voice said that he was going to ask me the same question. 'Mr. Teague?' I asked the dark. 'Yes. Miss Lamb?' the dark asked me. 'Yes,' I responded. He asked me what I was doing out in a shed when there was music and merriment inside. I told him that I was afraid that merriment goes stale very quickly when one is grieving. A silence followed and then there was another ember flare and the waft of cigar smoke with an exhalation that I could hear clearly against the chatter of insects disturbed by the storm. His voice in the dark said that he certainly understood, and he asked me if I was looking for something. I told him that I was looking for Papa's chest.

'One day we'll find that chest, don't worry. Now, about these guests. Do you think I could persuade you to favour us with a tune on the piano?' He said that if it mattered, that Jenny had asked it as well and that she had even brought down her 'fiddle.' The rain continued to roar. In a window of the great house, a man said something to two women, and they threw back their heads in laughter. On the lawn between the back porch and us, water was beginning to gather, as high as one's ankles. I looked at it and at the great house. 'Here,' he said, 'If you don't mind' and he put his great coat over me and lifted me. Then, he didn't run across the lawn and the rain but only purposefully strode. I could see his face from under the great coat, the scar within his beard, his nickel-grey eyes. His hair hung down wet over them both. So resolute, so dutiful a countenance in the face of the rain and the discomfort it brought, doubtless a reflection of his military days. I could easily imagine him moving thusly through a rainy encampment of soldiers. He set me down on the back porch, and we brushed water off our clothes. I followed him down the hall to a doorway, where he announced to the crowd of guests in the drawing rooms, which adjoin one another here at Mount Teague, 'Well, look here what I have brought in out of the rain! Perhaps she will favour us with an air or two!'

There before me was a new piano, a Pleyel like Chopin favoured! It is superb and plays divinely. However did he know? However did he manage to get it in the house without me seeing it? There was a cheer and a toast and a hear-hear, and I found myself seated at the piano. I played a few of the popular airs, 'Lorena,' and 'The Girl I Left Behind' and 'The Bonnie Blue Flag' and everyone sang along. Jenny joined in, and we played a Mozart piece that I learned with Mr. Nesbit and had taught Jenny. Everyone was silent, and when we ended it, there was a pause as if everyone had been somewhere else, and then there was hearty applause. Just then, Mr. Teague announced that everyone had been deprived of my 'fair visage' long enough, and he asked if it would be possible that I remove my veil. It embarrassed me, and I shook my head no. It seems that he does not know that this is a matter for the bereaved to decide. He seemed stricken by his own boldness and adopted an apologetic tone. 'Forgive my impertinence, ma'am. Whenever you are ready, then, we shall be also,' he said.

7 May 1871. The roadsides are lined with yellow-faced flowers, and it is a pleasant journey to and from church. Rev. Givens preached from the Acts of the Apostles. There was no music except for his fine tenor and the noisy gongs and clanging cymbals, that is, the voices of the congregation.

8 May 1871. Rev. Givens paid a call today here at Mount Teague. I supposed he had come to see Mr. Teague, and so I continued playing the new Pleyel in the ladies' parlour. However, our 'house girl' Ruthie saw him into the parlour rather than call for Mr. Teague, who was upstairs nursing a headache from the pollen of the Ligustrum. I stopped playing when Rev. Givens appeared in the doorway, but he bid me continue. When I was finished, he clapped, and I rose from the bench and gave a small bow. When I addressed him as 'reverend,' he insisted I call him by his Christian name, 'Henry,' and then he said something I remember Papa saying, that it is hard for a vicar to make friends and that it can be quite lonely at times. I asked him if I should get Mr. Teague, who was upstairs with a headache. My heart skipped a beat when he said that it was I he came to see and that he had a proposition to discuss with me. My head swam for a moment as I enjoyed the compliment of his visit and wondered what this proposition might be. He persuaded me to take a ride in his chaise, the same one that Papa and I used when he was vicar of St. Margaret's, and we did so in the fine, bright afternoon. This black veil was the perfect ruse for studying him. Such fine features, cheekbones, noble jaw and nose, golden curls. All the time, my mind raced with what his proposition might be. We stopped at St. Margaret's Church, where he had me play for him. Then, he sang, and his voice is truly a fine one, a soaring tenor in the quiet church. We discussed the liturgy and music for Sunday services. He is quite as handsome as has been said and perhaps more so. I admit to not a little distraction. In the end, his proposition was an offer for me to begin playing again for services at St. Margaret's. And I have accepted, my mourning veil notwithstanding.

11 May 1871. I set the girls on their studies and adjourned to take the trip to the vicarage for planning of the Sunday music service. We sang a duet, Henry and I, 'Jesus, Lover of My Soul.' When he excused himself to the vestry for a moment, I released my hair, and it fell golden from my black mourning bonnet. I draped it over my shoulders as if it had fallen there. A ploy, yes. I found myself daydreaming, wishing that he would raise my veil and look upon me and perhaps kiss me. He didn't, of course, but it still inhabits my daydreams. Perhaps Papa was right. The best ideas come to us in daydreams.

14 May 1871. I have resumed playing for the Sabbath. As I played the last of the selections Henry and I had chosen, 'God, My Father, Hear Me Pray,' I cried, though my tears were veiled.

16 May 1871. Mr. Teague continues to suffer greatly this time of year from the blooming of the privet hedges that our gardener, Mr. Luther, calls Ligustrum-bush. Mr. Luther says that some call it Devil Bush, because, though it might have a sweet smell, it provokes a plague of sneezing and phlegm in so many, Mr. Teague chiefly among them. The former Mrs. Teague was quite fond of them, Mr. Luther says, and had him put in a great number. Mr. Teague, however, complains about them between trumpeting blasts and dabs of his handkerchief. He emerges from the fine square of linen with a red nose and red eyes, muttering, 'That woman troubles me yet, with that *d—d* devil bush.'

19 May 1871. I found Ida and Lucy trying on my dresses, even the bustles! It was quite a sight, skirts and sleeves too long, bonnets set low over small heads. 'Oh, you naughty little monkeys!' I exclaimed, but I could not hold any expression, save a smile, for very long.

21 May 1871. The heat gathers each day and the windows of church are opened to gather a breeze. Light gathers as well and Rev. Givens, Henry, rather, is shown to me in lustrous silhouette. My mind wandered again as it did when I was a girl, and he had to clear his throat to remove me from my stare, which I must confess was at him, though veiled. Heads craned toward me behind the piano in the gaping pause, and I fear I panicked and hit some rather sour notes. After services, he asked me if there was something the matter. I replied that I was just thinking of Papa. That is a falsehood. I was thinking of the new vicar and not the old one.

24 May 1871. I find that the practise of arithmetic is aided greatly with the use of paper-dolls.

27 May 1871. Jenny persuaded me to go fishing, and I relented even though it provoked memories of fishing with Papa. It is quite different, however. Fishing in this style requires a negro servant to bait one's line and take the fish off when it is caught and then to rebait one's line again. Also, it is his task to retrieve ('fetch') lemonade from a tub and any other articles from the carriage one might require. Then, when the fish are caught, the servant is to clean and prepare them. One's hands never actually touch the fish or the bait. The only thing that is the same is the thrilling tug on the line and the anticipation pertaining to what sort of fish will emerge from the water. We had caught several fine perch (here, *sac-a-lait*) and bass when my line tugged again, and I pulled up something that caused me to begin crying, for in an instant it reminded me of Papa. 'Why, Miss,' the old grey-headed negro man said, 'Ain't nothin' but an old choupique.' How odd, that something like a fish might spur such a powerful, painful memory. A fish, an 'absolutely prehistoric' fish, the subject of Papa's fascination.

28 May 1871. Sabbath today. 'Name of Our Triumphant Saviour,' 'O God Our Help in Ages Past,' and 'Praise, My Soul, the King of Heaven.' Henry preached from the Gospel of St. John, in which Christ appears to his apostles. He says that I have been asked to play for a wedding Wednesday.

30 May 1871. The girls come on well as young scholars. We spent the morning on penmanship and the reading of French and Latin. As I tended my garden of three young flowers who blossom toward womanhood, outside the window, in the heat, Mr. Luther tends his gardens.

31 May 1871. Henry married a young couple today, a handsome groom and a beautiful bride. A random thought occurred to me, who would marry Henry and me, if it were to come to that? Henry had to clear his throat to prompt me toward the next selection. I was rather embarrassed by my lapse, but my blushing was behind a small curtain of black lace.

1 June 1871. This afternoon, whilst Henry and I practised selections for Sunday service, the door to the sanctuary opened and a long shadow stretched down the aisle. Henry stopped in the middle of the song, 'I Am Thine, O Lord,' and went to our visitor, an old friend of his with whom he served in the late war. They embraced as long-lost friends, in the manner, I'm sure, of two comrades who have faced hardship and suffering, even eminent death. He was introduced to me as Henry's dear, dear friend, Emil Hodge. I sat patiently as I considered my role in their reunion. After a time at the periphery, uncertain how to join their warm conversation, our practise was prematurely adjourned, and I departed, a little crestfallen.

4 June 1871. Mr. Hodge has departed to his family in Memphis. After services, the parish 'Dinner on the grounds' was held today on a splendid afternoon under the cool shade of the oaks, everything brilliant, deepening green and vibrant red and a light breeze to refresh it all over an emerald carpet. Rev. Givens was sitting at a table with several of the old hens who fancy themselves matchmakers. They begged me sit with them, and I did so. The vicar regaled us with stories of his youth in Memphis. He painted himself as quite a rogue to them, though this I cannot imagine. One of the hens asked him if he ever had a *belle* growing up, and he laughed it away. I could not tell if it was a yes or a no. Just then, the old cook announced that dinner was prepared, and Rev. Givens seemed rather relieved to rise and address the crowd in a blessing of our delightful repast. He is so handsome, so kind and good. Surely someone has broken his heart. Or perhaps he has not yet found his one true love. I must fight the urge to consider that I am she. I cannot gauge if he has any interest in me. I believe him to be quite shy when it comes to matters of the heart.

5 June 1871. I was going over lessons with Ida and Lucy when Mr. Howard arrived from the city, his greeting as flat and reserved as before. But as Lucy read from the primer and Jenny practised Mozart on the violin, I heard Mr. Teague and Mr. Howard laughing in his study. 'Well, Sam, it is just a matter of time. The Fairgrounds course has opened, and racing has begun. And then the Metairie Club will be no more.' Mr. Teague replied something along the lines of, 'Well, I guess you'll show up those pretentious bastards, even in death!' 'Especially in death!' Mr. Howard exclaimed, and they laughed long and loud until their glasses clinked in a toast. Mr. Howard added that 'they'll wish they had our 'new money.' Perhaps they feel the same pinch at being excluded from this 'Metairie Club' as Papa did in being excluded by the Linnaens, the elite excluding the unremarkable and then pushing them to the margin.

7 June 1871. Henry and I were going over the music for this Sunday. We paused a moment as he examined his notes for his sermon. I sat and waited next to him on the piano bench as he leafed through his remarks, so much like Papa used to do. A private conversation I was having with myself emerged into a question that I spoke aloud, quite on accident. 'Well, did you ever?' I asked. 'Pardon?' Henry asked as he peered over his reading glasses at his notes. Only then did I realise that I had spoken it aloud. 'What were you saying?' he asked as he looked to me. Realising that it was too late to recall my question, I asked it fully. 'Did you ever have a belle growing up?' He pursed his lips, something like a grin, and was rather evasive in his response. He took off his glasses and turned to me. 'I have always had female friends and have heartily enjoyed their society. Let us move on to the offertory song, shall we?' He replaced his glasses and took up his notes. And the matter was spoken of no more.

8 June 1871. Workmen arrived today at Mount Teague, and the sound of hammers and saws and workers calling one to another filled the grounds. I asked Mr. Teague what the new building is to be, and he would say only that it is to be a surprise. The men who are engaged in its construction paused only for ladlefuls of water from a wooden bucket brought by a servant. No one knows what the new building will be and there is much speculation that it shall be a new carriage house. Jenny approached the foreman to ask, and he would only say that he has been sworn to secrecy by Mr. Teague.

9 June 1871. During Ida's lessons, I overheard Jenny reading a telegram to her father, whose eyes still weep from the air of the Ligustrum bush. *'Sam. Metairie Club hard times. Deal bear fruit soon. Howard.'* She asked her father about it and he said it was his and Mr. Howard's affair. Then he chuckled to himself, and I smelled his cigar tint the air.

11 June 1871. Henry preached on the raising of Lazarus. 'The Sacred Day Hath Beamed' was the benedictory song. Afterwards, he adjourned for Sunday dinner with the Parrises.

12 June 1871. I adjourned to St. Margaret's today to return to the bench and keyboard. The heat had gathered sufficiently which made the air rather heavy. Feeling that I was quite alone, I lifted my mourning veil to continue playing. Light flooded in with the opening of a side door. I continued playing, supposing it was Mozie, but when I looked up, there was Henry. 'Alice,' he said, 'you are quite beautiful.' He said it as if he had not even imagined it so. Then he said, 'Such a shame that you must hide your light under a bushel.' At last he has seen me. Perhaps it is our beginning.

13 June 1871. Work on the building just beyond the gardens continues and appears to near completion. Mr. Luther said that he knows what the building will be, but that Mr. Teague has sworn him to secrecy. I can smell paint now that the Ligustrum have 'bout played out' as Mr. Luther says. The heat builds daily upon itself and is becoming quite oppressive. Mr. Teague has me read to him again as he says he enjoys the sound of my voice. I do not mind, though he has me read at length. I fan myself from the heat and pray for a breeze through the open window. The sugarcane is perhaps the only living thing that thrives in it.

14 June 1871. The identity of the building is now known. Midmorning, there was a great racket, and the quiet of the gardens was filled with huffing and belching. The workmen moved excitedly from one part of the building to the other. I caught a glimpse of the inside of one part of the building. There seemed to be iron machinery, pipes, valves, and a great wind of air being compressed and released. Men opened the door to enter, releasing the cacophony of the machinery which fell back into a growling hum when the door was shut again. In the afternoon, Mr.

Teague approached me in the garden where I sat and read Rousseau's *Confessions* on a bench. He carried with him a long box. He said that he had something for me and gave me the box. I opened it and was surprised to find a coat made from the softest animal fur. I held it up, as he rather proudly declared, 'Mink!'

'Mr. Teague!' I replied. 'I cannot accept this costly gift! I am only your children's governess!' But he said that cost was no matter and that it is a treat for him to give it to me and for me not to deny him the pleasure of it. I asked him, 'on what occasion shall I wear this? Certainly, it shall never be cold enough here in St. Matthew!' A smile broke on his face as if carved there next to his scar, and he bid me follow him to the new outbuilding, and upon entering, it was cold enough to see one's breath distill into a fog. Mr. Teague has had made an ingenious contrivance for the manufacture of ice, complete with an adjoining room into which some of the cold air is conveyed! This room is furnished with great windows that the sunlight penetrates but does not warm. Through the wall it shared, the hum of the engines drones like a cat, making ice, ice for Mount Teague and to sell at a profit to surrounding plantations. Without realizing it, I was clutching my waist and chest against the cold. Mr. Teague placed the mink coat over my shoulders and said, 'Here is a good occasion for this gift.'

15 June 1871. The heat gathers outside, but I remain inside in this cool cocoon. The girls complain of the chill in what Mr. Teague calls the Ice Parlour, but it is quite comfortable for an English girl who has endured the cold of Manchester. Nevertheless, at their insistence, lessons are held once more in the Ladies' Parlour of the great house.

16 June 1871. In my capacity as governess for the Teague girls, I am to travel with them to the mountains in what was Virginia before the late war and now is considered West Virginia. I am hesitant to leave Henry and Mozie, but it is my duty as governess, and I shall do it. Henry says he shall miss me when I am away, and that cheers me. Certainly, he has feelings for me after all and is only shy in them. My mind races to the calamity of losing him to the fever season, but I understand his steadfastness. It is what Papa would have done and did. Jenny is overjoyed that I am coming, as she said that last year her father was quite cross, having quarreled with several of the men, among them a Mr. Roddey, whom Mr. Teague regards as chief among all villains. We shall take the next few days to pack our belongings and be off early next week.

Sammy, 1982

Which room had been hers, he wondered, the girls' room or Quint's room or one of the other bedrooms? He slipped the deposit slip-bookmark into the diary, and the diary into the desk drawer. Pausing to stretch in the door of the study, he saw Quint sitting in front of the portrait of his grandfather's grandfather. An open textbook, *American History*, was in his lap.

"What are you studying, son?" Sammy asked.

"American history. The American Civil War."

Quint was still Canadian enough to call it the American Civil War, while everyone else called it simply the Civil War.

"Do you know where he was in the war?" Quint asked as he looked at the portrait of the man in the uniform.

"Your papere says that he was with the Army of the Tennessee, all the way through the defense of Atlanta. He got wounded in the hip." Sammy looked close at the portrait. "I wonder if that's how he got the blood stain on his sleeve, pressing on his wound, maybe."

The three Samuel Teagues gazed at each other. Sammy was thinking about the Pas Bon float at Mardi Gras with the mural of Mount Teague and the LA Dodgers shirts and the plastic hand grenade throws. Surely Quint now knew the whole story of why he had been born in Canada and spent the first years of his life there. Sammy wondered if Quint thought less of him, if his son considered his abandoned duty to be a tragic flaw in a man he otherwise admired.

"I'm going into Pierre Part to get some crawfish to boil," Sammy said. "Take a ride, son?"

Quint kept looking up at the portrait.

"I'd appreciate the company," Sammy added.

Quint closed the book and got his coat.

On the ride, Sammy said that, in the fall, Quint could take his place in a cane harvester, on the weekends, at least. Quint quietly looked out on the fields and tree lines. Sammy said that he was proud of his son's grades. Quint nodded and kept looking out the window. Sammy said that Nonc Claude and Tante Lucille were coming to eat crawfish and that if Quint wanted to invite a friend, they should get an extra sack to be sure. Quint said there was really no one he could think of to invite.

What he didn't say was that there was no one to invite because, at school, he was ostracized, that he struggled with the burden of the Teague name and that was why he threw himself into his schoolwork. That he had become a pariah by association, bearing the social consequences of the sin of his father. But he told his daddy that he couldn't think of anyone and left it at that.

Down Highway 70, the cane fields turned to swamp. In Pierre Part, they crossed the pontoon bridge over the bayou and listened to the singing of tires on the steel deck. They passed St. Joseph the Worker Catholic Church and the Blessed Virgin Mary on the island, the one that had been miraculously spared during a long-ago hurricane. They passed the Pierre Part store where a sign rightfully proclaimed, "If We Don't Have It, You Don't Need It." At a shed on the other side of town, they stopped and waited in a short line to buy two sacks of crawfish from men in white boots and overalls.

When they got back home, Teeter emerged from the metal shed to greet them, wiping his smudged hands on a rag. He took a sack from Sammy, and they dumped them into the smooth, white insides of an ice chest and rinsed them with the hosepipe. The tangled mass of dull brown creatures squirmed over each other, beady-eyed, some raising defiant claws. The pot was filled with water from the same hosepipe, and, with the click of a flame over the roar of propane, the water was brought to boil as Sammy's little girls practiced grabbing crawfish squarely on the back, out of reach of the pinchers, and teasingly menacing each other with them. The orange bags of spices were cut open with a knife and dumped into the troubled water, and the air smelled like spring in south Louisiana.

Sometime during the second batch, after the folding tables had been covered with newspaper, Nonc Claude and Tante Lucille drove up in an old Buick. She got out and went around to open the door to let Claude out. He pushed himself up, supporting himself on the door. Claude winced as he stood. Betsy asked him what happened, and he said, "Mais, I twisted my back jumpin' out a cake at one them bachelorette parties."

Tante Lucille swatted him and called him an ol' *coullion* and said that it was an old injury from when he was in the service. The *'docta'* at the VA in New Orleans had put him on 'some dat PT' for six weeks.

They gathered around the piles of red, steaming crawfish, flecked with yellow corn and white potatoes, and they ate. The women sat in lawn chairs with cardboard flats of hot crawfish. They peeled and ate and talked in English until the news became especially candid, and then they switched to French, finally dissolving into laughter, Betsy leaning her forehead into the back of her hand and squinting her eyes and shaking, Tante Lucille leaning back and chortling to the sky. Elizabeth, who knew very little French, pulled on Betsy's sleeve and asked, "What did she say, Mama?" Betsy shook her head, her laughter keeping her from speaking.

Pongeaux threaded her way through the legs of the gathering, waiting for a potato to fall or someone to peel a crawfish and toss her the small comma of meat. She sat on her haunches next to her boy, Quint, who was standing across the table from his Nonc Claude. Quint listened to his uncle tell jokes, most of them the kind of off-color jokes that uncles tell nephews in south Louisiana. After several rounds of laughter at tales unsuitable for the ears of women and children, Sammy asked about Nonc Claude's back, and Claude said that, as he got older, it gave him more trouble and he could thank the Japs for that. Quint had been peeling and eating by Nonc Claude the whole time, hanging on his every word. He asked his uncle what branch of the service he had been in in the war.

"The Marines," Nonc Claude said as he sucked the juice out of a shell and threw it in a can lined with a plastic bag. His fingers wandered over the pile of red bodies with curled-under tails, and he picked up another.

"The Marines!" Quint said. "Where?"

"The Pacific," Claude said without looking at his nephew. "We landed on an island called Tarawa."

"What was it like, to be in combat?" Quint asked.

Nonc Claude paused for a moment and said, "Well. They was palm trees on fire—" Then his voice trailed away. And then he said nothing. Quint stopped peeling and eating to look up at his uncle, whose orange fingers fidgeted with the same crawfish, as if he had forgotten how to peel. Quint held an empty shell in his fingers, waiting for the details of heroic military exploits. But Claude kept silently examining the clawed creature with the curled-under tail. At last, Teeter said, "I hear the Tigahs got themselves quite a recruiting class. Even got that Hilliard kid down Patterson, that runnin' back can't nobody tackle."

Nonc Claude seemed to slowly appear again. "I hear dat Hilliard kid is somethin', him," he said. "Maybe they beat Alabama this year." Then Claude told another joke, the one about Boudreaux' flatulent milking cow and how his friend Thibodeaux knew he had gotten her from Loreauville because Clotilde was from Loreauville, too, and everyone laughed and peeled and ate, and there was no more talk of war. Finally, he wiped his hands on a paper towel and went and sat on the porch. When he was off a suitable distance, Teeter spoke low to Quint.

"Boo, you don' never ask nobody dat. You can ask 'bout they drill sergeant or boot camp or stuff like dat, but you don' never ask about combat. Mais, they ain' no words for all dat." Teeter paused as he resumed peeling, trying to soften what he had said. "I know you jus' curious, Boo, thas all. I was curious once, too, me."

Claude returned, and the men gathered around peeling and eating, talking about fishing and hunting and the Tigahs and the Saints and the weather. But not war. One by one, the crawfish in the mound were reduced to shells and empty tails and the corn to bare, gnawed cobs.

Afterward, Teeter and Sammy took bags of shells and newspapers and cardboard flats to the trash. The women were inside making crawfish bisque with empty heads, and the girls were watching and waiting to be asked to help. Quint was holding a plastic trash bag and listening to Nonc Claude tell stories about basic training and a drill sergeant he had who had a voice like a tuba.

Teeter said, "Ya boy Quint, mais, he's fascinated with war and combat, like all us boys was. It's easy for a boy to fall in love wit dat shit."

As evening fell, Nonc Claude and Tante Lucille kissed everyone, male and female, on both cheeks, and got into their old Buick. It crumbled down the shell lane with the slightest of sways and turned onto the highway. The red and yellow and white taillights on the dark highway captivated Sammy. He felt a pull on his hand and saw that it was Elizabeth bringing him in. Everyone else had gone inside. He and his daughter went in, too, and his orange-tinted fingers opened the drawer and the old diary. And he read about the wedding of the apparition of his boyhood, Alice.

Alice, 1871

2 October 1871. Once again, my little friend, my confidant, I have neglected you. I realised on the train to Virginia that I had left you behind at Mount Teague. And there is so much to tell you now. I have been the recipient of a proposal. In Virginia, Mr. Teague kept to his own circles, former military men and personages of great importance. I was determined to perform my duty to his girls, whom I now consider my girls, like sisters to me. The mountains were truly a lovely place for those lucky enough to afford its luxuries. My mind and my heart, however, were constantly straying back to the ones I also love, Mozie and Henry, and I searched the southern papers daily for news of impending pestilence in the form of yellow fever.

We had been in the mountains perhaps a night or two when Mr. Teague instructed Jenny to see to the bedtimes of her sisters and asked me to accompany him on a walk through the grounds. We walked for quite some time with only small pleasantries to exchange. And then, under the first of the stars and the gazebo, he said it, not to me, but out to the gathering darkness. The suddenness of it quite put me out of countenance. 'I wish you would be my wife, Miss Lamb.' I was not at all expecting it and answered, 'Beg pardon, sir? Is this a proposal of marriage?' 'Yes,' he smiled, 'Yes, it is. I would like to marry you.' He said it in the way of one who always got what he wanted, one who was certain of the outcome. I could only say, 'I shall consider your offer, Mr. Teague.' He seemed to press like a barrister delivering his closing arguments. 'The organ at the church, the ice-house, a mink coat to wear in it, the Pleyel in the house,' he said, 'It's all been for you. Do you not see that? I can give you anything you desire. I can give you the world, and all that's in it.' Almost as an afterthought, he added. 'And my girls adore you.' I stammered that I adored them as well. I did not add that while I admired him in many aspects, I did not adore him in the same manner. It is a difficult prospect to reject a proposal from one's employer. So rather than reject him outright, I asked for time to consider it. The next day, he approached me as I read on the front porch and asked me if I had an answer for him. I said, 'Jacob laboured seven years for Rachel's hand, only to be given Leah's and labour seven more. Surely, you have a fraction of the patience of an old Jew, Mr. Teague?' He forced a smile like a man unused to being delayed, but with no other card to play in the hand. I was not ready to answer, and still I am not. Of course, the truth of the matter, my little confidant, is that I find myself in love with Rev. Givens. Mr. Teague has not mentioned it since, and it was a very quiet train ride home to St. Matthew.

3 October 1871. It was only a matter of time, but the proposition has again surfaced. Today, Mr. Teague came and asked me, 'Forgive my troubling you, but have you considered my proposal, my dear?' I posed a question in the matter, one that has been troubling me. I asked him, 'But are you not still married to Mrs. Teague, though she is absent? Would it not be bigamy?' He adopted a pained look, and I wished that perhaps I had not asked him. What he said next seemed painful for him to bear. 'I don't think she's coming back. I mean, the way she left. She just didn't want anything to do with these girls. My poor girls.' He turned away from me so that I might not see how distressed he was. It is especially sad when a great man's heart is breaking. At last, he cleared his throat and excused himself, and adjourned to his study for a cordial and a cigar.

4 October 1871. Today I read the *Picayune* to Mr. Teague, as his eyes are tired, and he cannot find his eyeglasses. Of course, I believe this a ruse for my company. Ruthie brought him coffee, and, to me, she brought tea. There is a report that most of the American whaling fleet has been crushed by sea ice north of Alaska. 'Which would be a more gruesome death, fire or ice? To freeze in the cold or be consumed by fire?' he asked with his beard over the lip of his coffee cup as he pondered the question. I told him that Papa always said that he feared drowning the most, as it removes us from the nourishment of God's air. At this, Mr. Teague frowned and grunted and stared out the window. 'Perhaps so,' he said rather vacantly.

5 October 1871. With the press of Mr. Teague's proposal, I found that I could bear it no longer. I had Reuben prepare the carriage but drove myself to St. Margaret's to speak frankly with Henry. Though the air was pleasant with the first cool of autumn and the cypresses were tinged a rusty brown, it was of little consequence to me. I entered through the big front door of the church to find him in the front pew facing the pulpit. The light from the windows was accompanied by the breeze that they admitted. I sat next to him, interrupting his prayer. 'Miss Lamb, he said, 'Why, I was just praying for you.' I asked the nature of his prayer for me, and he replied, 'For your happiness. That you might find a loving mate here, so far from your birthplace.' Words and tears suddenly came up in me like the flow of Vesuvius. I could contain them no longer. 'Do you not see how I look at you?' I cried, 'Do you not notice?' He looked around the empty sanctuary and took my hand, and I enjoyed how mine felt in his. He let me sob for a few moments, and then he said in an even lower voice, 'Miss Lamb, let me tell you something.' 'Alice, please!' I demanded, in a voice more insistent than I had intended. 'Alice,' he began again, 'I have something I must share with you. Something that I must tell you in strictest confidence.' He waved me back to the vestry, with the air of someone who has sent a message that he cannot call back. I followed him, thinking of what his secret must be. Perhaps he was already married and had run away from her. Perhaps he has a wound from the late war that might slow him in some manly manner. Perhaps he is tormented by ghosts from it. Perhaps, perhaps, perhaps, I thought. It was a very long walk to the sacristy. Once we were inside, he shut the door, and I sat in the chair I used to sit in as I waited for Papa to hang up his vestments. Rev. Givens pulled up a chair and sat across from me. 'I hope you will keep this as a great secret, Miss Lamb, for if you do not, I am ruined.' He paused again, studying the ceiling and then the floor. Again, he said, 'Please keep this in strictest confidence.' 'Surely,' I said as I thought of what terrible scar he must bear. I was now sure that the late war has left him so, as it did Mr. Phillips in Surrey and so many here. He drew an immense breath, as he does when he is about to mount a great note when he sings. And then he said it. 'I am afraid…that I have no desire…for female intimacy.' I sat silently. I could hear the very air in the sacristy. And having said what he must, it seemed to lighten and clear. I could think of nothing to say, nothing. 'It has always been so,' he added. Then, there was no sound whatsoever in this place so boisterous with organ and piano and voices on Sundays. The silence seemed as though it were trying to crush us.

'It appears that we have been the victims of misplaced affection,' he said quietly, almost as if we had been the butt of a joke. The silence still would not let me speak, so he drew another great breath and let it out quickly. 'The simple truth is—' he wet his lips nervously, 'The simple truth is, I have no interest in the fairer sex beyond friendship.' It was my turn to look from the ceiling to the floor. At last, I looked at him. There were tears in his eyes, blue circled pupils in red ellipses.

I said, 'Our friendship is a pearl of great price for me, and so you may know that you have my confidence, as I would have yours.' Having said what we must, Silence returned and enveloped us again, and we either enjoyed or endured it. At last he said, 'Do you wish to go over the Sunday selections today?' I shook my head in a sad refusal and then silently rose and turned to leave. He remained for a moment, contemplating the floor of the sacristy. As I neared the doorway, he rose and followed me. At the doorway of the church, he took my hand. 'Please,' he said, and perhaps he regretted telling me. 'Certainly,' I said. 'As you wish, Rev. Givens.' 'Henry,' he corrected me. And I said, 'Of course. Henry.'

I shall tell no one other than you, my little friend, my confidant.

7 October 1871. Though it is warm, and a hot breeze blows in from the south, Luther readies the gardens for cooler weather. The green citizens of his botanical sanctuary seem to understand his care and thrive in response to his efforts. Even at this transitional time of year, when winter seems poised at the gates, the gardens are a haven. He was raking leaves up around the trunks of the magnolias as tenderly as if he were attending the sick or putting a child to bed. The wind made the stiff green leaves above him crackle. I was afraid I would startle him, but even with his back to me, he seemed to sense my presence. 'Mr. Luther,' I said. He departed from his toil and turned silently to face me, looking briefly at me and then looking down and away. 'What are you about today?' I asked as cheerfully as I could manage. 'Be cold by tomorrow,' he said to the earth. 'Hot wind like dis bring rain, and rain bring cold. Yes ma'am.' I told him that his work certainly brings joy to many. He didn't smile, but only clutched his rake and said, 'Yes ma'am.'

'Mr. Luther, I wish to speak frankly with you,' I said a little hesitantly, for I had the question that has been troubling me. 'Yes ma'am,' he said, still looking off to the patch of ground beside me. His gaze did not stray an inch as I asked him what he could tell me of the flight of Mrs. Teague. He paused as he studied the ground and then said, 'I carried Miss Polly up yonder Dawsonville and put her off at the levee. Middle the night.' I asked him why she was leaving and where she was going, and he only told the ground, 'Don't rightly know, ma'am.' I asked him if she was good to him and he said, 'Yes ma'am, I didn't have nary trouble with Miss Polly.' I waited again for him to continue, but he simply stared away. The magnolia leaves shimmied and chattered in the breeze as the grey sky rolled over us. 'Yes,' I said at last, 'Very well. I don't wish to detain you further.' I looked up to the darkening sky. 'With the rain coming, as you say it will.' 'Yes ma'am,"' he said down to the dirt and the leaves and the magnolia trunk. And I ascended the stairs, turning at the top to see Mr. Luther pulling a skirt of leaves around the base of the tree.

8 October 1871. The Sabbath. I find I cannot look at Henry. I left church straightaway after the benedictory. Just as Mr. Luther said, the rain has arrived and with it much colder air.

9 October 1871. I read to Mr. Teague, as his eyes tire so quickly in the dim lamplight. The rain streaks the windows, cold and dense. Ruthie again brings us coffee and tea. I read at length from various newspapers, the *Compass*, the *Commercial-App*eal of Memphis, and the New Orleans newspapers. They arrive here regularly, as Mr. Teague is a voracious consumer of news, particularly that which involves commerce. The *Picayune* reports that a great fire has engulfed the city of Chicago. Many have perished, and much of the city has been lain waste. Here in St. Matthew, the cane towers again, and there is talk of storms in the Gulf, but only talk. Mr. Luther thinks we are done with any sea-blown weather this year.

10 October 1871. The rain continues, but so must the lessons also. The girls, who always study diligently, have been unusually quiet today. Then suddenly, during the middle of what we call 'mathematics hour,' Ida bolted from the parlour in tears and ran up the stairs. Jenny, usually cheerful and talkative, has also been reserved. I had dismissed this as influenced by the grey weather. But as the day has crept on, it felt as though the older girls and I were haunted by another issue. Only little Lucy has seemed the same to me. Finally, I asked Jenny what was the matter. The answer took me quite aback. She said that Mr. Teague is considering dismissing me, not for ill-performance of duty, but because it has become a source of amusement for St. Matthew that a young woman should share a house with a man presently wifeless. But surely, he is still married to Mrs. Teague, wherever she may be? But again, wagging tongues do not weigh evidence.

15 October 1871. Sabbath today. Weather cool and bright.

17 October 1871. Splendid weather. Mr. Teague has said nothing of dismissal, and so I continue lessons until that time.

20 October 1871. Mr. Teague called me into his study, and I feared the worst. It was only to read from the *Compass*, as he had misplaced his glasses.

22 October 1871. Henry is absent from the pulpit, away visiting in Memphis. A priest from New Orleans serves, a man with a voice like the hum of a mosquito.

26 October 1871. Rain again. Ruthie makes a sort of stew called gumbo which is served with rice. It is the sort of dish that could be eaten every day in the north of England, if they knew of it.

27 October 1871. The sun has returned, though the cold has remained to keep it company. Today the *Compass* carries the notice that Mr. Teague and the now former Mrs. Teague are divorced by decree of Judge Anderson.

28 October 1871. Talk is of cutting the cane, but the signal has not been given by Mr. Teague. Mozie says that the longer it grows, the more sugar it gives. She has been a balm for my soul and visiting her is a delight. I had come to visit Henry, but he had gone to Memphis for a visit to his old friend Mr. Hodge. Mozie says that the reverend left hurriedly and seemed agitated. 'Miss Alice, it ain't my place to say, but they keep to the same bed! They does!' I replied that they are just old friends, though, of course, I know the truth. Mozie said, 'You knows as well as I do that they another bed in this house! And why he don't take up with a purty thang like you? Many man round here be happy fo' that!' I wish I had had the words or sentiment to redirect her talk, but I did not.

29 October 1871. Henry has returned from Memphis, somewhat somber. He appears lovelorn. His sermon was from the Gospel according to St. John, the story of the woman caught in the act of adultery. I played 'Lord of Mercy and of Light,' on the great bellowing organ.

31 October 1871. Lessons continue. I have not been approached by Mr. Teague. Truly, my heart aches that I may have to leave these girls who are part sister and part daughter.

1 November 1871. A very happy day, the happiest in months! We are reunited, in a way. Today, Mr. Teague appeared in the doorway of the sewing room. He smiled as he braced himself on the jamb. He seemed quite like he had some big news, which was the case. 'Well, dear, at last we have found it! Your father's chest! It has been in a shed all this time!' And there it was behind him in the central hallway, borne into the house by Reuben and Simeon, who smiled proudly at their vindication. I could not hold my enthusiasm. 'You found it!' I exclaimed with the excitement of one rescued from a desert island. I jumped to my feet, spilling my embroidery hoop to the floor and giving Mr. Teague an embrace, which I had not intended to do but for the surge of emotion the discovery had elicited. There it was, the chest of old English oak! Papa's chest! I thought of the reams of papers, a lifetime of sermons, good advices, perhaps a witticism or two, that slumbered within the wood and past the lock. Mr. Teague smiled, saying that he had come across it in a shed as preparations were made for grinding and that it must have gotten misplaced there when I was moved to Mount Teague. He said he was waiting for an auspicious day to present it to me. Then he paused as one pauses before playing a winning hand at whist or a dramatic move on a chessboard. 'Perhaps as a wedding gift,' he said. I exclaimed that he had already given me so much. I looked upon the chest, where beyond the lock slept the words of my Papa. I was ecstatic, as I am yet. A part of him has been returned to me, a part that I thought was lost to me and the rest of the world. And then Mr. Teague said, 'Miss Lamb, I can give you so much more than a simple country vicar. I have made an offer of marriage to you—' He made a face like a blush and said, 'If you are not just the prettiest thing I have ever seen.' I found myself in a flawed moment, in a position of weakness. The truth had been distilled down to this single drop: Henry has no interest in me and never will, but this man who has been so kind to me does. This man with his adoring daughters who are like sisters to me. And so, I have accepted his offer. There, I am betrothed to Samuel Teague. I trade a mourning veil for a wedding veil. I pray that my decision is not an impetuous one.

Sammy, 1982

It was the same dream, of sheep gathered under a magnolia tree and red lights reflected in yellow and the slap of windshield wipers. He looked close through their sweeping arcs, through the wet glass, through the watery haze, all so real that he couldn't tell he was asleep.

He woke to the metronome clop of a pendulum and came downstairs. Pongeaux was at the window of the front parlour staring into the night and offering muffled barks into the starlit darkness of the oak lane. Sammy reached down to scratch her head, and she briefly looked up to him and resumed her vigilant gaze.

"Come on, gal," he said, and she reluctantly turned from the windowpane where her nose had rubbed little clouds into the glass. The two of them returned upstairs with the drum of his footsteps and the clack of her claws on the wood floor, and the rhythmic pop of the clock in the hall. As the man and his dog reached the top step, downstairs the ancient clock reported the hour with a soft chime.

The next morning at breakfast, Elizabeth said in her five-year-old voice, "Daddy, somebody painted your truck."

"Mr. Teeter did it," he said, "after somebody—" He changed the way he needed to say it. "After it got scratched."

"Somebody painted a word on it," she said, and she put her spoon into her cereal.

He looked at her, but she had said all she needed to say about the word painted on her daddy's truck. Sammy got up from the breakfast table and went outside, and there it was, spelled out in red spray paint on the aqua blue of the hood. He took a tarp from the back of the truck, small pools of rainwater falling from it, and he put it over the message. He went back in and resumed his breakfast.

Elizabeth said, "Did you see it, Daddy? Mama said that some people call cats that word and that whoever wrote that must like cats a lot."

"That's right," Sammy said.

"But they shouldn't have painted it on your truck," she seemed to be reasoning with herself.

"No, they shouldn't have," her daddy said.

"That's strange," Elizabeth said.

"Yes, it is," he said.

After breakfast, Betsy took the girls and drove Quint to school. Sammy went out to the metal barn looking for Teeter, but he wasn't there, though he had left a project half-finished, the disks of a soldier harvester disconnected and on a workbench. Sammy looked through a locker and found a can of spray paint, a light blue that didn't quite match the aqua blue, and he sprayed over the word. When he had most of the word concealed, the can ran out, and the P and the Y still showed, though faintly. It was a poor fix, but the best he could do. Teeter could do far better. Sober Teeter.

He drove to Teeter's house, but his truck wasn't there when he pulled up. An old Ford Mustang was in the yard up on blocks and partially covered with a tarp. Sammy got out. Behind a screen of laundry on a single clothesline strung between two trees, an outboard motor put-putted down the bayou. By the door, weeds were beginning to sprout around a statue of the Blessed Mother. Her blue robe and praying hands were spattered with dirt that the rain had kicked up. Miss Vessy opened the door after a long series of knocks. She was in her housecoat, and The Price is Right was on television. A ceramic ashtray held half-a-dozen cigarette butts, including one that still smoldered.

"Hi Miss Vessy. Teeter here?"

"Ain' seen him this morning," she said through the screen door. "I thought he was with you."

"No ma'am," he said. "I'll go see if I can find him."

They both knew where he might be. In the background, Bob Barker's voice announced that someone had won a vacation to Acapulco, but neither Sammy nor Miss Vessy was interested. Sammy left, and, as he started up his truck, he saw Miss Vessy smoking in the screen door and looking out at the sky. He backed out and pulled onto the highway.

On a shell road off Highway 70, there was a place called Tatootsy's Bar, a place made of cypress planks and tin roofing with PVC pipe gutters. Every few years, Bayou Corne tried to claim it, but it always came back, a place where oil field workers and crawfishermen who either didn't have families or had multiple families came to drink and smoke and play pool in the front room and bourré in the back room. Sammy pulled into the parking lot next to a pickup with chicken wire crawfish traps in the back. There were several other vehicles there, all trucks that were rigged for work of one kind or another. But none of them was Teeter's.

He entered the place and looked around. In the purple light, a girl danced in high heels and skimpy underwear and nothing else, holding a cigarette in one hand and holding onto a pole with the other. There was a twenty dollar bill she had put under the string herself, but no others. Several semi-interested men nursed beers and watched her gyrate her hips indifferently in the dim light while the jukebox sang, "If I Said You Had a Beautiful Body, Would You Hold It Against Me?"

One of the men at a pool table in the depths of the place came forward, still holding a pool cue, and, in French, asked Sammy what he wanted.

"I'm looking for Teeter Blanchard," Sammy said.

"You police?" the man asked, leaning his head back and picking up the pool cue in both hands.

"Just a friend."

The man relaxed and said, "Ain' around here, no. But you see him, tell him he got a ou'standin' tab wit the house."

"When was he here last?"

"Night fo' las'. Looked fucked up, real *cagou*."

"Did he say where he was going?"

"I ain' his mama. But we find him, mais, he gonna wish he paid his tab."

"I'll pay it," Sammy said. "How much does he owe?"

The man looked over his shoulder and yelled to a woman at the register. "How much dat Blanchard coullion owe da house?"

"The one got dat big nose?" she said as she put her cigarette in her lip and consulted a notepad by the register. In the purple glow, Sammy could see she had the tattoo of a panther down her arm. "Fitty-seven dollars," she yelled back. She lifted her bra strap up over the panther and under her leopard-print blouse.

Sammy gave the man three twenties, and the man folded them up and put them in his shirt pocket. On the plywood stage, the dancing girl removed her stiletto heels and tossed them to the side. She sat on the edge of the stage and used her foot to playfully massage the shirtfront of one of the men sitting there while she lifted the G-string in hopes that another twenty might roost under it. As Sammy left, the jukebox played Kenny Rogers' "Coward of the County."

The light outside was bright compared to the shadow world inside, and he put his hand to his forehead against it. He drove back into town trying not to worry about Teeter. Teeter had saved the Mount Teague crop a few years before by insisting that they plant more seed cane, and then, sure enough, a freeze had taken the cane that had already grown, the first and second ratoons, but the seed cane was spared and grew into an abundant crop. It was a genius move. But Teeter was also a man who, like a stray cat, would disappear for days at a time and then reappear as if nothing had happened. Occasionally, though, he would show up in the St. Matthew Parish lockup and call Sammy with his one phone call. Sammy always came and paid his bail. Teeter was good at raising cane, both good and bad. He'd show up in a day or two, Sammy was confident.

The aqua-blue truck with the light blue spray-painted hood pulled into the parking lot of the St. Matthew Parish Library. Sammy got out and looked at the hood again and the letters that slept under the light blue paint. He sighed and went inside.

In the *Archives* room, he pulled the box of microfilm that said, *St. Matthew Parish Compass, October 1871*, and loaded the film into the reader. The past came into focus, transactions, news of the day, advertisements, notices. He slowed down as the date neared, and then there it was:

> "Be it known to all men that Samuel M. Teague, of this Parish, henceforth enters into a state of divorce with his heretofore legally married wife, Paulina Hutchison 'Polly' Teague, on the grounds of desertion by said Mrs. Teague. Signed, Judge S. L. Anderson, St. Matthew Parish, Louisiana. The *Compass* is asked to direct that any and all persons who may encounter Mrs. Teague kindly convey this notice to her."

He rewound the microfilm and replaced it in the box and went home.

That night, he dreamed the dream again, of sheep under a magnolia tree and red taillights in the rain. He woke to the bark of a dog, and it took him a moment to realize that it was his dog, Pongeaux. He put his robe over his pajamas and went downstairs and out onto the back gallery. Pongeaux tried to slip through the door, but he kept her inside. She gave a faint whine, but he knew this was something he had to do himself, by himself.

He tuned his ears to the sounds of the Louisiana winter night. There were whispers and snickering and the shush of spray cans and the rattling clack of the ball inside them as they were shaken. Sammy felt shaken as well, shaken and angry and determined not to be victimized again. His slippers lightly touched each step and then left imprints in the frost. There was only a sliver of moon, and in the light of it, he saw what Betsy still called a *rateau*, a rake. He picked it up and tuned his ears to the night air, dense and cold. The sounds were out at the metal shed. He took a wide path so he could surprise whoever it might be.

He walked around to the back of the building and heard the voices and the snorting and the wheezing laughter and the exhalations of spray paint cans. He lifted the rake and crept closer. It was foolhardy and he knew it, but he couldn't stop himself. Two shadows were moving in the darkness along the back wall of the shed, pausing to shake their cans. Sammy took the rake in his hands like a baseball bat and drew it back. As he did, he thought, you could kill a man like this. But he didn't care. They were killing him, little by little. He could see how a man could be so angry, so violated, that he would scream a war cry and plunge a bayonet into another man. His anger was red-hot and ready to be satisfied. He had the rake all the way back, every muscle in his body tensed for the strike.

And then something fell on him and pushed him to the ground. The two shapes took off into the night, leaving their message on the shed half-finished and their spray paint cans on the frosty ground. One of Sammy's slippers fell to the ground, and he felt the icy grass against his bare foot. Against the night sky, he saw Teeter's face.

"Go back to base camp, Bawsman," he said. "Bravo company on the hill up yonda. They's VC all over here."

Teeter pulled Sammy up and gave him his rake and said, "Take your weapon, sojah." Teeter crunched off through the brittle grass toward the Twelve Arpent Canal.

Reason quickly came back to Sammy. He had almost killed a man for simple vandalism. He took a few deep breaths. He had to. He would have been put on trial for assault, possibly murder. He sat down right there on the cold grass behind the shed in his pajamas and his bathrobe. He had to.

After a while, he went inside and got a flashlight and came back to look at what they had written on his shed. In the circle of dim yellow light, the incomplete message on the back wall said, TRATER SUCK D. He aimed the light into the night. All he could only see were Teeter's footsteps trailing off into the frost. The light from the back porch flooded over the light of the flashlight. Betsy was on the back porch.

"Back of the shed this time," Sammy said as he came up the steps. "You go on to bed," he said as he kissed her. "I'm gonna stay up and read a little."

Alice, 1871

6 November 1871. A committee of ladies has gotten up a trousseau for me, and I must say I have never had a wardrobe as that which I now possess. Day dresses, evening dresses, hats, bonnets, the most fashionable of ladies' boots. Polonaise, silk sashes of all colours. And the most frilly and fussy of undergarments and petticoats, most of which I never even knew existed. Crinolettes and corsets with genuine whalebone, and exquisite bodices to put over them, and tunics to put over those. Everything fits as if it were bespoke. And the pinnacle of it all, a satin gown quite like the Queen wore when she married Prince Albert. I also have received a well-worn copy of a book by one William Andrus Alcott, *The Young Wife: Or, Duties of Woman in the Marriage Relation,* and a pamphlet, *Your Wedding Night: Advice to a Young Lady*, both given to me by a committee of ladies of St. Margaret's. The latter, *Advice to a Young Lady,* contains an explanation of the marital duties of a woman, including a description of something called the 'bud of passion.' O my! It is the cause of great blushing, even on reading it in private.

8 November 1871. Today was that most auspicious day in a woman's life, my wedding day. St. Margaret's was decorated handsomely, with flowers that had been brought in from elsewhere, as I know they do not grow here naturally at this time of year. Henry was in his finest vestments as the organ soared under the touch of an organist also brought in from elsewhere, the city or perhaps farther. I did not meet him, or perhaps I did, and I don't remember. The committee of ladies attended me, fussing and fretting over my hair and my dress. At last the wedding march sounded. There was a moment of consternation, and one of the ladies asked, 'O dear, who shall give you away?' 'I shall give myself away,' I replied at last, and I walked the aisle, my direction opposite to that which I traveled just weeks before, when Henry had followed me down it to get my assurance that I would keep his secret. I walked toward the altar and to Henry, and now Mr. Teague, my hesitant strides set to the booming, triumphant notes of the organ that trembled the flowers. The silk and lace skirts covered my shaking steps, the pearl and lace veil concealed my quivering lips. Those who could see my face might have thought that my nervousness was from joy. But truthfully, it was the loneliest moment of my life. In the crowded church, I could only think of who was *not* there. Papa.

Once at the altar, Henry dutifully asked us to confess our vows, and it all seemed to become so enormous then, as if the importance of the event had trebled itself, quadrupled itself. My legs trembled again, but I willed them to be still. Just as Papa used to do, Henry asked the congregation if anyone knew of any reason why Mr. Teague and I should not be joined as man and wife. And I waited for someone to say something (I know not why) and then with a blared fanfare of the organ that rattled the windowpanes, Henry pronounced us married, and *let no man put asunder what God has joined.* Mr. Teague raised my veil and smiled at me, and the scar within his beard frowned. Then he kissed me, and I tasted his morning cigar, and we turned to face the congregation, who clapped politely, though silently, rendered so by the bellow of the organ. The doors were thrown open and the sunlight crashed in and down the aisle with a rush of heavy, cold air. The weather had chilled considerably in the hour that had passed. A carriage awaited us, a fine white chaise with gold trim. Two superb horses, one white and one black, threw their heads about and shook their manes as they waited to pull it. Mr. Teague helped me up into it, surreptitiously running a hand down the small of my back and handing the bouquet up to me. We rattled down the lane through the churchyard, past Papa's tomb, and onto the bayou road to Mount Teague. All of St. Matthew Parish had turned out along the way, the men removing their hats and women cheering their congratulations. Behind my veil, everything swam as if in steam.

The crunch of white shells signaled that we had turned down the lane to Mount Teague. There it loomed, recessed at the end of the oaks in the stony twilight, the great house with its columns and galleries. I barely remember getting out of the carriage, only that I faltered a moment, and someone caught me. We ascended the steps to the front gallery, where we were toasted by guests on the lawn, one for the bride's health, one for the gallant groom, one for old Mrs. Teague who had come down from Missisipi *[sic]* and who smiled with thin lips and nodded. A dragon-breath belch from the gardens in the rear of the house announced a surprise that waited us—a hot air balloon. With some trepidation, I approached the basket, which came up to just over my waist. Mr. Teague lifted me up and over the side and into it, and the guests on the lawn of the gardens all clapped in approval. He himself pulled himself up on a rope and lowered himself into the basket with me. Above us, the fire belched like a dragon, and I felt us separate from the earth. The gardens and the well-wishers and even the immense house receded below us. The rope tether became taut, and we hovered in our wicker basket and looked out on the fields of other plantations that were changing from green to black patches with the cutting of each section of cane, though Mr. Teague has delayed cutting his. Ours, I suppose I should say. The serpentine bayou grinned and frowned and grinned over and over again along its tree-bristled course. The wind pulled at us, Mr. Teague's top hat and my wedding bonnet. We were above the water tower, the air was brisk and biting, and colder as we ascended. I hugged myself against it, wishing I had my mink coat. Down below us, the thrilling tableau, people as small as ants, animals as small as mites. The balloon pulled at the thick rope that tethered it. In the rushing wind, there were no other sounds, just my husband. How strange to write it: *my husband.* As we looked over his holdings, he said something that I fear quite put me out of countenance.

'You are to obey me, do you understand?' he said, 'If I say the sky is green, you are to say *yes sir.* If I say sugarcane is blue, you are to say, *yes sir.* Wives must obey their husbands, so the Bible says.' I was taken back by such words on such a propitious day, but I found my response. 'And husbands must love their wives as Christ loved the church, Mr. Teague.' 'Yes,' he said, 'If they are obedient. But first, they must obey.' He did not wait for my assent. It was for him an understood yes. He used a lever and the fire diminished, and we descended again. People and animals regained their normal size. And I daresay I was grateful for the earth under my feet once more. In the ballroom, a reception was held, and I was greeted by Mrs. Teague, now my mother-in-law, I suppose. She grasped my hand quite graciously, and I said, 'Well, then, I suppose we are both Mrs. Teagues!' 'Yes, and it is true, my dear,' she said in reply. A servant passed with a tray of cherry brandy cordials and I asked her, 'Will you have a glass of cherry brandy, then, my fellow Mrs. Teague? I hear it is a favourite of yours, and an elixir for one's health.'

'Cherry brandy?' she said, 'Why, there is nothing healthy at all about cherry brandy! A man could as easily drink himself to death with it as he could with whiskey.'

'But Mr. Teague said-' I replied.

'O, my son says many things. He was always a peculiar child. So very headstrong. So much like his late father. A nose for business, keen on the scent of money to be made, eager on collecting a prize.'

Instead, we had a glass of lemonade punch, 'My true favourite, not this cherry brandy my son speaks of,' she said. The rest of the day passed as a blur, a flurry of introductions and handshakes and embraces, of wedding cake uneaten or unenjoyed, of departing guests and tuneless serenades. And then I was left with my husband. *My husband.* So odd. Shall I ever get used to it? Or shall I always refer to myself, my true, inner self, as Alice Lamb? The light in his chamber, our chamber now, was honey-coloured, and it was as if the tall furniture stood guard lest I run away. My mind swam as I thought of Mrs. Teague, my predecessor, and I imagined she and my husband on their night. The process of the conjugal rite is so much rougher and quicker than I had expected. Mr. Teague goes to sleep straightaway upon its completion with a tremendous snore, and I am left in a state of agitation.

10 November 1871. Old Mrs. Teague returned to Mississippi this morning. Her granddaughters gathered about me on the front gallery as we bid her adieu. Mr. Teague was elsewhere, very likely overseeing the cane, as grinding season is imminent. Each gave their grandmother a polite embrace, and Mrs. Teague looked into each face with a grim smile, more like an appraisal than a show of affection. She at last came to me, looking up, as I am taller than the girls. 'Do be careful, dear. Won't you?' I thought it an odd thing to say in the light of such a promising time, filled with new beginnings. She alighted the carriage for Donaldsonville and the upriver steamer, and Reuben shook the reins a small snap, and the horse trotted away, and the carriage took Mrs. Teague off on spinning wheels, leaving another Mrs. Teague watching.

12 November 1871. My first Sabbath as a married woman. I sat in the Teague family pew with my girls, my step-daughters, I suppose they are now. And, of course, my husband. A man from Thibodaux was brought in, and he played the great organ passably, though I intend to return to the bench next Sunday.

13 November 1871. All here await the signal for cutting, which is given by Mr. Teague and him alone.

15 November 1871. A most horrid day. As it had been a year to the day that I lost my Papa, I made up my mind to look through his sermon chest. As I couldn't find the key, I had Mr. Favorite, the Mount Teague blacksmith, open it. Inside, I found that the chest was empty, yawning and empty. I fear I screamed or made some sort of animal noise. Mr. Teague came loping into the Ladies' Parlour where it had been placed. 'What is it, my dear?' he asked, taking his cigar from his lips. I could hardly form the words. 'Where? Where are Papa's sermons? His writings? His treatises? His letters?'

'Oh, I had the hands burn whatever was inside,' he said, rather flatly. 'It was just a bunch of old papers and such. But that chest, it is certainly a handsome one, now isn't it? Fine old English oak. Exquisite craftsmanship, wouldn't you say? It was such a stroke of luck that we found it!'

I am beyond words. It is as though I have lost my Papa again.

Sammy, 1982

It was the next morning. Teeter still had not returned to the shed, and new frost had covered over his footsteps in the night. The sheriff had come out to look at the new graffiti but had had no answers, no leads, and just a little sympathy. When he left, Sammy looked at the diary and began wondering what had happened to the chest.

Next to the ice barn, the second most terrifying place from his childhood was the attic. His sisters used to tell him that Alice the Burning Lady slept in the attic on warm nights so she could cool down because the hot attic was still cooler than she was. To make matters worse, animals would get in up there, mice or rats or racoons, and their scurrying feet would rouse him from his sleep, and he would spend the rest of the night listening for her, the Burning Lady, imagining her making noises up there. Once his sisters had locked him up in the attic, telling him that some beloved possession was up there and then letting the door shut on him and sealing him up in the dark heat with the dress forms and the boxes and the woman who was most certainly behind them. Miss Della Mae had rescued him and scolded his sisters, who had smirked behind her back.

This cold winter morning, Sammy had just gotten off the phone with his sister Charlotte, who had all but accused Betsy of having the sapphire pendant. He had some sharp words with his sister and hung up thinking of what his daddy had told him: "That god-damned thing. What good is a family heirloom if it causes such trouble for the family it belongs to?"

And so, he went upstairs to the second floor and climbed the first few steps to the attic. He looked into Quint's room and saw his son doing homework at the small desk in his room. Sammy looked up and ascended the steps and opened the door into the darkness. The flashlight glanced around the attic, flickering images of things, a dress form, an old baby carriage with a doll in it, boxes of ancient things that no longer held any purpose. The people who had thought them nostalgic or useful were themselves gone, and now the attic was a repository of the formerly mundane that was, at best, macabre. He calmly investigated the frightening things that had dwelled just above his head his whole life.

Just past the baby carriage with the porcelain doll in it, there was a trunk made of cracking leather and rusting latches, an old steamer trunk. He opened it carefully, not out of fear, but to keep from damaging it. The lid opened with a swirl of dust in the amber beam of his flashlight. On top of some old clothes was a list written in what he easily recognized as Alice's elegant script. With it was another note that said in some other feminine hand, *I know you're not coming, so I've returned your things*, and then the initials, *JT*, and the postmark, *LaHavre, France, January 28, 1873.*

He set the flashlight on its end with the beam pointed to the roof, and he turned back to the trunk. Under the notes was a green-and-black ball gown. It rustled as he reverently lifted it from its container, its crypt. Moths had long since sampled it and moved on, leaving it frayed. As he held it up in the glow, he thought he smelled something trapped within it, a fleeting scent. He put his nose to it. It still smelled faintly of smoke. He looked it over, thinking that perhaps the pendant might be within its folds, but he only found a label that read, *Madame Olympe, Canal Street, New Orleans.*

His fear and terror had been replaced by an odd combination of reverence and pity. He gently laid the empty ballgown aside as if the wearer were still in it. There were other things in the trunk. A tin cup with a fancifully embossed, *Krewe of Comus, 1873, All Hail the King.* Other dresses, a light blue ballgown with gold trim, and a few others. He wondered if all of them had belonged to her. But there was no sapphire pendant. He replaced everything in the trunk and fastened the lid. The flashlight beam swept around the attic. And then, in the corner, just over the eaves of the old house, he saw it, not the pendant, but something else.

He eased over to it, around other, more ordinary boxes. He rapped on the side of the chest to scare away any mice that might have found it a cozy habitat. In the beam of light, he read the inscription etched into the English oak, *John Clarke & Son, New Chapel Street, Guildford, Surrey. Bespoke chest for the Rev. Arthur Lamb, AD 1840.* Sammy opened the lid, which brought up another swirl of dust in the cone of the flashlight. The chest was, of course, empty. Old Sam Teague had seen to that.

And so, his great-grandson, Samuel Teague the fourth, pulled the chest to the door where the attic steps descended to the second floor, and he called from the top step for his son, Samuel Teague the fifth, Quint, to come and help him get it down. It was empty, but it was still heavy. Fine old English oak.

The top of Quint's head appeared from the door of his room, down in the light of the house.

"Yes sir?"

"Help me get this thing down, son," Sammy said.

"Sure, Dad."

From the attic, Sammy tilted the chest down onto the steps. They bumped it carefully, tread-over-tread to halfway down, and Sammy called down past it. "Got it, son?

"Got it," Quint said as he sat it on the floor of the hallway. Sammy realized that his son was now at least as strong as he was. Sammy turned and shut the attic door and came down the steps. They lifted the chest and Sammy said, "Downstairs. My study."

As they negotiated the stairs to the first floor, Sammy asked his son, "What were you studying?"

Quint kept his head turned to watch the steps they descended.

"Calculus."

"Sounds hard."

"Not really."

"You must get your math from your mother."

They struggled to get the old chest down the stairs. Sammy felt that his son was avoiding his gaze. Then, as they were turning into the study from the central hallway, Sammy saw his son's black eye and swollen lip. Sammy said nothing until they set the chest down next to the old desk.

"So what happened, son?"

"Prefer not to say, Dad," Quint said.

"All right," Sammy said. "All right, son."

With footfalls on the stairs, Quint returned to his room and his calculus. And his daddy transferred the documents from the white plastic Pierre Part Store bucket into the chest. He shut the lid to the chest and put the white bucket in the corner as if it were a trash can.

He went out to the yard to look at the sky, feeling the burden of one who has had his sin fall on the innocent, like something out of the Old Testament, the child paying the price of the father. He wondered who Quint had fought and why, but he was certain it had been someone who had insulted his boy's daddy. Sammy looked back to the great house and saw a faint light glowing from the two small windows in the attic. His heart rose and sank, but he was not afraid any more, only curious. He ascended the steps to the house and then the stairs to the second floor, past the room where his son and his swollen lip and eye looked from a calculus book to a three-ring binder and back, his pencil scratching out figures in the loose-leaf paper. Sammy ascended the stairs to the attic and opened the door. Inside, the light glowed and illuminated the rafters with a swirl of golden dust. The baby carriage and the doll and the trunk with the gowns sat bathed in the dim radiance of the flashlight he had forgotten. He retrieved it and clicked it off and descended from the darkness of the attic and shut the steps up in it. He paused and watched his son, who looked around from his homework.

"You sure you don't want to talk about it?" Sammy asked.

"Yes sir, I'm sure."

"All right."

Sammy went downstairs and sat in his study and looked out on the night sky and the emerging sugarcane, reflecting on this new emotion, the moment when a father first hears a man's opinion from his son and recognizes his right to it. He nodded his head in agreement with himself and opened the diary.

Alice, 1871

16 November 1871. The signal has been given to begin the cutting of cane. My husband gave a speech, nay, an exhortation, and men with cane knives and mules with wagons proceeded into the fields. The fires in the sugarhouse are kindled.

18 November 1871. The *Donaldsonville Chief* of the eleventh carries an inquiry from a woman named Sally in San Antonio, Texas, who looks for her family, slaves sold for the debts of a 'kind master' on his death, and so scattered, and now unknown to each other. How horrid. Shall they ever find each other?

21 November 1871. The marital rite again. I must confess to you, I do not appreciate the appeal of it. Perhaps it is the reason for the departure of the prior Mrs. Teague. I shall endure it, however, as it is my duty as a wife.

25 November 1871. A delightful day reading and playing music in front of a cheerful hearth-fire with my step-daughters. Lucy sings in a little chirp of a voice, so endearing.

28 November 1871. Papa's empty chest mocks me. His life's work up in flames and smoke. And so everything must return to ashes. I have only the things he had on his desk when he died, and so I keep those with me.

30 November 1871. My husband spends late nights supervising the grinding. When he comes in late, smelling of smoke and molasses, I feign sleep.

2 December 1871. The cutting and grinding go on during the day and then in the night by lantern light. The cane stubble is burned in the cut fields, and the hands move about in them like Lucifer's minions.

3 December 1871. We attended church again today, minus Mr. Teague who is 'getting sugar in.' Jenny sat with her sisters as I returned to the bench.

6 December 1871. The *Compass* says that the new synagogue in Donaldsonville is complete. It is said that it is the work of the same crew who built our Ice Parlour. There is no need to adjourn there at this cold time of year, so I read and did a little sewing in the Ladies' Parlour whilst the girls went about their lessons.

10 December 1871. After church today, I asked Henry about his visit to Memphis to see his friend, Mr. Hodge. He was reluctant to speak of it to any depth.

14 December 1871. The *Compass* estimates that over seven hundred people died in October in the fires in Chicago, Michigan, and Wisconsin. It is absolutely tragic to perish so.

17 December 1871. Church today, still without Mr. Teague. Advent music predominates. Henry preaches on Mary's visit to Elizabeth, and John the Baptist leaping for joy in her womb.

20 December 1871. My husband's eyes tire from the smoke of the grinding process, so I read the newspaper to him as he rests. The *Compass* believes that Governor Warmoth shall abolish the Louisiana Lottery, which it calls a 'chartered swindle.' Mr. Teague responded with decidedly unchristian language. This shocked me and I told him so, but he did not apologise for it.

22 December 1871. A day spent with reading and music. It is a small source of pleasure and a respite for me, and I am refreshed to be in the company of ones so loved. They seem so much like sisters rather than step-daughters. Jenny, of course, played splendidly. Ida comes on well on the piano, though her feet do not yet reach the pedals. I told her that I can remember it being so, and that one day her feet shall reach them, she may be sure of it.

Christmas Eve 1871. After church, Luther quietly assisted me in doing up the balconies and galleries with holly and cedar. The house smells so very festive. A large cedar was selected for the main parlour and the girls and I decorated it. Mr. Teague was not at all effected by the merriment and worried that we shall catch the 'house afire.' But the girls cried, and so he allowed us our celebration.

Christmas Day 1871. A holiday with my girls, exchanging gifts. Stationery, music, bows, new doll clothes for Lucy's Penny. Mr. Teague attended to sugar-making, pausing only for a quick Christmas Dinner before lumbering back out to the sugarhouse.

28 December 1871. Mr. Teague is quite elated that he is obtaining a yield of two hogshead of sugar per arpent.

1 January 1872. Black-eyed peas and cabbage were served for good luck and wealth in the coming year, as is the custom here.

2 January 1872. A very cold, bright day, which I spent with Mr. Teague in his study. He had me read to him, as he says he enjoys the sound of my voice, though I read until I was quite hoarse. 'The accent of ol' England. Why, it's like music to me!' he is quite fond of saying. In a room upstairs, Jenny played the Mozart concerto we have been learning. The violin sang happily, stopping very infrequently and retracing over an errant note. In each room, a hearth fire was kept against the cold. To my husband's compliment regarding my 'pretty little voice,' I smiled over the newspaper as I continued reading. In the *Compass*, there is the news that the Mormon potentate Brigham Young has been arrested for bigamy. It is said that he has twenty-five wives. 'It's an abomination!' Mr. Teague thundered. 'Just like that Roddey feller. Nothing people hate more than a bigamist. Can't be a hell hot enough for bastards like them!' I did not chide him for his language, lest I be considered shrewish. But I am aware of Mr. Roddey and of Mr. Teague's animosity for him. For Mr. Teague, bigamy is at the top or near the top of the list of sins a man may commit. It easily eclipses all others, particularly any of Mr. Teague's, whatever they might be. It is as Papa was fond of saying, 'only the sins of others do we find abhorrent. Our own sins are mere trifles.'

8 January 1872. A cold day with very little to mention, though the society of my girls cheers me.

14 January 1872. Advertisements appear in the newspapers for the theatres and shops in New Orleans. It would be grand to attend, but Mr. Teague shows no interest and I shan't go to the city alone.

10 February 1872. The *Picayune* says that the Grand Duke Alexis of Russia shall be staying at the St. Charles during his visit in the city for Mardi Gras. The *Picayune* also says that there shall be immense crowds. I should like to attend, but we have our own celebration here and my husband is the king of it. I suppose that makes me the queen.

11 February 1872. Henry is visiting his friend in Memphis, and so we again had a vicar from Thibodaux come for services. There is some whispering about Henry's absences from the pulpit. Surely the whispers would be shouts and tongue-clicking if they knew the nature of his visit.

13 February 1872. The Krewe of Jupitre passed today with my husband dressed as its king. What ideas Americans have of royalty! All fluff and pomp and exultation, all of it passing as wisdom. I watched it from the viewing platform set up in front of the St. Matthew Court House. Good King Sam stopped in front of the reviewing stand and offered his daughters and me and the rest of St. Matthew Parish a toast. He brought the brass chalice to his lips, and his beard pushed his mask a little, but one couldn't tell that his cheek is scarred unless already aware of it. Then, with a whip-snap and a sudden straining pull of the draft horses and a lurch of the wagon, the procession continued down the Thibodaux Road. Just down the parade route, Good King Sam was greeted by what I am told is the traditional cheer for the King of Jupitre: *Cet homme ca a jamais travaille un jour de sa vie!* Surely, he must know that they are shouting at the tops of their lungs that Mr. Teague has 'never worked a day in his life!' And certainly, he must know that over the massive haunches of each draft horse, embroidered in the green and gold satin livery is 'Good King Sam.' I suppose it is all in the spirit of carnival and he is a very good sport about it, waving to the crowd, one side and then the other as he receives the comic-cheering message about never having worked a day in his life, and the twin rumps eject muck from the parted folds in their fine livery under his name. Good King Sam.

18 February 1872. Henry has returned for the first Sunday in Lent, and it is a cold and rainy one, in keeping with the penitential season.

20 February 1872. Mr. Teague today had me compose (and sign for him, *Samuel M. Teague*, as he favours my handwriting), a letter requesting that the Union Army troops garrisoned here in St. Matthew be dismissed. *We are all reconstructed here*, I wrote for him, *as docile as kittens and God-fearing and law-loving as judges.*

25 February 1872. Mr. Teague has strongly requested that I stop playing for Sunday services. 'Why, I don't want the prying eyes of the congregation to become love-besotted with you, my beauty,' he says. Henry interceded, saying that it would be a shame to deprive the congregation of her lovely talents that are such a credit to the Teague name. Mr. Teague relented, for now.

28 February 1872. This afternoon I read the mail to Mr. Teague, as he complained of a headache and trouble with his eyes. This is a frequent occurrence, but I would rather take up the duty of reading than another duty which I shall not mention. Of interest, there was a letter from an address in New Orleans, the Argus detective agency with an emblem of the Great Seeing Eye. It held new intelligence on the former Mrs. Teague. An agent of Argus observed a 'voluptuous woman with red hair in a green dress' checking into the Willard Hotel in Washington, D.C. under the name Paulina Hutchison Teague. My husband suddenly sat straight up in his Campeche chair and exclaimed, 'That was her name before we married! Paulina Hutchison!' Then he nestled back into his chair and put his cigar to his lips and pursed them in a thoughtful pose. '*She paid cash for her lodgings*,' I read from the letter, '*which were for a period of three days, and ended with her quitting the capital and departing on the train north*.' He stared out onto the cane and puffed clouds into the air of the study. I set the letter down and said, 'Really, Mr. Teague, since you are divorced and remarried now, what does it matter where she goes?' I admit to a bit of jealousy here. Perhaps it is so, but, after all, I am Mrs. Teague now. Surely any wife would feel this pang of resentment. He pulled his cigar from his lips and adopted a tone of voice one might reserve for a child. 'My dear, when her money runs out, she may run up a bill in my name! Our name! She must be stopped! Why, you don't want her to ruin us, do you?' I suppose it is so, but I wish he would not be so troubled by it.

29 February 1872. Leap day, and so Ida and Lucy amused themselves and me by 'leaping' in honour of it. They are such little loves, as Mrs. Sullivan was fond of saying.

4 March 1872. Mr. Teague is quite fond of Latin, and the more martial, the more bellicose the saying, the better. Among his favourites is that of Caligula, *Oderint dim metuant*, 'Let them hate, so long as they fear.' Mr. Teague's pronunciation is not at all clear, however, and sounds rather like 'O dirt dim mesh want,' or something of the sort. Nevertheless, he smiles broadly as he repeats it, raising his chin as certainly the old Roman dictator himself did. I can almost fancy him in a toga with a wreath of laurels above his grey eyes and sandy beard and scar. As I read him quotes from *Riley's Book of Latin*, he practiced saying them over and over to himself, moving his finger in the air like a symphony conductor. Of course, he rehearsed the rest of his repertoire, including the one which is perhaps his favourite, *Nemo me impune lecassit*, Old King James' motto, *no one provokes me and goes unpunished.*

12 March 1872. The *Daily Picayune* arrived with news that the Russian Grand Duke Alexis is still visiting in the city and attended Mardi Gras celebrations. The Rev. Givens paid a call and we enjoyed tea on the gallery amid the jubilant gardens of Mr. Luther. They become more colourful and fragrant with each sunrise.

18 March 1872. Mr. Teague had me dictate a letter for him, and I must admit that I would prefer to write a thousand letters for him than to submit to the marital rite once. Please do not tire of hearing it, my little confidant—I have no one else to tell. The letter was to General Roddey, to whom Mr. Teague offered an olive branch. '*Dear General Roddey,*' it began, '*I hope that the new year finds you well and that we can make bygones be bygones. Really, sir, life is too short and dear for us to bear a grudge, one against the other. I send this letter written in the lovely hand of my wife, Alice—*' Here, he said in an aside to me, '*You see, I have but one wife at a time, as opposed to you, sir.* But don't write that, dear.' He snickered at his own cleverness and pressed on. '*I write you*—no, wait, dear—*it is our wish to invite you and your lovely wife Carlotta, or Fanny as she is also called, a rose by any other name, et cetera, et cetera, to come down to St. Matthew Parish and spend a few nights here to coincide with our annual ball held to celebrate the commencement of the spring growing season. The ball is set to occur the first week in May. We hope that you will favour us with your attendance.*' I asked him if he wanted me to spell favour with a 'u,' the English way, or without, and he looked at me as if I had asked him the circumference of the moon. 'Oh, any old way,' he finally said. Then he had me sign his name, as he says my hand is so pretty, just like my 'pretty little voice.' A 'gen-u-wine' thing of beauty.

24 March 1872. Palm Sunday, with the reading of the Passion of Our Lord. It is said that the Catholic citizens of this place burn the palms as a protection during inclement weather.

27 March 1872. The garden is again gaining her spring colours, and Venus looks out over it all. After setting the girls to their lessons, I read on the porch. It was pleasant, and the great house breathed in and breathed out the cool breeze that flowed through it. Another two months and the curtains shall be drawn against the heat, and I shall adjourn to the room off the ice-house which at Mount Teague is now called the Ice Parlour. Mr. Luther, the gardener, was on his knees scratching in the ground, and the smell of the dark, fecund earth lingered around him. I called to him, but he kept to his task. After another shout, he looked up. It is his way to look off from one's gaze when he is addressed. Mozie says it is the way of albinos and that it is something to do with their eyesight. I told him that the gardens looked exceptional, and he looked off to the cane fields and said, 'Thank you, ma'am.' I then asked him, 'What are you doing, may I ask you?' He stood up from his labours. His shirt was already wet from his exertions, though it was only midmorning. 'Got to get this soil opened up. Catch them weeds 'fore they get started. Gots to transfer them lilies fo' it gets too hot. Yes ma'am.' I tried to engage him further, but I could not. He is truly a man who insists on keeping his own counsel. Certainly, he must still hold an allegiance to the former Mrs. Teague and finds it hard to accept a new one. He was willing, after all, to help her escape in the middle of the night, though it is still difficult for me to believe that she would have trouble with the sweet society of the Teague girls. Mr. Luther still keeps the gardens, perhaps as a tribute to her. Now they are at their finest, vivid colours erupting from dark green leaves. All under his quiet labours.

31 March 1872. Easter Sunday. It was always Papa's favourite, even more than Christmas, the day that our Saviour rolled away the stone from his grave. And now Papa still sleeps in his. Rev. Givens gave a fine sermon, 'Someone Has Taken My Lord, and I Do Not Know Where They Have Laid Him,' and I played, 'Jesus Christ is Risen Today' though Mr. Teague still says that he would rather that I abandon playing for Sunday services. Perhaps some would find his jealousy gratifying. On our return to Mount Teague, a ham was prepared here as it is the tradition of this place on Easter Sunday. Also, there was turtle soup, brandied apples and pears, creamed potatoes, sweet potatoes, haricots, corn and a half-dozen other things I cannot remember. The girls are all very lovely in their finery, white and pink and pale blue and mint green and yellow.

3 April 1872. A letter arrived today from Mr. Howard inviting us up to the city for the races, and Mr. Teague had me reply that, yes, we shall attend. The azaleas have ''bout played out,' as Mr. Luther says. He has pruned them back for next year's blossoms. Venus pretended not to notice. I hear Mr. Teague's footsteps on the stairs. I fear he comes to me for the Rite. I shall submit to it, for it is my duty as a wife, but I daresay I shan't enjoy it. Such a penance, all for Eve's bite of an apple.

6 April 1872. I visited Henry today, and we went over the selections for tomorrow. I found him rather forlorn and asked him why. He said that it was the tenth anniversary of the Battle of Shiloh and that he still has vivid memories of it. He said that it occurred on a Sunday and that at the time he questioned the propriety of attacking on the Sabbath. Henry also said that it was the bloodiest day of the war up until then, though other battles would surpass it later, and that it rained that night, and flashes of lightning showed a field that writhed with wounded bodies and each clap of thunder drowned out the moans of grown men who called for water or their mamas or for someone to finish them. At last, Henry begged pardon for speaking of such a macabre subject, but that those who were there and witnessed it shall never be able to forget it. I reassured him, telling him that he was in the presence of a sympathetic ear. Nevertheless, his tale was most unsettling, but surely a trifle compared to having witnessed it.

7 April 1872. Sabbath. Fine weather, though such weather reminds us that the oppressive heat cannot be far off. This afternoon, I read to my husband, as he has misplaced his spectacles again. The *Compass* carries an article about the tenth anniversary of the Battle of Shiloh. Mr. Teague says that he was there, quite 'in the thick of it,' but remembers very little about it, for he was in many battles.

10 April 1872. The pecan trees have put out green shoots and one may plant a vegetable garden, so says Mr. Luther. A fine plot was laid out by Mr. Luther, and the girls and I assisted him, until Mr. Teague registered his objections to his daughters doing *n—* work. I responded with the Biblical passage about seeds falling on fertile ground. Mr. Teague did not seem to be familiar with it, and Mr. Luther was left to complete the garden by himself.

13 April 1872. Mr. Teague and I have come up to the city on Mr. Howard's invitation to see the inaugural race at the Fairgrounds race track. Mr. Howard met us at our room in the St. Charles Hotel, the same spacious suite that Papa and I occupied on our first night in America, and we rode in Mr. Howard's fine carriage to the racetrack at the end of Esplanade. The smell of earth and horses drifted on the fading breezes of spring. The magnificent animals, black and brown, sleek and shining muscular machines, gathered turf and flung it back, ears back, nostrils flaring, eyes wide, muscles and manes, all displayed in a gathering roar. Diminutive jockeys crouched low on the equine backs, crops in hands and under armpits, wildly coloured livery, checkered, striped, vivid, bold. The equally colourful women and more plainly clothed men of the crowd stirred with craning necks, all eyes on the finish line and the horses and riders that approached it. They crossed in a thunderous gallop that stirred its own breeze, and some of the crowd cheered and some of the crowd groaned. The Grand Duke Alexis of Russia attended, and the band played 'If I Ever Cease to Love' in his honour, as they have done since Mardi Gras several weeks ago. I wonder if he tires of hearing it. After a day of racing, we adjourned by carriage to Mr. Howard's home on St. Charles for a lengthy dinner in the twilight that became transformed into gaslight.

16 April 1872. We returned to Mount Teague to find a letter today addressed to both Mr. Teague and me. The Roddeys have accepted our offer and shall arrive for the Spring Ball in May. 'Excellent,' Mr. Teague says, though I think there is something disingenuous in his tone.

21 April 1872. The Sabbath again at St. Margaret's Church, and I am shocked to find a Mr. Mercer at the bench of the great organ. And so, Mr. Teague has had his way and replaced me. Henry glanced to me apologetically as if there was nothing he could do about it. Perhaps Mr. Teague could have told me that I would be replaced, but there would be no fighting it.

22 April 1872. The *Compass* carries a small paragraph on a recent sighting of the now ex-Mrs. Teague, in St. Louis, which is her native land. It reports that she appeared to the correspondent to be in fine fettle and her usual, boisterous, demonstrative self. Why does not Mr. Teague send someone after her?

25 April 1872. I am nineteen today. Papa always prayed with me and gave me a blessing on my birthday. On days such as this, I miss him dearly, more so than on other days. I adjourned to the banks of Bayou Lafourche, to the spot where he and I liked to fish, quite certain that my birthday would otherwise go unmarked. When I returned home, Jenny had had Ruthie prepare a cake for me and the girls serenaded me. Mr. Teague came in from the fields and asked what the occasion was.

28 April 1872. Dinner on the grounds after church. A young niece visiting from Mobile was introduced to Henry, and he politely took her hand in a greeting and endured the scheming. Mr. Teague and I were sitting next to the gathering, and it seemed to me as though my husband was trying to hold back a smirk, as if he knew of the futility of the proceedings and was quite entertained by Henry's discomfort.

30 April 1872. It has been a rainy, dark day, and Mr. Teague has kept to his study reading *Le Boussole de St. Matthieu*, the French version of the Compass. I asked him what the paper said, and he replied, 'Oh, same old nonsense.' Then, I said in French, '*vous me surprenez, Mr. Teague, je ne savais pas que vous pourriez lire le français,*' He closed the paper and looked at the front and asked me, 'What say?' so I repeated it in English, 'You surprise me. I had no idea you could read French.' He looked at the front of the paper again and quickly folded it and put it on his desk, saying, 'Oh, I don't read or speak French.' I did not ask him why he had a French language paper in front of him. Perhaps he was only using it as a ruse for a nap. I wonder again if he is aware of the joke about him not working a day in his life, or if he takes the cheering as empty adulation, a grand jest for carnival? Has someone explained it to him, or is he simply oblivious?

3 May 1872. The privet hedge has begun to bloom, and a sweet breeze strains through it that is pleasant and light. Mr. Teague is not at all happy about it. He has sneezed several times today, with increasingly unchristian language each time. He muttered that perhaps he should have the whole of the privet hedge trimmed back, or the entire gardens removed and returned into a vast lawn. 'I have a good mind to pull these gardens up,' he said as he dabbed his red eyes and watery nose. But, as they are surely a source of such pleasure to all but Mr. Teague, I asked him, 'But Mr. Teague, what of Mr. Luther?' I could not let it pass, Mr. Luther attends the gardens so lovingly, as a parent for a child. Mr. Teague gave me a look that bordered on an accusation and said, 'Well, I suppose he would just go back to cutting cane.' He said it as if he did not care what Mr. Luther did. 'But these gardens, they are the talk of the South! They are like a symphony, and Mr. Luther is the conductor,' I said. His mood brightened as one does with a happy and unexpected revelation. I continued to sway him, however. 'And Mr. Teague, let me tell you that several of our neighbours have told me in confidence how they envy them. They say also that they wished they had such an able gardener as Mr. Luther!' Mr. Teague pursed his lips and returned his handkerchief to his pocket. 'Well, I suppose we will keep them, then,' he murmured. I am sure that had I not intervened, Mr. Luther would have found himself swinging a cane-knife this autumn.

5 May 1872. The Sabbath. Mr. Mercer plays the organ competently, but it is difficult for me to endure the humiliation of being removed from it.

6 May 1872. Great excitement as Mr. Philip Roddey and his wife arrived this afternoon. (*One of his wives*, Mr. Teague snickered to me under his breath.) She introduced herself as Carlotta but said that she is known to her friends as Fanny. She is quite pretty and younger than I had supposed, perhaps a little older than I, whilst Mr. Roddy appears to be quite a bit older than Mr. Teague. They could almost pass as grandfather and granddaughter. As the servants took our guests' things to their lodgings, the beautiful blue bedroom at the southeast corner of the house, Mr. Teague (and I) took the Roddeys on a tour of our home. I couldn't tell if they were merely bored and polite or genuinely impressed, but there were raised eyebrows and gentle smiles and nods as each remarkable staircase, alcove, bedroom, window, door casing, fireplace, and mantle was showed off. At last we reached the ballroom. Everything in it, floors, walls, ceilings, mantelpieces, all gleamed white, the result of industrious cleaning by the servants in preparation for the Roddeys visit. White sunlight beamed in through windows past green ferns on pedestals. 'The biggest in the South, of course,' Mr. Teague proclaimed modestly. 'Is that so?' Mr. Roddey said, and then he said to his young wife, 'Fanny, my lovely, would you mind pacing the length of this immense space with those lovely little strides of yours?' He is a big, barrel-chested, walrus of a man, and, when he speaks, it is even more so. I can almost fancy two immense tusks protruding from his upper lip, bobbing as he talks. Perhaps I should get the servants to fetch him a fish later. Fanny held her skirts a little off the floor, the buttons of her fashionable shoes marching up her ankles to the tufted white of her petticoats. She strutted across the ballroom from the near wall to the far wall, counting as she went. When she reached the far wall near the piano, she announced, 'Twenty-one paces. Why, Philip, I believe it may be the largest in the South!'

'Certainly it is!' Mr. Teague exclaimed as if he had been challenged. 'Why, only the best and biggest at Mount Teague!' This, of course, my little confidant, is the battle-cry, the war-whoop, the marching slogan here: Only the best and biggest at Mount Teague. It does not matter if it is a ballroom or a guest bedroom or a formal garden or a chamber-pot or a mousetrap. It is understood to be the best of its kind. Later, as the men visited in the adjacent parlour in a haze of cigar smoke, Fanny and I did likewise in the Ladies' Parlour, though with tea in the place of cigars, of course. The day had grown warm, and the windows were up, permitting a breeze to stir the curtains.

Mrs. Roddey (Fanny) said that she could tell from my accent that I am English. I replied yes and said that hers was certainly not that of the South. She said that she was born and raised in New Jersey, where her father had been a merchant. I asked how she came to meet Mr. Roddey, and she said they had met in New York, where Mr. Roddey was a cotton broker. The servant came to get the tea-things, and Fanny and I adjourned to stroll through the gardens, along the privet hedge, which has finally given up its assault on Mr. Teague and his nose and eyes. At the end of it, we came upon Polly Teague's Venus. Mrs. Roddey stopped abruptly and said, 'Oh, my. Don't you find the Venus—' She put her hand on one side of her mouth and said in a lower voice, 'Exhilarating?' I replied congenially that I find her quite lovely and well-done. 'No, I mean, you know, exciting,' she murmured, and then she whispered, '*Erotic.*' I said again that she is certainly beautiful, trying to avoid the path that Mrs. Roddey was offering. I took her arm and directed her away from the marble goddess, saying, 'Our gardener, Mr. Luther does an admirable job, I must say. Let me show you the oleander. It is just beginning to flower.'

She took my arm and stole one last look over her shoulder at Venus. She seemed to be recovering from a 'state.' 'Forgive my reverie, Mrs. Teague,' she said, 'but that is one thing about being married to an older, more experienced man. The conjugal rite is so very—' It was as if she could not go on, being delayed by the nude statue of Venus and thoughts of the conjugal rite with her husband. I realised that she would not let the matter pass until I engaged upon it, so I asked, 'He has no war wounds to slow him?' 'Oh, no. Not at all,' she said with a somewhat vacant tone and a faraway look over the cedar hedges. It was almost in the way of a boast. We discussed being married to older men, and I said that I found Mr. Teague to be a good provider and that we wanted for nothing here at Mount Teague. She said that money had never been an object for her, as she came into marriage with money after her father died when she was young, and that she had benefited from wise investments.

I asked her if she thought they might have children, and she said that Philip was against it, that he says that he couldn't share his love for her with anyone else. 'That is why he insists on wearing those little rubber items the druggist sells.' This, of course, my little confidant, rendered me speechless. She repeated a question she had asked me and at last, I found my tongue. 'What about you and Mr. Teague?' she asked. 'What about us?' I asked in returned. 'Are you looking forward to children?' she repeated. I told her that we have no children of our own yet, though we haven't been married very long, and that Mr. Teague makes no pretenses about wanting a boy, 'a male heir,' he says, as if he were the king. Fanny replied rather coyly that it shall certainly be an enjoyable pastime trying, won't it? The frankness of our conversation had again gone too far for me, and I remarked, 'Let me take you to see our ice plant, Mrs. Roddey,' for I believed she could use some cooling off about then.

And so I close, my little confidant, as it has certainly been a very long day. As I write and Mr. Teague snores, I believe I can hear the Roddeys in the midst of the conjugal rite. Perhaps Fanny is correct regarding Mr. Roddey's capabilities. As for me, I am delighted that I must only endure Mr. Teague's snoring.

7 May 1872. Dinner with the Roddeys last night, and there was talk of the late war. Mr. Roddey spoke of his exploits as a steamboat captain and then as a soldier who came up through the ranks to general. Mr. Teague seemed a little envious. When pushed into the conversation by Mr. Roddey, he demurred. Today, the Roddeys kept to bed until midmorning (quietly this time). After a late breakfast, Mr. Roddey and Mr. Teague went for a long horseback ride along the grounds to visit the barns, sheds, and fields where the sugarcane is coming up almost as high as a man's chest. Mrs. Roddey and I followed in a carriage, the white one trimmed in gold pulled by the pair of dappled mares. We could see just over the verdant, leafy tops of the sugarcane as we drove along the lanes that transect it, as if we were Israelites traveling through the parting of the Green Sea. Mrs. Roddey was speaking, and I admit to not listening fully as she rambled. I was imagining walking over the sea of green like our Saviour walking on the Sea of Galilee. Suddenly, Mrs. Roddy remarked in a tone over the creak of the carriage and the clop of hooves and jangle of the traces. Our driver cast a glance over his shoulder, and his mouth wrinkled as he looked away. 'Do you and Mr. Teague engage in the conjugal rite frequently?' she had asked. 'Mrs. Roddey!' I exclaimed, but with a little effort, I was able to mitigate my shock with a smile.

'You said that Mr. Teague would like a son, didn't you?' she asked. 'Yes,' I said, 'but he has only daughters, and they are wonderful children. Perhaps God shall grant us a son.' Then I told her that my mother died in childbirth and, admittedly, the whole idea of it scared me. She said that she shared my sentiments and that she wanted nothing to do with such things as childbirth, and that is why she is happy that Mr. Roddey wears those things the druggist sells. Our husbands rode well ahead of us, mine pointing to things proudly and hers looking politely to where he pointed, then both of them trotting away. Mr. Teague invariably paced ahead of Mr. Roddey, only to turn his horse to wait for his guest to catch up. I tried to imagine Mr. Roddey putting one of those things the druggist sells on himself and could not do it without a shiver.

We spent the whole of the afternoon in this manner, until our conversation waned. The swaying of the carriage rocked us gently, and Mrs. Roddey and I fell into naps on opposite sides of the seat in the shade of the carriage bonnet, to the clop of the hooves of the mares and the tick-tick of our driver's encouragement of them. Whilst I slept, I had a dream that Mount Teague was ancient Rome and Mr. Teague was the Caesar. That is all I remember of it. I can only imagine what Mrs. Roddy was dreaming of. When I awoke, we were back at the big house. As I prepared for our dinner tonight, the mattress in our guests' chambers wheezed rhythmically. Certainly the whole house, servants and all, could hear their exertions. I leave you now, my little confidant, as guests are beginning to arrive.

8 May 1872. A quite volatile event occurred last night at our ball, which is normally proceeded with a finely prepared dinner. We stood at the door as our guests arrived, announced by the servant in a loud voice, even though we were right at hand and could see who entered. It is surely part of a spectacle done for form's sake. Colonel Pugh, Judge Anderson and his wife, Captain Someone (I did not hear, as I was engaged in conversation with several of the women at this time). At last, a familiar face from the city appeared. 'Charlie! Mrs. Howard!' Mr. Teague exclaimed before the servant could announce them. My husband took my hand and pulled me from the conversation I was having with Mrs. Pugh. 'Sam, Mrs. Teague,' Mr. Howard said with a nod. Hearty handshakes for the men, kisses on the cheek for the women. My husband asked where the Morrises were, and Mr. Howard answered that they had remained in the city and that Mrs. Morris was convalescing from the birth of a child a few weeks prior. Mr. Teague did not ask how Mrs. Morris was doing. He only asked if it were a boy or a girl. 'Why, another boy!' Mr. Howard murmured through his cigar and into the flame that Mr. Teague offered as a light. Mr. Teague grunted rather flatly as if his mood had suddenly soured. Recovering countenance a little, he said tersely, with a wiry, pushed-out smile, 'Then I suppose congratulations are in order.' As he took Mrs. Roddey's hand and bowed to receive her introduction, Mr. Howard said that he would certainly pass them along when he returned to the city. When a sufficient number of guests had arrived, we all gathered in the ballroom as refreshments of the alcoholic persuasion were served. Someone proposed a toast to Governor Warmoth, and then someone proposed a toast to President Grant. 'Grant,' Mr. Teague snorted, 'Son of a *b*— out to have his neck stretched.' One of the men said, 'surely you mean in effigy,' to which my husband replied, 'Why go all the way to this Effigy place? I say we the perform the service wherever it would be most expeditious.' There was laughter at what was perceived as a joke, though it appeared that Mr. Teague did not appreciate his own humour, as he failed to laugh. After the laughter subsided, one of the men removed to the piano and with one finger played the bugle calls from the old army, and the men took turns saying the message each one sent. When it came Mr. Teague's turn to guess, he seemed lost and offered the excuse that he was tone-deaf, something I never knew about him. One of the men asked, 'How did you ever know the call, sir?' Mr. Teague replied that his aide informed him.

Meanwhile, Mrs. Roddey and I made the rounds, and I introduced her to the wives and daughters that I knew. The conversation of men rumbled in the gentlemen's parlour amid the atmosphere of cigar smoke, which competed with the smell of the delightful repast which was being prepared and the sounds of the long table that was being set. Dinner was announced, and everyone took their places. The table had been ably and immaculately set, complete with centerpieces made of greenery and magnolia blossoms, the first of the year.

And then it happened, quite as suddenly as the eruption that consumed Pompeii. Sometime between the second and third courses, an unpleasant exchange occurred between my husband and our guest

General Roddey. The discussion had revolved, as it frequently does here, to military matters and specifically heroic exploits in the late war. One would think that the South was on the winning side. It is an old subject and a frequent one. Mr. Roddey asked my husband, 'Mr. Teague, you told me that you were an officer in the Army of the Tennessee. Do you ever hear from General Deshler?'

'Why, yes,' Mr. Teague said amiably, 'I received a letter not long ago.' 'Did you?' Mr. Roddey replied, 'That is truly remarkable, as he was killed at Chickamauga.' The guests nearest them abandoned their conversations. Teague took a slow sip from his wine glass and stared over it at Roddey who then asked him, 'What was the mascot of the 43rd Mississippi? This should be easy, sir.' Mr. Teague looked around nervously as if one of us could tell him. All other conversations had stopped, and all eyes were on Mr. Teague and Mr. Roddey. 'Why it was a, uh, racoon, was it not?' Mr. Teague fairly mumbled. 'A camel,' Roddey corrected him flatly. 'It was a camel, sir.' 'Yes, Sam,' Mr. Howard interceded, 'you remember, don't you?' 'Well, that was many years ago,' Mr. Teague protested, 'And my memory is not what it once was.' 'Perhaps your memory is poor,' General Roddey said, as he took a sip from the crystal goblet and set it down as he looked squarely at my husband. 'Or perhaps you weren't even there.' Mr. Teague rose from his seat and threw his knife and fork down. They bounced off the tablecloth and made a loud ring on a decanter of port. The silence begged for the tinkling of silverware and murmur of the conversation of our guests, but there was none. Instead all gazes were on General Roddey and Mr. Teague. Mr. Teague seemed to be looking through Roddey's eyes and examining the back of the man's skull. I wanted to slip under the table and slink out of the room like a cat. My husband growled, 'I was not aware that my service to our late country was any business of yours, Mr. Roddey. But your bigamy and your adulterous marriage—why, I will make it my business, sir. And it will be the business of every newspaper in Christendom!'

Mr. Roddey's face contorted in anger. He looked every bit the old warrior that he is said to be. 'Really, sir, I shall not bear this insult! Nor shall my wife!' he said as he backed away from the table with a loud scrape of his chair. He threw his napkin down on the floor. For a moment, I thought it might devolve into a fistfight, but Mr. Roddey seemed to talk himself out of it and said, 'Have someone fetch our carriage.' As he assisted Mrs. Roddey out of her chair, he thundered, 'I will not submit to this sort of abuse, and I certainly won't submit my dear wife to it!' Her burgundy skirts rustled after her as she stormed out of the dining room with her husband.

'This wife or the one you left behind in Alabama, sir?"' Mr. Teague called to them, smelling blood, perhaps, and forgetting the presence of his other guests, who were in hushed astonishment at this argument occurring in the midst of polite society. He limped after them, his lurching stride a receding series of bass notes on the floor, and we heard him call out the front door as the Roddeys alighted hurriedly into their carriage. 'Really, Teague, tread lightly and stick to your own business!' Roddey called up to the house as he and his wife were leaving. Mr. Teague, still with his napkin in his shirt front, called back to them, and, though they were on the path outside in front of the house, their voices were raised so that all could easily here them inside. 'I will make it my business, I will make it so, Roddey, and Mrs. Roddey, one of many! You may count on it! What I say, I mean to do. Every newspaper in Christendom, sir! For a bigamist, there is not a hell hot enough!'

As the carriage jangled away into the distance emitting the hollow notes of horse hooves, Mr. Teague limped back to the silent table. His chest rose and fell a little as he tried to compose himself. There was some talk of how in former days, this would have been an issue settled by dueling. Indeed, some of the older men mentioned it, but it otherwise received no serious consideration and was dismissed. Instead, someone told a joke to ease the situation, the old one about the Bible being against bigamy as it clearly states that 'no man can serve two masters.' There was relieved laughter and gradually the evening fell into a more comfortable manner, though an undercurrent still swirled. Servants came and removed the Roddeys' place settings as if this type of situation had happened for other guests in the past and that there was a protocol for it. After dinner, dancing was enjoyed, as if nothing had occurred. Whilst Mr. Teague and I danced, I asked him in a low voice, 'Really, Mr. Teague, was that called for?' At my question, there was the faintest look of betrayal on his face, and then he answered, 'He questioned my service to our dearly departed country, which was his mistake. You see, I have contacts who can find things out. One of them found out the truth on Roddey: he abandoned a wife in Alabama and took up with another, this Fanny.'

Surely, then, it is only a matter of time before Polly Teague is apprehended, hopefully before she accrues any more debt in our name. I did not mention this to my husband, fearing that Mount Vesuvius might erupt again.

9 May 1872. The guests have all departed, and the house is quiet again. The sugarcane is left to grow in the gathering heat, and the girls are allowed the run of the house again after being sequestered upstairs. And again, the act, the Marital Rite, as it is called in *Advice to a New Wife.* And again, if I am to be honest, I derive no pleasure from it, as it says I should and as Mrs. Roddey professes. I can only endure it. I know it is an old story, but bear with me, my little confidant, as I have no one else to tell.

11 May 1872. Lucy is ill. I am terrified that it is cholera, as took poor Papa, and I sit up with her. Mr. Teague came and wanted to know when I was coming to bed. When I said that I was going to sit up with Lucy, he said that we keep servants for such instances. Still, I insist on sitting up with the poor girl, as she is miserable, just as Mama and Papa sat up so many nights at my sick bed.

12 May 1872. Lucy was no better this morning, and I sent for Dr. McKnight. He came straightaway from church in his gig with the jet black mare and came at once to her room. He was of the certain opinion that this is a passing illness. By this evening, I see that he was quite in the right, and she has been able to take tea and toast and is more herself.

15 May 1872. Lucy is again completely herself, and the girls and I adjourn for fishing. We saw a snake winding across the bayou, and she squealed. I told her that it is just one of the Creator's creatures and that my Papa said that even the Garden of Eden had a snake in it. Of course, my little confidant, after six months of marriage to Mr. Teague, I can see how it would be so. The girls and I returned to Mount Teague with a pail of fish and clean hands. Our servants attended to all.

18 May 1872. A bill arrived in the mail today, forwarded through the Argus Detective Agency at the address on St. Charles in the city. Last month a Mrs. Samuel Teague incurred a bill of $135.78 at the Palmer House Hotel in Chicago. Included in the bill are several seven-course meals, bottles of champagne, and a suite overlooking Lake Michigan. Of course, it is not I, but the former Mrs. Teague. After I read it to him, I asked my husband if we are obligated for it, as I do not know of the laws of divorce in this country. Or any country, really. He said, 'I could easily pay it, but, on principle, I shall not! Not one cent of it!,' and he had me compose a note to that effect. He said that he shall post it later when he goes to the commissary, wherein is kept the post office of this place.

22 May 1872. The American Congress has passed an Act granting amnesty to those who took up arms for the old Confederacy. Those who betrayed the United States can again vote in its elections. Now the scheming may begin for the elections in November.

29 May 1872. A letter from Fanny Roddey arrived today. Upon leaving Mount Teague, they were guests of Mr. Randolph at Nottaway on the river above Donaldsonville. Mr. Roddey wishes to inform Mr. Teague that the ballroom there measures twenty-four of his wife's 'lovely strides' and is therefore bigger by three. Mr. Teague is furious and cursing rains down like hailstones. As a crescendo, he smashed a tumbler to the floor. And I confess to you, my little confidant that it is a small undertaking for me to suppress an urge to smile.

2 June 1872. The hens of St. Margaret's Church grow impatient in setting a match for Rev. Givens. Every visiting niece, young widow, and granddaughter coming of marriageable age is tried and each without success. Henry bears each overture with the patience of Job. His secret I keep to my heart and to you, my little confidant, convinced of its truth. Why does the Creator make some of us so?

7 June 1872. The garden planted by Mr. Luther now divulges its abundance, copious amounts of peas, beans, tomatoes, and other eatables. The girls and I enjoyed watermelon cooled in the Ice House.

9 June 1872. Fans fluttered in the congregation today like a flock of birds taking wing. Mr. Mercer sweated profusely, as he is from some northern place (Wisconsin, I think) and unaccustomed to the heat. If so, he is certainly in for a long summer.

14 June 1872. The weather was uncomfortably hot today, even in the shaded galleries of the porch, and I adjourned to the parlour of the Ice House and the pleasant coolness that it affords. I must confess, I fell into a nap on the settee in the alcove. I woke briefly to hear someone in the parlour with me. I raised an eye to see Mr. Teague open a door which I did not know existed, as it is blended in to seem a wall. I feigned sleep until he was done with his errand, 'waking' just as he slipped two small keys into the watchpocket of his waistcoat. 'Well, husband,' I said sleepily, 'I was napping on the settee here.' He said, yes, that I was like sleepy beauty, and I supposed he meant *sleeping* beauty, the fairy tale woman who woke on the kiss of the prince. I told him that was very kind of him, though he says kind things much less frequently now that we are married. He turned and eased through the door. When he left, I examined the dimensions of the building and concluded that there is a space in the middle of it that is not part of the room with the ice generating machinery and not part of the parlour which adjoins it. Along the wall I found a small latch, hidden behind the molding. When one presses it, a portion of the wall gives way and opens into a door. And behind this door sitting in the darkness is a safe, a black block of iron made by the Barnes and Burke Company of Pittsburgh, with openings for two keys to be used simultaneously. The keys that Mr. Teague put in his pocket must go to it.

16 June 1872. The Sabbath. I believe Mr. Mercer would play in shirtsleeves if it were allowed, or at least he would consider it.

19 June 1872. In the watchpocket of Mr. Teague's waistcoat I found keys that I guessed were to the safe. Knowing that Mr. Teague had gone into Donaldsonville on business, I left the girls sleeping and moved like a thief. I took the keys to the Ice Parlour and pressed the latch. It was as I surmised, the keys fit the locks. In Mr. Barnes and Burke's safe, there was a great deal of money, though I didn't count it. Hearing someone approach on the path that leads up to the Ice Parlour, I quickly arranged things as I found them, but not before I noticed a document that appears to be an exemption from military service in the Confederate Army for one who owned a sufficient number of slaves. At the very bottom are the signatures of the three witnesses and what are presumably my husband's initials, a backward S and a big-hatted T. Mr. Roddey was certainly in the right about my husband. Mr. Teague did not go off to war with the Army of the Tennessee or any other army. In a place where the honour of serving in the late war is so necessary for a man's standing, a document like this one would ruin his name. And so, I placed it back inside for safe-keeping (yes, a pun, my little confidant) and shut the latch to the secret room. The person was Mr. Luther, who was trimming 'shooters' from the crape myrtles. I clutched the keys in one hand and waved good morning to him with the other.

Sammy, 1982

Sammy took the yellowed paper from the oak chest and examined it more closely. There were the initials and the three signatures, only one legible, that of Judge Anderson.

THE CONFEDERATE STATES OF AMERICA

Samuel M. Teague **of** ***St. Matthew*** **County, of the State of** ***Louisiana***, **has applied for exemption of** ***himself*** **as a** ***farmer*** **under the 2d clause of the fourth article of the Tenth Section of the Act of Congress, approved 17th February, 1864, entitled, "An act to organize forces to serve during the war," there being on the farm or plantation of said** ***Samuel M. Teague*** **for which the exemption is sought,** ***one-hundred seventy-eight*** **able-bodied slaves between the ages of sixteen and fifty, within the meaning of said act; and which application is to be granted under the satisfactory execution of this Bond.**

All the lore of gallantry and duty to country, though a defunct one. All the tales of a dashing man in gray atop a muscular horse, a man pointing to a red-crossed banner flapping in air scented with bitter smoke, stirring men to rally under it and attack. All those legends of battle wounds gained at the hand of an adversary. All that high-minded nonsense he had been reverently taught as a boy and bragged of to his peers, all of it came crashing to an end, halted by a single piece of paper.

His great-grandfather had fought, but not in the war. He had fought to avoid it. Sammy took the paper and let it fall in the white plastic bucket in the corner, and then he sat in the central hallway under the scar-less portrait of the man painted in military trappings. And he knew how the Apostle Paul must have felt when the scales fell from his eyes.

Sammy palmed the beard on his own face and looked straight into the stern gaze of old Sam Teague, meeting it squarely. At last, he got up and went out to the shed and looked at the safe that had given up the secrets that were now making sense. Teeter wasn't there, but he had been there. The gate of a cane wagon had been taken down but not put back together. Sammy wasn't worried. Yet. After all, last year, Teeter had been gone for a week and a half before he came back, hungover and apologetic, just in time to off-barr the cane. He'd give him a few more days.

Sammy went back up to the house and his study, pausing to glare at the old paterfamilias on the wall, the man who was painted in nothing more than a costume.

Alice 1872

21 June 1872. A man with a debt to the Mount Teague commissary was apprehended at Donaldsonville trying to board a steamer to evade it. He was brought to Mr. Teague and me, though I was only in Mr. Teague's study at his insistence. The man stood before us as if we were the king and queen of this place. He gave me a dispirited glance, and I recognized him as a field hand, one of the galley slaves of this green-leafy ship, forever pulling, pulling, pulling, and going nowhere. Mr. Teague lit a cigar and puffed on it. After a while of observing the man, something I believe Mr. Teague thoroughly enjoyed, he said, 'Thou shall not steal. Why, it is written in the Bible. In the old days I would have you whipped. You know that, don't you?' The man said, 'yassuh,' and lowered his head and his voice, as if he expected to be whipped anyway, old days or not. And perhaps it would have happened, had I not interceded. I said, 'It is also written in the Bible that we are to forgive seventy times seven, dear husband.' Mr. Teague muttered through his cigar and its smoke, 'Foolishness, the world does not function thusly.' The man stood in the hallway with his head bowed. The tall clock ticked away, as if in thought on what should be done with him, a sort of Pontius Pilate of clocks. Mr. Teague continued to berate the man, saying, 'You have over a hundred dollars of commissary debt to me that you're trying to elude. Nothing escapes me. I always find out. Just like that Roddey feller. In the end I will most certainly find out. If the answer is on this earth, I will find it out.' In the end, perhaps because of a sweet glance to my husband, the man was released, though with his debt held fast against him and strict instructions to pay it. The man left with profuse, tearful thanks, to me and to Mr. Teague. And so, as my husband naps, I am off to the Ice Parlour and the secret room and its miraculous safe, and then the commissary to pay the poor man's debt, though I shall not tell my husband. As I go, I cannot help but ponder how Polly Teague is not found and held accountable for her debts, if Mr. Teague's influence is so far-reaching.

26 June 1872. Today the girls and I read in the Ice Parlour. I have completed Mr. Twain's new book, *The Innocents Abroad.*

30 June 1872. The Sabbath. The congregation thins as the populace begins to 'clear out' for the summer. I am quite certain that our northern organist would play in his underclothes if allowed and happily endure the public censure. He suffers so!

4 July 1872. Quite a holiday for the northern men who are garrisoned here. They drink beer and sing Yankee Doodle and other patriotic airs and fire their rifles to the sky. The sounds of it all reach Mount Teague through the breeze-less air.

6 July 1872. Preparations are made for an extended visit to the mountains again. Dresses, shoes, petticoats, bonnets, nightgowns, all are laid aside, and Lucy lays aside clothes for her doll, her beloved Penny. The clothes of this household are packed into great trunks like Napoleon planning for Moscow. This time I shall go as Mrs. Teague and not as Miss Lamb. I am hesitant to leave Henry behind, as he suffers greatly from anxiety. Perhaps it is the impending fever season, perhaps it is something else, I cannot say. I now see him as more of a sibling, a brother, and realise that he has always seen me as a sister. Filial love must suffice for me, as there can be no romantic love now. Tomorrow we shall bid adieu to Mount Teague and the vivid blossoms of the myrtles. When we return, they shall have lost their brilliant colours and faded.

8 July 1872. After a train ride in from Donaldsonville, we disembarked from the ferry across the river and into the city. Crowds of well-dressed people are everywhere, accompanied by trunks like ours and boarding trains and steamers on their way to quitting the city for the next few months. New Orleans seems to brace itself for the fever as if it might be an insult or a slap. Mr. Teague and the girls and I rode in the carriage Mr. Howard had sent for us, sheltered from the sweltering sun under the canopy as we clopped along, our carriage's horse easily outpacing the bobtail mules that stagger in front of the streetcars and their burden of passengers. From under summer bonnets of blue-and-white toile, the girls quietly studied the great buildings that sat drowsily under the boughs of the live oaks. The forward motion spurred a breeze that was welcome in cutting the heat. The afternoon clouds gathered from the steam of the town and the lake and the river, and poised overhead for just the precise time to fall back to earth again.

Mr. Howard greeted us on the front porch of his elegant home on St. Charles next to City Hall. The address seemed familiar to me, as if I had seen it before, but Mrs. Howard engaged me in conversation before I could think long upon it. She is a pleasant woman whose first name is Flora. In the gentlemen's parlour I overheard Mr. Howard tell my husband, 'Well, Sam, they have begun burying at the old Metairie Jockey Club.' Mr. Teague said that he knew that Mr. Howard would, 'get on top of them,' or something like that, and they clinked glasses and fell into a hearty snicker over their snifters, the crystal glittering in the looking glass between the two parlours. The sky grumbled outside, and the trees in the side-yard swayed in the draft of an afternoon shower. Mr. Teague raised his glass in another toast, this time to the 'good news' that he had persuaded the Federal commander to quit St. Matthew, though he was afraid the neighbouring parishes, Ascension and St. Martin and Terrebonne would still be under 'Yankee tyranny.' Mr. Howard said that was certainly something and perhaps when we return from the mountains, St. Matthew will be done with them. This must certainly be the fruit of the letters I have written, or rather, transcribed for Mr. Teague. Mrs. Howard (Flora) directed me back to our conversation with a question. I confess I didn't hear it, for I had been listening to the men. She repeated that her boys would like to hear me play an air or two on the piano and would I favour them with one. I happily obliged on the beautiful Steinway in the music room, which was right off the parlour. The Howard boys kept glancing at Jenny and, I suppose, at me. The oldest of the boys is around fifteen or so, about Jenny's age and just a few years younger than I. In between songs, I could not help but hear the men in the adjoining room. It seemed as though they had increased their volume so that I could hear them, though I am not certain of it. Nevertheless, I pretended to shuffle through sheet music while I tuned my ears to them and their conversation. The Howard boys had quickly fallen under the spell of Jenny and adjourned to the front porch with her and her sisters, and Mrs. Howard and I found ourselves alone in the music room.

In the gentlemen's parlour, Mr. Howard said, 'There's only this, Sam, a bill from Kansas City, from your wife—' He paused to correct himself. '—from your ex-wife, the *former* Mrs. Teague.' Mr. Teague patted his chest pocket and asked Mr. Howard to read it, as he had forgotten his glasses. Mr. Howard read that the former Mrs. Teague had accrued a debt there as well, at a dress shop, a hotel, at fancy restaurant. Mr. Howard remarked, 'Same sort of business, Sam, her *modus operandi*, run up a bill on your account and then abscond.' Mr. Teague grunted and asked Mr. Howard if he would be so kind as to take a letter and that he needed to put this matter to rest. In the looking glass, I could see Mr. Howard sit at this desk in the adjoining room and pull a blank sheet of paper from a slot and dip a pen into an inkwell. '"*Dear Sirs*' Mr. Teague began loudly, as if speaking to the entire house, pursing his lips in a thoughtful pause, '*Dear Sirs, The woman you refer to as having incurred these charges can longer claim the title of Mrs. Samuel Teague, as a divorce decree has been issued by Judge R. T. Anderson of St. Matthew Parish, Louisiana as of October 1871. Any debts claimed against me on her behalf are solely her responsibility. I refer you to my agents in New Orleans, Mr. Howard and Mr. Morris, if this does not settle the matter, signed, respectfully, Samuel M. Teague.*' Mr. Howard's reflection signed it for him.

'Mrs. Teague? Alice?' Mrs. Howard lightly touched my knee to get my attention. 'I was just telling you that Mr. Howard and the children and I are going to England for the season.' She said it as if it were the opera season or the racing season. 'It is fortunate for us that our husbands' business venture allows us the freedom to remove to Europe or the mountains,' she said. 'Yes, that is very fortunate indeed,' I said in a voice that bordered on a stammer, 'England should be quite lovely this time of year.' She said that Mr. Howard has arranged a little country house in the

Cotswolds. She went on to describe the 'little country house,' which, as she told it, sounded more and more like a manor house. I was thinking of Polly Teague, my fellow Mrs. Teague, though it is now I who wear the crown, and 'heavy is the head that wears the crown,' as Shakespeare said. As we left, I noticed the address over the door. There is something familiar about it. Now that we are on the train, I shall write it here for safekeeping, to ponder later.

121 St. Charles Avenue.

The Howards' chief house servant, an intensely black woman called 'Old Mama,' readies the house for its impending vacancy. She shall not be going to England with the Howards, but rather shall remain here in the city and hope for the best. 'Stay and pray,' it is called. And now, in the aftermath of the marital rite, I place you in my trunk for safekeeping. Mr. Teague seemed to be asserting himself this night. I was afraid the Howards and my girls would hear him. I am quite sore and have asked Old Mama to fetch some cold cloths. It shall be a long train ride tomorrow.

Sammy, 1982

Sammy woke from an after-supper nap and a ragged, mismatched dream, a dream so deep that for a moment he didn't know where he was. Night was falling, concealing the approach of the rain that the news had promised, and the last of the day's light asserted itself on him, seeping through the window of his study and onto the Campeche chair in which he had fallen asleep. Thunder churned in the west. He put the diary down under the lamp light and went outside. Twilight was past now, and night was falling with the rise of stars that were rapidly being obscured by the clouds that were pushing in. Among them both, the clattering, staccato thump of a helicopter passed overhead, workers coming in from the rig. The night swallowed the helicopter and the men it was carrying away.

Sammy came down off the back porch and walked out to the metal barn. Light fell through the big metal bay door on something Teeter had been taking apart, and it appeared that he had gotten distracted and left the thing disassembled. Sammy put his head in the barn and called out into the fluorescence, and his voice echoed among the green-and-gold cane harvesters sleeping in the humming depths of the building.

"Teeter?"

There was no answer, only the reverberation of the name off the cold corrugated metal walls and concrete slab. *Must've gone home to eat dinner with Miss Vessy*, Sammy thought. He rounded the back of the shed to see if Teeter was back there, and he came across what was left of the old ice barn, the ancient machinery of the ice plant itself that had been pulled out and salvaged before it was burned. He calmly examined it by the yellow light of the utility pole. It was the carcass of the monster that had once lurked in the shadows of the old barn, now reduced to mere iron pipes and flanges and bolts.

He inspected it, trying to figure out what had connected to what, a puzzle of valves and pipes, like some whimsical musical instrument, a series of turns and twists and straight sections, made from cast iron and held together by bolts and plates. He thought of the noise it might make, a deep-throated bellow like the organ at St. Margaret's. But a wren had already made her nest in the open mouth of one of them, and she chirped a hollow note from inside it. It was like a lion opening his toothy mouth but only squeaking. Sammy shook his head and snorted and laughed silently. Another helicopter flew overhead with a harsh stutter, barely visible among red and white flashing pinpoints as it sped north. Sammy looked up. Probably carrying workers home from the rigs offshore, maybe taking one of them to the hospital in Baton Rouge.

Over across the yard, the shadows of more grass were beginning to emerge in isolated clumps from the blackened earth where the ice barn had been. The winter rains had settled the soil and left an indention where the safe had come to rest in the aftermath of the fire. Sammy paced off the ground trying to remember the dimensions of the old ice barn, which he now knew once contained a sitting room called the ice parlour. Across the lawn and inside the house, the telephone rang, and Betsy's voice answered, small in the distance as she spoke a short while in French and then called through the screen door.

"Sammy, Boo, it's Miss Vessy."

Sammy trotted to the house and up the stairs. Betsy handed him the phone and looked into his face as he talked to Miss Vessy.

Mist' Teague, is Martin over deh? Ain' come home, no.

"Ma'am?"

My boy, Martin Blanchard. Teeter.

So that was Teeter's real name. He knew it wasn't Teeter because *M. J. Blanchard* was the name on the paycheck that Sammy signed every two weeks. But he never knew what the initials stood for. Sammy looked out the window to the metal barn.

"No, ma'am. He's not here."

Mais, you seen him?

"No ma'am. When did you see him last?"

Went down to Houma. Been two or tree days.

"Looks like he's been working out here, but I can't remember when I saw him last. Let me go look for him."

Sammy hung up and grabbed his jacket. The air was thick and cool, and wind was moving through the oaks and the cypresses. He thought of looking in the bars scattered around this part of St. Matthew, beginning with Tatootsy's, but, as he was pulling out, he spotted a pinpoint of light out by the Twelve Arpent Canal. He changed the truck into drive and drove out along the back paths between cane rows. Another few months and he would not have been able to see out that way.

It was beginning to sprinkle as Sammy got out of his truck. The door to Teeter's truck was open and the radio was on, KSMB from Lafayette playing Hall & Oates, "I Can't Go for That." On the front seat was a syringe and an old T shirt that had been wound up into a thick cord. There was a photograph of Teeter and two other men, and, in it, Teeter's helmet had a drawing of the rear end view of a raccoon with a lifted tail, the animal looking back with a devilish smile. One of his companions had the name 'Sparky' with lightning bolts, and one had no helmet, but had *Drumm* written over his shirt pocket. They all smiled with sweaty heads and cigarettes on their lips and dense jungle behind them. Sammy turned off the ignition, and Teeter's truck went silent as, on the radio, Hall & Oates sang a final, *no can do.* He looked out into the darkness. The rain was beginning to beat hard, on the top of the cab of Teeter's truck and the hood and the earth and the emerging cane. Along the bank of the canal under a tree, Sammy saw a slumping figure, and he ran to it.

Teeter was slouched back against a cypress knee. His eyes rolled around in his head, and Sammy patted Teeter's cheek, and the eyes stopped rolling and focused.

"Hey bawsman. Keep your head down. You know they's gooks 'round here?"

"Teeter. Your mama's worried about you."

"My mama," Teeter said blankly.

"Yeah, Teeter. She's worried."

"Tell her I jus' came out here to get away from them ghosts, bawsman." He flicked his hand as he referred to the ghosts. "Sparky, Drummer, all them, man. Tired a livin' wit' ghosts. Ready to pass on true to they world. Evvabody gotta leave this world sometime, right? Why not now, bawsman? I'm so tired, me. So tired a them ghosts. Won't leave me alone. They jus' won't leave me alone."

And he started crying, a gnarled, shuddering cry, an awkward expression of a festering emotion.

"So tired, bawsman, so tired."

"Come on, man," Sammy said as he cradled Teeter to his neck, just like he would do for any of his own children, like he had done for their bad dreams, trying to comfort a nameless, gnawing sensation. "Come on, man, it's all right."

The rain fell hard on the fields and the earth and the canal and the trees that lined it, and on the two men. One holding the other in a dense, jungle rain, trying to hold in his despair. Sammy lifted Teeter and carried the man and his secret burden back to his truck. Off in the distance was Mount Teague. He could never remember seeing it from this vantage point and at this time of night. The light on the utility pole cast a strange glow in the rain, and the metal shed cast a strange shadow almost as if the ballroom had been recreated exactly where he had been told as a boy it had once stood.

They drove to the emergency room in Thibodaux. Sammy had to keep patting Teeter's face or blow the horn or raise and lower the volume of the radio to keep Teeter from following the ghosts into another world. Teeter's head would roll back, and Sammy would grow frantic and look quickly from the road and yell, "Hey! Hey! Hey!" and Teeter's eyes would roll forward. In Thibodaux, he left his truck running and ran around to the passenger side and lifted Teeter over his shoulder and carried him into the bright lights of the Emergency Room. He put Teeter gently down on the gurney, and it was wheeled back to another room that attracted a flurry of nurses and doctors.

He called Miss Vessy from the pay phone and waited in the waiting room, sitting on the edge of one of the featureless plastic chairs with months-old magazines on side-tables and prints of bayou scenes on the walls. An hour later, Betsy arrived with her, and the three of them waited as a television played infomercials to the sterile space. At one point, an old woman was brought in by paramedics. Her expression was dazed, her gray hair wild, her face sagging into a transparent oxygen mask. Pneumatic doors opened, and she disappeared into the back. And the infomercials prattled optimistically.

Black night stewed beyond the windows as the overhead pager called for doctors to report here or nurses to report there. Miss Vessy waited with her arms crossed watching the television where a man talked excitedly as he effortlessly sliced tomatoes. One of her hands clutched a set of plastic Rosary beads that dangled onto her hip. Betsy had gone to use the payphone to check on Mr. Teague, who was watching the children with Quint.

"You ain' as bad as ev'body say," Miss Vessy grudgingly admitted.

Before Sammy could say anything, the voice overhead called for the family of Martin Blanchard. It was almost two in the morning. Sammy and Betsy and Miss Vessy rose and met a doctor in scrubs.

"Are you his brother?" the doctor asked.

"His friend," Sammy said.

"Well, you saved his life. He had enough smack in him, heroin, that is, to put down an elephant," the doctor said. "Got him stable, for now. We're gonna send him by ambulance to the VA in New Orleans. He's got a long road ahead of him."

Teeter was loaded into an ambulance with the Acadian flag on it. He looked like the shell of someone, the skin a locust might shed and fly away from. Miss Vessy kissed her boy on his unknowing cheek, and his IV bag was handed up into the back of the ambulance, and he was slid in. Miss Vessy cried, and Sammy and Betsy embraced her. But as the doors began to close, Miss Vessy got into the back of the ambulance, telling the attendants, "Ain' goin' wittout my boy, no." They didn't resist and let her inside. Before the doors of the ambulance closed for good, she gave Betsy her house key and asked her to go and get her things.

"And get my nightgown and robe," Miss Vessy said, "and t'ree or four pair a drawers, sha."

The doors closed, and the ambulance lights flickered red and blue into the black of the Louisiana night. Sammy followed Betsy home to get his own things, a change of clothes, his toiletries. And Alice Teague's diary.

Alice 1872

17 July 1872. You have ridden in the baggage car, haven't you, my little confidant? Hidden like a stowaway. Well, then, I must acquaint you with the current state of affairs. We have arrived at White Sulphur Springs to spend the remainder of the summer and the beginning of autumn. Mr. Teague says that when we return, it shall about be time to cut the cane.

The girls alighted from the carriage from the train station almost before it stopped, pulling me by the hand and looking about the grounds and the hotel like it was an enchanted place. It is quite as beautiful as I remember it from last year, nestled into a verdant valley ringed by cottages hidden under the trees that grow on the slopes. There is a springhouse wherein one might take the waters for rheumatism and similar agues and ailments. But the centerpiece here is the Grand Central Hotel, referred to by most as the 'Old White.' An attendant in black-and-red livery opened the immense front door for us, which gave way to a lobby with a forest of immense columns and trimmed in elaborate woodwork and filled with the smell of flowers and the hum of conversation. We Teagues approached the exquisite front desk where a clerk greeted us with a 'Good to see you again, Mr. Teague.' Then the clerk made an entry into the ledger and turned it round to have Mr. Teague sign. Just then, Jenny and the girls saw the grand piano across the lobby and pulled me by the hand to look at it. As I left, there was a certain, stricken look on my husband's face. And when I returned, on the line by his name, he had signed his two clumsy initials, a backwards S and a big-hatted T. Now I am almost sure of it. My husband cannot read or write beyond these two misshapen letters.

18 July 1872. There is great talk here of an accident on the railroad west of this place which occurred only a day or two prior to our arrival. A bridge collapsed and several were killed, all of them workmen. Perhaps this was the cause of our delay in arriving, though that is a small matter compared to the anguish of the families of the victims.

22 July 1872. A most lovely day touring the grounds here by carriage. The mountains were stippled green up to the tops of their ridges, and the sunlight that played upon them displayed every deep shade of it, all set beneath an intensely blue summer sky. As we returned to the stables at the hotel, Mr. Teague sent the girls under the care of Jenny to get sweets in the hotel parlour. I knew what he had in mind, so as we returned to our cottage (a gross understatement, as they are grander than most homes in St. Matthew), I claimed to be on my monthly issue. Mr. Teague's roving hands slowed and fell from my thighs and breasts. 'Yes,' he sighed in defeat. I, who have always told the truth and been brought up to do so, fall so easily into this sin. I fail not myself, but the loving God who made me and the dutiful parents who raised me to follow His commandments.

25 July 1872. Rain visits us this day, a dense, cool, mountain rain, much like the Himalayan rains of Darjeeling. We, the Teague family, enjoyed ourselves in the parlour of the 'Old White,' before its cheerful fire. I was enticed to play for those gathered against the elements, and a woman from Baltimore sang some of the popular songs of the day to my accompaniment. It was all quite pleasant and a delightful manner to spend a rainy afternoon.

2 August 1872. A sunny day again today, and the girls and I spent it in the fresh air playing at croquet on the lawn that is prepared for that purpose. When it is Lucy's turn to strike the ball, one of us must hold Penny for her. Judging by how Lucy cares for her doll, I believe she shall make a fine little mother one day. She and the doll are inseparable.

4 August 1872. We worshipped at St. Thomas' Church, and I prayed for my loved ones in St. Matthew Parish, Mozie, Henry, and even taciturn Mr. Luther. My heart bears a certain stain of guilt.

6 August 1872. Talk on the porches and in the hotel dining rooms and parlours are of military feats of the late war. There seem to be two camps of men in this discussion: Men who survived the catastrophe of the late war, through luck, heroism, and sheer will, and men like my husband who avoided it through guile, wealth, and deceit. Now that it is done and faded from the newspapers and into the annals of history, each might gladly exchange places with the other. It seems to have been a war fueled and fought by the sin of pride, though perhaps most wars are so. The conversation rumbles on in adjacent parlours:

'We marched them twenty miles that day!' Or 'There were perhaps eight artillery pieces on that ridge, I would say.' Or, 'We were under orders from our brigade commander, therefore, to clear out that cornfield.' And so on. They make it sound no more than an athletic contest, not an exercise that results in the maiming and killing of young men.

I could sense Mr. Teague feeling eclipsed. Perhaps it was his slouching body language or his vacant expression. He and I know, though separately, that his military career was a sham. He endured the boasts and swagger of the recounted tales of the other men present until he masterfully swung the conversation to commerce. On the subject of commerce, Mr. Teague is quite superior to all others. He certainly fancies himself to be so. For him, the pursuit of wealth borders on the religious.

'Well, gentlemen,' he maneuvered, 'Indeed, wars are fought and are over, but money, why, money continues like the beat of a drum. It rules everything, of course, in times of war and in times of peace.' He puffed out a cloud of smoke into the gentlemen's lounge. Someone asked in a bemused tone over a glass of port, 'But what do you mean, sir, rules everything?'

'I will be plain with you, sir,' Mr. Teague continued with an air of invincibility, 'Never underestimate the power of a dollar. A man will sell his soul for one if he's hungry. Or maybe if he's just bored. Oh, and make no mistake, money is also a love remedy. It can make an ugly man handsome, a dull man witty, a stupid man wise. Forget that foolishness about some Chinese root or a rhinoceros horn. Money is the only known aphrodisiac.' He pronounced this last thing, 'affer-deeshick,' or something close to that. Neither I, nor anyone else, corrected him. Upon the conclusion of Mr. Teague's soliloquy, each man hastily finished his refreshment and drifted away, and I was left alone with my husband and his perception of the truth. We left the hotel and made our way up the hill under a parasol in the rain, which has persisted through the night and given everything the feel of autumn. As we passed up the section of houses known here as 'Paradise Row,' a man with one leg and a crutch stood soaked in the rain at the foot of the steep steps to his cottage.

'Pardon me, sir, could you help a poor veteran up the steps here?' he asked us. My husband merely grumbled, more to himself, 'Help yourself. You're a hero, after all.' Then he moved us along in the rain under our umbrella. I looked over my shoulder to the poor man with his one leg, standing under the drumming rain. I thought he might be scowling at Mr. Teague's unpleasantness, but he only bore the downpour and examined the steps like Sisyphus from Greek mythology, trying to figure out how he could mount them and go in where it was dry. I broke from the protection of the umbrella and went to the man's aid. His wool suit was soaked, the empty leg of his trousers pinned up. I thought a random thought, is he required to buy a full pair of shoes, or just a left one? Could the right shoe be sold to someone missing the opposite leg?

'Allow me to help you, sir,' I said with cheer. He said that I was very kind, as he braced himself against me and we ascended the steps in the rain, which had not let up a drop. 'Your father seems to be in a rush,' he said to me. I told him that Mr. Teague was actually not my father, but, rather, my husband. Then I smiled and whispered, 'You must excuse him, sir, for he suffers from a chronic flux of his bowels which hurries him at times. It kept him from serving in the late war.' I was sorry that Mr. Teague wasn't there to hear the veteran's mistake. My husband is so vain about his age and the perception of his youth.

'Tasks that I took for granted,' the man mused at the steps as we ascended them one at a time in the rain, 'before I left my leg at Gettysburg.' We gained the top of the stairs and the sanctuary of the porch. 'May God bless you, ma'am, as He has certainly blessed me this day. Can I lend you an umbrella for your return?' I told him that it would be no matter, that I was already soaked through and that I should only need to return to our cottage for dry things and a cup of tea. He thanked me again, and I descended the steps. I found that the rain was not at all bothersome, and I tarried in the pleasant patter of it, much like I did when I was a girl in Surrey.

7 August 1872. A most robust day. The rain has traveled on, leaving a bright clear day in her wake. Mr. Teague went to take the waters for his leg, and the girls and I hired horses from the stables and took to the mountains. The air was clear and cool in the sunshine under a sky that was a colossal blue. How Papa would have loved a day such as this! And I have felt very near him on this day with these girls, as if he were sitting in a tree observing us. We had a picnic near a mountain stream and waded in it clutching our skirts above the clear flow and the smooth stones. A basket had been prepared with fried chicken and apple pie from the hotel dining room. As we lay on the blanket in the grass in the dappled shade, the river gurgled to us. We four, like sisters, toyed with each other's hair, and a school of white clouds swam in a blue sky over swaying leaves. We talked of the future as the last cloud scurried off to the east to join the rain clouds. It was all so easy, so relaxed, so possible. Ida said that she should like to be a teacher one day. Lucy said that she should like to be in the circus. 'Would you be the monkey?' Jenny teased, but Lucy said, no, she should like to be the lion tamer. 'Well, a tamer of lions! And what would you do if he roared at you?' I asked as I ate apple pie with my fingers, as we all did, licking our fingers of its tart, cinnamon, sweetness. 'I would roar right back!' she said, and she launched the most dreadful growl she could, but it was like the roar of a kitten. And we laughed, and she roared again, and I drew her to me and she drew Penny to her. The doll nestled between us as Lucy put her small arm over my waist and we reclined on the blanket. We listened to the river's wet chuckle and named the shapes of the clouds until there were none left, and the sky glowed blue. We fell silent to the quiet rustle of creation and babble of running water, and tree leaves and breezes and the glint of sun as the boughs moved to reveal the sky and conceal it again. And as we fell into a nap on our blanket, I had a wish that heaven would be half as fair as this. When we awoke, we waded in the river again, and soon it turned into a proper swim. Our bodies were perfectly outlined in our wet underclothes, dark-thimbled breasts, gentle curves of our bottoms draped with clinging wet linen. Dripping fingers and the backs of hands pushing and pulling wet hair from our faces before each laughing plunge. We dried ourselves in the warming sun and returned from the stables laughing arm-in-arm to the valley and the great 'Old White.' It was a perfectly tranquil & serene day, enough to satisfy one's curiosity about the nature of heaven.

12 August 1872. Today we played at croquet until we tired of it and have now spent the rest of the day on the grounds, though Ida wished to return to the place of our idyll by the river. As the day slides into evening, we stay close to the Old White and enjoy its great lawn. Daylight has intensified into a spectacular crescendo on the flowers that grow here in brilliant colours and are dotted by butterflies which 'flutter-by' as Ida jokes. They alight and pump their little hinged wings, and flutter into the breeze again, hovering as if trying to choose which flower is most worthy of a landing. As I write, the girls chase fireflies in the gathering darkness, calling them 'lightning-bugs' and cupping them in their hands and admiring them as if they were caught stars. Mr. Teague has missed all of it, having spent the afternoon at the telegraph office waiting on a message from Mr. Howard. You, my little confidant, have been a fine companion this day.

Sammy, 1982

He shut the diary. Across the room, Miss Vessy was praying the Rosary at her boy's bedside. Teeter was off oxygen and sleeping, but he still looked like a shell. His cheeks were hollow, sallow, almost like a corpse. She kissed the little plastic Jesus on the cross and genuflected. Then she rose and came and sat in the chair by Sammy. The two cups of government coffee sat between them in orange plastic government coffee cups. It was warm enough to drink but too weak to enjoy.

"I thought the day he left for the army was the worst day of my life," Miss Vessy said. "Now it's this one."

She took a sip of the VA's version of coffee and winced.

"He went tru' dat gate in his uniform. I knew he was scared, yeah, but tryin' not to show it, tryin' to keep me from seein' it. But a mama knows. She knows."

Someone paged someone else on the speaker in the hall. It sounded far away, like a voice coming from a cardboard box. Sammy took a quick sip of his coffee and set the cup down.

"I'm gonna have to find us some better coffee," Sammy said, hoping Miss Vessy would talk about something else.

She nodded and almost smiled. Then she said to the window, "You not as bad as evvabody say."

He debated leaving for coffee, but instead he spoke. "I left for my family," he said to the truth she had spoken obliquely.

"Lot a people had families, Mist' Teague. Ain' no excuse, no. No more for you than it would be for them."

He didn't say anything. He knew she was right.

"But thank you for savin' my boy. He looks up to you. He say it ain' right how people say about you. Him of all people, him come back so *cagou*, so messed up." She pointed to her temple and twirled her finger. "Teeter's a good boy, a good son. What I'm gonna do, Mist' Teague? What I'm gonna do 'bout my poor, broken boy? He's all I got dis world. What I'm gonna do?"

She cried a slow, leaking cry, tears that followed the channels in her sun-creased cheeks. Sammy reached over and took her hand in his, a hand that was thick and rough from working on the docks of Longueil on the St. Lawrence, the place in Canada where he had worked when he had dodged the draft. To save his family. And Miss Vessy took that hand in her rough hand, strong and firm from years of caring for hers.

"They say he might be here a while," Sammy said. "Let me take you back home for a little while, Miss Vessy."

"I ain't gonna leave my boy, no. You go, jus' come back and see 'im. He still looks up to you. He's gonna want to see you." And then she said without tears, "If he wakes up."

Miss Vessy's fingers lightly rubbed the wad of Rosary beads she clutched in her palm, and Sammy held the diary in his. He didn't realize it, but he was holding it just as tightly as she held her Rosary. Miss Vessy looked at it.

"Wha's that book you readin'?"

He looked down at it, the unfolding tale of Teague dishonor. Beneath its leather cover, Old Sam Teague no longer seemed brave or honorable. He didn't even seem ordinary or average. He seemed much less than even that.

"An old book I found on our place."

"Oh," she said with a nod, maybe waiting for him to elaborate.

Sammy looked down at the tattered old book. He didn't feel like talking about it right now. He didn't need to feel any smaller. And so, an intimate quiet took over in the hospital room. Outside the window, ships moved up and down river, their superstructures floating above the levee. Inside the room, soap opera actors silently mouthed their dialogue and gave each other concerned looks on the television mounted near the ceiling. Soon it was all far away.

Sammy dreamed of the white faces of sheep beneath a magnolia tree set in the middle of a cane field. A school bus was there, and it was raining, and he was a shepherd leading them onto it. One of the sheep spokc, and it was in an English accent. The rain pattered on the window glass of the bus and thunder pealed in the distance.

He woke to the sound of a medicine cart approaching with a muffled rumble in the hallway, and the door opened. Sammy quickly picked up his head to see the nurse look in at the three of them. Miss Vessy was sleeping, and the nurse held Teeter's wrist and looked at her watch and wrote the number down on a clipboard at the end of the bed. She checked the bedrails and said in a hush to Sammy, "If you need anything, push the call button," and she left as quietly as she had entered.

Miss Vessy didn't wake to the nurse's visit. She wasn't sleepy; she was exhausted. The Rosary had slipped from her hands and fallen to the floor. Sammy picked it up and placed it on the window ledge beside her and put a blanket over her. Through the window, the black city skyline of New Orleans was outlined against a blazing orange sunset in the distance across the river. He wondered how it must have looked a hundred years before. He left the sleeping mother and her son and went down the hall to use the payphone. The little sign outside the room read, *M J Blanchard, US Army. Service connected.*

An old Veteran shuffled by in a hospital gown and asked Sammy if he had a cigarette.

"Sorry, sir, I don't smoke anymore," Sammy said.

"That's smart, young man. I dodged German bullets for four years, and all the while the Red Cross was killing me with free cigarettes." The old man wandered down the hall to the nurses' station and tried flirting with the nurses, who politely tolerated it.

Sammy fed the phone six quarters, and it rewarded him with a buzzing ringtone. He punched in the number, and Betsy answered. In the background, his girls were giggling. It was a good sound that made him smile and made him homesick at the same time.

"What are they doing?" he asked.

"They dressed the dog up in clothes. I think she kinda likes it. Except for the socks. They make her walk funny. That's why they laughin'. How's Teeter?"

"Oh, stable. Hasn't woke up yet." He knew what he had to tell her. "Baby, I don't think I can go to Disney this weekend. I can't leave him. He and his mama don't have anybody else. But y'all go. I bet my daddy'll go with y'all. I hope the kids won't be disappointed."

"It's the right thing to do,' Betsy sighed. "These kids gonna be sad, yeah, for a while. But when they grow up, they gonna remember that their daddy gave it up to help a friend, and they gonna be better people because of it. Kids listen to half of what you say but watch everything you do."

Betsy was a woman who could see things like that, the long-term consequences, both good and bad that were waiting years down the line. It was one his favorite things about her.

"But I think I'll come home tonight," he said. "I need to be home."

"That would be good," she said. A serious tone crept into her voice. "I miss you."

"I miss you, too," he said, and then he asked, "Have I been a good husband to you?"

"Sammy, boo, why you ask me that? You been the best. You worked on the docks in Montreal and took care of Quint so I could finish school. You the best husband I know, the best I could ever have dreamed up. Bay, why you ask me that?"

"I just. I just needed to hear it."

"Well, don't you forget it, you ol' coullion." She smacked him a kiss over the phone. "Careful drivin', bay. I'll keep a little supper for you."

He dried his eyes on his shirtsleeve as he hung up. The person waiting to use the phone patted his back as he stepped away. They might have thought he was sad, but he wasn't.

It was late when he got in, and the girls were already to bed. Pongeaux slept on Judee's bed in the moonlight under the window. The dog was still wearing a Saints T-shirt.

He looked at his girls and felt again the sweet-sad emotion that every parent knows, made of equal parts fear and hope. One day, as surely as the earth tilts and turns on its axis and the tides rise and fall and the seasons change, we lose our children to adulthood. He kissed the little faces and turned off the lamp, and the Tinkerbell nightlight glowed cheerfully. Tonight, they were still under his roof.

That night, he dreamed the restless dream of the school bus and a little blonde girl and watery red lights and the letters APSB. He woke and went down to his study and the diary.

Alice, 1872

2 September 1872. I feared I had lost you, my little confidant. But why were you hiding in Mr. Teague's coat pocket? He was trying to decipher you, wasn't he? But you were just a mash of lines and circles to his grey eyes. He met me in our lodging with the book in his lap. Holding it up, he asked in a tone that was quite accusatory, 'Mrs. Teague, what is this book?' Thinking quickly, I replied, 'Why, husband, it is an old recipe book of Mama's.' He looked skeptical, and so I took it from him and paged through it, reciting, 'Scones and treacle…leg of mutton with parsnips,' and so forth, looking up and smiling with each turn of the page. After an initial look of suspicion, he became perfectly content with my answer. He is illiterate, I am quite sure of it. Mozie reads far better.

4 September 1872. Ida slipped away and was gone most of the day. As the sun began to sink to the tops of the mountains to the west, a fog nestled into the valley and the night became particularly dark. A little after sunset, a party was sent up into the woods. At last she was found at the area by the river where we had picnicked. A negro servant from the hotel came in with her on horseback, a blanket drawn over her as she rode and he led the horse. I expected Mr. Teague to thank the men for finding her. If he did so, I did not hear it. Their duty done, the search party disappeared into the fog, their horses loping off into the white mist, which dissolved the slow hoofbeats and neighing into nothingness. I thought Mr. Teague would get down on his knees and embrace his daughter, like the return of a prodigal, thanking heaven for the safe return of one who was lost. It is what Papa would have done and what most would do, or so I have always assumed. Instead, Mr. Teague thrashed her mercilessly. She cried loudly, her body twisting away from his smacking hand as she pled her case. Her hands tried to parry away her father's as she wailed, 'I was lost in the fog, and it settled over everything and I couldn't see the hotel.'

'You have been an embarrassment to me this day! *An. Em. Barras. Ment!'* he said with each popping blow of his hand. Jenny was crying, 'Father, stop, stop!' and Lucy was weeping pitifully. I could bear it no more and intervened between Ida and her father. After almost receiving a blow myself, I succeeded in wresting him from his exertions. At last he stopped and retired to his parlour, where I heard the tinkle of a decanter stopper and the tumble of liquid into crystal. As I picked up Ida to take her to her bed, I looked through our windows as the curtains in the windows of the adjoining cottages closed over the lights and the curiosities within. This morning, it was with Mr. Teague as if nothing had transpired, though Ida keeps to bed. Under her nightgown, her legs are frightfully bruised. I should consult the hotel's doctor but fear I cannot without angering Mr. Teague. Tea and rest must suffice for her.

9 September 1872. Ida is well enough to be kept in the watch of Jenny, and so Lucy and I went to take tea at the Old White. She was so proud of herself, little Lucy, telling Penny that she must be a big girl if she is to be allowed to take tea with grown-ups. She carried her little porcelain-skinned 'daughter' with her in one hand and held on tightly to mine with the other, her little gloved hand in mine. We were seated at a table with some ladies from Chicago, a Mrs. Corrigan and another whose name escapes me presently. They were good company and proud of their beleaguered city and its rebuilding after the Great Fire less than a year ago. I remarked that surely it is a relief that the Palmer House Hotel was spared. 'The Palmer House?' she exclaimed, 'Why it burned to the ground in the fire as well! And after being open only a short time! No, dear, there is no Palmer House now, though I have heard that there are plans to rebuild it.' Thinking of the bill accrued by the former Mrs. Teague, I asked, 'So there have been no guests since the fire? The woman replied that it was only open for a few weeks when it burned, and that she should know, for the fire began on her fortieth birthday, the eighth of October 1871 and burned for two days. She said that since then, there have been no guests, for there is no hotel to put them in.

And, of course, my little confidant, no bill for seven-course meals, bottles of champagne, and suites overlooking Lake Michigan.

12 September 1872. The nights cool quickly here, and the leaves on the uppermost part of the mountains are fading to yellow and orange. In the evenings in the parlour of the great hotel, Jenny and I play duets on the piano and violin for the guests. We have become quite the favourites to the other lodgers here on holiday. If a guest is to hum a little of their favorite song, we can play it convincingly and in fine style. Ida was able to accompany us, though she is still kept to bed most of the day and says very little. Lucy plays with her doll Penny in the room with Ida. 'One time *you* got a bo-bo too, Penny,' Lucy says to her doll quite sweetly. Mr. Teague spent a great part of the day touring the countryside on horseback. This evening, he sat and stared at a Bible in the lamplight as I re-read Rousseau's *Confessions.* When we retired for the evening, he placed the Bible on the table under the lamp. It had been upside down as he pretended to read it.

16 September 1872. At dinner this evening, we were seated with two gentlemen from New York, an older man and a much younger man with two different last names. I thought at first that they were uncle and nephew, but they admitted that they were not related and were just good companions. Afterward, Mr. Teague, in retiring from the night was removing his cravat and his waistcoat. His speech was thick from the bourbon whiskey he had consumed after our dinner. 'I believe those two men were a bit along the feminine persuasion,' he slurred. I said that I was not quite sure what he meant, so he said, 'Miss Nancy and Aunt Fancy, as they say.' He unbuttoned his collar and spoke into the dressing mirror to my reflection. 'Just as I knew also that our handsome Rev. Givens was a sodomite.' He said it as if he had elucidated a great truth out of an ancient scroll. 'Mr. Teague!' I said, and I'm sure my voice did not contain my surprise. 'Oh, don't look so shocked, my dear,' he said, 'why, the good reverend has no more desire for female flesh than a coon or a possum. That's why I insisted he was the man, and I say 'man' loosely, of course, for the position at St. Margaret's. Single men marry, married men stray, but men like him are completely safe when it comes to competition for the fairer sex. Anyone else would have been a rival in winning your hand. And make no mistake, no one competes with me when I want something. And it was you I wanted.'

I suppose I was to be flattered by this revelation. I am not sure, but my face may have adopted an expression that I had not intended. He let his nightshirt fall over his scarred cheek and twisted hip and leaned in to kiss me. I gave him my cheek rather than my lips. His breath smelled musky, like bourbon and cigars.

'The true way of things is not lost on me, dear,' he said as he slipped under the sheets and waited for me to undress. I tarried, waiting for sleep to come for him and to save me. The last of what he had to say spooled out in a falling tangle. 'I always find out. Always. No one pulls the wool over my eyes. No one. And if young Reverend Givens ever crosses me, why, his secret will be blared across every newspaper in Christendom. In big letters.'

For someone who cannot even read a newspaper, he certainly professes to have control over them. I undressed and came to bed, and waited for his overture into the marital impulse, afraid that I would be sick if he made one. But he only fell into snoring, and I was grateful for it. I find myself with this question which I asked silently to my sleeping husband as I pondered the ornate medallion on the ceiling: why, then, have you not found your second wife?

20 September 1872. The newspapers say that Yellow Fever stalks abroad in St. Matthew and the other southern parishes. I have sent several letters but have had no word in return. I fear for Henry and Mozie and all those I love there.

27 September 1872. A rainy stretch of days here in the mountains. The valley cools with each period of rain, and smoke from the cottage chimneys drifts into the cold, wet air. The green leaves of the mountain backdrop are beginning to change into their autumn colours. It is a quiet, satisfying day. I read all day to Ida who still gets around very little. Mr. Teague pretended to read.

1 October 1872. Today we packed for our return, like an army preparing to move. Our two gentlemen friends from New York came to call on the girls and me before setting off. I thanked them for their pleasant society these weeks and sent them off with good wishes. They are dapper men and good company. I wish I had gotten their addresses. They would have made delightful correspondents.

3 October 1872. We are on the train south. As we departed the station today, Lucy suddenly began crying for her doll, 'Penny! Penny!' Her little face reddened and contorted, looking to me and her sisters and out the window at the diminishing platform. Several of the passengers turned their heads. Mr. Teague looked off with a rather annoyed expression. 'Where is she, love?' I asked her in as calm a voice as I could gather. 'I left her in the station. We were looking out the window together and saying goodbye to the mountains.' The conductor came to see about her as the train was just creeping forward. He pulled his watch from his waistcoat pocket and told Mr. Teague, 'I can signal the engineer to stop and then I can run back for it, sir. We're still a little ahead of schedule.' As Lucy looked out the window and her reflection looked back to her, both of the little girls crying with twisted faces, Mr. Teague said coldly, 'It will serve as a lesson to the girl to keep track of her belongings from now on. I have cane in the fields that needs my attention. Let us press for home.' He turned his face forward, refusing to look in any other direction. The conductor reluctantly put his watch back in his pocket. The train gathered speed, and Lucy pressed her face to the window glass and sobbed until she slept, which she did restlessly. When she awakes, she remains inconsolable.

4 October 1872. Farewell, dreamy, autumn-coloured White Sulphur Springs. We continue on the train headed south through Tennessee, rocked gently by it as the engine blows up ahead with a sound much like a coo made by the distance. In each gentle curve I can see the great, big-wheeled iron beast belching soft black smoke at the head of a long banner of windows, and then the track straightens, and one can only hear it punctuate the rhythm of iron wheels on iron rails. Up and out, the mountains become greener and the air warmer with each southward mile as summer still clings to hope there. As soon as Lucy fell into a nap, I went to the baggage car to look for Penny in our trunks, but she wasn't in any of them. 'Po' lil' thang,' the negro attendant said, shaking his old grey head. Lucy sleeps fitfully, and when she awakes, I cheer her by telling her of the grand adventures that Penny is having back in West Virginia. 'What is she doing now?' Lucy asks, no longer whimpering when she asks me about her. 'Why, my dear,' I say, 'the kitchen staff at the hotel dining room is teaching Penny how to make the apple pie like we had on our picnic!' Lucy's countenance brightens but a little, and she says, 'Apple pie! When she comes home, she'll make us one, won't she Miss Alice?' I pull the little dear's coat around her and say, 'Of course, love,' though I haven't figured out how I shall make that occur. At our last stop, I posted a letter to the station and the hotel to look for Penny, but I fear that she has been taken as a plaything for another little girl or placed in a storeroom or closet. Does the doll miss her girl like her girl misses her, I wonder? Mr. Teague nods with the movement of the train as he fights with sleep. The girls gather on the green velvet seat draped around me as I write, though I do not let them see what I record. Ida is curious and tries to look over my shoulder, so I stop here. Her bruises show as dark blotches beneath her stockings like the darker clouds in an overcast sky.

5 October 1872. The girls sleep in their berths, and I take the time to ride in the dim light of the empty passenger car through the slumbering countryside. All day I have told Lucy of Penny's adventures. Penny has helped take care of the horses at the stables. She's led the people in the parlour in singing. She had a picnic with another doll who has become a particularly good friend. And then little Lucy said something that made my eyes wet with tears. 'Will she ever come back, *Mama*? It sounds as though she's having a grand time.' She has never addressed me as *Mama*, until now. I pulled her close to me so that she could not see my face, and I took several deep draughts of air so that my voice wouldn't falter. She looked up to me, and I looked away and out the window. Gathering my courage, I replied, 'Oh, I am quite sure of it, my love,' though I am not at all sure if this reunion shall occur.

6 October 1872. The Sabbath, and I read quietly from the *Book of Common Prayer* and pretend it is my Papa rocking me, though it is only the motion of the train. How I miss him and wish him near.

7 October 1872. In New Orleans once more. As there was to be a wait for the ferry to the train station on the west bank, Mr. Teague went to discuss a matter with Mr. Howard. I persuaded Jenny to take her sisters with her to see the Howard children, for I had an errand to attend to. I told Mr. Teague that I needed some necessary items for ladies. As soon as they were safely down the street, I went to Guéblé & Nippert's on Canal Street. In the selection of dolls on the shelves, I found one that is an almost exact duplicate of our beloved Penny. As the clerk gathered the new Penny for me, I heard a clerk say to a young woman at another counter, 'Will that be all, Miss Duplantier?'

The name was familiar, so I asked her, 'Would you be Emilia Duplantier?' She replied that she was. She had the eyes of the women here, dark and round and generously lashed, with lips that were full and well-shaped. Her figure was striking as well, short in stature but very well formed. Her kid-gloved hand held a small wicker basket that had several items, hair bows and ribbons among them. I asked her, 'Pardon me, mademoiselle, were you once a governess for the Teague children in St. Matthew?' Her look changed as she eyed me suspiciously and said, 'Yes, I was, but for a very short time.'

'And you left—' I said.

'It is said for drinking Mr. Teague's whiskey, isn't it?' she offered with a wry smile, 'but in that, I am falsely maligned.'

'Yes,' I said as I took inventory of her again. She was perhaps the soberest person I have ever met, clear-eyed and healthy in appearance. The facts suddenly did not bear the story. 'You do not seem to be very fond of drinking, Miss Duplantier.'

'Drinking? Pish-posh! I've never had a drop of liquor or wine in my life, apart from the Eucharist, nor have I wanted one. The truth is, my employer tried to have his way with me in a most ungentlemanly manner, and I spurned him with a slap of his scarred face! I quit immediately! If you are offered the same position, mademoiselle, well, I would advise you against it.' She seemed to be trying to recover herself. Her smile regained its throne on her apple-shaped cheeks, and she switched her basket and extended her hand and introduced herself. 'Emilia Duplantier. Forgive me, mademoiselle. That was very coarse of me.'

'Alice…' I paused, 'Alice…Lamb.' She looked at my purchase. 'That doll you have…it looks like the very same doll of the youngest Teague girl, Lucy. What a coincidence that we should be speaking of her. Penny, I believe we named her.'

'Yes, quite so,' and then I stammered, 'Or rather, that certainly is a coincidence.'

'Well, so nice to make your acquaintance, and good day, Miss Lamb,' she said. 'If you'll excuse me, I must be going. I am governess to a family on Esplanade, and one of my girls has a saint's day today.' She paused to turn and added, 'But do remember what I said about Mr. Teague.' I thanked her and said I certainly shall. She gathered her basket and alighted the omnibus. A gentleman gave up his seat, and she smiled and nodded her appreciation. And then the old mule bore them all away with trudging, patient steps. I returned to the ferry terminal to find Mr. Teague and the girls waiting. Their countenances brightened when they saw me, none more than little Lucy when she saw whom I carried. 'Penny!' she exclaimed, and she clutched the doll like a lost child, how any parent would clutch a missing child when she was safely returned from the foggy, mountain wilderness. Any parent, save Sam Teague. 'Where were you, Penny?' Lucy asked the cheerful little blank-faced girl in her petite arms.

'Why, I believe she just flew back from her adventures in the mountains! On a magic carpet like Aladdin and the Arabian knights!' I said. Lucy believed it wholeheartedly. It was a joyful reunion, though the joy wasn't shared by Mr. Teague. He scowled and lit a cigar. 'A lesson untaught, and a lesson unlearned,' he muttered. And then, as we boarded the ferry, he put his hand to the small of my back. It felt rather like a claw.

On the train into Donaldsonville, Lucy awoke from a nap and smiled at her doll. Rectangles of skewed light passed over them as swamp and cane raced by out the window. Lucy examined Penny, speaking to her in a small, motherly voice as she pulled the doll's hair up into a bow. Suddenly, she stopped and looked up to me. 'But Mama, Penny has a bo-bo behind this ear.' I suddenly remembered as she pointed to the smooth, pale porcelain behind her left ear where the scratch should have been. 'Why that is another remarkable thing about White Sulphur Springs!' I said, 'One of the porters at the Old White told me that there are fairies, kind-hearted fairies, who live in the mountains and perform good deeds for good children like you. I believe they have fixed Penny!' Lucy looked at Penny and then then at me with a look that held the slightest trace of doubt, the first gasp in the demise of innocence, the moment one begins to realise that Father Christmas isn't real, but rather an elaborate ruse. But she held the doll to herself, almost as if the doll had been the victim of the deceit and not she. How easily I lie now.

10 October 1872. We returned to St. Matthew to find that Death has visited this place, and many have passed. Much of the populace is in black, and many of the men wear black arm bands. New rectangles of earth appeared in every churchyard as we neared our home. I was relieved to find that Henry and Mozie and most of my loved ones are among the living, and Luther is preparing the gardens for winter. I tried to speak with him, but he was as reticent as ever. Mozie, however, was as genial as always. 'Oh, Miss Alice,' she declared, 'you should a seen them wagons pass with them dead folk! They must been fifteen or sixteen in a row! Revvin Givens, he had hisself a time keepin' up them funerals. Mens couldn't dig them holes fas' enough, no ma'am.' I inquired after the health of 'Revvin Givens,' and Mozie would only say, 'He seem so quiet, these days, but he sho' been worked hard, yes ma'am.'

11 October 1872. Now that we are home once again, Mr. Teague has fallen into the habit of taking absinthe in the evenings, as it was discussed at White Sulphur Springs as the new libation of a man of culture. The brilliant green liquid sparkles in his cut-glass tumbler as he stares out at the cane. But as much as he might strive, he can no more become cultured by drinking absinthe than he can become royalty by wearing a brass crown and silk stockings. There is no point in asserting it, however.

It would only anger him, and for no purpose. Henry rings the evening bells at St. Margaret's, the hard peals made pastel by the distance, each clanging reverberation seeping out, invisible over the countryside to meet the previous one and then the next reaching out for that one. It is a comfort to hear them. They are the perfect accompaniment to the vivid blue and orange sunset. I am anxious to see my friend.

12 October 1872. Papa has certainly gained new neighbours while we were away. Fresh plots of bare earth dot the graveyard of St. Margaret's, as it does others in St. Matthew, and I went among them to see if I could recognize any names of the recently departed. I placed new flowers on Papa's stone crypt and saw that on the graves of his neighbours, grass is beginning to cover the bare rectangles of earth. Weeds also encroach on Papa's crypt. I fell to my knees and pulled them away, and the soil relinquished the roots so unwillingly. I began weeping, why must it be so? Why is the earth so intent on devouring us, we who inhabit these temporary bodies? I cried for some time, enough time for a cool drizzle to fall and a brisk wind to drive it away and for the sun to return. In it, my shadow fell on the white tablet covering Papa, and then another shadow joined mine. I looked up to see the silhouette, a shadow that said, 'The children were the worst. Of the ones who died.' I shielded my eyes to see that it was Henry, in shirt sleeves and waistcoat. My skirts were damp where my knees had pressed into the wet ground. 'Let me tell you another secret, Alice. I wish I could join them sometimes.'

'Surely not!' I said as I swept the tears from my eyes with the heel of my hand and then brushed dirt from my cheek with the other.

'The ones who died were the ones who couldn't afford to leave,' he said as he watched the toe of his shoe push a clod of black earth. Straightaway, I said, 'I had a family to look after,' and it sounded as if I thought myself accused and was offering an apology. Perhaps I did, and I was.

'Oh, I don't blame you or any of the others. I suppose that it's only human nature, created as we are. But, like before, it's forever a rich man's war and a poor man's fight. Those who couldn't get away were left to contend with the pestilence. Like the plague of Egypt.' He sat upon a monument and traced the letters with his fingers, *gone from peril, safe in the arms of Jesus.* He stared at the touch of his skin on the cold marble and said, as if to his fingers, 'It serves as a reminder to us that one cannot master death any more than one can befriend it.' He looked off into the lengthening shadows. 'So much like the late war. Watching your friends and brothers and cousins and fellow townsmen die, bleeding into the mud and dust, as pale as a murmur. Except no cannons or smoke, only heaving and searing fever. But death is all the same, in the end.'

I have never seen Henry or any man, really, so despairing. Even Papa, with all his reverses, never seemed so abject. We parted company. I am worried for Henry and his flagging spirit.

13 October 1872. Among the departed resting in our churchyard is the organist Mr. Mercer, and the first Sunday since our return, we sing without accompaniment. Mr. Teague does not sing but pretends to follow along, not from the hymnal but from the Psalter. They are the same to him, two books with quizzical shapes in ink on paper, like all books to him, simple rectangles with paper centres. Afterward on the steps, Henry pulled both Mr. Teague and me aside. 'It is a shame about Mr. Mercer,' Henry told Mr. Teague, 'The magnificent organ you gave the church is silent.' My husband said, yes, that the music is diminished. 'Yes, Mr. Teague, and that is why I detain you. Your wife's skill is without equal here and a credit to the Teague name.' Henry knows enough of human frailty, and especially my husband's, to know that this small statement would find its mark. Mr. Teague suppressed a smile and his scar frowned in response. And so I shall resume the bench and keyboard next Sunday. I am quite looking forward to it. As I write, Lucy is sitting under a great live oak with Penny. She neither jabbers at the new doll, nor sings to her, nor plays with her hair, but only sits with her blank-faced playmate. The doll's sad eyes look to me through the window.

15 October 1872. Today, the girls were set to their lessons, and I read with them in the ladies' parlour. Through the window, however, I could see the new Penny outside under the magnolia, neglected in the rain with her pram beside her, also neglected.

16 October 1872. No bells tonight from St. Margaret's or perhaps I have missed them. Mr. Teague takes absinthe again, smacking his lips against the taste. I do not think he enjoys it. Perhaps he thinks that if he ingests enough of it, he shall be able to read.

17 October 1872. No bells again this morning, and I set off straightaway to see to Henry. I had Reuben drive me through waving cane fields to St. Margaret's and the vicarage. I knocked on the door of the vicarage, but there was no answer. From thence, I went to the sanctuary, opening the heavy doors with a strong pull and finding only empty pews and an empty pulpit. The vestry is empty also, surplices hung neatly and no sign of Henry. At last, I went to the bell tower, and there I found him, standing and looking through one of the spaces in the brick. A chair was under the clapper rope of the bell. 'Henry, what are you doing up here?' I asked, to which Henry replied, "He fears that he has been found out and exposed,' he said out to the live oaks and the cane. 'Who?' I asked. 'Mr. Hodge,' he said, 'My friend in Memphis. What am I to do? What am I to do, Alice?' I could not think of any good advice for my friend, so we looked out through the spaces in the brick at the sugarcane and endured the thick silence. All of us, Henry, the cane, and me, waiting for something.

20 October 1872. Henry takes to the pulpit again this Sunday. He tells me that he likens it to Our Saviour's ascent up Golgotha, though not just once, but once a week. His sermon this morning was entitled, 'Noisy Gongs and Clanging Cymbals,' the scriptural basis of it being Paul's letter to the Corinthians. The congregation seemed disinterested or unconvinced. Perhaps they would have enjoyed a reassuring talk on Retribution, or God rewarding the righteous with riches like Jabez from the Old Testament. It is as Papa was fond of saying, people don't want to know anything new, they just want to be told that what they already know is sufficient. Henry concluded by saying that we don't want to follow Jesus, we want Jesus to follow us. Afterward, the congregation filed past him without a word. Perhaps they believed there was no sense in what he said.

23 October 1872. I read to Mr. Teague who complained of his eyes, though this was certainly a ruse. We (I) read quite a bit of Latin, and to amuse myself, I dreamed of concocting nonsense phrases for him to repeat. 'All hail the conquering emperor' is really 'my cat has had kittens,' and so forth. I read until I was hoarse and he fell into snoring in his Campeche chair. I quietly closed Riley's *Book of Latin* and went to retrieve Penny and her pram from under the live oak. She has spent several days in the rain, and her features are partially washed through, her face speckled with earth.

24 October 1872. Henry called today. He appeared distracted and quite out of sorts. I was in need of the society of a friend, he told me, and I was happy to supply it. Cold weather returns.

25 October 1872. Mr. Teague has caught Jenny teaching the house girl's daughter her letters and became quite cross. 'What is this?' he said as he came in the back door. Jenny stood up, and the girl stood up with her. Jenny said, 'I'm teaching this young scholar her letters so that she may begin with words.' Mr. Teague answered in a growl, 'Why, they have no more business knowing how to read and write than a rooster has for socks! You will desist from teaching these *n*—! Do you hear me, girl?' Jenny was quite crestfallen, and her speech dribbled out of her, 'Yes sir.' He grabbed her shoulders and threw her back against the wall, hard enough to rattle the dishes in a cabinet along it. 'What?' he shouted. 'Yes sir,' she said again, a little clearer. He released her, and she made an anguished face but did not cry. When he had stormed off to his study, she whispered to me, 'He's like this sometimes.' I would have cried woefully. She must be quite inured to it.

27 October 1872. Henry preached today from the sixth chapter of Matthew, "It is impossible to serve both God and Mammon." There was a great deal of squirming in the pews, or perhaps I imagined it so. Henry seemed unaffected by the querulous looks from the congregants. No planter has yet given the word for his sugarcane to be cut. Everyone awaits on Mr. Teague whose judgment is widely held to be superior to others. The sugarcane shimmers in green, unaware as muffled thunder moans in the west. It is said that he is waiting for a series of dry days after a rain.

28 October 1872. Our kitchen girl Ruthie has let spoil a whole side of beef. Mr. Teague thundered as if it were an event so calamitous that it would put us all in rags for generations. 'Do you not know why I had an ice barn set up?' he seethed, 'as a place for the cool-keep of such items?' I wonder to myself if I am such an item. But I say only, in the girl's defense, 'The ice barn is a new thing, and we are all unused to it. I think we can forgive Ruthie her lapse. Mount Teague abounds with beeves. Let us have the butcher prepare us another.' Mr. Teague did not take well to my suggestion. 'I did not seek your counsel on this matter,' he growled to me as he glowered at her and she stared at a spot on the floor where she stood as if before Pilate. 'I have no choice but to take this out of your wages,' he said with pursed lips. 'Yassuh,' she said, 'I's show sorry.' Mr. Teague roared, 'What!' and she said a little louder, 'Yassuh, I sorry, suh.' She offered the servile, faltering apology to Mr. Teague, like all do here at Mount Teague. It is quite like the damned being forced to exchange pleasantries with the devil. We fawning underlings, we serfs of this verdant kingdom.

I am quite out of spirits tonight. I little thought that this would be my lot in life, the queen of a disheartened kingdom, married to its cruel potentate. And now I live between the beautiful lie and the ugly truth. The ugly truth is that I am married to Sam Teague, that charming tyrant. The beautiful lie is that I am in love with him. I am like a circus animal grown weary of performing my tricks. And Ruthie and I and the girls and all of us are marionettes, string-bound and despairing. Debt is as inevitable as death here. The entire population of St. Matthew is either debtor or creditor, with little chance of exchanging roles. And so as my husband snores in the embrace of an afternoon nap, I am off to offer relief for poor Ruthie. In gathering the keys to the safe, I came upon a letter with the Great Seeing Eye from several months ago, the one from the 'Argus Detective Agency.' It is a letter informing Mr. Teague of the debt in Kansas City of the former Mrs. Teague. The address of the Argus

Detective Agency is 121 St. Charles Avenue in New Orleans. I remember now. That is Mr. Howard's address.

29 October 1872. I dream ragged dreams, made from mismatched parts. In one of them, Polly Teague and I ride elephants. *Well, Mrs. Teague,* I yell to her, *here we are, off to Kansas City.* She answers, *why, you are also Mrs. Teague. We are both Mrs. Teagues now!* And then she is gone, and the elephants are gone, and Mr. Teague comes to me in my dream, dressed as a Turkish pasha. The dream seems to take place in an instant, and now I am suddenly awake, oddly both entertained and disturbed.

30 October 1872. Mr. Teague rose early today to ride the fields with the overseer, despite it being Sunday. He is anxious about the upcoming 'rolling season' as some call it, worried about weather and early frost and yield. It is the autumnal ritual here. Henry also seems preoccupied, though not with agriculture. He sits in prayer or thought, and if I see him falter during Sunday services, I repeat stanzas of the hymn I play. His sermons have abandoned the New Testament completely, and now he preaches on topics such as smiting and beheading. Today he preached on the slaughter of Dinah's lover and his people after their circumcisions. Henry says that he only tells them what they want to hear, and that they would be just as happy, or happier, perhaps, if there were no New Testament.

1 November 1872. The newspapers report that a woman, Victoria Woodhull, is running for president of the United States. Both the *Compass* and the *Picayune* are very much against it, as is Mr. Teague. 'A woman is no more fit to govern as she is to vote,' he interrupted me as I read to him. Neither the newspapers nor Mr. Teague seem to notice that a woman is governing the affairs of the British Empire. I want to say so to Mr. Teague, but I am sure he would call me insolent.

5 November 1872. Election day has arrived, and, having been restored with the right to vote, the men of this place gathered here in advance of going to the polling places. Horses were tied to branches or attended by negro liverymen, who now also may vote. Mr. Teague received the men of St. Matthew as they mounted the steps to the front porch, white hands clasping and shaking heartily, as if seeing each other after a long absence. Everyone wore a white camellia in his lapel, and I wondered at its significance. As all gathered in the gentlemen's parlour, Mr. Teague requested some music. 'Favour us with a diddy, won't you, my dear?' he said, gesturing to the piano. I did not tell him, but 'diddy' is Ancoats slang for a baby's soiled nappy. 'I would be delighted to present you with a diddy, dear husband,' I replied sweetly, and I played the first movement from Beethoven's Symphony No. 1. Judge Anderson asked for Rev. Givens to give an invocation for the success of the Democratic candidate, Mr. McEnery. 'As you wish, sir,' Henry said. Conversation dribbled away and there was a cleared throat in the gathering. When silence prevailed, Henry began his prayer. 'Loving and righteous God, we thank you for your aid in restoring our franchise, and earnestly pray that we shall you use it wisely, casting our votes with good sense and loving hearts, filled with kindness for our fellow man—' Eyelids were lifted from their reverence. Lips pursed. Eyebrows narrowed. Henry continued with eyes closed in supplication. His chin lifted as if raising his face to God and God alone. '—and not with the worst of our emotions or for the selfish purpose of improving our own purses.' When his prayer was concluded, there were no amens, and, in fact, all the heads were unbowed, as if Henry's prayer had no merit and no purpose. One of them added, 'And God bless John McEnery!' to which the others shouted 'Amen!' Coats and hats were redistributed to the men, and someone said, 'Well gentlemen, we are off to vote. May the best man win, which of course means McEnery!'

The men scampered down the steps of our home like boys off on a lark, white camellias in their lapels. Then they took the reins of their horses and mounted, off to the polls, hooves clattering on the white shells of our lane beneath the oaks. The negro liverymen then were off on foot, equally happy to have the vote now. Henry lingered for a moment on the front porch. I told him that his prayer sounded very much like a prayer Papa was in the habit of praying before elections. 'I would have liked to have met him,' Henry said, 'the world was diminished by his passing.' I responded, and I'm afraid somewhat morosely, 'My world certainly was.' Henry replied that our faith says that we shall all meet again. 'That is a consolation,' I replied more dryly than I intended, 'but until that joyous day, we must inhabit this diminished world without him.' Henry smiled sadly, and I recognized the pain of someone who fears that he might lose something loved exquisitely. He turned and was off to the polls himself.

Voting in America must take a very long time. Mr. Teague did not return home until very late last night and then woke me, smelling of absinthe and insisting on the marital rite. 'It is my right as a man,' he slurred. 'As a white man,' he added with a chuckle, as if it had been a running joke or slogan of the day. I could not help it, but as soon as Mr. Teague fell asleep, I vomited into a chamber-pot.

6 November 1872. Mr. Teague has held a council with his overseer, and the signal has been given. The cane is to be cut tomorrow. The bell rang and people emerged from cabins and cane and barns and assembled before *le bawsman.* Mount Teague teems now with men who appear as if from the very air or from the fields thick with cane, men who shall swing keen-edged cane knives and perhaps tell crude jokes in the shade of isolated trees during pauses for water. That is what Mozie says. Mr. Teague delivered his address to the field hands, grinders, and coopers today. The plantation bell was struck, and he took to the back of an empty cane wagon, haranguing the gathering with half an hour's worth of flatulent oratory under a crisp autumn sun. He quoted Latin, of course, all of the snippets that we have practiced and a few that he has known for years. He concluded his oration with 'audacious for tuna you bet,' a corruption of the Latin, *audaces fortuna iuvat* or, 'fortune favours the bold.' I think he sees himself as a general going off to war against a threatening army of sugarcane. The field hands responded with what is the traditional cheer, '*Cet homme-ça a jamais travaillé un jour de sa vie!*' He received the cheer with an upstretched arm wielding a cane-knife. Then he was helped from the back of the wagon, and, as he and I stood on the side gallery watching his field-hands descend upon the thousands of acres of green stalks, I asked him the meaning of the cheer, thinking that perhaps there is some subtle, alternate meaning of it. But he looked at me derisively and said, 'why, I thought you spoke French.' I replied that the accent here is different from the Parisian French that I learned. 'They're saying,' he said as if explaining to a child, 'Here's to a bountiful harvest!' Of course, my little confidant, they are saying 'That man there never worked a day in his life.'

7 November 1872. Henry has gone to Memphis on a personal matter, so there is no music practice this week. Mrs. Parris arrived, unannounced (to me, at least) for a visit today. 'Oh, Mrs. Teague…you're home,' she said when she saw me. Mr. Teague and she and I took tea. It was a strange visit, something about it strained and uncomfortable. Long pauses found their way into our conversation. It was almost as if she was not expecting me home and resented my presence here.

8 November 1872. The Harvest Ball was held again tonight with what seemed to be an ever-enlarging collection of guests. A parade of carriages reminiscent of the Strand in London at holiday time streamed under the oaks and down our white-shell lane. Horses shook their heads impatiently as each carriage disgorged another packet of guests, and then each carriage was parked under the oaks. The fine horses which pulled them were set out to graze, perhaps trading secrets of households, secrets known only to horses, illicit liaisons and misdeeds. Night fell in the blue and orange and purple shades of autumn sunsets, and Mr. Teague and I greeted our guests as they ascended the steps between the lanterns. Twin flurries of moths, clouds of frantic wings, crowded around the glassy amber lights that flank the front doors. And the night slipped by with string music from the quartet, a different one than the one we had for the Planters' Ball in the spring. We dancers went through our paces in various quadrilles and waltzes as the conversationalists and intriguers and gossipers and connivers traded juicy tidbits of 'news,' whilst also managing to discuss the Sunday sermon somewhere in the midst of the more salacious fare. Henry did not attend, and among the gossip is the whispered insinuation that his bachelorhood is a ruse for his true nature. I launched the counter-rumour of his having a true love, a lovely girl in Atlanta, the daughter of a cotton merchant. Or that is what I've heard, I said. It is the key to believability of any rumour, to add *that is what I've heard.* It lends a little credence to even the most preposterous of news. I hope it shall be enough to quiet the wagging tongues of this place. But again, I bear false witness, though for a noble cause.

The Kenners are in from across the river in Ashland and staid the night, as did a host of others. As the night advanced, I looked around for Mr. Teague, but I could not find him. He wasn't in the gentlemen's parlour, nor on the front porch nor back porch, nor among the scattered knots of guests in the lantern lights hanging from oak limbs on the lawn. I was about to check upstairs when I was offered another drink of rum cordial, and soon I forgot about Mr. Teague. I was asked to dance by Mr. Morris who stamped about, joking again, 'it is as if I have but one leg,' though after another glass of rum cordial he seemed quite capable. We danced one tune and then another and then someone persuaded Jenny to play with the quartet and she ran upstairs to fetch her violin and I ran after her and I had a notion to retrieve something from our bedroom but it seemed as if the door was locked and then I thought perhaps I had the wrong room and I thought what a remarkable thing rum cordial was.

Jenny descended the stairs in quick, excited steps, holding her violin and her bow. Downstairs, she tentatively pulled the bow across a string, and then she played a selection from Chopin, her favourite and one at which she is most adept, and she rendered it rather flawlessly or perhaps it was the rum cordial that gave it its perfection. Everyone clapped enthusiastically, nodding to each other with murmurs of admiration. She played another and there was more applause. And then Mr. Teague appeared on the stairs with the lovely doe-eyed wife of Mr. Parris or Patterson or Parker, or something of that nature, I did not remember, and we all stopped and listened to hear Jenny play again. There was great and enthusiastic applause again, and Jenny blushed, I believe, but I was rather insensible to my surroundings, and even more so when the violinist from the quartet approached her and asked where she has trained. She blushed again, which I could only tell by her mannerisms, a sinking chin and a reticent smile, perhaps, as the light was low, and she said that she has had a teacher here and there, but that she is largely self-taught. I listened to them and became aware that there were others listening. I felt as though we were all underwater in the gaslit ballroom. And then the quartet played again, and there were fewer dancers and more couples were engaged in conversation.

Now I have crawled into bed exhausted to find that it has come unmade. I am sure that it was made this morning or perhaps it wasn't, overlooked with all the preparations for the ball. Still, it is not at all like Ruthie to let something like this go undone. But it is no matter, as my exhaustion prevails. I have managed to remove my dress, a brilliant green, the colour Mr. Teague prefers, and I have crawled within the elegantly carved posts with the silk canopy top still clothed in just my petticoats. I cannot be bothered with removing them and putting on a chemise. Sleep is too near. My hand has encountered something wet, like the aftermath of passion, though I cannot be sure, and sleep is so close that I can elude it no longer. I have moved to the edge to avoid the wetness. If I were not so tired, I would have Ruthie change the sheets or change them myself. I find myself barely able to complete this entry.

9 November 1872. This morning I have an aching head. The thought of having gone to sleep in an unmade bed greeted me as I woke in bright autumn sunshine. I remembered the wetness and threw back the covers, but the mattress was dry. Perhaps the rum confused me, and I dreamed it all. Downstairs, bottles and glasses clinked as they were being picked up by the house-servants. I made my daily toilet and went downstairs. Morning moved along, our guests all yet sleeping, but Mr. Teague was up and sitting quietly in his Campeche chair and looking away, out the window and onto his empire which is being managed with cane knives, shorn like a sheep for its wool. Morning sunlight fell upon his nickel-grey eyes as white smoke from his cigar wreathed his head. He tilted his head back as he let it go, and then his lips thoughtfully pulled on his cigar, the tip glowing orange before another cloud of white smoke rose. I fancy he thinks the obscure thoughts of a cat plotting to get inside a butter churn. Ruthie brought me toast and treacle (molasses, rather) and an egg, and I took it in the Ladies' Parlour in small bites until my stomach gave its assent for more. Jenny came down in her dressing gown. 'We shall have guests downstairs soon,' I said, 'perhaps you should dress,' but she was too excited to go back up just yet. She had to tell me what occurred after

I went to bed. She sat on the divan opposite me and said that a Mr. Masac, a member of the quartet last night and the President of the New Orleans Conservatory of Music, asked Jenny to play, and she did, first anything, then from sheet music, and then a succession of notes he hummed. She played them all, and *without a single flaw*, she said excitedly, as she grasped my hand. She said that her father had sat and listened to her impromptu recital, and I can imagine that it was with an expression bordering on a scowl, as if someone were bartering with him for something he was reluctant to give up. And then Jenny said that Mr. Masac asked her, 'My girl, where did you learn to play in such a manner? Your notes are so pure and lilting!' (Jenny tells me this twice.) She told him, 'We had a man that worked for us once. He showed me.'

Even now, she is like a boiling pot whose lid is rattling, she is so excited. 'Well, your potential is astounding,' she said Mr. Masac told her, and then he said to Jenny's father, 'Mr. Teague, with a little more formal training, surely your daughter would be a credit to you and your name!' And then I knew it at once. That was the key that fit the lock. *A credit to you and your name.*

10 November 1872. The pulpit this morning was occupied by the vicar from Donaldsonville, a rather short man with wooly-white whiskers that gave him the appearance of a sheep but with a voice almost as booming as the organ, which is silent this Sabbath. Mr. Teague has made no further overtures for the marital rite, save one, since we returned from West Virginia, and certainly I haven't. Perhaps there are many wives who would be disappointed. I myself am relieved. I am certain I have made a mistake. I would ask for a divorce, but I fear angering him. And what would become of these girls? I am as a mother or older sister to them, and they are as sisters or daughters to me. The wedding veil is lifted, and I see him plainly now. There is something feral in Mr. Teague, something that crouches in the darkness and waits. He is a man who, if he fails by persuasion, succeeds by violence. The malignant genie is out of the bottle.

11 November 1872. Of all the Louisiana parishes, St. Matthew is one of the only ones in which McEnery prevailed. It is also the only one which the Union troops have abandoned. Mozie tells me that the men of her family, and indeed, all those of colour, were prevented from voting by men with white sacks over their heads. A polling place was burned by them, the inhabitants (all negroes) quitting it only just before it erupted. I find the long day and late night of our election party no small coincidence.

12 November 1872. Ida and little Lucy said goodbye to Jenny today as she embarked for the city and her education at the New Orleans Conservatory. I told them that I shall be home in a few days, after I get Jenny settled and that this shall be a grand adventure for their sister. Then Jenny and I took the train into Algiers and then the ferry into the city. The city suddenly seemed so big to me, knowing that I would leave her here alone in it. The sound of it was quite like a machine, with horses and wagons and streetcars for gears. Mr. Teague has stayed behind in St. Matthew to supervise the cutting and grinding and barreling of sugar. I am sure that he believes that in his absence, sugar might be stolen from him. In New Orleans, Jenny and I were met by a friendly face, Mr. Morris, who offered his assistance if trouble arises, and it cheered us somewhat. Jenny remained quiet, and it appeared as if the city were new to her and the prospect of a new course of study was not as compelling an idea now that it is put into practice.

The New Orleans Conservatory of Music is on Baronne Street and conveniently shares space with a Mr. L. Grunewald's music store. There were perhaps a dozen or so pianos, Pleyels, Chickerings, Steinways, all polished to radiance, and glass cases of stringed instruments and horns. Truly, it was a confectioner's shop for musicians. A Mr. and Mrs. Masac greeted us, and I recognized Mr. Masac as a member of the quartet at the Harvest Ball. Jenny absently gave him her hand when he offered his. Around us, music floated in snippets of various length, horns, pianos, violins, violincellos, voices of singers, all in the process of being mastered. The Masacs were kindly, amiable people, and Mrs. Masac told Jenny that she may call her 'Miss Melanie,' if she pleases.

'You will be under the tutelage of—' Mr. Masac said before he was interrupted by a shout from a back room. A violin faltered to a stop, but the other instruments and singing voices in the grand room continued forth without a pause. '*Nein, nein, nein!*' A voice shouted in a pointed, erect German accent. 'Someone! Someone call der police! Puhr Mr. Beethoven ees beink muddered!' A young girl with mouse-brown hair and a red plaid frock hurried past us, red-eyed, holding her violin and bow in the same hand. She pursed her quivering lips as she rushed by, quite as if she were fleeing the last judgment. Miss Melanie broke from our group and hurried to catch the girl, and when she did, she put an arm around her and consoled her in a voice which we could not hear. Mr. Masac looked from the back room and then to us and said, almost apologetically, 'You will be under the tutelage of Mr. Herman Braun.' A man I assume is Herr Braun emerged from the room which the girl had departed. He is completely bald (a head like a cue ball, Mr. Teague would say), with sunken eyes and a pointed chin which seemed to try to support his scowl. One hand and then the other moved over his bare scalp as if he were trying to rub himself back into a fair countenance.

'His temper is…mercurial,' Mr. Masac said to us in a low tone, 'But he is the best. He demands perfection.' And I feared for my girl Jenny, being subjected to this tyrant, until she raised her chin and said resolutely, 'Then perfection is what I shall give him.'

My Jenny. She has the doggedness of her father but with a kind heart. She must have received that trait from her mother.

13 November 1872. Jenny is boarded and began lessons today, but I tarried so I could see her after her first day. Perhaps it is maternal or sisterly instinct, but I cannot leave before I see that she has withstood the first day of the 'tutelage' of Herr Braun. While she was in class, I was the guest of Mr. and Mrs. Howard, and we took a carriage out to the Fairgrounds Race Track. He was anxious to show us his racehorse, of which he is quite proud. The track was heard before seen and smelled before heard. The earth surrendered bits of turf as the shining, muscular animals plowed it up one hoof-full at a time in rapid successions. The jockeys hunched down on them with flexing knees, crops tucked under arms, a blur of bouncing colour. At the end of each run, they bent to half-standing in the stirrups and turned their animals, who took prancing trots.

'There she is! Say! But isn't she grand?' Mr. Howard shouted, an unexpected show of emotion from this taciturn man. He pointed to a chestnut mare, ridden by a man in a red blouse and blue cap. The horse seemed as big as an elephant when compared to the little man astride it. After another run, the animal slowed to the pull of the reins with a shake of her head and a great flash of her mane and flying clods of turf. Behind her, there was a man sketching the horses, looking up from his sketch pad to the horse and back. He looked to us. Then, our eyes met, and he dropped his pencil and almost dropped his sketchpad. He reached down to get it and wiped the dirt from it, and, as he did so, I looked away. I pretended to watch the trainers attend to Mr. Howard's horse, but from the corner of my eye, I could see the artist eyeing me. When I looked to him, he resumed looking from his sketching to the horse and back. 'Who is that? That man with the sketchpad in the sailor's cap?' I asked Mrs. Howard. She said it was a young man just arrived from Paris, the nephew of a cotton factor, a Mr. Musson. We adjourned to the stables to see Mr. Howard's horse (Elsinore, I believe she is called) put up, and then we took our carriage back into the city, pulled by a much more ordinary horse. We turned onto the lane, and there I saw the artist walking away, perhaps to his lodgings, his satchel at his knee.

14 November 1872. A few lines this evening on the train for home. How difficult it was to leave my girl in the city, though I shall be both cheered and needed by the other two. They depend on me, perhaps more so than Jenny, who is quite capable of managing herself. The train seems to take forever in both leaving the Algiers Station across from New Orleans and arriving in Donaldsonville.

15 November 1872. How dreadful. How hateful of Mr. Teague. I arrived at Mount Teague to find it yawning and empty of all, save Mr. Teague and the servants. He was in his study looking out on his sugarcane and the lines of men who 'hacked and stacked.' I asked Mr. Teague where Ida and Lucy were. He said that he has sent the girls to stay with their grandmother, Mrs. Teague, 'for their betterment.' I asked him how long they would be away, and he said that they shall tour Europe with his mother for several months, and then they shall likely reside with her in Mississippi. He turned from the window, and I thought I could see his scar frown, though I couldn't tell if he smirked or stifled a belch. 'Could you have consulted me first?' I asked, trying to retain my composure. He replied rather pointedly, 'You are not their mother, any more than you are their sister.'

I felt as though I had fallen into a hole, and I am sure my countenance reflected it. And then again, there was the slightest twitch of my husband's scar as he suppressed a smile. Tonight, the rain rises to a murmur and chatters off the eaves. And this house grows colder, this finely appointed house, full of furniture and pianos and tapestries and vases and marble and frieze-work. But for me it is empty of everything except quiet. It rains violently, and Ruthie sets a fire in the Ladies' Parlour. How are my girls faring? Are they warm? Are they dry? How shall I know if they make their journey safely? To make matters worse, it is the anniversary of Papa's passing.

16 November 1872. Today, a package arrived from White Sulphur Springs. It is Penny, Lucy's doll, her original one. It was found behind a chair in the hotel parlour. There is a chip in the porcelain behind her ear. I put it in Papa's sermon chest with the new Penny, which Lucy has left behind.

17 November 1872. Sabbath or not, I could no longer bear the silence of this tomb, and so I told Ruthie that I had come across Jenny's favourite bow. I did not say if it was for her hair or her violin. I left a note for Mr. Teague saying that I shall be going back into the city and that it is quite possible that I shall extend my visit and perhaps pay a call on the Howards while I am in. I have instructed Ruthie to tell him that the note is for him, though, of course, I am certainly aware that he won't be able to read it and shall have to have another do it for him.

18 November 1872. I have arrived in the city and taken a room, not with the Howards, but in the City Hotel, away from the Howards and the Morrises and the other prying eyes who might be in league with my husband. I did, however, pay a call on Jenny. I found her in the midst of the large music room, populated by the sounds of different musical instruments, like a forest of birds and other animals. Her face intently followed the score in front of her, her bow sliding across the strings in the middle of the menagerie. She looked up, and when she saw me, she was so gladdened that she forgot her task altogether, and she ran to me still holding her violin and bow and threw her arms around me. I didn't tell her that her sisters were off to Europe and wouldn't be home for Christmas. I couldn't bear to spoil the moment. Lessons for the day concluded, and then there were introductions made to teachers and classmates. She seems to get on quite well with all of them, and, indeed, she appears to have become quite a favourite with them. 'Come with me, Sister,' she said as she put her violin and her bow in the case, carefully, as if putting a child to bed, laying a polishing cloth over both. 'I've been playing for a ballet school on Rue St. Philip. Mr. Masac arranges opportunities such as those for us so that we might become accustomed to playing in front of others. And, Alice, I can make a little money. Such a feeling to earn one's own!'

In all candour, I was hungry and a bit fatigued from my journey, but she begged me come, and I was so happy to see her that I relented. She talked excitedly about the city and the people she has met, the girl from Natchez who plays the flute 'simply divinely' and the boy from Montgomery in Alabama who plays the cello and is a nephew to Alexander Stephens, the vice president of the late Confederacy. We crossed the great High Street, Canal Street, amid the passing of omnibuses, gigs, phaetons, and other conveyances and the mules and horses which conveyed them. She asked if her father had come with me, and I told her no, that he was consumed with rolling season and sugar that must be got in. 'Yes,' she said, 'I hope that when Christ returns for the rapture, it won't be during rolling season. Everyone in St. Matthew would be too busy to go with Him!' She took my arm with her free arm, and we descended down into the Old Quarter, where the French language predominates, and the sound of it colours everything. My French returned to my consciousness in snippets, tittles and jots, words of conversations about the lives occurring beyond open windows and shop doors: *theatre, marche, poulet.* We walked along the streets in that part of the city, among the old, large houses that lounge in the sun, the windows letting escape the smell of cooking and where fashionable women lounged on the balconies in patches of sunlight. We passed a magnificent building with stately columns and curved ends, and Jenny said that it was the French Opera House and that there are whispers that it is poorly managed and that there wouldn't be any programs there this winter.

And then we turned down a street called 'Rue St.Philip,' and through an open window I heard the shuffle of feet and the clap of a single pair of hands and instructions in French, *prepare well, my girls* and *five minutes, we begin when the music arrives!* A door opened for us, and we entered a room where there were perhaps a dozen or more girls about our age or younger and in the typical stages of bodily development, some whose bodies were tall and full and winning the race to womanhood, and some whose bodies were flat and short and hopelessly behind. All were stretching and going through their repertoire of movements as an older woman in bare feet moved through them. She turned to us and said, "*Ah! La musique est ici!*' Jenny addressed her in English, 'Madame Renain, this is my sister, Alice. She plays the piano.' There was a piano in one corner, and I stood by it with my fingers touching the magic ivory keys. On the stand was a stack of musical scores.

'We are rehearsing *La Sylphide,*' Madame said, 'Do you think you are up to it?' I nodded to her and said, 'Oui, madame, *avec pleasur.*' She nodded back to me and turned to arrange her girls as I sat at the bench and looked through the music for *La Sylphide.* The girls were assembled, and Jenny and I nodded to each other and to Madame, and we began. The quiet shuffle of feet on the planked floors began with the piano and the violin. Madame moved through the dancers, examining footwork, making sure chests were out and chins were up. Occasionally, she would scold them, '*Non, non, non! Vous ne piétinez pas les raisins!*' In English, 'You are not stomping grapes!'

I looked up from the keys of the piano, an old Chickering, to behold young girls in blossoming but confused bodies, most of them dancing rather flawlessly. They moved as if in response to the keys of the piano and the strings of Jenny's violin, like figures on a music box. For a musician, it was splendid. 'Tendu! Plié! Arabesque!' Mme. Renain called, and each attitude was executed, slippered feet shuffling across the planks of the floor. She paused again to scold one of the girls, and the girl nodded assent to her error and raised her chin and arms in the ready position to prepare again. And then with a nod from Madame, we resumed the music once more, the shuffle of slippers resumed on the creaking wood floor, 'Tendu, plié, arabesque!' We played as the dancers moved more or less harmoniously to the clapping of Mme. Renain as she kept time with the music and watched the movements of her girls.

There was a knock upon the door, and Mme. Renain strode over to it, still voicing instructions to the girls over her shoulder. She opened it and said, 'Bonjour, Monsieur,' and admitted a man. When he entered, I recognized him as the artist who had been sketching at the race track. She greeted him amicably and showed him to a seat, and he set up a chair and began sketching. He couldn't see me from behind the raised top of the piano, but I could see him. We began the music again, though I must admit to you, my little confidant, that I had to keep my eyes from straying to him.

I didn't realize that I had stopped playing, and Jenny was carrying the tune alone on the violin. She cleared her throat to prompt me, and it took me a moment to read our place in the song, from *La Sylphide*, the part in which the sylph approaches young James. I found it, and the piano joined the violin once more, but I found it hard to concentrate. The artist still seemed to have failed to notice the lapse in the music, but instead was intent on the movement of the dancers, eyes going from subject to sketch and back again. Finally, he saw me and seemed to smile in a way, though it was not a proper smile but something a little more reserved. My piano faltered again. Mme. Renain signaled for a break by rapping on a metal watering can used to settle the dust on the floor.

During the break, Jenny continued to play a few reels for several of the girls, mainly the younger ones who still had the energy to dance and seemed to enjoy the freedom of dancing as they pleased. I was watching them when a voice distracted me, and I turned to find the young man by the piano. It was a good thing that he appeared so suddenly, for if I had seen him approach, I would have lost my tongue completely. He nodded and said in French but with a very noticeable Parisian accent, 'You and your sister, you two are very adept musicians.' It was very charitable of him, for my distraction had affected my playing most unfavourably. I did not correct him by telling him that Jenny is my step-daughter but instead thanked him. My conscience whispered insistently that this, my little confidant, was a deception. He said that we followed Madame quite well, as well as the musicians follow the dance-masters in Paris. This, too, was charitable, considering the missteps my fingers had made. I asked him, 'You were at the stables, weren't you? Last week, monsieur?' His face brightened, and he said that yes, he was, and I favour myself that he was pleased that I had remembered.

'I saw you there,' he said, 'With your husband?' I answered quickly. 'No,' I said, 'With friends. I don't live here in the city. I'm only visiting,' and then I added, 'my sister.' Just then, Mme. Renain rounded up the girls with handclapping and genial scolding. The jigs and reels were put away as the girls returned to the more serious and refined movements of ballet. Mme. Renain called out, 'Places, girls! Heels forward, wrists in the air! Begin!' The next half hour crawled until our glances met, and then time sprinted to the next glance. His smile, at first reserved, was broader with each look we exchanged. I missed a note, and Mme. Renain looked over her shoulder at me. I found my place, but almost lost it again when, from across the room, I saw him purse his lips in a smile at my error. He seemed to have put away the idea of sketching altogether.

When the class was over, and the girls were bundling up against the November evening chill, he took an old paint-splotched canvas satchel and put away his sketchpad and approached as Jenny talked to Mme. Renain. This time, he came with much the same posture of a stray dog waiting outside a door for scraps. He removed his hat, not a topper or a bowler, but a hat much like the sailing men wear, and bowed slightly and said, 'Edgar Degas.'

'Alice,' I said, 'Alice Lamb.' It was not a lie but certainly less than the truth. A half-truth, I suppose. 'Well, Miss Lamb, it is my pleasure to make your acquaintance.' He said it in English, in the practiced cadence of a non-native speaker who is struggling to learn the language and has found a new phrase, a useful new nugget of speech. And may God forgive me, but I did not correct him. I allowed myself to be Miss Lamb rather than Mrs. Teague. And then he asked me, with the candour of a Parisian, 'And may I ask you, Miss Alice Lamb, do you have a beau? Or is it that you cannot decide which beau on whom to bestow your favour?' 'No—that is, I mean—' I said, quickly, impulsively, and quite undone. He smiled rather impishly and asked, 'Do you mean, no, I may not ask you, or no, you do not have a beau?'

'Forgive me,' I blushed, 'I do not have a beau.' This, of course, my little confidant, is also half-truth. But a husband is not a beau. And he didn't ask if I had a husband. And so, I have split a lie in two and told it as a pair of half-truths.

'Yes, well, then,' he said, as if he had suddenly lost his nerve, 'It was such a pleasure to meet you. And I should consider myself lucky if we might meet again.' I said nothing, though I wanted to, and should have. Jenny approached with her case in hand, and as she did, all I could say was, 'Yes, perhaps we shall Monsieur—'

'Degas,' he prompted me. As Jenny and I departed toward Canal Street, I looked over my shoulder. And his glance met mine as he made his way toward the opposite end of the street.

Sammy, 1982

Sammy marked his place in the diary and put it away in the desk drawer. He looked around himself at the study, the fallacy of old Sam Teague's library, the showpiece of books of a man who couldn't read a single sentence in any of them. His great-grandfather had only passed himself off as wise, the King of Jupitre dressed up as fake royalty in a sequined mask, silk tights, and a brass crown. The wall of books in the study was just a façade of learnedness, a case of ignorance passing as wisdom. In the central hallway, Sammy looked up at his great-grandfather's portrait. The awe he had once felt for the old patriarch in the uniform had now melted away into something between shame and anger.

Sammy stroked his beard and sat in front of the portrait of the man. As Sammy sat there, the great-great granddaughters of the man in the Confederate uniform came jabbering down the stairs in tutus and leotards. They hugged their mother, and it made Sammy think of the Teague girls of a hundred years ago, Jenny, Ida, and Lucy. They had climbed the same steps and gone through the same doors. What ever became of them? he wondered. Had Alice ever greeted them like Betsy greeted their girls, stooping to kiss and hug them?

They climbed into his truck, and they rumbled down the lane of oaks over the white shells. As his girls chattered on the front seat next to him, he drove and thought about his cane and what needed to be done, which fields should be cut first, which should be skipped, fields of first stubble cane, fields of second stubble cane, signs of disease on the emerging green stalks and Johnson grass pushing up between them. His mind scanned the ten-thousand acres and at last came to the metal shed. The things that Teeter had taken apart were still a collection of nuts, bolts, screws, and brackets. He hoped that Teeter would be well enough to have them back together before the cane got high. And then he hoped that Teeter would be well-enough, period.

The P and the Y of the graffiti insult that had been written on the hood was still faintly visible through the light blue spray paint that Sammy had hastily applied over it. Judee and Elizabeth sat next to each other on the front seat beside him, and he listened to them talk as if he wasn't there.

"Mama said we're gonna go to Disney this summer instead of next week 'cause in the summer they got fireworks every night," Elizabeth said to her sister. Elizabeth's little hands rose, and her fingers opened as she made firework noises.

"Is Mickey Mouse there in the summer?" Judee asked, brightly and suspiciously.

"Every day, Mama says," Elizabeth said. "And in the summer, they got ice cream."

"I like ice cream," Judee said.

"Me too. Everybody does. That's why we goin' in the summer instead of next week."

Sammy knew that Disney had fireworks and ice cream every night, year-round. He also knew that Betsy had told them they were going to have to postpone their trip, and that, after a moment of big bottom lips and watery eyes from the girls, Betsy had cleverly, effortlessly, redirected them to an even greater adventure that involved the bonus of fireworks and ice cream. When it came to children, she was a genius. Like Alice explaining the absence of a missing doll.

They pulled into the white shell parking lot with the prefab metal building called *Miss Kayla's School of Dance.* Under it was written, *Jazz-Tap-Ballet.* Miss Kayla had been a Golden Girl at LSU and on graduation had an offer to dance in New York, which gave her an element of celebrity in the parish. But she had fallen in love with and then married a boy who worked at one of the chemical plants, and now she taught dance to children in a prefab metal building on the edge of a cane field. Though she had had her brush with stardom, she was content with her purpose. St. Matthew Parish was home, after all.

She greeted each girl who came in as if she were her own daughter or niece or little sister, stooping to take their little arms around her neck. The girls in pink leotards and tutus ran in ballet-slippered feet, dusted with the powder of the shells in the parking lot, and the girls in the mirror along the back wall ran to them, and the girls and their reflections took their little bags off their shoulders and set them down by the wall in perfect synchrony.

Miss Kayla's ponytail shook as she clapped her hands, just like Alice had described Mme. Renain doing. Without being told, the girls lined up according to height, girls as young as Judee and girls tall enough to have confused bodies that were beginning to push out against their leotards. Miss Kayla raised her arms, and the room fell silent, though a big truck grumbled past on Highway 1, and the room was silent again. Miss Kayla padded over to a tape deck and pressed the tab and pre-recorded violin and piano music filled the studio.

There were no young women to play the violin and piano, no watering can to keep the dust down, no clop of mules or clatter of wagons outside windows that were kept open to fetch a breeze. But the girls and the attitudes they performed were the same, however, *tendu, plié, arabesque.* The older girls were crisp in their movements, even the waving of their ponytails was identical, but the younger girls were more varied, and no two executed the moves the same way, most of them checking each other in sidelong glances, small heads with ponytails and buns peeking with arms over heads, bending knees at various angles, wavering on one leg in shallow arabesques. Miss Kayla passed between, correcting a pose here, illustrating a pose there, the little faces beaming up with looks of pure admiration that are seldom found on a Broadway stage.

In a distant corner was a piano, though it was now supplanted by a tape deck and cassettes. Sammy thought of how an English woman might play it and how a Parisian artist might sit in the metal-and-plastic folding chairs and sketch the dancers and how the two might exchange looks, flirting without meaning to. He wondered if Mme. Renain had moved like Miss Kayla, launching up on the balls of her feet to show an arabesque and then moving among her girls, giving encouragement to the younger ones and quietly scolding the older ones. He imagined Miss Kayla passing a young artist and speaking a word in French to him. *Bonjour, Monsieur Artiste*, she might say as she moved along to correct a dancer's form.

Sammy fell so deeply into the daydream of it that he could almost hear music coming from the upright piano facing out from along the wall, though he couldn't see anyone behind it. He watched the mirror, and it dimmed, and in the darkness, he saw that the chairs and the studio were empty. He rose and wound his way among the places where the mothers had been watching their girls dance. He still heard them whispering, however, as young feet whisked across the floor to the sound of a piano and a violin. He approached the piano, the back of it facing out into the darkened room and the keyboard and the bench obscured behind it. The sound was grainy like that of tape-recorded piano music from a ballet; perhaps it was from *La Sylphide*, though he wasn't sure.

He approached the piano, and he was sure that, when he looked over it, he would see her, blonde hair flowing over a dress of a style no longer worn, her fingers pressing the keys into music like a line of birds singing their notes. He wanted to see her, to say something to her, to make peace with her, to forgive her for the terror she had caused him. The music rose to a climactic rush. The steps of the dancers had faded, and he was alone with the piano. He heard Mme. Renain clap her hands, and her voice murmured as if it were coming from a deep, dark well, so distant that he couldn't tell if she were speaking English or French, only echoes. As he placed his hand on the back of the piano to look over it, to make himself look, the music suddenly ended with a clap.

He opened his eyes to see his daughters' faces. Their bags were over their shoulders.

"Daddy's sweepin'," Judee whispered to Elizabeth.

Over the bubbling conversation of girls and young women who were being collected by their mothers, Miss Kayla clapped her hands and said, "I need your costume forms! Recital is in four weeks!"

Sammy walked over to the piano and looked down at a closed keyboard cover and an empty bench. He looked around, cloudy with half-sleep, and finally walked back over and took his girls' hands. As he approached the door, he took one last look at the piano in the corner and his reflection in the mirror. The reflection of the three of them, a cane farmer and his daughters, receded through the door in the mirror and into the white-shell parking lot beyond that, deeper into the mirror.

Judee leaned into Elizabeth, and Elizabeth leaned into her daddy as they followed the winding highway along Bayou Lafourche and then crossed it. They were still too young to know the stigma he had earned them. How long would it be, he wondered, before the girls had to deal with mean-spirited talk and jibes against them and their cowardly daddy? Would they think less of him? Would they think less of themselves?

They turned onto the long white-shell lane of oaks, and Pongeaux greeted them halfway down, barking wildly at their return, an orange-brown blur launching herself in long strides with her ears laid back. The dog barked and slapped her front paws on the ground and turned in circles and wiggled as Elizabeth knelt and rubbed her belly. As his girls ascended the steps, one at a time, and their dog waited at the top like a patient nanny, he opened the door and then followed them inside. With a kiss for their mother, he adjourned to his study.

Alice, 1872

19 November 1872. Jenny is at school again. Though the threat of an illness called 'horse flu' hangs over the city, carriages are still available, and I hired one and amused myself with a long ride through the city. I directed the driver to drive along the street where I last saw M. Degas. Along the way, my nose was subjected to the rapidly shifting kaleidoscope of good and bad smells of this city. The sweet wafting of flowers at the market, the ejected matter of horses and mules, the pleasing aroma of cooking in the fine restaurants, the emptied stomachs on the sidewalks outside the saloons, washed away with buckets of water by men in suspenders and dingy, collarless shirts. I saw much, but I did not see my Parisian.

20 November 1872. My conscience spurred me, and I succumbed to its pressure and paid a call on the Howards. An old woman, as dark as any I have seen, greeted me with a grim, 'Yes ma'am?' and then retreated down the central hallway whilst I peered into it. From down the length of it, I heard her say into a parlour, 'Miz Flora?' Mrs. Howard appeared, setting her embroidery hoop on the hall table. Within the ring of it, a floral scene was emerging. 'Mrs. Teague, how nice you should call,' she said with what seemed to be only a meager amount of enthusiasm. Tea was prepared, and Mrs. Howard and I took it in the gardens adjacent the house, behind the stone wall that separated them from the street. Our conversation was polite but restrained, and the sound of wheels and hooves serenaded us as our conversation faltered. The ancient negress called 'Old Mama' attended us at the beck and call of Mrs. Howard.

Old Mama, bring us shortbread!

Old Mama, please arrange our chairs, this patch of sun has gotten hot.

Old Mama, that will be all.

And Old Mama supplied all with a drooping head and downcast eyes and a yes, ma'am.

Mrs. Howard confirmed that the Opera in this city is suspended for the season. She has heard that it is due to financial reverses. I was hopeful that I had spent sufficient time to conclude my visit, when Mrs.

Howard insisted that I stay with them, and I could think of no reason to refuse. She said that her husband is away on business and should return in a week or two. Unable to think of a reason otherwise, I was sent with a servant to retrieve my things from the City Hotel.

21 November 1872. I once again attended dance class with Jenny, resolved to follow the tune this time. It was no issue, as M. Degas did not attend. It is lucky that the music was both easy and familiar to me, as I spent a great deal of time daydreaming, and you, of course, my little confidant, know about whom. Jenny asked why I was so quiet, and I said that it has been two years since Papa died, and the thought of it sets me melancholic. But that is only part of it. I feel I am under a spell, that magic is being worked upon me. Were I not a married woman, it would be delightful. Such foolishness, such folly!

22 November 1872. It is a day much like spring, and if there were no calendar to consult, one might think it April. The Howard children animate this place on St. Charles, attended to almost exclusively by Old Mama and the tutors that come to instruct them. In the garden, I found myself thinking of him, his hands and how they must feel, mine in his, his on my back. I dream of him sketching me, enjoying his appraisal of me as we silently share the same space. His quiet, brown eyes, his mouth and how it broke into a smile from within his beard, only to return to a thoughtful repose. Who is he, this quiet, thoughtful man? What has prompted him to journey across the sea to be here? How is he able to make a living as an artist? My thoughts dare to wander, and the dream transforms itself, and I am in the bare pose of the odalisque, light falling on uncovered breasts, reclining thighs crossed in repose. Surely it is madness, forbidden madness. Such thoughts must be banished, and I do, but once again they intrude.

23 November 1872. A most dreadful surprise today. Mr. Teague has come for a visit to the city. I suppose he is willing to risk stolen sugar.

I returned to the Howards to find his hat and gloves on the hall table and to hear his voice in the parlour where he was speaking with Mr.

Howard. He did not rise to greet me, nor kiss me on my cheek, nor take my hand. He only said, 'Hello, Mrs. Teague,' to which I responded, 'Hello, Mr. Teague.' He is in town with the same concern as much of the populace, worried that the vote shall be incorrectly counted and that the wrong outcome given. The newspapers have daily called for a fair count. That is, one that ensures a victory for McEnery.

The Howards have given us the use of their box at the Varieties tonight, and my husband said that we shall attend. It was not an offer, nor a question, nor a proposal. It was, as most pronouncements from Mr. Teague are, a command, a summons. 'Yes, husband,' I said, which was the only proper response. And so, as the night fell on the city, the Howards' driver took us to the Varieties Theatre for the performance of a play entitled, 'Man and Wife,' featuring a Miss Clara Morris of New York, no relation to Mr. Morris of this city. As the lights dimmed and the orchestra filled the hall with music, Mr. Teague quickly fell off into the Land of Nod. The curtains opened to reveal the stage, and the audience was flooded with light. And then I saw him. My Parisian.

He was sitting in the balcony in a private box of seats with a group of women and men who had the comfortable of air of family about them. The music crescendoed and fell, and the actors began their lines. Jenny's raptured face captured the lights of the stage, as did Mr. Teague's sunken face as he slumbered in them, his scar curling and writhing in his beard like a worm with each exhalation.

And then I felt eyes upon me, and I looked over to the balcony, and there he was, looking at me. We exchanged a nod, and then, thinking the same thought, perhaps, we turned our attention to the stage. The plot was lost on me, the pretense of the dialog forgotten and of no consequence. My palms were sweating, as they sweat now as I record these events. We traded surreptitious glimpses and stolen smiles. At intermission, the house lights came up, and my Parisian left his box with several others. I stayed in ours and listened to Jenny chatter on about the performance, under the spell of its make-believe. My eyes strayed to the balcony, and as the lights dimmed to announce the second act, Jenny quieted, and I waited for him to return and take his seat. I was afraid that Monsieur had abandoned the performance, but he returned and took his seat during the first scene of the second act, casting a glance to me with a mock pout during a downpour of laughter from some onstage joke. I became aware that he had waited for me in the lobby at intermission, and I became aware also of a forbidden aching in my body, and when I gathered the courage to look over to him, he looked off to the stage rather than meet my glance. Jenny whispered something to me, presumably about the play, but I heard none of what she said, and if I had heard it, I would have been insensible to it, and so I only inclined my ear and smiled weakly.

The play concluded, unappreciated by Mr. Teague, who roused from slumber with the brightening houselights, and by me, who stood with the rest of the audience and clapped. We the audience applauded as each member of the cast came and took a bow, the applause reaching a peak as at last Miss Clara Morris took her bow and graciously gestured with an open palm to her supporting players. We rose and made slowly for the stairs. My weak legs could scarcely support me. 'Oh Alice, wasn't that just capital?' Jenny said. 'Yes, quite,' I said, though I had not the foggiest idea what had transpired on the stage, having been involved in my own, private tableau. I still ached in those certain, secret places, and the steps were a difficulty due to it.

Jenny asked her father if he had enjoyed the performance, and Mr. Teague said that he had found it rather droll, though I know this was a falsehood to match mine. He had not heard a word of it either. 'Waste of a good evening,' he said.

'But it was certainly charitable of the Howards to allow us the use of their box,' I offered, though rather feebly. We descended the carpeted stairs, and I tarried to let Jenny and my husband trail ahead in the crowd, which was shoulder-to-shoulder, a forest of hats and bonnets and shawls and greatcoats preparing to depart from the gaslight and enter the night cold. I scanned the egressing crowd, and I saw him, engaged in conversation with several others, men and women, one of them clearly expecting a child. Our eyes met once more, his brown eyes on mine, and he smiled and perhaps I did. And then the crowd bore me away into the cold, where my husband waited impatiently by our brougham, sent by Mr. Howard and waiting in the queue of carriages. I took my seat under a blanket with Jenny. The carriage tilted and squeaked with Mr. Teague's entry, and he said, *forward* to the driver. I looked over my shoulder to see my Parisian, Edgar—yes, his name is Edgar—emerge from the crowd and recede to the dense rattle of hooves on the cobblestones. Later, the conjugal rite, and Mr. Teague commented that I was certainly a 'a spirited little philly tonight!' He drifts away and into a snore now and I ask myself this question: 'Do the wandering thoughts of another, imagined during the conjugal rite, constitute the sin of adultery?'

25 November 1872. Mr. Teague and I visited Jenny today at the Conservatory on Baronne Street. He maintained the air of a man checking on the progress of an investment. We arrived to find an impromptu recital in progress. The students were arranged in a broad semicircle, and Jenny was among them, listening with her violin and her bow in her lap. I could not tell if she had played or was waiting her turn. A young man, rather frail in appearance, was seated at the piano, navigating his way through Mozart's *Piano Sonata No. 11, the Andante Grazioso.* He sweated with a worried look on his brow, his pink-circled eyes frantically searching the pages of the music. I thought back to the day of my first public performance in Surrey, and how Papa told me to imagine the listeners as animals. I sought to give the young man my best encouraging countenance, but his terrified gaze remained locked onto his sheet music. His fingers mistepped and hit a sour note, and he appeared on the verge of tears. Mr. Teague snorted and grinned. Just then, Mrs. Masac came and sat next to the young man and said something reassuring. He took a deep breath as she turned the page, and he began again. When he was done, he stood up with a scrape of the bench and bowed to polite applause. He took his seat among his classmates as quickly as he could.

'Miss Teague?' Mr. Masac said, inclining his head to my step-daughter. Mr. Teague looked up from the spot on the wall he had been contemplating and raised his chin in anticipation. He crossed and then uncrossed his arms. And then our Jenny rose and faced the gathering. She put her instrument under her chin, softly squeezing it there and looking to Mr. Masac. He nodded, and she took a short, confidant breath with a quick nod of chin and violin. The bow pulled across the strings and the sublime piece began. It was a nocturne I had not heard before, a lilting, soothing strain, simply magnificent. Eyes were closed, heads were bowed. It was as if no one wanted to breathe, lest the meager sound of moving air across lips disturb the music emanating from the violin. Mrs. Masac stood at her side, turning the pages of music as quietly as she could, but closing her eyes to the tune, almost like the sighing face of an angel. When Jenny was finished, there was no applause. The air was completely still, as if waiting for the tune to continue, and then finally, after that moment, which held its own eternity, applause arose like a whirlwind of birds, and the students and teachers rose from their seats, and my Jenny blushed. Mr. Masac approached, also clapping, and whispered into her ear. I saw his lips trace the words, *take your bow.*

She did so with violin in one hand and bow in the other, once and then again and again. Finally, she took her seat again, cradling her instrument and its bow on her lap, and at last her hands shook a little. Two other students performed, not badly, really, but they sounded somewhat dissonant in the wake of Jenny's performance, a large boy with an acne-pocked face who played Strauss' *The Beautiful Blue Danube* on the tuba and a girl who played a popular march on the piano. They were both passably done, but nothing near the sublime effort of Jenny, something I say in total candour and without favouritism. The recital adjourned, and as instruments were put away, Mr. Masac asked if he might have a word with Miss Teague's father. I stood and waited as the two men talked, and it appeared as if Mr. Masac was trying to sell Mr. Teague something. Mr. Teague pursed his lips and furrowed his brow. Mr. Masac paused, and they looked at us, or rather, at Jenny who was speaking to the boy who had played *The Beautiful Blue Danube* on the tuba. Mr. Teague scratched his beard thoughtfully, his thumb absently tracing over his scar. At last, Mr. Masac offered his hand to Mr. Teague, who hesitated and then shook it. When I asked my husband what he and Mr. Masac were discussing, he said only, 'Oh, I would say that it is not your affair,' and he limped along, placing his hat upon his head. I felt quite dismissed.

26 November 1872. The night is warm for this time of year, like a summer night in Surrey. I write in a square of light cast from inside the house on the front gallery of the Howard's and listen to the conversation of the men in the parlour. Night traffic has fallen off on St. Charles, though an omnibus passed a few moments ago like a shadow amid the resonance of mule hooves on the pavement, sound and shadow receding away into the night. Then the boil of voices inside the window emerges again to the forefront.

The talk inside is of the election. The votes are counted at last and McEnery is defeated by Kellogg for governor much to the chagrin and grumbling of a large portion of the populace here. Great is the disappointment. All is in danger on this turn of fate—ebbing fortunes, negro overlords, confiscated property, the rape of wives and daughters. Upset voices declare, this won't do! It shall not pass! There are shouts of agreement. They are the sounds of the disappointed, the dejected, and the angry. The *Picayune* reported this morning that Warmouth, who is the sitting governor, appointed a State Returns Board which has found for McEnery, but a rival board, set up by the Union occupiers, has found for Kellogg and his negro running mate, a Mr. Antoine. The voices inside declare, 'McEnery is *our* governor, not this Kellogg, carpet-bagging bastard and his saddle-coloured lieutenant governor Antoine. Grant's puppet, pulled by scurrilous Yankee strings—' The voice of my husband emerges among them, clear, certain, convincing. His is a voice that seems to light a fuse, the sizzle of a spark that races along a wick, searching for tinder to ignite. There was talk of taking up arms again, against this outrage. Other voices interceded, however, and a decision was made to pursue the matter in the courts, though there was considerable opposition. Now men are leaving, driven home by the negro servants that terrify them so. One by one, they fade into the shadows on the hollow notes of the hooves of the beasts of burden that bear them away. And so, I close for the night, my little confidant.

27 November 1872. Jenny and I attended church by ourselves at St. Paul's, as Mr. Teague has returned to St. Matthew to supervise the grinding of his sugarcane. He is convinced that whole barrels, nay, whole wagon-loads of it, may find their way from Mount Teague to be sold by others. Stolen sugarcane is not the only concern in the city. The talk of stolen elections has found its way to the pulpit, and there were surreptitious prayers, not that God's will be done, but that the guilty should be punished for violation of the commandment, 'thou shall not steal.' Apparently, this commandment extends to elections as well. I wonder if Moses was aware of it.

After church, Jenny and I walked back to the Howards where Sunday dinner awaited. She asked why I didn't tell her that her sisters had gone to Europe. I told her that her joy was so great to be in the city that I hadn't the heart for it. She asked if I could get Mr. Teague to recall them, and I stated the obvious, 'Your Father does as he pleases.' Of course, she knew the truth of it and said, 'I suppose there is nothing that I can do about it. I was hoping that we would all be together for Christmas.' It is true that this shall be the first Christmas that the sisters will be apart. We both miss them terribly, but there is nothing that can be done about it.

28 November 1872. As it is a Monday and Jenny resumes studies at the conservatory, I took breakfast with Mrs. Howard. Old Mama prepared a delightful meal, seemingly with little effort. Mrs. Howard was under the weather and returned to bed, and I went for a stroll in very agreeable temperatures. The city was going about its business, and I pretended that I had business in it as well. And then, on Carondelet, I heard my name, 'Alice!' I paused and looked all around, into the faces on the street, though none looked to mine. 'Mam'selle Lamb!' I heard, and then, 'Up here!' I put my hand to my eyes to shield the bright sun. There he was, what I had secretly been hoping for, if I am to be honest. My Parisian, resting on his elbows on the ornate iron railing of the second floor of a business called, 'Musson & Prestidge, & Co., Cotton Factors.' He bid me wait right where I was, and he entered the window on the balcony and in a moment was on the street before me, mildly out of breath.

'You were at the theatre,' he said as a greeting. 'Yes, I saw you,' I said, 'and I wished to speak with you, but the crowd bore me away.' He said he thought I was being coy, but he pronounced it as a Frenchman might, 'kwah,' and I laughed and corrected him, 'coy,' like 'boy.' I added that I had not intended to be either coy or kwah. He laughed quietly, and then he gave me a look of such tenderness, such kindness, so vulnerable and soft-hearted, that words failed me, to a point that I did not care that they had failed me. I was only half-aware that he was studying me, and I was studying him, brown eyes, lashes, lips. The moment began to weigh heavily and so I spoke to relieve the tension of it, for I am sure he laboured under it as well. 'What are you sketching?' I asked as if I were coming up for air from the dreamy underwater world of that moment. 'My Uncle Michel's brokerage, come,' he whispered as if waking, and I realized again that we were standing in front of a brokerage, a place of commerce and not on a cloud. He put my arm in his and we ascended the stairs to the second floor, to a room in which a group of men orbited around a table piled high with cotton samples. On an empty chair was his sketchpad, and on it was the room, drawn with the men in it. 'See here,' he said, gesturing from the sketch to the subjects, 'Here is my Uncle Michel, my brothers, Rene and Achille. My cousin's husband, Mr. Bell. Here, Mr. Prestidge.'

'I can see them. I can see them thinking and moving,' I said, 'You have rendered them so well, they seem to have motion, they seem to be alive. How do you do it?' He shrugged his shoulders and said, 'I just draw lines, and then I draw more lines.' He smiled as he looked at me again, and I became aware that he might be looking at me in the same manner, how he might draw me with lines and then more lines. I was aware of my breath and my beating heart and nothing else. His voice came from faraway. 'Did you and your sister enjoy the performance?' his lips asked. His voice seemed separate. 'Yes,' I lied. In truth, I had but little noticed it, 'did you?' He was more truthful and said, 'I was distracted.'

'I'm sorry to hear that,' my ragged voice trailed away. I could feel the blood rushing in my ears, hear my breath and his, and if he had tried to kiss me I would not have stopped him, and I wished he would try to kiss me so that I could fail to stop him. The air around us was glowing, though the men in the room seemed unaware of it. How could they not notice, something as rare and magical as that? The space we shared, we shared alone, and it was compressed, or expanded—I couldn't tell and was unconcerned anyway. It was not a cotton office on Carondelet Street in New Orleans but the very center of the universe. 'There was someone in your box,' he said in a low, struggling voice, in such a way that I could tell that he also was under the spell, as if both resisting it and protected by it at the same time. 'Was it a gentleman? I could not see him well, only his shadow when the lights were just so.' My conscience screamed at me to be forthright and tell this man that the person in the box was my husband and the girl was not my sister but my step-daughter. But instead, I told him the shadow belonged to our father. The commandment is broken again, and to this innocent person. I find false witness so easy to bear, as light as a feather.

He escorted me downstairs, and at the bottom of them, on the banquette of Carondelet, he asked if he might call on me, but I told him that my father was very possessive of us, his daughters, and that he discouraged gentleman callers. 'Well, he is welcomed to bring you for a visit to see my Uncle Michel,' and from his waistcoat pocket, he presented me with a card with his address. 'I am sure my Uncle would enjoy a visit from your father, as I know I would enjoy a visit from you.' The strange light glowed around us and the calling card my white gloves held. My fingers traced the embossed address, No. 372 Esplanade, the dwelling place of this man and his Uncle Michel. At last, I said, 'Well, your subjects must be moving about up there. Perhaps I should let you return to your work.'

'Yes,' he said, with something almost like dejection, and he entered the building again. I should have turned to leave, to make my way down the banquette, but I didn't. And he should have continued up the stairs to his work, but he didn't. Rather, he turned around, and we looked at each other briefly. And there was no mistaking that he felt the same sensation that I did. It was like being touched by a flame.

29 Nov. 1872. I gathered my courage and walked to the opposite end of the French Quarter to find the address of my Parisian. The trees in the strip of ground in the center of Rue Esplanade bore whitewashed trunks, repeating off into the distance away from the river. Each block passed, and the numbers of the fine houses increased until at last I came to it on the left side of the street, No. 372 Esplanade. It is a fine, large house with a broad front porch and an upper gallery that span the length of the house. A few houses down from 372, two boys were throwing acorns at blackbirds. I retrieved the note that I had made in pencil and gave each boy a nickel to carry the message to M. Edgar Degas at 372 Esplanade. '*Monsieur*,' it read, '*if you are not otherwise engaged, please meet me this afternoon in the square in front of the cathedral. I shall be sitting on a bench in front of the statue of General Jackson. Signed, your friend.*'

The boys scurried up to the doorstep and rang the bell hanging by a small chain. One threw the rest of his acorns off the porch, and, when the door opened, the boys took off their hats. The figure of the woman who answered the door stated that she was obviously expecting a child. It also appeared that, by her mannerisms, she was blind or partially blind. She looked off and away, much like Mr. Luther, our gardener at Mount Teague, though much more pronounced. She thanked the boys with a smile and took the note inside with her. She seemed to be examining it with her fingertips.

I returned to the Howards where Old Mama prepared a lunch for me, but I had little appetite for it. I tried to nap but could not. I tried to read but could not. The minute hand scraped slowly over the faces of the clocks and the pendulums swung painfully unhurried. A little past one, I departed the Howards and walked down to the square and amused myself watching the pigeons strut. At half past one, a priest in a long cassock came out and scattered a handful of bread crumbs to them. We greeted each other with a nod, and the priest went back into the cathedral, leaving me with the pigeons. Their round, glowing eyes regarded the bread and me, and their shimmering necks pumped. When the ground was pecked clean of bread, their fat bodies strutted away. The sun shifted, and at a quarter till, so did I, to a patch of shade opposite from where I was sitting. There I waited nervously in the shadow of the great general who had, oddly enough, defeated the English below the city some sixty years before. I checked the clock on the cathedral again and again. I had almost made up my mind against my folly, a married woman rather scandalously meeting this unassuming man, when he appeared a few minutes before the clock tower struck two. He removed his hat with a slight bow. His eyes were sad and brown and kind. 'I am hope that it is you who send the message,' he said in faltering English.

'It was,' I said as calmly as I could, though my heart was beating wildly, and I took a breath trying to slow it. He said something else, and I sensed the frustration of someone struggling with a foreign tongue. I asked him if he preferred French or English. He complimented me on my French, and I told him that I had a teacher when I was younger who called French 'la belle langue.' He said that she had taught me well, that I got on quite well in la belle langue, but that he thought he should at least try English so he could improve. 'One must do so to get along,' he said.

I told him that his uncle has a rather large house. 'Yes,' he said, 'and filled with family!' And so, we spoke of his family. He is visiting from Paris, staying in the house of his Uncle Michel, who has been a widower for a year or so. In the house with them are his cousins, three women. Two are married and have families, and the house is full of children. He described it as chaotic, but truly, it sounded like heaven to me, a house full of family. I asked about the woman who answered the door, and he said it was his cousin Estelle, who is also his sister-in-law, married to his brother Rene. 'Such a hard life she has had! She is a *veuve de guerre,'* he said.

'A war widow?' I asked him in English, and he made an attempt to begin again in it. 'Yes,' he said, 'and now she goes blind. But how she makes her way around the house! As if her fingertips are eyes! She never suffers a—' He searched for the term in English again but failed. 'A *faux pas,'* He said at last.

'A misstep,' I offered the English for him. 'Merci,' he said, 'yes, a *misstep*. 'She is a lovely person, lovely enough to be both cousin and sister,' he said in French, and then he asked me about my family, and I found myself speaking of them rather vaguely, and I hoped that my speaking in French served to hide it. I rather obliquely told him about Jenny, Lucy, and Ida, whom I referred to as 'my three girls.' I told him that the younger two were in Europe with my *belle-mère*. His brow wrinkled as he repeated the term, *belle-mère,* French for mother-in-law. My heart skipped a beat, and I recovered by saying that sometimes words jumble for me in *la belle langue*, and then I laughed at the colossal absurdity that my grandmother Mrs. Teague could be my mother-in-law, and he laughed with me. 'Yes, it is the same for me in English,' he said reassuringly, 'one word slips in the place of another, and the result is quite entertaining, sometimes. But it is a very good thing to have a family, to have good children.' I asked of his parents and if they still lived in Paris, and he said that his mother died when he was thirteen, and I exclaimed, 'as did mine!' We looked at each other and wondered at this coincidence. He said that it had been the worst day of his life, and I responded that losing my mother was the worst day of mine, though, my little confidant, the day that I married Mr. Teague might rival it. May heaven forgive me, but, truly, it does.

Edgar said that his father lives in Naples where he is a banker, and that he wanted him to become a banker also, but that he had chosen art, though really, art had chosen him. 'I work very hard at it, to prove that I can make a name, or at least a living, at it.' I asked him if he had had much success, and he said that he manages a small living, though the Salon in Paris, 'has little use for me. It is discouraging, sometimes.'

I was so at ease with this man's pleasant company, that an outcropping of truth emerged from the bare soil of this pretense, and I said, 'It was the same for Papa and the Linnaen Society in London. They had little use for him as well.' I said it rather absently, and as soon as I did, I regretted it.

'What prevents him?' he asked, 'do they reject him because he is an American?' His question brought me back to the present. 'Perhaps,' I said, realising that the truth had seeped over into the lie. And so, I changed the subject. I told him that his sketch of the cotton office was very good, and that I could get a good idea of their motion, their thoughts. 'I could almost tell who was hungry and who was not!' I said. He threw his head back and laughed. 'They are probably always hungry, those men!'

He suggested we take a walk. 'Come,' he said, 'I fear that if we tarry longer, we shall be arrested as vagrants!' He gave me his arm and I took it, but we hesitated on which direction to pursue. The day had become warm, and we kept to the shade of the store fronts. He said that in England and Paris, people would be bundled up against the cold and perhaps trudging through snow. 'New Orleans is England in her best mood, wouldn't you agree?' he asked as he smiled to the warm air. 'Yes, quite,' I said, 'I have often thought the very same thing.' As we walked, I pretended to look in shop windows, but really, I was watching him, watching him as he watched everything else. Pigeons strutted and scattered, and Edgar watched them, taking in the green and purple heads and necks, set on the drab grey bodies, the sudden burst of wings as they went from begging to flying. The movement of people and animals. Faces, gestures. He seemed to be trying to elucidate what their motion looked like, truly looked like, and perhaps how he could portray it. We reached the river and the forest of masts there and the clouds of smoke from the engines.

A drayman's horse stood waiting for his cart to be loaded, and Edgar found a fallen apple and stopped to pick it up and gave it to the horse. He stroked her sleek brown withers and whispered something soothing to her in French as her block teeth worked on the apple. When she finished, she motioned her long forehead for more, but he cooed, 'I have no more for you, I am sorry, but I wish good health and no horse-flu for you, my friend,' and we proceeded down the levee.

A ship was coming in bearing the flag of some foreign place, the tug tending her billowing black smoke as wavelets washed the muddy banks. Crewmen lashed the boat to the cleats of the dock with massive ropes as the wood of hulls and docks neared each other. Edgar watched the play of the winter light on the waves lapping the bank, and I wondered if he was supposing the colour of water and light. He held his hand up to his eyes as the jagged rays glanced off the water. He said that his eyes suffer sometimes as his cousin's do. I asked him if he feared for his sight, and he said, 'Yes, it is a concern for me. I have so much I want to see and paint. They had wanted me to be a sharpshooter in the war, but when they found out about my eyes, they put me in the artillery instead.'

'You were in the war? Between France and Prussia?' I asked. I recalled reading about it in the newspapers, but the people involved in it were abstract to me then. Meeting a soldier from it made it all so very real. He said that yes, he had, and though I waited for him to tell me more, to expound upon it like the veterans in the parlours of the Old White in Virginia, he only rose and said, 'let us venture back into the city, shall we?' We turned from the river and the masts and smoke and descended into the city. The warm winter sun of this city was moving high into the sky, and the shade was welcome. I watched his face as his eyes opened in the cooler dark. At times, he would stop with me on his arm and watch a scene, a team of horses trotting by, a woman with a basket on her head and great hoop earrings from her ears, men in darkened shirts unloading barrels from the back of a wagon. His eyes scanned everything that moved and put it away somewhere. We moved along, going nowhere in particular, up a street, down a street, arm-in-arm. In this man's company, I began to see the city as he saw it, a place blossoming in a thousand separate motions, all part of the whole. If I could have pretended that I was not married, I would have been at complete peace.

We walked until we heard the croon of a fiddle. We followed the sound and at last found it at the corner of Rue Bourbon and St. Louis. As Edgar studied the angles and gestures of man and instrument and bow and their movement, I studied the man himself, and I recognized him as the Irish fiddler on the *Chrysolite*. As he played, a weightlessness, a giddiness consumed me like the warmth of a hearth fire, and I was taken by the urge to dance the jigs and reels that they had inspired on the ship, and I could almost feel the sway of the ocean. Impulsively, I took Edgar's hand, and in a moment of pure joy, I danced. Several others had formed around us and clapped as the fiddler played a dusty old air and Edgar and I danced. Or, I should say, I jigged and reeled, and he rather shyly held up my hand. I felt as carefree as a schoolgirl. The tune was done, and with the croon of a fresh note, the slow crawl of a bow across a string, the old Irishman launched into another. His ruddy face smiled at me, and he and his fiddle nodded, and I grabbed the hem of my dress and twirled myself under Edgar's hand and those gathered in a small circle on the street corner clapped. Faces whirled about in my happiness, and especially Edgar's face, his brown eyes placid and beatific. The tune ended, and I found myself breathless. Coins clinked in the Irishman's hat, and he said, 'thankee' and began another, 'The Rocky Road to Dublin,' I think it was. A little girl took her place in the center and began dancing to the clapping of those gathered.

As I recovered my breath, from the corner of my eye, I saw a young woman coming down the street. She carried something in her arm, and when she paused to look in a shop window, I saw that it was a violin case. Her face was concealed by the brim of her bonnet and the slant of light on it. The music was far away as I watched her, and I became aware that the music had paused, and the crowd had faded away. The fiddler was taking a break, mopping his face and neck as he stooped and retrieved the change from his hat. The young woman continued to approach, pausing to raise her hands to her brow to look in shop windows. She turned again, and I put my hand to my own brow to block the sun, and then I saw it was Jenny. 'Monsieur,' I said to Edgar, rather impulsively, 'Certainly the light is difficult for your eyes.'

'Yes,' he said, and he turned to me. 'But I have had a delightful day. I suppose I must get home and paint a little while my eyes are still up for it. May I accompany you home first?' I suddenly felt the eyes of the world on me, as if Mr. and Mrs. Howard and Mr. Teague were all watching me from upstairs windows. I fear I stammered a bit as I told him that I had some errands to attend and that I hated to detain him further. But I asked if he would meet me in front of the statue of General Jackson again tomorrow, at ten o'clock. And my Parisian said that he would be waiting. He appeared to want to kiss me but was too much of a gentleman to be so bold, so soon, though I am quite sure that I would have let him. But he left me and proceeded up Royal Street, and I turned onto Bienville. At the corner, I tarried in front of a shop window, a stationer, I think, though my head was swimming. From down the street at the corner, Jenny's violin joined the Irish fiddle, soon finding a beautiful counter melody. The Irishman beamed in the company of this pretty young accompanist, and I thought I heard him say, 'and so you come again today, me garl' and the two played a song or two. Passersby dropped coins into the hat of the Irishman as he nodded without breaking his tune.

I should have turned and gone the other way from my shop window, but my spirits were soaring and the music was beguiling, and I wanted to hear my sister, my step-daughter play. So, I turned back to the corner and the music. She saw me and smiled, and I returned it as she played with the old fiddler. The reel folded and refolded itself, the two musicians and their instruments weaving a beautiful vine of music around itself until at last it ended with a long pull of each bow.

The old fiddler asked me, 'And where is yer fella off to, then, me garl?' At this indictment, I demurred. 'Pardon, sir?' I said, 'surely it must have been someone else.' The old fiddler furrowed his brow and said, 'Oh, 'tis sure, 'twas you, such a beautiful garl as yerself and pardon me, ma'am, fer tellin' the truth, then.' I mumbled, 'I'm sorry, sir, but surely it was someone else,' and with a doubtful look, he tucked his fiddle under his chin, and he and Jenny began playing again. She looked as though she were thinking or worried, and I did not dance this time, lest he be sure that it was me earlier. I listened as people came and staid and went, until the old fiddler tired and the instruments were put away, and then Jenny and I walked to the Howard's. As Jenny and I walked arm-in-arm, she said, 'Please don't tell Father that I am playing on street-corners like a common street performer.'

'Oh, you seem to enjoy it so, and it was lovely, sure,' I said with an Irish accent, like old Mrs. Sullivan, and we laughed, though my laugh was but a meager one. I was thinking that Jenny and I both have things we don't want Mr. Teague to know. We walked toward the American part of town, and from time to time, I looked over my shoulder hoping to see my Parisian but did not. As I retire for the night, I find that I can think of nothing else.

30 November 1872. I did not sleep well at all as guilt and desire competed for the attention of my dreams. When the sunrise found me awake this morning, I had resolved to forego our liaison this morning and forget all of it as madness unbecoming a Christian lady. Instead I made up my mind to offer to accompany Mrs. Howard on her errands. And so I sat and waited for her in the downstairs parlour and read through a day-old copy of the *Picayune.* I had read perhaps half of the newspaper when I looked up from it to see Old Mama come from upstairs to tell me that Miz Flora (Mrs. Howard) was confined to bed again with 'lady-trouble' and would not be up to her errands and that she suggested that I visit the shops on Canal Street if I would like. I resolved to do so, but as soon as my feet touched the cobblestones of St. Charles, I found myself with the unbridled desire to cross Canal and head for the square. It was as if my feet decided for me. I followed Rue Chartres breathlessly, my heart beating like the frantic wings of a moth, and I found him on our bench, reading. The clock on the cathedral said twenty minutes past ten. 'Forgive my tardiness,' I said in French, 'but I was detained.'

'It is certainly worth the wait to see you,' he said, 'I have spent the time with M. Rousseau.' He showed me the book he was reading, Rousseau's *Confessions.* I said that I had read him both in English and in French and asked how he liked him. 'I find his candor refreshing,' Edgar said, 'even when the truth paints him in an unflattering light. Honesty is the most appealing of virtues, is it not?' I felt a sting from his comment about candor and the truth, though certainly it wasn't intended to hurt me. He rose and placed the book in his coat pocket and said, 'A book is a small companion who may follow us anywhere, a whole different world in one's pocket,' he said, and I thought of you, my little confidant, who have followed me for so long, you, the scribe of my days. 'Your English is a little better,' I said, 'have you been practising?' He said that, yes, he had, though he was afraid that he was becoming tiresome to his cousins. Then he patted his coat pocket and said that he had no temptations of passing himself off as an Englishman as young Rousseau did. We passed a street vendor who proclaimed the merits of her raspberries, '*Framboise, framboise, les bijoux du bois.*'

'Let us try some of these, *jewels of the woods*,' I said, and we bought a small paper box of them and ate them, though they stained my white muslin gloves red. We walked along and chatted in a mixture of French and English, though mostly French. We passed the French Opera House, and he remarked that it was a shame that there would be no opera this winter. He apparently is quite a devotee of the opera, having attended in Italy when he was studying there, and in Paris, though Paris has been in quite a state in the wake of the Commune.

As we walked, my eyes scanned for Jenny, though I knew she was at class at the Conservatory, or Mr. Howard, or Mrs. Howard, relieved from her 'lady-trouble.'. The sky was grey, but under it we were content, content to be arm-in-arm. A dog approached us, and Edgar called his name. The dog rolled onto the banquette and Edgar scratched his belly with fingers stained red from the raspberries. 'Do you know this dog?' I asked him. 'Yes,' he said, 'This—' he moved his hand from the dog's belly to his ears, '—this is Vasco. He may look the part of a mongrel, but what talent he has! Here, see!' The dog regained a sitting position and canted his head and put his ears in an attentive posture. 'Vasco, fetch.' He threw a stick and the dog looked at it. Then Edgar said, 'Now, Vasco, roll over.' The dog just looked at Edgar with a perplexed grin. Edgar repeated, 'Vasco, roll over.' Still the dog did nothing but twist his head into a canine question. 'See?' Edgar said, 'I have taught him only this trick—to ignore me!' I laughed and said, 'You have done well. He ignores you every time!' and we laughed, and Vasco rolled over to have his belly scratched again, and we laughed even harder. We found a little tea room, leaving Vasco outside. When we were done, the dog was gone, and Edgar said that he had probably wandered home or was exploring, true to his namesake, the Portuguese explorer, Vasco da Gama. We parted, agreeing to meet again Monday morning, day after tomorrow, in the square. And I had even fewer misgivings about it, fewer than the day before, and much fewer than I should.

1 December 1872. The Sabbath, and I prayed for right judgment and self-discipline. Sunday dinner with the Howards. I do not wish to be a poor guest, but honestly I found it tiresome.

2 December 1872. He was not there today. I went to the square and found the only familiar personage there was the general atop his horse. I spent quite a bit of time, wishing I had brought a book as the cathedral bells chimed hour after hour. But as the rain began to move in, I quit the square and returned home where I write now. I suppose it is true that absence makes the heart grow fonder. I have spent the time writing a letter to Henry. I have not heard from him in some time and I fear that he believes I have forgotten him.

3 December 1872. He was not there, and perhaps this is the answer to my prayer. I suppose I should return to Mount Teague, like an animal returning to a darkened burrow.

4 December 1872. Another day with a square empty of my Parisian. The weather was a little cooler today, and I spent the time rereading Rousseau's *Confessions*, afraid that if I left for even a moment, I would miss him. If he is not there tomorrow, I shall either abandon this madness. Or send another note to Esplanade.

5 December 1872. The Howards' house here on St. Charles is quiet except for the subdued play of children upstairs, under the care of a servant girl. Mr. and Mrs. Howard have gone to dine at M. Arnaud's. They extended an invitation, but I begged leave, saying that I was feeling a little under the weather and would likely play the piano for a while and then turn in early. This is not the truth, and of course, you know it, my little confidant. You are nothing if not a little volume of veracity. I do not lie to you, though it seems that there are fewer persons each day that receive the truth from me. But here is what happened today.

I was elated this morning to find Edgar again in the square under the statue of General Jackson on his prancing horse, both the general and his horse made of bronze and hence unconcerned with the horse disease, though it is thought that it is now passing the city. I was about to turn around and quit the square and the idea of this man for good, when I saw him on a bench in the shade. He stood with a tip of his hat and greeted me with a phrase of practiced English, 'Please accept a good morning from the general and me,' and Edgar took off his hat like the man in bronze in the center of the square. 'Where have you been, my friend?' I asked, trying not to sound perturbed or sullen. 'I have been ill, for a day or two,' he said. 'I am sorry to hear it,' I said, 'I trust your health improves?'

'Yes, much. In a house with so many children, one is bound to catch something. And if you were wondering, it was not the horse flu,' he said. This made me laugh beside myself, and then we laughed together, under the bronze man and his horse and the twin cathedral spires.

When we had recovered our breath, we talked of what he was working on, paintings of his family, mostly, though he says it is difficult to get the children to sit still, and perhaps more so for adults with babies in their laps. The sun seemed to speed through the sky as if pulled by the Greek chariots of mythology. We both seemed reluctant to part company. 'I have a wish for you,' he said, his brown eyes full of candor, 'I wish I could see you more often. Perhaps you could accompany me to the theatre?' His honesty affected me, and I answered him with it, before I could think about such things as propriety and sensibility, 'Yes, I should like that very much.'

He said, 'Then perhaps I shall call for you at your dwelling-place?' My mind raced with worries that the Howards or Jenny or my husband would see me with this handsome man and know the truth of the tender feelings I have for him. Or perhaps they would merely regard him as an acquaintance. I thought of how the verse from Proverbs is proven true: 'The wicked flee when no man pursueth.' In the end, I replied, 'Perhaps I should meet you there. My father discourages gentleman callers. Since mother died, you see. He is quite possessive.' Such a twisted falsehood. 'Certainly,' he said. 'But one day, surely I must meet him.'

'Yes,' I said, rather distantly, imagining the calamity of such a meeting. We bid adieu, and now I am in this half-empty mansion, with the sounds of children being prepared for bed, about to prepare myself for something illicit, something that could evolve into calamity. I must stop here.

Sammy, 1982

Sammy laid the diary aside and stroked his beard, thinking of being young and in love in those days when everything is uncertain except the attraction of one for another. No one knows where it might lead, that feeling like gravity. It had led Sammy to a house with the smell of supper and the sounds of children playing and the music of another generation upstairs, the young listener to it waiting for that same attraction himself.

It led Sammy downstairs to the kitchen where Betsy was at the stove. Her hair was up in a ponytail like when she was younger. He moved to her and put his arms around her and kissed the back of her neck through wisps of fallen hair, and she turned back to kiss his cheek. She stroked his beard, her hand smelling of onions, and said, "You ol' cave-man."

He closed his eyes and held her from behind, remembering how circumstances had denied them each other, the rich boy and the poor tenant girl. She was wearing one of his button-down shirts, untucked, with the sleeves rolled halfway up. Inside the collar of the shirt, the leather straps of her scapular fell over her collarbones. He picked at one of them.

"What's this?"

"The Miraculous Promise of Our Lady of Mount Carmel," she said.

He tried to remember the Miraculous Promise but couldn't, so he leaned in close and kissed the back of her neck again and cupped her breast through bra and shirt. She sighed and closed her eyes and whispered in his ear, "They children in this house, boy."

One of those children, the oldest, came in the kitchen, and Sammy moved his hands to Betsy's waist. Quint took a pinch from the pot of rice and hurriedly put it in his mouth, and his mother swatted his hand. "Be ready five minutes," Betsy said. "Go get your sisters."

He kissed his mama's cheek and went upstairs. His lip was normal size now, and the bruising around his eye had faded to purple and green. If he had told her how he had gotten it, she hadn't told Sammy.

After dinner, Sammy showered and made an overnight bag, though he wasn't sure how long he would be gone. Betsy packed a Delchamps bag with a thermos and two cannisters of Mello Joy coffee. When she went to the kitchen for an old coffee maker, he put the diary in the bag with them. She returned to the central hallway under the portrait of the original Samuel Teague. Sammy put his arms around her waist.

"I'll try to come home tomorrow for a little while."

"Whenever you can," she said. "Tell Miss Vessy I'm makin' a novena."

She kissed him and opened the door for him. As he was about to go down the steps to his truck, Elizabeth came downstairs with her hand on the bannister and her eyes on each step. In her free hand, she held a piece of paper.

"Daddy, Daddy, wait! Give Mr. Teeter this," she said.

> mr. Teeter, I hope you feel better soon and
> that your tummy gonna feel better soon

too so my daddy can go with us to see
Mickey Mose. elizabeth T.

She had put the missing u above Mose and then signed it with a merry parade of vowels and consonants because she knew all the letters in her name now: Elizabeth T. They marched along in a faltering line with big happy grins on the e's.

He kissed wife and daughter and threw his overnight case and the paper bag on the front seat. As he cranked the truck, Sammy looked down at the Get-Well note. Betsy had told the girls that Mr. Teeter had a tummy ache and that's why their daddy had to go see him in the hospital. They couldn't begin to comprehend things like 'addiction' and 'overdose' and 'withdrawal.' He drove down the lane and turned onto LA 308, thinking of Old Sam Teague gazing out of his frame in the hallway of his house. This letter from a child had more letters in it than the stern man in the portrait ever knew.

His eyes followed the road, but his mind wandered. Alice had made the same journey to Algiers to catch the ferry into the city. He imagined a young golden-haired English woman, barely past girlhood and taking the train into the city, tortured by regret in having married his great-grandfather, the ancestral hero of the Teagues and St. Matthew Parish.

The lights cast by the lampposts along the highway slid by in rectangles over the spray-painted hood and the front seat with the bag that held a coffeemaker, a thermos, and two cannisters of Mello Joy coffee. And a woman's diary from the 19th century, with a Get-Well card from a child of the 20th tucked within its pages.

At the VA in Algiers, Sammy found Teeter's room empty and his name taken off the door. A nurse's aide was washing down the mattress. He went to find Miss Vessy in the waiting room, but she wasn't there. He went back to the room and stood there with his overnight bag in one hand and the paper bag with the coffee and coffee maker in the other.

"Where is Mr. Blanchard?" he asked the lady in the room.

"I don't know, sir. I'm just changin' the sheets. You go ast the nurse."

It was change-of-shift, and the nurses were in report, a conversation taking place in a side room about IV rates and meds and who needed restraints. Finally, they exited the staff room, and Sammy asked one of them, an older, heavyset woman in straining white polyester and a nurses' cap, "Where is Mr. Blanchard?"

She eyed him suspiciously. "Are you family?"

"Yes," Sammy said. He might as well be. The Blanchards had no one else.

"I'm sorry, sir. Sometimes the pushers of these OD patients will come in to settle up the debt before their customer…you know. Anyway, they took him to Charity. They had a bed in the unit there."

"Thank you," Sammy said, and he walked away.

He got in his truck and crossed the river. The lights of ships were reflected in the black water far below him. Across it, the city skyline towered with the low, broad mushroom of the Superdome nestled down in it. The rain, which had been a light patter, began to fall more heavily. It limited his vision, and traffic stalled on the down ramp and herded him onto Camp Street. As the rain plummeted in white sheets, the shells of other poor, ruined people, mostly men, slept under the eaves of buildings out of the downpour. An ambulance passed, and Sammy followed it down Common Street to the monolith on Tulane Avenue, Big Charity. Its gray wings rose into the night sky that pelted it with rain as police and ambulance lights swirled and sirens blared at its base.

Sammy parked on the street and fed the meter, but he had forgotten his umbrella and was quickly soaked. Patients in hospital gowns crowded under the eaves and smoked cigarettes behind sheets of water, some of them holding onto IV poles. Sammy ran past them with his flannel jacket over his head, clutching his overnight case and his paper bag. He paused for a moment to look up. Over the main door of the hospital was an aluminum art deco mural of a human figure that seemed to be bound in the center of a web of other human figures. He ran under it, and the noise of the rain diminished as he entered the building.

A man entered with blood covering half of his face, his hands pressing on whatever wound he had. The security guards seemed only mildly interested and pointed the man to the emergency room. Sammy asked one of them where the ICU was, and a woman security guard who sucked one of her teeth and picked at her hair with her little finger pointed to the elevator and held up four fingers.

The elevator lurched upward and then jolted to a stop, and he got off and followed the arrow to the ICU. Down a hall, he got as far as a set of tightly closed pneumatic doors. Inside the narrow strip of window, he saw nurses and residents and suggestions of patients, forms under bedsheets attended by machines that breathed for them and tubes that emptied their bladders for them. He turned and looked for the waiting room, and there was Miss Vessy. She saw him and rose and embraced him as if she had been rescued. She sobbed in his arms, and he could smell the cigarette smoke on her. He waited for her to separate from him, but she held him and whimpered, *oh, Mist' Teague, my boy, my boy, my boy,* over and over.

At last, they sat together, their cane-country eyes wide at the collection of odd, urban people in the waiting room with them, rough people with cigarettes behind their ears and homemade tattoos and unkempt hair and gold teeth. Someone was drinking. They could smell it.

When he felt she was calm enough, Sammy left her and got up to get them each a cup of vending machine coffee. He gave one to Miss Vessy, and she took it in two hands with a pitiful attempt at a smile. He sat next to her, and they each took a sip of their coffee. Miss Vessy looked at Sammy and took his coffee, and she pitched both of them in the trash. She sat and looked onto the city nightscape, the points of streetlights glistening in the rainy darkness. The sounds of new sirens floated up from below, and a red wash of light reflected on the buildings across the way, as the ambulances and police cars waited to complete their errands so that other ambulances and police cars could come and complete theirs. As Miss Vessy looked out into the dark, damp night outside, maybe thinking of nothing and maybe thinking of everything, Sammy reached in the paper bag and took out the diary.

Alice, 1872

6 December 1872. I hastily commit to paper these unsayable things, these emotions like whirlwinds, this urge like the pull of gravity. It is hard for me to recount this, even to you, my little confidant, but I shall, as there is no one else to tell. My conscience screams less at me now, only a rumble in the background of my thoughts, as if it is only quietly shaking its head and clicking its tongue at the folly it is forced to bear with me. But my heart is so full, so weary, so burdened, so exalted.

When I returned to the Howards', I was on the front gallery, pretending to read, when Mrs. Howard asked if I would care to accompany them to Arnaud's for dinner. I declined, saying that I wanted to spend the evening in, perhaps playing the piano or reading or both. I made a joke that I hoped I wasn't coming down with the horse flu, and she smiled and almost laughed. 'Very well,' she said, 'perhaps we should have Jonas prepare some poultices for you.' Jonas is the liveryman for the Howards and has kept their horses in fine shape, perhaps with some of these poultices she mentioned. I played for a while, a few simple pieces, waiting for them to leave. When they had done so, and I was sure they were gone at last, I retired to my chamber and began dressing. It was still early, but the situation of the horse-and-carriage shortages gave me to believe that I might have to walk to the theatre. In preparation for my rendezvous at the Varieties, I confess I took extra care at my toilette, selecting the green dress with the black polonaise. I was in it and seated at my dressing table, trying to arrange my hair in the looking glass, when, in the gaslight, Old Mama's face appeared. She asked if I needed 'hep' with my hair, and I told her yes, if she didn't mind. She did not ask where I was going. There is a modest wisdom about her. Her black fingers laced through the gold of my hair, and if I would have not been in such a state of anxiety, it would have been a source of pleasure. She skillfully arranged my coiffure into a shape quite fashionable, taking her time and never once asking where I was going or why I was taking such care in my appearance. When she was done, she only showed me my reflection in the looking glass and said, 'Now ain't you a picture!'

I left without an explanation, walking into the night and worrying that time would fall short for me and that I would keep my Parisian waiting. The night was warm enough to forego the carriage, but I waited for a hack to the theatre anyway, lest I be seen as a girl of easy virtue on the streets at night, plying my vocation. At last, there being no carriages that did not already have occupants, I fell in with a crowd of theatre-goers who were walking to the Varieties. I arrived just as the orchestra was finishing its preamble.

And there he was in the gaslight of the lobby, dressed in an evening coat with a starched white shirt and a red silk cravat, his beard neatly trimmed. His kind, brown eyes widened on seeing me and he took my hand and kissed it and whispered into my ear, 'You astonish me yet with your beauty.' From there, we ascended the red-and-gold carpet of the stairs. On opening the door to his box, I found several members of his family there, including his Uncle Michel, an older man with spectacles, and his brothers Rene and Achille, and his cousins, Desiree (Didi, I think she is called), and Tell, blind and expecting, and Mathilde, and her husband, Mr. Bell. I do not recall his first name. The men rose and took my hand, and the women nodded. Scarcely had we made our introductions than the lights dimmed, and the orchestra began. The curtains opened to applause, and I scanned the audience, who clapped in anticipation. The Howard's box was empty, of course.

In the second scene, during a song by the lead character, I glanced over to the Howard's box to find it being readied. And then in the dim light I saw Jenny and the Howards sitting down. Jenny said something to Mrs. Howard, who handed over a pair of opera glasses. Jenny put them to her eyes and scanned the stage and then the orchestra. I panicked inwardly and turned my head from their direction and to the door of the Musson family box. Edgar's gaze met mine for a moment and his smile radiated, and I met it with my own, and he turned to the performance. Tell's dim-sighted eyes surely couldn't make out the people on stage, so she stared at the opposite wall of the theatre as her ears followed the dialogue. I looked back to the Howards, and I thought I saw Jenny glance away from our box, but it may have been my conscience whispering its indictment of this folly. The performance was scrolling out the story, but I found that I paid no more attention to it than I did to the last one when I was sitting across the way in the Howards' box. The air seemed hot and dense. Edgar turned to me and asked in a whisper, 'Are you well, Alice?'

'Yes,' I murmured, 'I am a little overcome. Perhaps I just need a little air.' I rose and was met by the glances of his cousins, Mathilde and Didi, and the ear of Tell, whose eyes uselessly looked for us. I heard Edgar whisper to Didi in French, 'She is a little flushed. We're going to take a draught of air.' Didi nodded and turned back to the stage, and her face glowed with its bright light, and the bright light glowed in the lenses of Uncle Michel's spectacles. Edgar rose and took my hand and opened the door to the box just enough for us to exit. The door closed and the sound of the players on the stage diminished. The audience laughed a muffled laugh behind the door.

'Are you well?' he asked again once we were on the landing of the stairs. He looked at me like he might kiss me, and I confess to you again, my little confidant, that I wanted him to, more than anything. I yearned for my wish would be granted, and more so. I responded to his inquiry, 'Yes, but sometimes I find the air of public places so close. Perhaps a little walk would help.'

'Yes, of course,' he replied, and he helped me down the carpeted stairs. I paused on the last step, just before the stairs gave into the lobby, not because I was overcome, but instead, to make sure that Jenny or the Howards had not come down to the lobby also and would see me, a married woman, the wife of both friend and father. There were only a few knots of people, mostly men who had been summoned to the theatre by wives and had no interest in the performance. I surveyed them for a moment to make sure that none of them were acquaintances.

'Here, let me assist you, *ma belle*,' Edgar said, and he helped me from the last soft, step. The doorman opened the door to the street with a tip of his cap, and I found us either free, or approaching the center of a beguiling snare. The fog had stirred itself into a drizzle. I took Edgar's arm and put my head to his shoulder, the cool dampness of the mist was welcome on my burning face. After a short walk, Edgar asked if I was feeling better. 'Yes,' I replied, 'the fresh air helps.' Just then, the drizzle began to thicken into a proper rain. Edgar took off his coat and placed it over my head. We walked down the street, in a direction I knew not, when at last we came to a saloon, much like the public houses of England. It was peopled not by theatre-goers but by a more common set of men and women. 'Perhaps a refreshment would help,' I said.

'Yes, as you wish,' Edgar replied. We entered the dim interior, like a cave, perhaps, where shadowy forms laughed and conversation rumbled.

Bottles lined the shelves in the gaslight. A man and a woman sang a horribly out-of-tune duet somewhere in the dim depths of the place. As they finished to sarcastic clapping and cheering, I spotted a bottle of green liquid. The luminous colour fascinated me. I asked Edgar if he had ever tried absinthe.

'The Green Fairy, some in Paris call it,' he said as he pondered the glowing emerald bottle and its glowing emerald reflection in the glass behind it. 'Yes,' he said, 'once or twice. I find it rather bitter.' He turned his head and gave me a questioning look. I nodded, and he summoned the keeper and held up two fingers and said, *absinthe, pour deux, s'il vous plait.* We held up our glasses and admired them.

'Well, then,' he said, 'I give you the Green Fairy, the colour of the Seine,' and we clinked our glasses and sipped from them. We made horrendous faces at the bitterness and laughed at our reactions, but then took another. The taste of each sip improved, the last sip forgotten. A spell ensued, and in that enchanted world, our lips approached each other like dancers in a minuet or a waltz. I was only vaguely aware of the other patrons in the salon, of the dim lights and bright shadows and conversations and tink-tink of glasses or that the rain had stopped or that we were in America or New Orleans or the earth. Or that Edgar had paid the man.

'Are you ready to return?' he said, 'we might be able to see the second or third acts.' I responded, 'No,' rather quickly and more plainly than I might have otherwise.

'*Moi non plus*,' he said in French, *neither do I*, and we kissed again, and I wondered if the other patrons took notice of us and the whole notion of whether they did wasn't worth a thought. Our inclinations for each other were suddenly and nakedly obvious. We walked out on the street, and as soon as we were safely down it, we threw our arms around each other's necks, and our lips spoke plainly on each other, tracing a secret alphabet. The barman and the other patrons were far away, but we needed a world in which there were no others. No others at all, anywhere. I mumbled something to him at which now, even in the calm light of day, I blush at having to write here. '*Amène moi quelque part*,' I whispered into his ear.

Such a wanton, irresponsible thing to say, *Take me somewhere.* We began walking hurriedly, and then running hand in hand, crossing streets in the mist, at last coming to the house on Esplanade. He bid me wait on the porch as he entered, but then he returned. He was too excited for even a try in English, so he said in French, "*Ils sont en haut. Venir vite.*" *They are upstairs. Come quickly.*

We entered the house and passed a staircase. Edgar kept his eyes on the top as we passed through the library to a room near the rear of the house. By the scent of oil paint and turpentine and the easel set up in the corner, I knew it was his. He secreted us into it, locking the door behind us. Our lips played on lips and necks, our hands roamed. Our breath was uneven, staggering in and out of us. I was dizzy with excitement, and perhaps he was as well, but he seemed to force himself to be calm, resolute. But his hands shook as he unbuttoned my blouse, and my hands shook as I unbuttoned his shirt, fighting my gloves and his silk cravat. Finally, I plucked the white cotton away, finger by finger, and he pulled the red silk cravat and we flung them away, cravat and gloves. Everything swam, and the small steps of children thumped distantly upstairs. I lost track of where we were, and then I remembered that we were in New Orleans, that great back door to America, that great, throbbing nation, this country of steam engines. We were in his room, in the house of his uncle and his family, but where were they? And without realizing it, I asked it. 'They are at the theatre, remember?' he murmured into my neck.

'Who is upstairs?' I panted to the ceiling. My eyes rolled closed to whoever might be up there as he kissed the softness under my chin.

'The children,' he said between kisses, 'My cousins' children. With the servants.' He kept kissing but exhaled into my ear, 'Shall we stop?'

But our hands and lips continued, and I knew they would not stop. The small voice of my conscience shrieked for us to compose ourselves and forget this foolishness, but the scream faded into a receding pinpoint and was replaced by my racing breath, a small, puffing breath that might blow out a small candle but instead ignited a bonfire. Stockings, corset, crinolette, all fell away. Pants, shirt, underclothes, all, and we were naked in the darkness. And in that moment, I wanted this man more than anything I have ever wanted, more than a family, more than peace, tranquility, comfort, more than heaven itself. We surrendered to the strange arithmetic of our bodies, the interposed and complementary geometry, and the chaos of attraction. His lips found my breasts and I made a sound quite involuntarily, and then his flesh found mine and I enveloped him, and I made the sound again, louder and he shushed me and whispered, *upstairs.* Upstairs and the rest of the irrelevant world were forgotten, and our bodies moved on each other. And then suddenly my torso writhed, my hips quaked, my arms tightened around the small of his back, my fingers locked over his buttocks, and we made the sounds of wounded animals and fell together from heaven to earth, onto a single bed in the house of his uncle on a street called Esplanade in a city called New Orleans in a country called America.

After a time entwined naked on top of the bed, a minute or an hour, we became aware that the night had become colder, and Edgar pulled the covers back for us to warm ourselves under them. My conscience urged me to dress and run, and quickly, but I slipped under the covers and nestled in close to him. The glow of the absinthe had left us, but the glow of the aftermath of our passion had not. It began to rain violently, and our blinking eyes contemplated it in the dark.

We heard the noise of a family returning home in the rain, feminine and masculine voices, hurried footfalls on steps, the shake of umbrellas, and Edgar got up to test the lock. My eyes strained to see his naked body but could only get an obscure sense of it in the darkness. He returned to our bed, a waft of cold air as he pulled the sheet back, and the return of warmth as he drew near and kissed my cheek. I turned to him and I felt us begin to surge, but there was a quiet knock on the door and a voice that called softly, 'Cousin, are you well?' Edgar's lips broke from my neck and he told the door, 'Yes,' then he kissed my neck again and said, 'My friend was not feeling well, so I saw her home.' The voice behind the door said, 'She was very lovely, a very beautiful woman.'

'Yes,' he said, 'I will pass along your compliment when I see her again.' The shape of our kiss changed, and I knew we were grinning. 'Come tell us about her,' the door asked. He adopted a very sleepy voice and a yawn that was somewhat theatrical. 'I would love to, and I will, cousin, but I am very tired,' he said. His fingers lightly found me, and I shuddered, pressing my sweaty palms into his chest. I had to remind myself to breathe deeply and keep quiet. I did not hear the rest of the conversation he had through the closed door, and if I did, I do not remember it. I only remember the drum of the cold rain outside and seeing him in a brief flash of lightning. He was astride me, and then within me, and I was grateful for the sound of the hard rain as it rushed over the sound of our desire and covered it.

Later, I emerged from sleep to the quiet of a sleeping household, the snoring in a nearby room of an old man whom I assumed was his Uncle Michel. The rain had stopped, and all was quiet, as if the rain had scoured away all sound except for the faint snoring of an old man. A candle flared in the darkness and illuminated the trailing smoke of the match that set it, and I saw his face in the candlelight, Edgar, my lover.

'Forgive me,' he murmured, 'I had to light a candle. So I could look at you.' We kissed, but it was only a kiss this time and not a preamble to anything more. The candle on the night stand burned as we embraced, the flame swaying in the slightest draught. I felt his breath on my arm as he slept, as light and pleasant as a spring zephyr.

I woke again to the blanching of the eastern sky, fearing I would hear the morning sounds of a household, the deep thumping of footsteps, the light patter of children, something cooking over a coal fire, coffee being made. But all was still silent. He slept yet, and I eased out of bed and gathered my clothes. I found all except one glove. I searched for something to write a note, but I found nothing suitable, which on a moment's reflection was fitting, as there was nothing suitable to say. So instead, I quietly opened the door that led to a back gallery. I eased out, resisting the urge to wake up my lover, this innocent man, hoping I could still turn back and resume some other life, that he would be my former lover, that God might find a way to absolve me of this sin or at the very least give me the strength to avoid committing it again. I left as the cold air crept into his room, and he pulled the covers over himself in his sleep. I broke away and trotted as if pursued. And then I ran as if the world were tumbling down on me.

I ran down Esplanade until I came to Rue Royal, and I turned onto it and began walking, avoiding puddles from the night's rain, panting cold air in and out of my lungs. The city was awakening to a chilly bright morning. Maids emptied night water from balconies, and I had to cross the street from time to time to avoid them. I blocked out thoughts of Edgar, though I could not block out the evidence of our passion clinging to the secret places of my body. With each step I felt smaller and more exhausted, the weight of two separate lives pressing on me, an impossible burden, but a burden that I chose. Or a burden that chose me. Morning traffic was beginning, the first of the omnibuses, the initial deliveries to businesses, mules and horses and people exhaling steamy breaths. I pulled my shawl tightly around my shoulders and remembered that I had left a glove behind. Still I hurried ahead, down Royal toward Canal and the American part of town.

Up ahead, two soldiers approached. They leaned into each other, though it was impossible to tell who was supporting whom. One's uniform tunic was opened, the dark blue with columns of brass buttons parted to reveal his grey undershirt. His friend had taken off his tunic completely and held it slung over his shoulder. His suspenders hung limply at his knees and he alternated pawing aimlessly for them and hitching up his pants. They paused from a drunken rendition of 'The Girl I Left Behind' to tip imaginary hats to me, and one remarked that they must have left them behind at 'Miss Sadie's' and that her girls would surely keep them there for when they returned. 'What about our dear sergeant?' the other asked, 'don't you think he'll want us to have our hats?'

I left them working on the problem of their hats and their sergeant, though they abandoned it for another chorus of 'The Girl I Left Behind." I crossed Canal Street behind the statue of Mr. Clay who looked away toward the river. As I neared the house on St. Charles, I became more and more worried that the Howards might be up and that they would be aware of my absence last night. I paused at the side door, hesitating to open it. Suddenly it opened and my heart jumped. It was the kind, black face of Old Mama, who was up and waiting for me. She had been cooking, and the smell of it welcomed me. She asked me with a grin and a wink, 'How you sleep, ma'am?'

'I was sitting up with a sick friend, last night,' I lied to her, a sin unto itself. 'Yes ma'am,' she replied, 'and that's a good deed, tend to folks when they sick, yes ma'am.' But I knew that my absence was not a work of charity, and I suspect that she knew. She poured me a cup of coffee, and in its blackness, I contemplated myself.

What have I become, then? A harlot? A temptress? A High Street tart? A kissing Judas? The chief character in the drunkard's' song about the vicar's daughter? I, who as a girl scarcely had anything worth confessing, now carry a spot that my soul struggles to bear. Dear God, take pity. Another commandment is broken, not smashed on the rocks of Sinai like Moses, but chipped away one by one, like a sculptor with a chisel. And yet I contemplate taking up the commandment against adultery and smashing it, over and over again, to dust. The girls of easy virtue do not seem so far below me now. My late night has found me at last, and I write this before I search for sleep. But I fear that my lover will not relinquish my dreams, as he has not relinquished my thoughts.

7 December 1872. Thinking of no suitable reason to avoid it, I spent the morning attending the shops of this city with Mrs. Howard. None of them interested me, not even the music stores with their glistening black pianos and sheets of music, neither the popular scores nor those of the masters. I paused in the door of an artist's shop, filled with blank canvasses and brushes and pigments. There were shop-goers there, but not my Parisian. Nothing in it held my interest, and I didn't spend a farthing. Cent, rather. Mrs. Howard, however, spent prodigiously, and when I mentioned it, she said with a rather surprised look, 'Oh, Mrs. Teague, you know our husbands can afford it!' And so, our errands continued. Jewelers, clothiers, a fine noontime meal of which I ate very little. My mind was elsewhere. My mind and my heart and every other part of me, elsewhere, in the distant heaven of his embrace and the ecstasy that it brings, and it continues so. Behind the closed doors of my room, I am driven into fits of self-pollution, hoping it will break the spell, but I find myself only deeper in it. The urge to find him is ever-present, and I must fight it constantly. I do not sleep at all well, and when I do, my dreams are filled with him. It is a madness worthy of Bedlam. And now this.

This evening, Jenny came to the Howards with great elation, bearing a letter from her father. Of course, though it may have been nominally from him, it was most certainly written by another. I have it here before me. It is in the customary creamy beige envelope with the embossed MT and the heading of the stationary that proclaims the motto of Mount Teague, *Mount Teague sugar, sweetest—purest.*

My dear wife, it begins, *I trust you are having an enjoyable stay with our friends the Howards*, etc, etc, and it goes on to say *Mr. Masac and Mr. Braun at the New Orleans Conservatory have informed me that they have given all the instruction they can to my daughter Jenny* (he leaves out that she is also my daughter, or at the very least, step-daughter, but of course, he is not one to share credit), and that *a position has been arranged for her at a school in London in 'jolly old England' which shall more keenly challenge her abilities. It will be necessary, therefore, for you to accompany her on her voyage. I fear also for your safety in the city of New Orleans in these uncertain political times….*

By this he (and she) mean the dueling governors and legislatures that Louisiana now bears. Daily there are hints of violence. Then, it says that I may stay in England as long as I wish and that he encourages me to do so. *My mother, Mrs. Teague and my daughters* (our daughters, he forgets*) will meet you at the port of Liverpool. Mr. Howard has arranged passage there on the Fire Queen, to depart December 11 from the Liverpool Warehouse on the river in New Orleans to Liverpool, thence by rail to London.* And then there are some meager pleasantries, which I hear in the voice of my husband, though written in this feminine hand, the writing delicate and practiced. I have strong suspicions that it is that of Mrs. Parris. The slant of her characters is very distinctive, the way of her T's, the tails of her G's and Y's very particular, like the subtle uniqueness of a face. The letter remains here on my desk. The thought of leaving Edgar is my first one on reading it. I feel ill at the prospect. I cannot think upon it, and only with great effort can I re-read the letter. Jenny approaches with news of dinner's readiness, and so I must close you, my little confidant. Please remember to keep our confidences. Pray that it shall not be like King Midas' barber whispering his secret into the ground.

I return to you, my little intimate, after dinner has been served and I prepare for bed in my room, this splendid space in this splendid house, marble mantelpiece framing a coal fire, throwing a light that lightly bounces off the high ceilings and curtains and magnificent bed. Dinner was attended by Jenny and me, and Mrs. Howard and her children. The boys ate like little tavern-goers, to the gentle scolding of Mrs. Howard. The little girl was quite picky and sat defiantly with her arms embracing herself and a scowl on her face. Old Mama brought her a biscuit and cut it up into pieces, and the little girl released herself from her embrace and ate it with her fingers. Mrs. Howard said that her husband is away in the northeast on business, trying to persuade the legislatures there to sanction the selling of tickets for 'our state enterprise,' the lottery of Louisiana, I am certain she means. Then the talk was of the courts and the fate of our government. There has even been some talk of taking up arms again if the results are not satisfactory.

Jenny steered the conversation away from such unpleasantries and to our trip to England, an enchanted wonderland to her, replete with knights and castles and a queen, and Dickens tales and a snowy Christmas. I don't have the heart to tell her about the mills of Ancoats and Miles Platting in Manchester. She asked about the theatres in London, and I told her, though I have never attended them, I have heard tell that they are both numerous and magnificent. Then, she said, 'Oh, I keep forgetting to tell you. Last night at the theatre, I saw the artist who sketches at Mme. Renain's dance studio. There was a lady in the box with him.' She cut her meat daintily. 'In the light, she looked so much like you, Alice.'

'Really?' I asked, and I realized my fork was raking across my plate. 'Yes,' she said, 'but the lights dimmed and when they came up again, she and the artist had left.' I placed my fork by my plate and took up my spoon, perhaps feeling I might get on more convincingly with it. 'How odd,' I remarked as dryly as I could, 'I retired early and spent the evening in my room, reading Rousseau's *Confessions*. Oh yes, I remember, Old Mama had biscuits made when I arose. Isn't that right, Old Mama?' She had come into the dining room with a warm basket of bread. 'Yes ma'am,' she said in her plodding monotone as she waited on us. I knew it would be a safe maneuver. I don't think that Old Mama ever tells anyone no in this house. 'Mrs. Teague,' Mrs. Howard said just then, 'you've barely touched your beef. It's another one of Old Mama's best dishes, second, perhaps, only to her biscuits. Are you feeling well?'

'I admit that I have slept poorly, as of late,' I said, 'I am missing my little ones.' This, of course, is true, but there is much missing from my life, as of late. Peace and contentment, among them. I waited for Jenny to press the issue of the woman in the Musson's theatre box, but she happily moved on to the subject of Mozart and the music she was learning and her friends. And the prospect of Christmas in London with her sisters and her grandmother. And with me.

8 December 1872. Another sleepless night ending in an early morning. Day has dawned grey with a sky that speaks of rain but does nothing toward it. I awakened with the tossing, fitful bedfellow that is my Conscience. It has presented its case all night like a barrister.

Miss Lamb, do you know with what you are charged?

Yes, my lord, bearing false witness.

And what else?

Even in my dreams, I cannot say it. The vague face lifts its chin and scowls under the white wig.

Adultery, my Conscience says.

Yes, I murmur.

Say it, my Conscience insists, *say it!*

Adultery, I would sob, but it is a dream and I cannot.

Say it! He yells so loudly that I recoil and the white curls of his wig shake. *Say it to the court!*

And there they are, arranged on benches like Parliament, men in black robes and frilled collars and white-curled wigs. The fog of my dream fades to reveal two familiar figures sitting among the others of the court, Mama and Papa, sad-faced and disappointed. I am aware that also in the gallery, though I could not see him, is Edgar, with an easel placed. He is painting the whole tableau. And then I realize I am naked in the witness' box, and I cover myself with my arms but to no avail.

SAY IT! The barrister screams, and I awake with the word on my tongue.

Adultery, I murmured, now awake and clutching myself tightly. And I found that I had uttered it to the canopy of my fine bed in my magnificent room in the Howards' on St. Charles. Outside, the morning air was heavy, uncertain if it would burn away to sunshine or simply rain. I rose, resolved to find Edgar and confess all, so that he may resume an honorable life, and I can somehow attempt to do the same.

I dressed in the black-and-white dress and burgundy opera cloak and walked down to the square in a fine mist. I hoped to find him in the usual place before the great general who defeated the English at the turn downriver. As I approached, the rain began to fall, a patter that caused others to hasten their steps and draw their umbrellas. I pulled the hood of my cloak against it, and as the rain increased, I waited under the eaves of the cathedral. The rain beat on the square and the general and the smokestacks and masts in the river beyond him. Stevedores in oil-cloth slickers continued their work to and from the boats along the levee as auras of white rain rose from them. My eyes strained, and then there he was, sitting under the bloom of a black umbrella on the very bench where we met, not reading, not sketching, only sitting quietly under the silk canopy. White drops of rain bounced up from it and made circles in the water at his feet. He saw me and I saw him, and he beckoned me to come sit with him. I took a deep breath and pulled the hood of my cloak over me, the burgundy darkened almost to black, and I ran through the puddles of the square. As I sat next to him, I pushed back the hood of my cloak. He pulled something out of his pocket and gave it to me. It was the glove that I had left behind.

'You look a little drawn,' he said as his hand caressed my jaw. I closed my eyes to his touch and confessed, 'Yes. I have no appetite.' He sighed. 'Nor I,' he said, and then he added, 'I am obsessed with you. Forgive me, but I am.' It was the very thing I feared he would say. The rain continued around us, no thunder, no lightning, no wind, just a patter of nourishing rain like I can remember it raining as a child in Surrey. Everyone else had been driven indoors by it, and we were alone with the general and his horse in the square. I put my head on Edgar's shoulder.

'The rain is picking up,' he said, 'perhaps we should go inside, somewhere,' and I thought that going inside somewhere would be both wonderful and disastrous. And then I thought, *there is something painful I must tell you. Something incredibly painful. Something that might destroy you, and both of us, if I were to speak it, but I must. You see, I am married, and you have been deceived. You are a good man, and you have been deceived long enough.*

But the thing I needed to speak remained only a thought. I could not do it. There was no breath in my lungs that would support it. A hack was waiting with his horse and brougham on the edge of the square, reading a newspaper under the eaves of a shop as the rain pelted off the brown flanks of his horse. We ran to him through the rain. The man folded his newspaper and drew away from the wall he had been leaning against. He opened the door for us, and I stood there for a moment, and a strange feeling came about me, a feeling that if I entered that carriage, things would never be the same again.

'You are getting wet,' Edgar said, and I got in and he followed me, and the driver shut the door behind us. When we were inside, Edgar folded the umbrella. The carriage shifted as the driver took to the buckboard, and then a small window slid open. I could see the side of the driver's face as he looked off into the rain and awaited his directions. Edgar said, in faltering English, 'Rue Esplanade. Three. Seven. Two.'

The driver nodded, and the window slid closed, and the carriage lurched forward as the rain drummed on its roof, and hooves clattered on cobblestones, and wheels splashed through puddles. The carriage swayed us like the movements of our passion, gently, back and forth. We were sequestered from the world by glass and pleated curtains, and I felt that I had but one fleeting moment to speak my awful truth. 'Monsieur,' I said, 'There is something I must tell you—'

'I am mad for you,' he said before I could finish, and we kissed. After a time, our lips parted, and he asked me, 'What is it you must tell me?' And I spoke a truth even more simple. 'I am mad for you also, I think of nothing else.' And our hands roamed over each other's bodies and his lips found the soft skin of my neck. Our breath was ragged. His eyes looked at me, and I looked at his. But I had to turn away, lest I fall there and become lost and irretrievable, though, to be honest, my little confidant, that is what I already am, lost and irretrievable. I looked again, but he was pulling the edge of the curtain, looking through the small gap in its pleats at the shapes of houses that scrolled past, indistinct in the condensation on the glass. I leaned into him and rested my head on his shoulder. And to the window he murmured, *"Je te desire. Je suis obsédé par toi."*

I want you. I am obsessed with you.

My breath caught somewhere in my chest, and my hands pressed into the black leather of the seat cushion. My finger toyed with the button in the tufting and when I became aware of it, I stopped and put my hands in my lap. He innocently reached for my hand, and it was if a spark was ignited with the simple touch of fingers and skin. My thighs parted, and my hand pressed his hand into me, and I shut my eyes and whimpered to his caresses. Our unseen driver quietly ticked to his horse—perhaps he is accustomed to the sounds of a tableau such as ours. Edgar's lips kissed my neck, my chest heaved like a violent ocean, my hips moved on the black leather of the carriage seat. We were concealed from the world by simple pleated curtains and unaware that we had stopped. A throat cleared itself, and the driver's voice outside the glass said, 'Pardon me, but here we are. Esplanade, 372.'

Through the gap in the curtain, I saw a dim shape. I wiped the moisture from the window, and there it was, the house on Esplanade, the house of his Uncle Michel, the number *372* painted neatly above the door. 'Will you keep driving, sir?' I asked him. The driver replied that he didn't intend on driving his horse aimlessly through the streets in the rain all afternoon, for he didn't want his animal to catch the horse flu. And so, Edgar gave him a different address, and the driver snapped the reins and yipped at his horse. Hooves clopped, and I felt us change direction. I reclined into Edgar, and he toyed with my hair, wrapping his finger in a golden coil and examining its sheen. I wonder now if he was judging how he might mix its colour to represent it on canvass. The rain had slackened, but the streets still sounded unpeopled and bare. We continued on through them, perhaps another fifteen minutes. When we stopped again, I straightened my skirts as Edgar got out and then helped me down. He paid the driver, who then vaulted back up onto his seat and, with a pop of his whip and a tick-tick, was off down the street. I watched him go, and I wondered if he had taken away the remainder of my sense and right judgment. Yes, an odd thought, my little confidant.

'My brother Achille's apartment,' Edgar said in a voice between a murmur and a whisper, 'he is away on business.' Edgar picked up a loose brick to reveal a key and unlocked the door with it. The paneled door with peeling, green paint swung open, and we bounded up the narrow stairway to a simple, one room apartment, furnished with a bed and with empty wine crates as a night table. In short, the habitation of a bachelor. I was looking around the room, trying to get a sense of its usual occupant, the brother of my lover, when I felt Edgar approach from behind and put his arms around me, a hand sliding low and one sliding high. I gasped and shut my eyes. Restraint faltered quickly and was cast aside and forgotten, and our hands sought the shapes of each other's bodies, clever, delightful riddles in the dim afternoon light of an overcast day. We faced each other, and slowly removed our clothes. And the commandment was broken again.

Afterward, we lay naked, listening to the noise of the outside world, steam whistles, carriages, people, cathedral bells. The rain came and went outside our window, and I dozed with the sound of Edgar's heart singing in my ear. A heart that I did not have the heart to break. I woke to find him dressed and contemplating me. I was still naked, and the sheets had rearranged themselves in my sleep to partially uncover me. I rose and dressed as his silhouette turned to contemplate the street outside. The rain had stopped. We descended the stairs, and he locked the door behind us, carefully replacing the key under the loose brick. We turned up the street, arm-in-arm, and he walked me as far as Canal Street. He made a motion to kiss me near the statue of Mr. Clay, but I felt the eyes of the world on us and whispered, 'My father may get word. He is possessive beyond reason.' I did, however, smile and touch Edgar's face lightly, feeling the softness of his beard under my glove. The smooth white cotton of my thumb traced his lips for a moment, and then we parted, each of us pausing to turn and look at the other. '*Au demain*,' he shouted, and then in English, '*Tomorrow*.' I nodded yes. My errand was left undone. I said nothing of leaving the city this Wednesday. I cannot release myself. So this is it, this is love, the thing into whose hand we willingly climb, even though it might crush us.

10 December 1872. Edgar and I spent yesterday and then today at Achille's apartment, though Edgar says that his brother will be returning in a few days from his business upriver, well in time for Christmas.

I shall be gone then. I still did not have the heart to tell him. I left again with the promise to meet him tomorrow. That promise is an empty one, as I am to sail with Jenny to England on a ship called the *Fire Queen.* We packed our things tonight, a trunk for me, a trunk for Jenny. She chattered without ceasing, sometimes gently scolding me for having forgotten to put something in my trunk.

'Alice, shouldn't you bring your bonnet for church? Are bonnets worn in church there?'

'Yes,' I said.

'Alice, here are your favourite pair of gloves, neglected in the bureau.'

'Yes,' I said.

'Alice, how long shall we spend in Liverpool before departing for London?'

'Yes,' I said.

'How long?' she asked again.

'I'm not sure,' I said.

'Alice, I can't wait to see Lucy and Ida! Won't it be grand to see them?'

'Yes,' I said.

And then, as she was folding a petticoat for her trunk, she turned and said, 'You seem sad. Aren't you excited to return to your native land?' I told a colossal lie: 'I fear I shall miss Mount Teague and your father. He is, after all, my husband.' She continued to speak excitedly as she packed, 'Father will be so preoccupied with rolling season. Why, you know how he is about his sugarcane! And in the meantime, we'll be in London seeing magnificent things!' And she chattered on about the ocean voyage and the ship and what she will read and that she might play for the other passengers on her violin. 'Do you think we'll see snow, like in a Dickens tale? Tell me about Trafalgar Square and the National Gallery!' I told her again of the statue of the English hero, Admiral Nelson, as my thoughts strayed to the statue of the American hero, General Jackson, and the sad Parisian who shall be left on the park bench under him. I almost fell to tears. 'There, there,' Jenny said, 'maybe when the cane is in, Father will join us in England, and we can take a trip to the continent, all of us together. Paris, perhaps!' I fell into a proper cry, a gentle sob, and she came and put her arm around me. 'It's just that—' I muttered into my hands, '—the last time I was in Liverpool, it was with Papa.' She stayed at my side on the edge of the bed, and then she rose and finished packing for me and for herself. When she was done, we went to sleep in the same bed. She did not say anything else about our journey.

11 December 1872. I write this in far different surroundings than the fine mansion of the Howards on St. Charles. I confess I did not sleep well last night, not in anticipation of our journey, nor disturbed by the delighted tossing and turning of Jenny as her dreams anticipated our voyage, but after a night of wrestling with my conscience and the plot that my desire for Edgar has concocted.

This morning, we bid adieu to the Howards and they wished us a safe journey to England. Again, they asked if they could offer us a ride to the wharf, but I told them not to bother with getting the carriage harnessed, and that we would say our goodbyes there on the steps on St. Charles and hope to see them soon. I began to say that I have had no trouble in finding a carriage recently but finished by saying only 'I hear that carriages are not so difficult to find now.' One appeared soon after, and our things were loaded onto it by a negro man with greying hair. He drove us to the levee, where the forest of masts rose into the sky, one ship in particular waiting for us at the Liverpool Warehouse. The city was living its life, commerce taking place, newsboys shouting the news that Mr. Pinchback serves as governor now that Mr. Warmoth has been suspended. The white populace wore an anxious countenance, and there is fear for the future, all for the change in colour of the governor. Perhaps, I thought, it is best that I should go.

As the wooden spires and beams of the ships approached and loomed larger, Jenny asked me if I ever got seasick and what one should do for it. 'A little tea and plain crackers,' I mumbled, 'failing that, laudanum. One asks it of the ship's doctor.' I could almost hear my heart breaking. I could certainly feel it.

The carriage swayed with the steps of the mule who pulled it, and I closed my eyes to the thought of the love act it inspired. And then the sounds of river and ocean commerce were upon us, ships' bells, the bellow of steamship whistles, the shouts of men exhorting huffing stevedores and their heavy steps on gangplanks under enormous loads. Our trunks were taken up and placed on board, men bearing them on their backs like ants effortlessly carrying off enormous morsels. Jenny and I were assisted out of our carriage, she with her violin case, me with my portmanteau. Of course, my portmanteau is where I keep you, my little confidant. I carry you everywhere, and you are a comfort to me. She held her violin case in one hand while holding onto the dark hand of the steward with the other. Before stepping onto the gangplank, their hands rose as if they were about to make a turn in a minuet. Our trunks were already loaded down into the hold, and Jenny turned to the city. 'Well, I suppose this is farewell to the United States of America for a while!' she exclaimed with a wave to the city. I looked to the square and the distant general there, and at last I could go no further, and I understood the terror that makes a frightened horse balk on being loaded aboard a ship.

'There is something I must tell you, sister,' I said to her. She turned to me and the steward turned, just as they were preparing to step onto the gangplank. Passengers were behind us, waiting their turn to embark. I could feel their impatience. 'I can't leave with you," I said at last.

'Can't leave?' Jenny asked. There was both surprise and something pleading in her voice.

'I can't leave your father in the middle of rolling season. I have been absent from Mount Teague long enough. I would love nothing more than to go with you, but a wife belongs with her husband, and a girl your age is entitled to her own adventures. And this is your adventure, not mine. Your sisters and your grandmother will meet you in Liverpool. Send them my regrets.'

'But. But Alice,' she implored, and I almost changed my mind. Surely, I did. Almost.

'What about your trunk, ma'am?' the steward asked, 'it already down yonder that hold, other folks' trunks on top it.'

I breathed deeply. 'Oh, send it along,' I said, 'perhaps I shall join you later, when I can persuade your father to join us. But a wife belongs with her husband.' Such lies I tell! And so convincingly! Even though I know her to be naturally gregarious and she is sure to be a favourite of her shipmates, my conscience bid me ask her, 'Are you sure you feel competent to travel alone?'

'Yes,' she said, 'though I wish you would come, too, Alice.'

'Yes,' I replied, 'and I would love nothing better, but your father tends to get melancholy in the winter. And if something were to happen to him, there would be no one to look after Mount Teague.'

'Mr. Labranche would,' she said.

'Mr. Labranche is just the overseer,' I said, 'Your father and I feel it should be family. And so, I must return to St. Matthew. I feel that I have neglected my duty long enough.'

The steward, a kindly, grey-headed man took her hand again, but she hesitated. At last, she turned away, and they walked up the gangplank. She held her violin case limply at her side. At the top, she handed it over to another steward, even older and darker. He took it and assisted her onto the deck. Other passengers were going up the ramp. She disappeared into the small crowd on deck, and I waited there on the levee for her, the brown wavelets of the river washing the dark mud bank. But she was either in her berth or on the other side of the ship, looking at the river, perhaps. I tried to console myself that she had already found a friend on board and that such was her nature to make acquaintances quickly and easily. The gangway was taken up, and the tug pulled the ship out into the river and the passengers waved to us on the bank. My eyes strained for her, the young woman who is both sister and daughter to me. At last, she walked to the near side of the ship, and I waved to her as cheerfully as I could. But she did not wave back, and only clutched her violin case tightly like a child. And then she was taken away from me by the river, to be given over to the ocean and the land beyond it.

I know that I have betrayed her, as I have betrayed all that is proper and honourable, Mama and Papa, the loving Christian parents who raised me so carefully to do what is right. And, of course, my husband whom I have sworn before God to love and cherish, and, of course, to obey. I have betrayed them all. But the one for whom I feel the sting most of all is my lover, this innocent man who adores me so fully, as I adore him. I turned from the river and into the city, and I walked back to this dwelling, and I lifted the brick to retrieve the key. I have recorded all of it here, like Rousseau and his confessions. I close my eyes and I can still see Jenny, my dear Jenny, sailing away with the look of betrayal on her face, as bitter as it is subtle.

12 December 1872. I woke this morning to a knocking on a door. It seemed to come from the dream I was having, forgotten now, but it became more insistent until finally my eyes opened, shutting out the tableau that had been playing in my slumber. I sat up and covered myself with the sheets, bewildered by waking in a strange room, finding not an exquisite marble mantel but a rather plain wooden one, and not fine damask curtains but plain muslin ones. My eyes wandered the room, and I remembered that I was in the apartment of Edgar's brother. I felt as though I had slept a century.

'Monsieur?' a woman's voice called up distantly.

'Non,' I called down, *'Je reste ici en tant qu'invité de Monsieur Degas pendant son absence.'*

The voice replied with a clear Irish brogue, 'Sorry, but I don't speak no French, ma'am.'

I repeated in English, 'I am staying here as a guest of Monsieur Degas while he is away.'

The voice said, 'Oh. Very well. Are ye decent, then?' She said *decent* in the Irish manner, *'day-cent.'*

I called down, 'Give me a moment, will you?' and I rose quickly and dressed hastily. 'All right,' I said as I buttoned the last button on the dress I wear now, the blue velvet with the deeper blue silk bodice. Steps treaded heavily on the stairs with the sound of water sloshing in a vessel, and an older woman appeared. She held an armload of neatly folded sheets and a bucket. Her hair was a mousy brown, and she had a little spot of a nose like a turtle.

'Mrs. Coogan, ma'am, here to clean for Monsieur Achille,' she said in the way of an introduction.

'Please to meet you,' I said, though I didn't give her my name. Her eyes were so blue as to be almost transparent.

'Is he still away?' she asked as she sat down the bucket. It sloshed a small tongue of soapy water. I realized that she must have thought that he might be up here with me, perhaps in some private moment.

'Yes, that is what I hear,' I said as I pushed my hair back out of my face, 'Give me a moment, and I shall be out.' I put the few things I had removed back into my portmanteau and left her to straighten the apartment, singing softly to herself amid the clinking of empty wine bottles. As I left, I said, 'Please don't tell monsieur that you saw me here today. It is all part of a surprise.'

'Surely, ma'am, and ye can have me word upon it, then,' and she winked at me with her pale blue eyes, and I could tell at once she was a lover of secrets and intrigue. Perhaps I shall be the whispered talk of the servant class, the butt of some ribald tale. It is no matter and no consequence, however. What is done is done, as Lady Macbeth said.

I descended the stairs and the cold light of morning met me. It was still early, though not so early that the city wasn't attending to its errands. And so, I did also. In a coffee house on Chartres, I bought the morning edition of the *Picayune* and read it with a cup of tea and a biscuit (American, not sweet as are English biscuits). Several others were doing likewise, a dapper man with a cane and a top hat, a woman in a plain day-dress, two men who discussed bales and so forth. Bales of cotton, no doubt. The newspaper buzzes with the uncertainty surrounding the prospect of competing governments. Governor Warmoth has been suspended from office, and his lieutenant, a negro man named Pinchback, has been sworn in his place pending the inauguration of a new governor. From Washington, President Grant has offered force to Mr. Pinchback so that, 'the state will be protected from domestic violence.' Already, two companies of U.S. infantry have arrived at the Mechanic's Institute where the legislature meets. The newspaper says that more troops are expected. In the meantime, minutes of both legislatures appear on the same page of the same newspaper, each conducting business as if the other did not exist.

The news is rife with vitriol, as if the earth were to be consumed by flames, that a negro man should be given dominion over white men. The paper goes on to say that Mr. Pinchback will serve until the elected governor is seated, whether it be Mr. Kellogg, he of the Union occupiers and the faction called the Republicans, or Mr. McEnery, he of the Fusionists and the golden idol of my husband and his contemporaries.

The cotton men at the table next to me must have been reading the same news. One of them remarked with a chuckle, 'Why, Old Howard and his boy Teague ain't gonna know which legislature to bribe!' which elicited a guffaw from his companion. I listened to hear further news about Mr. Howard and 'his boy Teague,' but the men said no more on the subject and finally left. On the next page appeared the transcript of a speech by outgoing Gov. Warmoth, certainly one of his last in office, in which he proclaims that the true statehouse shall be at City Hall on St. Charles, where Mr. McEnery's legislature is set up. This is just next to Mr. Howard's home. Perhaps 'Old Howard' shall begin with bribing them. But at last, I moved on to more pressing matters. On page five, there were notices for rooms to rent. I folded the paper and circled suitable prospects. When I finished the last of my tea and biscuit, I set off to find a new dwelling-place.

The first place, on Chartres, would not rent to a woman, either on principle or from fear that I would earn my living in it at the expense of my virtue. The second was rather small and dingy with poor lighting. The third, the landlord was not in. And so, I kept moving, to the fourth, which I have settled upon. This place is on the top floor of a former great home on Ursulines. There are two large windows facing to the south and east, which should give a splendid view of the river whilst protecting the eyes from the harsh light that slants southward this time of year. There is also a black-marble mantle for a cozy fire on cold nights.

I entered the bottom floor of the house, and the landlady greeted me. She was a lady with elegant features and bearing, streaks of gray in her lustrous black hair. She seemed to have no objection to renting to a woman, and to a solitary one at that. We climbed the flights of stairs to the fourth floor, pausing for her to think or catch her breath or both. As she opened the lock with a key, she said, 'I have had to subdivide our old house, a thing that my husband would never have allowed when he was alive, before the war. But the times and my situation demand it now that I am alone in this world.' She paused as if waiting for an old emotion to surge, but it seemed to have burned down to nothing, and she was able to stifle the remainder of it with a simple sigh. There was little doubt about the cause of her new 'situation.'

She stood with one palm pressed into her hip and the other on her forehead. I can imagine her striking the same, stricken posture when she received news of her husband's passing on some distant battlefield. She required that I pay two months in advance, ten dollars a month. I did so and told her that perhaps I should like it for a longer term, if I decided to tarry in the city past carnival season and into the spring. 'As you wish,' she said, and she handed over the key. Almost as an afterthought, she asked who would be renting it. I paused for a moment and then said, quite deliberately, 'Mrs. Teague. Polly H. Teague.'

She left me in the apartment alone, and I paused at the window facing the river, squinting at the thin grey ribbon slicing towards the horizon. I stood there, feeling the absence of my girls, and especially for Jenny, all borne away by the water that wound itself off and away. I turned and took stock of my new residence, and then I left to purchase new things for myself and my home, all in the account of the former Mrs. Teague, to be billed to Mount Teague Plantation, St. Matthew, Louisiana. She is apparently the only person whom my husband has difficulty in finding. I shall risk discovery by the Argus Detective Agency, an operation that I am quite convinced is a humbug.

13 December 1872. I sent a boy with a message to Edgar at his Uncle's house to meet me at this address on Ursulines. From high on the balcony, I watched the street for him, my Parisian. Far below, the life of the city moved in linear directions, parallel and perpendicular. Wagons and carriages passed. A soldier smoked on a street corner standing on one leg and leaning against a building, the sole of the other foot pressed into the brick wall and his rifle propped against it also. Draymen's' carts passed. Each person perhaps only dimly aware of the others, caught up in private thoughts, qualms and pleasures, doubts and certainties. Fashionable creole women under parasols or behind veils, a policeman in blue with two rows of brass buttons speaking to a shopkeeper by a cart of bananas. A group of nuns chatting and smiling, habits stirring as they walk, rosaries hanging around large waists, rounding the corner by the policeman and the shopkeeper who pause in their conversation only to bow slightly to the nuns.

And then I saw him, a distant figure approaching, his gait now so familiar to me, pausing and shielding eyes to compare the addresses to that of the note. As he approached, and I raced down the four flights of stairs in time to greet him at the street. I stepped out of the doorway and onto the banquette.

'I have a surprise for you,' I said, trying not to sound breathless from my descent, 'Close your eyes. Take my hand.' He smiled and took it. 'Your eyes,' I repeated, and he shut them. We entered the doorway and ascended the stairs. After the first two flights, he asked through squinted eyes, "*A quel étage est la surprise?*"

'The surprise is on the fourth floor. Remember, no peeking,' I said to the slightest relaxation of his narrowed eyes. At last we reached the top floor, and I released his hand to turn the key in the lock. The door opened to a space in which morning light fell in skewed squares upon the bare planks of the floor. The sky to the south was a brilliant blue, and a subtle breeze stirred the curtains to cause a ripple in the shadows that framed the windows. It appeared even more splendid than when I had run down the stairs a few minutes before.

'All right,' I said, 'open your eyes.' He opened them and blinked in wonder. 'A place for us,' I said, 'The light should be about right for an artist, don't you think?' He approached the window and looked up to the sky and off to the river and said in uncertain English, 'Light from the south. Well, it is perfect for an artist. *Les meubles?*'

'There will be furniture tomorrow,' I said, and then a moment of hesitation found us as we realised that we were alone, truly alone, with no one to interfere with us. Without speaking, we undressed patiently in this empty room, pausing only for kisses and caresses. And then it became clear that a passion such as ours doesn't require a bed or a mattress or a divan. A wood floor suffices.

Afterward, as we lay together in a nest of our clothes, Edgar said that it was a good thing that I had taken an apartment when I did, as his brother Achille had returned early from Natchez. Had I not been awakened by the cleaning lady, I would have been discovered by him. Edgar said that he wondered if Achille would have thought me an intruder or a gift from heaven. We laughed at that and reclined in the ample southern light that fell through the big windows, away from St. Charles Avenue and Esplanade, high above the world that would frown so ignorantly upon this attraction, so simple and undeniable. The bells of the convent chimed as soft as the southern breeze, which lightly pushed and pulled the curtains over the window sills. Over the rooftops, a thin sliver of sparkling river wound off into the distance.

14 December 1872. We spent the night sleeping on a pallet of bedclothes. This morning, the furniture was delivered, a divan, a pair of chairs, a bed, a small table. All was purchased by Polly H. Teague, that mysterious woman who is as generous as she is elusive. I lay now in the big bed and write as Edgar paints by the windows. The feeling of soft cotton sheets against my bare skin is a pleasure unto itself. Across the room, he works on a painting he is calling 'The Song Rehearsal.' I can see that it is set in a yellow room, and in it there are two women, whom I believe will be his cousins when they are fully painted in. They hold songbooks as they appear to be enacting a scene from a play, or an opera, perhaps. One holds her hand forth as a protagonist, while one seems to shield herself from the other's message. A man whom I do not recognize plays the piano for them. It may be Edgar's brother Rene.

'A piano would be nice,' I sit up and murmur, absently pulling the sheets over my breasts. 'I miss playing.'

'Pardon?' Edgar asks, his eyes still on his work.

'A piano would be nice to have,' I repeat, 'here, in our nest. But there isn't enough space for one.'

Or money, really, I think to myself. I wouldn't want Polly Teague to overextend her credit. Too much spending, even by a profligate like her, might arouse suspicion. Edgar touches his palette with a brush and then touches the canvass.

'Perhaps it is time for you to pay a visit to my Uncle's house. A proper visit," he adds as he looks over his shoulder. His lips break into an unintended smile, and he turns and touches the canvass again. 'He has a piano, you know. This one,' and he points with his brush at the piano that is emerging in black strokes. 'Both Tell and Rene play, and the older children are learning.' He dips his brush in a glass jar of turpentine and cleans it on a rag mottled yellow and orange and brown. He studies his canvass, again testing it in the light with sidelong glances. Then he sets the brush down and comes wiping his hands on the rag. He has come to sit down next to me.

He has gotten up again, and I resume. He has told me that tomorrow is Sunday, and his family shall attend Mass. His cousin Didi, who plays the role of lady of the house in place of her dearly departed mother, Edgar's Tante Odile, insists upon attendance by the entire household. The only one excused is Tell who is expecting a baby any day.

'The chore of sitting through Mass with a horde of squirming children is worth it,' Edgar says, 'Sunday is the best day to be a Creole. After High Mass, there is always a grand dinner and then amusements.' As an illustration, he points to the painting on which he was working with its singers and pianist. He is sure that they will be as enchanted with me as he is. I confess to a fear that they shall not. Most certainly they would not if they knew the true nature of my situation.

Sammy, 1982

He felt a jolt on his shoulder that was firm enough to shake his head.

"Mist' Teague, they movin' him," Miss Vessy said.

He looked for the diary and couldn't find it. He eyed the other people in the waiting room suspiciously as he got on his knees and looked under the pressed plastic chairs in which he and Miss Vessy had spent the night. He found it and stood and stretched. Only the knees and elbows of his clothes were still wet. She put out her hand, and he helped her up.

The pneumatic doors opened, and an orderly wheeled Teeter out of the ICU. He was bundled in sheets and blankets with only his face, mostly nose, showing. Miss Vessy followed by the side of the gurney with Sammy right behind it. They moved him to a room with three other patients, all unseen behind curtains. The orderly locked the wheels of the stretcher, and Teeter moved to the bed next to it. Under the sheets, his legs were spindly. One of his calves had a tattoo on it, one that Sammy had never seen before. A nurse came and looked over the chart at the end of the bed and then left without introducing herself to anyone, and the three of them were alone in the curtained-off space. Through the window, the Superdome loomed in the distance.

"Hey, my boy," Miss Vessy said tenderly.

"Hey, Mama," Teeter whispered, and then he closed his eyes and cried so hard that his teeth showed, clinching white between stretched lips. "I'm so sorry, mama, I'm so sorry, so sorry, so sorry, oh, I'm so sorry."

He opened his eyes and looked to Sammy.

"I'm so sorry bawsman, I let you down, *mais*, I'm so sorry. I let y'all down. I just couldn't tell her no. Couldn't tell her no."

His cheeks were still wet with tears as his lips went slack and he fell into an exhausted sleep.

"Who he couldn't tell no?" Miss Vessy asked as she tried to dry her eyes.

Sammy knew.

"Madame Dope," he said.

And Teeter slept, chin back and open-mouthed, and then Miss Vessy slept in the chair by his bed, her chin on her chest and her head tilted to one side. But Sammy couldn't sleep.

Alice, 1872

15 December 1872. Sunday. A most enchanting day spent in the company of the Bells, Degas, and the Mussons and their houseful of children. And of course, my Parisian. I attended Catholic Mass at St. Louis with all, including a perpetually moving assortment of children who fidgeted constantly along the length of our pew despite the stern looks and shushing of Edgar's cousins. A line of nuns sat in the foremost pew like the birds on a telegraph wire, and I imagined them all representing the same repeating note. The altarpiece was magnificent, soaring upward with colourful statues of saints, though the Latin made no more sense to me than it would to Mr. Teague. But let us not speak of him, my little confidant. I have happier things to discuss.

Afterwards, to the triumphant chiming of bells onto the square and General Jackson, we adjourned to the Musson's home on Esplanade. This time I entered as a known and welcome guest, not creeping in, but walking proudly and upright. I found the house was only vaguely familiar without the hazy cloud of absinthe. Several servants waited on us whilst we were at table, including a man named Joseph who patiently shucked oysters at a side table. The smallest children sat on the laps of mothers, fathers, aunts, and uncles, as conversation bubbled equally in French and English.

Edgar's Uncle Michel and I have taken an instant liking to each other, as his ways are so much like Papa's. There is an air about him which I recognize, as if he continues to be burdened by the mourning he endures for his late wife. After dinner, as he polished his spectacles with a napkin, he remarked that he had heard that I play the piano, and so I was persuaded to do so on their fine Pleyel in the drawing room. I played for quite a while, without thinking, and scarcely breathing. The adults and the older children all listened, and then Mouche began to sing, a beautiful soprano. After a while, another voice joined hers, and I looked up from the keys to see that Tell had risen from her nap and had joined her sister in a duet. Estelle, or simply, 'Tell' is blind, or nearly so, and her sightless eyes trained on an unseeable point as her voice rose from within her. It was quite lovely, so expressive, the trickling of an emotion that none of us could know and I expect none of us could bear even if we knew it.

When her song was concluded, she smiled blankly to the pattering applause of the family and gave a small nod. Then she adjourned to a settee, one hand resting on her expectant midsection and the other holding the hand of her daughter Jo, a girl who seems to be about my age when we left Surrey, ten years-old or so. The girl was persuaded to play, the same simple things that beginners learn, and she was quite passable.

I took my leave as night fell, gathering a shawl about my shoulders against the night chill. The men of the house, Uncle Michel and Rene and Mr. Bell (Will) were on the front gallery smoking cigars and watching the Sunday evening traffic trot by the white-washed tree trunks on Esplanade. On seeing me leave, Uncle Michel placed his cigar on the railing where its glowing tip burned. He grasped my hands and bid me adieu, kissing me on both cheeks and telling me, 'You make my family happy, then you make me happy. Your invitation is an open one, extended by all in this house.' I saw my reflection in his spectacles amid the flame of the gaslight as he reached to pick up his cigar. Rene and Will each nodded and told me how pleased they were to make my acquaintance and that they hoped to see me again. Edgar accompanied me home, here to our nest on Ursulines, but returned to Esplanade for the night so as not to impugn my honour in the eyes of his family. And in these quiet rooms, I feel the weight of the lie descend. I do my best to ignore it, to pretend that I am not married, that there is an honourable future for us. I close still waiting for the success of such pretense.

16 December 1872. Edgar has come this morning. He tells me that everyone was absolutely enchanted with me, none more so than his Uncle Michel, who Edgar says refers to me as *La Fille D'Or*, the Golden Girl. My Parisian has now dressed again, though only to his trousers and undershirt and suspenders. He works against the backdrop of windows that look out onto a cool, overcast day, his brush thoughtfully painting in colours to the sketches he has made previously. The smell of oil and turpentine have become to me the smells of love and passion. How odd, how thrilling. I have passed a pleasant morning reading the newspaper and drinking the tea that Edgar brought for me when he came in, though we were delayed in drinking it and it has cooled a measure. I suppose I shall rise and dress again soon.

The *Picayune* carries news of a tumultuous world, writhing in turmoil. It is so distant from the tranquility of our nest, even the people passing on the street four floors below us seem faraway and dealing with faraway problems. The *Picayune* says that a fire in New York at the Fifth Avenue Hotel has left sixteen dead, all burned beyond recognition, all of them female domestics. None of the guests were harmed, but the thought of those poor girls huddling together in the smoke! How very frightful! The newspaper also tells of competing legislatures here in New Orleans and carries the minutes of their sessions, replete with the shouts and postures each assumes to ensure its supremacy. Indeed, in order to gain an upper hand, the McEnery faction, of which Mr. Teague is a member, has sent a 'Committee of One Hundred,' to Washington to persuade President Grant to give up the 'Kellogg Usurpation.' My husband is not listed as part of the committee. Literacy must be a prerequisite. Certainly, Mr. Teague keeps to St. Matthew and the production of sugar, and I am certainly happy for his absence. His is one less face to avoid here in the city. There is also news in the *Picayune* that the *Fire Queen* has cleared the Southwest Pass and has made the open water of the Gulf. It is my hope that Jenny has forgiven me or will do so with time. The pain written on her departing face still haunts me, but it is diminished by the joy I feel in the presence of this man, my Parisian. Still, my joy has a chip in its veneer like that of Lucy's porcelain doll, what is her name? Yes, I remember now, her name is Penny.

17 December 1872. A close call today, a stark reminder of the precarious position I maintain and the need to take greater care. Edgar and I attended the races, which are just up Esplanade near his Uncle Michel's house. The air buzzed with fog which was quite thick, and we wondered if we would be able to see anything at all. Edgar assured me that the races are held in all sorts of weather, even rain. He carried his sketch pad in a satchel as we walked along in the fog. The white-washed trunks of the oaks stood as sentinels, their canopies rising into the mist. The sound of hooves and the smell of manure and earth announced the track to us, and then we came upon the grandstand looming in the fog. Edgar presented our passes to the man at the gate, a gentleman in a red waistcoat and jacket and black trousers and top hat.

The horses were going through their preliminaries in anticipation for the first race, the sounds of hooves on turf swelling and falling as they approached and then returned into the fog. We had an excellent place, right on the finish line, courtesy of Mouche's husband, Mr. Bell, who serves on the board of what is called the Louisiana Jockey Club.

The bugle sounded for the horses to gather somewhere in the fog, and, after a moment's hesitation, there was a bell, and the distant gallop of hooves began somewhere in the dense swarm of whiteness. The shouts of the crowd moved with the horses, as only the crowd closest to the pack could see them. The rumble of horses and commotion of men began to approach, and then they were upon us, a thrilling rush, a spray of earth under thundering hooves. I clapped like a girl of eleven and looked at Edgar, who paused from his sketching to give a bemused look at my girlish delight and to kiss me. The sound of the horses and shouting faded, and everything else might have faded, as it does when we kiss, but we were in the company of others. Then, just as we broke from our kiss, I heard a voice that jostled me. My ears tuned to it as Edgar resumed his work, his mind replaying the forms of the horses, his pencil capturing muscle and mane surging for the finish line.

It was a man's voice, a familiar one. It approached, saying something about it being the last day of the fall season and how lucky they had been to come through the horse flu unscathed. With that, I recognized the voice's owner. Luckily, he was turned and talking to another man as they walked along the rail. I turned my face away as he passed. When he did, I saw that it was Mr. Howard, with his unmistakable small pet of a beard.

How careless of me. I had forgotten that he is also on the board of the Jockey Club. I opened Edgar's umbrella to shield my identity from those who had no need of it. Edgar looked up from his drawing and asked if I felt rain.

'No,' I stammered, 'but one can't take chances. I wouldn't want your sketch to get wet.'

He smiled at my thoughtfulness and kissed me. If he had kissed me again, I would have lost all propriety and forgotten about horses and patrons and Mr. Howard. But Edgar resumed sketching, the powerful flanks of his horse seeming to heave toward a finish line somewhere in the paper. The next race began with the bell, and then the next, though worry prevented me from enjoying them as fully as the first. The fog burned away quickly, and I spent the day using the umbrella to shield myself from Mr. Howard. Once, he and his companion passed again just in front of us, and Mr. Howard and Edgar exchanged a greeting.

'Do you do portraits, sir?' Mr. Howard asked. I could see his expensive boots pressing into the turf, his gray wool trousers with the fine cuffs holding specks of mud. Edgar took a breath, as he does when he is about to say something in English.

'Generally, no, monsieur. Only friends and family.'

Mr. Howard gave Edgar his card, *Chas. T. Howard, Louisiana Lottery, St. Charles Avenue, New Orleans, Louisiana,* and said, 'Let me tell you, sir, that price is no object for me and my friends, if you're looking to make some money.' Edgar took it with a polite, *merci, monsieur.* Mr. Howard paused for a moment and said, presumably to me, 'Are you enjoying yourself today, ma'am?'

'Oui, monsieur,' I said, and there was another pause, as if he was waiting for me to say more, or to show myself. Indeed, his hand with its great ring nudged the edge of the umbrella, but I pulled it away. A man's voice in the distance announced the next race.

'Au revoir, then, ma'am,' Mr. Howard's voice said.

'Au revoir, monsieur,' I returned. Then Mr. Howard's fancy boots and trouser legs moved away from the canopy of my umbrella.

'Nouveau riche,' Edgar chuckled as he put the card in his pocket, and then he asked if it would trouble me if we left early, as the light was beginning to be a bother to his eyes. I said, not at all, but of course, I was relieved beyond measure and could not leave soon enough. He put his work in his satchel, and we left. I kept to the cover of the umbrella, clutching it tightly with one hand and holding my hem above the soggy turf with the other. As we boarded the omnibus and headed back into the city, at last I folded the umbrella and gave it back to Edgar. My arm was fatigued from supporting it all day, and, though it had been overcast, it had not rained a drop. I write this now as the rain has begun in earnest outside our nest, beating on house tops and smoking chimneys and the masts and smokestacks of the ships in the river. We have satisfied our thirsts for each other, and he has fallen into peaceful slumber. And I have taken Mr. Howard's card from Edgar's coat pocket and burned it in the flame of a candle. I put you away now, my little confidant, and move under the covers with him as I watch the lazy plumes of smoke trail up into the cool, grey damp of the city.

18 December 1872. A rainy day spent indoors. Edgar and I have read and loved and napped in equal measure. The day has been sufficiently dark to require candles for reading. Loving and napping, of course, do not require them. My Conscience also naps, and well it may nap forever.

Earlier today, however, Edgar said that he should like to meet my father. He said that his Uncle Michel doesn't know a planter in St. Matthew named Lamb, but that this is not surprising because his uncle is a cotton broker and more acquainted with the planters in the northern part of the state and in Mississippi, where cotton is grown. I told Edgar that perhaps in time they shall meet, but that my father is consumed this time of year with making sugar, which sets him in a very bad humour and that he becomes quite agitated and remains so through much of the winter, until rolling season is done, and the sugar is to market.

'Yes,' Edgar sighed, 'But for my own sake and for my family's honour, I must do what is right. For the love of his beautiful daughter and for his decency as a man, I owe him my respect. You don't think I am dishonouring you like this?'

'Nonsense,' I said, and I kissed his forehead, and then his lips and then his chest and then we were consumed by the white flames of passion. Of course, I am putting him off. The truth cloys within me, though my Conscience no longer complains. Perhaps it has given up on me.

19 December 1872. An overcast day with a wind that played upon the windowpanes of the Musson's house on Esplanade, a place to which I now have an open invitation. Not thinking that the wind would be so stout nor so cold, I decided to walk there and found myself bundled up against it. I was contemplating hailing a hack for the remainder when the Mussons' dog Vasco greeted me on the Bayou Road and walked with me like an old friend, pausing to sniff and leave his scent for other dogs to sniff whilst looking up to me with that friendly grin of dogs. Every puddle was an occasion to stop for a drink, every row of wet shrubs a forest to be walked through and investigated. When we arrived at the Musson's, he shook himself, and when the door was opened by one of the servant girls, he felt he was entitled to admittance. He darted past her through the cracked door and clattered into the house. He skittered across the floor to the delight of the children until he had gone through the house to the back gallery. Another servant took my coat and shawl and went to fetch a mop and a bucket.

Using the commotion as a diversion, I walked through the library to Edgar's room, where I found him working on a painting in which Tell is arranging flowers. He saw me and lay down his brush and approached in his mottled smock. At the doorway, he looked past me and then both ways. Seeing that his cousins were occupied, he gave me a kiss, and I traced my fingers through his beard until we heard footsteps. We separated quickly as Mouche appeared and exclaimed what a delightful surprise it was to see me, as Didi was upstairs reading to Tell, the men were all at their offices, and she was 'quite alone with the children and this aloof man.'

Mouche and I sat and chatted with Edgar as he painted in detail on the canvas. Mouche said that the doctor has put her sister, Tell, to bed, as her day is imminent. Edgar pointed to Tell's expectant midsection and its occupant and said that he is to be the *parrain*, meaning the godfather. I asked him if he thought it was going to be a boy or a girl, and he guessed that it would be a boy. Mouche laughed that it is quite like a man to believe all babies to be boys. I laughed as well, though my laugh faltered as I thought of Mr. Teague and his quest for a male heir, a prince for the Kingdom of Mount Teague.

I turned and looked out the window at the children playing in the field beyond the garden, Vasco barking and bowing, chasing the children and being chased and tugging on the same stick. On a swing suspended from an oak limb, Jo moved like a pendulum, legs reaching and tucking, the movement of air playing with the length of her dark hair. Edgar appeared at my side holding his palette, mottled with paint.

'It is really a good thing to have a family, good children,' he said.

'Yes, yes it is,' I said, for in truth, a family is all I have ever wanted, to be part of a whole that is to be both enjoyed and endured. That is, it is all I have ever wanted until I met this man. Of course, I thought this but did not say it. Instead, I whispered in his ear, 'Come by later,' and he smiled and pursed his lips at me, a small, surreptitious, telegraph of a kiss. I returned it, and as I did, over his shoulder something caught my eye.

Across the garden and the field, a familiar figure exited the side door of the house in the distance. I stole another quick glimpse. Now, later, as I write this and wait for Edgar, I am almost sure that the figure was Edgar's brother Rene, emerging from the house across the field.

20 December 1872. It seems that Tell's day has arrived at last. This morning at the Mussons, the servant girl Virginie escorted a small-framed negress upstairs. Mouche whispered that it was *l'accoucheuse*, the midwife. A growling cry erupted from time to time, punctuated with shrieks, followed by low singing in French, a lullaby, and then more howling. The blind agony of it all. One of the servants came downstairs and went back up with a pair of scissors. Mouche looked up from her Rosary that she was praying with Didi and whispered knowingly, 'Put the scissors under the bed, and it will cut the pain.'

Edgar seemed quite ill-at-ease with the screaming upstairs, and so I offered that he and I might take the older children to Mr. Barnum's circus, which is in town. Indeed, it seems as though there are broadsides announcing it from every telegraph post, tree, and wall in the city. Sea-cows and sea-lions. A lady in a fancy dress and crinolette and ringlets, but with a beard as full as a man's. Horses galloping side-by-side with feathered headdresses. Elephants, tigers, so forth.

We left the younger children in the care of the servants and walked to the circus grounds at Tonti's corner with Canal. As we neared, we saw men wading and pulling up stakes. The whole of the enormous lot was underwater from the recent rains, and the tents were being taken down. I asked one of the men what was going on, and he answered me, to my surprise, with a Yorkshire accent. 'Too wet for a circus today, mum,' he said as he wiped his face on his upper arm, 'Mr. Barnum's got us a place uptown near Tivoli Circus.'

'Circle, you mean?' I clarified.

'Yes, mum, that'd be the one,' he answered. I thanked him, and he waded back into the water with his mallet over his shoulder. Though it was cold, his undershirt had sweated a dark patch that encroached on both sides of his suspenders.

The man's accent had been too much for the children to understand, and certainly too much for Edgar, though I'm sure he knew that it was too wet. A circus cannot be held in such a setting. It was too deep for the animals and too shallow for the sea-lions and sea-cows. I took him aside and told him our predicament.

They will be heartbroken,' he said, and he seemed on the verge of tears at the prospect of having to tell them. His heart is so pure. So, I leaned to the children and broke the news to them. I told them that the man had told me that they knew we were coming, and in our honour, they were moving to an even grander place near Tivoli Circle, but they need another day to prepare it for us. Jo turned to Carrie and Pierre and said, 'Did you hear that!'

And so we took them for a long walk down the bank of Bayou St. John. As we watched the children throw shells into the water, Edgar whispered that I shall make a wonderful mother one day, and I replied in a whisper to him that he shall make a wonderful father. I imagined Edgar and me with our own children, calling us Maman and Papa and holding our hands, and returning home and reading to them and putting them down to sleep in little feather beds and kissing them goodnight and turning down the wicks on their lamps. And going to bed ourselves to petition God for more children. We returned this afternoon and were greeted by a quiet house and the news that the Musson household had increased by one, a baby girl, the newest Degas.

Sammy, 1982

Fireworks and ice cream and a command performance by the circus. Alice had done the very same kind of thing with the children of the Musson house that Betsy had done with his, skillfully redirecting them to something better. The Musson children had returned home that winter evening to find a brand-new cousin, a little thing wrapped up in blankets, tongue and eyes probing for the world and met with the tentative and curious touches of cousins. Sammy thought back to the day in Montreal when he and Betsy were handed their baby and the wonder that whispered, *Here. Here is a new person.*

He looked over at Missy Vessy who was reading a copy of *People* magazine while her little boy lay in the bed battling demons in his sleep.

Sammy imagined the day that little Martin Blanchard was handed over to his mother, before he had earned himself the nickname *Tête Dur*, hard-head, and before it had been twisted into Teeter. There was a solitary card on the metal-and-pressboard nightstand, from a child, a card that said, *dear mr Teeter, I hope your tummy gonna feel better soon….* There were no other cards with it, only a plastic cup and a water pitcher that sat in the wet ring it had made on a paper placemat. Sammy got up and excused himself to make a call at the payphone by the elevator.

Hello? The woman's voice answered, and the operator's voice replied, *collect from Sammy, will you accept?*

Yes ma'am, the woman's voice said. A click signaled the departure of the operator from the conversation.

"Hey," Betsy said. In the background behind her voice, his household laughed and shouted and barked. He was glad to hear it.

"Hey," he said.

"How's Teeter?"

"Still alive. Not sure how happy he is about it."

"Novena must be working, then," she said. *Just a second*, she said to someone. A little breathy voice got on the phone and said, "hey daddy," and then another got on. He thought it might be his youngest, Judee, who was still shy about phones. She breathed in and out through her nose and made a small static over the receiver. *Say hi daddy*, Betsy's voice encouraged in the background, *say hi.* At last, a little voice breathed right into the phone, "hi daddy." Then the sound of two little girls squealing and running through the house receded from the phone.

"Everybody okay?" Sammy asked. "Any more trouble?"

"Another chicken in the tree. I got it before the kids saw it."

"Good. Good," he said, though it wasn't completely good, and they both knew it.

Two people in the waiting room got into a loud, garbled argument, and Sammy turned his head and put a finger in his ear. He heard his girls giggling in the background.

"Girls not upset about Disney?"

"Already forgot about it. Got the dog dressed up again."

He told her he loved her. And she told him. An orderly and a security guard broke up the two fighters, two women, and escorted them onto the elevator. One of them held the other's wig in her hand. Sammy returned to the room.

In the Blanchard section of the curtained room, the television played, but no one watched it. Teeter had wakened and was looking out the window at the city skyline. Miss Vessy had put down her *People* magazine and was looking out the window with her son.

"Miss Vessy, you need to get out for a few minutes? For a smoke break or something?"

"Naw," she said, and she looked at the pack of Marlboro Lights in her purse. "Maybe I quit them things," she said.

The television droned on with soap opera dialogue, a serious conversation between a television doctor and nurse in a hospital coffee shop, definitely not the coffee shop downstairs at Big Charity. The scene ended with a single, somber note of a French horn.

A woman strode by the door of Teeter's hospital room, a tall woman in white with a flash of blonde hair. As she passed, Sammy heard an unmistakable English accent. He got up and looked up and down the hall. She was walking away, in all white with white stockings and long, wavy golden blonde hair. He followed her and lightly touched her shoulder.

"Excuse me," he said.

She turned, and he saw that she was dark-skinned. Her hair was either dyed blonde or was a wig.

"I'm sorry, I thought you were someone-"

"Well, I am someone. You sayin' I ain't nobody?" she scowled as if she had been challenged.

He apologetically returned to the room. A commercial on the television ended with a woman speaking in an English accent about "pu-uhre luxury," as chocolate drizzled into the form of a candy bar. It had been a commercial. He shook his head at himself and sat down and opened the diary.

Alice, 1872

21 December 1872. The weather was colder and clearer today, and unhurried plumes of smoke rose up into the blue sky from the chimneys of the Musson house, out over the gardens and the rooftops and chimneys of other houses on Esplanade. I was escorted upstairs and received by Tell who held her new baby, a small loaf of blankets, really. Tell stared vacantly across her chamber and touched her child lightly as if trying to see her with her fingertips. The servant woman Miss Petinque had a fire going in the fireplace, and the room glowed with the warmth of it. As we approached in the hall, Tell said to the wall, 'Mouche? And is that Alice and Edgar with you?' and I marveled that she could know us by the sound of our footsteps. She smiled at wherever she thought we might be and opened the blankets to reveal a small pink face which moved its lips in a twisted yawn. I approached and said, 'She's beautiful.'

'Is she?' Tell asked the air between us. I said yes and asked if she had a name. Tell smiled into the air and said, 'Jeanne. Her name is Jeanne.' I dared not ask to hold her, but it was what I wanted more than anything, to hold this new creature, unencumbered with the nonsense of the world. But Tell seemed disinclined to let the pleasant little bundle go, and I didn't ask her. So much like the day that Alice Latham brought her new baby to the church in Manchester and bid Papa marry her and its father. That baby should be walking and talking now. Where are they, I wonder? I suppose she is Alice Pennywaite now.

Tell cooed to her baby, something low and sweet and French, the sort of blessing that only a new mother can give. We sat for a moment in the soft sounds of a winter morning and the quiet crackle of a fire set against it until the scampering rumble of children coming up the stairs broke the idyllic moment. Pierre climbed into bed with his mother, who knew him by his scent and by his voice and by the weight of him in the bed beside her. He pulled back the blankets around his sister's tiny face and asked if baby Jeanne could go to the circus with us. Tell told him softly and with a placating smile that Jeanne is only a baby and that the circus was for big boys like him who can mind Cousin Edgar and Demoiselle Alice.

And so, we left Mouche reading to Tell, and we bundled up for the circus. In the style of a good Creole woman, I placed my new veil over my face as we went outside so that from behind the lace I could watch the suspicious world in the bright winter sun. I wrapped in a woolen shawl and was mindful to keep the children wrapped up as well. We splurged in hiring a fine brougham to take us to the circus, in no small part due to the degree of anonymity it afforded us, though I said it was to cut the wind and cold from the children. The bright crystal streets clattered by outside.

At Tivoli Circle, we stepped out to the buzz of curiosity-seekers gathering around the enormous tents in the field off the roundabout, under the twin spires of the Jewish temple. With small hands held tightly in ours, we spent the afternoon touring the menageries, going first to the animal tents. White camels and polar bears, a black rhinoceros and panther, tigers, lions, and, of course, elephants. We saw the sea-cows, and little Pierre asked where its horns were. The lumpy creature floated amiably in its enclosure, nibbling on kelp that a man forked in from the side. Edgar said that it was a sea-cow and that only sea-bulls have horns, and it was explanation enough for Pierre.

We came across a whale in a colossal vat of water, a great 'marine monster,' according to Mr. Barnum, a creature so much like the one Papa and I saw in our crossing. I stared into the great blinking eye. How sad a thing it must be, separated from the sea! Just then, it respired through the hole in the top of its held, sending a plume of cold spray up and out, and causing the children to squeal and laugh. As well as live animals, there were stuffed ones, some of which appeared to be the skillful amalgamations of two or three other animals. There was a preserved specimen of a mermaid, which to Edgar and me appeared exactly as it was, the clever marriage of some sort of monkey head to the tail of a fish. To the children, however, it was most certainly a mermaid.

Jo stood on the railing next to the exhibit with a boy and a girl her age, gawking and discussing it among themselves in the friendly manner of small children. I touched her shoulder to tell her we were moving on to the next tent. As I did, her little companions turned, and they looked so very familiar to me. Just then a voice in the crowd said, 'Chirren, get away from over yonda.' I turned to see the square, black face of Old Mama approaching and realized that the children were the Howards' two youngest, Annie and her brother, whose name I can't remember presently. I pulled my veil nervously, as if it were too small and I was trying to make it larger. The two children took her dark hands, and they disappeared into the crowds. Of course, they would want to attend the circus, I thought. They live not a mile away from here, and they are children, after all.

I was a little shaken, but we continued to the next tent. In it, there were snake-charmers, jugglers, tight-rope walkers. There was a collection of Feejee cannibals, ransomed, it was said, by Mr. Barnum himself from a King Timbuktu or some such. Rather than dine on the flesh of humans, the bored-looking trio of cannibals ate ham-sandwiches and gawked back at us patrons. Down past the cannibals was an exhibit in which an enormous man played the fiddle and, when he did, his equally enormous wife tapped her fat foot and leg to the tune. They shared a tent with the other oddities, among them a man who did the most grotesque of contortions.

We saw but a half of it, wandering between the sounds of music from the various bands set up on the grounds. The children ate salt-water taffy and peanuts and a sort of hand-pie whose name I forget now. Our hands were sticky from the hands of our little ones. The shadows of tents and people grew long, and a man made his way through the crowds with another man blowing a trumpet, announcing the Grand Entry Procession, and we were gathered into the largest of the tents.

We took our seats in the day's failing light, into the illumination of some of the five thousand gas jets of which Mr. Barnum boasted on the broadsides. The largest of the bands began a pompous march, and through a flap in the canvas, the parade entered. The performers filed in to the martial airs of the band, entire squads of Turks, Mamelukes, Tartars, Greeks, and others, all in colourful costumes. The band, several dozen strong, played a brassy marching air to the procession. The air in the tent flashed to life with the entrance of stilt-walking fire-breathers who held torches to their mouths and belched out flames to the gasping astonishment of us all. The gaslight was low enough that I quit my veil, and we watched the acrobats and bareback riders of Signor Sebastian's Circus, including a Mlle. Lucilla Watson and Young Romeo, and an acrobat who did a double somersault over no less than ten horses. The children were captivated, every spectacle doubled and tripled in their little eyes, which opened wide in the struggle to take it all in and remember it forever. A woman in a sequined costume performed acrobatic feats, at one point suspending herself from a harness by her teeth and spinning, spinning, spinning, until I thought that I should be dizzy myself.

This is only a part of it, my little confidant, I cannot remember it all. But when it was over, we carried two sleeping children whilst the third walked along side of us rubbing her eyes. It was a quiet ride home in the dark, in a plainer carriage, bundled together under a blanket which smelled of horses. Mouche met us on the porch of 372 Esplanade, telling us she was beginning to worry. At the back door, we stepped over Vasco, who raised his head from a drowsy repose and put it down again. The children were put to bed, and Edgar saw me home to our nest on Ursulines. Rather than fall into the arms of Venus, we fell asleep like two weary children.

22 December 1872. Edgar rose before sunrise and returned to his uncle's house to dress for Mass, and then I met them at the cathedral. He asked me, surreptitiously, how I slept, and I told him very well, like a child. And we exchanged a subtle look of mischief at our secret. The Musson pew was its usual squirming line of fidgeting children punctuated by adults who gave them stern looks of admonishment whilst jiggling babies into restless sleep, save Tell, who still keeps to bed with the new baby. Mouche's boy Sidney, not quite two years old, sat nestled into me, his little eyes vacant and contemplating slumber as he picked at the folds of my skirts. His fair little finger traced the burgundy silk as the Latin droned softly. By our golden hair, other worshipers might have thought us mother and son. Those who slumbered were awakened at the close, including Uncle Michel, who again insisted that he had been resting his eyes, to which his daughters said, bien sur, *of course*, Papa, though Mouche winked at me. On our way out the doors and onto the square, Jo, in her favourite lavender dress, held Carrie's hand in the way that I have seen Ida hold little Lucy's at Mount Teague. Ida and little Lucy, how do they get on now? What are they seeing of the old country? Do they think of me?

Over Sunday dinner, talk turned to carnival season, and Rene told of a surprise that a certain Pickwick Club was concocting for Mardi Gras, and that it would be a grand joke on the Yankees and their puppet government, but that he wasn't at liberty to discuss it any further than that. Mr. Bell, who seldom speaks, said, 'I hear that folks down in St. Matthew Parish have been freed of U. S. Troops, largely from the efforts of a man named Teague. We could use a man like that here.'

'Undoubtedly,' Rene said between bites. 'Kellogg will be the ruin of us.' The conversation turned a while on this axis, and I let it spin but did not engage in it. Apparently, the men of this household, like my husband, are devotees of Governor McEnery. Edgar was silent also, and I fancy it was a disapproving silence, though we have not discussed American politics and I believe he has but little interest in it.

After dinner, as the servants cleared the dishes, Rene played the piano and Mouche sang. Edgar sat at the table as Pierre drew Vasco, and if the poor dog had seen it and could make sense of it, he would have run under the house and hid. But Edgar praised it effusively.

'Why, Pierre my boy, I can almost hear him bark!' Edgar said, which was more charitable than candid. This evening, when we returned to our nest on Ursulines, I rested my head on Edgar's bare chest as my hair fell golden upon it and he stroked my bare back. I told him it was generous of him to praise Pierre's drawing. 'Art is easy, until you know how,' he said, 'If he sticks with it, it will get harder for him. Let him enjoy it while he still can.' My Parisian has fallen asleep now as I write, despite his intending to return to his room at Uncle Michel's. He and I still glow from our love, and I contemplate waking him for another go. But we have exhausted each other enough, and so I shall wake him early so that he might sneak into his uncle's house before his family wakes.

23 December 1872. We woke early, though not as early as we had intended, and dressed hurriedly in the cold, without making a fire, and returned to Uncle Michel's great house on Esplanade. Over breakfast, Edgar told his uncle that he had risen early to go with me to see the sunrise on the river. He did not say that we had risen from the same bed. Uncle Michel said that Rene had already departed and that it is a busy time of year if you are a wine merchant. We decided to pay Rene and Achille a visit at their Commission House on Common Street, under the placard that announced, *DeGas Freres Marchand du Vin.*

We arrived to a crowded shop, to hear Rene telling a man in a frock coat, 'We have some lovely claret, sir. Several cases of good cheer for you and your family.' Commerce was so brisk that Edgar and Rene only exchanged waves and we departed without a proper visit. Edgar said that his brothers Achille and Rene are making a name for themselves, and their success delights him, as their father wanted them all to be bankers like him. He spoke of fathers and expectations and asked me if my father would be expecting me home for Christmas. I told him no. I thought Edgar would be taken back by my not spending Christmas with my 'father' in St. Matthew, and so I concocted a tale of a house empty of sisters and a man consumed with worry, preoccupied with getting his sugarcane in and to market in the face of horse flu and freezing weather. Edgar said that he could see my father was a very driven man. I replied, 'Yes, very much so. To the point that he neglects his daughters.' Of course my little confidant, this is true. But bear with me. I find I must mark it down here to keep track of what is true and what is not.

People made the shops on Canal in increasing numbers as across the street in the American part of town, gifts shall be exchanged, whilst on this side, they are not exchanged until the first day of the New Year, that is, at least among Creoles like Uncle Michel and his family. Nevertheless, Edgar and I attended the shops on the High Street, Canal Street. He says that perhaps I should stop referring to it as the High Street, unless I want to appear as English.

'Well, that is the matter of it,' I said. 'Under this creole veil, I am, after all, still English.' Edgar said, that is true, but asked me if I didn't want to blend in. 'How you talk with your Parisian accent!' I laughed, and we moved along.

There was a sense of ease behind my veil, a strange and comforting anonymity. I could see everyone, though they could not see me. We spent a happy morning along Canal High Street, visiting Mr. Holmes' great store, and Mr. Moody's, he of the famous shirts, and Madame Olympe's Dress Shop, where I must confess I was captivated by the elegant dresses in the window. I looked to see our reflections in the glass, and parted my veil for a moment, and rather than a bored man strung along on a woman's errands, I saw in Edgar's face a man as happy to be in my company as I was in his. And here I shall say it, my little confidant: I saw the faces of two people in love. People were passing as reflections in the glass, but they were as spirits in another world.

'It shall soon be carnival season,' Edgar's reflection said as we pulled away from the window, 'You would look even more captivating in one of those ballgowns.' I pursed my lips in a kiss toward his reflection and pulled my veil to, and we resumed our places in the real world. I put my arm in his and squeezed his forearm as we moved along. We came to the toy store, Guéblé & Nippert's, and I saw an old acquaintance from a time that seems decades ago, though it was only a few months. I touched her shoulder softly with my gloved hand. 'Miss Duplantier?' I asked.

'Yes?' she replied to my veil. I had forgotten that I was wearing it, so I parted the white lace and she said, 'Why, Miss Lamb.' I replied that I saw she was making her holiday errands.

'Isn't it a wonderful time of year to be a child?' she said, 'It certainly is to be a governess. Such joy in those little faces!' and she smiled a smile that hinted of rapture and goodwill. And then she asked me, 'May I ask you how your niece liked her doll?'

'Oh,' I said, 'she was quite beside herself.' Falsehoods escape my mouth so effortlessly. She looked to Edgar who was watching the movements of the store, the way a little girl stood on her toes and pointed, the manner of a woman retrieving her pocketbook, the clerk who leaned on the counter in his shirtsleeves, the girl who must be his daughter who attended other shoppers. I watched Edgar whilst Edgar watched all of it. Miss Duplantier's voice startled me.

'Miss Lamb, forgive me for mentioning it, but I hope you have taken my advice regarding a certain planter in St. Matthew.' I told her, 'Yes, I have been avoiding him at all costs.' That of course was the truth. We parted with holiday wishes, and I thought, and still think now, that she and I could be great friends under different circumstance, one in which the truth could prevail completely. But that is not the world I inhabit now. As she departed back out onto the banquette of Canal Street, Edgar asked who she was. I told him that she was an old acquaintance here in the city and a governess for a family uptown, and we took again to the banquette, moving along like any other creole couple. Miss Duplantier's admonition about my husband lingers yet on my mind, like that of the angel in the Magi's dream, warning them of King Herod and advising them to take another way. Perhaps this is the other way.

Christmas Day 1872. The children had little trouble enduring Christmas Eve Mass, subdued by the candlelight and greenery of the cathedral. The Bishop conducted the services in vestments much like an Anglican bishop, the gold trim glimmering in the sway of candlelight. It was all lovely, the shadows and dim light and soaring voices, the faces of these ones I have come to love, and I believe have come to love me, the contented face of Uncle Michel as the scene played in the small circles of his glasses. Mouche with Sidney leaning into her side and Willie on her lap, Tell's Odile and Pierre nestled into their Tante Didi, their mother still to bed on Esplanade with baby Jeanne. And Tell's oldest, Jo, sitting between Edgar and me, like a diminutive chaperon, not so much supervising a courtship but enjoying it. She is of the age at which a girl begins to recognize things like romance and affection.

My mind wandered, as it has always done during church, perhaps trying to avoid the secret I keep, a secret reminded to me by the finery of the surroundings and the Latin. The cloying secret that I am the wife of another, a man who has a penchant for fine things and bellicose Latin sayings. The people in the pews rose, and I thought in my nighttime-daydream that they were leaving me, but Edgar whispered, 'The benediction. Rise.'

We left the Cathedral to the ringing of the midnight bells. On the corner, two soldiers, tall boys with hair so blonde it was almost white, were singing *Silent Night* in German. It was a beautifully done duet, filled with a longing for home, certainly a home in the north surrounded by snow and a warm hearth and loved ones. At Esplanade, Miss Petinque had the hearth-fires burning and the house glowing and a fine table set. After our meal and stories and prayers, the children were put to bed, and we, the adults stayed up playing the piano and singing.

There was talk of the neighbours, M. and Mme. Olivier, coming by, but they never did, and Rene remarked, 'That husband of hers! So joyless.' Edgar frowned, though I could not tell if the cause of it was Rene or Mr. Olivier. Mouche gave her glass to Rene to be filled and said, 'And that is a shame, Mme. Olivier has been so attentive to Tell.'

'And to my brother,' I think I heard Edgar mutter, though this was after a glass or two of café brulot and another of wine. Rene passed around bonbons and dried fruit, imported from Paris to a shop on Canal Street, Hebert-Miret & Pinsard, *the best in the city!* he declared. He also had fine port and wine from Bordeaux and Malaga in Spain, and there was a bottle of cherry brandy, the elixir that my mother-in-law may or may not believe is good for one's health. It all flowed a little too freely, and our glasses rose again and again. Outside, pistol shots to the sky sounded in celebration of the birth of Our Lord, and there was talk by Mouche of us doing the same, but it was abandoned and forgotten.

Rene was himself quite under the spell of his wares, and he proposed yet another toast to his older brother, a quote from Ecclesiastes, 'Let us now speak of famous men! Edgar Hilaire Degas! Surely he shall hold first prize at the Paris Salon!'

Our glasses rose, though Edgar's did not rise as high as ours. He said something about not being the caretaker (guardian, I think was the word he used) of such things as the Salon, and I heard the same trace of bitterness that I would hear when my Papa spoke of the Linnaen Society. Uncle Michel, who had consumed more brandy than café brulot, said that I was becoming much as another daughter to him, and he hoped I would someday be a niece and that he was a good judge of character. 'Why, just look at this happy family assembled under my roof!' he said, rather unevenly. Everyone in the gaslight raised their glass, and Rene proposed a toast to *La Fille D'Or,* the Golden Girl, and then another in my honour. 'To Venus! The new Aphrodite, the warmer of cold hearts!' he said up to the raised glasses that twinkled in the light of the chandelier.

The attention was embarrassing and would have been so even without the secret I bear. To deflect it, I moved to the piano and, mindful of sleeping children upstairs, softly I played 'Lo, How E'er a Rose is Blooming,' and then Rene insisted on playing, though in his state he made frequent mistakes. Achille made a joke about Rene needing lessons from Mme. Olivier and everyone laughed, save Edgar. Didi came down the stairs in her night-dress, hissing about the noise, and everyone retired.

Because of the hour, I was put to bed with little Carrie and Jo, and during the night I woke with the sense that they were Ida and Lucy, and then I pretended that they were. My thoughts turned to my girls, far away in England or somewhere on the continent, celebrating the holidays without me. And on this joyous night under the influence of the cherry brandy that their grandmother says is not healthful, I wept silently, for I had not wished my Teague girls so much as a Merry Christmas. I felt rather lonelier than I should have in that house with that family. Perhaps because I feel myself a sham, a fraud. And certainly, I am right to feel so.

27 December 1872. I have returned to our nest on Ursulines and spent a night in the embrace of Venus with Edgar. A very cold day has followed the very cold night, cold enough to necessitate a night-dress for sleeping. This morning Edgar painted in his chemise, working on a picture of Tell sitting on the side of a chaise. The brilliant light outside framed his silhouette in the window, and if I were a painter, this would be my subject. In between thoughtful brushstrokes, he spoke of the theatre tonight, though I would be content staying in by a coal fire in our hearth. I looked at the canvas and said from the cocoon of sheets, 'Tell looks unhappy.' Edgar kept painting, and I wondered if he was absorbed in his work or if his hearing was damaged from the artillery he manned in the Prussian siege of Paris. After a moment he looked to me and asked, 'Did you say something, my love?' I repeated that I thought that Tell looked unhappy.

'Perhaps. Or perhaps just blind. That is the thing about art,' he said, washing his brush in a small glass jar of a clear liquid, turpentine, I believe, 'Some might see blindness, some unhappiness. Some might see both.' He wiped his hands on a rag and kept examining his composition as if waiting for Tell to say if she were unhappy or blind or both. He said that the first time he had painted her was just after her husband, her first husband, Joseph, was killed in the war. She had just had Jo a few weeks after that, and then she and Didi and his Tante Odile came to France to escape the northern occupation of the city.

He came and sat on the edge of the bed and I put my head in his lap and he stroked the golden length of my hair. 'Chromium yellow no. 3, zinc white, perhaps a shade of red,' he murmured as he examined the colour of it and tried to elucidate how to mix it. He held a strand of it up to the light that came in through the window. 'What does the newspaper say today?' he asked it.

'There is a foot of snow on the ground in New York,' I said as I folded the paper and laid it aside. He asked me if I missed having snow and let the strand of my hair fall over my face, and I brushed it aside. I said yes, that I've always found it enchanting as it falls. 'Do you?' I asked him.

'No, not really,' he said, 'I saw enough of it the winter of the siege. It is one thing to view it through a window, sitting before the warmth of a blazing hearth, and another to stand in it and wait for an enemy to send shells at you.' He stood and lifted his chemise and slipped it over his head. There were no scars on his body as it came for mine. Perhaps they are on the inside.

28 Dec. 1872. We stayed indoors and in bed all day and let the coal fire of the hearth simmer. Heat is no issue. We have each other for that. Edgar has gone out to get us bread and wine, a true Parisian.

29 December 1872. A quiet day in our nest. We napped as Adam and Eve must have napped in the garden, unconcerned with things like sin and nakedness. The breeze off the river blew and the boats bellowed, and faraway people had faraway conversations. Nothing else mattered in the bliss. I awoke and picked up the sketch, a study for the painting that Edgar is calling 'The Song Rehearsal.' He seems to be considering a change to the identities of the women. They are no longer Tell and Mathilde, but another woman, drawn in both roles, protagonist and antagonist, a woman with dark lashes and hair and a rosebud of a mouth.

31 December 1872. The Krewe of Momus, the god of ridicule, shall hold a parade tonight that is to end in a grand ball. Mouche and Mr. Bell are among those invited, and she has excitedly shown me the fancy invitation, left by an anonymous hand which is the way of this 'Mystick Krewe.'

The envelope is green-tinted, and bears a knight on horseback, raising his hand, castle ramparts behind him. A cherub frolics in the sky behind him among an elaborately enter-twined K and M. Also in the snare of these letters is a winged figure, naked and holding a staff, and looking suspiciously like the Republican governor Kellogg, so hated among much of the white populace of this place. Written in a banner across the defiant knight is the motto of this 'Krewe,' *Dum Vivimus Vivamus,* 'While We Live, Let Us Live.'

Rene and Tell are also invited, though Tell is in no condition to attend, and I wonder if her sight permits her to ever dance. Mouche has asked Rene to allow Edgar and I to use the ball tickets, but Rene said that he might attend with Achille. It is just as well. I have no suitable gown, as my finery is in a trunk somewhere in England now.

All is to begin with a procession this evening. Indeed, talk along the high streets has been of nothing else, and shops closed early in preparation for the passing of the pageant. And so, the old year draws to a close and vanishes without telling us where it shall go, and a new year takes its place without telling where it might take us. Farewell, old 1872!

Sammy, 1982

The walls were beginning to close in. Or, actually, the curtains, pressing in on him like a shroud or a net. The family on the other side of them was eating something fried as a game show played loudly on the television, smells and sounds that ignored the curtains and filled the entire room. Someone had just won a new car, and everyone, including the announcer, was ecstatic. Sammy had had about enough of all of it.

"Anybody want a Lucky Dog?" he asked Teeter and Miss Vessy. "I'm buying." They looked at him with vacant expressions, so he said, "I'll get all the stuff on the side, you can put what you want on it."

Miss Vessy gave a faint, fading nod, and Sammy left the room as the game show theme music played on the TV and the audience clapped rhythmically and an announcer babbled the show's sponsors. Sammy took the elevator down and walked out the front doors to Tulane Avenue, looking for the nearest Lucky Dog cart. He crossed Lafayette Square and paused at the statue of Henry Clay, the same one that had once greeted Alice and Reverend Lamb on their arrival to the city over a hundred years before. Mr. Clay had been on Canal Street then but had been moved to Lafayette Square for some reason. A pigeon sat on the statue's head, and the Great Compromiser pretended to be as comfortable with the bird as St. Francis of Assisi would have been.

Sammy crossed Canal Street in the wake of a streetcar. The day was brilliant blue after the passing of the rain, and it was almost warm enough to take off his flannel coat, but a wave of cool air blew down Chartres Street, so he kept it on and followed the breeze. He was enjoying the walk so much that he passed the Lucky Dog vendor at the corner of Chartres and Bienville.

He came to Jackson Square and sat in one of the benches at the base of General Jackson, vanquisher of the English. The cathedral bells chimed, and the hooves of mules and roll of tourist carriage wheels sounded and a tugboat whistle mimicked the ancient sounds of the old century. Sammy closed his eyes and imagined himself sitting on the bench in the winter of 1872. In his imagination, a man and a woman were sitting on the bench next to him and falling in love. He had almost convinced himself that it was all true when a car horn honked and broke the spell, and it was 1982 again.

He rose and stopped at the cathedral doors of St. Louis. The Mussons and Alice and Edgar and the children had passed through them, stopping to dip their fingers in the font and genuflect before settling into the pews for the scent of incense and the incantation of Latin. The sound of the old century returned. A carriage turned the corner from St. Ann onto Chartres, and he followed it as the tour guide turned in his seat and spoke to the camera-wielding tourists in the backseat. It turned onto St. Phillip, but Sammy kept walking down Chartres, down to the old Ursulines Convent. He stood outside its walls and looked up and around. And then it connected.

Alice said that the apartment was on the fourth floor near the intersection of Ursulines and Chartres, the only four-story building in the vicinity. She had written that it had two windows and that she could see the old convent from them, down and to the left, and the river over the rooftops. Sammy looked up and across the street, and there it was, a four-story building with a balcony facing out to the river. With two windows.

A horn blasted him with an admonishing blare, and Sammy broke from his trance to realize he was in the middle of the intersection of Ursulines and Chartres. He waved an apology to the driver and stepped onto the banquette, but he kept his eyes on the balcony as he walked down to the front of the building's ground floor entrance. A man was testing the lock with a set of keys.

"Excuse me," Sammy said. "Do you live here?"

The man looked up from the key in the lock.

"Honestly, I'd be embarrassed to say I did. Old apartment building. Place is a dump. Hopefully whoever buys it can do something with it. I'm the realtor, Mr. Giacomo." He took a hand off the bundle of keys and offered it to Sammy, who shook it. Sammy released Mr. Giacomo's hand and looked up through the wrought iron balconies.

"How old is it, would you say?" Sammy asked him.

"A hundred, a hundred-fifty years, or so. Built by a man named Voorhies who didn't come back from the Civil War. His widow divided it into apartments."

"Did you say Voorhies?" Sammy asked, shielding his hand against the sun and the bright blue sky. He looked back to Mr. Giacomo.

"Yeah. That's right. Voorhies."

"What's on the fourth floor?"

"It's just an old storeroom. Kind of an attic with windows."

"Do you mind if I take a look?"

"Ah-right, I guess," Mr. Giacomo said as he jiggled the keys and turned the one in the lock. He put his shoulder into the door to open it. "Not much to it, though."

They walked up the first two flights of stairs before Mr. Giacomo tired and rested on the landing. Sammy kept going. On the fourth floor, he arrived at the only room there. The door was an old frame-and-panel, and the hardware looked to be original, ancient tarnished brass, both knob and lock. He put his hand to the knob and twisted it. The door welcomed him with a wheeze, and then there he was, in the room with twin windows that looked out onto the rooftops of nearby buildings. A black-marble mantel was on the wall to the left, just as Alice had described. Out the window and down below, across Chartres and Ursulines, was the convent of the Ursuline Sisters. Over the rooftops, a thin sliver of sparkling blue-gray river wound away south. The room was piled with boxes and smelled old despite the orange shag carpet. Mr. Giacomo's steps labored up the stairs, and he joined Sammy in the room, out-wheezing the door and leaning over to put his hands on his knees.

"Big for a storeroom," Sammy said.

"I don't think there's been a tenant for five, ten years. But I bet they had a cat. You can tell from the carpet."

Sammy moved sideways through the boxes to the twin windows. He opened one of them, and a breeze pushed in. The sounds of the street were far below and as small as the people on the sidewalk and cars on the street. He turned to Mr. Giacomo.

"Is anybody interested in the building?"

"We're hoping someone takes the place and does something with it. A hotel or one them bed-and-breakfastes, maybe. Not much interest, though."

Sammy leaned forward on his hands, looking out the window and trying to imagine Alice and Edgar looking through it, exhausted and satisfied in the wake of their passion. He could almost see their silhouettes, Edgar in his painter's smock and the light from the window falling on the canvas and the paint, Alice rising in bed sheets, coming to admire her lover's work. The river breeze sighing through the window.

Mr. Giacomo cleared his throat. Sammy stood up and rubbed his palms together.

"If you're interested, here's my card," Mr. Giacomo said.

They passed through the door and onto the landing. As Mr. Giacomo shut the door, Sammy craned his head to look over his shoulder into the room one last time. He followed the man down the stairs, keeping his eyes on the door until he had descended the stairs and it was out of sight.

Sammy returned to Big Charity with three Lucky Dogs. The visitors on the other side of the curtain had left, and their loved one slept. Teeter, Sammy, and Miss Vessy ate amid the late evening sounds of a hospital putting itself to bed. Then Sammy reverently wiped mustard from his fingers and opened the diary.

Alice, 1873

1 January 1873. The first morning of the new year finds me in paradise, curled up with this man whom I have loved from the very first moment of our meeting. I write as he sleeps, exhausted from our exertions.

Last night, we saw the knights of Momus parade through the city. A great commotion and light came off the levee at the foot of Esplanade, and a detail of mounted policemen began to clear the way in the torchlight. Edgar and I waited with the other onlookers, and though it was night, I kept under a veil and parasol, but, of course, there were others who did so as part of the revelry.

The procession turned at Royal, and we watched it pass. Mounted men, knights in suits of tin armor, clattered down Royal, where it was said they would cross Canal and be toasted on the steps of City Hall by Mayor Wiltz. Edgar asked if I wanted to follow the procession to see the toasting and hear the speeches, but I remembered that City Hall is next to the Howards, and so, I declined, and we adjourned here to our nest on Ursulines, whilst Mouche and Mr. Bell danced and welcomed the new year at the Opera House.

Perhaps it was a look Edgar and I exchanged, or a touch, a brief trail of fingertips, or an understanding which is beyond any of the senses, but suddenly we felt the need to be alone, away from all the crowds and all the madness. We strained through the merrymakers, some with masks, some with parasols, all singing, all drinking. We breathlessly wove around them, exasperated with their inertia, their surprised looks as we struggled to get back to privacy and the intimacy it afforded.

At last, we turned on Ursulines, and, at last, we found our doorway and the steps. We bounded up them, the four flights seeming like eight, finally making the top and our door, panting more from anticipation than from exertion. My hand rattled the key in the lock, Edgar's hands on my breasts and my lower stomach. I pressed my face into the door, and we almost gave ourselves to each other right there on the landing, without regard to the landlady who might come up or wayward revelers or anyone else. If we had had anything at all to drink, we would have. I am quite sure of it. But my shaking hand turned, and the door opened, and we fell through it and I can only vaguely remember it closing. I don't remember if I closed it or Edgar did. I looked to light a candle and then forgot about it. The torchlights of the revelers on the street below gave off enough light to cast shadows on the ceiling and walls of our loft.

My heart rose to my lips, and I presented it to him soft and wet, and we undressed and fell together. *Hurry, hurry, hurry, oh hurry*, I murmured, and then the sensation again as my back arched and everything released and expanded and squeezed and my fingertips pushed into his back and my mouth pressed into his shoulder and my eyes squinted tightly against a world that would deny us this pleasure. Then the sensation of rapture, of falling and clinging together.

And again, we found ourselves washed upon the shore, breathless amid the smell of oil paints and turpentine and a stained smock on a hanger. Far below on the street, the warm night air carried the sound of revelers and even further, the sound of the orchestra at the Opera House. We listened to it all in the darkness, and then we slept, Edgar and I, content in our nest, far below the fireworks in a winter sky and far above the streets and their revelers.

And so, I awake in the early dawn, with a giddiness that consumes me and flirts with the memory of our intimacy, our ecstasy. It is delirium, blissful delirium. I cannot forsake it. It is wrong, but I cannot. I am captive to it. Any sigh of resignation is quickly replaced by a sigh of ecstasy. I shall never, ever be able to give this up. Indeed, I cannot think upon it long, lest my heart break. I shall not let a cruel fate hand me a desolate life with Samuel Teague, that charming tyrant. I end for now, my little confidant, to awaken Edgar.

2 January 1873. Very warm today, like a summer day in England. A little rain, also. It has warmed considerably since yesterday, the first day of the new year. I arrived at the Musson house New Year's morning to find that Didi was up and overseeing the servants in the supervision of the Bell children, as William and Mouche were still abed after a New Year's Eve of revelry. Edgar gave no explanation for his absence from the house last night, and none was asked for. Perhaps his family thinks he rose early to go and fetch me. I shall leave it at that.

The first day of the new year was celebrated at the Musson house and in all the houses in the city and the world, a new year fresh with possibility. Everyone exchanged gifts, as is the Creole fashion on this day, though Rene outdid all in his generosity, giving his brothers, brother-in-law, and uncle fine English watches purchased from Mr. Buckley's shop on Camp, 'the best in the city!' Rene proclaimed. Uncle Michel exclaimed that the wine business must be very good as he opened the gold cover and examined the dial with the fine black numbers. Rene replied, 'Well, Uncle, this time of year, the spirits must flow!' Edgar has said that his brother has always been very generous with his gifts and that he has the tastes of a baronet.

Edgar and I gave the children a book, *The Nursery Treasury* by Harriet McKeever, handsomely done with coloured illustrations. I gave Edgar a French-English dictionary, and he presented me with a book about the life of the composer Mendelsohn. A wonderful dinner was prepared, stuffed peppers, *piments vert farcis*, réchauffé Bonaparte, oysters a la Poulette, gombo aux Crevettes, and more. Mouche and William (Mr. Bell) came downstairs during dinner, begging pardon for their tardiness and making the rounds kissing cheeks and wishing everyone a *bonne année.* They sat and were served and gave us a recount of the tableaux of the ball.

Mouche told Rene that she and Mr. Bell looked for him at the ball and gently chided him that if he wasn't going to attend, the invitation could have been given to us. Rene looked up from his gumbo and said that he was there, though briefly, but business at the shop detained him and that it was a very busy time of year. The faintest look of a cornered animal flashed over Rene's countenance as he looked at his Uncle Michel for corroboration of the briskness of the wine trade.

'Besides.' Rene added, 'I didn't want to attend without Tell.' Tell neither smiled nor frowned. It was as if she were deaf as well as blind.

Mouche said, '*Bien*, Monsieur Olivier was there without Mme. Olivier. She told him that in her present state she could not attend either and for him to go on to the ball without her.' Mouche sipped a small spoonful of gumbo and said, '*Mon cousin Rene*, you could have made a pair. You and Monsieur Olivier, I mean.'

The children had finished and were fidgeting at the table. Rene took the opportunity to ask for a serenade for the adults as they finished eating. Jo and Carrie jumped up from the table and played a traditional tune, and Carrie sang along in her petite voice. The song was one that Mme. Olivier had taught them, 'Compère Lapin,' about a mischievous rabbit. Edgar hummed along and waved his fork as he chewed. His eyes were on his brother.

3 January 1873. A Committee was dispatched last month to persuade the government in Washington of the legitimacy of the government headed here in Louisiana by McEnery. News today in the *Picayune* says that the committee was unsuccessful and that it is proof that President Grant is in league with the Republican 'bayonet' government. There are cries of 'chicanery, fraud, and violence.' It as if these people still do not think themselves citizens of the United States, and perhaps they are not considered so.

The *Picayune* also carries the usual hodgepodge of comments and disjointed facts, among them, the news that in England, suicides are always buried at night. This is true, though they are no longer buried at crossroads, as in the past. Edgar sketches and paints whilst I read. I suppose we should dress. We are much like Adam and Eve in the garden, before the serpent and the apple.

4 January 1873. I journeyed to the post office today on two errands. First, I sent a letter to the postmaster in Liverpool, with a message for him to send back the enclosed letter to Mr. Teague (and of course, Mrs. Parris, who shall surely read it to him). I have asked the postmaster in Liverpool to be sure and postmark the letter as coming from there, as it shall be a great keepsake for Mr. Teague, who is a quite an admirer of 'jolly old England.' The letter is full of fallacies regarding my visit in England, telling how glad I am to be in the home country and how much has changed and how much has stayed the same and the many memories that have been stirred. I say that Mrs. Teague and the girls are off to the continent as I have decided to tarry in England, visiting old acquaintances and reminiscing. I close in asking Mr. Teague to pass on to Mr. and Mrs. Parris my regards and to thank them for the example of affection and fidelity that they give to the people of St. Matthew. Of course, this is all a falsehood worthy of Mr. Barnum's Menagerie, a fat lie, large and grotesque, that plays the fiddle whilst its fat wife taps its foot.

The second errand was to request that all mail that is addressed to me, Alice Teague, St. Matthew Parish, be held at the post office here in New Orleans, as I shall be staying in the city for the near future. Thus, I hope to at least hear word of my girls in Europe and perhaps from Henry. A very vivid thunderstorm passed through the city this evening, ripping awnings to shreds and blowing down signs, including that of Rene and Achille's business, *DeGas Frères, Marchands du Vin.*

5 January 1873. A cool Sabbath day with a worship service replete with incense and Latin. What a shame the Bishop of Manchester could not attend! The conversation at the dinner table this Sunday centered around the beginning of ball season. It commences tomorrow on Twelfth Night, or 'Épiphanie,' as it is called in this house. I wonder, however, if it is ever anything but ball season in this city. Mouche insists that I get a new ballgown or two, as Edgar is an excellent dancer and shall most certainly be taking me. She and Mr. Bell attend them without fail, she said, and she gave me the name of a Mme. Olympe on Canal. Mr. Bell laughed and said that I must make sure and bring my pocketbook along as well.

6 January 1873. A cool morning spent indoors by the fire. Midday it warmed enough to open the windows to let a southerly breeze enter, though our bare skin rose in goosebumps to it. Our private nest lends itself to the act of love, which I give into with noisy fervor, quite forgetting myself. In the aftermath, with the noises of the city and the river murmuring in the air, a small voice shouted up to our window. It was one of the sisters from the convent. She called up to us in French, 'Is everyone all right up there?' Edgar rose with the sheets around his waist and went to the window, though his buttocks were exposed to the room. He called down to her, 'Yes, Sister, perfectly so!' He turned back to me, grinning like a pirate, and he fell back onto the bed as we expired with laughter like two schoolchildren who have played a joke on the headmaster and gotten away with it.

7 January 1873. Late yesterday evening, the Twelfth Night Revelers paraded through the streets under the theme, 'The World of Audubon.' The topic is bittersweet, as it reminds me of Papa. What has become of the book I gave him? Did Mr. Teague burn it along with his sermons?

I was thinking this when Edgar called my attention to the 'Lord of Misrule,' who wore a scarlet robe with silver lettering upon it. He was followed by a statue of Audubon, the artist son of a Creole woman like himself, Edgar said. Then came the enormous Twelfth Night Cake and a parade consisting of men in different bird costumes, a parrot teaching school to a macaw wearing a dunce-cap, a sick owl attended by a doctor who was a duck (a quack, I suppose the joke was), a cardinal marrying two doves, a kingfisher's banquet, and so on, all accompanied by bands that played frolicking music. A pelican and her three chicks were the last of the parade, which concluded at the Opera House, where, according to the *Picayune*, the curtain went up on a forest scene with the birds grouped around the statue of 'their master,' Mr. Audubon himself. The Twelfth Night Cake was then carried about the assembly and at last cut into pieces and distributed to the ladies present. A Miss Mary Zacharie found the large bean in her piece, and a Miss Pelie the smaller one, and they became the Queen and Maid of Honour of the ball, respectively. Dancing then began and continued into the night, according to the *Picayune*. We were content to stay the night in our nest, away from those other 'birds.'

Sammy, 1982

His great-grandfather had not burned the vicar's copy of Audubon's *Birds of America*. It was in the chest back at Mount Teague. The artfully drawn specimens of Audubon, an artist with a Creole mother, compiled in a book that had enticed an English vicar to travel halfway around the world with his daughter to a place he thought was the Garden of Eden. Where he had died of cholera.

He placed the diary in his overnight case. For the first time in several days, Teeter wanted to get up and walk. Miss Vessy had been persuaded to leave the bedside long enough to go down to the cafeteria to get something to eat. Sammy wondered if she had also gone down to smoke, but she had left the gold-and-white package of Marlboro Lights in the window. He gathered up Teeter's IV pole and pushed it as he walked next to him.

"They sendin' me to one them halfway houses, bawsman," Teeter said to his slippers as they shuffled over the tiles in the hallway. "They say I'm gonna be there for a while. Over off Elysian Fields someplace. Ain' nobody gonna be able to stay with me, jus' visit during the day. Mama's some upset. She don' need that."

"Betsy and me'll be looking in on her, don't worry," Sammy said.

"She says she'll sleep on the streets before she leaves the city without me."

They returned to the room. The patient who was on the other side of the curtain had been discharged, and the aide was wiping down the bed and bedside table, humming to herself. Teeter and Sammy listened to her, some gospel something, low and heart-felt. Teeter got back in bed and turned on his side to look out the window.

Sammy got up and went to the payphone and called Mr. Giacomo. They met that afternoon in front of the building on Ursulines Street.

"I'd like to rent that top apartment for a friend," Sammy said. "She's having a hard time."

"A lot of hard times have come and gone through that place," Mr. Giacomo said. "Don't see why she can't stay there until it's sold. We'll have to get the lights and the water turned on, and them boxes out."

"I'll get some furniture brought in. Her son is—" Sammy paused. "—her son'll be staying off Elysian Fields. She'll be glad to be near him."

They exchanged the rent check for the key and shook hands.

"It's not that half-way house for vets is it? On Elysian Fields?"

"Yeah," Sammy admitted.

Mr. Giacomo gave Sammy his check back.

"Let me do this for you. For him. And his mama."

Sammy stood there with the check in his hand. Mr. Giacomo looked him in the eye, and Sammy could see the look of someone who knew what duty was, what honor was, what compassion was. And how one soldier could have it for another.

"I was in Korea, Mr. Teague. I know it's never as clean as the monuments make it out to be. Let me do this, and let's not say any more about it."

Sammy started to thank him, but Mr. Giacomo simply put his finger across his lips, almost a salute, and then put a cigarette in them. As Mr. Giacomo brought the flame of his lighter up to light it, Sammy asked him a question.

"Listen, Mr. Giacomo, I was reading about a house that was on Esplanade in the 1870s. The address is listed as No. 372, but the old U.S. Mint is there."

"That's because the streets were numbered different then. Three-seven-two would be…" He thought with one eye closed. "…the twenty-three hundred block, nowadays. That's the block with the old Musson house, or houses, in it. Some famous painter-guy stayed there with his uncle one winter, went back and made a name for himself in France or Spain someplace. In the twenties they cut the house in two and moved it onto separate lots right next to each other so they could get two separate rents for 'em. Corner of Esplanade and Tonti."

They shook hands again, and Sammy watched him head up the block toward the back of the Quarter. Sammy could almost see something military in how Mr. Giacomo walked, something subtle, almost like a march.

The next day was Saturday, and Sammy brought Quint up, and they moved the boxes downstairs and pulled up the orange shag carpet. The last tenants must have had a cat. Under the carpet was a beautiful old plank floor, and on it, near the window, were the faintest traces of hundred-year-old paint stains. They went to Goodwill and got second hand furniture—a chair, a side-table, a lamp A mattress without a frame, with spare sheets on it. It was a simply and hastily arranged dwelling-place, just as Alice had arranged a century before.

After the morning's work, Sammy and his son rested by the fourth-floor window, sitting and eating roast beef po-boys on the old wood-plank floor that held the faintest of paint stains, random drops of yellow and orange and red, washed away by a century of scrubbing, though not completely. Soft drinks in Styrofoam cups rested on the black marble mantle.

When they were done, they crumbled the white paper stained with gravy and put it all in the bag. The double windows breathed a breeze off the river, in and out. Quint sat and read Twain's *The Innocents Abroad* on the floor of the old apartment while his daddy read from the diary of the woman who had lived there over a hundred years before.

Alice, 1873

8 January 1873. Cloudy and cool with a north wind off the lake today. Edgar paints and sketches whilst I read the newspapers. The *Picayune* says that the two legislatures promised us have both set up in this city, only a few streets apart. For now, they do battle only in the newspapers. The Metairie Cemetery Association advertises for landscape architects and gardeners, and I think of Mr. Luther, who would certainly be acceptable for those purposes, were he not chained to his labours at Mount Teague like a figure from a Greek myth. How does Mount Teague and St. Matthew Parish get on in my absence? And my dear, kind Henry, what of him? The old year seems like a hundred years past.

9 January 1873. Edgar and I spent another night in 'the Arms of Venus,' but rather than a contented slumber, I slept rather fitfully, dreaming of barristers and accusations again. And again, Papa appeared in my dreams, but without the usual encouraging countenance I remember. It was more a neutral expression, which by comparison, seemed harsh and critical. I was relieved to wake and find Edgar propped on one elbow and looking at me.

'Your sleep was restless,' he said with brown eyes full of kindness. His dark hair was disheveled around his smile as he traced the outline of my lips with his finger. 'You spoke of your Papa,' he said, 'You must miss him.'

I was still not quite awake, and I spoke still thinking he meant my Papa, my real Papa, my English vicar Papa. 'Yes,' I said, 'Even after all this time, I still miss him terribly.'

'Why don't we go for a visit?' Edgar suggested, 'I am so very anxious to meet him.'

I found myself suddenly and fully awake, and I said, "Oh. Yes, him, I miss him, but he is still in the midst of grinding,' and then I added, 'It—it consumes him. As if he were a bear that disappears during the winter.'

Edgar chuckled and said, 'To hibernate in a field of sugarcane!' and he kissed the soft skin at the base of my neck. 'I would love to meet your family, any of them, really,' he said, 'Sometimes it seems to me as if you have no family, as if you have fallen from heaven and into my arms.'

He kissed me softly, and I thought that it is true. I am a fallen angel, one that has plummeted and broken into pieces, and this man holds them in his hands as if they were a treasure. Like the broken glass of a chemist's bottle becomes a sapphire in the eyes of a little girl.

10 January 1873. A cold, clear day. The only blemish to a brilliant blue sky is the smoke from the city's chimneys. Within the black marble of our mantle, a coal fire warms us and sends smoke up into the blue with the rest of the city's hearth-fires. Edgar recognized the name 'Napoleon' in the English language *Picayune* and began reading, though slowly, the report that the French Emperor Napoleon has died in exile in Chislehurst in England. He read a few sentences before I read the rest to him, translating into French the account of the Emperor's last hours. Edgar said that Napoleon III was responsible for modernizing and beautifying Paris, and in the last days of the siege, the Emperor walked among the shells of the Prussians, wishing for death rather than surrender. How could one be so despondent, I wonder, to wish for death? Edgar paints this morning. This afternoon we shall visit *la famille* on Esplanade.

11 January 1873. Today was a day perhaps even more beautiful than yesterday, made so by warmer temperatures borne on the soft breath a south wind. As Edgar dressed this morning, he announced that he should like to visit a sugar plantation, to see it being ground into syrup and made into sugar. As he tied his cravat, he cast a glance to me and suggested that perhaps we could pay a call to my father in St. Matthew. My mind squirmed like a fox or a weasel caught in a snare.

'What was that, my love?' I asked as I slipped my petticoat over my head. My mind was still working, desperately searching for a moment more. He repeated that he would like to see a mill in operation, before grinding is finished.

'Why don't we go and see your father?' he asked.

'Oh, now would not be a good time,' I said, 'It takes the better part of a day to get to St. Matthew, the roads would be full of cane wagons, and we would miss Mass and dinner tomorrow with *la famille*.'

'We can tell them that we will be visiting, and certainly they have a church there?' Edgar said. I felt myself on the verge of panic, and when I finally was able to speak, my words were a bit strangled.

'Really, love, I'm afraid that grinding season would not be a favourable time to visit Father,' I babbled, 'He remains anxious through it all and becomes cross so easily. He might resent your presence when there is sugar to be made.' I put my palm to Edgar's cheek and caressed it and cooed, 'And I want your first meeting with my father to be an auspicious one,' and I turned to resume dressing. 'But this time of year, he is best left alone to work. Fasten my corset, would you, love? He spends so much of the day in the fields. Let us leave him to his business. We shall meet him later.' It was great work to keep my voice from trembling, a performance worthy of the stage, as the prospect of Edgar meeting Mr. Teague fills me with terror.

Instead, we visited an acquaintance of Uncle Michel's just beyond the outskirts of the city at the plantation of a M. Millaudon, where grinding is also taking place as it is at Mount Teague. The ride out was pleasant, the smell of earth and horses and woodsmoke and burning cane vivid in the crisp air, brown leaves still hanging beneath the colossal blue.

We were met by M. Millaudon, who greeted us warmly, though in muddy boots. He shed his soiled leather work-gloves and shook Edgar's hand with a slight bow and took mine and did the same. Off in the separate distances, in the sheds and in the fields, there were the shouts of men in French and the crack of whips and the bray of mules. The rattle and hum of big gears and the crackle of burning cane and the smell of smoke and the seething steam of bubbling liquid. All of it made me think of St. Matthew Parish. The field hands with cane knives and smoky breath in the chill air, chanting in French, songs for cutting, mules straining against impossibly full wagons they pulled down cold mud lanes, littered with spent cane stalks like straw, the looming mill stacks belching sulfurous smoke into the winter sky, and the iron wheels taller than most housetops, with even rows of immense cogs like teeth. It was all just like Mount Teague, and I confess to finding myself ill-at-ease because of it.

Edgar said, 'Mademoiselle Lamb is from St. Matthew Parish. Her father is a planter there.' M. Millaudon asked, Is that right? 'Forgive me, what is the name again?' I pulled at the breath that was trying to escape. 'Lamb,' I croaked my former name, and the word felt cross-ways in my throat. It is a question the barristers in my nightmare ask me, *tell the court, what is your name?*

'I know most of the planters in St. Matthew, but I don't know a Lamb,' M. Millaudon said. I lied and told him that our place was rather small, several hundred hectares. Actually, it is ten times that, but this was no time for boasting, had I even wanted to. M. Millaudon asked me if my father still had cane in the field, and I replied that I believed he did, but I wasn't sure and that I was in the habit of leaving him to his task when it comes to his cane and that he becomes quite snappish when it is grinding season.

'You are quite correct, mademoiselle,' M. Millaudon said, 'Especially for smaller planters, it is desirable to leave the cane for as long as one can in order to increase the yield. I know a man in St. Matthew named Teague who does that and is quite good at it, though he is by no means a smaller planter. Do you know of him? He has his own ice plant. Quite proud of it, as he is of his whole operation.'

I shuddered but forced myself to smile. 'It seems as though I have heard the name. An ice plant is certainly not necessary on days like today,' I said, trying to move the topic to something other than my husband. M. Millaudon toured us proudly through his 'whole operation,' a sugarhouse filled with conveyor belts, huffing steam engines, great throbbing iron pipes, enormous tanks of liquid. The smell of burning cane hung over all of it. After our tour, we were treated to a meal on the rear gallery, dining there thanks in equal measure to Monsieur's muddy boots and the agreeable weather. Edgar and Monsieur looked over Edgar's sketchbook, more than half-full of drawings of M. Millaudon's sugar-works.

Then, amid shadows that fell away from the winter sun, we took a carriage back from Millaudon under a blanket that covered us against the chill of the evening air. The trees along the lane held beards of grey moss, and I told Edgar that I imagine them as beards in the backroom of the Linnaen Society. He said the Salon in Paris is much the same, old men who fancy themselves the Keepers of Art and Science, to be kept away from infidels. It was only then that I sensed his rejection, of someone who labours in obscurity, someone who waits for the blaring trumpets of fame and only receives silence. Papa endured much the same and died rejected still, and always to be so.

'Well, my love,' I said, 'I believe that you are the greatest artist in the world. You are certainly the greatest artist in *my* world.' I put my head on his shoulder and felt him stroke my hair. He murmured as he curled wisps of gold around his finger, 'Chromium yellow no. 2, zinc white, and as the day's light fails, perhaps a bit of raw umber, just a bit.' I was enjoying the gentle pull of his fingers in my hair. I whispered a memory to him, to raise his spirits. It has only been a few short weeks, but it seems like a lifetime, though the memory still burns brightly for us.

'Do you remember our first ride in a carriage together?' my lips spoke quietly into his ear.

He smiled as the carriage shook like a mother gently rocking us, and he leaned into me and put his lips to my ear. 'Constantly,' he whispered, and he kissed the lobe.

And I as well, I thought as my body leaned and drifted. It was a thought that remained only that, a thought, for before I could say it, or even sigh it, our lips met and our mouths pressed together and I couldn't say it, I couldn't say anything. Our hands unclasped beneath the blanket that covered us and began to roam. The dark was descending rapidly, the trees and their grey bearded limbs only silhouettes against an eastern sky that was moving in transit from sky blue to midnight blue and every colour in between, colours known to this man, colours he could mix as deftly as he could stir my body.

The driver stopped and lit the lanterns on the postillions of the carriage and adjusted the harnesses of his horses. He alighted back onto the buckboard, and the carriage moved forward again. The air was colder still, but I was insensible to it, as I'm sure Edgar was, taken by the aching of our bodies that exuded a strange and pleasurable heat under the blanket that obscured us from the driver and the grey beards in the trees and the midnight blue sky. We exchanged kisses as one feeds a fire, keeping it kindled enough so that it may ignite into a blaze with time. Several times I neared ecstasy, but pushed Edgar's hand away, lest I let escape an exclamation and we be found out by the driver.

The lampposts of the city began to appear, and we held our breath as each passed us. The driver stopped to extinguish his lanterns as the presence of the city lights had made them unnecessary. The drive was still painfully slow, excruciating, as our bodies ached for each other but could do nothing toward it. Edgar said something in French to our driver, but he replied in an Irish accent, 'I don't speak no French, mizzure, sorry, sir.'

'He says we are hoping to make the theatre tonight,' I said in English, 'He would appreciate a little more speed.'

The Irishman said nothing, but only shook snaps into the reins. The horses accelerated but only meagerly, or so it seemed. We passed the

Howards' great home on St. Charles, and I was only dimly aware of it. We crossed Canal and the statue of Henry Clay, cold and bronzed, and then behind the Opera House where the windows of the upper stories glowed yellow-orange against the night sky. The cathedral bells chimed an hour that was unrecognized by us, and then, at long last, we were before our door on Ursulines. My wavering hand paid the driver, an amount which was surely generous, as he said, 'Thankee, ma'am,' and tipped his hat.

Edgar vaulted out of the carriage. The blanket was thrown off, and through the layers of my dress, the cold air found the wet linen, soaked to my petticoats. I did not hear the Irishman and his team pull away, I did not hear the sounds of the city, I did not hear anything but our footfalls on the stairs, four flights-worth of an excited, desperate rumble and the jangle of a lock and a doorknob and the wheeze of a door and the clack of it against the wall as it rebounded. Our lips and arms and chests met, and our hands wandered. My body leaned and drifted and weakened and my spirit went willingly up into the air with a cloud of sighs like chimney smoke. Coats, cravats, scarf, skirts, petticoats were wrestled from our bodies which trembled and panted.

And ecstasy found us ready again. It found us and we laughed at the rush of it, a force equal to gravity. Loving him is so natural, so necessary. Were it not for him, I feel as though I would break or wither. I feel as though I should always be touching him, that the parting of our flesh, the separation of our skin, is a small death. Outside the windows the stars are stony specks in an impartial midnight blue. And now I must lay down this pen and put out this candle.

12 January 1873. Sunday services at the Cathedral. Down the length of the Musson pew, children were canted in repose against the nearest adult. In the middle of our group, Uncle Michel sat with his top hat in his lap. With each drowsy phrase of Latin, his chin fell slowly toward his chest, and upon reaching it, rose and fell and rose with his breathing. With the first serrated snore, Didi prodded him, and his chin lifted, and his finger pushed his wire spectacles from the tip of his nose back to the bridge. And the liturgy droned on, quiet echoes of it filling the alcoves and chapels and moving over us as if we were in an ocean of Latin and

French. How wonderful it is to say 'we' and 'us,' to be included, to be part of a whole, an 'us.'

The *Picayune* says that tomorrow, two separate legislatures are to be seated and two separate governors are to take the oath of office, in meeting halls just streets apart. It was the talk over our Sunday dinner, as I'm sure it is over most Sunday dinners in this city and state. All of the stated opinions of this house are in favour of the government of Governor McEnery and squarely against that of what is felt to be the false government of Mr. Kellogg and the Republicans. It is a sentiment they would share with Mr. Teague and his cronies.

'This family has lost so much in the late war," Uncle Michel said as he cut his eyes to his daughter Tell, whose widowed gaze looked out onto nothing, 'They have taken so much from us. How dare they take our duly elected government as well.' The men and women at his table nodded in agreement to the click of silverware and the quiet passing of servants. Edgar, however, kept quiet on the topic of politics. He favours the topic of art and especially music. 'Perhaps the new governor can arrange a fine French opera at the Opera House,' he finally said, 'I would support that.'

'That,' Mouche said with a raised glass, 'would be welcome.'

Mr. Bell, her husband, was intent upon the subject of Yankee occupation and the Republican 'Bayonet Legislature' it backs. 'Well, down in St. Matthew they have a man name of Teague who has gotten the Yankees to quit that place with just one well-composed letter,' he said, 'If he could do the same for us here in the city, well, then, that would be a promising start.' I paused a moment to make sure my countenance was also well-composed, reassuring myself that they could not possibly know that the scribe for that 'well-composed letter' was sitting at the table with them.

Edgar said, 'Monsieur Millaudon spoke of him, that he is a hard man, a man of nerve, a man who gets things done,' Edgar's voice was distant to my guilty ears as he continued, 'He says that Teague has lost a wife to death and one to divorce, and now he has a beautiful new wife half his age.'

Mouche's voice startled me. 'Alice?' she asked quietly, 'Where is your appetite?'

'Oh,' I said, emerging from my trance, 'I was just hoping that everything is settled peacefully. This country has seen so much violence.' Edgar raised his glass in a toast and said, 'Yes, I, for one, have seen enough of it. Violence only begets more violence.' And only Tell, the widow of the late war, raised her glass in response. The rest seemed not to hear.

After dinner, the children persuaded me into a game of blindman's bluff. I thought this might offend Tell, but she said with a beaming, blank countenance, 'Perhaps I can take a turn. I can be trusted not to so much as peek from under my blindfold.' There was a pause as no one knew whether to laugh or not at this frank admission. 'It is my situation now,' Tell added wanly, 'and I must make light of it to keep it from crushing me.'

I offered to be the first protagonist in this parlour game. From within the red scarf that covered my eyes, I could hear the giggles of the children in the room and Miss Petinque's feet scurry as she removed vases from their pedestals, and the French voices of this house discuss me in whispers as if my ears were closed as well.

She is so lovely, so kind to our children, so good to Edgar.

She has made him bloom like a spring rain does for thirsty flowers.

Uncle Michel's deep voice could not be contained by a whisper, 'She is becoming like another daughter to me. Am I a good judge of character!' And so, I deceive him as well, as if he wears a scarf over his eyes.

13 January 1873. Louisiana either enjoyed or endured two inaugurations today. Businesses were closed out of a sense of propriety, or perhaps, fear, as the city held its breath. The streets were filled, more so around Lafayette Square, where a platform had been erected. Edgar and I attended and were among the throng who watched outgoing Governor Warmoth rise and make his way through the crowd toward the podium on the platform. Before ascending the steps, he paused and shook hands with several men, among them Mr. Howard, a sight which made me tug at my veil. Mr. Howard and Governor Warmoth shook hands vigorously, and their feathery moustaches wriggled at one another as if they were two small animals engaged in some sort of courtship ritual. Then, Mr. Warmoth gave an address that lasted perhaps half an hour to the gathering of mostly white men. Then he surrendered the podium to the new Governor McEnery. One of our new governors, I should say. He addressed the crowd of top hats, stopping occasionally to be serenaded with hurrahs and applause, and then continuing for the white faces who beamed up to him in adoration. His speech being much like the one before it, Edgar and I walked up the street to the Mechanics Institute, where Governor Kellogg was finishing his address to a crowd of mostly black faces, many of them Union soldiers. As he descended the podium, he was greeted by none other than Mr. Howard, who gave him a hearty handshake and a bow. Mr. Howard knows he must keep in good graces with each side. It is well for him that there is not a third government. He would be prostrate with exhaustion. And so, we now have two governors set up just streets apart. Edgar says it is like when the church had two popes. He says that no man can serve two governments and repeats the old joke that the Bible is against bigamy because a man cannot serve two masters. But of course, neither can a wife serve two husbands.

14 January 1873. There was fog early today, but the weather turned warm and fair, a day that hinted of springtime. As Edgar painted Mouche on the balcony upstairs, I contented myself with reading on the back porch and watching Mr. Gardener attend to the camellias and roses. Midmorning, the fog was burning away when a lady approached the house from Tonti, wearing a yellow muslin dress with black dots, with a red shawl over her shoulders. Even from a distance, it was quite noticeable that she is expecting a child in another month at most. Vasco rose from his place on the porch and barked a muffled note and went to meet her with a wagging tail. Setting a hand to her lower back, she stooped to stroke his head and ear, and he turned from her and came to me as if he were arranging our introduction.

'Bonjour,' she said as she approached under a parasol struck against an emerging bright winter sun. One hand grasped the curved handle and the other rested on her protuberant midsection. The woman put her hand to her eyes to shield them from the sun, then extended the hand and said, 'You must be the famous Alice of whom the children speak so much.'

'Yes, and you must be Madame Olivier,' I said as our gloved hands clasped. Her pale skin intensified the black sheen of her hair. Her fair face had a mouth with a red rosebud of lips and eyes that were all lashes like a brush (*'tous les cils comme un pinceau,'* Mouche has said).

'And you, mademoiselle,' she said, 'you have the slightest of accents. French is not your first language?'

"*Non*," I said as we continued in French, 'I am originally from England, but I have spoken French from my youth.' Her red bud of a mouth put forth a pleasant smile as she tilted her head a bit and said, 'Your French is still very good. I hear also that you are dear cousin Edgar's belle?'

'I suppose the children have told you,' I said, and, as we walked to the house under the shade of her umbrella, she replied, 'Children tell everything. Those little tongues cannot help but wag.'

I said, 'That is certainly the truth, especially among the brood of the Musson house.' The dog escorted us along the path of the garden, pausing to sniff and mark, though he always returned to Mme. Olivier's side. She switched hands on the umbrella and pulled the ends of her red shawl together as she leaned down to scratch his ear again. I told her that Vasco seemed quite delighted with her, and she said that he is certainly a dog that lives up to his explorer title, the dog of the whole neighborhood. She said that she grew up with dogs and would love one, for her husband, M. Olivier, works very long hours and she would find the company of a pet very pleasant. He will not allow it, she said, as they have a little girl, Lou-Lou, and he doesn't trust dogs around children.

'Well, that is a pity,' I said, stroking Vasco's side, 'They are very good companions. Dogs, I mean.'

'Yes, but a good wife must obey her husband,' she replied, and the faintest trace of a sigh fell into a silence between us. The silence was broken by Vasco's deep bark. The girls were on the back porch, waiting for Madame Olivier. 'Bien,' she said, 'Josephine and Carrie are waiting for their piano lessons. Rene says that he would like to begin Pierre as well, though I think he is a little too young.'

I said that perhaps he could begin on something simple, and Mme. Olivier said that she heard that I play quite well, and she asked me if I had any suggestions for simple pieces for Pierre. I told her that I shall think upon it and that it was a pleasure to meet her. She closed her parasol and set it by the back door, and Vasco sniffed it. I sat down again on the chair on the back porch, and he lay at my feet. Inside, the piano keys were stirred in the tentative preliminary exercises one learns as a beginner. And I looked out on the garden of roses with blossoms like bright-red mouths, and the Oliviers' house beyond it, and thought of lonely wives and the companionship they might seek.

15 January 1873. A wonderful day spent in our nest high above Ursulines Street, like a day spent in the rapture of heaven. The sounds of the city serenaded us, as vague as the scent of coffee and bananas being unloaded at the river, the sounds of softly bellowing steamboats, distant tapping of hooves, and voices, laughing, shouting, calling. All of it, so far away and hardly worth a thought. This morning Edgar worked on the painting of his uncle's cotton office.

'Your Uncle Michel seems distracted,' I said to the painting, and I pulled my dressing gown over my head.

'His office is seldom as busy as this,' Edgar said, 'These days, so much cotton is sent to England by rail through other ports, without passing through the city. And so, he worries that his office will fail, and that he will be left to be ruled over by Yankees and negroes. That is what Didi says.' He stippled the white of the cotton on the table, and it seemed so soft that I could almost feel it with my eyes.

'Have you heard from your father?' Edgar asked, 'Has he gotten all of his sugar cane in?' I told him that I had not heard, which of course, my little confidant, is the truth. A rarity from me these days. He kept his eyes on his canvas, and I thumbed through a book of sketches to find that he has drawn me as I brush my hair and that I can see my movement in it. He has also drawn me bathing, my breast and buttocks round and soft, and I can almost hear the splash of trickling water from the cloth I hold and am about to wring out. And, rather than embarrassed, I am flattered by his attention. So much so that I lift my gown over my head and lead him to bed. He has no time to wash his brushes or hands, and now my breast and buttocks are painted again, though literally this time.

16 January 1873. Mouche sat again for Edgar on the balcony, and I visited with them before excusing myself to enjoy the fine weather in the garden. Jo came running from the house to me, and Vasco loped along with her and barked. She sat in the swing and asked that I push her, and Vasco went off to sniff under the camellias and roses which bloom with wide-eyed vigour. Jo's white-stockinged legs pulled under and then out, her hands grasping the rope. I thought of when I was her age and womanhood was so much closer than I could ever have believed.

I met every backward arc of the pendulum, gathering the space between her shoulders and giving her another gentle push. I asked her how she liked her new sister, and she replied that baby Jeanne is really only her half-sister. She cheerfully said that her real Papa was a soldier who died in the war and that Yankees had killed him. I found that I had to think upon my response. At last, I said, 'That is what your cousin Edgar has told me.' It did not seem enough of a reply to such a weighty matter. I thought again and told her that my Papa had died also.

She asked if he was in a war, and I replied that, no, he had died of cholera, which is an illness. 'Like yellow fever?' she asked. I said that it was something like it, and she asked if I had been sad. I said, 'Yes, very, as I still am sometimes, though not as much.'

She continued through several more arcs, and I sat on a bench and watched her. Her lavender dress rippled in the breeze stirred by her swinging. Jo remarked that Mme. Olivier was their neighbour and that she was going to have a baby and that Tante Mouche said it would be in a month or two. Jo put her feet down to slow herself and, when it was still, brushed off her dress. She came and sat on the bench next to me and asked me, 'Mam'selle Alice, are you and Edgar in love?'

I could only smile at her and her little-girl notions of love and romance. 'Come,' I said, offering her my hand, 'Show me how you can play Monsieur Liszt' Liebestraum.'

'It means 'love dream,'' she said as she took my hand, 'Tante Mouche says that you and Edgar are in a love dream.' I could only blush. Our free hands swept away the dust from our skirts and walked back to the house, hand-in-hand. As we entered the back door, stepping over a sleeping Vasco, we heard the accomplished playing of Tell, a nocturne by

Chopin. Despite her blindness, she does not miss a single note, nor commit a single 'faux pas.'

17 January 1873. We passed a lazy afternoon in our nest, drinking deeply of each other. In between fits of passion, we lay naked in the sheets with a cartonette of raspberries between us. 'You know,' Edgar said, examining a raspberry and putting it in his mouth, 'I should have been in Paris by now. I have much business to attend to there, but I have stayed in New Orleans for one reason-' He selected another raspberry and placed it on my lips, '—you,' he smiled.

My puzzled expression accepted it, and I chewed it absently. It tasted bitter to me.

'But I won't be able to stay in New Orleans much longer,' he said, 'I must return to Paris sometime.' I asked him why, and I'm afraid my tone was somewhat like that of a petulant child. 'At my heart, I am a Parisian,' he shrugged. He gave me another raspberry, and my lips sequestered it into my mouth where I held it passively. An idea seemed to seize him, as if he had been suppressing it and it had finally escaped.

'You would make me the happiest of husbands. I will ask you no more than this.' He said it with such resolve that he never considered that I would say anything but yes, and quickly.

I told him there is nothing I desired more. *Did he just propose marriage?* I thought, and *did I just accept?* The raspberry seemed like a stone in my mouth, and I swallowed it with a bit of difficulty.

'It is only a matter of Father,' I said when I had found my tongue, 'He is so possessive. His preoccupation with grinding season has been a sweet respite. I fear sometimes that my life shall be as Didi's, growing old caring for an old man.' Edgar put the cartonette aside as he pondered my fear of growing old in the service of the old.

'Perhaps he will marry again?' Edgar asked.

'He is so particular,' I said, 'A match for him would be very difficult.'

Edgar pursed his lips as he considered it. 'But Paris is my home,' he said at last, and he rolled over, and the sheets twisted and exposed his bare back. He kissed me and smiled that smile of his, his hair hanging in his eyes until he dismissed it with a hand across his forehead. 'And I want you to come with me, to Paris. I am anxious for you to meet my friends,

Tissot, Manet, Mme. Morisot. We will get on splendidly. I will paint, and you may play music, perhaps for one of the dance schools, or give music lessons, perhaps. There is much opportunity in Paris. She is already rebuilding herself after the war and the Commune. And perhaps there will be a house-full of children.'

It sounded splendid, really it did.

'But what of Father?' I asked in a murmur, 'I cannot leave him.'

'Yes, your father,' he frowned, and then the sunrise of an idea broke over his face, 'Why don't we take a visit? Surely grinding season is over and—we can go tomorrow, if you please! I have a very important matter to discuss with him.'

'Oh—' I said, 'Yes, grinding season is over and he— I didn't tell you? He has gone to join my sisters and his mother—our grandmother—in England.'

Edgar gave me a look that was half surprise and half indignation. 'He has left you here? Without so much as a visit before departing?' I shook my head slowly and turned away as my mind worked.

'I think he favours my little sisters,' I said, but on this, of course, I lied. The truth is that Sam Teague only favours himself.

'How could he?' Edgar pleaded, 'You are the loveliest person I have ever met!'

How untrue this idea is, and how deceived this man is.

'I cannot explain it,' I said, 'But he dotes on them. Perhaps because my mother died in my birth.' But I remembered that I said she died when I was thirteen and that I had younger sisters, so I said, 'Almost died, I mean. But she was very ill the rest of her life.'

'Well, then,' Edgar said, 'Come to Paris with me, and let us find your father. Perhaps we can cable him! Tell him we will meet him in Paris. Or London, if you prefer! And I can ask him for his permission, as one man to another. It is the honorable thing to do. And if a man has no honour, what does he have, then? What is he?'

I remarked that it would be simply wonderful but that I would like for us to postpone it until later in the spring, that I would rather him meet Father here in America than in some other city or country. Edgar agreed, and his departure is delayed.

How long can I keep up this ruse? I am consumed with remorse, and it is not because I am deceiving my husband. Of course, that is not it. It is because I am deceiving my lover.

Sammy, 1982

He had been discharged, and Teeter had walked out of Big Charity, blinking away the bright sunlight. The aluminum mural over the door, of a man caught in a web of people, was behind him. He asked Sammy a question which could've been about both the day and the rest of his life.

"Where I'm gonna go from here, bawsman?"

"Up," Sammy told him. "The only way there is from here."

They walked with Miss Vessy to his truck, parked on Tulane Avenue, and they got in. Old Teeter would have stopped and examined the spray-painted hood where Sammy had tried to cover the crude insult. Just the ends of it showed now, the P and the Y. Old Teeter would have said something like, "You did a shitty job with that paint, bawsman." He would've said, "If you want a job done right—" and Sammy would have answered, "—then I should've just let you do it."

But New Teeter didn't say anything. Instead he held the door for his mama, who slid into the middle, and then he got in. Sammy shut the door and went around and got in the driver's side. The three of them looked out at the new world over the hastily spray-painted hood. Teeter looked like he was about to burst into tears, but he always looked like that nowadays.

Miss Vessy held her boy's manly hand as he looked up and out at the buildings that towered up. They turned onto Camp Street, passing the shells of other people sitting and lying on the banquette. He watched them slip by, men and women who had been courted and seduced by Madame Dope and left to rot under cardboard and newspapers. They waited unwashed and hopeless, desperate for her return, part of a slow and ongoing rape.

Teeter put his face to the glass. Across Canal in Jackson Square, happy tourists wandered the streets under wrought iron balconies with daiquiris and enormous beers in their hands, whimsical hats on their heads, T-shirts with jokes on them on their backs, and cameras around their necks. Teeter and his reflection in the window glass blinked at each other. Miss Vessy held his hand like she had done on his first day of school.

On the far side of the Quarter, foot traffic was sparser. The truck crossed Esplanade, and Sammy paused at the light to watch it stretch away from the river to the fairgrounds under the shade of live oaks, past the witness of the houses that had lined it for over a century. The light changed, and they drove a little further and turned onto Elysian Fields and then onto a side street.

The halfway house was unmarked but recognizable by the young men who sat on the front balcony and smoked. They looked like Teeter, men just past youth, once strong, but now with a certain fragility to them, men who looked down or away or a thousand yards off or deep inside themselves.

Sammy opened the door for Teeter and Miss Vessy, and they got out. Teeter held his simple valise and looked up at the men on the balcony. One of them raised a hand with a cigarette in it and then put it to his lips again. He was the only one to acknowledge Teeter. A button on the wrought iron gate asked that visitors ring, and Sammy did. A lady in a turtleneck sweater and a gray wool skirt opened the door and came down the steps. She had short, gray hair and wore a cross around her neck. She didn't look like a nun.

"I'm Sister Theresa. You must be Mr. Blanchard," she said. She took Teeter's hand in hers.

"Yes ma'am," he said.

"Well, come with me, Martin. We have a bed waiting for you. I'll explain the house rules."

Miss Vessy started in the gate when it was opened, but Sister Theresa politely denied her entrance.

"I'm sorry ma'am. Residents only inside the gate."

"But tha's my boy, sister."

"Yes ma'am, and we're going to take good care of him. Just like the child of God he is."

Teeter walked up the steps and paused and looked back. He forced a smile to his mama and Sammy and turned back to the door. After the slightest hesitation, he stepped through it with the tentative steps of someone entering a machine that would rework him, a booth that would change him.

Sammy waited while Miss Vessy quietly cried into her hands. The men on the balcony looked away, up into the oak tops or the sky or down the quiet street, almost as if she were their mother, and they had let her down, too. Then Sammy put his arm around her, and they walked the few blocks to the apartment on Ursulines. From there, it was just across Esplanade, no more than ten minutes.

All that was yesterday. Sammy had dropped off Miss Vessy at the apartment, picked up Quint from there, and returned home. And then he slept in a bed, his own bed next to his wife, for the first time in several nights.

He returned to the city the next day and parked on Ursulines. He used his key for the lock downstairs and then climbed the four flights with the thought of two breathless lovers falling up them, hands eager for the touch of each other's bodies, something he had always assumed didn't happen back then. But of course, why wouldn't it be? People have always been people, inhabitants of bodies that both hunger and thirst.

He knocked on Miss Vessy's door, but there was no answer. He waited a moment and knocked again. Finally, he used his key, speaking softly through the crack before opening it. The light from the south and east greeted him, just as it did Alice and Edgar. His eyes adjusted, hoping he would see them, their silhouettes, hoping to hear the briefest word of their conversation. Hoping there were such things as ghosts.

But it was empty. The mattress on the floor was neatly made. He put the vase with the spray of spring flowers Betsy had sent with him down on the black marble mantle. He thought the place would smell like Miss Vessy's cigarettes, but it was still scented with the ancient patina of old wood and the coming and going of a century of human beings. He turned and locked the door behind him and descended the stairs. Down Chartres at the corner of Esplanade, he saw Miss Vessy. They crossed together and met in the neutral ground under an oak.

"I got to see him. They havin' that therapy group now. He looks pretty good."

"How are you making out?" Sammy asked her.

"Boy, them stairs are somethin'. But I'm grateful Mist' Teague."

"How did you sleep?" he asked her, but what he really wanted to say was, *did you see or hear anything? Any ghosts?*

What she did say was, "I ain' never slept better, no. Not since Martin was born. Mais, I slept deep-deep."

It was Lent, so they had catfish po-boys from a shop around the corner. He thought she might go back to see about Teeter, but she said that visiting hours were over for the day and that she was going to go back to the apartment and begin a Novena because that's what Sister Theresa said she should do. Miss Vessy hugged Sammy like he was her own son and kissed him on the cheek. He walked her up the four flights of steps, and she moved like she was thirty years younger and thirty pounds lighter. When he saw that she was settled, he shut the door behind himself and stood for a moment looking at it, the old frame-and-panel door with a tarnished brass knob and lock.

He drove up Esplanade to the 2300 block, to the broad avenue's intersection with Tonti. He looked at the old house there, split in two and resting on two different lots, according to Mr. Giacomo. The half-house on the right had a wrought iron balcony with a distinctive oval pattern. He sat in his truck and looked up at the house, trying to imagine women with veils and fans and necklaces worn tight to the skin of their pale necks. He tried to imagine the dull clop of hooves and the rattle of carriage harnesses. And the sound of a piano and singing inside on days when the weather permitted open windows. And the smell of food cooking behind the house. He tried to will a young golden-haired Englishwoman to come out of the front door, so he could talk to her or, at least, exchange a wave.

A curtain parted in one of the windows, and Sammy strained to see who it was, but whoever it had been had retreated into the inner parts of the house. Loud rock music had been playing inside, but it diminished after the lady had moved away from the window.

A few minutes later, a New Orleans Police Department cruiser stopped and asked what he was doing parked there. Sammy couldn't begin to tell him everything, so, as the policeman looked at his license, Sammy told him he had felt sleepy, so he stopped to rest his eyes. The policeman gave him his license back and told him to move along. Sammy thanked him and turned the key in the ignition. As he pulled away, he took one last look at the balcony and the repeating wrought-iron ovals. He turned onto Chartres, and, as he crossed Ursulines, he looked up to see the light on in the fourth-floor apartment.

He stopped at the mall in Metairie and browsed the art section of *B. Dalton Bookseller.* And there he found it, under the quiet whisper of mall-muzak and the distant, sporadic laughter of preteens awkwardly flirting on the benches of the promenade by the Orange Julius. His fingers touched the spines of the books about art and the Impressionists, Renoir, Monet, Manet. And then, there it was, *The Complete Works of Edgar Degas.*

He bought it, with some children's books for his girls and a book about gardening for Betsy. In the mall parking lot, the first lamp came on to signal the night, like the first rooster to crow is for day. Under its light, he took the book out of the bag and opened it to the painting of a woman sitting on the front porch on Esplanade. Behind her was the distinctive pattern of repetitive wrought-iron ovals. The caption said it was the artist's cousin, Mathilde Musson Bell. She had the very impish, spit-fire gaze he had expected, and he said her name out loud.

"Mouche."

He closed the book and started home, anxious to get there and see the family that was waiting on him. And anxious to resume reading about the one on Esplanade.

Alice, 1873

18 January 1873. At Mouche's insistence, I visited *la modiste* Madame Olympe's shop on Canal on the errand of procuring a gown for ball season, which is serious business in this city. Madame is said to keep on hand a large and varied selection of taffeta and silk and lace and beads, bonnets, veils, capes, an array of finery 'equal to any to be found in Paris or New York,' as her advertisement in the *Picayune* proclaims. I found her at *le comptoir* of her shop, looking over samples of muslin and lace. She is a woman who is somewhere between having brown hair with grey streaks and grey hair with brown streaks. As I entered, she took the spectacles off her nose and greeted me with *bonjour, mademoiselle.*

On either side of the shop, bolts of fabric rose in tiers of shelves that lined the walls, rainbows of colour all the way to the ceiling and in every conceivable texture. Mannequins stood guard in dresses in various stages of completion amid spools of lace trim and beads and ribbons. At the rear of the shop, there was a short hallway with curtained alcoves for taking measurements. At the end of the hallway, in a back room, there were no less than half a dozen seamstresses of every shade of white and black and every age from old to young. I watched through the doorway as they measured and cut and sewed silently amid the quiet whisper of scissors and the clacking of sewing machine treadles pumped by plain black boots. No sooner was the yard measure applied to the fabric than it was taken up again and the scissors did their work.

In the grand front room, more of a parlour than a shop or a workroom, Madame took my coat and gloves and my veil, and placed them on the back of a chair, one tufted in a rich burgundy velvet with a matching settee nearby, all arranged around a fireplace with a marble mantle, unlit except on the coldest days, I'm sure, to keep the smell of burning coal out of the fabric. I told Madame that I was looking for a new ball gown, and she said, 'yes, of course,' and produced from behind the counter a collection of books from Emile Pingat and the House of Worth in Paris, all current volumes, but already well-worn. As we looked through the plates, she asked me what I might like, something to bare the shoulders or something a little more modest? I told her that I was inclined to the former.

'Yes, of course,' she said again, 'One must dress so when one is young, while one still can.' Dress after fancy dress flipped by, worn by elegantly drawn women with fashionable hair and poses and parasols. They were all tall and pretty and placed in elegant country scenes. Some even had fashionable little dogs who played at their fashionable heels. I fancied how Edgar would look at me in dresses such as these, an enchanted look of rapture, how he might paint my movement in them. I imagined him removing them in the candlelight of our nest, pausing to kiss the skin that would become exposed as it rustled from my body. I began to breathe deeply and stare vacantly. Madame cleared her throat.

'Mademoiselle, *s'il vous plait*, may I ask you to adjourn to one of the rooms to be measured, and think there upon your selection?" she said, with the faintest trace of annoyance in her voice. Her eyes were on someone or something up the street on the banquette. She ushered me rather hastily to a booth, where I sat and waited, either for Madame or one of her girls to come and put the measure to me. I again imagined buttons being unbuttoned, hooks being unhooked, things fastened becoming unfastened. I closed my eyes and leaned my head against the wall and took another deep draught of air. My reverie was broken by the tinkle of the bell on the shop door and a familiar voice.

Bonjour, Madame Olympe.

'Ah, Madame Howard,' Madame Olympe gushed, 'so good to see you! I have some things that are just perfect for you, and how is Monsieur Howard?'

In a sudden panic, I searched the room for my veil, so I could put it on and leave, but I remembered that I had left it on the back of the fancy chair with my coat and gloves in the main parlour where Mrs. Howard was speaking to Madame Olympe. I resolved to wait it out. I had no other course. If Madame Olympe or her girl came to the door to inquire, I would say *I am still deciding. Please give me a moment further.* Thinking that perhaps this wouldn't do, either, I nervously put a copy of *Godey's Lady's Book* to my face, thinking I might use it as a veil, or more properly, a shield to wear whilst retrieving my veil from the back of the chair. My mind was keenly working through the dilemma, like the mind of a fox must work when caught in a trap or surrounded by hounds. At last, I feigned difficulty with disrobing and called out through the door in French, 'Can you help me, Madame Olympe? I am having trouble with my corset. I must have put on weight.' Of course, this is not true. I am as slim as ever. Perhaps the love act has kept me so.

She broke from her conversation with Mrs. Howard, one that gushed with glowing superlatives and flattery on the part of Mme. Olympe. 'I will send the girl to help you,' Madame Olympe called back to me in an annoyed tone, before resuming her homage to Mrs. Howard.

'I shall need your opinion, however,' I called out again, disguising my voice with a thick French accent so that it would fool the ears of Mrs. Howard. I heard Mme. Olympe exhale in exasperation and tell Mrs. Howard, 'Forgive me, madame, but, for you, to avoid distractions I shall close the shop and come pay you a call, in person and at your convenience. I shall come with two trunks of samples and my complete inventory of plates, such as are carried by the House of Worth in Paris. Do accept my apologies.' There was low conversation, and then I heard Mrs. Howard's voice say, 'Very well, madame,' or something of the sort. The bell jingled, and the door closed. And I was relieved.

I heard the dressmaker snipe at her assistant, 'That was only Mrs. Howard, married to one of the wealthiest men in the city.' Madame pulled back the velvet curtain to find me in my petticoats, pretending to struggle with my corset. 'What is the trouble here?' she said with a look that silently added, *you silly girl.* My hands searched my back, my fingers feeling for the seam of my corset, 'I'm afraid the hooks on my corset are misaligned.' She looked over her nose and her spectacles at my corset and said, 'No, they are perfectly straight, Mademoiselle.'

I adopted a rather haughty tone and said, "Thank you, but it is Madame, and perhaps I should take two of these dresses rather than one. I favour the green with the mother-of-pearl, but the light blue with the brocaded silk taffeta and the gold trim appeals to me as well. I shall take both, I suppose. And the matching bonnets and wraps, of course.'

'The workmanship of either is very involved,' she said in a voice one might use for a child, 'It will be, perhaps, too expensive.'

'Oh, expense is no impediment,' I replied, 'My husband is one of the wealthiest men in the state. I can expect these to be ready within the week?' She smiled at me, as if I had said a secret word, the countersign that gave me admittance. My selections were made, and my measurements were taken, and on the invoice with the fancy *Madame Olympe & Co., 144 Canal Street,* I signed as that most profligate of spenders, Paulina H. Teague, St. Matthew, Louisiana.

19 January 1873. Over Sunday dinner, Uncle Michel inquired about the health of old Mr. Bell, William Bell's father, who resides in this city, though I have not met him. Toasts were given for fathers living and dead, with genuflections added for the dead. Jo, so eager as children are to be part of adult conversation, said that her father died, too, and that he was a brave man who died for his country. She was pleased that another toast and genuflection were offered, though Rene, her step-father, continued to eat. Elated with her inclusion in the conversation and her offering ending with a toast, Jo then raised her glass and innocently proposed another toast, 'To Mam'selle Alice's Papa, for he died, too.'

The adults stopped eating. Edgar put down his fork. 'When?' he asked, his eyes suddenly sadder than usual. 'In Europe?'

I quickly became aware of the incongruency of the truth and the lie, and my mind wiggled like a worm dodging a hook as I concocted yet another one.

'Oh, that was my *grand*-father,' I said. The space and its silence yawned and begged for me to fill it, so I added, 'Cholera.' Everyone resumed eating, though quietly. 'The child simply misunderstood,' I said into the insatiable pause, 'Cholera,' I said once more to the subdued clank of silverware and porcelain.

'Cholera is an awful thing,' Mouche said at last, 'We trust that he did not suffer and that he has gained his rest.' Everyone set down their silverware and paused to genuflect and then resumed eating. And the silence resumed.

I simply could not get the conversation to another topic fast enough, so I asked Jo about her toe. She still wore a look of confusion at the sudden improvement of my father, but she managed to say that it still hurt her, especially when she tried to press the pedals on the piano. Tell said with a blank gaze to the fireplace that tomorrow she would send for the chiropodist, Dr. McCoy. Didi said that Jo's shoes were too tight, as she grows at an alarming rate and they can't keep up with her. Talk began to steer away from the subject of fathers, and I was grateful for it. After dinner, as we reclined in the parlour and listened to Jo and Tell play a duet on the piano, Edgar said in amusement, 'For a moment I thought you meant your father had died! We all thought it. How stoically you bear such bad news, I was thinking!'

'No,' I said, feeling quite small, 'It was my grandfather who died,' and I weakly repeated the pitiful lie, 'Cholera.'

20 January 1873. Dr. McCoy came to see Josephine and her ailing toe. He is a balding man with a furry thing of a moustache, as if his hair has slipped from the front of his scalp and come to rest on his upper lip. Miss Petinque answered the door and saw him in with his bag and took his great coat to put aside on the hall-tree. Jo sat waiting for him with a book in her lap, dressed in her favourite lavender dress and fearfully trying to put her mind on reading.

He examined her toe, pursing his lips and narrowing his eyes. He then stood and asked that she be given a whiskey toddy with a little honey and orange zest. Whilst she took it, sipping carefully at its bitterness, we adults chatted over the news of the day, including the matter of dual legislatures and governors. At last, she grew sleepy, and Edgar carried her upstairs and Dr. McCoy followed, and I played Jo's favourite, Beethoven's Piano Sonata No. 15 in D Major, on the piano downstairs.

He was done in less than half an hour and came downstairs to collect his hat and coat from Miss Petinque and a grateful *merci, docteur* from Tell. Jo slept the rest of the afternoon, until the winter sun fatigued and fell into the west. I went up to see her as the day's last lights crept away into the night. She slept with the sweet eyes of a lamb, her dark hair splayed over her pillow and her lips parted slightly in deep sleep. I kissed her forehead and went out on the balcony. The smell of cigar smoke was in the chilly shadows of Esplanade. Below me, two men were talking, and I recognized the voices as Edgar and his brother Rene. One of them spoke with a hissing anger in his voice that I have never before heard in this house.

'Mon frère! Elle est un femme mariée!'

She is a married woman!

I held my breath, certain that I had been found out. The air was painfully silent, filled only with the smoke from Rene's cigar. 'Un *femme mariée!*' the voice repeated indignantly.

The other voice spoke, 'Her marriage is so unhappy, married to that braggart, that—that tyrant!'

I closed my eyes. The weight of shame and guilt pressed on me. I began calculating ways to leave the house to escape them.

'That is no excuse!' the other said, and I realized that it was Edgar who was scolding Rene. Rene shushed him, but Edgar said, lower, though I could still hear, 'And you are a married man!' Rene tried to shush his brother, but Edgar continued in a low tirade, 'How dare you come into this man's house—our dear uncle—and soil his honour and the honour of his daughter, your wife, your family!' A cloud of cigar smoke rose like another grey night shadow.

'Edgar, how you exaggerate!' Rene said. 'Like you always do, like you have always done, since we were boys! Mme. Olivier and I are friends, and only that. And her marriage is so unhappy, married to that boor, and she needs friends. He won't even allow her the companionship of a dog, Edgar.'

'She needs friends,' Edgar hissed, 'but she does not need a lover!'

'Mon frère!' Rene said, 'You insult me, and you insult Mme. Olivier!'

'The truth insults you both,' Edgar said. The door opened and shut, almost a slam. I sat in the haze of Rene's cigar smoke, thinking that the conversation could just as well have been about me. It is a truth that Edgar would abhor, if he knew it. Poor, blind Tell. She has suffered enough for two lifetimes. Tonight, I put off sleep, fearful that I shall dream of barristers and accusations again.

21 January 1873. I saw today in the *Picayune* that a Rev. Henry Givens is listed as checking into the City Hotel. I left Edgar in half-sleep and told him that I was going out to find the lady who sells raspberries, those *bijoux du bois.* He grunted assent from the sheets and rolled over.

'Do not let a homesick soldier steal your heart, or I shall have to go back to war,' his muted voice proclaimed from within the sheets. I pulled back the sheets and kissed him and whispered resolutely, 'Never!' And I pulled the sheets over his head again.

At the City Hotel, I sent a message up with the bellman and waited on the circular settee in the lobby, tracing the tufted velvet with my fingers and watching the crowd come and go from within the lace of my Creole veil. A few minutes later, Henry came down the stairs, looking older than I remember him, but still tall and fair and decidedly handsome. He held the message in his hand as he scanned the lobby. I realized that my hair was pinned up under my bonnet and my veil concealed my identity, so I approached him. 'Hello, old friend,' I said.

'Alice?' he asked. I pulled my veil briefly to the side and then let it fall into place again. 'Alice,' he repeated, 'I thought you were in Europe. Apparently not.'

'Apparently not,' I said, 'and it is to be our secret.'

'Yes,' Henry said, 'Of course.' He escorted me to a quiet corner of the lobby, where we sat together on a sofa of red-and-gold toile. We talked of St. Matthew and Mount Teague. The seed cane is being laid in, and the first ratoons are ankle-high. Carnival season is spoken of, to the pleasure of the populace there. Then, he offered this. 'Alice,' he said, taking my hand, 'it is a sin to engage in gossip, but as a friend I feel I must tell you something.'

'Mrs. Parris spends a great deal of time with my husband, does she not?' I said, rather flatly.

He seemed surprised that I knew. 'Yes. Yes, that is it,' he said as his face relaxed.

'And well she may have him,' I said.

He seemed bewildered and asked if it bothered me, and I replied, 'Very little,' to which he merely raised his eyebrows. He did not ask why I was still in town, and I did not ask why he was. He only said that he was headed to Memphis for a fortnight or so, and that the vicar of Thibodaux would be in the pulpit of St. Margaret's. Surely, there has been no small amount of grumbling about Henry's absences, and surely, Henry is going to see his friend Mr. Hodge. I told Henry to write me in care of the post office here in the city, and then I said, 'My friend, our secrets must remain our secrets.'

'Certainly,' he nodded. I returned to our nest on Ursulines without bringing back *les framboise*. Edgar was up and painting, working colour into the portrait of Mouche on the front balcony on Esplanade.

'Where are the raspberries?' he asked after he gave me his lips, and I kissed them. I realized that I had forgotten all about them, and so I told him that I couldn't find the lady who sells them. Nature and a Christian upbringing have given me the aspiration for honesty, but circumstance and desire have taken it away, and so one lie is as good as another.

22 January 1873. A letter has arrived for me from Jenny, held at the post office here in New Orleans per my instructions. I've read her letter, once in the lobby of the post office, and again here on the back gallery of the Mussons as the rain moves in and falls and the sky rumbles like the low E note of a piano.

Jenny sends word of her sisters, who have taken in all the sights of London and Paris, and who are moving south to Geneva and Milan and the rest of Italy with the coming spring. She says that her sisters ask her that she wish me *bonjour* and *Joyeux Noel* and *bonne année* from France and hope to see me soon. She says also that they shall return in the summer and then go directly to the mountains in White Sulphur Springs. Thence, they shall return to Mississippi with their grandmother for an extended visit. Jenny confides that she wonders if they shall ever return to Mount Teague and that it is just as well. Her sisters are happy and thriving, though Lucy still asks for me and Ida now walks with only the slightest of limps. They all want me to go to Mississippi to see them when they return.

She also says that her father insists that it is I who have requested that the girls now live with their grandmother because I find them a bother. She says that she does not believe it for a minute. When I return to the nest on Ursulines, I shall compose a note for her, verifying her thoughts and sending my affection to all. She says they shall be in Venice in a month's time, so I shall send it there in hopes that it shall find them.

It is quite apparent to me that the world of the Teague girls and the world of the Mussons cannot coexist. For now, however, the rain falls, and I sit on the back gallery and listen to it and the noises from the house that compete with it, the sounds of the little ones, Odile and Sidney, playing, and the sounds of Jo at the piano as Carrie sings 'Compère Lapin.' Outside in the garden, the grey sky leaks onto the cheerful faces of camellias and roses. Servants hurry from the kitchen to the house and back. They cannot stop for the rain. The house has now grown quiet on this sleepy afternoon. The smoke of chimneys mixes into the grey, damp sky, and the house and its people nap, and even Vasco is curled up at my feet fidgeting in dog-dreams. Just inside the door, Edgar paints, and my tea has gone cold, but I am content. Vasco raises his head at the small sound of a door opening across the garden and the field. Two figures leave through the side door of the Olivier house and move in together under the umbrella they share as they approach. The dog recognizes the figures across the way and thumps his tail. It is Rene escorting Mme. Olivier, who is coming to give the children their music lessons. I recognize her by her red shawl. The way they look at each other under the sanctuary of their umbrella, I see it. The umbrella tilts and they stop walking, and their faces are hidden, but their legs draw near each other under it. Then they separate a little and the umbrella tilts upward, and they are smiling as they approach the house. I begin to see what Edgar sees, though I also see what he cannot. That is, I am as guilty as they are.

23 January 1873. A nice long visit today with Tell in her quarters upstairs. The open armoire held the fine suits and cravats that Rene wears. The bottom had rows of men's shoes and boots that are also *au currant.* On the table were gold and silver cuff links, and on the hat tree, a variety of *chapeaux*, top hats, hats of all sorts, hats for every occasion. Tell and I sat and took coffee, the ritual before every ritual in every Creole household. I held baby Jeanne on my lap until she became fussy and Virginie came to get her to nurse. As she took the baby away in her brown arms, the little face brushed across the woman's bodice, the little pink mouth searching for the dark nipple on the brown bosom.

When the child was quieted in the next room, Tell said, 'My cousin, Edgar, and you. Everyone sees how you look at each other. Even I can see it.'

She smiled wanly at her joke, a smile that trailed off toward some invisible something as the light of day beamed through the window and illuminated her face. 'He wants to ask you to marry him,' she continued, 'but he won't do it until he speaks to your father. He feels that you keep putting him off.' She set her cup down tentatively on its saucer, listening for the clink of china on china, and then she said, 'Alice, forgive me for asking you, but do you belong to another?'

I felt accused, though I don't believe that was her intention. And I suppose I did feel accused, though from within. However, I managed to reply, 'No. Certainly not.'

'Yes,' she smiled, 'Certainly, you don't.' Her fingers searched for her demitasse cup and curled around the tiny scrolled handle. 'My Jo adores you,' she said, 'Everything is 'Miss Alice, Miss Alice.' She is my heart, my last connection to Joseph, my first husband. She is named for him.'

I waited for her to cry, but she didn't. Perhaps blind eyes don't, or she has cried all she could long ago, and there are no tears left in the account set aside for that particular sadness. She put her hands together on the warmth of her cup and said, 'After Joseph was killed, Mama took Didi and me to France for the rest of the war. Mouche stayed in the city, waiting for William to return from the army, which he did,' she sighed, the heavy sigh of the blind and weary, 'But, alas, there would be no homecoming for me. Edgar met us in France and was so kind to me then. Tell me, Alice, are his eyes still caring and patient, like those of a faithful dog?' Yes, I said, they were, as the clock in the parlour downstairs chimed the hour and motes of dust swirled in the morning sun, but of course, she could not see them. Perhaps she could feel them on her face, a downy tap on her skin. 'We've only recently told Jo about her father,' Tell said, 'She wondered why her last name is Balfour and not Degas, so we told her everything. Children deserve the truth, no less so than adults." The clock finished chiming and she sipped the rest of her coffee. She set her cup down on its saucer, moving the cup into the circular place for its base, and she asked me, 'Would you mind reading to me?'

'Gladly,' I said, 'In English or French?'

'Either,' she said putting her hands together in her lap, 'Your accent in both is beautiful.'

And I read to her from Rousseau's *Confessions*. Downstairs, Mme. Olivier gave Jo her piano lesson, a hesitantly rendered version of one of Chopin's simpler nocturnes.

Sammy, 1982

He closed the diary and curled his finger around the handle of his coffee cup, the last of the old Teague family china cups, the rest of them broken and swept away over the decades. Over a hundred years, a fine old age for a china cup. He wondered about the different lips that had pressed to its rim, maybe even Alice's. The tall clock in the hallway marched its arm in the endless circle with clunk-clunk steps. The piano played in the hallway, bright notes contrasting to the insistence of the clock's mechanism. Quint was giving his sister Elizabeth a music lesson.

Middle C, Quint said in the central hallway as the ringing note faded. *And there's a C here.* A note as if sung by a tenor. *Here.* A note like a soprano. *And here.* The highest C, the tapping of glass. Or an old china cup.

He listened to the patience in his son's voice. That hadn't happened by chance. Children don't learn patience that way. They were good children who didn't deserve the stigma of bearing the same last name as a draft dodger in such a small place as St. Matthew Parish. But would they even be here if he had gone? He went to the kitchen to refill his coffee and kissed them both on the cheek on his way.

The new pot was gurgling the rich, black smell. Sammy waited and looked out the window at the bare backyard. He was unsure where it had all been, the gardens, the statue. Grass had even taken over the black cinders where the ice barn had been. Now it was just more to mow. Whatever became of Mr. Luther, the architect of it, and his patroness, Paulina Teague, his great-grandfather's second wife? She was talked about even less than Alice, his third wife, but maybe because Alice had died a sudden and tragic death, which carried with it an element of the interesting and the entertaining. And maybe the reason that Paulina was so little spoken of by the family was because she had tricked Old Sam Teague, stealthily departing in the middle of the night. He had been forced to divorce her and then bear the smudge of it in a time when divorce was rarely practiced. Whatever became of her? Did she remarry, perhaps an even wealthier man? Assume a different name? Wherever she had gone, she had made a clean getaway, never seen or heard from again.

Sammy looked out the kitchen window to the spreading grass, brilliant green with the increasing daylight of lengthening days. Who did away with the gardens and statue? His daddy never saw them as a boy. He wondered if his Grandpappy, Sam Teague's son and successor, had them taken up. Were they too much trouble to maintain? Had they fallen out of vogue? Had they simply been unenjoyed and fallen into weeds and then abandoned altogether?

The coffee was ready, and he poured himself a cup and returned to the hallway. Elizabeth had tired of her lesson, and Quint was playing something soft and thoughtful. He squeezed his son's shoulder and went back in his study. On the desk, *The Complete Works of Edgar Degas* was opened to a painting of the artist's cousin, Estelle Musson Balfour Degas. Tell was arranging flowers, by texture and scent, he supposed. Her black dress and shadows hid her pregnancy, but, when he looked closer, he could see the swelling, the new baby they would name Jeanne. Amid the dark colors, the oranges and greens and reds of the flowers burst as Tell blithely set them into place. By texture and by scent.

Sammy opened the diary and lifted his bookmark, a deposit slip from the St. Matthew Planters Bank. It was becoming worn. He took a rippling sip of strong black coffee from the last of the original Teague china cups.

Alice, 1873

24 January 1873. In our nest on Ursulines, I read to Edgar from the newspaper as he painted, translating the English into French. The *Picayune* says that it snows heavily in the east, Washington and Philadelphia. He stopped painting for a moment and looked out the window at the New Orleans winter, cold, yes, but barely a winter at all.

'I saw enough snow the winter of the siege,' he murmured as he peered up to the sky. 'Bazile died that winter,' he said to the canvas and to me, 'He was a tremendous painter. And friend.'

I said that I was sorry, such a small thing to always have to say to something as huge as death, especially a premature one, but it must suffice, as there is nothing else to say. He shrugged and said, 'People die every day, though more do it on days when there is a war.' He touched the canvas with his brush with the lightness that he touches my secret places, and I shivered, and he asked me whilst looking at his brush touch his palette, 'Do you long for snow?' I told him that it snowed when I was a girl in England, and in the mountains in India. He stopped painting and turned to me. 'You've been to India?' he asked, a little perplexed.

'Yes,' I said, and I fear I stammered a measure, 'Father went there to—to help them introduce sugarcane.' I thought he might ask me about India, but he let it pass. Perhaps when one is in love, details such as trips halfway around the world, to India, slip away unnoticed, like a clever thief.

25 January 1873. For appearance's sake, Edgar spent the night with *la famille*, and I awoke alone this morning with a troubling thought: If the gowns arrived at Esplanade, then the deliveryman would ask for Mrs. Teague to sign for them, and if I received them as her, the Mussons would rightfully suspect that I was not who I said I was. And if Mme. Olympe has the Musson's address, and if Mr. Teague or Mr. Howard would come to her shop to pay the bill, then they might coerce her into divulging it. My bold move now seemed a foolhardy and reckless one. I resolved that I would simply rise and go and fetch the gowns from Mme. Olympe's shop myself and tell her that I had given her the wrong address.

I hired a carriage to drive me from Ursulines to Mme. Olympe's shop on Canal Street. The winter sun was well in the sky as the city was already up and on its feet. Vendors were crying in various languages, wheels of wagons and carriages and carts were creaking, hooves were striking cobblestones, food was cooking, men and women walking on the banquette absorbed in errands, all of it occurring beyond the concealing curtain of my veil. I could not imagine any of them having a more pressing errand than mine. We turned onto that great chasm of the city, Canal Street, into the traffic of more carriages, carts, and wagons. I alighted and pressed through the crowd on the banquette, turning sideways to pass, even separating a couple to whom I gave an over-the-shoulder apology. At last I arrived at Mme. Olympe's shop, and when I opened the door and entered, she greeted me as if I were a daughter she had not seen in ages.

'Ah, Madame Teague!' she said as if I were a duchess, a baroness, or a queen, 'I have just received the perfect bonnet for you! The dimensions and colour would suit the shape of your face and your complexion perfectly! A royal blue, just in from Paris! It is still in the box—I have shown it to no one!'

I thanked her and told her perhaps another time, but that I had come to collect my prior purchases. 'Oui, madame,' she gushed, 'and they are ready, and they are simply splendid, splendid. Your taste is impeccable! Your husband Monsieur Teague shall be so pleased as to buy you two more! I predict it! I have just sent the delivery man to bring them to you,' and she consulted a ledger and read, 'Three-seventy-two Esplanade, *n'est-pas?*'

'Yes," I stammered, and then, 'No, rather. I mean, they are to be a surprise, and I don't want them delivered there. I was hoping to just pick them up. And that is—that is not our address.'

She looked into the ledger and then pointed to the entry, 'It is the address you gave, not even a week ago.' A trace of condescension had crept into her voice, as when before she knew I was the wife of a rich man, and again I felt as though she might add, *you silly girl.* My reply was almost babbled.

'Yes, we recently moved, and—and I was mistaken as regards to the house number,' I blurted.

'Oh, my, then,' she said, 'The deliveryman has just left. He should be at that address shortly. Perhaps you can catch him. Whoever is at this address would be delighted to have such exquisite ball gowns as those!'

'Let us keep this transaction a secret, shall we?' I said as I opened the door to make a hasty exit, 'Well, then, *merci* and *bonjour*, Madame.'

I quickly climbed into the carriage without assistance as I instructed the driver to proceed with great haste down Canal and then Tonti, and he did so, shouting warnings to children who played by the street, *garde-la!* and going around milk wagons and butchers' carts. We passed through intersections, barely missing cross-traffic. And then, up ahead was a fine delivery van, painted white, pulled by two white horses with plumed headdresses of green-and-blue peacock feathers and driven by a finely-liveried man in a top hat and a swallowtail coat.

My driver, who himself was rather plainly attired, said to me, 'Here he is,' and called to the deliveryman in a coarse French, 'You there, monsieur, my lady says you have a package for her and that I am to save you the trouble of calling.' Madame's deliveryman slowed to a stop as we pulled aside. On the side of his carriage in fancy black-trimmed gold letters was an elegant, *Mme. Olympe & Co., 144 Canal Street, N. O., La.* From the back of my carriage, I could see the pitch of the Musson's roof through the trees.

'Paulina Teague?' the deliveryman read from his invoice. His face was young but wrinkled, and his pale eyes had dark circles under them.

'Yes,' I said, turning my gaze from the Musson's roof which was half-concealed in the branches of trees, less than a block away. I told Mme. Olympe's driver that I would take possession of his delivery, and I signed Paulina H. Teague, and he saw that the signatures matched. The two boxes were loaded onto our carriage, and I tipped the deliveryman and told him not to tell a soul of his errand, as it was to be a surprise for a certain gentleman, and to only say that the goods had been duly delivered to Mme. Teague. And I forced a smile, which I'm sure was a vague one behind the lace of my veil. Then my driver took me and my packages to the nest on Ursulines and even brought them up, pausing as if he were waiting to see what precious thing could be inside. I sent him off with a tip and with his curiosity unsatisfied. Now I only hope that Mme. Olympe can keep the address a secret, and that it cannot be bought from her, should anyone try it.

26 January 1873. My arrival each Sunday morning has become a source of great excitement for the children of the Musson house. Pierre and Sidney run around the parlour shouting, 'Mam'selle Alice, Mam'selle Alice!' whilst little Odile comes running directly to me with her arms out for me to pick her up, and when I do, she gives me a big kiss and won't let me put her down. Jo comes to me with ribbons for her hair, and I must put Odile aside so that I can gather Jo's hair into the satin strands. In the carriages to the cathedral, the children nudge each other to ride in the one with me and their mothers gently scold them that they must share Mam'selle Alice. In church, they nestle into my sides and sit on my lap as their heavy eyes fight falling into slumber from the murmur of Latin.

Afterward, during Sunday dinner, Pierre will not eat his petit pois except at my insistence, and Odile won't eat anything if I don't spoon it into her mouth. And after dinner, I read to them in French and in English until I am hoarse, and Carrie says, 'Mam'selle Alice, your hair is like Goldilocks,' and 'Mam'selle Alice, you are like the princess and Edgar is like the prince.' When they fall into their afternoon naps, I listen to the breath of deep sleep that only children may enjoy. And then I nap, and I awake on the divan thinking Carrie is little Lucy. How I wish this is how it could be forever, seeing these children grow up in this house, Edgar and I as aunt and uncle, husband and wife. But as no man can serve two masters, nor can any woman. Difficult decisions cannot go unresolved, though I shall put them off as long as I can, a day, a week, a month, forever.

27 January 1873. A notice, an advertisement, really, appeared today in the newspaper that gentlemen readers must go to Walshe's so that 'they may make a good appearance in the court of the King of Carnival, if they are so summoned.' There is also an announcement that a ball is to be held in two weeks' time at the French Opera House. Mouche is quite certain that she can gain admittance for Edgar and me, and so Edgar has gone with Rene to buy a new evening suit with Mr. Walshe, as Edgar has left his in

Paris, and it is possibly out of style, as it was well before the war and the siege that he last wore it. Rene told Edgar that evening coats with tails and darker waistcoats are *au currant* and to leave the talking and buying to him. Edgar replied that he was happy to do both, as he has neither the fine tastes nor the pocketbook of his brother. When they had left, Mouche asked me if I have anything to wear, and that she would gladly loan me a dress, were we the same size. She is quite petite, however, and I, of course am quite tall, almost as tall as Edgar.

'Oh, I have a couple of things,' I said dismissively, though I admit to you, my little confidant that I tried on the dresses last night while I was alone, as Edgar reluctantly spent the night again here at Esplanade. Both the green-and-black and the blue dresses were every bit as splendid as Mme. Olympe said.

'Well, then,' Mouche said, 'I can't wait to see them, as I'm sure Edgar can't wait. While he is out, let's see what he is painting.'

I can tell that when her mother was alive, Mouche gave her great fits, as she now gives her father, Uncle Michel, great diversion. We rose and went through the library to Edgar's room and studio. We were surprised to find Uncle Michel there, taking coffee and reading *L'Abeille d'Nouvelle Orleans.*

'Is the office closed today, Papa?' Mouche asked him.

'No, *mon coeur*, business is slow just now, and so I pretend to be a man of leisure,' he said. He set his spectacles on the end table and lifted the newspaper like it was an old rag in referring to it. 'Business may be slow, but not for our governments. We have more governors and legislators than are necessary. And now we have two more senators for Congress. Our two legislatures have elected one each.'

Apparently, it is among the rules of this country that the state legislatures convene to elect the senators that are sent to Washington. Not surprisingly, they have elected two different men, and now there is no small controversy on which should be seated in the Senate in Washington. Uncle Michel replaced his spectacles on his nose and shook the paper open again and said to it, 'Perhaps Mr. Barnum should return to the city and take the whole lot away with his menagerie.' We left him reading about surplus governors and legislatures and senators and entered the buttery scent of Edgar's room and studio, a place of oil paints and turpentine and colour. On an easel was the painting of Jo and Dr. McCoy. Edgar has made remarkable progress. All but the border is complete.

'Edgar is really very good,' Mouche observed as we peered into not just the painting, but the room with the girl and the chiropodist. Looking into the canvas, I could hear the stillness, the ticking of the clock in the room where Jo was draped in a sheet, her favourite lavender dress on the back of the divan, the dress that she would outgrow soon. Her hair was down, her face somnolent from the whiskey toddy given to calm her. I could hear the quiet words of Dr. McCoy as he spoke to the girl and her foot and its troublesome toe. I could almost hear myself playing Mozart's *Piano Sonata No. 15* on the piano downstairs.

28 January 1873. A quiet day in our nest on Ursulines. Edgar was sitting in the armchair and sketching again. Always sketching, that man. 'These boxes, what are they?' he asked as he pointed to them with his pencil.

'They are new clothes, a surprise for you,' I said. He replied that he already had his suit for the ball. Certainly, he was teasing. I rose and sat on his lap, and he set his sketchpad aside. 'They are a surprise for you,' I said, 'but they are *my* clothes.' He asked if he would have to wait for the ball to see them, and I asked him, rather coyly, 'Would you like to see them now?' and he replied, 'Yes, I think I may.'

'Well, then,' I said, 'turn to the window, and no peeking.' His outline waited at the window, looking down at the street well below us and trying to make it seem as interesting as my dressing. First, I put on the green-and-black. My hair had been carefully swept up, in the way of Creole women, but in putting on the dress, a few small strands fell onto my neck. I checked my reflection in the looking glass and decided to leave it as it was. 'Now,' I announced, 'You may turn around.'

He turned, but I could not see his expression, as he was in silhouette. 'Are you pleased?' I asked his shadow.

'Yes,' he said, though he seemed a bit out of breath, 'Very much so.' He approached, and his finger swept up a wisp of golden hair and replaced it behind my ear. He murmured, 'You astound me. How could you become more beautiful?'

I blushed and told him, 'I have another. Turn, and I shall try it on, and you can judge which you like best.' He turned, and I could tell he was trying to resist turning back to see me dressing. 'Don't look yet!' I admonished him as if he were just a boy. I admit to some delight in making him wait. I looked at my image in the smoky reflection of the looking glass. My hair had fallen even more, so I shook it all loose and let it go completely. 'Now you may look,' I said. It was the light blue dress with the gold piping and the silk brocade. I turned in it, keeping my eyes to his, my head pivoting like a ballerina in a slow revolution with her face toward the dance-master. 'Which do you favour?' I asked, 'This one, or the other?'

He stood there with his chin in his hand and his elbow on his chest, a thinking posture. 'I cannot decide', he said, 'Let me think upon it.'

'Turn around again' I said. He turned and I added, 'And no peeking, either.'

'Is there a third?' his silhouette asked the light in the window. I said nothing, but only let the light blue and gold dress fall, and then I let my petticoats fall, let my chemise fall, everything, and I was naked, like Eve in the Garden. 'You may turn around, monsieur,' I said.

'Well,' he said with a smile and the faintest trace of a blush, 'it appears as though the empress has no clothes.'

'Nor should the emperor,' I said, just as an empress might say it. He stood speechless as I undressed him, and then he began helping me, and we were slowed in our efforts only by kisses. We watched our bodies as they followed their nature, the movement of smooth skin on smooth skin.

He compared my nipples to the cartonette of raspberries, tense and red, and we fed them to each other, grinning like fools, my head snapping in laughter and shaking my hair. He beckoned me to sit astride him, and I gasped as our skin met and my flesh enveloped him. I inclined to him and braced my hands on the bed on either side of his head. Golden hair and ivory breasts and pink nipples fell toward his chest and swayed. The push and pull of sea and sky, our movements the respiration of the ocean and the heavens, the earth and the wind.

We passed the day in an embrace without saying anything or having to say it. Right and wrong have become as significant as right and left, two hypothetical choices of no real consequence, like guilt and atonement, sin and repentance. They all slip through my fingers, like sand, water, dust, air. In this blissful aura, they have no meaning and no purpose. When we are in the embrace of Venus, Mount Teague seems an imaginary place from long ago, as remote as Rome or Greece.

29 January 1873. A cold grey morning indeed with a wind that pushed the plumes rising from every chimney, all the smoke of all the city's chimneys pushed southward by the insistent north wind to join the grey of the sky. A carriage ride was a necessity rather than a luxury. I knocked on the door and was ushered in by Johanna this time, her French, '*C'est Mam'selle Alice, Madame*' tinged with Irish brogue. Didi came forth from the parlour and said, 'Alice, you don't have to knock, anymore, our house is as good as yours.' Inside, beyond the parlour, the older children were gathered around the dining room table engaged in their studies.

'I'm glad you're here,' Didi said as she drew me back into the parlour, 'My sisters and I have a proposal for you.' She lowered her voice so that the children could not hear. 'Monsieur le docteur has put Mme. Olivier to bed for the remainder of her time. We were hoping you would continue the children's lessons, and especially the music lessons. I am afraid that I have neither the temperament nor patience, Mouche hasn't the aptitude, and Tell, well—'

'You needn't explain,' I said, 'I would be delighted.' And, truly I was.

'The children would certainly be delighted as well,' Didi said. Edgar came into the parlour with paint-covered hands and leaned in to kiss me on both cheeks, though I could feel his lips linger surreptitiously on my skin.

'I thought I heard your voice,' he said. I told him that I was to be a governess, and I almost added, *again*.

Didi said that if I wished, space in the house on Esplanade could be found for me to inhabit, but I replied that I didn't mind the travel, really, and that the walk is quite enjoyable when the weather is clement. A relieved look came over Edgar's face, for we both know that if I stayed here in the house, there would be no time or place for us to enjoy our love. And so, I immediately set about the studies for the children.

I spent an hour learning what the children, Pierre, Carrie, and Jo, were studying, and then reviewed where we might expect to be in a month's time and then beyond. I would set one about a task, and then the next, and then the next, and then it would be time to tend to the first, and so on. The morning went quickly. At one point or another, I would look up to find Edgar looking at me, a face of gentleness and admiration. I would look up again to find that he had returned to his studio, and I would miss his presence there, so I would leave the children for a moment and go to his room to watch him paint, and I wonder if he saw the same portrait of tenderness on my face that I had seen on his.

Late in the morning, Edgar came into the dining room, and we stood before the fire and warmed ourselves as we watched the children pursue their lessons. Jo performed mathematics problems, multiplication and division and fractions. Carrie read from the primer, half an hour in English and half an hour in French, and Pierre earnestly traced his letters, fat, looping vowels and wavering sticks of consonants. Even after a day, he is more proficient than my husband back in St. Matthew.

Edgar announced that he had a surprise for me, two tickets to a Mr. Rubenstein's piano concert tonight. He said that I might like to hear him, and he himself was dying for music. I put my hand to Edgar's face and told him that was very thoughtful. 'Wear the green-and-black dress, will you?' he whispered as he put his hand to my waist and his mouth to my ear. And I smiled coyly.

30 January 1873. We had seats last night in the second tier at the Varieties for Mr. Rubenstein's performance. I allowed myself the thought that Edgar and I might be man and wife, out for a night of rest after tending a houseful of children and hoping to return to that house to find them already asleep, and then engaging in the heavenly business of love. Nevertheless, I kept Uncle Michel's opera glasses tight to my eyes, more as a disguise than anything else. I found myself scanning the theatre constantly, looking for the Howards, or, worse, my husband, but neither made an appearance.

Mr. Rubenstein gained the stage to enthusiastic applause, bowed, and began playing a selection of the old favourites, Beethoven, Mozart, low notes like the stomp of an elephant and high notes like the fall of icicles from the eaves of a roof, and every note in between. Gusts of applause rose with the end of each piece (as Mr. Nesbit in old Guildford used to call them), and Mr. Rubenstein rose also from the bench and bowed to us before sitting once again to continue. At the end, he received a standing ovation and generous hurrahs as he played selections of a M. Gottschalk, a native of the city and an obvious favourite. As Mr. Rubenstein stood by the bench and the piano, taking yet another bow, Edgar leaned into me and whispered, 'He is quite good, but I believe you play as well as this fellow.' It was a generous thing to say, though an exaggeration, I should think. But perhaps to Edgar's ears, it is correct. And perhaps that is the way of love.

'He plays a Steinway,' I whispered to Edgar as we, the audience, clapped enthusiastically, a rain-shower of applause, and I put the opera glasses away in their case and replaced my veil. 'I have never played one, but I would love to,' I said into his ear under the applause.

'Perhaps one day I will be able to buy you one,' he said, and I took his hand in mine as I wondered how that could ever be. But it was all forgotten in our loft on Ursulines, as he removed the green-and-black dress from my body and my golden hair fell in golden candlelight and we fell into the embrace of Venus, and I wished with all my heart that we could be man and wife always.

31 January 1873. Edgar spent the night with me on Ursulines. We cannot be apart long, though he fears that evidence of our lying together would besmirch my honour if his cousins, the sisters, were to find out. He thinks his brothers would understand, and perhaps Uncle Michel. He, too, was a young man once, Edgar says.

Again, however, I had the dream of the barristers and their accusations. They were more insistent for me to announce my crime to the gathering of white wigs and frilled collars and scowls, and I looked up from the witness box. I was naked, and I saw my Papa's face in the gallery when I spoke my crime.

I awoke with the word on my lips, and as I did, I saw Edgar's face. He was in his sleeping chemise, lying next to me and propped on one elbow, his fingers stroking the angle of my jaw.

'Adultery,' I thought I heard you say,' Edgar said, 'So, you are aware of it, the sin.'

I was sweaty and agitated. The dream was the most real one yet. I could not speak at first but, finally, I managed it. 'Aware of what, dear?' I asked innocently.

'It is no matter,' he said as he looked off and through the window.

'No,' I insisted, 'aware of what?'

Edgar looked to the ceiling and sighed and said, 'My brother. Rene. I suspect that he carries on with someone.' Edgar would not say anything further, but I am quite certain that it is Mme. Olivier.

We rose and dressed, and went to the house on Esplanade, where Edgar made a great show of presenting me as if he had risen early and gone to Ursulines to fetch me.

'Well, cousins,' he said as he made the rounds of the breakfast table, giving each of the sisters a kiss, 'I woke early and went to gather up an English rose!' And I made the rounds giving each a kiss as well, and all the children also. Didi called for Virginie to set two more places.

After clearing the dining room table of the breakfast dishes, the lessons continued, and, again, Uncle Michel kept to his library with coffee and *L'Abeille* and the *Picayune*. As the children were set about their scholarly tasks, I played a piece by Chopin, one that I know Uncle Michel favours.

Midmorning, two men arrived whom I recognized from Edgar's sketch of the Cotton Office, Mr. Prestidge and M. Livaudais. Uncle Michel rose and greeted them, and they adjourned to the library and closed the door. I resumed asking the children questions to which they must raise their hands if they know the answer. They enjoy the competition to be the one called upon and soon became quite boisterous. But Uncle Michel came and asked if the children could not be allowed to run and play in the garden for a while. 'Certainly,' I said, and he kissed my cheek in appreciation, though he looked sad. Lessons were suspended and the children ran pell-mell through the back door to the happy barking of Vasco. Three more men whom I did not know arrived, and Joanna took their hats and coats and saw them to the library. After a half-hour, the meeting in the library adjourned. One of the men put some documents in a valise as he left.

'It will be announced in the newspapers, then, in the morning,' one of the unknown men said. There was a round of handshakes and subtle bows among the men, and Joanna gave out hats and coats. They departed in separate carriages, leaving Uncle Michel standing and looking at the door that had closed behind them.

'Would you play something for me dear Alice?' he asked, 'Nothing too happy.' And so, I played the adagio from Mozart's *Piano Concerto No. 23, in A*. And Uncle Michel poured himself a tumbler of bourbon, even though it wasn't yet noon. I have seen the look on his face before, on the face of my dear Papa. It is the look of a defeated man.

1 February 1873. The *Picayune* carries the announcement this morning that the cotton office of Musson, Prestidge, & Co. is dissolved. A Mr. Graham and a Mr. Hardeman shall be its successors.

2 February 1873. Candlemas. Only 3 years ago Papa and I celebrated it aboard the *Chrysolite*, and now he sleeps in a crypt far from England. Who would attend his grave if I did not? Perhaps Mozie. Do I betray him, even in death? Do I betray his memory?

I paused in dressing for church, and suddenly, like a rogue wave on the ocean, these thoughts overwhelmed me, and I began crying. I sat down on the edge of the bed and put my face in my hands, and I wept for how far I have fallen, especially when judged by the noble nature of my Papa. Edgar was at the window of our nest, looking out onto the rooftops of a sleepy city and listening to the ring of drowsy church bells. He turned from the window and sat down next to me, taking my hand and putting his arm around me. 'What's wrong, love? What?' he asked, and he searched his pocket for his handkerchief and gave it to me. I shook my head as I wept until I could say, 'It's just that, sometimes, I miss my Papa so.'

'Don't worry, Alice,' Edgar said, 'Certainly, he'll be back in time for spring, when there is a crop to be tended.' And again, I realised that for Edgar, my Papa was only in Europe, and so I said, 'Yes, but Papa trusts that to our overseer.' Edgar seemed confused. He said, 'Forgive me, but for one so intent on getting in a good crop—'

Recovering from my error, I shrugged and said, 'That is just what he does.' Edgar must believe my father to be a very complex and peculiar man. Little does he know. And now we are off to church, where I shall pray for forgiveness from my heavenly father, for sins that have become so commonplace for me, sins that I have neither the desire nor the ability to forsake.

3 February 1873. All in this house went to Mass again today, as it is the feast day of St. Blaise, and it is very important in this household, and perhaps all Creole households, to have one's throat blessed on this feast day, to prevent sickness. All went, even servants, though Edgar and I tarried and enjoyed the blessing of each other's bodies in his room-and-studio on Esplanade, his *atelier*, he calls it. It was a quick rendezvous, and we replaced the clothes which were removed for it and lay exhausted on his bed. We talked of small matters as we waited for the family to return. Edgar is thinking of reworking the painting of Didi. Mouche has gained us admittance to the ball later this week. Jo's toe is completely healed, and she runs about with no trouble. Carrie turns six today and there shall be cake. The weather has been mild, and the azaleas are to bloom in the next few weeks.

And as the first spring breeze stirred through the shutters that look onto Tonti Street, we spoke of Mme. Olivier and how she gets along now that Monsieur le Docteur has put her to bed.

'But of course, he is not the only man to put her to bed,' Edgar said with a hint of disgust.

'Edgar!' I said, swatting his chest rather playfully. He seemed not to notice. He only clicked his tongue in abhorrence of the entire matter.

'Such a dishonor, to bed another man's wife,' he muttered.

There was nothing I could say upon the subject. We straightened our clothes and hair and rose without a word to sit in the garden and innocently await *la famille's* return from having their throats blessed.

4 February 1873. The weather being pleasant, I dismissed the children at noon, and they happily took to the outdoors where spring is quietly dropping hints at her arrival. I adjourned to the back gallery to watch them play in the garden. Just inside the door, Edgar painted, occasionally breaking from his work to come and watch the children with me and to steal a kiss. When the children adjourned for naps, and Jo, for her piano practise, I read the *Picayune*, and in the arrivals section, there is word that a

Henry Givens is listed as having arrived at the St. Charles Hotel. I told Edgar that I was going out on an errand, and that I should be back soon.

I alighted from the carriage in front of the St. Charles, securing my veil as I did, as the hotel is just down the street from the Howards, who still believe me to be in England. As I looked up the steps, I saw Henry at the top of them with a man whom I faintly recognized as Mr. Hodge. The city gets more crowded every day with the approach of carnival, and I made my way up the steps through the swarm of black wool coats, and shawls and bonnets, at one point losing sight of Henry and Mr. Hodge. At last, I found Henry's blonde hair when he went to remove his hat. After a half-dozen *pardon, madams* and *excuse me, sirs*, I was able to reach them. From behind my lace, I called his name.

'Yes?' he asked as he turned. I lifted my veil, and, on recognizing me, he said, 'Alice!' As I withdrew from a filial embrace with Henry, I addressed his friend, 'And you are Mr. Hodge, am I correct?'

'Yes, but how did you know my name?' he asked. Mr. Hodge's tone was that of a man who felt himself pursued, as if he had been accused, and I fear that his name is something I should not have known or should not have told if I did know it. I told him that we had met in the past, in St. Matthew, to which he stammered, 'Perhaps, perhaps so.' I said that Henry and I are very dear friends, like brother and sister, and that his friends were my friends. I grasped Mr. Hodge's hand warmly, and even through my glove, his hand felt soft. I secured my veil again, and the three of us walked down St. Charles to Canal Street and then crossed it. A Metropolitan policeman in the distinctive blue suit with brass buttons paused traffic for us to cross. Thence, we turned up Canal and walked along the banquette, moving away from the river. Henry and I talked, whilst Mr. Hodge kept largely silent. He seemed ill-at-ease, but perhaps that is his nature.

In front of Mr. Holmes' store, I saw a woman ahead of us walking with the help of another woman beside her. The woman who was being helped looked up and away, perhaps admiring the buildings along the street. They did not walk as fast as the three of us, and as we neared them, I realised that it was Didi and Tell. I slowed and quieted, as I suddenly found my old and new lives within feet of each other. I pretended to look in the windows of Mr. Holmes' store, but Tell stopped abruptly and lifted her gaze and turned her head as she held onto Didi to detain her.

'Alice,' Tell asked the sky, 'Is that you? I believe I hear your footsteps.' I suppose that a veil will not conceal one from the gaze of the blind.

I could say nothing more than, 'Yes, Tell, you are quite correct.'

Didi asked, 'And who is your gentleman friend?' and I replied, 'This is my brother, Henry, and his friend, in for a visit from Memphis.' What I didn't say was if they were both from Memphis or just his friend was. Details were not necessary.

'It is a pleasure to meet you both,' Tell said as she sent her wavering hand out into the space between them. Henry, and then Mr. Hodge, took it lightly with nodding heads, and then Didi offered her hand.

'Well, Mr. Lamb,' Didi said to Henry, 'you and your sister certainly favour.' I was afraid that Henry would refute the assertion that we were brother and sister, but he said, 'Yes, we both favour our mother.'

"God rest her," I quickly added, lest Henry mention that she was still living, and that he and Mr. Hodge were off to visit her.

Didi and Tell genuflected, and Didi asked, 'Have you met Edgar, Mr. Lamb? He is our cousin, and my sister's brother-in-law.' Tell's blank expression smiled broadly as she said, 'And Edgar is Alice's—'

'—Edgar is my friend I was telling you about, Brother,' I said quickly.

Henry gave me a sidelong glance and said, 'No, madame, I have not had the pleasure of meeting Edgar, though I hope to one day soon. He sounds like a very particular friend. But it will have to wait another time. Mr. Hodge and I have a train to catch later today. We were just off to Mr. Holmes' here, to purchase a few sundries. Perhaps later.'

Didi said, 'Very well, Mr. Lamb, 'but do come visit us, when you are in the city again. Our house is on Esplanade,' and she gave Henry a calling card with the name and address, *MUSSON, 372 Rue Esplanade, N. O., La.* Henry thanked her and put the card in his waistcoat pocket.

'Tell Edgar that I shall be along later, as soon as I see Brother and his friend off,' I told Didi and Tell.

'Certainly,' Tell said with a smile, off and away, over the traffic of Canal and to the rooftops. Didi and Tell turned and were already engaged in conversation, and I wondered if they were discussing the strange fact that my brother had a distinctly southern accent and not an English one like mine.

'My, but what a web, Sister,' Henry murmured to me, and rather facetiously.

'Yes,' I sighed, and he said nothing more of it. Mr. Hodge kept nervously looking up and down Canal Street. Perhaps he was wishing for a veil. We returned to the steps of the hotel, and Mr. Hodge excused himself and hurried up the stairs, muffled footfalls on the red-carpeted treads. As he disappeared, Henry embraced me and said, 'What a pair of spiders we are, you and I,' and then he held me tight and whispered in my ear, 'Pray for me, Sister.'

5 February 1873. Edgar was quite disappointed to have missed meeting my 'brother,' almost as disappointed in not knowing that I had one in the first place. 'You have never spoken of him,' he said as he touched the canvas with his brush.

'Henry is a few years older than I. I seldom see him,' I said, a puny truth.

Edgar left it at that and painted most of the day in his room-atelier on Esplanade, whilst I employed myself in the instruction of children in the dining room of the house. After supper, he returned with me back to Ursulines, the light of a lengthening day sending our shadows well across the Bayou Road. After submitting ourselves to the goddess of love, we lay exhausted, though I thought I might write in you, my confidant, for, as you can see, there was much to tell. I could not find my pen, and, as Edgar had risen, I asked him to find it. He looked through the side table, and then my portmanteau. Suddenly he stopped and said, 'Alice, there is a wedding ring in your portmanteau.'

My heart skipped. 'Yes,' I stumbled, 'It is, well, it is—' I swallowed, and I fear almost audibly. '—it is my mother's. One of the few things I have of hers. I bring it with me always.' I exhaled and wondered if he could tell, as if a lie might have a peculiar colour or odour as it hangs in the air.

'She must have been exactly your size,' he said, holding it up to the light of the window.

'Yes,' I said, 'I take after her strongly.' That part is true, of course. How refreshing to be able to tell even a small truth. He still held it in his fingers when he came to slip it on my mine to compare.

'Well, look at that!' he said, 'A perfect fit!' He looked into me with his kind, brown eyes and said, 'How I should like to slip a similar one on that finger one day.' He embraced me, and then leaned back and held me by my shoulders to look at me. I was almost in tears from fear that I had been found out. I was trembling, and he tenderly asked me what was wrong.

'Yes,' I said, 'it's just that—I miss her terribly.'

Edgar sighed and shook his head, 'And your father, so indifferent to your suffering. When we finally meet, it will take some effort for me to be civil,' Edgar said.

Yes, when you two meet, I thought, *and may God forbid it.* Edgar lovingly shushed me and held me, stroking my hair until the colour faded with the light, from golden in the twilight to the grey of night. When we went to sleep, I removed the ring and put it on the washstand by the basin. Sleep is long in finding me this night as I feel my Conscience scowling and hissing at me in the dark.

Sammy, 1982

Whatever happened to it, Alice Teague's wedding ring? He supposed it had been consumed in the flames of the ballroom on the night she died and was left in the cinders and rubble, now covered over by earth and grass, a hundred years' worth. Or perhaps it had been the one piece of evidence that had helped identify her remains. He looked down at the manuscript, the fine hand of an Englishwoman showing the slightest wavering on upstrokes, the faintest quivering hesitancy in the rounding of vowels. The staggering weight of living one life while hiding another.

Upstairs, his girls were talking in tiny conversation, peppered with giggles. He replaced the deposit slip bookmark and put the diary in his desk drawer. In the central hallway, he paused in front of the portrait of his great-grandfather, and the two bearded Teagues pondered each other, one in a soldier's uniform, one in the denim shirt of a cane farmer. Sammy turned and went upstairs.

On the floor in the middle of their room, his daughters were holding a tea party. Their invited guest, the dog, sat on her haunches with a scarf over her head and tied under her chin. Her whiskered snout protruded from the scarf, her brown eyes blinking and twitching. She sat politely, willing to endure anything for the promise of a morsel of scrap that the girls had culled from the refrigerator.

"Hi Daddy," Elizabeth said.

"We habbin' a tea porty," little Judee exclaimed, looking up to her daddy with an exaggerated smile and squinting eyes. Using two hands on the plastic teapot, Elizabeth poured invisible tea for her sister and the dog.

"That's a love-a-ly jew-ler-ree you have, Mrs. Pongeaux," Elizabeth said.

Mrs. Pongeaux blinked her eyes, shivering for the next bit of treat. Judee held it above the dog's head, and the dog daintily lifted her neck and took it off her girl's little fingers. That's when Sammy saw it, the sapphire pendant around Mrs. Pongeaux's neck.

"Where did you find that necklace?" Sammy asked. Mrs. Pongeaux sniffed his fingers as he lifted the pendant from the orange-and-white fur of her neck.

"I found it in your desk drawer. Um, *Judee* found it in your desk drawer."

Sammy took the pendant off the dog.

"Show me where." He paused and grinned at his girls. "I'm not mad."

Sammy and his girls got up and went downstairs to his study, and Mrs. Pongeaux took the opportunity to raid the plastic bowl of treats and empty it completely.

In his study, Judee went to the desk drawer and opened it. Inside, there were receipts for fertilizer and cane-cutter parts and invoices. Behind them was a latch, and Judee's little fingers pressed it to reveal that it was a false back with a tray behind it.

"Well, look at that!" Sammy said, and he ruffled her hair, black like her mother's. "You found a secret compartment!" He held up the sapphire. "Aunt Charlotte and Aunt Marilyn have been looking for this!"

And fighting over it like they were your ages, he thought. "Won't they be proud of you for finding it," he murmured to them as he looked closely at the pendant. "Why don't we go down to Cato's and get Mrs. Pongeaux some fancy new jewelry?" Sammy asked his girls. They hoorayed and went back to their room to break the good news to Mrs. Pongeaux. Her stomach full, she was already napping in a patch of sunshine. The scarf had slipped onto her snout.

He gathered up his keys, and he and his girls went into Thibodaux. And then Sammy Teague amazed himself by buying twenty dollars of costume jewelry for a dog who only attended the tea parties for the companionship of her girls and the scraps of food they gave her. But so it is with fatherhood.

Later that day, he went back into Thibodaux to see the jeweler, Mr. Dupuy. The sign in his shop on St. Patrick Street proclaimed that he was a licensed gemologist and a member of the Better Business Bureau and the Thibodaux Chamber of Commerce. In the window, surrounded by a display of necklaces and bracelets, a beautiful, delighted young woman accepted a ring from a handsome young man against a festive background of blurry lights. Sammy entered the red-carpeted shop amid glass cases with twinkling rings and shining strands of pearls. He introduced himself to Mr. Dupuy and showed him the pendant.

"*Garde-des-don*," Mr. Dupuy muttered to himself as he put his jeweler's lens to his eye. He repeated it in English in case Sammy hadn't understood. "Look at that."

He examined it for a few seconds and then took his jeweler's lens from his eye and took a deep breath and sighed. "I don't know how to tell you this, Mr. Teague, but your family heirloom is just blue glass, in a setting that's, well, okay."

"Is that right?"

Mr. Dupuy put his lens back in his shirt pocket and looked at Sammy. "I thought you might be disappointed, but you seem amused."

"How much would it cost you to make another?" Sammy asked.

"I'd be ripping you off if I charged you more than twenty dollars."

"I'll take two then. How long will it take? Is a week too soon?"

"Oh, I'll have this for you in an hour or two."

"All right. I may just wait, if you don't mind."

"Just don't tell anyone you got it here, all right?" Mr. Dupuy said. "We may be down-the-bayou, but we still have a reputation to uphold."

"Sure," Sammy said. "I'll be out in my truck."

As Sammy opened the door to the dull ping of the electronic shop bell, he heard Mr. Dupuy say to his assistant in French, "Run down to K&B and get me a bottle of Milk of Magnesia. The one in the blue-glass bottle."

And Sammy went down to a bench by Bayou Lafourche and read from the diary. It was a nice day for it.

Alice, 1873

6 February 1873. Edgar has received a letter from his friend Tissot in France and is quite elated. He read it as we lay in bed, my bare inner thigh draped over his legs, my head on his shoulder, my golden hair splayed over his chest. The writing on the trifolded paper that Edgar held was in French, of course, though Tissot lives in London. I moved in to read it with Edgar, and as I did, my breast changed shape as it nestled into his chest. Edgar's eyes squinted into the paper, his friend Tissot's handwriting crisp and exact, which is how Edgar says his friend's painting is. I read with my face over Edgar's shoulder, something for which Mama always scolded me, but it is no issue for me and this man. Any excuse to keep our skin pressing into each other. The letter began as from any friend to another, *I send you my greetings from England and hope you are well, etc., etc.*

I turned from my lover and the letter from his friend and took the cartonette of raspberries from the night-table. I sat up in bed next to him, my breasts changing shape again, and I made no attempt to cover them with the sheets. Honestly, I was hoping he would set the letter aside. I fed him a raspberry, which he took on his lips at the side of his mouth whilst keeping his eyes on the letter. I gave myself a berry, the smooth-tense texture on my lips, the sweet-succulent eruption on my tongue. I gave him another which his lips fumbled, and it fell, and I rescued it from the sheets and put it to my own lips before selecting another from the cartonette and giving it to him as he turned over a page and continued reading. I fed him another raspberry and traced a finger on his chest. He was at the conclusion, the closing salutation ending at mid-page. My breath betrayed me, and our lips met with the taste of raspberries on them. He reached to put the letter on the night-table, but it missed and fell to the floor. And I offered the tense sweetness of a nipple.

Afterward, we spoke in the quiet eddy that follows the turbulent waters. The sky was scented by the smell of coal smoke and horses as the sounds of the city murmured faraway outside the windows. I was still astride him, where I had come to rest like debris from a storm. He spoke to the golden tresses he examined, holding them up and contemplating them.

'My friend Tissot has completed his work which he calls, 'Gentleman in a Railway Carriage,' and he is anxious for me to see it.'

I said nothing. Instead, my silence spoke for me.

'He is quite proud of it,' Edgar said to the yellow strands between his fingers. I answered with a facial expression and a nod that said, *Yes, is that so?* 'He thinks I should go back to Paris,' Edgar said finally, 'There will be an exhibition in March at the Salon, and he thinks I should be there. He says I should come as soon as I can. He thinks the painting of the Cotton Office would be the very thing and that I should hurry and finish it.'

All I could say was, "The painting of the Cotton Office is quite good.'

Edgar must have sensed my ill-ease with the talk of Paris and the thought of being without him, and he said, 'I don't want to leave without you. I won't.' Relieved, I kissed his cheek and moved from him and to his side. But he talked of Paris and fountains and monuments and the Tuileries Gardens and the smells of bread baking and coffee roasting. I confess here to you that it begins to appeal to me, a life with him and without a veil or the need for one and so I listened to him.

7 February 1873. Edgar sleeps now, as we have returned to Ursulines after the ball and have loved. Sleep does not come for me tonight, however, as I begin to fear that perhaps Mr. Teague's reach is as great as he says.

Earlier this evening, in our nest on Ursulines, Edgar and I prepared for the ball held tonight at the French Opera House. I held up my hair as he fastened my corset, and then I slipped on my dress, the light blue one with the gold trimmings. As I turned, pulling my hair from within the back of it, he said, 'Is it possible for you to get any more beautiful?'

'Oh, you Parisians, such a way with words,' I said, and I kissed him. I sat at the looking glass, aware of him watching my image in it as I put up my hair. I moved slowly, enjoying the artist's gaze, his appraisal. When I was done and my reflection turned her head this way and that, he came behind me and slipped his hands into the dress and the cups of the corset. I closed my eyes and exhaled and said, 'You'll undo everything, and I shall let you, if you persist.' But before I could sink (or rise) further, I pulled up his hands and kissed one and then the other. 'Well, I suppose we are ready,' I said with a deep breath.

Edgar looked absolutely at his best, *au currant* in an evening suit and four-in-hand tie. His image departed the looking glass and returned to it. 'And now, our masks,' he said, and he presented one to me. We placed them on our faces and laughed at their equal blankness, vividly coloured but expressionless.

We left our nest and descended the steps where, on the street, we hailed a carriage, though it was only a matter of a few blocks. Edgar wanted the grandeur of an entrance by carriage, as, I confess, did I. And, as you know, my little confidant, carriage rides hold a certain charm for us now. In the carriage, we kissed with our masks on, but finding it awkward, we removed them and kissed again. Our hands embraced as we looked out the windows at the recession of finely dressed men and women who, like us, were on their way to the Opera House and the ball. I put my head on Edgar's shoulder and watched as we passed them.

The driver let us out to a grand entrance on Royal Street, and we donned our masks and went up the stairs. Inside, the music had already begun, the floor teeming with dancers in disguises like us. The Grand March was played, and so Edgar and I faced each other, and it occurred to me that we had never danced before. The men and women separated and circled the floor, and my eyes strayed for him, looking for him as we women moved in our revolutions and the men did likewise. I was touched by a mild sense of panic until I recognized his benevolent, brown eyes before me in the openings of his mask. I began to relax again as the music moved us into a quadrille.

A man was in our group of eight, and, at once, there was something familiar about his height and the irregularity of his stride. We approached each other and then receded back, as called for by the dance, and then the other pairs did likewise. My eyes continued to follow his figure as we dancers moved about each other. The music called for *Le Cotillon*, and I found myself face to face with him again, this man with the limp, our faces masked, but the curl of a scar only half-concealed by his. Of course, my little confidant, by now I knew exactly who he was. I feigned missteps in our dance, and apologised in the little German I knew, making sure my accent was thick. 'You must be a Dutch gal,' he said in English, and his voice was unmistakable. *Ja*, I said, but I pretended not to understand the rest of his flirtatious nonsense.

The dance called for us to separate, and I adjourned to a quiet alcove, trying to quiet my breathing and slow my heart. I looked around for Edgar and saw him talking to two men, one of whom, from the reddish tinge of his receding hairline, I judged to be Mr. Prestidge, Uncle Michel's now former partner. I breathed deeply, and my composure slowly returned to me. The sconces flickered amber light, and I wished that the lamplight would darken further and that I might take Edgar and escape this place. But I sat in my quiet recess, and as I did, I heard two men talking.

One said, 'Howard, I can't understand a word these folks are saying, all this French jibber-jabber. You think that if they were Americans, they'd learn to speak English.' The other, Mr. Howard, replied, 'Sam, let me remind you that we're their guests tonight and that they do speak English, but only when they're conducting business. An enterprise such as ours needs all the friends it can get.' The music rose over their conversation, so I positioned my chair closer to the corner so that I could hear them. Their voices were now quite recognizable, though they seemed from another era, as remote as Greece and Rome. My ears searched, and I understood their conversation. Mr. Howard said, '—I tell you, Sam, she's at it again, this time right here in New Orleans.'

'Who?' my husband asked. I was close enough to smell his cigar, close enough, in fact, to hear him strike the match for it.

'You know who,' Mr. Howard said, 'Your former wife.'

My husband asked, 'Is this more of our humbug, Howard?' and Mr. Howard replied, 'No, Sam. This time it's bonafide. A woman, the proprietress of a dress shop on Canal, says that it was a lady who spoke perfect French.'

Mr. Howard paused to puff his cigar to life. When it was well-lit, he continued, 'Said her name was Paulina Teague and that she was married to a wealthy man down in St. Matthew.'

My husband said that was impossible, to which Mr. Howard replied that this time it was no humbug, and that Mrs. Teague had charged two very expensive ballgowns to Mr. Teague at the fancy establishment of a lady named Madame Olympe on Canal Street.'

Mr. Teague snorted, and I could see his hand tap an ash into the tray. From behind and to the side, I could just see the edge of his scar crawling out from under his mask. It wriggled as he said, 'Well, you and I both know that that can't be, Howard, old boy. It just can't be.'

'I'm telling you, Sam,' Mr. Howard said, 'The bill came in yesterday. Invoice signed by Paulina H. Teague.'

Mr. Teague said that this was a concern, then, that this couldn't possibly be Polly Teague, and that it had to be someone. I looked down on one of those gowns that Paulina H. Teague had charged, the light blue one, silk as blue as a robin's egg, trimmed in gold piping. Admittedly, she has very good taste. The next song began, and the men around the corner rose and went back to the ballroom without stating what their next move would be. Edgar passed by them and exchanged a casual greeting with them, and then came into my little alcove and pulled me up. We stole a kiss, though from within my mask, my eyes looked for my husband and his friend. All that was left where they had sat was the butt of my husband's cigar, smoldering in the ashtray.

'Take me home,' I whispered in Edgar's ear, putting my hand on his chest.

'Do you tire so quickly?' he asked with a grin, perhaps thinking that I wanted his hands in the cups of my corset again, and more, and that I could wait no longer. We gathered our coats from the valet, and as I put mine on, I glanced through the foyer into the adjacent ballroom. Among the throng of masked dancers, I recognized the lunging stride of a man who most certainly my husband, dancing with a woman whom I should wonder was Mrs. Parris. Edgar touched me on the small of my back, and I shivered and forgot about them instantly.

8 February 1873. Edgar and I rose early and returned to Esplanade Street under the usual pretense, that is, that he had risen early at his uncle's and come to Ursulines to fetch me. We arrived to hear someone playing a lovely nocturne and found that it was Tell, her fingers roaming the keyboard confidently as her eyes examined the opposite wall. She barely slowed as she called our names and gave us her cheek to receive our kisses. The children came downstairs and rushed Edgar and me, and we picked them up one after the other.

Mouche came down straightaway after them, looking rather bleary-eyed. She said that she and Mr. Bell had stayed late at the ball and had looked for Edgar and me. 'What a crowd!' she said, 'And such a convivial bunch. There was one man, a rather tall gentleman who gamely danced despite a pronounced limp. And what a flirt he was!'

I replied rather flatly what a remarkable fellow he must have been. Edgar and I adjourned to the back gallery where he set up his easel and, through the open door, we listened to Tell play in the parlour. The children played in the garden, taking turns swinging high on the swing and lavishing affection on Vasco who bore it patiently. Jo came and sat with me while Edgar worked, painting in colour for 'The Song Rehearsal.' I asked Jo where her Papa was today.

'He has gone to pay a call on Mme. Olivier,' she said, 'Madame is going to have a baby and Monsieur le Docteur says that she must remain home and in bed until it is time for it to come.' I told her that is what I have also heard, but Edgar said nothing and continued to fill in colour on his painting. The walls of the room in the painting, 'The Song Rehearsal,' were becoming yellow and brown, the molding and settees white, the piano a dark umber edging to black, and a shawl draped over a white chair emerged into red. Jo and I looked into the room in the painting where the song rehearsal was taking place, the Musson parlour. I asked Jo if she might read to us, Edgar and me, and she replied yes, and what might we like for her to read. 'Oh,' I said as I squinted one eye thoughtfully, 'Something from the Bible, perhaps.'

She ran to get the Musson Bible and sat with me and opened it. It fell to the eighth chapter of John, and she began reading. It was the story of the woman caught in adultery, a story I have heard all my life, but never in French and not since it might be a story about me. Jo's small voice merrily recounted the tale of the crowd of men armed with rocks and Jesus quietly drawing in the sand as the crowd asks what should be done with the woman. 'That is enough,' I said as cheerfully as I could, 'You read very well, mademoiselle.'

Edgar continued to paint quietly, and I noticed that he had reworked 'The Song Rehearsal' so that the two women who are singing are unmistakably Mme. Olivier. I recognized her red shawl painted onto the divan in the foreground. On the left, the expectant version of her raises her arm in song at the other Mme. Olivier, who stands by the piano and shields herself as if from an accusation or some other unwanted admonition. Rene looks to them both as he plays blithely.

Jo swung her legs and asked Edgar innocently, 'Cousin, what does *adulterie* mean?' He paused and thought, sipping from a cup of coffee. Then he made a small stroke of dark umber on the figure of Rene and said, 'Go ask your Papa.' Of course, my little confidant, I could have told her the meaning of *adulterie* as well.

9 February 1873. Sunday Mass, and I am aware that Rene and Tell sit, not together, but on opposite sides of their children in the pastel aroma of incense and the murmur of Latin. On the cue, we take to the kneeler and pray. I would pray for forgiveness, but I wouldn't know where to start, as I have neither the ability nor the intention of abandoning my sin. After Sunday dinner, I nap in the parlour, falling into the strange dream that Uncle Michel was rejected by the Linnaens and Edgar has painted the portraits of the Teague girls. I wake to find that little Odile is nestled into my side on the settee.

10 February 1873. My hand only now has stopped trembling so that I may write this. I was giving Carrie her piano lesson when I heard someone ascend the steps outside. The person rang the bell at the door, the friendly little jingle of it distracting Carrie, and I made her laugh by playing the high E note with each ring. Miss Petinque answered the door and exchanged greetings with our visitor. The door opened with an advancing shape of afternoon light. Carrie and I began again on the piece we were working on 'Georgie's Waltz' from the children's lesson book, 'Eight Little Scamps.' In the looking glass of the music room, I saw Miss Petinque take the hat and coat of our visitor and place them on the hall table. And then I recognized the scarred cheek above the beard. It was Mr. Teague. My husband.

My first inclination was to run up the stairs, but there was no way I could do so, as he was between me and them, as also were my veil and bonnet. Carrie blithely, carefully plodded through her lesson, oblivious to the visitor. I told her to continue, that I only needed a little air and that she sounded marvelous, which was charitable, as she is only six and her playing is what one would expect for a six-year-old. I hastily walked through the library, where Didi was engaged in embroidery. She raised her face from her needle and thread as I rushed past her and said, 'Need a little air.'

She rose on the message from Miss Petinque that we had a visitor, a Mr. Teague from St. Matthew Parish, enquiring about his former wife, Paulina Teague. Edgar was painting in his room-atelier, typically absorbed, and I rushed past him as well, gaining the relative sanctuary of the rear gallery. I sat in a chair and looked away from the door, encapsulated in fear and desperately wishing I had my veil. There was conversation from the front of the house which I could not discern. And then I heard the lurching stride of Mr. Teague across the floor of the house, this sacred place, this place of happiness, and then the conversation between Didi and my husband, in English. How strange it was to hear her speak it, she has only the trace of an accent. The door was open, and I was terrified that he would come onto the porch and see me, but it was too late for me to go further.

'And this, sir, is my cousin Edgar,' Didi said, 'He is an artist, as you see,' and then she asked Edgar, in French, 'Monsieur wants to know if you know anything of a Paulina, or Polly, Teague.'

Edgar seemed a little exasperated at being interrupted but politely shook his head and said, directly to Mr. Teague, 'Non, monsieur.' Mr. Teague extended his hand to Edgar, but Edgar showed him his paint splotched hands and said, '*Pardonez-moi, monsieur.*'

My husband grunted his familiar grunt, and then said, 'That's a purty good picture, there, mizzure.' If Edgar replied, I did not hear it on the back gallery. Perhaps he didn't understand Mr. Teague's accent.

My husband's steps clumped toward the open door. He could not have been more than ten feet away from me. He paused and spoke as I breathed deeply and looked out over the garden to the Oliviers' house across the field.

'Tell your cousin the artist that the gardens are very beautiful,' Mr. Teague said, 'He should paint them.'

Didi did not relay this message, but only said, 'Perhaps I shall, sir.'

Mr. Teague let out a rather complicated sneeze, and, when he had gathered himself, said, 'Very beautiful, ma'am, but my hay fever has a time with the scent.' Didi said that was certainly a shame for him, and, with that, she escorted him to the front door. Their conversation, pleasantries about weather and carnival season, receded with them.

I cautiously rose from the porch and went through Edgar's studio, aware now that he had been working on a painting of a woman sitting in a theatre box, a woman with golden hair whom I am sure is destined to be me when finished. Thank goodness it is not even half-way complete. Mr. Teague would have easily recognized his wife. I listened from the library for Didi's farewell to our guest.

'I am sorry we could not help you, sir,' her voice said from the front of the house, 'If I hear of a Paulina, or Polly, Teague, I shall send word to you at this address on St. Charles, as you wish.' The door closed, and Didi returned to her embroidery in the library.

'Who was that?' I asked innocently as I returned from the rear gallery.

'A Mr. Teague from St. Matthew,' Didi said, 'He was looking for his wife. Or former wife, rather.' She handed me the calling card, *Chas. T. Howard, St. Charles, New Orleans, La.*, and said to me as I looked at it, 'You are from St. Matthew, Alice. I should have thought to introduce you two so that he could ask you. Are you familiar with a Mrs. Teague?'

I summoned just enough breath to reply, 'I have heard the name, but that is all. Let me go upstairs. I might catch a glimpse of him.' I raced up the stairs on legs that even now tremble, and I peered through the lace curtains. Mr. Teague was standing in front of his carriage while his driver, a young negro man, waited. He examined the front of the house, and I doubled the lace curtain to conceal myself further. He took one last look at the house and got back into the carriage. He said a word to the driver, who gave a small snap of his whip and the carriage surged forward and bore my husband away down Esplanade. Perhaps Mr. Teague is correct. No one can long elude him, and nothing escapes him.

Sammy, 1982

It took Mr. Dupuy a little under an hour to make two new sapphire pendants, the stones made of blue glass from a bottle of medicine used for constipation. He held the trio of pendants up on a dowel for Sammy to inspect. The two replacements weren't replicas. They were duplicates.

"Here's the original," Mr. Dupuy said. "Now don't tell anyone I made these for you. In fact, don't ask me to gift wrap them in a box with my name on them. Just put them in your pocket."

"Don't worry about that," Sammy said. "Anybody asks me, I got them at Cato's. I'll come back at Christmas to get something nice for the missus." Mr. Dupuy winked at him and shook his hand.

When Sammy returned to Mount Teague, he put the original pendant in the middle drawer of his desk next to the diary, and he searched the other drawers. He had hoped that perhaps he might find the keys to the safe or some other old artifact, but everything in them belonged to this century. The keys were useless now, anyway.

He looked through *The Complete Works of Edgar Degas* and came to *A Cotton Office in New Orleans.* He recognized Uncle Michel seated in the foreground of it, a sad, bespectacled widower left with hands full of cotton and a heart full of grief. Tante Odile had been dead a little over a year when the painting was done, and his nephew's young belle, an English girl he called *la fille d'or*, the golden girl, had brightened his spirits.

At dinner that night, Sammy watched his daddy eat at the same table where he had eaten thousands of meals with Sammy's mother, sometimes just the two of them and sometimes with family crowded around. His mother was gone now, sleeping in the Teague vault in the distant grove of cedars. His father bore the same loneliness as Michel Musson, the loneliness of one who loses half of himself and is forced to carry on and make do with that. Though Sammy's daddy might complain of quarreling daughters, politicians, football coaches, and young-people-these-days, he never complained of the loneliness he felt. It was too intense to talk about, too painful to mention. But that look of loneliness—there was no mistaking it. It was the identical look, subtle and somber, that Uncle Michel wore in the painting his nephew had done, *A Cotton Office in New Orleans.* The countenance of a widower.

Sammy helped Betsy in the kitchen, part of their marriage-dance, an intimate ritual of plates and running water and soap. She hummed the songs that he knew would have French words if she sang them. Sometimes she did. When they were done, they put their hands on each other's hips and kissed, their palm prints leaving spots that were barely wet.

He went out into the blue-black night of the side-yard, where a fire blazed in the sugar kettle. His daddy took a log from the woodpile and tossed it in. It fell with an eruption of sparks that cackled and rose among the tree limbs. Sammy handed his daddy a beer, and they opened them and threw the caps in the fire. They took a few sips before Sammy could no longer hold the news.

"Look what I found," he said, and he pulled the pendant from his coat pocket. His daddy pulled his glasses from his coat pocket and put them on. He focused on the pendant.

"Where?"

"In the back of a drawer in the old desk. Secret compartment."

His daddy couldn't contain his look of surprise.

"Well I'll be," he murmured as he looked at it, through his glasses, over his glasses, and then through his glasses again.

"I had it appraised," Sammy added.

His daddy looked from the pendant to his son, waiting for the announcement of some fantastic sum.

"It's glass."

"Glass?"

"Glass. Blue glass."

And then his daddy shook, and his mouth opened wide, and he began laughing. He took off his glasses and laughed for five solid minutes, squinting, struggling for air, pressing the pendant, worthless and coveted, into his forehead as he shook with seismic laughter. Father and son laughed into the fire and the night sky and the whirl of sparks and cinders.

"So I. So I," Sammy fought for the breath to tell the rest. "So I." Father and son were red-faced as they snickered together. "So I had the man make. I had him make." He pressed his palms into his eyes. He could barely say it. He feared he would expire with laughter before he could get it all out.

"Two. More."

He pulled them from his other pocket. The yard was a whirlwind of laughter, a hurricane of guffaws. Deep laughter from throats whose muscles ached at having to give it up, this sacred laughter.

"Here," Trey said as he held out his hand and wiped his eyes. Sammy handed the two identical pendants to his daddy.

"How much do I owe you, son?"

"Twenty bucks."

Another eruption of laughter soared with the fire in the old sugar kettle. Sammy thought his daddy would split in two from laughter. He didn't tell his daddy they had been made from a Milk of Magnesia bottle. Any more laughter and his daddy would have died. He was sure of it. He would tell him later.

When they had recovered, Trey Teague told his son, "This solves a lot of problems. Life just got a lot easier for this ol' boy."

They raised their bottles and clinked them together and finished their beers.

"Well, Daddy, let me go in and help mama get these children to bed." He threw his bottle in the fire and went inside. As he walked through the door, Betsy handed him the books the girls had picked out for him to read.

"That must've been some joke you tol' your daddy out there," Betsy said.

He kissed her cheek and went upstairs. From the central hallway, he chuckled, and then his voice called back through the house, "Yes it was." And the stairs squeaked with his footsteps. Upstairs, he read to two shampoo-scented, damp-headed little girls and kissed them goodnight.

The next day, Trey Teague composed two identical notes, "*I want you to have this, just don't tell your sister. I'm sure she would be jealous.*" Then he put them in fancy boxes and mailed one to Marilyn and one to Charlotte, an act worthy of a Nobel Peace Prize.

As Trey Teague headed to the post office, Sammy adjourned to his study. He thought of putting the original pendant back on Mrs. Pongeaux, but he was afraid his sisters might see it, if they were to visit, so he put it back into the false compartment. Then he opened the diary, pausing to chuckle one more time.

Alice, 1873

11 February 1873. I arrived again this morning on Esplanade to the delighted shouts and small embraces of the children. Edgar was already upstairs preparing to paint Tell. His easel was set up before her as she waited whilst he went downstairs to fetch his palette and brushes. She wore the same grey dress with black spots and sash, and her eyes were blank under arching eyebrows, eyes that seemed to be looking for something that she could not find. She sat with her hands in her lap and looked away into the light from the window that illuminated her face and neck and the back of the settee. As she heard my steps reach the top of the stairs, she smiled into the infinite distance and said, 'Ah, Alice, *bon matin,*' and she gave me her cheek to kiss. Edgar came up with his palette, and we met at the top of the stairs. Our small greeting-kiss wavered toward a more involved kiss until I broke from it and excused myself to go down and get the children started on their lessons. Miss Petinque had cleared the dishes and set out a new linen cover, and the children were rounded up to come and sit for their lessons. We began, and there were never any children so single-minded about the process of learning.

I wish the same could be said of their instructor, for every time there was a knock on the door, I scampered up the stairs, where Edgar would look up from his painting, or I fled into the library, where Uncle Michel would look up from his newspaper. But I could not help it. I cowered with every sound of footsteps on the porch, with every passing of a shadow in the window. The laundress returning the clean and taking the soiled. The milkman. The coal-man. Every knock was like a hammer blow, every jingle of the doorbell an accusation.

The children pursued their lessons untroubled by shadows and footsteps, and we concluded at noon. I told Edgar that I was returning to my apartment, and he stole a kiss from me and said that he would be by later. Tell smiled, either at the message or the mere whisper in which it was delivered, both a small intimacy between two people in love.

On my way back to Ursulines, I stopped by the post office and found there a letter from the Teague girls. Jenny writes the majority of the letter, speaking of London and the shops and the Thames, which she says is ten times as wide as Bayou Lafourche but that the Seine is much smaller and a greenish colour and is crossed by bridges that are both old and beautiful. Ida's penmanship is less refined than Jenny's, and she mentions snow on the ground in England and also in France. Granny Teague is strict, she says, but not as strict as her father and she is able to walk about all day with no limp whatsoever. Lucy writes a single sentence in the comic hand of a small child, 'We saw the Loove,' and she draws a pair of pictures, two simple circle-shaped faces in rectangles, our portraits. Under them she has labeled, 'me' and 'you.' And then it is the writing of Jenny's fine hand again, telling me that they are all quite taken with Paris and shall remain there for another month or two and then proceed to Geneva and Milan. She says that she and her sisters miss me terribly, but that it is noble that I should want to stay with their father. Nevertheless, she says, they hope to see me soon, here or there.

How I miss them, once I remember to think about them. They believe that I am with Mr. Teague, and Mr. Teague believes that I am with them. And the spider steps lightly upon her web.

12 February 1873. We rose from the same bed this morning but left for different places. Edgar went to the American side of town to make some sketches for a portrait of a woman, and I rose and went to the house on Esplanade. I thought we might have lessons in the garden, but then I became worried that if Mr. Teague returned, he might see me well before I saw him and recognize me by my figure or mannerisms, veil or not. The girls were quite taken with the idea of lessons outdoors and were disappointed when I said that it looked like rain. Jo said that it was only partly cloudy, and she was right, but in the end, lessons were held in the dining room. And it is a shame, as it was a day which enjoyed the lingering kiss of spring.

Midmorning, a stout, red-headed man named Mr. Ogden arrived with a knock on the door. It startled me and I dropped the book I was holding. My veil is always at hand now and when there is a knock on the door or a bell-jingle, I quickly put it on, even when I am indoors. Jo asked me why, and I told her that sometimes I am shy around gentleman I don't know. She said, 'But Mam'selle, it's only Mr. Ogden, Uncle Will's partner.'

'Yes,' I said, 'But I don't know him well,' and I kept behind my little curtain as Miss Petinque showed him to the library, where Uncle Michel sat and drank coffee in his white shirt and braces ('suspenders,' rather, here in America. Three years hence and I cannot break from the English term for them). Mr. Bell's brother-in-law Mr. Witherspoon arrived, and then several others. The knocking fists and jingling bell were becoming excruciating. Then Rene and Edgar's other brother, Achille, came in without knocking, and the sudden, unexpectedness of their appearance was perhaps even more frightening. Several more men arrived, raising the bubble of conversation in the library to an absolute boil, and I pronounced lessons done for the day. The girls joined Virginie and the younger children in the garden, welcomed by the barking and prancing of Vasco. As the number of men in the library increased, so did the stirring noise of their conversation behind the closed door. I tried to make out the voices and the topics, but it was all a distant rumble and hum.

Until I heard my name. My real name. Teague. I approached the door and leaned toward it. Mr. Ogden's leathery voice was the most prominent, and I believe it was he who mentioned my husband's name. 'Things are coming to a head, I tell you, Mr. Musson, sir,' Mr. Ogden said, 'The election was stolen by these carpetbaggers, and I fear we shall not be able to retrieve it except by force.'

'Come now, sir, haven't we learned enough from the late war?' Uncle Michel said in English, which was remarkably crisp, so much so that I did not recognize it as him at first. As is the case with Didi, I have seldom heard him speak it.

'I beg your pardon, sir,' someone said, possibly Mr. Ogden, 'but what we have learned from it is that we were not made by God to be subjugated to the negro. Enough is enough, wouldn't you say? We cannot have our rights trampled by the Yankee and his negro ally. What would we become? A race of mongrels?' Voices rose in acclamation, *yes, that's right, hear-hear.*

There were then some profane utterances, and Uncle Michel's voice said, 'I will thank you not to speak in that manner in my house, sir,' and whoever had said it apologized.

'Now, what of this man Teague?' someone else asked.

'Veteran of the late war,' Mr. Ogden's voice said, 'A clear thinker and a man of nerve. He's been able to persuade the troops to quit St. Matthew, though he says that he was perfectly willing to fight it out, if it had come to it.'

Someone said that he sounded like the kind of man we could use here, and there was more acclamation, and then Mr. Ogden spoke again, 'I say we give them to the end of the month, and if there is no respite from this tyranny, then, by God, we shall take back our government if it means fists, bullets, and blood.'

'Speak for yourself on that one,' someone said, and I am quite sure it was Uncle Michel's voice, 'We've had enough bloodshed.'

A hand touched my shoulder and I pushed a shriek back in my mouth with my palm. I turned, and there was Tell smiling blithely.

'I don't suppose they're discussing carnival,' she said softly.

'No,' I replied, and we adjourned to the parlour and played duets on the piano until the men left, gathering coats, capes, and top hats as they went, sent off by Uncle Michel in white shirt and braces. Suspenders, rather.

13 February 1873. This morning, we rose and threw open the windows to a day that is more like spring than winter. 'Like a summer day in Paris!' Edgar exclaimed to the sunlight and the rooftops, 'If it were like this year-round, one would be tempted to stay here.' He turned to me and told me what I already knew. 'But I am a Parisian. In my heart I am, and I always will be.'

I said nothing. The mere thought of it sets me melancholic. He turned from the windows and said, 'Tissot expects me to be leaving this week. I didn't tell him that I wouldn't be.' He looked out over the rooftops to the masts and smokestacks of the ships in the river, ships that could, anyone of them, take him away from me. I rose and embraced him from behind, and he put his hands over mine. At last, I said meekly, 'You should let him know, I suppose.' He stared out the window. One of the smokestacks bellowed a bass note, I believe a throaty low C.

'Yes, I should,' he said, 'To even be considered for the Salon, I will need to be there. But the truth is, I don't want to think about a Paris that doesn't have you in it, nor will I return to one.'

If he awaits an answer as to my return to Paris, I cannot give him one. I have become quite certain that Mr. Teague would find me even there.

14 February 1873. St. Valentine's Day, and Edgar presented me with a black velvet choker with an ivory medallion with the embossed head of Venus on it. He placed it on my neck, and it contrasted darkly to the paleness of my nakedness. He kissed me there.

'I have nothing for you, monsieur,' I murmured facetiously and rather coyly, and Edgar replied, 'How can a woman who is everything for me have nothing for me?' And then we celebrated the day of love and romance in a most fitting and simple fashion.

After we exhausted ourselves, we fought the urge to lay abed all morning, and finally we rose and made our morning toilette and returned to Esplanade for Edgar to paint and for the children to receive their lessons. As we approached the house, we caught a glimpse of Rene opening the garden gate, headed to the Oliviers'. He carried with him a bouquet of roses, intense red mouths and lips set on dark green stems. Edgar, who had been talking excitedly about ideas he has for a new composition, fell silent and stayed so until we reached the house.

We entered the house to the shouts of children and the bark of Vasco, who was chased out of the house by Virginie and Johanna. As Miss Petinque went to fetch a mop for his muddy tracks, Edgar went to his atelier to get his easel and palette.

Tell was sitting on a settee in the parlour holding a single red rose. She heard my footsteps and looked up and out and greeted me, more absently than usual. She held the rose in front of her as if it were a small wildflower, the kind that used to grow on the Down in Surrey, the kind we would string together as girls to make necklaces. She put it to her nose and made no attempt to smile, as if it no longer had any scent or perhaps never did at all. She closed her eyes and then opened them again, and I wondered if she ever opened them with the hope that they would suddenly see again. Her fingertips lightly traced the silky red folds of the rose, her mind trying to see its shape.

'Alice, am I still beautiful?' she asked with wandering eyes. She closed them once more and put the bud to her nose and withdrew it. 'Do you think men still find me attractive?'

I told her, 'I am sure of it,' and it was the truth. She handed me the rose as Edgar returned to the parlour to paint her, and I went to the dining room to begin the children's lesson.

15 February 1873. A day spent in idyll high above Ursulines. Edgar painted in a speckled smock whilst I read the papers and had tea. A roaring fire would have also been nice, but the weather was simply too warm for it. The *Picayune* said that one legislature has passed a law prohibiting the other from collecting taxes. An absurdity worthy of a child's nonsense rhyme. I tired of the newspaper and wrote a letter to Jenny telling her of the events of Mount Teague and that her father's health is excellent, and the cane begins to sprout, and Mrs. Parris came for a visit and I closed telling her that I miss my girls madly and hope to see them either in Europe or in the mountains of Virginia this summer. And then I asked myself, shall I ever see them again? But of course, I did not write it. The letter was a sham, anyway.

16 February 1873. We rose early on Ursulines and returned to Esplanade, repeating the complicated ritual of appearing to sleep under two separate roofs. After church and the carriage ride home, dinner awaited us, the servants taking coats and hats and bonnets whilst parents told the children to wash hands. Conversation moved about the table with the dishes of grillades and maque choux and haricots. Rene said that a pianist, a negro called Blind Tom, shall be playing at the Masonic Hall every night this week and that the *Picayune* says that he is quite a musician and can voice any sound given him to mimic. I could not help but to look at poor blind Tell who sat next to her husband as he made his pronouncement. Really, it was quite a callous thing to say and was followed by a silence peppered with silverware clicking on porcelain.

Mouche broke it with a change of subject. 'The *Picayune* also says that Mme. Alabau on Conti has all types of costumes,' Mouche said, 'You don't want to be at carnival without a mask. A veil simply will not do!'

You have no idea, I thought.

There was a discussion of costumes and masks and balls, and Didi dutifully reminded us that Lent follows Carnival and one should also give thought to what penance one is take up. Jo said that she shall give up sweets and pray the Rosary every day, and then Carrie said that she would do so as well. Pierre stumbled for something to give up, but Didi said that he was excused from *Carême* (Lent) because he was still little. Desert was served, an apricot glacée, and Uncle Michel said that with such deserts as Miss Petinque could prepare, that would be a penance to give them up, indeed.

After dinner, Edgar rose and playfully used his napkin as a matador's cape as Pierre rushed it and the family shouted, 'Olé!' After a few playful passes, Edgar told Pierre to run and play, and that perhaps Pierre could be the matador and Vasco the bull. Pierre took the napkin with him out the back door, shouting for the dog.

Edgar and I adjourned to the back gallery where he set up his easel, and I watched the children play in the garden. Inside, Jo played the piano with her mother. The girl has quite improved, though the difference between her play and that of her mother is still altogether noticeable, Tell being so much more accomplished. Edgar worked again on the scene from the Cotton Office, working on his brother's figure, slouched in a chair and reading *L'Abeille du Nouvelle Orleans.*

'Rene is a cad, sometimes,' Edgar said, 'Tell puts up with him with the patience of a saint. But what choice does she have, a blind widow? What are her prospects?'

I said, 'Certainly they still love each other.'

'Yes,' Edgar replied, 'but I don't think they love each other like we love each other.'

I had no reply to this. I don't think any two people have ever loved each other like Edgar and I do. But perhaps all lovers think thusly.

'I must go by memory now,' he said to the Cotton Office that was taking shape on the canvas, 'now that Uncle Michel's office is closed, I mean.' Edgar shrugged and dotted something. "It is no great issue. It is how I tend to do it, anyway. From memory."

'It is coming along splendidly,' I said, 'I can see the movement in it, hear the men discussing things.'

Edgar pointed to the canvas with the handle of his brush and then dipped it into a small puddle of umber on his palette. 'Tissot thinks that Agnew may be able to sell it to Mr. Cotterel.'

'Yes, I remember them from Manchester,' I said, before I caught myself, 'Or rather, I have heard of them. Read about them in the newspapers, I mean.'

Of course, my little confidant, Sir William Agnew is an art dealer and Mr. Cotterel is one of the mill barons in Manchester. I recall that they are two men who go about the coal-hazed town and its belching smokestacks in fine chaises with elegantly dressed wives whilst children push spindles in the huffing machinery of the mills.

Edgar touched the canvas with his brush again, a small spot of colour, and it changed everything about the picture, the balance, the hue, the movement of the subjects, everything. In the painting of the Cotton Office, Achille leans onto the windowsill on the left. Edgar has captured his nonchalance, like a man with the mannerisms of a cat. Mr. Prestidge and Mr. Livaudais work grimly as if trying to keep the business from foundering on the rocks. Uncle Michel examines a bit of cotton in his hands, and I see quiet dejection captured in his expression. He looks so sad, staring into a handful of cotton, so much like Papa, defeated by the world but still forced to live in it. And how sad Papa would be to see me now, stripped of all virtue, sadder than a handful of pale-white, unsold cotton. I was thinking thusly when Edgar's voice startled me.

'—and so, I told Tissot that I would be leaving for Paris last week, that I was going to catch a train for the east, and sail from New York. He's afraid I'll miss the exhibition in Paris in March.' Edgar looked around for a second and then leaned over to kiss me a quick peck on the lips. 'Of course, it was never my intention of leaving on that train.'

'I'm afraid that I keep you from your advancement,' I said. He paused from his work, and his brown eyes, as sincere as they are languid, looked to me. 'I cannot bear the thought of a Paris without you,' he said.

'And I cannot bear the thought of anywhere without you,' I replied, and I wanted to kiss him again, slowly, generously, and would have, but Didi came out onto the gallery.

'Well, Edgar, your brother says that Mme. Olivier's day is close at hand,' she said, 'And he has offered to let her little one, Lou-Lou, play here when the baby arrives, so that Madame may rest with the new one.'

'My brother seems very concerned with her,' Edgar said, mixing umber and red and yellow with a palette knife, and I recognized the sharp-edged precision in his voice when something angers him.

'Rene says that Madame's husband is very driven,' Didi replied, 'He says that M. Olivier neglects her and his daughter.'

'I don't know enough of him to say one way or the other,' Edgar said, 'But it sounds as if he is only trying to earn a living for his family. Hard work is not a sin.'

'Rene says that Monsieur takes time to march with Komus,' Didi said, and I couldn't tell if she was taking up for Edgar's brother or was simply enjoying the argument for its own sake.

Edgar touched a thin line along the windowsill in the painting. He kept his eyes on it as he asked Didi, 'Isn't he allowed a bit of recreation?' Didi replied that certainly Mme. Olivier becomes quite lonely or something of that sort.

Didi does not see as Edgar sees, but he is more acquainted with the ways of both the world and men. But she and I sat quietly and watched as children shouted and Vasco barked and Jo lifted and tucked her legs in the swing that swung like a pendulum from a limb. And Edgar used darker colours to finish the figure of Rene in his uncle's Cotton Office, his brother's figure sitting slouched in a chair, reading the newspaper, whilst his uncle's livelihood slowly sinks.

17 February 1873. Today's *Picayune* says that the fire at M. Toulande's killed three men who were living there. One of them was M. Toulande himself. What a horrible death, to perish in flames.

This morning the children were set about their lessons, and I adjourned for a moment to sit with Edgar, who worked again on the Cotton Office. It is nearing completion, as if emerging from a cloud, or, ironically, a nest of cotton.

'I may be able to sell this one, and for a good price,' Edgar said, 'Tissot liked the sound of it, as I have described it to him. He says that it would be of great interest to someone like Mr. Cotterel or another of the mill owners.' I told Edgar that one day his paintings shall be in the Louvre and in the homes of collectors, and that I was sure of it, and with that, I kissed his temple, my lips lingering there. The smell of oil paints has become an aphrodisiac for me.

'For now,' Edgar said, 'I would be happy to be shown in the main gallery of the Salon, rather than some back hallway.'

I said that certainly his work shall be there, trying to make it sound undoubtable.

'If that comes to pass, say you, too, shall be there!' he replied, 'Then we shall stroll the galleries arm-in-arm and look at them. And I will show you the places I sat before my easel and copied the masters. What days they were!'

He put down his brush and put his arms around my waist. 'Just think how we shall be, two sets of old bones tottering down the sidewalk by the green water of the Seine, under the changing leaves of the trees in the Tuileries.'

'Yes,' I said, though in all candour, I cannot allow myself the luxury of such reverie. Just then, Jo appeared at the backdoor and said she had finished her lesson. She asked if she should practice her piano now. I moved Edgar's hands away from my waist and said, 'Yes, play that selection from *Madame Angot* you play so well.' And she did, and it was rather well-done. Truly, she has gone from merely competent to lovely.

I reclined and listened and thought as Edgar resumed painting: What if I left with Edgar, to France, and became Alice Degas? Would my aching conscience be soothed? Or would my Conscience whistle and shout more than it does now, bringing new charges against me, charges of bigamy? And would that path eventually lead to madness? Do both paths lead there? And would my husband find me, even there? He has come quite close to finding me here. Perhaps it is only a matter of time, and I would be better off fleeing.

18 February 1873. Edgar has finished the Cotton Office and has left it to dry in his room-atelier on Esplanade. He spent the rest of the morning sketching Mr. Bell's army uniform of the late war, a grey thing with elaborate piping on the sleeves. There is a rusty stain on one of the cuffs, possibly the blood of a dying comrade, though Mr. Bell never mentions anything of it, and perhaps that is the way of those who were there and endured it all.

Carrie and I practised arithmetic by using paper dolls, as I remember doing as a girl with Mama. I set Jo to reading to Pierre, so that both might feel useful. Pierre is at the age that he simply must be included with his older sister and his cousin, and though his letters are crude, fat vowels and backwards consonants, they are still far superior to my husband's, both in number and in quality. Herr Gardener worked all morning in the gardens, and I thought of Mr. Luther at Mount Teague. Certainly, he prepares his as well. The azaleas must be blooming, the camellias past their time. And the sugarcane must be almost knee-high by now.

At noon, with the children's lessons completed for the day, Tell said that she felt like getting out and asked if I would accompany her. 'I am in a corset and crinolette again, and I must get used to wearing them,' she whispered to me so that Edgar would not hear, and then she asked him, 'Cousin, we're going to town. Would you like to join us?'

He was looking over the sketches he had done, and he spoke without looking up from them, 'I have a woman coming to sit for a portrait.' I felt a pang of jealousy.

'I thought you were of a mind not to take commissioned portraits,' I said, and he must have noticed the voice in which it was rendered. Perhaps our love is at that level, that depth, the tone of our voices begins to carry such a weight with each other.

'Let me show you her picture,' he said, shuffling through the sketches. He took me through the sheaf of drawings of his subject, a woman well into her fifties. I was relieved to find her quite a bit older and rather plain. As he showed them to me he said, 'She wants to appear as she did when she was a young woman, and she is willing to pay, and so I bowed and said, 'As you wish, madame.' Edgar seemed to be making light of something that bothered him, as if, instead of an artist, he had been treated as a chimneysweep or a stable hand or any other hired man. We looked through the sketches and it seemed that with each one, age was melting away from her and beauty was adhering to her, as she asked for revision after revision.

'Will it be difficult for you? To paint her younger?' I asked.

'Such magic?' Edgar shrugged his shoulders without looking away from the sketches. 'Not for a magician like me. Besides, hard times drive a hard bargain,' he said, 'I also have several veterans of the late war lined up. If you paint one veteran, then word gets out and you must paint another. It is easy, quick work. Paint the same uniform and paint a different head each time. And it pays well.'

Tell and I left him and walked down to Rampart, slowly along the banquette, arm-in-arm. We would approach a place where a tree root bulged the path, and without me telling her, she would raise her step to clear it. At Rampart, her ears seemed to see the mule as it clopped forward with the omnibus. When it stopped, we ascended the step and sat down together. She smiled into the breeze that our motion stirred.

'He seems to be trying to be cheerful about it,' Tell said as the houses drifted by. I asked her what she meant, and she replied, 'Painting portraits. But I know he detests it. Before, he would only do it for family.' The mule's hooves went silent, and we stopped to collect a passenger at St. Peter. When we moved forward, Tell leaned and whispered, 'Edgar pays my husband's debts, now that my father can't do it.'

I didn't know what to say to her intimation, so I said only, 'I had no idea.'

'It is very important for Edgar to do the honourable thing,' she said, her voice rising out of a whisper.

She and I alighted from the Rampart car at the juncture with Canal. A man in a bowler hat said, 'Watch your step Madame, and Mademoiselle,' and then we moved arm-in-arm down the banquette. On the corner of Dryades, two barbers passed the time between customers, one sitting in a chair reading the newspaper, the other standing by the door. Both were waiting patiently for hair to grow, much as planters wait for the cane to grow. Down Canal Street, the statue of Mr. Clay, the Great Compromiser, stood small at the other end, either welcoming people to the city or defending it. Or, from his posture—his hands are at his side—perhaps he is surrendering the idea of compromise.

'Alice,' Tell said as we moved along with the crowd on the banquette, 'I was wondering. How did an Englishman like your father end up growing sugarcane in Louisiana?'

I was suddenly struck by the absurdity of it. I paused, and I fancied she could hear me take a deep and deliberate breath. 'Oh, he. He. He inherited it. From an old uncle,' I said.

'How fortunate for him,' Tell said, 'Or unfortunate, given the summers here, compared to England.'

'Yes, he was a fortunate man,' I said, 'Is, rather.'

'I hear it is hard work, and luck is needed in addition to it. To be successful at cane farming, I mean,' she said. I was afraid that she might ask more questions regarding my father and cane farming and St. Matthew Parish when we came upon Mme. Alabau's costume shop, and so I said, 'Oh, Tell, let us stop here. Edgar and I are thinking of dressing as King Louis and Marie Antoinette for carnival.'

'Oh, Alice, he must love you so!' she smiled, 'For a man of his reserve to don the mask for carnival, he must love you dearly!' And we entered the shop and I looked at the rows of masks, shelf after shelf of false identities.

19 February 1873. And there, so it is done. In a moment of weakness, in that breathless moment of ecstasy, I agreed to return to Paris with Edgar, telling him, yes, yes, I would, yes, as my body contorted in rapture and my soul heaved with bliss. Yes, yes, a thousand times, yes. Afterward, he asked me if I really meant it. I believe he said it facetiously, as my passion made it quite emphatic that I would go. And, of course, I could not withdraw it, nor, at the heart of it, did I want to.

'Yes,' I said, 'but only until after Mme. Olivier has had her baby and fully convalesced, April, perhaps. The children could use some constancy with regards to their studies. And when we get to Paris, we shall look for my father and sisters.'

Or pretend to, rather. By then, my Jenny and the girls and Mrs. Teague will have quit Paris for Italy. And then perhaps I can invent one last falsehood for Edgar, that my father has perished at sea on the return home or some similar mishap. Or simply vanished like Polly Teague, abandoning family and debt. Falsehoods: I have become quite proficient with them.

The Teague girls would be another matter. How could I explain their absence to Edgar? Would Edgar want to visit them, or have them visit, when I am Alice Degas? It would not be possible, and so the curtain would have to fall on them as well. And that sets my heart melancholy, though that emotion is overwhelmed by the love I feel for Edgar and the rapture of its expression.

20 February 1873. In the lazy morning light of a day that pondered the idea of spring, Edgar and I talked of Paris again. I find that I begin to allow myself the enjoyment of thinking upon it. I only need a month or two to pass for the Teague girls, and my mother-in-law, to quit Paris for Italy and so avoid any chance encounter there.

Edgar has been nothing but giddy since I agreed that I would come with him. He talks unceasingly of his artist friends, and I tell him that I cannot wait to see Paris and to meet them. There is someone named Manet, and this fellow Tissot, of whom he has spoken before, and a Mme. Morisot and her daughters. There are several others, but he rattled their names with such glee that I had no chance to hear or remember them.

'Surely they shall be as enchanted with you as I am,' he said, and then he kissed me, on the lips and then my neck. Then this man, who is normally rather taciturn, said, 'And we will have to send word for your father to meet us in Paris, or take the train and meet them in Lyon, if he prefers. We have so much to discuss, your father and I. So much so that I shall have to work more on my English!'

Of course, that is a discussion that need never take place. My mind twirls, working like the mechanical looms in the mills of Miles Platting, thinking of what I hope shall be my final falsehood, one that must be my masterpiece, a lie to eclipse all others. Perhaps I shall tell him that my family has been lost at sea or buried by an avalanche in the Alps or perished in a train wreck in the Carolinas, anything suitable. For when I am Madame Degas. Certainly Mr. Teague could never find me there, in Paris, an ocean away and under the name, Alice Degas.

Could he?

The notion that I should forget all this madness with Edgar has long since passed. It is much too late for it now. The heart that beats beneath this bodice and corset breaks with the truth, so I ignore it, knowing that I shall remember it always, until my dying breath, come what may. It cannot be helped.

21 February 1873. Today, whilst I was out, Edgar had a sitter come to Ursulines, another of the veterans of the late war, coming to ensure that a measure of his immortality is committed to canvas. There are perhaps six or eight portraits along the base of the walls of our nest now, many of them different veterans, all wearing Mr. Bell's grey uniform. I find it unnerving that they watch us as we partake in the love act, so Edgar has turned them away and to the wall.

As Edgar prepared for yet another veteran to come and sit this morning, I excused myself to give the lessons on Esplanade, though between the expectation of Mme. Olivier's baby and carnival, I found Jo and Carrie to be quite uninspired when it came to scholarly pursuits. After a rather fruitless morning, I arrived home to find Edgar cleaning his brushes on a rag. An easel was set to the window to take advantage of the light. I approached him and he approached me, and he leaned in with his lips and we kissed. How I could get used to this small ritual, and repeat it daily, forever! Outside the window were the sounds of traffic on the river and traffic in the city, mules and hooves and bells and smokestacks and voices and laughter and shouts, all on earth, far, far below this heaven.

Sammy, 1982

He woke having nodded off and with the notion that he had dreamed of the school bus again. Like before, it had been raining, smearing the red of the school bus lights. The rain was hard enough to bend the cane at its tops, and there were no other cars, just a stretch of rainy highway in the middle of cane fields, green fronds pelted by the sudden, intense rain of a south Louisiana summer afternoon. Neither his truck nor the bus was moving, just the slap of wiper blades against the cascading rain. Then, without getting wet, he was on the bus, and it was empty. He walked the center aisle, his hands on the backs of the seats as he made his way to the rear. When he came to the end of the aisle, he turned around. At the front of the bus, he saw the little girl wearing a navy-blue dress with a white pinafore. Her golden hair fell from under her bonnet, the brim obscuring her face. She looked up at him plainly, as if she was about to say something. Her mouth moved, but he couldn't hear her over the slap of windshield wipers. The repetitive clack, over and over and over.

And then he woke to the tapping of the pendulum of the clock in the central hallway. His hands rubbed his bearded face as he looked down at the diary in his lap. He slipped the deposit slip back into his place and got up to make coffee. It was a cold gray afternoon, maybe the last one until November.

When coffee was made, he sat down in the central hallway with the last Mount Teague china cup on the yellow padding of the armrest of the settee, steam curling up from the black surface. It was once difficult, but now he could look old Sam Teague in the eye, man to man. The unknown painter had been a man who had traveled up and down Bayou Lafourche with paints and blank canvases and called at all the houses of any size because the people in those houses were the kind who had the pocketbooks to afford portraits and the egos to desire them.

Sammy wondered when it was painted. There was no scar on his great-grandfather's face, so certainly it must have been done well before he had married Alice. Sammy rubbed his beard and traced a finger over his cheek where his scar would be if he had one. With just a little more time, his beard would be as thick as old Sam Teague's. It still itched, though, and he wondered if it was even worth it. It had garnered him no respect. In fact, sometimes he heard the word *hippie* whispered as he passed. He wondered if it would ever be spray-painted on the hood of his truck or one of his barns, *Hippie.* Elizabeth's voice startled him.

"Mama says you the rugarou."

She sat next to him on the bench across from the portrait of her Papere's grandfather.

"No," Sammy said, his hand still stroking his beard. "I'm not the rugarou. Your mama just likes to tease me."

"I didn't think so," Elizabeth said candidly, and she whispered, "you're too nice." She hugged her daddy, who was not the rugarou, and she scampered up the stairs as quickly as she had appeared. He thought about trying to nap again, to summon the dream. He closed his eyes, but it was no use. He wasn't sleepy, so he opened them again, and then he opened the diary.

Alice, 1873

22 February 1873. I fall into sleep so easily these days! And such vivid dreams! I awoke from a dream in which Edgar and I left a church, and vaguely, it seemed as though it was in Paris. Yes. Yes, in the dream it was Notre Dame, though it didn't look like the pictures I have seen of Notre Dame. It also seemed that Paris was quite small, perhaps the size of Napoleonville. And then I came upon the Teague girls as beggar children, bare-legged in the cold with tattered gloves and stringy hair. Someone was playing Irish reels on a violin, and I thought, how odd that I should hear such a tune in Paris. I awoke, relieved that it was only a dream, but troubled that I had had it in the first place.

23 February 1873. This morning, before Mass, a servant came running across the field holding a little girl by the hand, at last picking her up and carrying her to the backdoor with the news that Mme. Olivier's time had come. The girl was met by Mouche who said, 'Well, now, Lou-Lou, you are to be a big sister today!' The girl looked around, wide-eyed with anxiety at having been spirited away from her own home. She is a remarkably pretty girl who is about Pierre's age, with dark lashes and a small rosebud of a mouth, just like her mother. Jo came forward and led her by the hand and said, 'Here, Lou-Lou, come and let us read a storybook to you and Pierre.' The little girl took Jo's hand but glanced back to the house whence she had come.

She was not the only one out of sorts. Rene was quite nervous today and paced as the news of the impending event was delivered at the back doorstep along with little Lou-Lou. As the day wore on, he snapped at the children for being noisy, as if Madame would be disturbed by their play from across the field and the garden, and he spent all day in his waistcoat, staring there, listening for any sounds of agony or a baby crying or both.

Didi and Uncle Michel attended Mass and then returned straightaway after. But instead of a leisurely Sunday dinner, cold-meat sandwiches were prepared and then only half-eaten, abandoned for the various pre-dieu scattered around the house where the sisters nervously took to their knees and fumbled the beads of Rosaries. Rene even briefly joined them, though he is famously irreverent, but soon his nervous energy summoned him elsewhere. I waited on the back gallery, also imagining the drama that was going on in the house across the way.

Edgar painted as Lou-Lou and Pierre played in the garden, picking azaleas and putting them in their hair like Tahitian Islanders. Then they became tired of that and played the game that Pierre now calls Olé with Vasco and each other, and then they became tired of that. Pierre ran onto the porch and past us into the house to reappear a moment later with a handful of galettes. He gave some to Lou-Lou as Vasco sat patiently on his haunches, and they took turns feeding the dog and themselves. The day crept by and still there was no word from the house beyond the gardens and the field.

Sunset fell, and Didi and Mouche and I had tea by the fire as they sewed and we waited news of Mme. Olivier. The children had at last been put to bed, though Lou-Lou became tearful and said she missed her Ma-Ma. Shortly after the children were put to bed again, for good, this time, there was a knock on the door. One of the servants was there with the news that the baby had arrived, and that Madame had done splendidly, though it had been a long day. And that it was a boy, Victor Frederic Olivier.

24 February 1873. A fine day spent with the children of this house on Esplanade, as Edgar painted portraits in our nest on Ursulines. Lou-Lou is now quite accustomed to the Musson household, though later in the day she became sad and was allowed to return home to go and see her mother and her new brother.

Every day Jo seems more and more attached to me. Today as I looked through the sheaves of music on the stand above the Pleyel, she asked me with a blush, 'Mam'selle, do you and Cousin Edgar ever—' she reddened and giggled, '—kiss?'

I leaned in and whispered to her, 'Sometimes. But you shan't tell. You won't, will you?' My tone was quite facetious, and she giggled again. 'No, Mam'selle! I would be too embarrassed!'

'As well you should,' I said in a voice just above a whisper and an expression just below a smile. 'Now play that piece from *Madame Angot,* the new one, and let's hear your improvement.' And she played, looking quizzically into the notes perched on the lines like birds on wires, and willing her fingers to transform them into sound. And I remembered being her age, when a kiss was the zenith of romantic love, and the secret purpose of willies and hoo-hoos was talked about but scarcely believed.

25 February 1873. Mardi Gras today, and Edgar and I don the costumes I arranged from Madame Alabau. No time to write, my little confidant, as today promises to be a lengthy one. *Dum Vivimus Vivamus*, let us live while we are yet living, for tomorrow is ashes.

26 February 1873. Ash Wednesday. I wear the ash today, as do all the foreheads in this household and this city, and I dare say many or most of those heads aching from revelry. Carnival arrived at last, and lessons and all else in the house on Esplanade were suspended as everyone looked forward to a carefree day of gaiety. Even Edgar took time off from painting, and we took to the streets with other revelers. The men of the house, save Edgar and Uncle Michel, masked with Comus and promised a great trick upon the 'occupiers and usurpers,' that is, the Union troops and the Republican government of Gov. Kellogg. For the first time, costumes had been made here in New Orleans in the style of ones which Rene and Edgar saw in Paris. I wonder at the cost.

I persuaded Edgar to costume, and he and I dressed as the late King and Queen of France, complete with wigs, and, for Edgar, knee breeches. He looked down at them and the bows at the knees and looked up at me and sighed, 'Ah, but what a man does for love.' We looked at our reflections in the smoky depths of the looking glass in our nest on Esplanade, our outrageous other-selves looking back at us. I feared the day would become too warm for such costumes but resolved that it was all in the sake of fun and so we were off to Esplanade to pay a carnival call on *la famille*.

We appeared in the front door and were greeted by Mouche and the children. 'Ah!' she said, holding up her hems and curtseying to us, 'Marie Antoinette and old King Louis, except still in possession of their heads!' Uncle Michel emerged from the library with *L'Abeille* in his hand. The other men of the house were already off to prepare for the parading of the Mystick Krewe of Comus and their 'grand surprise.'

'Well! Royalty in my humble home,' he said, and he flourished a bow deep enough to cause him to push his glasses back onto the bridge of his nose with a finger when he was done. 'I'm surprised you persuaded this old soul to dress up,' he said, and he put his hand affectionately on the shoulder of Edgar's royal coat. The children gathered around us with giggles at our attire, and Jo said into the parlour, 'Aunt Didi! Come look at Cousin Edgar and Mam'selle Alice!' In the parlour, Didi read the *Catholic Messenger* to Tell, a column on what may be laid aside for Lent. Mouche made trumpeting sounds like a fanfare as we stepped into the doorway of the parlour. 'Very nice costumes.' Didi said, looking up from the *Catholic Messenger*.

'Whom do you portray?' Tell asked the wall.

'Yes, who are you?' Didi seconded.

'Well, let's see if you can guess,' Edgar said, more to Tell than Didi, 'I wear clothes of the old century, knee breeches and white stockings, a shirt with ruffled collar and sleeves, and a coat of fine linen with costly jewels sewn on it, and a wig, since I still have a head to put it on. Alice wears fine silk skirts of the most royal blue, and a bodice to match, with fanciful embroidery upon it, and a wig of the last century as well, with the beauty mark of a mole upon her cheek—'

'—King Louis and Marie Antoinette!' Tell said quickly.

'Yes, exactly, cousin!' Edgar exclaimed, and he kissed her on both cheeks. 'Though, I admit, the jewels are not costly at all but are fake ones instead.'

His words echoed for me, *fake ones.* Edgar smiled at me and I smiled back, or, rather, forced myself to. After the shouts and giggles of the children and wishes of Happy Mardi Gras, Edgar and I made our leave for the crowds of Canal and St. Charles.

The parade of Rex, King of Carnival, was held in the afternoon, and Comus last night, each followed by a ball. We took a carriage and something about the scent of the leather seats or the enclosure or the curtains ignited us. We kissed, once and again, and my heavy face powder and the mole on my cheek became smudged, and Edgar's wig was out of place. Fearing that things would ignite even further, I pushed his hands away and touched his nose.

'Perhaps later, you randy boy,' I whispered in his ear before pulling at the lobe with my lips.

'Oh, but just think, my queen, tomorrow begins forty days of abstinence, even for royalty like us,' he said with a mock-pout.

'Well, then, perhaps later. But only if you are a good king,' I said. Honestly, I was quite close to having the driver take us back to Ursulines. Along the streets, banners and flags hung from every window and balcony. At Canal, we emerged from our carriage and waited with the crowd under the awning of Mr. Holmes' Store, where a large green-and-gold pelican had been placed in decoration. Spirits were already flowing freely, and we were greeted with bows and addressed as 'my liege' and 'my queen' as other revelers recognized us. Cups were shared, as were wishes for a merry carnival.

Late in the morning, a small hurrah rose across town, as Rex arrived by barge at the foot of St. Joseph Street. A murmur went through us as we anticipated his arrival, but there was another wait, and someone said that King Rex always stops at City Hall to be toasted by the Mayor. The sun broke free from the clouds and the heat rose, and I was tempted to remove my mask and wig, but just then the sound of a band grew, and then a vanguard of the Metropolitan police appeared, led by their commissioner Colonel Badger. They were followed by a band of three or four dozen which made quite a sound. They blared past us, gleaming brass instruments and buttons against the soldiers' blue uniforms.

As the parade filed by, it seemed as though half the city was in the parade whilst the other half watched it. A large banner read, MAKE

WAY FOR THE KING, and then there he was, Rex, King of Carnival. He wore a shining gold breastplate and an Egyptian frock and waved beatifically as he was escorted by Federal troops dressed in colourful costumes reminiscent of Arabs and Turks. The band began the song, 'If I Ever Cease to Love,' the first of dozens of times it was played yesterday. Then there was a succession of royal standards, heavily adorned with fringe and tassels, the most prominent announcing KING OF THE CARNIVAL.

The procession took most of the morning, with personages such as 'the Earl Marshall of the Empire' and 'the Lord of the Carriages' and 'the Lord High Master of the Horse' passing, each likely some banker or commission agent on other days of the year. The Boeuf Gras passed, an enormous steer adorned with golden apples and blue ribbons and garlands, surrounded by men dressed as butchers in white aprons and caps and carrying meat cleavers. The animal plodded along, either unknowing or resigned to his fate.

More carriages passed by, all of them bearing fanciful coats of arms, all facetiously concocted. Shakespeare's Seven Ages of Man were depicted in seven separate wagons, referred to as floats, which carried more masked revelers, everyone shouting and waving and bowing to everyone else as regimental bands marched along giving brassy accompaniment. We fluttered our handkerchiefs in the air and shouted and hurrahed as each float passed. Everything was stirred by a whirlwind of noise. A squadron of police brought up the rear to signal the end of the parade, and they passed us and advanced down Canal toward the parade's end, to adjourn to the ball with Rex and his invited guests.

It was late afternoon by then, and the emerging sun had made Marie Antoinette's mask and wig become quite hot. I removed them, and Edgar and I adjourned to Ursulines to rest and to indulge our flesh and to replenish it in true Parisian style with bread, wine, and cheese. My voice was just a little husky, and I realised how much shouting and cheering I had done.

As we mounted the stairs, I whispered something into Edgar's ear, something wanton, something unbecoming a vicar's daughter, something I wanted him to do to me. Feverishly, we wrestled ourselves from the low-neckline dress of a dead queen and the knee-breeches and splendid cape of a headless king. We fell to the bed, the powder of our faces caked with our sweat from the heat of the sun and the heat of our shadows. We shared the feeling of rising into the sky and the heavens and the thrilling bliss of crashing to earth again, landing together on the mattress of a bed in a fourth-floor apartment in a city called New Orleans in a country called America. We held each other in ecstasy and expired with laughter.

Down below, the crowds boiled with conversation and shouting, and the music of horns and fiddles, all isolated, none of them playing a complete tune, all of them falling into drunken laughter within a few bars, fiddle strings trailing off into hoarse notes, horns snickering into the sounds of flatulence. And then more laughter, the laughter one might find in the halls of Bedlam. And ours joined theirs, those whoever-people far below us.

'Well, *Carni Vale, adieu to the flesh.* I suppose that will have to last us forty days,' Edgar said at last.

'I suppose it shall,' I murmured into his neck, though I doubt if we shall make forty hours, much less forty days. I could hear Edgar' heart beat within his chest below my ear. 'Let's just stay in. I am quite fatigued,' I said.

But Edgar said that he had promised his brothers that we would attend the procession of Comus and the ball. He said that he was anxious to see the subject they've been so secretive about. He stood, naked, and pulled me up, and we dressed once more. King Louis again put on his royal finery and straightened his wig, and I re-powdered my face and dotted a small mole on my cheek.

We emerged from the bottom of our stairs onto Ursulines, both refreshed and exhausted. Sunset had occurred, and revelers were already falling by the wayside, empty and half-empty bottles lying by them, boot-toes of the occasional Metropolitan policeman gently nudging the sleeping forms to judge the quick and the dead. As night had fallen, calcium lights were struck along Canal and the crowd was gathering under them, seething with its collective motion and simmering in conversation.

A man with a stack of tin cups made his way through the crowd, and Edgar bought us one. On them was stamped, *Mystick Krewe of Comus, 1873.* We revelers shared the contents of bottles and jugs and became one happy family, and more so with each sip. Off in the direction of

Lafayette Square, a band began, and an excited murmur rippled through the crowd of us gathered on Canal. A guard of Metropolitan Police came marching in the lights that flickered between the buildings on St. Charles, illuminating the façades of storefronts as the music filled the avenue and spilled onto Canal Street. Negro torch-bearers, *les flambeaux*, came capering under their fire that joined with the calcium lights. The blare of brass instruments and the rattling beat of drums echoed down Canal, and then, there he was in the lights. Comus.

He rode in a carriage pulled by ponies outfitted in plumed headdresses, one of the ponies ridden by a cherubic figure. As Comus made his way between the crowded banquettes in the illuminated night, he lifted his golden cup, smoking with incense, and saluted the crowd, who cheered back at him. He pretended to drink from the cup and lifted it again, and we all lifted our cups and bottles and jugs, and he gave us a slight bow. The incense from the golden cup was sweet-smelling but tinged also with a bitter aroma, but it seemed to blend with the absinthe that someone had poured in our cup. Behind Comus, written on an altar set on poles and borne by men dressed as Egyptian foot soldiers was the theme of the procession: The Missing Links to Darwin's Origin of Species. Perhaps it was the absinthe that was being shared in our little gathering of strangers on the banquette, which had developed among the throng, but I clapped rather wildly and involuntarily at the subject of the parade, feeling that Papa would be delighted that something of his interest might be the subject of such a grand spectacle, a thing that would be impossible in England.

They marched past Mr. Clay's statue, whose gesturing hand seemed to be introducing each passing section of the parade, each section preceded by a banner and on each, a word that I had heard before from Papa: Zoophytes, Mollusca, etc. Under the lights of a flambeau, each character marched by. A sponge with a big red nose. Coral and sea nettles. A sea anemone. Their papier-mâché heads were enormous and grotesque under the flickering flames held aloft. The faces had human features, and it soon became apparent that each was a mixture of a creature both animal and human. The Mollusca and Crustaceans paced past us, followed by fish, a whale, a seal, a walrus as the bands played jaunty airs. And then came the plants, the feet of the hidden participants disguised as roots.

In front of us, nearer the street, a man and a woman watched the parade. They seemed familiar, and my curiosity bid me approach closer. The man said, 'What does it say? I don't have my glasses.'

It was the kind of thing Mr. Teague would say, and I looked at the woman to see if she resembled Mrs. Parris or perhaps some other woman. My eyes, I'm sure, were wide behind my mask and under Marie Antoinette's head of ringlets as they searched the man's cheek for a scar.

'Oh, you and your glasses,' the woman said, and she produced a pair and gave them to the man who placed them on his nose. To my relief, he read the entire poem on the banner that approached and then passed in the torchlight. The man turned to say something to the woman, and I saw that his cheek was scar-less and smooth. He took his glasses off the end of his nose, and she said, 'Keep them on, Frank, there'll be more banners coming.' And I breathed again, especially when I thought that even if it had been Mr. Teague and Mrs. Parris, they could not have recognized me dressed as Marie Antoinette. But certainly, as far as my husband was concerned, I was still in Europe.

The crowd's great voice went up into the night again as the next division approached. Edgar shouted into my ear, 'Rene said he would be among the insects. Now I understand what he was speaking of.'

And on they came, costumes of beetles, spiders, moths. A grasshopper jigged along with a fiddle and a bow. I allowed myself to enjoy the spectacle, safe behind the anonymity of my disguise. Surely no one knew it was me, except for Edgar. As I relaxed, safe and concealed against the world, a tobacco grub appeared, an exact rendering of the American President Grant, except with an insect's body and tail. He bowed to us, and from within the head, a muffled voice said, 'Mon frère, Mam'selle Alice.'

'Ah!' Edgar said with both surprise and delight, 'Rene, you old dog!' The tobacco grub president bowed again and put a finger over his papier-mâché lips to safeguard his secret and marched off with the other insects. Rodents were parading by in the quivering amber light, the crowd noise rising in delight with the passing of each papier-mâché creature, squirrels, rabbits, then rats and mice. And then the ruminants processed by, sheep, buffalo, zebras, giraffes, camels, and then the carnivores, boars, racoons, bears, tigers.

A dog dressed as a policeman walked by turning to both sides of the street and brandishing his club at the crowd, who booed him. Someone called out, 'Why there's old Badger!' They meant Colonel Badger, the head of the Metropolitans Police. Then a hog dressed as a cook, a horse dressed as a jockey, and several other animals who had seemingly reversed the roles of hierarchy.

It occurred to me that there was a point to all this madness. Then a gorilla strutted by playing a banjo and someone called out, 'Look there! It's that old *n*— Pinchback!' Other monkeys paraded past us. Far away, down at the foot of Canal Street, a shout went up, followed by an uproar that swelled with anger, shouting and counter-shouting. Heads were craning away from the parade, and even some of the maskers in the procession stood on their tiptoes to see down Canal. The music from the last band fell into a muttering of horns.

'Wait under this streetlamp,' Edgar said, 'I'm going to see what the matter is.' I put a hand out to him, a weak attempt to detain him as he pushed through the crowd toward the foot of Canal. I watched him disappear in the sea of heads and shoulders whilst I held fast to the lamppost.

Under its light, a man sat with his head in his hands with the worried look of someone who is on the verge of sickness, the look that I have seen before in the public houses of Miles Platting. His fingers were laced through an unkempt shock of white hair. The crowd continued to seethe around us, craning their heads to see what was happening at the end of the street. I leaned down to the poor man, and when he looked up, I was quite taken aback. He looked so much like Papa that I even said it, 'Papa,' as I put my fingers over my lips. He opened his mouth to speak, and I waited for an English voice to emerge from it. The crowd shouted at something down the street, and I couldn't hear what the white-haired man said. The shouting diminished and I waited for the man to speak again, but he vomited. He wiped his mouth on the back of his hand and looked at me again. I fell into tears as I helped him to his feet. He pressed his weight into the lamppost and slurred, 'Well, I thank you, my beautiful daughter, but it seems as though I have 'shook the man's hand.' This, of course, is American slang for having gotten sick from the drink, and it was given with an American accent. It was most certainly not Papa. And of course, my little confidant, how could it have been?

The torches of *les flambeaux* had receded away, and the light had faded and then it was hard to discern the man's face. He looked up from the shadows, and I heard my name called. I was reluctant to answer to it, until I realised that it was Edgar returning from the foot of Canal Street.

'Oh, there you are,' he said, 'A mob has stopped the parade, and so everyone is parading back to the Varieties, for a presentation and the Ball.' He held out two fancifully engraved billets. 'My brother, the president of tobacco grubs, has given us two tickets for them.'

We moved against the crowd, up Canal to the Varieties Theatre and showed the doorman our tickets. Through the doors, the lights were dimmed into a reddish glow, and we stepped into it. As we entered, he said to me, 'Masks off, madame, only the krewe is masked at the Ball.' He turned his attention to the next couple, and I pretended not to hear him and kept my mask on. We sat at a table in the smoky glow of cigar-scented red air. Other ball-goers were there, only shapes in the dim light before the curtains that concealed the stage. Fans fluttered away in the shadows.

The curtain rose with a blare of lights and horns, and there before us was an underwater scene filled with the sea creatures that had marched down Canal. Seal, walrus, alligator, sea anemone, all waved as if in gentle currents. Then the curtain fell, and the audience clapped enthusiastically.

There was a short pause, and when the curtain rose, the tableau had changed, and the gorilla had been crowned king, a monkey his queen, and an Orang-Outang was his ambassador. All the other creatures bowed to the new king, except for Comus, who struck a defiant pose in the tableau. The grasshopper began playing his fiddle, and the creatures of the tableau descended from the stage and onto the dance floor.

I began to feel sick at the perversion of Papa's high scientific ideals being reduced to twisted political satire. A man approached and told me again that only members of the Krewe could remain masked. But I could not relinquish my mask. I felt that if I did so, it would be the same as if I relinquished all my clothing. Every grotesque mask seemed to conceal a Mr. Howard, or worse, a Mr. Teague, though certainly he was back in St.

Matthew, portraying the god of the gods in the Krewe of Jupitre. I refused to give up my mask, and the man reached for it. As he did, I turned my head, and he pulled my wig instead, and Marie Antoinette's fanciful curls came off in his hand. My own true hair fell around my mask as I held it close to my face.

'I don't feel well,' I mumbled, and suddenly it seemed as though all the eyes in the theatre were upon me, and I rose and fled outside. I could no longer breathe with the mask over my face, and I flung it away as I moved down the street. Drunken forms lurked in the alleys, the sounds of belching and heaving stomachs. I heard the song about the vicar's daughter, and I began crying, and I lifted the hem of the skirts of the French queen I was not, and I began running, my heels clicking in the muffling fog, my shadows running forward and then away. I heard my name called, and it seemed a pronouncement, an accusation. Nausea welled up in me, and at last I fell to my knees by the side of the street and wretched and splattered. A hand lifted my hair out of my face, my own hair, golden in daylight, but silver in the night shadows. 'There, my dear,' Edgar cooed quietly as I heaved, 'You have only had a little too much to drink.'

Perhaps I had, or perhaps, I had not had near enough.

Sammy, 1982

His fingers traced the embossed Old English characters, MKC, for *Mystick Krewe of Comus.* He put his nose into it to see if it smelled of absinthe, but the licorice scent was long gone. He raised it to the light, imagining it being raised on Canal Street as the King of Comus passed. He traced the rim with his finger. Their lips had touched it and then surely touched each other. He carefully put it back into the chest and looked out the window.

The yard was delirious with the abundance of rain and sunshine. The grass had grown thick enough to mow, islands of clover with white flowers mounded up like swales in the sea of green. The weather was too nice to put it off another day. He set the diary aside and went out to the barn.

On the turning of the switch, the tractor pulsed to life, muttering and coughing gray smoke through the flap in the exhaust pipe. He lowered the mowing deck and trundled out to the yard, the fringe of chain swaying at the bottom. The tractor paused at the usual starting point, like the first step in a dance. And then it moved forward.

Each mowed swath brought a sense of satisfaction, of order. The jumble was ejected from the mower, green and fragrant, leaving behind smoothness, stability, consistency. He knew the yard like no one else, what spots retained water, what spots were most likely to raise a cloud of dust when it failed to rain. Once he had mowed over a moccasin, sending its pieces flying. It had been oddly satisfying.

At the edge of the lawn, the cypresses and pines held wisteria, as lavender as Jo's favorite dress placed on the back of the couch in Degas' *The Pedicure*. The tractor rumbled over the lawn, and he wondered about her, Jo, what kind of woman she became. What became of her beloved dress, the favorite garment of a child? Handed down to her cousin Carrie? Given to charity or the children of servants? Cut up and used to polish silver? Thrown away? The lavender of the wisteria remained, but, within a week, it would also be gone, replaced by insistent green tendrils that explored ever higher into the trees. The tractor moved from the bright green of the sun-swept lawn to the dark green of the oak shade and out again. Sammy wondered how Edgar would have painted it.

The tractor turned sharply into another pass, over the spot where the ice barn had been. There were barely any black cinders left in the green tang of grass. The fringe of chain swept over the patch, jingling and swaying over it like the veil of a dancer. He wheeled the tractor around to make the final pass, looking over the hood at the division between order and chaos. He glanced up to the house, and then he saw him.

A man was standing at the foot of the steps leading up to the back porch. His hair was cut, and he had gained a little weight. The perpetual stubble he had worn before was gone, and his face was smooth. Sammy stopped the tractor and got down and then reached up to kill the engine, which he had forgotten to do in his haste. The world went quiet, and he walked briskly over to Teeter, and they shook hands. And then they embraced. Sammy paused a minute, unsure if it was a question that should be asked, but then he asked it.

"How you doin', man?"

"Another day clean, bawsman. I'll see about tomorrow when it gets here." Silence settled for a moment, a clean, calm silence, and then he said, "Wanted to say thank you, bawsman."

"I believe you can do it," Sammy said.

Teeter looked away and wiped his eyes on the back of his hand.

"You think so?"

"I know so," Sammy said.

The quiet of a south Louisiana spring day seeped in again. The sigh of a passing car on the distant highway and then the peppering of bird-song in its wake. The whisking of a spring breeze over the knee-high cane tops, the brushing of that same breeze in the oak bows, and the kaleidoscope of light under them on the white-shell lane and the newly mowed lawn as oak limbs waved over the sun. They had each been raised with these things, these sights and sounds amid the scent of bitter-green grass under a spring-blue sky.

Finally, Teeter said, "I saw that paint-job on the hood of your truck, bawsman. Whoever it was did a shitty job. Mais, if you had wanted it done right—"

"—then I should have gotten you to do it," Sammy said.

They headed off to the patch of shade where Sammy's truck was parked. On the back porch, Pongeaux raised her head from a twitching sleep and gave a tongue-curled yawn. Her claws clicked down the steps, and she followed the two men. The tractor sat idle in the yard, resting in the sunshine in front of the final unmowed swath of grass and clover mounds.

Teeter's fingers examined the spray paint and the P and the Y lurking below the blue like something below the flat smoothness of bayou water, a vague shape. He crouched down and looked across the surface of the hood, and his fingers again danced over the aqua-blue metal. They were as steady as Teeter's gaze. Teeter held his hand out to Sammy.

"Keys, bawsman? Gonna move it into the shed."

Sammy gave him the keys, and Teeter moved the truck into the shed, next to the safe with its lock resting in a cut-out circle. Teeter plugged a grinder into an extension cord and flipped down his welding hood.

Sparks flew like cinders, like stars, as Sammy watched Teeter calmly and patiently enjoy the thing that every good man craves: a purpose.

Sammy mowed the last strip of lawn and pulled the tractor under the awning on the side of the metal shed. Inside, he could hear Teeter working to remove the graffiti on the hood of his truck. Sammy paused at the shed door and watched him. And then, he turned and went back up to the house.

Alice, 1873

27 February 1873. Everyday life returned today after Mardi Gras and *Le Mercredi des Cendres*, Ash Wednesday. For Didi, it is certainly one of the High Holy Days.

'On peut trouver le temps pour les plasirs du Mardi Gras, mais quand il s'agit du Bon Dieu, on oublie bien facilement,' she said, 'One can find time for all the pleasures of Mardi Gras, but when it concerns God, one easily forgets.'

Lessons were held, and the men went back to their offices, save Uncle Michel. Didi went to Mass. Mouche says that attending daily Mass is part of her sister's Lenten ritual. Tell went with her, the devout leading the blind. Edgar painted in his quarters, and I began lessons in the dining room.

After I set my young scholars to their tasks, I went to steal a kiss from Edgar whilst Uncle Michel dressed in his chamber in preparation for a meeting with some men who were coming to the house. I looked into the painting at Edgar's brothers, Achille standing at the left, leaning against the sill of an open window, and Rene sitting and reading a copy of *L'Abeille du Nouvelle-Orleans*, in English, the *New Orleans Bee.* Edgar saw me looking at the subtle changes he had made, including changes to his brother Rene.

'And that, my dear,' he said, 'is a visual pun. The Bee of New Orleans, read by the bee of New Orleans, a man who merrily flits from flower to flower.' My reaction to his joke was a smile that may have seemed wry, but really, it was rather forced.

As Uncle Michel emerged, dressed as if he were going to the setting of the painting, Edgar and I separated so that his uncle would not see us alone and displaying affection in Edgar's room. There was a knock on the door, and the servant Johanna went to answer it and announced, 'Monsieur Michel, there is a Mr. Teague to see you.'

That moment was one of great and almost overwhelming indecision, a moment of supreme inertia, a moment in which resignation or something like it grasped me. Perhaps it was the weight of fatigue from perpetuating this ruse. I quickly shook it off and retreated into the nearest sanctuary, Edgar's room. He followed me in as Uncle Michel went to the door to greet Mr. Teague.

'Alice, are you well?' Edgar asked.

'I feel a little dizzy, suddenly,' I muttered.

'Let's get you upstairs, then. My family would see it as improper for you to lie in this bed—' he began.

'—no,' I said, 'I mean, let me just rest here for a little while. I don't think I should try the stairs just now. And I don't want to lay about the parlour with company here.'

Edgar caressed my forehead and said that he would dismiss the children from their lessons and that the dining room chairs would be needed in the library anyway. But he shut the door to his room.

Through it, I listened to the greetings exchanged between Uncle Michel and Mr. Teague (must I say it? My husband?) as I lay on top of the duvet of Edgar's bed. It smelled like Edgar and was a comfort to me, as much so as the smell of oil paint and turpentine. It was almost enough to calm my nerves and slow my heart, which beat rapidly like a cornered mouse's. Without straining my ears, I could hear their conversation in the library.

'I seem to have visited this house before,' Mr. Teague said, 'My ex-wife, Paulina Teague, had some dresses delivered here, I believe.'

'Well, it must have been a mistake, monsieur,' Uncle Michel said, 'No dresses were ever delivered here, for anyone but my daughters, sir.' The smell of cigars seeped around the cracks in the door.

I heard footsteps, light and feminine, enter the library, and Uncle Michel said, 'Mr. Teague, this is my middle daughter, Mathilde Bell, Will's wife.' Mouche and Mr. Teague exchanged greetings, and Uncle Michel asked Mouche, '*Ma fille*, do you know of a Paulina Teague? Mr. Teague says that she is his ex-wife and that she had some dresses delivered here.'

Mouche answered, 'No, Papa, we never received any dresses here for anyone but us. Do you remember their colour? Mr.—'

'—Teague,' my husband said, and I held my breath, worried that he would describe the dresses that I had worn. Mouche had been almost as proud of them than as if they had been her own. 'No, I, I don't remember,' Mr. Teague said, 'They were from a dress shop on Canal, though.'

Mouche answered politely but I could hear a trace of sauciness in her voice, 'Well, Monsieur, there are many shops on Canal, but none of them sent dresses here to anyone but my sisters and me. I am quite sure of it.'

Other men began arriving, and their voices stirred the air in the library and made me tuck my legs in, and I grasped them, hoping I could roll up into a ball and disappear. My husband's resonant voice mixed with the others, his voice defiling this house, this haven, this sacred space, and I became certain that his reach is as extensive as he has always boasted. It was quite like finding a serpent among one's rose bushes.

I heard the voices of Mr. Livaudais, Mr. Prestidge, and Mr. Weatherspoon, Mr. Bell's business partner and brother-in-law. Men were still arriving, and it sounded as if there were two dozen or more men packed into the library. I heard Rene and Achille, as well, and then Mr. Ogden called the meeting to order.

'Gentlemen, tomorrow's *Picayune* will have a call for a militia to be formed for the express purpose of seizing key assets of the occupiers. As leaders and right-minded men, I felt that you needed to know this in advance.'

I heard the voices in the next room and saw them in the painting before me. It was quite odd.

'Isn't there hope for a more peaceful solution?' Uncle Michel asked.

To this Mr. Ogden replied, 'There is always hope, but the question remains, is it a *reasonable* hope?'

Several voices rose to add their answers to the question, but the responses fell into a whirlwind of discussion, and I could only make out bits and pieces of it. Someone was trying to make a point and spoke over the rest. It was some sort of military point.

'And how do you know that would work?' another asked him.

'Well, during the late war, I served in the Army of the Tennessee, under General Roddey—'

My husband exploded with the most uncivil invective. I shall not write all of it here. 'Roddey? That *G— d—d* bigamist?' he snapped. A chair scraped across the floor of the library. I felt as if it did so as well inside my head.

'I will defend the honour of my commander, sir!' the man challenged Mr. Teague. Voices rose as men tried to calm other men, my husband included.

'Let me remind us of our common cause, gentleman,' a voice said. It was deep and leathery. I believe it was Mr. Ogden. The room fell silent again, though I could easily imagine the sulking look that surely had come across my husband's face.

'So we are agreed? We give them through the weekend?' someone said, though I could not tell whose voice it was.

'Aye,' the collective voices said. They left much more quietly than they had entered, as if they thought that posterity might one day record the moment that a small band of patriots had met in a house on Esplanade and made a courageous decision to form together to rescue their country and their dignity from the hands of those who would keep it from them. When they were gone and the house was silent except for the play of children out in the garden, the door eased open and Edgar appeared with a cup of tea and a galette.

28 February 1873. A much more normal day, reassuring in its mundaneness, a pleasure in its routineness. Uncle Michel read the newspaper to Tell and me, leaving out the call for militia. Instead, he read all the other news from across the country and the world. There was a notice that the State Lottery shall begin again with a drawing in April.

'Well, perhaps we shall be winners,' Uncle Michel dryly proclaimed before closing the paper and gathering his coat and hat for a trip downtown.

When he was gone, Tell said, 'He's never been interested in the lottery before.' I said that perhaps he sees it as an idle amusement. 'Perhaps,' she smiled, though there was something unconvincing in it.

'Alice,' she said, 'Does Mme. Olivier's baby look like her?'

I was unprepared to answer, but I managed to say that I have heard that he looks just like her husband, M. Olivier. This, of course, my little confidant, is not so much a lie as a hope.

'Yes,' Tell said flatly and with another unconvincing smile, 'Yes, and why wouldn't he?' She seemed to be asking it of herself.

I picked up the newspaper and resumed reading it to myself. The *Picayune* cries for a militia to be formed up and assembled by the statue of Mr. Clay on Canal. Edgar fears for his family's safety.

'The same hot heads of secession and the Paris Commune and every war since Cane slew Abel. No one ever learns anything,' he said.

1 March 1873. Our abstinence has lasted as long as it could, and the Lenten vows for it have been broken. It has only been three days, but what a feat of self-denial it has been. Our bodies were matted with our passion as he turned in bed and sat up on one elbow. We are so comfortable with our naked bodies now, like Adam and Eve must have been in the garden, before the snake and before the apple.

He pointed to the portraits that sat on easels facing the window and said, 'These portraits pay well, though they are tiresome, committed to canvas more as a servant than an artist. Americans, they are so concerned with how they are portrayed! And the wealthier, then the more so. But they are always willing to pay.' Edgar rolled over on his back. 'I once painted a peasant farmer in Normandy who had lost an eye while haying. I asked him if he would like me to paint it in for him. *Certainly not!* he cried. He seemed appalled that I would even suggest it. *Our scars make us,* he told me, *they are proof that we have lived.*'

Edgar sat on the side of the bed, the sheets gathering around his naked waist. 'But here,' he pointed to the back of one portrait, its unseen subject facing the window and the revealing light, 'here this old widow wants her hair black again, and so I say, *Oui, madame, it is difficult, but for a few dollars more, I can do you great credit.*' And this fellow, this wealthy man in his uniform of the late war, he wants the scar on his cheek painted out. His beard isn't serving to hide it, and so I say, *Yes, my dear sir, I shall paint it as you wish. But of course, it will be more.* And so he crows like a cock at dawn, *Money is no matter! Only the best!* And the *coup de fin*? He doesn't even want me to sign the front! He says if I must, then sign the back. And I shall! After he has paid me I shall!'

This canvas was also facing away to the window to take advantage of the light. A horrible thought occurred to me, so dreadful and certain that it put me on the edge of tears. I had to look at this portrait, but I had to look at it alone.

'Edgar,' I said, 'Would you go and get us some more of those raspberries, *les bijoux du bois*? The lady who sells them is on Rue Bienville today, I believe.'

He kissed me and said, 'Oui, mon coeur.'

The back of his fingers trailed lightly over my nipple, and it responded with tense pleasure, separately from me, as if it had no concern over whose portrait was looking out the window. I closed my eyes and breathed deeply and forced them open again. We walk on a precipice, Edgar and I, in danger of falling into rapture at any moment. I held my balance with deep breaths. He kissed me again, but I broke from it with a forced smile.

'Those raspberries,' I murmured with a smile and a quick, light touch of a finger to his nose.

'For you,' he kissed me, 'I would swim to Paris for them.' He rose and dressed quickly, and when he left whistling a tune down the steps, I wrapped my bare body in the damp bedsheets and rose. My bare feet drummed over the wood floor within the shroud of linen I carried on my shoulders. I looked out the window and took a deep breath, as a man on the gallows might take as the drum rolls and he awaits the simple work of the trapdoor. I turned to the canvas, and there was my husband's scar-less face looking sternly back at me and my draped nakedness.

Sammy, 1982

The clock pendulum clicked in the hallway to a silent house. Betsy had taken the girls to dancing lessons, and Quint was still at school. Sammy's daddy was in Houma on errands. Pongeaux was out in the metal shed with Teeter. Sammy was completely alone with the portrait of his great-grandfather, Old Sam Teague, the illustrious patriarch, the old warrior and man of letters. Not long ago, Sammy could barely look at the portrait. Now his hands grasped the elaborately carved wood frame, painted gold. *Only the best at Mount Teague*, he thought. He lifted the painting from its hanger and carefully set it on the wood planks of the floor of the central hallway.

He briefly thought of hanging it up again without looking, but there was no going back now. He turned the painting so that his great-grandfather was looking into the wall. A hundred years of dust had accumulated on the back, obscuring everything. He carefully swept it away, gray snowdrifts falling to the floor and raising a swirl of motes in the light coming through the transom and the sidelights of the front door of the great house. He sneezed and waited and sneezed again, becoming aggravated at having to pause. The sneezing stopped, and his hand continued to wipe away the drifts of dust. At the middle, he found it, the trace of letters. They didn't make sense at first, but then he realized they were in French. Of course they would be. The gray dust fell with the subtle pass of his palms. And then there it was on the back.

À Monsieur Samuel Teague, un plus grand cretin n'a jamais vécu,

He quietly mouthed the inscription in French, and then his mouth curved into a tight grin. He read it again in French and broke into laughter as he said it aloud to himself in English.

To Mr. Samuel Teague, a bigger imbecile never lived,

And under it, five simple letters, the five-letter signature of the famous French artist, inscribed in charcoal pencil:

Degas

He replaced it on the wall and swept up the dust and returned to the study and the diary.

Alice, 1873

2 March 1873. Sunday. Mass at the cathedral was only half full, as was the Musson pew. Tell and the children stayed at home, lest violence erupt, and they be caught in the middle of it. The service seemed to take twice as long without the quiet antics of children in the pew, little fingers tracing words in Missals and the lines along the backs of adult hands, and the soft weight of them leaning into you as they fight sleep under the melodious incense of Latin and French. Perhaps there is some mathematical formula to it: the emptier the pews, the longer it seems services take. After a smaller and quicker than normal Sunday dinner, the women of this house took to their pre-dieu and recited the Rosary, the beads passing through fingers to the whispered prayer. Even the children were subdued, and only read and napped. I could hear Jo upstairs playing the role of eldest cousin.

As I write tonight in our nest, the heavens have finished exploding into thunderstorms and have left us only the pattering trickle of rain. After our passion and the projection of it in the shadows on the wall with each lightning flash, Edgar sleeps now, and sleep is not far away for me, either. With each sudden illumination I can see his sleeping face, followed by darkness. Then as the storms move off with distant echoes, I found myself praying for another flash, but the storm has passed, off and east, over the English turn. And so I hold the candle to see his peaceful face. How I long for Paris so that I may begin living the rest of my life with him. Upon Mme. Olivier's return, it shall be so.

3 March 1873. I have kept to bed today, as I have not slept well, and find myself exhausted and nauseated. I have sent a message to Esplanade that I shall not be in today. Perhaps the cheese and bread have gone bad, though Edgar suffers no effect from it. He returned having delivered the message and brought the well-wishes of *la famille.* He said that traffic in the city was light, and everyone seemed to be concealing a certain agitation. He spent the morning sketching and waiting on me. Midmorning, there was an insistent knock on the door, and Edgar rose and answered it. I heard the voice of Mr. Teague, and I curled up and pulled the sheets over myself.

'I'm here for my portrait, sir,' Mr. Teague said, and there was a rustle of money. 'Forty dollars, did you say?' There was a pause as Edgar strove to understand his meaning and formulate his answer.

'No, one hundred dollars, sir,' Edgar said, much more cordially.

'You said forty,' Mr. Teague bellowed.

'Non, monsieur,' Edgar replied with a voice that was measured and resolute, 'one hun-der-ed.' I cowered in the sheets facing away, both eyes and ears listening. On the opposite wall, two shadows played, one my husband and one my lover.

'Forty! We said forty!' Teague exclaimed.

At this, Edgar's English failed, and I wondered if he was becoming flustered. In French, he said, without the least bit of passion, 'One hundred, or I shall run a knife through it, monsieur.' I knew his English would not serve him much further, so I spoke from the bed, from under the sheets, taking on an exaggerated accent.

'He say that if you do not give it to him the hun-der-ed, he shall run a knife through eet, before your ver-ee eyes, monsieur.'

Edgar's voice asked me, in French, 'And tell him I must sign it,' and I told Mr. Teague thusly.

Suddenly a wave of nausea gripped me, and not wanting to get up and reveal myself, I was sick over the side of the bed opposite them and their argument. There was a moment of quiet as Mr. Teague paused and said, 'All right, he may sign it, but on the back, not the front.'

Sur le dos, I told Edgar from within the sheets as I wiped my mouth. There was another short pause and the scratch of a charcoal *crayon,* and Edgar said again, 'One hun-der-ed, monsieur.'

I heard the exasperated rustle of money, and cursing of the foulest kind, and the slam of a door, and when I peeked from within the sheets, the easel was empty, and my husband and his portrait were gone. Edgar came and kissed me on the forehead, and if he was puzzled by my accent, he said nothing of it. All day he has attended me, cleaning my face and hands and the floor with a bucket and a rag that smells of oil paint and turpentine. This selfless man. I am undeserving.

4 March 1873. I was hesitant to get out of bed this morning, worried that my husband would greet me at the foot of the stairs or be standing around the corner. And even though I have changed to the black veil of Lent, I feel as though he would look right through it and see his wife. Instead, I sent word to Esplanade that I would be out again, and I stayed abed and read the newspaper that Edgar brought back. Within the pages, the legislatures battle again, and there is the sense that it is only a matter of time before the conflict shall spill from the newspapers and the courts and into the streets. I lay the *Picayune* aside with its bad news and vitriol, and Edgar stepped away from the easel, wiping his hands on a rag, to come and cuddle. He spoke of Paris again, the Café Guerbois, the Louvre, the Luxembourg Gardens, the promenade by the Seine, the Tuileries. Edgar is sure that his friend Tissot, a lover of all things English, shall be as enthralled with me as he is. Edgar murmured excitedly that we must visit his father in Naples straightaway, as he is getting old, and surely he would love to see the prize his eldest son brings to him.

'Am I a prize?' I asked him as he stroked the smooth skin of my back.

'Without question,' he said, and he kissed the back of my neck and I wanted so much to believe him. 'Just a few more weeks,' he said as he gathered me in his arms and pulled me closer. 'As soon as Mme. Olivier returns to oversee the children's studies, you and I shall be off to Paris, where I will do my best to transform you into a Parisienne. I think you shall take to it quite admirably.'

We silently watched the sky as birds scattered into it, and as the cathedral bells of St. Louis tolled the hour, I let myself believe that they were the bells of Notre Dame.

5 March 1873. Not wanting to miss three days in a row, I went to Esplanade this morning for the children's lessons, Edgar and I returning together to the house and *la famille.* The perpetuation of the hoax that we sleep under different roofs has long become second nature to us. As part of it, Edgar announced to his cousins, 'Well, look who I have gathered up this morning!'

'You certainly are an early riser, cousin,' Mouche said over her demitasse of coffee, and I wonder if she is wise to us and our arrangement, and sympathetic to it.

'I enjoy the sunrise upon the river,' Edgar said, 'before the harsh sting of full sun.'

I marvel how this lie seems so small when measured against mine. The children came down the stairs, little Odile and Pierre running to me and each hugging a leg, and Jo and Carrie hugging my middle. Jo seems to have gained a foot in height in the last month and has at last outgrown her favourite dress, the lavender one.

In the parlour, Mouche was asking Didi if turtle is considered meat and if it is considered acceptable during Lent. I believe Mouche carries on facetious arguments with her sister, who doesn't realise it and easily falls into consternation. The children were very well behaved indeed, so as a treat, we read fairy tales from *La Collection de Conte de Fées.* How lovely it shall be when Edgar and I begin our new lives in Paris, or I should say, our life, as ours shall be a single life, seamlessly together.

As I was leaving, Mr. Bell came from the library to tell me in a hushed voice to keep to my dwelling-place tonight, and that it is very important. Indeed, an air hangs over the city like a pall, the same breathless air that hangs over it when it waits for fever season. Shops closed early, and judging by the traffic, the theatres are poorly attended. This evening, as the sun sets and I write, I think of Mount Teague. There are things there, remembrances that I should like to have, Papa's *Book of Common Prayer*, his copy of Audubon's *Birds of America*, his empty chest, and others. But apart from those, I have no use for that place and no meaningful business there. And so I blow out the candle as Edgar sleeps in the wake of our ecstasy. We cannot keep from it, no more than we can avoid gravity.

6 March 1873. In the city this morning, there were no street peddlers, no musicians, only the chiming of the cathedral bells onto empty streets. The mischief that Mr. Bell warned against has transpired.

A little after nine o'clock last night, there was the boiling sound of a mass of angry men, followed by shouting and then rifle shots. Edgar and I burrowed under the sheets, listening to the sounds of upheaval, shouts and running footsteps and breaking glass. He stroked my hair and made soothing sounds and reminded me that we shall be in Paris in a matter of weeks, that this shall all pass, pass away, and then we shall be together. He said that we must begin our lives there soon, as we shall only have forever in which to be together. A cannon fired and then there were cries and shouts coming down Chartres. I began crying and pushed my face into his chest. There was a flash like lightning and another cannon blast and the shouting swelled, and it sounded as if it dispersed. The measured pace of soldiers marching rose and faded below on the street, and Edgar quit our bed to go to the balcony and watch them pass. I fell asleep and woke to the dim grey light of morning.

Edgar had gone to fetch the newspaper, and I read from the *Picayune* to him, translating into French. It said that two men have died in an attack on the police station in Jackson Square and that over sixty have been arrested. No sooner had I read it to him than he was dressing to go find Rene and Achille and Mr. Bell. He is quite certain that they were involved. I begged him not to go, and that later, perhaps, we would go to Esplanade, that surely his brothers and Mr. Bell would be there.

'Perhaps,' he said, 'but I must go and see now.' I once again begged him to wait, but he paused for a moment to look into my face and said, 'It is what one does for family.' And so, I wait alone for him to return, worried for his safety.

Sammy, 1982

There was a blank page after that. The house seemed blank, too, dormant in the glow of the kind of light that sparkles in the dew of a spring morning, the only sound the pecking of the hall clock. The older children were at school, Betsy and Judee were visiting her Nonc Claude and Tante Lucille in Labadieville, and his daddy was fishing from the bank of the Twelve Arpent Canal. In the big house, it was only Sammy and the portrait of his great-grandfather.

He rose and sat across from the Degas in the hallway. Now he could almost hear his great-grandfather's voice admonishing the artist, the man who now had paintings in museums around the world, in cities like Paris, New York, and London. Old Sam Teague's stern voice growling between puffs on his cigar, 'paint out that scar' and 'make sure you get my good side.'

Sammy looked at his namesake in the portrait, a man who had offered the Father of the Impressionist movement forty dollars for his portrait when a hundred was what they had agreed upon. Sammy wondered how much it was worth now as his hand absently caressed his face and beard. It was becoming second-nature to him now, almost a tic, stroking the beard that was about the same color and length as his great-grandfather's, the man who was neither a war hero nor a man of letters. Now, Sammy saw him as he truly had been, a blusterer and a bully.

The light dimmed across the face in the portrait, across the borrowed gray uniform, across the sandy-brown beard and scar-less face and nickel-gray eyes, identical to those of his great-grandson, Sammy Teague, who now sat before him. And then, there was a knock that seemed like a rifle shot, and a silhouette appeared in the sidelight of the door, an eclipse against the morning sun. Sammy's workboots drummed hollow notes on the wood planks of the hallway as he got up to answer it. Teeter's nose and eyes withdrew from the sidelight as Sammy opened the door.

"Hey, bawsman, that hood's ready for paint. You want to go with the same color, that sea blue?"

"I was thinking, why don't we paint it all another color?"

"Throw the sumbitches off?"

"Yeah."

Sammy reached for his flannel coat on the rack by the front door but realized it was too warm for it. Under the oak limbs and the piccolo notes of birds in them, Teeter's truck sat, old, but clean and shining. It had been washed, and, when Sammy got inside, he noticed that the seat and floor mats had been vacuumed. The Rosary and Scapular still hung from the rearview mirror. The little plastic Jesus on the plastic cross watched the road with them as the truck crunched down the white shells on the oak lane. The weather was perfect for leaving the windows down, and, once they made the highway, the air rushed by in coarse static as the green cane fields rushed by in silence. The crucifix on the Rosary twisted and twirled with the flurry of wind.

"How about midnight blue?" Sammy shouted over the noise.

"I like that. Look sharp," Teeter shouted back.

Sammy picked through the eight-track tapes in a plastic rack on the floor. He selected one that said *Agents of Fortune* and *Blue Oyster Cult* and pushed it into the player under the dashboard. Over the ragged wind, he tried to listen to the words of a song that the cover said was called "Don't Fear the Reaper." It seemed to be about a woman contemplating suicide, but he wasn't sure because of the wind and road noise. He looked at Teeter, wondering if he still had moments when he felt that way, sad enough to end it all, to set down a life that had become too heavy to carry anymore. As Sammy watched him out of the corner of his eye, Teeter smiled out to the road, playing the steering wheel as a guitar and then as the drums. Sammy looked out the other window and smiled, too.

They slowed to cross the bridge onto the Highway One side of the bayou. Teeter's fingers played the guitar solo in an interlude of the song, and the wind shuddered across the windows again as they moved onto the highway and the interlude came to a close and the guitar and the bass and the drums drove the whole song home. Clusters of buildings announced the town of Napoleonville, the church waiting for Sunday, a snowball stand waiting for warmer weather, cane in the fields behind town waiting for fall. Beads were still on the ground and in trees from the Mardi Gras parade.

The beauty shop slid by and then Mr. Clyde's barber shop with the red-and-white striped pole. Mr. Picquet was sitting on the bench outside, watching traffic go by and picking at his nails. He looked up and scowled at Teeter and Sammy, the Loser and the Dodger, and then he receded in the rearview mirror.

The truck crunched into the shell parking lot of the hardware store. They entered through the door that was half-covered in handwritten public service announcements. The KC's were selling fish dinners this Friday and every Friday during Lent. Someone was selling Catahoula puppies; there was a number to call if you were interested. A girl at St. Matthew High, "an A-student," was available to babysit.

Sammy opened the door for Teeter, and they went into a world with the chemical smell of lawn fertilizer, bags of it stacked on a pallet for display. They passed an aisle with lines of rakes and shovels and hoes and brooms, bins of nuts, bolts, washers, hooks, screw, and nails, all in zinc, nickel, and brass.

In the back, in the automotive section, they looked at the grids of paint colors, each one a subtle change of the one next to it. They chose "No. 3182, Midnight Blue Poly." The colors on the grid looked so much like an artist's palette, and Sammy imagined Degas dipping a brush into each square and touching them onto a canvas as shapes emerged, dancers holding pirouettes, children fidgeting as they posed, Creole sisters fashionably dressed, a room full of cotton merchants, a jockey and a racehorse.

Sammy looked up, and Teeter was already heading to the front and the register with the paint. Sammy turned and walked quickly down the aisle past mops and metal buckets and air conditioner filters. Teeter had the paint on the counter and had pulled out his wallet, but Sammy stopped him.

"Let me do this, bawsman," Teeter said. "After all, you saved my—"

"—I believe that midnight blue's gonna look good," Sammy quickly interjected. "What you think, Mr. Boudreaux? For an old Ford truck?"

"Dark-blue, mais, that's a classic, that," Mr. Boudreaux said. He pulled a pen from his red apron and totaled up the bill of sale.

Teeter paid for the paint, but Sammy stuffed a twenty into Teeter's shirt pocket. Outside, the south wind was picking up, bringing heat off the Gulf. Teeter put the paint in the bed of the truck, but, instead of getting in, he crossed the highway and went to look at the bayou. Sammy let a car pass and crossed the highway behind him.

Teeter was looking down the bank of the bayou, a spot where cypress trees rose with beards of gray moss hanging from their branches. On the black-and-gray surface of the water, hyacinth was blooming, blossoms as lavender as Jo's dress floating over a mat of thick green leaves and bulbs. Another car passed on the highway to their backs.

"Sometimes, when things were really bad over yonda, I'd think about things like this," Teeter said. "Pretty things, peaceful things." He gestured to the bayou and the hyacinths. "If I was a painter, mais, I'd paint that."

"Maybe you ought to paint. You might be the next Degas."

"Who?"

"Degas. French painter. I got a book on him at home. Let you borrow it."

Teeter pursed his lips and nodded. After a short silence, he and Sammy crossed back and got in the truck. The coarse roar of the highway and the ripping wind resumed their duet. Mr. Aucoin's old store was up ahead.

He had been a character in the childhoods of almost every boy and girl in this part of the parish, a man with thick glasses who listened to a radio that murmured and hummed songs in French. He had been a man of small kindnesses, a source of quiet encouragement and penny candy, a bantering laugh, a man who knew the name of every person who came in and called them by it. It was said that, if a carful of drunken teenagers came by late in the evening, he would close his store and drive them all home and walk back by himself in the middle of the night, even in the rain. It was all done with a quiet humility, and Old Mr. Aucoin was a man who was rarely noticed until he was gone. Sammy and Teeter had been out of the country when he passed away, Sammy in Canada and Teeter 'ova-yonda.' His store had sat vacant for a while before a Vietnamese family had bought it.

The scent lured Teeter off the highway, the smell of spring in south Louisiana, the red, pepper-sharp aroma of crawfish. Sammy and Teeter followed it into the store, their hands now the hands of men and not boys, opening the screen door. The tinny, mosquito-hum sound of fiddles and accordions and triangles on Mr. Aucoin's radio was replaced with the smacking and snapping vowels and consonants of the Vietnamese language, a language entirely different from English and French. The young Vietnamese woman behind the counter exchanged a look with Teeter. She was cheerful and sincere about being cheerful. Her hair was coal-black, shining and straight, pulled into a long ponytail, out and away from a face with two lovely doe-eyes. Her figure was simple and lithe, like her fingers, which rested on the edge of the counter.

"Hey Meesta Teeta, you want crawfish? We got ball-crawfish," she said proudly.

Teeter's big nose sniffed the air, and he said, "Gimme ten pounds. Corn and potatoes, too, mademoiselle. And two pop rouge, s'il vous plait. Merci, beaucoup."

She blushed and scooped from an old ice chest that steamed out more delicious scent when she opened the lid. As she filled the plastic bag inside the paper bag, she looked back to a middle-aged Asian man who was reading the *St. Matthew Compass.* She winked and gave Teeter an extra scoop and put her finger across her lips. Then Teeter pulled the twenty out of his shirt pocket and paid for the crawfish and left the girl with the change. As they backed out, Teeter looking over his shoulder for traffic, Sammy waved to the young woman, who had come to the screen door. She waved back.

Under the shade of the Mount Teague oaks, the two of them ate the crawfish from cardboard flats. They were good, perfectly seasoned and big, and Teeter and Sammy made quick work of their ten pounds. When they were done, Sammy took their flats of empty shells and put them in the garbage on his way back to the house while Teeter went into the metal shed where Sammy's truck was parked.

Sammy sat down at the old desk in his study. He thought for a moment and stood and reached for a volume of Kendall's *History of New Orleans,* a relic from the 1920s. His fingers, orange and crawfish-scented, searched the index and found what he was after, "The First Battle of Jackson Square, March 5-6, 1873." He read over the events of that night, when a scared Englishwoman watched her lover go looking for his loved ones.

On the night of March 5, 1873, it said, a militia of citizens under the command of a General F. N. Ogden, occupied Jackson Square and fired upon the Third Precinct Police Station. They were poorly armed and prepared, however, and found themselves too exposed, and so they retreated to the shelter of the walls of St. Louis Cathedral. Reinforcements arrived at the corner of Toulouse and Chartres, but U. S. General Longstreet, oddly a former Confederate general, sent the Metropolitan police to Chartres with a twelve-pound cannon and drove the militia back to St. Peter. Then U. S. troops arrived, and the militia was given an ultimatum: disperse or face annihilation. The militia dispersed.

Two men in the militia had been killed and several wounded, among them General Ogden, who was shot in the shoulder. The next day, it said, the McEnery legislature was marched out of the Oddfellows Hall on Lafayette Square. The 'Bayonet' legislature had prevailed.

Sammy shut the book and replaced it on the shelf with the other volumes. He wondered if the man in the portrait in the hall had had the guts to have been there with the militia. Sammy doubted it. He figured Old Sam Teague had spent it right where he had spent the Civil War, right here at Mount Teague. Right where Sammy was sitting now.

He retrieved the diary from the desk drawer and opened it with orange-tinged fingers, like the tips of flames, and removed the deposit slip from The St. Matthew Parish Planters Bank. Alice's handwriting had changed drastically. Her punctuation was erratic, dates were left off. Something had happened. Something catastrophic, something horrible.

Alice, 1873

Traitor! Betrayer! Leather-bound Judas! You were separated from me, doing your worst, and you have done it! Oh, you have done it, and everything is in shambles. We have been found out, you and I, and I have a great urge to cast you into the fire.

March. Oh, why

March. I could not cast you in the fire. You are my only friend, the only one left, my last.

March 1873. It is not your fault, my little confidant. It was I who misplaced you, and you fell into the wrong hands. Come, let us make amends. You are truly my only friend now, and I have no other to tell these things. Forgive me and let me tell all.

After Edgar left our nest on Ursulines on the morning of the 6th, instant, I waited. Time moved slowly, gunshots were lessening but the streets were still largely deserted, though occasionally men ran down them. Church bells rang out onto empty streets, and even the dogs of this city stayed in the shadows. And still I waited, worrying that Edgar had been detained, or injured, or killed.

Midday, I heard uneven steps on the stairs and heavy breathing. I thought at once that Edgar had indeed been injured and was struggling up the steps, near death. As they approached and I heard the laboured breathing, I became sure that when I opened the door, he would fall at my feet and die in my arms. There was then loud, insistent knocking, and I ran to the door and opened it without thinking that it could be anyone else.

And there was my husband, Mr. Teague. In retrospect, surely he had recognized the flight of stairs from when he retrieved his portrait. And on seeing them, he had bolted it up them, like a fox pursued by baying hounds.

'Oh, Alice, they will hang me!' he blubbered, a truly appalling and pathetic display for a man who fancies himself a champion. He cried like a schoolboy whipped by another, his face contorting in emotion. He didn't ask me what I was doing there. I suppose that he simply was too overcome with terror. I provided a chair for him and he sat in it, whilst he ran his fingers through his hair and beard and sniveled in a most cowardly manner. His presence seemed to defile this sacred space, and it was all made worse by my suspicion that his ordeal had led him to foul himself.

I became afraid that Edgar would return any moment and find me here, and that Mr. Teague would let it slip, in no uncertain terms, that I was his wife. He stood and began pacing and stroking his hair and beard. I almost sat down upon the edge of the bed but caught myself before displaying any familiarity with the habitation. Instead, I turned, and I saw my wedding ring by the basin on the washstand. As he paced, I quietly placed it on my finger. It had been some time since I had worn it, and it felt strange against my skin.

'They will hang me,' Mr. Teague kept saying, his hair and eyes wild, 'They will hang me.'

There was agitated conversation on the street, and again a rumble of footsteps on the steps, the urgent sound of men doing their duty, and then an angry knock. My first thought was that it was Edgar returning, perhaps with Rene and Mr. Bell, and my breath caught within me, and it seemed as though I had to force air into my lungs. The knob rattled, and the door shook in its jamb but stayed closed.

'Who is it?' I asked the door.

'Metropolitan police!' a stern voice said behind it. It was the authorities, hounds on the trail of their fox.

'Just a moment,' I called to them. Mr. Teague had stopped his pacing and was sitting in the simple wooden chair. He looked up at me, his grey eyes begging me not to answer it. I leaned forward and said to him in a whisper as the men knocked on the door again, even harder this time. 'If you want to live,' I murmured to Mr. Teague, 'you shall do as I say. Or else, you shall wear their noose, and I shall be a widow and your daughters, orphans. All of us shamed by the Teague name.'

He swallowed forcefully and nodded. There was a smell, a wafting odor, and it was unmistakable how frightened he had been and was. The swell of nausea rose in me, but I suppressed it and took a sheet from the bed and put it around him, leaving his pitiful head exposed. The knock on the door was so loud this time that I thought they might bring it down. 'Police!' the voices said, 'With United States troops!'

'Coming!' I answered, casting an admonishing glance at my husband's wretched form. I straightened my hair and my countenance and interrupted the next knock as I opened the door. There were several blue uniforms. Two of them were soldiers, the others were Metropolitan police. 'Looking for men who participated in the disturbance, ma'am,' the policeman said, 'So they can be charged and tried.'

'And convicted and hung,' one of the soldiers said with a look brimming with mirth.

'A man was seen running along Ursulines. Would this be him?' the policeman said.

Perhaps it was basic Christian charity. Perhaps it was pity. Perhaps I have become so accustom to lying that I can no longer avoid it, even when the truth would serve me better. But no matter the reason, I intervened, though it was most certainly undeserved, and, as I found out later, unappreciated.

'This heap of a man?' I held forth with an exaggerated laugh, 'Why, it is widely known that he is not fit for any sort of military service!'

I admit to the enjoyment of saying this aloud and the fact that my husband could say nothing against it, lest he ascend the steps of the gallows and half-fall through its trapdoor.

'Father here was struck in the head by a mule when I was just a girl. It has rendered him quite slow-witted, and he requires attendance constantly. He is never to be left alone.' I looked to my husband and added, 'Why, he is no more capable of violence than a coon or a possum.'

The policemen grinned and seemed satisfied with this pronouncement. One of them sniffed the air around my husband and was convinced. Their tone changed, and they apologised for the disturbance and tipped their hats and apologised again and then left. The rumble of their steps was quieter on leaving.

Why did I not turn him over to the certainty of the noose, one might ask? Now that I reflect upon it, it wasn't charity or pity, nor was it Christian forbearance. It was solely because of his daughters, who would have had to bear for the rest of their lives the stigma of a father hanged for insurrection. I could not place this burden upon them, as long as I had the power to prevent it. They were destined to lose another mother, and I didn't want the girls to lose their father, albeit this poor example of one. I had lost mine, and I knew the vacuum that it leaves and what such an absence feels like. But no, the telling of this falsehood was neither charity nor pity. It is second nature to me now, really.

I began to fear again that Edgar might return any moment, and so I told Mr. Teague that he should quit the city as soon as possible. He readily agreed, but he begged me not to leave him, to get him home, home to Mount Teague. He all but fell upon his knees and embraced mine. He said he would not venture back onto the street without me.

'Very well,' I said, 'but I must leave a note for the artist, saying I shall call upon him later.' And I explained to Mr. Teague that I had come to the artist's studio to see him about having my portrait made, a present to my husband on my return from Europe. It was to be a surprise, but the artist was away, and the landlady had me wait for him in his lodgings. I sat and composed a short note for Edgar. In it, I said that I would be going home to St. Matthew for a few days, as Papa had just arrived from Europe. I told Edgar that I would see him on my return, in a fortnight or less, and that I loved him very much, as much as it is possible for one person to ever love another. And that was the truth, a truth that yet endures.

I put the note under a book which I thought was Rousseau's *Confessions*, to keep it from flying away with the draught of the opening door. Then I took my portmanteau, and we descended the four flights of stairs down to the street.

Mr. Teague and I made our way through the streets and alleyways. Up ahead of us, a group of the Metropolitan police and their blue-coated allies approached us, kicking over refuse bins and looking down alleys. They paused and looked at us. I had the urge to yell to them, 'This man is an insurrectionist!' and turn and run and leave Mr. Teague to their mercies, but I stayed. They paused as we approached, my husband's lurching stride accentuated by his terror. They lowered their bayonets at us and called us to halt. And if Mr. Teague's limp did not fully convince them of his infirmity, then his odour did.

'Were you among the rabble?' one of the Metropolitans asked. The soldiers, two negroes, brought their bayonets close to Mr. Teague's chest. I repeated the tale of Mr. Teague's imbecility, and our confronters could smell the truth of it and let us pass.

In front of the cathedral, people were beginning to take to the streets and examine the trees in the square for bullet holes. We left them probing their curious fingers into the bark and continued down Chartres, where the smell of gunpowder still hung in the air. On Canal, the bronze statue of Mr. Clay, the Great Compromiser, had his back turned to it all. We made our way to the Howards and were greeted by Mr. Howard. He had had the good sense to remove himself from the dirty part of this business.

We stayed there that night, though at least a half-dozen times, I contemplated leaving and returning to our nest on Ursulines, but I was afraid that in his state, Mr. Teague wouldn't make it back home. Or that I would be presumed abducted and searched after. In hindsight, I wish I had left. How differently things would have turned out. But perhaps it was shame in how I had dealt with my girls, Jenny, Ida, and Lucy, and how they would certainly feel abandoned by yet another step-mother, that compelled me to complete my task and deliver their father safely home. There were also some things of Papa's at Mount Teague that I wanted to retrieve and bring with me to Paris. And, of course, New Orleans was still not completely secured, and so I resolved to return when the climate was less volatile. I thought of Edgar constantly and woke wondering if he was also waking and thinking of me. I would look at the moon, and wonder if he was looking at it, too. I wondered if he was sketching, painting, reading. And I wonder yet, and I believe I shall wonder every day, and forever.

We were fed the next morning by Old Mama, but I ate almost nothing, consumed with worry for Edgar. We were ferried across the river, and I looked back once more on the city, hoping I would see him wave from a street corner. But the streets were still largely empty. We crossed into Algiers and caught the train for Donaldsonville.

Mr. Teague had recovered some of his senses and retrieved his portrait from the Howards. He and the warrior he claimed to be rode together in a bank of seats on one side of the aisle and I on the other. The train jostled the three of us equally. I began to congratulate myself on gaining the upper hand and felt that it might prove a propitious time to ask for a divorce when I had him safely back at Mount Teague.

Ruthie and the other servants greeted me warmly on our return, but they seemed uneasy, as if I was not expected, which I wasn't, as I found Mrs. Parris reading in the ladies' parlour. She rose and left rather hastily, though she left her trunk in Mr. Teague's bedroom. I suppose it is my bedroom as well, but rather than share it with Mr. Teague, I occupied the girls' old room, still populated with most of their things. It was the only part of the house where I felt the least bit welcome.

Mrs. Parris was not so bold as to stay with my husband under the same roof as me, though perhaps it is only through great restraint or to avoid gossip. The latter, I suppose. Mr. Teague did not come for me for the conjugal rite, perhaps still feeling undone by his ordeal. I felt that I was a nuisance to them both, and that, of course, gave me a small sense of pleasure.

It was then as I settled in to write in you that I discovered your absence. I searched everywhere, including Mr. Teague's study. I thought perhaps that Mrs. Parris had taken you. I tried to remember the last place that I saw you and remembered that it was at the apartment on Ursulines and that it was you that I had placed on the note for Edgar and not Rousseau's *Confessions*. I resolved that I would come for you on my return to the city and my Parisian.

I dreamed in fitful sleep, the quiet of Mount Teague oddly disconcerting after so many months in the city. The small bed was enormous without my lover, and I comforted myself by clutching pillows close to my body and trying to recall his scent.

My Conscience gave me an ultimatum that night: seek a divorce and quit this place. Go forth and live the life meant for you, surely it is not too late. Everything had happened as it should, only out of order, a misstep, a faux pas. Those things I could bear. The only pang I felt was for my girls, my adopted daughters who were as sisters to me. But I had endured this arrangement so long for them, and I could endure it no longer. I was resolved to leave, come what may. Mr. Teague had been humbled, and the time would never be so favourable. And even though I would leave, he would not be alone for very long, if at all. His only problem would be circumventing Mr. Parris, that other cuckolded husband, but I would be gone and that would be his concern. Dueling has fallen out of favour, even here in America, and the matter would be one for the courts. I simply could not bear falsehoods any longer, the most preposterous among them being that I loved Mr. Teague and considered myself his wife.

The following day, I woke with a new resolve. I dressed and made my morning toilette as I rehearsed what I would say no less than half a dozen times. Downstairs, Mr. Teague was in his study, taking coffee and smoking a cigar as if nothing had happened.

'Mr. Teague?' I asked at the door.

'Yes? he said rather gruffly behind the newspaper he was pretending to read. I know this, for it was upside down. A cloudy puff went up behind it like an Indian smoke signal one reads about. I took a deep breath. It was suddenly harder than I had imagined it, which is not to say I thought it would be easy. He folded the newspaper sloppily and set it on his desk. I set my chin as stone.

'May I have a word with you?' I asked.

He motioned for the chair across the desk, and I sat in it, almost as a dog performing a trick. His lips pumped two quick breaths on the cigar, and he tapped an ash in the ashtray. My hands wrung themselves in my lap.

'Mr. Teague,' I inhaled deeply, hoping the air contained courage, and at last I said, 'I wish to divorce you.'

I thought he would be angry. Devastated, perhaps. Or that he would be grateful for me sparing his life and reluctantly release me, so that then he could openly pursue Mrs. Parris. But now that I reflect upon it, I should have realised that he is incapable of the virtue of gratitude. Rather than penitent or contrite, he seemed all the better pleased with himself for having come out alive. He began laughing until he was red-faced and continued chuckling as he tapped out another ash.

'Is that so?' he said, 'Let me tell you something. I will not divorce you, and you should know that Judge Anderson will not allow it, nor will any other judge. He will not grant you a divorce because he is a friend. A friend who knows who butters his and everyone else's bread here in St. Matthew.' He stood and stretched and looked out the window. 'Nor will you leave. I have been left once, and I will not be abandoned again. So, I suggest you buckle down and make the most of it.'

I wondered at this. Certainly, his romance with Mrs. Parris had suffered a reverse with my return. Still, I was trembling but defiant, and so I said, 'Sir, if your reach is so extensive, why have you not found the former Mrs. Teague?'

He turned, and his look was vastly different from the self-soiled wretch I rescued from the city. He looked at me as if I were the imbecile now.

'Didn't you hear?' he said, 'The last Mrs. Teague is in custody in—' he drew on his cigar and narrowed his eyebrows, as if his mind were wandering through possible locations, '—Baltimore or Boston, I believe. It was in all the newspapers.'

I wanted to doubt it. Certainly, he could not read a single newspaper, let alone all of them.

'You see, Mrs. Teague,' he pointed to the sky proudly, 'It might take time, but the hounds always get their fox.' His cigar had gone out, and he relit it and shook out the match and puffed triumphantly. The embered tip glowed, and he opened his mouth to let the smoke escape into a ring. The orange light in the smoke made his visage grotesque.

I was utterly defeated, and I left in frustration. All day I pondered the matter. Had he read the news of Paulina Teague, or had it been read to him? Or was it a falsehood? Suddenly I felt lost in them, a towering forest of lies and deceit, most of them from seeds I had planted.

However, divorce or not, I resolved to return to New Orleans and Edgar, and to risk the title of bigamist. I thought that with time I could tell him, or that a French court would grant me a divorce. Or that I would never tell him, and I would simply and quietly become known as Alice Degas.

I gathered the few things I cared for, Papa's surviving papers, his books, and other sundries. Then I told the servants that I had left some items in New Orleans, and that I would return soon after I had retrieved them. Our parting betrayed the announcement of this trivial errand, as I looked into each face as if it was a tearful last good-bye. The carriage to Donaldsonville and the train to Algiers and the ferry into the city all seemed to take an eternity. The distance from the ferry landing to our nest seemed league upon league. I stopped and bought raspberries, those jewels of the woods. My body was aching in anticipation of our reunion.

I breathlessly ascended the stairs to the apartment on Ursulines, sure I had left you there, my little confidant, but you weren't, and I began to worry that you had been left on the train or dropped on the street and pitched into a rubbish bin or that you were still at Mount Teague somewhere and that with time, you would be found there and read to Mr. Teague. I knew that if that were the case, I could most certainly not go back to Mount Teague. And that was quite all right with me.

I waited a few moments in our nest on the fourth floor on Ursulines. How different it seemed. Perhaps Mr. Teague's presence had robbed it of its magic. Edgar's things were gone, his easels, his paints. It was so empty. The curtains languidly twisted and fell in the breeze that pushed and pulled through the window. I could only bear a few moments of it before I took a hack to the Mussons' on Esplanade.

I rode with my portmanteau in my lap and rested my hands upon it, and they fidgeted almost uncontrollably. My palms sweated and dampened the cotton of my gloves. Every spot along the street held a memory, the time he made me laugh here, that time he kissed me there, how Vasco had merrily escorted us along this block. I could hardly wait to see my Parisian, and I could hardly wait to quit the city and begin a new life with him, wherever that might be, Paris, London, Naples, anywhere, anywhere with him.

I alighted from the carriage, forgetting to pay the man until he reminded me. I turned to the house as the driver snapped the reins and pulled away. Mouche was sitting on the balcony fanning herself. I called up to her, but she looked away and continued fanning herself. Somewhere inside a baby cried, and she rose and went in.

'How unlike her,' I thought as I mounted the steps. I knocked on the door, my portmanteau in hand. And then it all twisted apart in one hideous moment, a moment that plummeted with broken wings and died halfway in its fall to a broken heart.

Didi answered it, letting escape the sound of Jo practising the piano and the giggling of the little ones and the smell of Miss Petinque's cooking. Didi looked at me with quiet indignation and shielded the door, as if I might dart through it like Vasco. She spoke not in French but in clear, pointed English.

'Edgar has returned to France. He has no desire to see you again. Nor do we.' And she handed you over, my little confidant, and addressed me with a look of pure contempt, 'You may remove the veil now, as you are proven false, *Missus* Teague.'

And the door shut. Oh, the door shut on all of it.

I turned with you in my hands, my little confidant, and walked down the steps, missing the last one and almost tripping. I looked up to the empty balcony. Inside, the crying baby was being quieted by a lullaby in French. I couldn't tell if it was little Jeanne or Willy, but I suppose it is of no importance now.

I turned down Tonti and walked along the side of the house. I found that I could not pass without looking in Edgar's window one last time, as one looks in a casket before it is closed. I set my case on the ground and peered through the glass. The bed he had pretended to sleep in so many nights was gone from the room, and there were crates stacked along the wall, on them stamped *DeGas Freres, Commission Merchants of Fine Wines, Common Street, New Orleans, La.* The room is being used for storage again, as this family erases its memory of me.

And so, I have returned here to our apartment, a nest that is without its chicks, as if robbed by a serpent. I had not noticed it when I first returned, but the looking glass is cracked. In it were two versions of me, one on each side of the crack. There was a small smear of dried blood, surely from the calm hand of an artist whose anger had been roused and had broken the surface.

15? March 1873. The raspberries have spoiled, taking on a coat of grey fuzz, and I have thrown them out. I was not hungry for them, anyway. I am not hungry for anything. I spend my time in the room I rent, the room in which Edgar and I spent our days in the blissful embrace of Venus. He has vanished from my life and from my world, and this blissful heaven has become an anguished hell. When I summon the energy, I walk down to the Square and sit in front of the triumphant equestrian, General Jackson, vanquisher of the English. Pigeons attend me, pigeons and the prostitutes who attend the soldiers.

March 1873. The Cathedral bells toll more vigorously today. Perhaps it is Sunday.

18 March 1873. I called at the Post Office today, hoping that there would be a letter from him, but there was none, there was nothing. Hope visits me less each day. The clerk said it is the 18th, a Tuesday.

19 March 1873. Last night I attended a performance at the Opera House. I sat in a balcony box and waited, but the Mussons did not attend. Surely money is tight for them now. I left at intermission, chased out by the manager who thought I was a woman of easy virtue, looking for customers. I had no interest in the performance, anyway.

20 March 1873. I saw her today. So odd to see her in the dress of the girls of the Ursulines School and not in her favourite lavender dress. Surely, she has completely outgrown it, and it is now cast aside or perhaps put up for her cousin Carrie when she might grow into it. I called to her, and on recognizing me, her face brightened. But she subdued the glow and said to me, '*S'il vous plait, madame*, I am not to speak with strangers.' It was delivered as a line rehearsed. I stood along the line of girls as they walked single-file, much as we used to do when I was a girl at the Guildford School in Surrey. The line began to disappear into a side door of the convent where certainly a classroom awaited them. When it was her turn to enter, she broke from the line of girls and ran to embrace me. Her lip quivered and she put her arms around me and sobbed. And then I sobbed as well. One of the nuns called from under her great gull-winged bonnet, 'Josephine, fall in with the other girls.' My little one replied to her, 'Oui, Sister Marie,' and she ran to join them, and they marched inside. Jo gave me one last weepy, red-faced glance, and I saw her no more.

21 March 1873. Why, Edgar? Why? Was our love not larger than these earthly circumstances? Oh, why

22 March 1873. I float like a ghost in this world, this city, a place where I no longer belong, though there may be no place where I truly belong. Each new place is as empty of him as the last. But I wander them, and I presently found myself on Common Street, around the corner from the now closed Cotton Office of Musson & Co.

The sign over the door said, *DeGas Frères, Marchands du Vin*, and then in English, *Wine Merchants.* It is Lent, and there were no customers for wine, so the sign on the door said, '*fermé.*' Closed.

I put my face to the darkened window and saw Rene inside. He slouched in a chair and drank wine from a bottle. He motioned for me to enter, and I pushed open the door to the coarse rasp of a tarnished brass bell.

'I suppose you have heard,' he said as he tipped the bottle up, 'My brother has left for home.'

'Yes,' I said. I have gone several days without using my voice, and it cracked when I spoke. And emotion took whatever speech I might have had left. I could say no more, but there was nothing left to say, anyway. He offered me the bottle, but I shook my head. He took the sip he had offered me.

'It is our lot in life, you know, you and me,' he said, 'To inflict pain upon others with our appetites. It is a duty for people like us. There will be no changing us.' He took another sip, and I left him, knowing that I would never see him again, but his pronouncement followed me down the street. *People like us.*

23 March 1873. The heavens erupted tonight, and with each flash of lightning I looked for Edgar's face in the fleeting moment of light, but there were only rumpled sheets and an empty bed. Nausea and fatigue attend me. The post office has nothing. The hard-metal clang of cathedral bells. Do the Mussons attend Mass this morning? Is it my affair?

24 March 1873. I went to see a doctor on Camp Street for what I thought was a nervous condition or melancholia. Why did I not see it? I am with child.

25 March 1873. It is Tuesday. The *Picayune* carried an announcement of unclaimed letters in the post office, and I was stirred out of indolence by the sight of my name among those listed. My heart glimmered with excitement as that fickle vapour, Hope, whispered that it was surely from Edgar. I moved with a speed that I have not possessed in weeks, simultaneously exhilarated and wary. Perhaps it would be an explanation or a sad goodbye, which would be preferable to no goodbye. Or perhaps it would say, 'Come to Paris! I am still mad for you, there is only you for me in this world. All is forgiven!'

The letter was merely this:

REVERN AINT ET NOTHIN AN HE SHO LOOK BAD. COM SEE BOUT HIM MISS ALICE YO HIS FRIN. MOZIE COUSINS

There is nothing else for me to do but to go back to St. Matthew. Hope, that vapour, whispers, *What if he comes back and you are not here?* In the confines of our tomb of a nest, I shout at her, *Cease! CEASE!* And then in a lower voice, to myself as much as Hope, I say the truth.

He's not coming back. Ever.

26 March 1873. If I had any resolve, I would have left yesterday for St. Matthew, but I am as directionless and inert as a ship becalmed at sea. I keep to the nest on Ursulines all day and all night, for days on end. There is nothing to eat, but I desire nothing. This morning, there was a knock on the door, and I rushed to rise and answer it, still in my linens. I was certain that it was Edgar, but when I opened the door, it was Madame Voorhies, the landlady, coming to see if I shall be staying on here, as the rent is due for April. She says that I have been a good tenant, though my gentleman friend, *or friends*, she said, and I have been rather noisy at times. I answered her in English, as I have resolved not to speak in French until the moment that Edgar returns and I speak it with him. But a fact announced itself to me again, like the sudden toll of a bell. That moment shall never come, and all is lost, all. But still, I answered her in English, and she understood.

'No,' I said, 'I shall be moving on.'

'And what of the furniture, ma'am?' she asked.

'Keep it for your trouble,' I said, 'I have no use for it now.'

She thanked me, in English. But before she shut the door, she asked me, 'Forgive me, ma'am, but I must ask it. Are you a woman of the town, and have you been plying your trade here under my roof? I would not fault you for it. We all must do what we must do.'

'I shall be out within the hour,' I said without giving her an answer, and I shut the door on her and her question. Perhaps there was a speck of truth in it.

27 March 1873. I write this on the ferry to Algiers as I turn my back on the city and return to St. Matthew. Mr. Teague shall find me anyway. He found me in New Orleans. He found the former Mrs. Teague. His reach is truly all-encompassing. There is no spot on this earth where he could not find me, not even Paris. I am quite sure of it.

28 March 1873. I arrived at Mount Teague with the half-truth for my husband that I had left some things in the city and had gone to retrieve them. The whole truth is that I left things in the city that can never be retrieved, among them, Love, Innocence, Self-respect. I also told him I went to see the artist, but he had quit the city and returned to France and so I shall have no portrait for him. It seemed no loss for my husband. He is only interested in his own portrait.

He had me sit in front of it as he expounded upon it like a guide at the National Gallery might do. Of course, he said it as if the quality of his portrait had everything to do with the subject and very little to do with the artist. There it was on the wall of the central hallway, his head painted seamlessly over the image of the uniform borrowed from Mr. Bell. My husband's scar-less face, resolute and duty-bound. And false. He waited for me to praise it.

'Yes, that is quite a rendering,' I said into the pause. But truly, my heart breaks to look at the painting and know that Edgar spent time before it. Mr. Teague went back into his study and left me contemplating his false image whilst he whistled a tune of nonsense notes, no melody to it at all, an odd crossing of 'Turkey in the Straw' and 'The Vicar's Daughter.'

After spending a few moments in quiet adoration of his image, I put my things away. Then I came back downstairs and told Mr. Teague I felt like going to play the organ in the church. He made no display of affection, but only said, 'Certainly, certainly, as you wish.'

I had Reuben drive me out to St. Margaret's, as I am out of the habit of managing a carriage and quite distracted anyway. On the Thibodaux Road, we met the fancy carriage of Mrs. Parris, pulled by two fine chestnut geldings and heading for Mount Teague. We did not speak but only exchanged nods and then turned our faces out to the knee-high sugarcane. She seemed quite surprised at seeing me and must have been perturbed by my reappearance. But she retains her prize, and well she may have him. Reuben tipped his hat to her and shook the reins as we passed each other. His waistcoat was open, and his elbows rested on his knees. He had very little to say, other than, 'It show is good to see you, Miss Alice,' which he must have said three or four times on our short trip to the church. He seemed to treat me as someone who is unaware of a plot, the unfortunate and unsuspecting butt of a cruel joke, though I was quite aware of what had just passed us in the road.

The red brick church under the live oaks was surrounded by budding azaleas and the bright green of spring leaves, all made brighter by the sunshine. In the past, upon hearing my approach, Henry would emerge from the vicarage, but this time he did not. It was Mozie who came out to greet me, wiping her hands on her apron and embracing me. I felt like crying but didn't. I am too exhausted for it, there are insufficient tears for it. She ushered me into the vicarage, and its memories rushed about me like curious ghosts.

I found Henry in the study. He was staring out the window, much as Papa used to do when he was composing a sermon or pausing in the middle of writing a letter. Though Henry's eyes were red, he did not cry, either.

'Hello, Alice,' he said.

'Henry,' I said, 'What is it?'

He drew a great breath and announced to the churchyard, 'Mr. Hodge is dead.'

I paused, incapable of sufficient emotion to comfort him.

'Why? How? Was it fever?' I asked, though I knew it wasn't the season for fever.

'No,' he said, 'he could not live with his secret. Our secret.' He pointed to his desk, 'That letter. He wrote it before he took his life.'

I picked it up and looked to Henry.

'Go ahead and read it,' Henry said out to the azaleas and live oaks and the cane. Glorious Spring was asserting herself, but I knew then that for Henry and me, it shall always be winter. Winter, forever.

'My dear Henry,' it began, *'we have been found out, the abomination we commit, the sin we bear…'* The rest I did not have the heart to read.

'He had a wife and young child,' Henry muttered, and then he put his head in his hands, fingers lacing into his yellow hair. 'His blood is upon me. His widow and child bear our sin.'

And the child I carry and I shall bear mine, I thought.

If I am to stay here and tolerate this situation, perhaps it shall be fair and blonde like me, and not dark-eyed like Edgar. I saw my image in the silver teapot that Mr. Teague had given Papa and me. In it, I was bulbous and grotesque, though really, I have grown quite lean and pale. Henry's image was smaller in the rounded silver. I turned from our reflections and put my hand on his shoulder rather awkwardly, as if I no longer understood the purpose of milder forms of affection.

'Please, Alice, if you would, I would like to be alone now,' Henry said.

My old self would have thought of some encouraging thing to say, but that self has vanished, so I put my cheek to the top of his head, and I turned and left. I returned home without playing a single note.

I write now on the settee in the Ice Parlour. I shall keep to these quarters from now on. Across the way, workmen are enlarging the ballroom 'three dainty steps.' Whatever became of Fanny Roddey and her husband? They seem as remote as Egyptians.

29 March 1873. Amid the hammering and sawing of the men working on the ballroom, my old trunk arrived after being sent to Europe without me. A note accompanied it, written in the hand of Jenny.

'Alice,' it reads, 'I know you're not coming, so I have taken the liberty of sending back your things.' It was postmarked from LaHavre in France.

Will the Teague girls ever return here? I find it unlikely, and I pray for their safety that they do not. And even if they did, would my guilty conscience poison my dealings with those girls who advance to womanhood, closer every day? Can one return to a weedy, neglected garden and expect to find fruit?

30 March 1873. Word is that Rev. Givens is ill with melancholia, and the pulpit was occupied this morning by the vicar of Thibodaux. I did not attend, lest God see me, and I go up in the flames of His wrath. The ballroom has a solid roof and the walls are shaped. The men work today at Mr. Teague's insistence even though it is the Sabbath.

31 March 1873. Ruthie came to get me in the Ice Parlour today. I was strangely elated, thinking for some reason that Mr. Teague had reconsidered and would grant me a divorce. Though it is too late now, I felt that at least I could move along and start a new life somewhere else.

He was in his study, sitting in his Campeche chair, smoking a cigar and gazing out the window.

'You deceived me and betrayed me,' he said to the gardens and the feathery green fields beyond them.

'Sir?' I said.

'You deceived me,' he repeated. He calmly blew out smoke and put his cigar to his lips again and then blew out new smoke. I stood perfectly still and said nothing, like a rabbit in tall grass with the wolf nearby and sniffing.

'You've been paying off commissary debts behind my back,' he said, and he stood and looked out upon the gardens and the cane. Venus stood bared and stony-white among the magenta buds of the azaleas. From the angle it appeared as though she were looking down and away.

I was relieved that it was only a matter of commissary debts and nothing more. The thing that was much, much more, bigger than the satisfied debts in a plantation commissary.

'Oh, dear husband—' I began as I moved to him. And he turned to me, and I had never seen a face like that on another human being until that moment. Anger welled up in it and then radiated out, hot and glowing. And then Mr. Teague struck me.

The taste of warm iron settled on my lips and my eye began to slowly shut against my will. I stood there with my hand to my lip and my fingers on my eye. The world swam and tilted as if I were at sea again. He hit me once more, an open palm, a slap, I believe, though I didn't see it. I fell to my knees and I began crying, bitterly, wretchedly.

I thought he might feel a sudden remorse, the shame that any gentleman would feel in striking a woman, and, particularly, his wife. But he only said, 'You're a sight less appealing to me when you cry. I'd advise you dry it up, dear. Now get out of my study.'

If he had known the whole truth, the truth of my lover and me and the child I carry, he would have killed me. I am certain of it. It is only a matter of a week or two before my secret shall grow to be apparent to most, and, although my husband cannot read, he shall certainly know the arithmetic of it.

1 April 1873. My face remains swollen to twice its size, and my reflection in the looking glass appears to me like that of an inhabitant of the back-most tent of a circus, an oddity, a curiosity worth six-pence a peek. The servants quickly attend to me and then leave. No one craves my society nor long endures it. They fear any association with me.

2 April 1873. Mr. Teague sent a box for me to the Ice Parlour, via Ruthie. I took it and sat back on the settee without opening it.

'He want you to open it, Miss Alice,' Ruthie said uneasily.

My trembling fingers worked away the bow and the ribbon. It was a pendant, an exquisite sapphire. Surely it was intended as a gift for his new paramour. No one simply keeps a sapphire pendant like this on hand for no reason. I suppose it serves as an apology, as he cannot speak it, as certainly he cannot write it. Or it is a gift to keep me silent and his gentlemanly character among the citizens here intact. That is more likely. Ruthie looked out the window of the Ice Parlour and cast a quick glance at me.

'He want you to put it on yo'self,' she stammered.

I removed my veil, and she looked away from my face, which appears quite like a plate of overripe fruit on the verge of rotting. I took the pendant and asked for Ruthie's help in fastening it behind my neck. Her eyes kept tightly to the clasp and the back of my neck. Once it was secured, I gazed into the looking glass.

So lovely. The colour highlights my bruises. But it means no more to me than the blue glass of a chemist's bottle.

'Please send my thanks to Mr. Teague,' I told Ruthie.

'Yes ma'am,' she said, and she quickly scurried back up to the house, past the workmen who were completing the last of ballroom's walls.

3 April 1873. I sat today on a bench in the gardens, which are well past peak, the blossoms fading to brown and falling. I looked up into the face of Venus, never changing and forever beautiful. I thought I heard her voice say, 'Miss Alice?'

Yes? I asked the marble woman.

'What happen yo face, ma'am?'

With that, Mr. Luther stepped from behind a hedge of cedars at Venus' back.

'It appears as though I have taken a fall, haven't I?' I said quite flatly, still looking at the Goddess of Love. Behind her, the last azalea buds were open in splendorous white, clinging to what is left of their beauty before falling to the earth. Their caretaker, their conductor, looked up to Venus as he asked, 'I have a word with you, Miss Alice?'

This time it was I who stared at the ground and not Mr. Luther. He sat next to me on the bench and placed the hedge-trimmers between us.

'I tol' you a stirry, Miss Alice. You been so good to us, here.' He shook his head at the shame of it all. 'You been such an angel to us.' A bird landed on a bough of the azalea bushes and chirped, and then flew away with a rustle of branches. Mr. Luther wrung his hands nervously. His lips quivered. His blank eyes stared at the patch of ground where my eyes had fallen.

'I never did take Miss Polly to the boat up Donaldsonville,' he said as he wet his lips and laced and unlaced his thick, calloused fingers. 'You been so good to Marse Sam's chirren,' he said, 'You been so good.'

He did not want to say what he was about to say. His lips quivered and pursed, and he began to cry.

'He kilt her. He did. Drowned her in the canal. Miss Polly, she struggle and struggle and he kept puttin' her head under. I seen it, I seen it all in the moonlight. It was a night so quiet, so still. You could a heard a pin drop on cotton. Show could. I heard it, that water gurgle and her head go under and her face so scared and then it go under. And I seen it, and I'm always gone see it till the day I pass. God seen it too. God seen it and marked it down in his book.'

The scene he described, the dark night and the black water, was in such contrast to the bright green and red and brilliant white spring air in which we sat.

'He made me bury her where that ol' ice barn at,' he said to his feet, 'She under there.'

He put his yellow face into his yellow palms. Wet tracks trickled down his great forearms as we sat in his masterpiece, Marse Sam's showplace garden.

'You a good person, Miss Alice,' Mr. Luther whimpered, 'You ain' never harmed no-body. No ma'am.'

I began crying, the first time in days, and I took his yellow hand in mine, and it seemed to release more of the truth from him.

'And that limp?' he said, 'He got that right here in St. Matthew. Somebody shot him, they did, but they ain' never caught that man shot him. Weren't in no war, no ma'am. Ev'body hate Marse Sam. Somethin' wrong that man. Somethin' bad wrong. Ev'body wish he dead, white folk, black folk, ev'body.'

He stood up. 'Anybody ask, I ain' tol' you nothin', no ma'am,' he said, and he disappeared behind the cedar hedgerow and left me staring at the ground. I now wonder if he thought I had heard him or, even if I had, if I had understood.

4 April 1873. I was summoned to read to Mr. Teague, as he again claimed that his eyes were tired. We sat in his study together, and it was quite like a cat and a mouse sharing the same room. He asked me where the pendant was, and I silently retrieved it, carelessly adorning myself with it. I believe it might have been askew, but I didn't look at it, as if it is the ransom-price of my soul. He looked out of the window and had me read again from the newspapers and then from *Riley's Book of Latin Quotations.* I lifted my mourning veil to read, so that the sapphire's blue light could play off the pink and grey bruises. He didn't want to look at me and my bruised face, so he looked out on the velvet green of his sugarcane instead.

As I turned a page in *Riley's*, I asked Mr. Teague rather blankly, 'Should we expect the Parrises for the Planters Ball, husband?'

'I believe that Mr. Parris is away in Kentucky, looking at horses. Foaling season,' he said, 'But Mrs. Parris may attend.'

I believe? Of course, he knows where Mr. Parris is. A rake always knows when the cuckold is away. And, of course, Mrs. Parris shall attend. I continued, reading more Latin quotations to him, including all of his favourites.

Let them hate, so long as they fear.

I came, I saw, I conquered.

It never troubles the wolf how numerous are the sheep.

My voice was unanimated and flat, in time to the slow, steady tick of the clock in the hallway. He had almost fallen into a nap when I had a new quotation for him, one that aroused him from his near-slumber. I confess to you, my little confidant, that I made this one up. But, like all the others, he simply parroted it like a macaw. He is quite fond of his new phrase, and I'm sure that uttering it makes him feel like the learned man that he most certainly is not.

Submersus sum uxor mea, he said, over and over again. *Submersus sum uxor mea, Submersus sum uxor mea.*

I told him it means, 'Military Might Bows to Wealth.' We practiced it until his pronunciation was perfect, immaculate. A Roman emperor could not have pronounced it more clearly. I insisted upon him repeating it into perfection, cooing and boasting from within my hideous bruises, praising his flawless enunciation. Certainly, he shall spout it every chance he gets, at his forthcoming Planters' Ball, in gatherings of learned men over port and absinthe and cigars, dressed in finery in the gaslights of his fine mansion. Eyebrows will raise to his pronouncement in Latin which he shall speak flawlessly, as we have practiced it over and over until he can utter it impeccably.

Submersus sum uxor mea—submersus sum uxor mea—submersus sum uxor mea. Why, he was such a willing pupil. He just couldn't repeat it enough, the sentiment of it was delicious on his lips and delightful on his tongue. It may well become the new motto of Mount Teague. *Submersus sum uxor mea.* Military Might Bows to Wealth. Of course, you, my little confidant, know what this simple bit of Latin really means.

Sammy, 1982

The book was one of the oldest in the study, with a worn spine that bore the gold-embossed letters, *Riley's Latin Quotations.* His orange-tinged, crawfish boil-scented finger carefully tilted it out of its place on the top shelf next to *The Rise and Fall of the Roman Empire* and the volumes of *Kendall's History of New Orleans.* Other Teagues had read them, but not Old Marse Sam.

Sammy sat with the old book at the ancient desk, the pilot-house of that great, green ship, Mount Teague. Someone had made notations in the margins, and he recognized the handwriting as Alice's, like seeing a familiar face in a crowd. In the index at the back of *Riley's*, he looked up each word, which was made easier by the tick-marks she had put by them when she had composed the saying his great-grandfather had found so appealing, Submersus Sum Uxor Mea, *Military Might Bows to Wealth.* He followed her marks, piecing the words together until the true meaning floated up to him like a photograph in a developer's basin.

Submersus. Sum. Uxor. Mea.

And then, there it was.

I drowned my wife.

He closed the book with his finger in the place and then opened it again and read and then closed it again. He stared out the window at the shivering green tops of the sugarcane that were darkening in the spring twilight. His fingers held the book closed as if the dreadful secret might get out.

"Dad, Mama says dinner's ready."

He looked up to see Quint, Samuel Teague the fifth, at the door, a teenager in jeans and a T-shirt. Sammy stood up and put *Riley's Latin* back in its place.

He was quiet during dinner while his daughters chattered pleasantly, legs swinging under the table. Twice, Quint asked him something, and twice Sammy had to be reminded of it.

"You not hungry. Musta been all them crawfish," Betsy said with the trace of a grin. He looked up to her from his trance.

"I saw the shells in the trash," she explained.

"Must've been," he muttered. There was more to it than that, of course. She rose and kissed his cheek and picked up his plate.

"Next time, you bring me some," she said as she went in the kitchen.

He rose, too, and went with her and scraped the plates his children brought him. Betsy ran dish water, her wedding ring on the window ledge above the sink. The ring sat there like Alice Teague's ring on the washstand in the nest on Ursulines, and he wondered if Alice's ring had once been Polly Teague's ring, too, taken off her lifeless body and given to the next Mrs. Teague. He looked beyond the window to the shadows in the backyard where the gardens and the ice barn had been. She was out there, under the ground. The second Mrs. Teague.

"Bay, you all *cagou* here lately," Betsy said as she handed him a clean, wet plate. He dried it and put it in the cabinet. "You all right?"

He had wanted to tell her about the diary, but he felt too embarrassed, afraid that she would feel embarrassed, too, ashamed of bearing the same last name as that charming tyrant, Old Sam Teague. So he told Betsy, yes, he was all right.

And then they talked about everything else, about Quint and how he was getting along in school, about the girls' dance recital, about Teeter, about the Vietnamese that ran Aucoin's now and how they had seasoned the crawfish perfectly. He talked about anything but the ugly secret buried in the backyard. But his eyes kept straying out the back window looking for the spot where she might be.

Was it a crime scene, he wondered? After a hundred years? Maybe it was just a set of buried bones, a hidden stain on the family name, the name he shared with the cherished people of this house. They already bore the public stain of the disgrace of his neglected duty to country. They didn't need the weight of a murder added to that scandal. None of them did.

After the dishes were done, the girls were bathed and their hair was combed and they were put in pajamas and read to and kissed goodnight. He was persuaded to read *Madeline* one more time, and they giggled again at the line, "To the tiger in the zoo, Madeline just said, pooh-pooh." He sang them the song about Itsy Bitsy Spider and their small breaths slackened into quiet night-breathing and he turned off the lamp and turned on the nightlight. In the next room, he squeezed the shoulder of the boy who studied under a lamp at the desk. *Love you, Dad*, his son said, and Sammy said it back and went downstairs on the old wooden stairs of the ancient house. Betsy was watching *Knots Landing* and clipping coupons. He kissed her on the cheek, and she smiled down to the scissors and the newspaper. In the amber glow of the lamp in his study, he picked up the diary again. There were just a few pages left.

Alice, 1873

5 April 1873. After practicing his new Latin pronouncement again this morning, I read the newspaper to Marse Sam. He asked me if I would, as he seemed to have misplaced his glasses again, that charming tyrant. Last week's *Picayune*, just now arrived, carries a report that in England, a woman named Mary Ann Cotton was hanged last month in Durham Gaol for poisoning her husband and stepson. It said that the symptoms were at first thought to be cholera. I quickly skipped over this article, and instead read Marse Sam a few merry anecdotes about simple negroes and dimwitted Irishmen.

6 April 1873. No services for me today, as I only crave the society of one person, and he is halfway around the world. I believe it is Palm Sunday, though it matters as little as anything else. Yesterday afternoon, Mr. Teague came to the sitting room, perhaps for the conjugal rite, as he had doused himself with cologne. I smelled him before I saw him, and so I left through another doorway and adjourned to the Ice Parlour, locking myself in and feigning sleep as he knocked on the door. Perhaps I fell into a proper sleep, for it sounded as if the knocking transformed itself into thunder or the rolling of empty barrels. I awoke later with only a passing sense of it. The ground had been stirred by a multitude of horse hooves, and it occurred to me that was the sound to which I had dozed off. The smell of sweet cologne had faded from the air, and I returned to the main house, stepping lightly and looking cautiously in each room.

'Some mens come for Marse Sam,' a voice said, and I jumped and turned to find Ruthie there. 'They say they got trouble up yonder nawf in a place called Call-fax. They all lef' in a hurry, all of 'em wearin' a white camellia on they jackets.'

7 April 1873. From across the lawn, the scent wafts from the new ballroom, the smell of oil paint and turpentine, a smell that frankly is bittersweet, an aroma that awakens my heart and then puts a knife in it. So I adjourned to the Ice Parlour and read today the passion of Christ in Luke's Gospel: 'For, behold, the days are coming, in which they shall say, blessed are the barren, and the wombs that never bore, and the breasts which never gave suck. Then shall they begin to say to the mountains, fall on us; and to the hills, cover us.'

That day has arrived for me. And so, I beg God to erase me, for the mountains to cover me, for the sea to devour me, for flames to erupt and consume me, to disappear from this earth. It shall be a relief.

8 April 1873. In Mr. Teague's absence, I have taken the liberty of having Mr. Luther transplant the privet hedges of Ligustrum to a place under Mr. Teague's bedroom windows, as many as he could fit and have them thrive. I want Marse Sam and his hay-fever to enjoy them later in the spring, after I am gone. It has taken him two days, but Mr. Luther did admirably. They are planted quite thick, and knowing his horticultural skills, the air under the Mr. Teague's windows should be dense with the sweet fragrance of their pollen in a month or so. He shall be so overcome as to be in tears. Such a pity that I shall not be here to see and hear him enjoy the sick-sweet smell of them.

The rest of the fine garden I have had Mr. Luther raze. All else, the azaleas still with the last of the clinging blooms, the sweet olives, the cedar hedges, all has been cut down, piled high and burned as if it were a funeral pyre rising into the bright spring air. There is nothing but scorched earth there now, like cane fields in autumn, save the Ligustrum, which is still green and thriving under the windows of Old Marse Sam's bedroom. The statue of Venus has been trundled away by a team of oxen to the Twelve Arpent Canal, exactly at the site of Polly Teague's departure from Mount Teague and the earth that night. It toppled end over end, and she came to rest with her head just above water. Thus, she shall be ready to greet Mr.

Teague when he returns from his errand in the northern parishes. It was a small stroke of luck that she landed just so, her gleaming white marble head glaring above the waterline toward the bank, and I am hopeful Mr. Teague shall appreciate it.

9 April 1873. I have sent letters to the Teague girls via their grandmother's address in Mississippi for when they return from their tour of Europe. I have told them what a blessing they have been to me, and how I shall always be watching over them, but I am ill and do not think I shall live long. I would want to see them one last time, but it is well that they are not here. I have enclosed a lock of my hair in the book of stories that little Lucy and I have sat and read on so many sleepy afternoons. I hope that she shall find it one day and that it shall kindle a glowing memory. But I fear for what I must do, and I don't want them to be here when it happens.

10 April 1873. There is a commandment I have not broken, the fourth one, Thou Shall Not Kill. My little confidant, you are quite aware of how I have broken most of the others, and so I go to see about this one.

11 April 1873. I felt remarkably well yesterday, and so I had the carriage prepared for a trip along the Bayou Road into Napoleonville. I felt so good that I drove myself and alighted along the main street and tied up to the hitching post. I floated from one store to another, the clerks asking me in French if I might be helped. I answered in English that there was no longer any help for me and thanked them for their concern and endured their questioning looks. In the chemist's, the druggist here in America, rather, I looked at the rows of blue and brown and white and green bottles. There I recognized an old friend dressed in sparkling green glass among the bottles.

'Is that absinthe in the green bottle?' I asked the druggist, a man with spectacles much like Uncle Michel, though this man also wore a thick wooly mustache.

'No, madame,' he chuckled, and then he said amiably, 'Paris green.' He looked over the small oval lenses and read the label, 'Copper. Acetate. Tri. Arsenite.' He looked up at me again trying to discern my face, hidden behind my black veil. 'Arsenic solution for rats, pests, vermin, so forth,' he said, 'Most people use cats or these little terrier dogs to keep down the mice and rats nowadays. This Paris Green is just so deadly. Difficult to use safely, so it's really fallen out of favour.'

I asked him how much he had.

'Oh, still about half a bottle or so. Lethal to people as well as rats,' he reminded me with an upstretched finger, 'so we sell very little of it, and you have to sign for it.'

There was a little black-covered ledger that accompanied the bottle. He opened it to the page where a cord marked the place of the last sale.

'Last time we dispensed any of it was several years ago to a feller down the bayou a ways. Said he had a problem with pests.'

There on the last page in an entry marked *November 7, 1870* were the carefully, carelessly drawn initials, the backward S and the big-hatted T of my husband, ST. And then the date, November 7, 1870, written in the even hand of the clerk. The date was a week before Papa died.

'How much you want?' the clerk asked.

'How much does it take? For a rat, I mean?' I asked in return.

'Oh, that I don't know,' he replied, 'Much as you can feed 'em, I suppose.'

'Well, then,' I said, 'I shall take all you have. More than enough for one good-sized rat. And I shall see that he receives it.' And I signed the ledger, Paulina H. Teague.

12 April 1873. It seems as though I have drunk half of my husband's bottle of absinthe. He shall be very angry indeed. Here, I shall replenish it with this solution of Paris Green that I purchased at the druggist in Napoleonville.

There, the bottle is full again, full of green liquid. He shall never know. My little confidant, my Parisian called this bottle of absinthe the Green Fairy, but I know it is an elixir to quench a rat's thirst. Forever.

I sat one last time and played the piano, something that I have not done in weeks, since I sat down to the Pleyel on Esplanade. I performed Liebestraum all the way through to the end, the last note I shall ever play, a slow ringing A. I have removed my lovely sapphire pendant, a gift from my husband, that charming tyrant. Certainly, he shall want to give it to his next wife, that unfortunate woman.

Treachery is my only recourse. This shall be my last entry in you, my little confidant, the last words of my life's humble chronicle, begun as an innocent child in a loving home. My metamorphosis has been in reverse, from lovely, silk-winged butterfly into a grotesque caterpillar. It is quite like the story that little Carrie Bell loved so, about the lady spider who becomes entangled in her own web. Little Lucy loved it also. Poor Lucy. To be so young and to lose yet another mother. But it cannot be helped.

The people of St. Matthew see me as one might observe a star, bright and glowing, an object of distant beauty and fascination. They speak of me the way in which children might sing, 'up above the world so high, like a diamond in the sky.' But if they could approach nearer, they would see the truth about stars, that they are a sphere of intense flame, a swirling chaos. It is so like the beautiful world offered to me by Mr. Teague, though all that I have left of it is the flaming, hellish centre. Papa once told me when I was a girl in Surrey that a rabbit, under great duress, may scream. I can now see how it would be so. In the ballroom, the painters have left turpentine and linseed oil, the old nostalgic scent of my lover, reminders of all that is combustible.

This, of all dark nights, is the darkest I have ever known. I have the laudanum for my nerves. I have the kerosene for the ballroom. And I have the matches for the kerosene. May God forgive me for erasing myself and the life within me, as I have forgiven Him for ever having created me in the first place. Mr. Teague may soon join me, as I have fortified the last of his absinthe with arsenic.

Night falls and it is fitting, for it was in the darkness that I first saw who he truly was. Now the curtain must drop on Mount Teague and me forever. I shall not be buried at a crossroad nor at night. I shall go up in flames and not be buried at all. Surely Hell cannot hold half as much anguish as this vacant earth. My little confidant, you have been my companion through this life, and now I consign you to the protection of Mr. Barnes' miraculous safe, thiefproof and fireproof, and I bring the keys with me. It is I who must be cast into the fire. You were only my accomplice. And so I begin my last hour.

Sammy, 1982

A strange panic took hold in him, as if something had been taken from him. His hands frantically pulled things out of the chest and put them in the white plastic bucket with Pierre Part Store stamped in red on the side, hoping to find another volume to the diary. Then, in turn, he dumped the contents of the bucket onto the study floor and then just as frantically searched the pile as he put everything back in the bucket. Nothing.

He rubbed his beard for answers, looking up to the bookshelf. He took down the book *Stories for Children by Cousin Sarah* and looked at the lock of golden hair in the red ribbon. Through the window, moonlight bathed the emerging cane, which grew indifferently toward the night sky, only concerned about tomorrow's sunlight and the prospect of rain. He went through what had once been the parlour, now the living room, where Betsy had fallen asleep on the couch during the ten o'clock news. On the sofa table in the lamp light, there was an uneven stack of coupons under the scissors. He eased out the back door and crossed the lawn in the cool night, past the spot in the yard where the ice barn had been. Grass had claimed the cinders and erased them. It was truly just a memory now, and, even if it had still been there, he would not have been scared of it anymore.

He rolled up the door of the big metal shed and threw the switch inside it, and the fluorescent lights hummed to life. His truck still had the glass taped off with newspaper over the windows, but the midnight blue paint gleamed in the bright lights. He saw his bearded reflection in the depths of the paint. Off to the edge of the light, the safe sat with a circular hole cut into its front. Sammy fell on his knees before it and swung open the iron door and looked into its emptiness, searching for something, anything. A handwritten note in the same hand as the diary, any note. But there was nothing, no scraps, no jottings. The safe was *as empty as the garden tomb*, as Miss Della Mae used to say when a canister of flour or a bottle of milk had run out. He snapped the light switch, and the shed fell into darkness, and he rolled down the metal door and locked it.

In his study, he shut the door and turned down the lights. He didn't like for his children to see him cry, nor did he want Betsy to see him.

How would he explain that he was grieving for a woman he had never met and who had died a century ago?

But she appeared at the door of the study. His head was in his hands, and he looked up to see her. He handed her the diary and looked out the window.

"I already read it," Betsy said. "I been readin' it this whole time." She sat sideways in his lap and put her arms around him and nestled her head under his chin. "I didn't want to tell you 'cause the more I read it, the more I thought this was something you had to feel like you were readin' by yourself."

"Sorry you had to know about this. This lie. This name. Our name."

She straightened up and looked him in the eye. "As if! Let's get one thing straight. Old Sam Teague is *defan*, dead, and New Sam Teague has to make his own way now, make his own decisions and victories and mistakes and then more decisions. And it ain't no burden, no. It's my decision. You a good man, Sammy Teague." She put her head back under his chin and murmured, "A good man."

They listened to the footsteps of their oldest on the floor overhead and the faint sound of his light clicking off, and then their household was quiet. The old bones of the house creaked a little and went silent again, leaving the quiet rapping meter of the clock in the hallway. After a while, she pivoted on his lap and put her legs on either side of his. She opened the book, *The Life and Complete Works of Edgar Degas*, and they looked through it. There were crisp, shiny pages of dancers and racehorses and then family portraits of the artist's Italian relatives. And then they came to a section entitled, New Orleans. The people in the portraits were familiar to them. It was almost like looking through a family album.

In *A Cotton Office in New Orleans*, they easily recognized Uncle Michel, a pensive, bespectacled man sitting in the foreground, his hands pulling at a sample of cotton in his lap. The room was full of men, and Sammy and Betsy consulted the explanation in the margin. Achille leaning against a window. Rene reading the newspaper. Everyone else was working.

"The Bee of New Orleans, read by the bee of New Orleans, happily buzzing from flower to flower," Sammy said.

Betsy eyed the text in the margin as her finger pointed out the others. "Mr. Bell with the hat. Mr. Prestidge. Mr. Livaudais. I wonder if they knew the office would close in a few months."

"I wonder," Sammy said quietly, and he turned the page to *Children on a Doorstep in New Orleans.* There was no explanation as to who in the painting was who, but Sammy and Betsy were able to piece the identities together. She pointed to the dog in the lane in the garden. Vasco. Sammy pointed out the oldest of the children, Jo, and then, Pierre. Carrie, standing, with the bonnet. Little blonde-haired Sidney, and the yellow-haired smudge next to him, his baby brother, Willy. The briefest shadow behind Sidney: Odile, maybe. Betsy pointed to the dark woman at the left edge of the painting, "This must be Miss Petinque."

In the background was the side of the Oliviers' house, the front facing Tonti Street.

"I guess Rene walked between these houses a few times," Sammy mumbled as his finger traced the path.

"For true," Betsy said. "Ready?" she asked, and she turned the page to *The Pedicure.*

"There's Jo and her lavender dress," Sammy said.

"It looks a little more like pink to me," Betsy said.

"I guess it was the light. Or maybe his eyes were a little bad, and that's how he saw it."

Betsy nodded, and the small shake of her ponytail rustled against his beard. He reached up to scratch it as she turned the page. On it was *Woman Seated on a Balcony.* Mouche sat on the front porch in a white-and-yellow, low-cut, off-the-shoulder dress with a black choker necklace. Her hair was up, and her shoulders and neck were creamy-pale. Her hands held a fan in her lap. Betsy flattened the page to remove the glare of the desk lamp. "She musta been some *canaille*, this one. Mais, just look at her! A pistol!"

"This house is still there." Sammy said as his finger traced the repeating ovals of the balcony railing. "They cut it in half at some point and put it on adjacent lots. I went down Esplanade and found it. I recognized this oval pattern in the balcony railing."

"I want to see it," Betsy said.

"I'll take you sometime," Sammy said.

They paused as each silently wondered what had happened to the people in these paintings. Had they lived to an old age, still close with each other, a big, extended family that enjoyed holidays, weddings, Sunday dinner? These portraits were just snapshots, a sample in time, like water scooped from a river that had come from upstream and continued to move downstream. Finally, Betsy looked to Sammy and turned the page.

It was the portrait of Tell arranging flowers. It wasn't clear whether she was looking at the flowers or looking where their scent was. The blooms were bright orange, red, and white in a dark room. Her left hand braced herself on the table while her right hand held a green stem. Between them was the swelling of her expectant midsection.

"Must have been baby Jeanne in there," Betsy said, and she turned the page.

The next picture was also of Tell, *Portrait of Estelle Musson De Gas.* She was wearing a gray dress with black spots and a wide black belt, sitting alone and looking off across the room. Her eyes were as blank as the wall behind her. One of her hands rested on the other in her lap.

"She really looks blind in this one," Sammy said. "Just look at her gaze. So vacant."

"Yeah. And in this one you can tell she and Mouche are sisters," Betsy said. "Do you think she ever knew about her husband and Madame Olivier?"

Sammy read the accompanying text. "It says here that her second husband, her cousin Rene, Edgar's brother, eventually left her for their neighbor, the children's piano teacher."

Betsy turned the page. "Well, well. Speaking of."

There she was, Madame Olivier, singing a duet with herself while a man played the piano, a man who was most likely Rene. The version of Madame Olivier on the left was as pregnant as Tell was in the flower arrangement painting, and she was singing an accusation or a warning to her non-pregnant self who stood next to the piano and Rene. Her red shawl was on the back of a white chair.

They continued looking through the pictures that Degas painted after New Orleans. There were scenes from the ballet and dance rehearsals, and one entitled, *L'Absinthe*, a picture of a sad young woman and a burly, bearded man in a cafe. Then there were more dancers and milliners, laundresses and prostitutes. There were several of a blonde woman in mundane scenes of her daily routine, all of them capturing the subject's motion.

"I wonder if any of these pictures are of Alice?" Betsy asked.

"I wonder that, too. This lady bathing and the one who's combing her hair. But their hair is more red than blonde."

"I'd like to know what she looked like," Betsy said.

"Me too."

But the book didn't say who the woman was who was combing her long hair and bathing and dressing. It did say that Degas was known to paint from memory, working and re-working a canvas and rarely painting spontaneously and that, as his eyesight declined, he experimented with sculpture. It said he became bitter in old age and difficult to be around, and gradually he lost most of his friends. His niece, the daughter of one of his sisters, cared for him until he died at age eighty-three. He never married.

"Mais, that's sad," Betsy said. She yawned and leaned back into Sammy, and he closed the book. On the front cover was a self-portrait of a frank and unsmiling young Edgar Degas. The artist looked up at Mr. and Mrs. Teague in the amber light of the study. To anyone else, he might have looked self-assured. To Sammy and Betsy, he looked like he was trying to conceal a broken heart.

Sammy, 1982

He was there the next morning when the librarian turned the key in the lock, and they went inside together. She snapped on the light in the small room that said *Archives.* He went immediately to the gray metal cabinet with the thin, wide drawers and chose the one that read, *Compass, 1871 through 1875.* His finger tapped over the little boxes, history neatly put to bed, months and years sleeping soundly together in little paper boxes. His fingertip hovered over the timeline, January, February, March, and then he pulled out the one that said, *St. Matthew Compass, April 1873.* His hands shook a little as he threaded the film in the projector, politely declining any help from the librarian, afraid that she might ask him what he was interested in or look over his shoulder. At last, it was on track, and he flipped on the projector light and turned the reel to the title frame, *April 1873.*

He scrolled through, pausing to look at dates, knowing that she was alive here, in early April 1873, but terribly sad, despondent, really. The newspaper told of events that were occurring as she struggled, things for sale, news from around the world, witticisms tucked in between it all to make up the space. And then he found it, his own name. He stopped the reel on an article called, *On Dit*, the society column of Saturday, April 5, 1873, a few days after his great-grandfather had struck his young wife:

> For reasons unknown to the Compass, Mrs. Samuel Teague has again taken on the mourning veil.

Sammy read the illuminated words projected through the microfiche onto the flat white screen. Around the small, simple sentence were other announcements—who had been born, who was marrying, who was baptized, who had died, who was visiting, who was arriving, and who was departing St. Matthew Parish, by train, steamboat, birth, or death.

He moved past the date and further into April 1873. The writing blurred over the clean white smoothness of the Formica backdrop of the reader. Below it, in his dirt-tinged denim lap, the diary was opened to the final words of her final hour. Her handwriting was emotion-tossed, jagged and distorted like the tracing of a breaking heart, a far cry from the beginning of the diary and the self-assured script of a young Englishwoman embarking proudly upon her life.

The images of April 11th, April 12th, April 13th, all passed by, and then there it was, a special edition of the St. Matthew Parish Compass, printed on Monday, April 14, 1873. The headlines eclipsed all else, and the details scrolled out below it:

Terrible Conflagration!

Young Wife of Sam Teague Perishes in Fire!

Early Easter morning, Alice Teague, wife of Samuel M. Teague of Mount Teague of St. Matthew Parish, succumbed in an inferno that consumed the ballroom being constructed on his place. Field-hands and servants responded to the blaze at approximately 1 a.m. Easter morning and formed a bucket brigade from the Twelve Arpent Canal, but the flames quickly outpaced their exertions, and all was lost. After the fire was extinguished, far too late, a woman's charred remains were discovered and promptly interred in St. Margaret's Cemetery behind the church, Rev. Henry Givens officiating the service. A sapphire pendant was found in the grass, the gift from a husband who now grieves her loss.

Mrs. Teague was a native of England and a talented pianist, having served as accompanist at St. Margaret's until her marriage. In addition to a grieving husband, she leaves behind three stepdaughters who loved her like their own mother. They are presently touring Italy and it is not known if they are aware of her passing. She is preceded in death by her father, the late Rev. Arthur Lamb of Guildford, Surrey, England. Her remains were interred next to him in St. Margaret's Cemetery.

The ballroom, once thought to be the largest in the South and destined to surely be so, was erased in the flames of a single

> night, though the stately home on the Thibodaux Road was saved with only minimal damage. The blaze is thought to have begun from errs committed by the work crew. Mr. Teague, who is away on business in the northern parishes, has telegraphed that he is returning by train and that he vows to sue.

Sammy scrolled slowly forward until he reached April 19, 1873, and an account of a disturbance in Colfax in Grant Parish in north Louisiana. A hundred or more 'negroes' were trapped in the courthouse, which was set on fire. When they fled the burning building, most were shot by the mob of whites who had laid siege to it. The article ended saying that the river landing was strewn with the bodies of colored men. The rest of the page was of cotton and sugar prices, advertisements for carriages and medicinal tonics, and merry anecdotes about simple negroes and dim-witted Irishmen.

Sammy had a pretty good idea what his great-grandfather's "business up nawf" had been in this place called "Call-facts."

There was no other word on the fire at Mount Teague, as news of it settled into the past and was covered by the dust of newer topics. He scrolled forward, a little deeper into April 1873, the projected newsprint running in a blur of articles and advertisements. And then there was this, complete with another error, 'morns' instead of 'mourns.'

Cholera at Mount Teague

> Sam Teague is now in danger of joining his late wife whom he still morns. Their neighbor, Mrs. Parris, has also taken ill and has succumbed while her husband Mr. Tom Parris is away in Kentucky. No others have been afflicted as of yet, but more are feared to follow.

And then, on May 5, 1873, *On Dit* carried this news:

> The *Compass* is happy to report that the health of our dear Sam Teague improves daily. All here along the bayou are grateful that God has spared our local champion and pillar of St. Matthew.

Our dear Sam Teague. Sammy could only shake his head. He took the microfiche and put it back in the box and returned to Mount Teague.

The smell of coffee greeted him as he came in the backdoor, and he filled the old cup, the last of the original Mount Teague china. He brought it with him to the central hallway and sat down on the settee across from the portrait like a heavy, weary traveler, slouching and looking at the great non-warrior across from him. They now wore identical beards, both in length and sandy-brown color. Now he could see how a man could be so angry as to spit in another man's face. But he refrained. It was a Degas, after all. Instead, he swept his hand over the end table next to the settee, and the last Teague china cup crashed and tinkled into pieces. Betsy came running.

"Bay, what happened?"

"Guess it just slipped out of my hand," he said, and he went to get the broom and dustpan and a mop.

Sammy, June 1982

It was in the mail when they returned from Orlando with a backseat of sleeping children, including two little girls with mouse-ear hats. The postmistress, Miss Jeannie, had him sign for it, a creamy legal-size envelope with a red, white, and blue airmail stamp on it from an address in London. He sat in his study and opened it, running his fingers over the embossed lettering. He took it and went straight into Thibodaux, paying extra and waiting to have it framed immediately. He also paid extra to have a slab of marble prepared with a new, more fitting inscription, expedited so that it could be set in place with the least possible delay.

When the stone was ready, the workmen settled it into place over the crypt, where its marble whiteness looked up through a cloudless sky to heaven. At the margins of the cemetery, the cane grew chest high. There were no more cool days, and it was just a matter of days before there would be no more cool mornings.

Sammy shook hands with the men from the monument yard in Houma. The two men, one black, one white, walked back to the oak-shade of the parking lot. Betsy and Sammy stayed behind. When the flatbed truck pulled out onto the highway, they were alone. Sammy pulled a piece of loose-leaf paper from his pocket and unfolded it. He began to read from it.

"The Soldier," he read aloud. He faltered. "The Soldier," he repeated. There was a long pause as he tried to gather himself. Finally, Betsy held out her hand, and he gave it to her. They drew near to each other in front of the fresh-white marble, and she read from the paper. It was "The Soldier," by Rupert Brooke, the English poet who had died during the first World War. A poem written by an Englishman, read by a woman with a Cajun accent.

> If I should die, think only this of me:
> That there's some corner of a foreign field
> That is forever England.
>
> There shall be
> In that rich earth a richer dust concealed;
> A dust whom England bore, shaped, made aware,
> Gave, once, her flowers to love, her ways to roam,
> A body of England's, breathing English air,
> Washed by the rivers, blest by suns of home.
>
> And think, this heart, all evil shed away,
> A pulse in the eternal mind, no less
> Gives somewhere back the thoughts by England given;
> Her sights and sounds; dreams happy as her day;
> And laughter, learnt of friends; and gentleness,
> In hearts at peace, under an English heaven.

"Rupert Brooke," she said, and she folded up the paper and put a small British flag into the ground by the headstone. Etched in the smooth marble, cold-white and mottled with faint cool flames of gray, was a new inscription:

IF I SHOULD DIE, THINK ONLY THIS OF ME:
THAT THERE'S SOME CORNER OF A FOREIGN FIELD
THAT IS FOREVER ENGLAND

And below it,

MOST REVEREND ARTHUR LAMB,
FELLOW, ROYAL LINNAEN SOCIETY

Betsy and Sammy were quiet for a while. The sounds of the highway came and went. A dog barked to another dog in a backyard somewhere. An outboard motor chuckled hoarsely down Bayou Lafourche. Everything was so far away. It was just the three of them, Sammy, Betsy, and the Reverend Arthur Lamb, Fellow, RLS. Sammy broke the silence, reading from the certificate:

Be it known on this day, April 25, 1982,

Arthur Lamb,

of St. Matthew Parish, Louisiana,
United States, is posthumously
granted fellowship into the

Royal Linnaen Society

They looked at the date on the proclamation and then at the marble obelisk with the name, Alice Lamb Teague, and the date of her death, April 13, 1873 and the date of her birth, April 25, 1853, and he remembered it was the birthday of the vicar's beautiful daughter, Alice Lamb. He hadn't realized it, but she had died less than two weeks shy of her twentieth birthday.

They walked up to the vicarage and gave the plaque to the current vicar, Reverend Armstrong, who waited with a hammer and a nail so that it could be hung on the wall of the study in the vicarage.

Sammy, June 1982

Everything that could be done for it had been done, and now the cane had been laid-by. The rest was up to the sun and the rain.

Music was playing from a radio in the metal shed. Pongeaux jumped up and followed Sammy down the back steps. The grass was cut, but, at this time of year, it would need it again in just a few days. A fan blew air across the sunlit concrete. Inside the big bay door on the concrete floor, Teeter sat on a workbench in front of a painting resting on a homemade easel. There were other paintings and sketches on similar easels, made from cast-off pallets and 2x4's. Each work seemed to be a little better than the last. He looked over his shoulder at Sammy and the dog and then looked back to his canvas and said, "Hey, bawsman."

"Hey, man. You've really come along."

Teeter watched his brush dip into a small puddle of yellow on his palette.

"Somebody tol' ya boy Degas when he was first gettin' started that all he had to do was draw lines and then draw more lines. So that's what I did." Teeter's brush paused over the canvas as he stared at the results of the latest stroke.

Sammy leaned back against the workbench and put his hands behind himself. Pongeaux lay on the cool concrete. Her tongue curled in a massive yawn that made her shake her head and smack. Teeter touched his palette, puddles of green and blue and yellow on the lid of an old K&B ice cream container. He paused with his brush and said, "Then, after he started doin' it, paintin', I mean, Degas said that paintin' is easy until you know how. Then you don' leave nothin' to chance. Every brush stroke," Teeter paused and touched the canvas, "Every brush stroke got a purpose. Every one of 'em got to say somethin'. Mais, I'm startin' to see it, me."

The painting he was working on was of a soldier sitting up in a tree, smiling beatifically.

"Who's the guy in the tree?" Sammy asked.

"That's Drumm. He was the first person to save my life."

"How?"

Teeter dipped into a little sky blue and touched the canvas above Pfc. Drumm's head.

"He changed places with me that day and walked the point. The mine caught him instead of me." The brush worked a blue stroke into the pause. "We had to get him out of a tree to send him home to his mama and daddy. His body, I mean."

Teeter's brush arched a big blue stroke above Drumm.

"He saved my life." Teeter put the brush in a glass jar of mineral spirits and picked up a different one. He touched a puddle of green on the palette and put it in the leaves of the tree. "Then you saved my life, Bawsman."

Teeter didn't even look away from the canvas as he said it, as if it was a well-known fact that Sammy had saved him. Sammy didn't say anything. Instead, he picked up a sketch of two Vietnamese girls on a street in a city, Saigon, maybe. One looked familiar.

"Is this the girl in Aucoin's?" Sammy asked.

Teeter stopped and looked at the sketch with Sammy and then resumed painting Drumm in the tree. "Yes, sir. That's Lilly."

"So you know her name now?" Sammy said with a smile. Teeter pursed his lips to conceal his. He dipped his brush again.

"I believe she's the reason you and Drumm saved it." Teeter painted the green leaves with a cloud of short brushstrokes. Drumm was sitting up in his tree as proud and happy as the Buddha.

"You need your Degas book back, bawsman?"

"Keep it as long as you want."

"Merci beaucoup," he said. "Degas was a sculptor, too, you know, bawsman. Sculpted statues of dancers and naked women."

"That's what I read," Sammy said. "When his eyes got bad."

Teeter didn't say anything. He was absorbed in the canvas where a deep green jungle grew under a blue south Asian sky. Sammy didn't say anything, either. He was thinking about statues of naked women.

Sammy was alone in a bateau in the Twelve Arpent Canal. He thrust a pole downward, and it sunk into the bayou and the mud below it. He stabbed here and then there, pushing the pole as far down as it would go. It made sucking noises when he retrieved it. The top layer of water had long since muddied up with clouds of gray-brown silt swirling against the clear surface. But Sammy kept probing the bottom.

And then he struck something hard. He moved over a little and missed again and then moved back and struck it again. He measured the depth on the pole. From the surface of the water, the mark was well over his head, seven or eight feet under. He tied a string with a red-and-yellow fishing cork on the cypress limb just above the spot.

He returned with divers from the St. Matthew Parish Volunteer Fire Department and a truck with a winch. The divers flipped their masks and put their regulators in their mouths and went down. Sammy followed their bubbles in the canal. He counted to ten. He counted to twenty. A breeze swayed the smallest branches of the cypresses, including the branch with the fishing cork marker, and the cane rustled at his back. He stopped counting and just waited. Quint had come down to the canal and stood talking to the younger brother of one of the divers, a classmate of Quint's called Albie.

At last, the two divers surfaced and flipped their masks back and took out their mouthpieces and pushed water away from their faces. "She's down there," one of them said. Though he wasn't dressed for it, Sammy waded out into the cloudy water and handed them the end of a set of chains, and they descended back into the canal. They surfaced a while later, and one of them gave a thumbs up. Sammy attached the chains to the winch on the back of the truck, and the spool slowly took up the chain, link by link. A century of mud and silt boiled away as she emerged, parting the surface, brown water clearing in her wake, emerging like Botticelli's *The Birth of Venus.* Patches of black mud clung to her contours, filling the recesses in the hollow of her neck and her eyes. Sammy started the winch truck and pulled the statue up onto the grassy bank and then stopped.

The divers emerged from the water and clumsily slapped their flippered feet up to the bank, walking like clowns. They unshouldered their tanks and took off their flippers. The men crowded around her. Her blind, blank marble eyes gazed to the Louisiana sky for the first time in over a hundred years.

She made her way back to Mount Teague not in a wagon drawn by oxen, the way she had departed, but carefully trundled back to the house in the scoop of a bulldozer. Pongeaux trotted along excitedly, barking instructions to the men, who ignored her and did as they saw fit. Sammy eased the statue down on the spot where the old ice barn had been, and then it took the strength of all of them to lift her to the vertical. Sammy shook the hands of the firemen, and then Quint and Albie washed her down with the hosepipe and pretended not to study her nakedness. The statue of Venus had been found under a century of bayou mud.

Sammy, July 1982

The girls giggled on the back porch, watching their grandfather, Trey Teague, scan the backyard with a metal detector. Every time it would crackle into the earphones, the ones that his granddaughters thought made him look like Mickey Mouse, he would stop and dig with a shovel. If he had known he was making them laugh, he would have been pleased. Every so often, he would pause from his side-to-side sweeping to put down small, wire-flag markers, mapping out underground cables and pipes. The outline of the flags worked out the puzzle of what was underneath the soil, including a multitude of square nails from where the ballroom must have once been. Trey Teague had a whole bucket full of them, along with a few old coins, the head of a hammer, its handle long since rotted away, and a pair of keys that went to some unknown locks.

After they had eaten lunch, Trey Teague studied the ancient blueprints on the back porch, looking up at the pattern of flags. They were the original plans for the gardens, found in the attic of the house under a century of dust. They were from the landscape architecture firm of Olmsted, Vaux, & Co., and signed by Frederick Law Olmsted. The name was familiar to Sammy, so he looked him up in the World Book Encyclopedia. Olmstead was the man who designed New York's Central Park. His son had designed Audubon Park in New Orleans.

Only the best at Mount Teague.

As his daddy resumed his mapping of the backyard, in preparation for the rebirth of the formal gardens, Sammy looked through the bucket of metal artifacts. He pulled out the two keys and rinsed them off with the hosepipe. When they were clean, he took them out to the metal shed where Teeter had welded the circular island with the lock back into the safe's iron door. He had done it carefully, like an artist, and it was a seamless, perfect repair. Sammy took the two keys and looked at them, took a big breath, and pushed them into the slots. They fit perfectly, and, when he turned them, the bolts moved without the slightest hesitation.

After a few days and a few trips to the nursery in Thibodaux, they were all in the backyard with rakes and shovels, working the earth in areas marked by stakes and strings. A backhoe with a power-auger was boring precisely aligned holes in the gathering heat. Old Mr. Teague drank iced tea and studied the original blueprints for the exquisite 19th century gardens, old, fragile pages held down by books on the wicker table on the back gallery of Mount Teague. Everything was there, waiting with bundled roots ready for the holes in the earth, cedars, jasmine, oleanders, hibiscus. An arbor with lavender wisteria. *Magnolia fuscatum*, sweet banana-scented blossoms, a magnificent orchestra of blossoms and scents. At the base of the statue of Venus, hostia with variegated leaves like peacock feathers. The only new addition would be the bank of peace roses, fragrant yellow-pink on the south wind.

Everyone was working on the re-creation, Quint, Albie, Betsy, Miss Vessy. Judee and Elizabeth wore garde-soleil bonnets and picked at insects that wriggled from the fresh earth. Teeter was there, also, with Lilly, though that was her American name. Her real name was Sang, Vietnamese for morning. She was a lovely woman, a blithe spirit who smiled easily and often and who seemed to crave the feel of Teeter's hand in hers.

Sammy went up to Miss Vessy who was teasing a plant from a plastic pot to put it in a hole. The oak had thrown shade over the spot, and, across the yard, Teeter and Lilly were working side by side in the sun. Miss Vessy straightened up and looked over to them.

"He looks like he's doing good," Sammy said.

"Oh, Mist' Sammy, that Lilly, though! *Pauvre bête*, she talk a little funny, yeah, but she's sweet-sweet. And Cat-lick, too! Got my boy goin' Mass ever Sunday and even them obligation-days!"

She stooped and put the plant in the hole and shook it to loosen up the roots. Sammy shoveled dirt in around it. Miss Vessy stood up again and slapped dirt off her hands. "Mist' Sammy," she said, wiping her fingers on each other. Sammy rested on his shovel for a minute and looked into her face. It was finely beaded with droplets of sweat.

"The first night in that apartment you rented in the city, that one on the fourt' floor. I had this dream, mais, it was so real. There was this lady. She was tellin' me somethin', I don't remember her sayin' it, wit' her mout', I mean. I just remember her tellin' me and me knowin' it. You ever have a dream like dat?"

"Yes ma'am. I have. What did she tell you?" Sammy asked.

"She said I was gonna be okay and so was my boy. I never heard her talk, no, but it's like she had an accent."

"Was she tall and blonde?"

"Yeah, now that you mention it, maybe she was. Why? You saw her too?"

"No ma'am, I don't believe I did, but I believe you did."

He smiled at Miss Vessy and walked out into the sun.

Later that afternoon, Sammy, Quint, and Teeter were the last ones working in the new garden. Their shadows were beginning to creep toward the east, the silhouettes of unusually tall men reaching to the cane far beyond the yard. Sammy was centering the auger for one of the posts for the arbor, when Betsy appeared on the back porch. She called to him, and he put his hand to his forehead to shield away the late afternoon sun that slanted in over the roof of the old house.

"Boo, Mr. Adrian's here to see 'bout the desk."

Sammy said something to Teeter and took off his work gloves. Their shirts were sticking to their bodies. Something was cooking in the kitchen, and they were all beginning to think about what it was. Quint and Teeter passed a plastic Igloo jug back and forth as Sammy and his long, trailing shadow walked up to the house.

Mr. Adrian stood looking out at the gardens that were forming and the statue of Venus that would preside over them again from where the old ice barn had been. Sammy ascended the steps and shook his hand.

"Boy, that's gonna be nice," Mr. Adrian said.

"We found the plans in the attic and the statue in the canal. We're using them to re-create the gardens as they were in the last century. Thought we'd give that old desk a facelift while we were at it. Come on, it's in my study."

Sammy opened the backdoor, and Mr. Adrian and Betsy went in. Pongeaux weaved around Sammy's leg and went in before him. When Betsy stayed in the kitchen to attend to supper, Pongeaux sat on her haunches on the mat at her feet.

In the study, the desk had been emptied of its contents, which were in cardboard boxes stacked against the bookshelves and placed in the old Campeche chair. Mr. Adrian approached the desk and ran his hand over the top and then squatted and checked the levelness of the top. His fingernail checked for dings, dents, scratches, maybe not to repair them, but to inventory them. They were, after all, part of the history of the desk.

"Oh, that's a nice one, Mr. Teague."

"Belonged to my great-grandfather."

"I heard he was somethin'," Mr. Adrian said, lifting up his glasses to examine a detail more closely.

Sammy put it more succinctly.

"A real son-of-a-bitch," he said.

"I didn't want to say it," Mr. Adrian chuckled as he lifted up his glasses to peer under them at the workmanship, cock-beading, dovetail drawers, finely detailed molding. He pulled out a drawer and said, "You know sometimes these old pieces have hidden compartments."

"We already found one, a false back to this drawer." Sammy opened it, and Mr. Adrian looked at it over his glasses.

"Mm-hmm, mm-hmm," he said. He took the drawer out of the case. His fingers probed the back compartment. Then he turned the drawer around and lifted his glasses to look at it closer.

"Come see, Mr. Teague."

Sammy drew in closer, and they looked at the back of the drawer. Mr. Adrian pushed a latch and tilted the drawer, and a letter slid out.

"A false bottom," Mr. Adrian said.

The envelope was a time-warmed beige, and there was no return address on it, only the words, *Samuel Teague, Mount Teague, St. Matthew, Louisiana*, and a postmark, *San Francisco, California, April 30, 1906*. Sammy opened it and found another envelope and a short note.

Dear Mr. Teague,

If you have learned to read, then I advise that you read this in private in order to avoid embarrassment. If you still cannot read and someone else is reading this to you, which is more likely, then I would strongly suggest that you leave the inner letter unopened.

A.L.T.

The inner letter was opened.

"Well," Mr. Adrian said. "You're Mr. Teague now. I suppose you should read it."

"I suppose I should," Sammy mumbled, but he put it on the shelf and helped Mr. Adrian trundle the desk out of the study and the house and down the steps to Mr. Adrian's truck with the magnet sign on the side, *Jay's Upholstery & Refinishing, Bayou Vista, La.*

The sunset cast a strange light through the bows of the oak lane and made the white-shell lane look a smoldering, ashy gray. Sammy balanced the desk while Mr. Adrian maneuvered it on a hand-truck. When it was loaded, Sammy said, "Do you think we ought to check the other drawers for compartments?"

"You know, we probably should."

They climbed into the back of the truck and checked every drawer for false bottoms and false backs. But there weren't any. The desk had given up all its secrets. And so, Mr. Adrian shook Sammy's hand and said something. But Sammy was staring off to the house, his house, a fiery gold in the rays of the sun. It seemed to glow.

"What's that?" Sammy asked.

"I said, I can have it refinished and back in about ten days. Look good as new," Mr. Adrian said.

"Oh, the desk. Sure. Yes sir. That'll be just fine."

Sammy watched the old desk move off in the back of the delivery truck, under a tarp and a mover's quilt, headed off to its refurbishment, to return renewed and spotless. As soon as Mr. Adrian turned onto 308, Sammy ran back up the stairs and to his study, now emptier without the chair and the desk.

Then, like Achille Degas in the painting, *A Cotton Office in New Orleans*, Sammy sat down on the window sill in the empty study with the letter, as the engine of the power auger muttered in the backyard. He removed the time-yellowed letter from the time-yellowed envelope. The edges were fraying, but the handwriting was familiar.

San Francisco, California
April 30, 1906

My dear husband,

No doubt you have at least heard (if you still cannot read) of the great upheaval that has lately befallen my adopted home, San Francisco. I survived the earthquake and subsequent fire, barely escaping my home early on the morning of the 18th instant. I wandered then and found relief in one of the Army hospitals in Golden Gate Park, and thence to the home of a friend where I now convalesce. My uncertain health has compelled me to write you, in case I do not survive. It is thought that I have typhoid, as it has stalked this place in wake of our recent twin calamities, earthquake and fire. Of course, this is not the first fire that I have survived. The first was in St. Matthew Parish in 1873, over thirty years ago.

If this letter would have borne a return address, it would be from a lot that is now missing its house, as a fire has engulfed it much the same as the fire engulfed your magnificent ballroom years ago. It may come as a shock to you, Mr. Teague, that the same fire did not engulf your wife.

I have only vague, laudanum-and-smoke scented recollections of that night, the crashing of timbers, ceilings, walls, and of window glass, of being carried over a shoulder, of being laid in the cool spring night-grass. The kindness and concern on those moonlit faces convinced me of the folly of ending myself and, may I add, the life within me. When one receives a kindness of that depth, an act of compassion of that magnitude, well, then, it must be repaid, if not to the bearers of such kindness, then to others.

I was put on the first passing steamer by those benevolent people with a few belongings and a false name. The steamer, whose name I also withhold from you, took me to Kansas City and St. Joseph, from whence, I took the train to here, San Francisco (much of which now lay in rubble and flame). I had plans at the time that I left St. Matthew Parish of traveling to Australia to find my distant cousins, whom I was always told were dwelling there. But I could barely remember their names, and I realised that I didn't even know where in Australia they lived. And, as I was almost out of money, I stayed in San Francisco and began to create a life here.

The man known in St. Matthew Parish in those days as the Rev. Henry Givens and I have led a rather ambiguous life together here in San Francisco. Did you not find it odd that he quit St. Matthew Parish soon after preaching my funeral? Or that your gardener, Mr. Luther, also departed at that time? The

California air was much to their liking. And Mr. Luther, before he passed some ten years ago, was responsible for many of the fascinating botanical displays at Mr. Woodward's Gardens which gave joy to so many here in the city.

And what of Mozie, who was never again seen after that night? She was the only one of my rescuers not to get out alive that night. I take solace in the fact that she died a kind and literate person. Can you say that you will be able to do the same, Mr. Teague? When it is your time to depart this earth?

To some, Rev. Givens and I have been as brother and sister, to others, an old husband and wife. The former is closer to the truth. All these years, I have dutifully endured the shackles and chains of celibacy. After all, Mr. Teague, you and I are still married, and bigamy shall not be on the list of my transgressions in St. Peter's ledger, as it will be for you. In the meantime, I expect forgiveness for my sins with more hope than confidence.

Forgive me the proud boast when I say that I am a person in this city whose counsel is trusted, a person known for her sagacity. (That means wisdom, Mr. Teague.) There is not a civic endeavor nor charitable undertaking in San Francisco about which I am not consulted. It has also been so for the former Rev. Givens.

I left behind the beautiful sapphire pendant you gave me, the ransom for a guilty conscience. Truly, it surprised me that you should be capable of remorse for anything, including twice striking me that day. Perhaps your liaison with Mrs. Parris was turning sour, and you wished to reconcile with me and felt that sapphire trinket would serve. More likely, you wished to avoid besmirching your reputation as a gentleman by having it known that you struck a woman, and you felt this shallow act would both placate me and absolve you of your guilt. In any case, the pendant must have fallen from my neck and gone up with the ballroom. Nevertheless, it is well. I would not have brought it with me, such a pathetic attempt to regain my favour. Knowing you as I do, I am almost certain you gave it as a gift to the new Mrs. Teague.

Among the meager belongings which I did bring with me when I arrived in San Francisco was the unfinished manuscript of Papa's last sermon, one entitled, "All Hail the Queen, or, What Must Pass for Wisdom." He was working on it when he died, of cholera or arsenic poisoning, only you and St. Peter can be certain. It is a lovely sermon and would have been among his best, had he finished it. Allow me to quote from it:

> The Queen of all virtues is Wisdom. Truth is her scepter, Humility is the chief diadem in her crown, Kindness is her robe. But despite all her magnificence, two things must pass for Wisdom to ascend her throne: Ignorance, and her consort, Arrogance. These things must pass for Wisdom to reign.

Those are the last words of my father's long and faithful ecclesiastical career. I can't but wonder, how many people are the better for it? I favour myself with the belief that they are numerous indeed. Nevertheless, I can add a third thing that must pass for Wisdom, and that, Mr. Teague, is the sad-eyed child, Innocence.

I think of Papa often and hope for a happy reunion with him in a land of bliss wherein 'every tear is wiped dry.' I think also of Mrs. Sullivan and Mama, Mr. Luther and of course, dear, courageous Mozie, all of whom have preceded me in death, and I look forward to seeing them again. Of course, it is only my hope that I should assign them and myself heaven. Such issues do not belong to us. Your eternity, Mr. Teague, shall be a matter bartered for by God and the devil.

If I see you in the next life, then either something has gone incredibly wrong for me or else you have had an astonishing conversion, and God is much more merciful than I could ever have imagined. As for me, I have pled guilty to my sins and await His forgiveness. My faith is my only hope that it may be so.

In the meantime, this flesh is fleeting, our souls strain against it. But certainly, it shall pass, as shall Ignorance, Arrogance, and Innocence. None of us lives forever. This is such a simple truth—surely even you are aware of it, Mr. Teague. Our lives are written as if in chalk on slate. We are not permitted the permanence of ink on paper. We walk the face of this earth, and then we disappear from it, leaving traces, Mr. Teague, only traces. And then, nothing.

Until then, we are still married. This means that you, Mr. Teague, like Mr. Roddey, are a bigamist. (I am aware of both your marriage and your new children, having subscribed to the *St. Matthew Parish Compass* for thirty years. It arrives weekly, and I read it faithfully.) You have said more than once, and always most vehemently, that there is nothing people hate more than a Bigamist. I disagree with you on that point, Mr. Teague. I am of the belief that there is nothing people hate more than a Hypocrite. But, of course, you are both.

If I die suspiciously, I have left word with the executor of my will that news of your bigamy be published in 'every newspaper in Christendom,' as you once put it to Mr. Roddey. This is also true if anything suspicious happens to my son, a remarkable boy who has grown to be a remarkable man, a man who has given me an array of grandsons and granddaughters as numerous as the children of Abraham. They all have the dark eyes and hair of their father (my son) and grandfather (my lover, a certain Parisian), not the nickel-grey eyes of the Teagues. My Parisian lives yet and has made quite a name for himself in the artistic world, though I have not seen him in over thirty years. I fear he feels yet the sting of my betrayal, and I have made no attempt of approaching him. I deceived him, and so the least I can do is to let his wounds heal privately. Nevertheless, if anything suspicious were to happen to him, the private news of your bigamy would become very public, very quickly. The transoceanic telegraph is a remarkable advancement.

Your daughters, of course, are estranged from you and have been for many years. This is no secret to anyone from St. Matthew Parish, though none should be so bold as to speak of it. It has been so long that quite possibly you would not recognize them if you saw them, but I can tell you that they are beautiful women and you have some lovely grandchildren by them. They have no need for your money—they have made their own way in the world.

They visit us here in San Francisco quite frequently. They will only say to their children that Henry and I are old friends to them, though your grandchildren have always treated us more as grandparents, or at the very least, a beloved old aunt and uncle. Fortunately, these loved ones had left after a lengthy visit just before the earthquake struck this place. I will not tell you where they reside. Your daughters insist upon it. They have no desire for your society and, in fact, are repulsed by the very mention of it.

Up until now, I have withheld public announcement of your bigamy, more for the sake of the fourth Mrs. Teague and her children than for you. She doesn't deserve the public censure that it would promote like you deserve it. Nor do your children from this poor woman. They, of course, would rightfully be considered bastards. However, do not be disheartened, Mr. Teague: bastards have ruled the earth, or at least small parcels of it, for centuries, ever since the first self-important Neanderthal raised a flaming club and pronounced himself thus. I am sure it will continue to be no different in St. Matthew Parish.

I have received nothing in the way that I wanted as a girl, but everything that was meant for me. Consequently, I have resolved to want that instead. It has been the key to a productive life, full of happiness and contentment. Papa was fond of saying that we stop breathing when we die because the Creator shows us something that takes our breath away, and that it may be splendid and beautiful or hideous and frightful, but it is the reflection of what we were in life.

And so, I leave you with a little friendly advice, Mr. Teague: go and reform. Night shall fall for you as surely as it falls for all of us.

(Still) your wife,

Alice Lamb Teague

Sammy, July 1982

They had taken turns reading the letter, over and over silently and then aloud, asking the same questions of themselves and each other. Did she die then, after the earthquake and fire, of typhoid or dysentery? Or did she live for years after? She was only fifty-three at the time. And what about Rev. Givens? Did she take his name, or some other name? She was more of a mystery now than before.

Finally, Betsy fell asleep in the light of the bedside lamp. Sammy reached over her and looked at the scapular that was lying on top of the letter. He picked it up and ran his finger on the leather strings and the pouch with the cloth facing with the blessed promise of Our Lady of Mount Carmel stitched in it, *Whosoever Dies Clothed in This Scapular Shall Not Perish in Everlasting Fire.*

He put the scapular back on the letter and kissed the cheek of his sleeping wife as he clicked off the lamp. The golden lamp-light fell to silver moonlight, and his sleepless face was bathed in the pale gleam. The night sky glowed with it. Insects vibrated monotonous songs in it. Sleep tarried and then came for him.

The next morning, he rose early and called information for the San Francisco Historical Society. Then he drank a pot of coffee and watched the clock. At eight, he called the number but got a recording that said office hours were nine to five, Monday through Friday. He waited. He called again at nine and got the same recording and realized that there was a two-hour time difference between Louisiana and the West Coast. The girls were up by then, and Betsy took them to swimming lessons. And

Sammy waited some more, poking around the metal shed and the safe and the study and Reverend Lamb's sermon chest. He walked out to the Twelve Arpent Canal and then back again.

He called again as the hall clock struck eleven. A neutral, female voice answered the phone and asked that he hold. While he waited, the phone played a small, compressed version of Liebestraum, and his fingers pressed the notes on the side table. After a minute or so, a Ms. or Mrs. McAllister answered. Sammy suddenly realized that he didn't know what to ask or how to ask it.

"Yes." He cleared his throat. "Yes, I'm, uh, I'm looking for some information about a woman who was involved in philanthropy in San Francisco in the late 1800s through the turn-of-the-century."

"And who is this?" she asked.

"Sammy Teague, calling from Louisiana."

"Can you be a little more specific, Mr. Teague? About this person?"

"She had one child and lived with a man who was either her husband or her brother."

The woman seemed to be writing something down.

"Anything else?"

"She was kind of tall, from what I've read. And blonde. Golden. Golden-blonde."

"Oh-kay," the lady said with a doubtful tone.

"Let's see," Sammy stumbled, "she had an English accent. She was an accomplished pianist—"

"—Alice Cousins," Mrs. McAllister said, her voice suddenly animated. "Of course. There was a lady, Alice Cousins, who lived with her brother, Henry Givens. She only had one child, a son, but tons of grandchildren and great-grandchildren. She and her brother were involved in everything, Orphan Society, Longshoreman's Relief Fund, Opera Guild, you name it. She left her mark on a lot of the good of San Francisco."

"Yes," Sammy said. "That sounds like her. What can you tell me about her? Are there any pictures of her? And her brother?"

"Very few. For all her philanthropy, she was fairly shy."

"What else do you know about her and her brother? Did they die in the quake?"

"Oh, no, they both lived into their eighties, I seem to recall. But I don't know much more than that. Mr. Teague, was it?

"Yes, Sammy Teague."

"Yes. Sammy Teague." Her voice changed, and Sammy imagined she was writing down his name. "But let me give you the number of an acquaintance of mine, Mr. Teague. Her name is Ida Fulton. We serve together in the Flower Guild at Grace Cathedral."

He scribbled the number down and asked her, "Do you think Mrs. Fulton might know anything about Mrs. Cousins?"

"She should. She's Alice Cousins' granddaughter."

Sammy thanked Ms. or Mrs. McAllister and hung up. Immediately, he dialed the number of Ida Fulton. The phone rang until the machine answered with an older woman's voice. He chose not to leave a message and hung up. It wasn't an introduction he wanted to make via a machine.

He called again in an hour, and the same old voice on the machine-message answered.

"Hello?"

"Hi, is this Ida Fulton?

"It is. Who is this?"

"This is Sammy Teague. I live in Louisiana. Mrs. McAllister at the Historical Society gave me your name and number. I was wondering if I could talk to you about your grandmother, Alice Cousins."

"Did you say your name was Teague?"

"Yes ma'am."

"When I was a girl in the 1920s, there were three elderly sisters who used to visit my grandmother and my Uncle Henry. We called them the Teague sisters, though that was their maiden name and they all had married names, but I don't remember them now. The Teague sisters. One of them was a very accomplished violinist who played across the United States and in Europe. I have such wonderful memories of them. In fact, I was just thinking of them. Funny you should have the same last name."

"Yes," Sammy said. "Funny."

"We called them all 'Aunt.' Aunt Jenny, Aunt Ida, and Aunt Lucy. Aunt Jenny and Grandmother used to play duets on the piano and violin. Very lovely. I'm named after Aunt Ida, in fact."

"They were the daughters of my great-grandfather and his first wife," Sammy said.

"Well, the world just got a little smaller, didn't it!" she exclaimed.

He wanted to know everything at once. What happened to the Teague sisters? Their children? There were so many questions whose answers were pending, but the one he asked Mrs. Fulton was, "What do you know of your grandmother? Before she came to San Francisco?"

"Well, she was English, you could tell it from her accent, and her father was an Anglican minister, but, beyond that, she was very reticent to give details. She always said her memory of that time was very dim compared to the wonderful life she had with such loving family and friends. She was very skilled at redirecting any conversation away from the details."

"I might be able to fill in those blanks," he said.

"And how is that, Mr. Teague?"

He paused, thinking of the best way to tell it. After all, Mrs. Fulton's beloved grandmother had been an adulteress who bore an illegitimate child, Mrs. Fulton's father. It might be too much for her. Suddenly, he felt like he might be an intruder, a messenger with unwanted news. But it was too late to turn back.

"I've come across some information from when she was a young woman."

Mrs. Fulton paused. "Well," she said.

"I understand that, that she was a patroness of the arts," Sammy said.

"Yes," Mrs. Fulton returned from speechlessness. "Yes, she was. She was particularly fond of the Impressionists and especially Degas. There was a man named Mr. Crocker, one of the richest men in the City, and the world, for that matter. Well, he had a painting of Degas' called *La Fille D'Or* that was rumored to be Grandmother herself, though I hear it was difficult to tell from the pose of the subject. She always wanted to buy it from him, but Mr. Crocker would never sell. We always doubted the rumours. It was a nude, you see, which would have been so unlike her, and she never went to Paris, that any of us knew, so how could she possibly have sat for Degas? And in the nude, no less!"

"Yes," Sammy laughed half-heartedly. "Where is it now? Can I see it?"

"It went up in flames with most of Mr. Crocker's art collection when his mansion on Nob Hill burned after the earthquake in 1906. I never saw it, of course. I wasn't born until 1912."

"So she survived it?"

"Oh, definitely. She and Uncle Henry. I remember them quite well."

"Do you have any photographs of them?"

"Yes, quite a few, in family albums. I have a lovely one of me next to Grandmother in her rocking chair. I've got the big bow in my hair like little girls wore then."

"I would love to see them."

"If you came out, I'd would be happy to show them to you. Oh, and Mr. Teague. You'll bring the information you have, won't you?"

"Certainly," he said. "I can be there tomorrow, if I can get a plane ticket."

"I'm certainly looking forward to meeting you."

"Yes ma'am, me too."

They hung up, and Sammy stared out the bedroom window at the live oak limbs. Mount Teague seemed suddenly devoid of her presence, emptier. Even her ghost was no longer there. He read the letter one last time and put it back in the desk drawer of the bedside table with the scapular and the Rosary. When he looked up, Betsy was in the doorway to their bedroom.

"I just talked to her granddaughter," he told her.

"Whose granddaughter?" she asked.

"Alice's."

"For true?"

"For true."

"Sammy, that gives me the *frissons*," she said as she shivered and hugged herself. She sat down on the bed next to him. They leaned into each other and lay back on the bed. The ceiling fan mixed the midday summer air, and Sammy spoke up to it.

"She says she has pictures of Alice and Henry. They lived into their eighties. She said I could come out and look at them and she would tell me more. I've got to go into Thibodaux and get a plane ticket. Why don't you come with me?"

"I think I ought to stay with the children. But you go. She haunted you, after all."

Sammy was quiet for a moment. "I only thought she haunted me," he said. "All these years, I only thought she did."

He left and returned later that day with the ticket, a last-minute seat on a last-minute flight to San Francisco with a connection in Las Vegas.

The next day, he put his suitcase on the front seat of his truck and ran up the steps to kiss her and hug her one more time. He had more than enough time, but he hated to be late, and this was a flight he dared not miss.

"Call me when you get to Las Vegas, and then when you get to San Francisco," she said. The summer sun had already burned away any notion or hope of coolness. She stood barefooted on the porch in a plain white-print dress. Inside the screen door in the central hallway, the girls were sitting on the piano bench in their swimsuits and randomly pressing keys.

"I wish you could go," Sammy said.

"The girls got swimming lessons."

He accepted her excuse, though he knew she was afraid to fly, perhaps the only thing she was afraid of. Even after all these years of marriage, he craved her company, and being under a different roof from her was never easy. He got in the truck and started it up and blew her one more kiss.

In the midday July heat, Betsy watched Sammy's truck stir up white dust from the shell lane under the oaks. Then she waited on the front porch until Sammy was gone and the dust had returned to the earth. Pongeaux returned from escorting him down the lane and vaulted up the steps. Though Betsy was a little unsettled about Sammy going, she hadn't said anything. She wasn't one to yield to vague misgivings, and she was just as anxious to know what had happened to Alice as Sammy was. After all, Alice Lamb had been a Mrs. Teague also. She turned and went in the house to get two little girls ready for their swimming lessons.

He watched the plume of white dust boil behind him and then checked traffic and turned onto LA 308. Clouds were gathering in the sky, distilled off the Gulf and sent racing northward on the south wind. To pass the time, he turned on the Cajun French radio station, listening to the DJ banter with the people who called in. Before Donaldsonville, he got caught behind an old couple, gray heads just visible over the front bench seat of an old Plymouth churning along at barely twenty miles an hour. Every time he tried to pass, another oncoming car would appear, and he would have to duck back into his lane behind the old couple. After twenty minutes, he finally reached a straightaway and gunned the diesel Ford. Another car suddenly appeared, closing the distance rapidly and passing just as Sammy ducked in. The ancient man in the car behind Sammy pried an old hand off the wheel and waved to him. Sammy waved in the rearview mirror. The car he had barely missed gave a long trailing honk as the old couple in the Plymouth receded to a dot in his mirror. With an eye on the road, Sammy reached down to get his suitcase from the floorboard where it had slid.

The Sunshine Bridge loomed ahead like the bones of an immense dinosaur, spanning the wide river before setting its feet down on the east bank. There was a line at the tollbooth on the west bank, and a man with sun-browned arms and a cigarette on his lips shifted in his seat as his hands explored his pockets for change. The woman in the toll booth accepted the fare piecemeal, pushing the coins in her palm and calmly giving the man the count. Sammy checked his watch. The heat had stirred up a heavy balm through the window of the Ford. He was considering just walking up and paying the toll for him, when the man scratched through his console and finally came up with the coin that made the difference.

The man's car puttered to the right lane, and Sammy paid his toll and passed on the left. At the top of the bridge, he checked his watch again and laughed at how Betsy teased him about being compulsively early.

The girls were swinging in pendulum arcs on the swing-set in the backyard. Legs tucking and straightening, tucking and straightening. Betsy paused and thought of Jo Balfour Degas and the other children in the Musson house and then folded the last of the empty Delchamps bags and put it into a drawer in the kitchen with the rest of them. Pongeaux was outside with the girls, sleeping on her side in a patch of shade. Betsy was thinking about what to make for supper without Sammy and his appetite. The last soap opera of the day was on the television in the den.

The news bulletin broke through in mid-sentence of the television actor. Betsy closed the kitchen cabinet to go and see what was happening in the world. The announcer's voice was grave, and, on the television screen, fire hoses sprayed flaming wreckage, like the night the old ice barn was burned.

Again, repeating this breaking story, Pan Am Flight 759 has crashed on takeoff from the New Orleans airport into the Morningside Park neighborhood of Kenner. Emergency personnel are on the scene, but it is feared there are no survivors….We'll have more details and expanded coverage at six.

The soap opera returned with the false drama of false characters that paled in comparison to what was occurring under her own roof, in her own life. Her mind would not allow it. Surely it was another flight, she thought, not his. She checked where he had scribbled the flight number on the calendar. She read it, *Pan Am flight 759, gate 3*, and her knees crumpled, and she leaned into the kitchen counter.

Outside the window, the girls played in the backyard, swinging high in the air on the swing set, mouths wide and singing to the tops of their lungs, still in their swimsuits. Upstairs, music was playing from Quint's room. She sat at the kitchen table and put her face in her hands, suspended in that moment that holds its breath, before the trains with excited travelers collide or the earthquake hits the peacefully sleeping town or the tsunami consumes the beach of carefree bathers. And she began sobbing as she thought of how she would tell her children that their old world had just ceased to exist, and they would have to begin living in a new one.

After he passed the man who had scraped together his change, Sammy made the top of the Sunshine Bridge. He kept his eyes on the road and held his breath. Ghosts no longer scared him, but big bridges still did and likely always would. Down below, on the east bank, the cane undulated in green velvet, waiting under the graying sky for the afternoon wind and rain.

On the downslope of the bridge, he allowed himself to look away from the road, and then he saw it. The smoke from it lifted up over the cane fields, billowing in monochrome into the clouds the same gray color as the smoke. A charter bus was smoldering on the highway under the bridge, and jagged flames were beginning to kindle under it around the tires, illuminating the pavement in the gloom of the impending rain, a skyful of it. He glanced from the road before him, descending from the apex of the bridge, to the tiny road by the levee far below the bridge. The bus was smoking, but there was no one there yet; there weren't even any sirens. He looked at his watch again. When he got to the bottom of the approach, he made a U-turn onto the access road and headed for the levee road.

He parked well behind the bus, which Sammy could now see had hit head-on into one of the live oaks that crowded the edge of the highway. The bus was burning now, shadowy figures stirring inside. Sammy pried open the door to find the bus driver, a large man whose uniform strained to contain him, pale and drooping over the stirring wheel. His black tie was splayed in two and curved over his gut. Sammy stepped onto the top step. The bus was full of white heads and eyeglasses, and sweaters despite the heat of July.

"Come with me. Quick!" he shouted.

When an old man went to get his bag from the overhead, Sammy snapped, "We don't have time for that." The man gave him a startled expression, and Sammy added a softer, "Sorry, sir. We don't have time."

They filed past Sammy, old hands steadying themselves on headrests as they tottered down the aisles.

"Meet under that magnolia," he said.

"Which one would that be?" a woman's voice asked. It was distinctively British.

"That one there with the big white flowers."

The bus was half-full, then half-empty, and then there were just a few people and then just one person in the back. Sammy could see and feel the flames through the windows of the bus now, and the air was smoke-scented. The woman was sitting in the back seat, knitting calmly, though she had tears in her eyes.

"Come with me ma'am," Sammy said rolling his hand. He was halfway to the back of the bus, farther than he wished, farther than he felt safe. The old woman looked up to him.

"What if I want to stay?"

"What?"

The air was even denser now with an acrid haze.

"What if I want to stay?" she asked with a trailing cough.

"Then I'm gonna come get you and drag you out. Come with me."

He grabbed her arm. She rose, and her knitting fell to the floor. She reached down to retrieve it. Plastic on the seats was beginning to melt. The inner ticking was burning around the springs.

"Come. With. Me." Sammy shouted over the flames as he threw the woman over his shoulder. The smoke was so dense now that he had to look at the orientation of the seats to tell which way was forward. He felt the sting of the flames as he stepped out of the bus with the woman over his shoulder. The air was cool despite the summer heat, and he wondered if the rain was upon them or if it only felt cool after the intense heat of the bus. He put her down under the magnolia and went back to the bus.

The driver was still slumped over the wheel. Sammy checked his pulse. It was weak, but it was there. He fumbled with the seatbelt and noticed that the man had vomited down his shirtfront. Sammy pulled the driver out by the shoulders as the last of the flames took the bus. Sirens began to overtake the crackle of flames.

Red light whirled in the oaks and over the cane fields as Sammy set the driver's shoulders down and fell to his knees. Firemen hosed down the live oak and the charred bones of the bus that rested against it, like the carcass of a whale. Sammy's palms pressed into his knees, which pressed into the roadside dirt. He looked up. A fireman was slipping an oxygen mask onto the face of the bus driver. More people had made it to the scene. The sheriff turned from the fireman and the driver he attended and walked over to the group of people who rested under the magnolia. Their white hair gave them the appearance of a flock of sheep, lounging in a meadow. One of the old people under the magnolia pointed to Sammy, and the sheriff came to talk to him.

Sammy remembered none of the interview, only that suddenly the sheriff had filled out several pages of yellow legal pad. The sheriff spoke into a walkie-talkie, saying something, something far away and indistinct except for one thing.

"Yeah, chief, down here under the bridge cross from Donaldsonville. Looks like the bus driver had a heart attack, hit a tree. Outfit out a New Orleans called Gemstone Tours. Full a English tourists come down to see plantations." There was a squawk of a voice from the small speaker, and the sheriff replied, "This bus is called the..." He checked his handwriting on the yellow pad, "…the Chrysolite."

The squawk replied, and the sheriff raised the walkie-talkie to his mouth, pushed a button, and said, "Ten-four."

He walked over to the shade of the magnolia, hitching up his khaki pants and replacing the radio into a holster on his belt. The spray of the hoses was behind him as he calmly gave instructions to the old people under the tree. It was beginning to rain, the first metallic drops pocking the waxy, green leaves. The tree was large and dense enough to shelter all of them, almost two dozen.

"Bus on the way for you folks now," the sheriff announced. "Take y'all up to Gonzales. Red Cross meet y'all up yonda, get you some fresh clothes, somethin' to eat. Tour company gonna get y'all home then."

There were a few questions asked in polite English accents under the green leaves and white blossoms. The sheriff answered them in a big voice. "In Gonzales, they gonna have phones to call your families back home. We'll have one of the pharmacies in town see to your medications." A man asked him something, and there was a small, relieved round of laughter.

"Yeah, they got beer in Gonzales. Ain't no dry towns round here, no," the sheriff smiled. Someone asked a question, and the laughter stopped.

"Don't know. Took him to the hospital up in Baton Rouge. Not sure yet. Say ya prayers."

Sammy looked at his watch. When he looked up, someone snapped his picture while another person asked him some questions. He couldn't remember any of them, only that they were the same questions the sheriff had asked him. The old people filed one by one onto the yellow bus, *Ascension Parish School Board* written in black under the windows. Some of their clothes were singed, their faces smudged, and Sammy realized that they were the ones in the back of the bus, the last ones to get out. He looked at his watch again. He still had enough time to make his flight.

He climbed into his truck and took one more look at the bones of the bus resting in a smudge of ash on the shoulder of the highway. Off the road, under the magnolia, a woman sat. She was the one who had been hesitant to leave, the one who had been knitting. She rested with her hands clasped in her lap, looking out at the field and the cane which patiently bore the rain. Sammy turned off the truck and went to sit under the leaves of the magnolia with her. She was sitting Indian-style, remarkably spry for someone her age. The rain clattered off the leaves above them and kept Sammy and the old woman dry. Finally, she spoke, though she looked away.

"I suppose I should thank you," she said.

"Thank me?" It still had not sunk in what he had done. It was as if someone else had done it.

"For saving my life," she said in a voice that carried a touch of indignance.

"You sound ambivalent about living," Sammy said out to the cane field across the highway. Cars were slowly passing the burned-out skeleton of the bus resting against the live oak.

"I just lost me husband in Lancashire. Life has been a bit of a struggle without him. We were married fifty-three years, after all." The rain picked up. "I wouldn't have minded just goin' up with the bus. Just headed off on holiday with me knitting in me lap."

And then she cried, her grief having fought its way out in a circuitous path and at last finding her eyes. "This was a holiday we had planned to take together."

She blew her nose and then cried for a while.

"He was always so enamored with the American South. Plantations and chivalry, great houses. We both were. We had saved up for it and were so looking forward to going." Her grief rattled and shook her and leaked from her eyes. "Together."

The school bus waited with the door open. The sheriff was wearing a yellow vinyl poncho with APSO on it. He ran over to the magnolia.

"Ma'am, we're ready for you."

She stood up, her graying-blonde hair specked with flakes of soot. He could see that she had once been a strikingly beautiful woman. She gathered her purse and boarded the bus. Sammy stood by the door as she disappeared inside. The sheriff approached and extended his hand, and Sammy shook it.

"All right, Mr. Teague," the sheriff said.

"How did you know my name?" Sammy asked.

The sheriff looked into Sammy's face incredulously.

"I just took a three-page statement from you, sir."

Sammy went back to his truck and started it up. The school bus pulled ahead and turned onto the highway, its red-and-yellow lights blurred in the rain. The woman's face looked back at him through one of the rear windows, and then the bus disappeared into the distance. The wipers pushed away the rain as the truck pulled onto the highway toward I-10 and the airport in New Orleans. He checked the ticket again, Pan Am flight 759, departing at 4:05 pm. He checked his watch. He would make it easily.

Betsy sat on the front porch waiting on the rain and waiting for the visit from the St. Matthew Parish sheriff, but within earshot of the phone for when the call came, if that was how these things happened. She practiced what she would say.

Yes, officer. Yes, I heard the news on the television. No, I'm alright. I have my children with me. I'll be alright. I'll tell his father old Mr. Teague when he comes back from playing golf.

The rain began to fall, clicking off the leaves of the magnolias and the oaks and the statue of Venus, and beating the white dust of the shell lane back into the earth. As she heard the girls come in from playing, she was hoping she wouldn't cry before she told them what she had to say. But she wasn't sure if she could, so she decided that she wouldn't say anything to the children until she heard something definite, though she had no idea when that would be. Tonight? Tomorrow? A week from now when they found some vestige of him in the rubble? Or when he simply never came home? At last, she opened the screen door and went inside.

In the kitchen, she looked into a cabinet, presumably thinking of what to make, but really, she was just staring. Quint came in and kissed her cheek and asked her what was for supper. She moved her head behind the open door of the cabinet, her face close to the cans lined up inside. She bit her lip and cleared her throat. "White beans and ham? That sound good?"

The phone rang, and he said, "Sounds good to me," as he moved into the hall to answer it.

She held her breath and listened. It rang again, though to her it was like the searing rasp of a sawmill blade cleaving a log in two. And then another time. Quint interrupted the next ring. Betsy shut her eyes and felt the tears well up behind her eyelids.

"Hello? Hey man!" Her son paused. "Yeah! Sure!" His voice called to her from the hallway. "Mama. Albie wants to go fishing on Belle River tomorrow. Can I go?"

"Yeah," her voice faltered and regained its strength as the back of her hand wiped her eyes behind the cabinet door. "Yeah, baby, that sounds great." She blew her nose into a paper towel. "Just bring me back some fish."

"She said yeah, just bring back some fish," Quint told the phone. "All right, man. *Early*," he stressed. "Before it gets too hot."

Betsy braced herself in case he came back into the kitchen, but his footsteps drummed up the stairs and into his room. She wrestled the black iron Dutch oven onto the stove and chopped an onion and a bell pepper, some ham. She scraped them in, and they sizzled and waited for the cans of white beans lined up by the sink. She could barely smell or hear them. The girls chased each other around the house and through the front door, giggling and still in swimsuits. Betsy went and shut the front door to the rain and the arched oak limbs and white shell lane and the trouble that was headed down it.

He drove and thought of her and what she might look like in the old photographs he would be handed and whether he would recognize her. The windshield wipers pranced back and forth in a monotonous dance, straight lines pushing away circles. The cane swayed in the breeze in its own dance, joyous in the rain, bristling as sheets of it pushed through and over the green velvet, unconcerned and unaware of things like autumn and harvest. Up ahead, traffic on the interstate pulsed on the overpass. He got in the right lane to maneuver for the on-ramp. As he veered into the eastbound lane, he checked the ticket again, Pan Am flight 759, leaving New Orleans at 4:05 pm. His watch said it was only 1:10.

She was a Cajun girl. Onions didn't make her cry.

But she was crying as she made her kitchen make kitchen sounds, trying to drown out an encroaching world of sorrowful news. The girls laughed at something on television and sang along with Oscar and Big Bird. She was grateful that LPB didn't have news that might break into the programming. Still, she said, "Girls, that's enough TV. Go upstairs and get on some dry clothes. Shoo, now." They giggled and sang and scrambled up the stairs in their wiry little swimsuited bodies.

She decided that she would let them be happy for now. For just a little while longer. For as long as they could. She cut up the okra and put it in the skillet, and it hissed as the wooden spoon pushed along the black-iron bottom and tapped on the side. Her lips grasped the elastic ring as her hands tried to put her hair into a ponytail, but they shook so much that she gave up and let the cable of black hair fall loose again and put the ring on the window sill. The girls came downstairs, chattering together, small young patter on old stairs. Betsy was still trying to convince herself that there had been some mistake or that it had been a bad dream.

The girls came into the kitchen in wildly mismatched shorts and T-shirts and announced that they were hungry. Little Judee leaned into her mama's leg and hugged it. Betsy hastily wiped her eyes and turned her head away from them.

"Go upstairs and get your brother, Elizabeth," she said. "Judee, baby, help me set the table."

Elizabeth's small footsteps drummed through the hallway, and then the stairs creaked lightly under little feet. Betsy gave Judee a handful of forks from a drawer and pulled down plates from a cabinet. They set them out, Judee following her mother and placing the forks carefully next to each plate.

"That's real good, my baby," she said to Judee as she straightened them. She gave Judee a glass from the cabinet and told her youngest, "Now, let's put one next to each place." The little girl took the glass in two hands as if she were bringing an expensive, delicate gift to the baby Jesus, and she put it next to a plate.

"This glass for my daddy," Judee said.

Betsy realized that, out of habit, she had set a place for Sammy. There would be one less place-setting from now on. Elizabeth appeared in the kitchen door with her brother.

"Why are you crying, Mama?" Quint asked.

Betsy turned and washed her hands at the kitchen sink, wiping her eyes with her forearms and looking out the window at the falling shadows.

"Them onions, boo, they get me every time."

She took her time in washing her hands while her children sat and waited for her, and then she sat down and forced a smile.

"Woo. Them onions," she repeated, and they said grace and genuflected, Elizabeth doing an elaborate version, a cross-and-a-half, and Judee copying her big sister in a gesture that was more like someone describing a swarm of bees. They ate, and Betsy silently bore the unbearable, behind a smile that was so delicate and so breakable that she feared it might shatter with the slightest touch or the mere mention of a husband and a father. She steered the conversation away from him.

She ate almost nothing and rearranged her food with her fork to look like she had. When supper was over, she asked Quint to clean the kitchen with his sisters while she sat on the back porch and watched the early evening shadow of the house creep over the gardens and toward the statue of Venus. Like every summer afternoon in south Louisiana, the rain had fallen hard and then passed away to allow a vivid sunset.

The ticket rode nestled inside the diary on the front seat next to him, the flight number, 759, and the destination and part of the connection, *San Francisco via Las-* showing near the spine.

On the interstate, he got behind a tanker truck with the words *Flammable Liquid* written along the side and end of the tank. A drop of cartoon flame with eyes and a smile and a round body with a pointed head waved a friendly warning for him to stay back and leave plenty of room. Sammy thought it was a truck headed to or from one of the chemical plants along the river. The windshield wipers slapped back and forth at the rain, and the big tires of the tanker raised a mist off the pavement. It was white, like old hair, and he thought of the white heads on the bus, like sheep, like lambs, and the British accents. Like the dream he had had. The green-and-white sign approached and said, *Sorrento, US 61*, and then one just past it said, *NEXT EXIT, 25 miles.*

The shadow of the house had reached the base of Venus, who stood stony-white in a patch of evening sunlight. Betsy looked at her and thought of Alice, the Mrs. Teague who had looked at her a hundred years before and staggered under an awful weight. Inside the house, through the kitchen window, she heard her three children working together, glasses tinkling, the chatter of silverware in the sink. The sound of the last moments of their former childhoods.

She was sure that old Mr. Teague's round of golf had been delayed by the rain, and he was probably just finishing up. When he got in, she would tell him first, and then he could help her tell the children. Then she supposed there would be a trip to the funeral home. Maybe an attorney would be involved. She wasn't sure. Maybe there would be people who would say to themselves, good riddance. Maybe there would be people who would say it out loud. She wouldn't hold her tongue, then. She would tell them that her late husband was the most courageous, giving, loving man she would ever know. She might even scream it at them. The phone rang inside the house in a dreamy trickling tingle, and Quint answered it again.

"Mama, telephone."

She went in the door and picked up the phone where he had left it.

She cleared her throat and closed her eyes and calmly waited for the impact.

"Yes?"

It was Mr. Teague, Sammy's daddy.

"Come home," she said without giving him a chance to speak. Though she didn't say why, her shaking voice betrayed the urgency.

A little while later, a swirl of red-and-white lights illuminated the limbs of the lane of oaks. She got up and went to the window and saw the St. Matthew sheriff's cruiser coming down the lane. The white dust was red and blue in the twilight. There was a truck behind it, most certainly her father-in-law. She stood at the bottom of the stairs and waited for the sheriff to tell her and her family what she already knew.

It wasn't panic; it was a sense of uneasiness that made him veer off at the last minute, cross a lane of traffic, and rattle over the warning bumps at the exit. He turned and drove over the overpass, pausing to watch the tanker truck disappear east with its skirt of mist and the friendly drop of flame. He signaled another left turn and got on I-10 going west.

When he got to Gonzales, he followed the signs to St. Theresa's Catholic Church. The Ascension Parish School Bus was in the parking lot, so he pulled in beside it and got out. The Parish Hall was next to the sanctuary, a plain brick building with patches of clinging moss and mildew. He opened the door to the quiet sound of old, British conversation and the smell of tea brewing.

A nun greeted him. She wasn't the wool-skirt and sweater kind of nun who ran the halfway house in New Orleans. She was an old-style nun with a black-and-white habit. Sammy recognized the Scapular she wore with the Blessed Promise of Our Lady of Mount Carmel. He knew it by heart now, *Whosoever Dies Clothed in This Scapular Shall Not Perish in Everlasting Fire.*

The Englishwoman was sitting by herself at a table in the Parish Hall, looking at her lap and her hands and the gleaming white floor. The other old people spoke with each other in quiet, old English voices that murmured among the steel-and-plastic chairs and tables. The woman looked up to Sammy as he came in, but she didn't smile or frown. She just looked at him. She had grown exhausted from the events of the last year of her life and then completely done in by the events of the last two hours. Sammy pulled up a chair and sat next to her.

"My name is Teague," he said, "Sammy Teague."

The woman maintained a blank look. Then she mumbled, "Beatrice Pennywaite. Bea."

"Nice to meet you, Bea."

Bea looked out the window and said nothing.

Pennywaite, Sammy thought. The name struck a note.

"Miss Bea, is Pennywaite your married name?"

"Yes, it is."

"What was your husband's name? First name, I mean?"

"Bertie. Why do you ask?"

"Named after his grandfather, or great-grandfather? And was he a railroad man on the Great Northern?"

"Why, yes, he was." She turned to Sammy as if only now interested in what he was saying. "How did you know that?"

He couldn't begin to explain, so he said, "My family has an old plantation home across the river. We've had it for over a hundred years. I want you to come and stay with us. I have a teenage son and two young daughters who would enjoy meeting you," Sammy said. "And my wife, Betsy. We would enjoy having you as our guest."

The woman seemed to warm a little and to break the surface of whatever sorrow she was under.

"How old are your girls?" she asked.

"Five and four," he said.

"Ah!" she said. "What little loves they must be."

"Let me get your things," he said.

"I don't have any things. They've all gone up in flames!" she laughed sardonically and then fell to sobbing and put her face in her hands.

"Come on, then," Sammy said. "We'll see to that, too."

He took her arm and went to speak with the nun.

"Sister, I'm Sammy Teague from St. Matthew Parish. I'll be taking Mrs. Pennywaite to be the guest of me and my family. We have a place down on Bayou Lafourche." And he wrote his name and address down on the back of a church bulletin. The nun studied it for a moment.

"Teague," she said in wonder. "Where have I heard that name?"

"I'm the guy down in St. Matthew who dodged the draft. The one they make fun of."

The rain had moved through as if nothing had happened, leaving only puddles in the parking lot and a slow, brown trickle in the ditches. Mrs. Pennywaite looked up at the sky as if perplexed at how it could rain so hard and then the sky become blue again in a matter of minutes. Sammy helped her into the cab of his truck, and, when he got in the driver side, the smell of smoke was amplified by the small space. She looked at the diary on the front seat between them and opened it and read the first page to herself and then closed it again and placed it on the seat.

"I kept a diary when I was a girl." She looked around at the cab of the pickup. "You Americans and your lorries," she muttered. Then she noticed the suitcase.

"A suitcase? Were you going away on holiday just now? I hope I'm not keeping you."

"No ma'am," he said. "I was just heading home."

They picked up the interstate and crossed over the Sunshine Bridge. He explained to her that it was named after the song, "You Are My Sunshine." She broke into a wistful smile and looked out the window at the big, brown swath of river and the ships that sat in it.

"Bertie used to sing that to me."

When they crossed the St. Matthew Parish line, a sheriff's cruiser emerged from cane rows and followed them. Sammy checked the speedometer. He was just a few miles over the limit. After a quarter mile, the cruiser hit its lights and Sammy pulled over. The sheriff got out of his car and walked up to Sammy's truck. Sammy rolled down the window. Twilight had fallen, and the rain had made the air thick.

"Are you Samuel Teague?" the sheriff asked. He was a man with an intensely black face.

"Yes sir," Sammy answered.

"I thought I recognized you from the times you bailed Martin Blanchard out of jail. I remember how good you were about it. How's he doing?"

"He's doing well. Was I speeding, officer?"

"Oh, a little. But that's not why I stopped you, Mr. Teague. I stopped you because I got a call on the radio from over in Ascension. Word's got out about what you done. I'm here to give you an escort home." He tipped his hat to Mrs. Pennywaite and said, "Ma'am."

Then the patrol car pulled ahead, and Sammy and Bea Pennywaite followed its flashing lights along 308 until the lane of oaks led them to the glowing home at the end of them. He had missed his flight, a last-minute, impulsively bought flight that had cost them a lot of money. He hoped Betsy wouldn't be mad.

She braced herself as the sheriff parked in front of the house. When the red and blue and white lights fell, she saw that it was Sammy's truck. Her first thought was that they had already retrieved it from the parking garage and were returning it. She put her hands over face to force it back into a happy, or at least a neutral, expression. Elizabeth ran down the steps with Judee to the truck. From behind her hands, Betsy heard a little girl exclaim a word that saved her life. And all of their lives.

"Daddy!"

Betsy took her hands from her face. And there he was with his suitcase. And an old woman. And a St. Matthew Parish sheriff.

"Your husband was a hero today," the sheriff called up to the house.

She still didn't understand.

"But he's a hero every day," she said.

The sheriff shook Sammy's hand and touched the brim of his hat to Mrs. Pennywaite, and then he got in his cruiser and disappeared in a white dust cloud under the branches of the oaks. Sammy looked up to the porch. The yard and the oaks and the cane had fallen into night. He was standing in a circle of amber light.

"Baby," he said. "This is Bea Pennywaite. From England. Bea, this is my wife, Betsy."

As his girls hugged his legs, Betsy ran to him and hugged him, and he asked her, "What's wrong? Why are you crying, baby?"

"I was already missing you. I'm glad you're home." It was all she could say.

Quint came down the steps and asked to take Mrs. Pennywaite's bags.

"I haven't any," she said.

They went inside the house. In the central hallway, Mrs. Pennywaite looked around herself. She looked into the study and the parlours that shared doorways with the hallway. At last, she turned to Sammy and asked, "Mr. Teague, do you believe in déjà vu?"

Before he could answer, she pointed to the piano and asked, "Who plays?"

"I do," Sammy said. "And my son, Quint. He plays quite well."

"I was a music teacher back home in Lancashire. May I?"

Bea seated herself at the bench and began playing Beethoven's *Moonlight Sonata* from the yellowed sheet music that had once belonged to Alice Lamb. And then, in wildly mismatched clothes, Elizabeth and Judee sat next to Bea on the bench as if they had known her all their lives. When she finished, Bea looked to the girls on either side of her.

"Ah, what little loves you are! I always wanted children, but Bertie and I never had any."

"Miss Bea," Elizabeth said earnestly, "you smell like smoke."

"Well I should then, like a chimneysweep, I suppose it is!"

She looked up to the painting on the wall.

"And who is this chap?" she asked.

"My great-grandfather," Sammy said. He felt uncomfortable, almost embarrassed.

"Hmm. Looks to be in the style of Tissot," she said as she pulled up her eyeglasses and squinted under them. "Or Degas, perhaps. Very well done." She looked at Sammy and back to the picture. "You have his eyes. And the beard, of course."

She turned back to the piano and chose another selection, *Liebestraum*, Love dream. "Lovely sound, it has," she said as she played, and his daughters danced in the central hallway, comic dances in the carelessly chosen clothes of summer children.

When Bea had finished playing, Mr. Teague came in with his golf clubs. As he opened the door and maneuvered them in, he was asking, "What was the sheriff doing—" And then he saw Mrs. Pennywaite and said, "Now who is this?"

It had taken Sammy two showers the night before and one this morning, but the smoke-scent had not quite left him. It had permeated the sheets and the pillows, and he had not slept well, even though Betsy had spent the night cuddled right next to him.

He rose mid-morning, something unheard of for a cane farmer. In the yard, Quint and Albie were cleaning fish, filling bulging freezer bags with filets. Pongeaux sat on her haunches and watched.

He wandered through his house, confused a little until he remembered that Betsy had taken Miss Bea into Thibodaux to get her new things for a new life. His daddy had gone with them, talking nonstop to their guest.

Sammy looked into the bathroom mirror, trying to figure out how to trim a beard. Finally, he put down the clippers and dressed and drove into Napoleonville. The cane was growing tall again, drinking July morning sunshine and waiting on July afternoon rain, unaware of things like autumn and cane cutting and grinding and boiling. Growing like it would grow eternally, up past the trees and forever.

On the bench in front of the barber shop, Mr. Picquet sat reading the *Compass* with the headline on the front,

St. Matthew Parish Man Hailed as Hero

And there Sammy saw himself, ash-faced and hair askew with a cinder-flecked beard. It didn't look like the photograph of a hero. It looked more like a DWI mugshot. He looked perplexed and disoriented. But if the paper said he was a hero, well, then, so be it.

The picture and article shared a page with the news of Flight 759. It had crashed on take-off from the New Orleans Airport, en route from Miami to Las Vegas and San Diego. One hundred forty-five on board had died, with no survivors. Eight on the ground in Kenner had also died.

Betsy hadn't said a word to him about it.

He felt his knees weaken.

Mr. Picquet pretended he didn't see Sammy, even when Sammy sat next to him and looked out over the highway and the hot, brown water of Bayou Lafourche and the green trees lining it and the blue sky above all of it. Sammy was thinking.

What if the old couple on 308 had turned off and allowed him to go on? What if the man at the tollbooth of the Sunshine Bridge had had correct change? He would have passed before the accident had occurred and made his flight and been in a bigger accident himself. And he would not have come back, and he would not be here today, hailed as a man who had risked his life in the service of others. The pendulum swings, and sometimes it misses.

Sammy's mind wandered for a few moments, and then he realized he had put his hands on top of his head. He stood up and left Mr. Picquet hiding behind the *St. Matthew Parish Compass*, reports of heroism and disaster separated by the thin white space between the columns of newsprint. He opened the glass door and felt the cool air of the window unit fall on him.

Inside Mr. Clyde's Barber Shop, the old men in the chrome-and-vinyl chairs each stood up and put down their papers and magazines. They shook Sammy's hand and patted his back vigorously saying things like, *you a hero, you,* and *bon fait*, and *mais that was somethin', that*, and *ida crapped my draws, me, swearda Chris'*.

Sammy sat in the end chair in the line to wait his turn, but someone said, "Heroes first."

He stepped up into the swivel chair, and Mr. Clyde draped him in black and snapped the collar around his neck.

"Mais, you still smoky. Ima have to put some smell-good on you, baw. Usual, Mist' Teague?"

"Mr. Clyde, I been thinkin'" Sammy said. "Let's take this beard off. I've decided it just ain't me."

"Mais, Sammy, I been tryin' to tell you, boo. That beard ain't nobody."

And the old men laughed over the *Field and Streams* and *Louisiana Conservationists* and *Popular Mechanics* they held, and the stiletto-heeled calendar girl in the red bikini holding the wrench, *The Tool You Can Trust*, gave a seductive, approving smirk as Sammy leaned back and gave Mr. Clyde his throat. And Mr. Clyde put a hot towel over it and stropped his razor on a leather belt. Sandy-brown hair slid off the black cape and fell in clumps on the black vinyl tiles of the floor.

Acknowledgements & Gratitude

I am grateful to my editor, Katie Schellack, for your unvarnished assessment, on this and previous books. I have come to both rely on and look forward to your judgment and candor.

I am also, as always, grateful to my test readers, the last line of defense between you, the reader, and this book. Thank you, Flavia Lancon, Nan Murtagh, Gloria Landry, Gina Lobue, Emily Aucoin, Steve Feigley, Liz Parker, MaryBeth Garic, Dawn Jelks, and Lindsey Fontenot.

Thank you to Catherine, "wife of my life," who listened to the random ideas for this story while knitting as we sat around the lamp at night like an old English couple.

Thanks to Daniel Mattingly, a Louisiana cane farmer who filled in the (rather large) gaps in my knowledge regarding the cultivation of sugarcane.

Thank you to the staff of The Historic New Orleans Collection for your help in elucidating the geography of 1872 New Orleans. Before I could tell this story, I had to know where everything was.

Thank you to sisters Micey Moyer and Joan Prados, great-nieces of Edgar Degas and docents at the Degas House on Esplanade Avenue in New Orleans. They are also the great-granddaughters of Edgar's brother Rene. I appreciate their candor about their great-grandfather. You can visit the Degas House and even stay overnight in the rooms where the Degas, the Musson, and the Bell families once lived. The house had fallen into anonymity until someone noticed that the distinctive oval railing was an exact match of the one found in Degas' portrait of his cousin Mathilde ("Mouche") in *Woman Seated on a Balcony.*

Samuel Johnson said, "The greatest part of a writer's time is spent in reading. In order to write, a man will turn over half a library to make one book." It is certainly so.

Especially helpful in preparing this novel were Christopher Benfrey's *Degas in New Orleans: Encounters in the Creole World of Kate Chopin and George Washington Cable*, Leonard Huber's *Creole Collage: Reflections on the Colorful Customs of Latter-Day New Orleans Creoles*, John Smith Kendall's *History of New Orleans*, also, *Degas' Letters*, edited by Marcel Guerin, and John C.

Rodrigue's *Reconstruction in the Cane Fields: From Slavery to Free Labor in Louisiana's Sugar Parishes, 1862—1880.*

Much of the day-to-day occurrences found in this story are drawn from the archives of the *New Orleans Picayune.*

Thanks also to associate curator Christina Johnson of the Fashion Institute of Design and Merchandising in Los Angeles for providing me with a copy of curator Kevin Jones' presentation on Mme. Olympe, "A French *Modiste* in an American City: Olympe Boisse & New Orleans."

Which reminds me. Many of the people in this story were real.

The Bishop of Manchester, James Prince Lee, died on Christmas Eve, 1869, and was replaced by the new bishop, James Fraser. Bishop Fraser was an opponent of the Oxford Movement, an element of the Anglican church which sought to bring back some of the vestiges of the Roman Catholic liturgy. He also had little respect for the theories of Darwin, saying that they were "merely guesses, conjectures, and inferences resting upon remote analogies." Rev. Arthur Lamb is based in part on Rev. Sidney Faithorn Green, incumbent of St. John's Church in Miles Platting. Rev. Green was imprisoned for twenty months for violation of Parliament's *Public Regulation of Worship Act of 1874.* There was a right way and a wrong way to worship in the Queen's church. Parliament said so.

The *Chrysolite* was an actual ship which was captained by a man named Gill. It sailed between Liverpool and New Orleans in the 1860s and 1870s. For that matter, so did a ship called the *Fire Queen.*

Philip Roddey was indeed a Civil War general. And a bigamist. He left his wife and family in Alabama and married Carlotta 'Fanny' Shotwell, a woman twenty years his junior. Later, he stole from her, but set her up as the thief. You can read about it in the July 22, 1874 issue of the *New York Times,* "A Farce Ended: Carlotta F. Shotwell Acquitted." Roddey fled the country and died in England. His body was returned to Alabama for burial. Fanny Shotwell wrote a tell-all account of the whole incident, *A General Betrayal: The Sufferings and Trials of Carlotta Frances Roddey.*

Charles T. Howard founded and was president of the first Louisiana Lottery. He is a man with a murky war record, as there is no tangible evidence that he ever served, as he said he did. He did, however, make a fabulous amount of money from the lottery, only to be excluded by the Metairie Jockey Club for being, it is said, 'new money.' He also bought them out when they fell on hard times. If you look at aerial maps of Metairie Cemetery, you'll see it retains the oval shape of a racetrack. Mr. Howard himself is among those buried on the infield. He died in a carriage accident in 1885, and one can only wonder if the 'fractious beast of a horse' was a gift from Sam Teague.

The Masacs, Theopilus and his wife Melanie, ran the New Orleans Conservatory of Music in the 19th century. It was located on Baronne Street in the same building as Mr. Grunewald's music store about the time that Louisiana had two governors and two legislatures.

During the administration of Governor Warmoth, a former Union officer who stayed on in Louisiana after the war, two different return boards were set up to count the votes of the 1872 election. The reason for this is unclear to me. Two different governors and legislatures were elected, and the legislatures elected two different senators. Back then, the Constitution of the United States called for the state legislatures, rather than a popular election, to elect senators to send to Washington. The competing legislatures did battle in the papers and the courts until it all came to a head the night of March 5, 1873. Two men were killed, and several dozen were wounded, but no one was hung, though Sam Teague feared that he would be. The following year, there was even more loss of life at the battle of Liberty Place, Sept. 14, 1874.

The late fall-early winter of 1872 saw the advance from north to south of an equine illness called the "horse flu." Though generally not fatal, it was as crippling as a gasoline shortage would be today.

Mme. Olympe Boisse ran a high-end boutique at 144 Canal Street in the 19th century. She would spend part of each year in Paris (I imagine the summer months) and then would return to New Orleans with all the latest. She was by Kevin Jones' account a masterful saleswoman. She eventually moved back to Paris and little else is known of her.

Michel Musson and his family lived on Esplanade through most of the 1860s and 1870s, and it was here that his nephew Edgar Degas, the son of his sister, visited in the winter of 1872-73. Edgar's cousin Estelle (Tell) was married to Edgar's brother Rene. Tell and Desiree (Didi) lived well into old age. Mathilde Musson Bell (Mouche), however, died in 1878 of Yellow Fever, as did her niece Jeanne, the baby Mouche's sister 'Tell' had in December of 1872.

Tell's daughter Jo died of scarlet fever in April of 1881 at the age of nineteen. Her little brother Pierre had died the week before of the same thing.

In the spring of 1878, Rene Degas and the children's piano teacher, America Olivier, ran off together and got what was then called a 'Utah divorce.' They married and left for Paris, never to return. Michel Musson threatened to shoot Rene, his nephew/son-in-law, if he ever saw him, and for years after Rene's abandonment of their cousin Estelle, Edgar didn't speak to his brother. Edgar did, however, sell many of the paintings from his private collection to pay off Rene's debts. Edgar died in 1919 in Paris. Rene died there in 1921.

Edgar Degas never married, though he continued to paint, and, as his eyesight declined in old age, sculpt. One of the ballet students described him as "a kind old man who wore blue spectacles." He once said he never married because he was too involved with his art.

You can find the Mussons in the paintings of Degas, particularly *Children on a Doorstep* and *A Cotton Office in New Orleans.* I believe that Mme. Olivier and Rene Degas are the people portrayed in the painting *The Song Rehearsal.* But you can decide, and I encourage you to look for yourself.

Also by C. H. Lawler:

The Saints of Lost Things

The Memory of Time

Living Among the Dead